Published by
Adhyaksha
Sri Ramakrishna Math
Mylapore, Chennai-4

© Sri Ramakrishna Math, Chennai
All rights reserved

I-2M 3C-8-2013
ISBN 978-81-7883-633-1

Printed in India at
Sri Ramakrishna Math Printing Press
Mylapore, Chennai-4

AF815814

SWAMI TAPASYANAN
As We Knew Hin

Reminiscences
of
Monastics and Lay Devotees

Sri Ramakrishna Math
Mylapore, Chennai - 600 004

Publisher's Note

Within a short period of time, the Ramakrishna Order has produced a number of spiritual stalwarts whose sterling qualities have been greatly inspiring and deeply influencing countless spiritual aspirants all over the world. Revered Swami Tapasyananda Maharaj was one such phenomenon in the intellectual and spiritual world whose personality embodied a plethora of values – a sharp intellect yet tender heart, high thinking yet simple living, learned yet humble, humorous yet grave, devotional in temperament yet rational in approach, strict with himself yet generous with others, an erudite scholar yet practical administrator. In short, his life was a confluence of several noble values worthy of emulation.

This volume provides interesting and illuminating insights into the life and personality of Revered Tapasyananda Maharaj through the biographical sketches and the reminiscences of both monastics and lay.

The volume is divided into three sections. Section I deals with biographical aspects of Revered Tapasyananda Maharaj. We have also included brief biographical sketches about his mother who herself led an exemplary life of religious fervour and who had pleaded with Swami Brahmananda to bless that her son may become a monk of the Ramakrishna Order, and his brother who had blessings of some of the direct disciples of Sri Ramakrishna and was a spiritual co-traveller of Revered Maharaj. Letters of Swamis Brahmananda, Shivananda, Saradananda, Nirmalananda, and Vireswarananda to either Revered Tapasyananda Maharaj's mother or to his brother and letters of Revered Tapasyananda Maharaj to his own family are also included in this section.

Sections II and III contain the reminiscences of Revered Tapasyananda Maharaj by monastic and lay respectively. The distinguishing feature of the reminiscences is that they come from a wide spectrum – monastics who either lived with Revered Maharaj or were closely associated with him and devotees from all walks of life, from learned professors to workers and flower vendors, from intimate disciples and devotees to professionals who met him occasionally – providing a kaleidoscope of myriad perceptions these people had about Revered Maharaj.

Since Chennai, Mumbai, Thiruvanthapuram, Kozhikode, Thrissur and Kolkatta were called Madras, Bombay, Trivandrum, Calicut, Trichur and Calcutta in Revered Maharaj's time, we have retained those names in this volume.

Following Revered Tapasyananda Maharaj's style of diacritical notation, words like Moksha, Diksha, Shiksha, Shashi, Darshan etc. are spelt Moksa, Diksa, Siksa, Sasi, Darsan etc. in this volume.

The words Revered Maharaj or Maharaj in this volume generally refers to Revered Tapasyananda Maharaj unless otherwise contextualized.

The letters, reports, articles included in the Biographical Section and Appendices have been reproduced in this volume as found in the original and we have not made any changes except for aligning the text for uniformity.

We offer our reverential pranams to Most Revered President Maharaj, Srimat Swami Atmasthanandaji Maharaj, and to Revered Vice-president Maharaj, Srimat Swami Smarananandaji Maharaj, for sending us messages of benediction and to Revered Vice-president Maharaj, Srimat Swami Prabhanandaji Maharaj, for sharing his reminiscences of Revered Tapasyananda Maharaj.

Swami Asutoshananda (Manager, Sri Ramakrishna Math, Chennai) has coordinated the preparation of this volume. Swami Tyagananda (Minister, Ramakrishna Vedanta Society, Boston), apart from sharing his reminiscences of Revered Tapasyananda Maharaj, has also sketched the biography of Revered Maharaj. Swami Atmashraddhananda (Editor, *The Vedanta Kesari*) has helped in editing a few reminiscences.

The major portion of the work – compiling, editing and giving shape to the book – has been done by Swami Lakshmidharananda, a monk of the Ramakrishna Order.

We gratefully acknowledge the active support of Sri Udayanan and Smt. Indira Krishnakumar, both relatives of Revered Tapasyananda Maharaj, for sending us the photographs, letters, and relevant information pertaining to Revered Maharaj's pre-monastic life. We also profusely thank Smt. Indira Krishnakumar for her efforts in collecting and translating from Malayalam to English the relevant information from the diaries of Revered Maharaj's brother, Sri K.P.A. Menon, and for contributing invaluable articles and reminiscences about Revered Maharaj. Our heartfelt thanks to Smt. Lalita Menon who has taken the trouble of meeting many people associated with Revered Maharaj and compiling their reminiscences and impressions about him when he was in Trivandrum.

Our heartfelt thanks to Smt. Pushkala, Smt. Bragada, Smt. Usha Ganesan, Smt. Yamuna Subramanian, Sri Kannan, Sri K.K. Venkataraman, Sri Mohan, Ms. Mavillapalli Rajyalakshmi and a few others for translating the reminiscences in Tamil or Telugu into English.

We heartily express our gratitude to Ms. Sorna Kumari, Sri S. Raghunandan, Smt. Radha Govardan, Selvi Alamelu, and Selvi Jwalini for sparing their valuable time for proof reading. And above all, our wholehearted thanks to those who have shared their reminiscences of Revered Maharaj.

The intention of bringing out this volume portraying the illustrious life and personality of Revered Maharaj is to place it as a beacon of inspiration to spiritual aspirants, present and future.

We are happy to bring out this volume on the occasion of 151st Birthday Celebrations of Swami Ramakrishnananda. We earnestly pray that Sri Ramakrishna, Holy Mother Sri Sarada Devi, Swami Vivekananda, and Swami Ramakrishnananda may shower their blessings on the readers and all those who have contributed to the preparation of this volume.

Sri Ramakrishna Math, Chennai
4 August 2013

Contents

Section II
Reminiscences by Monastics

Appendices

....

A Dedication to Swami Ramakrishnananda, the Founder of Sri Ramakrishna Math, Chennai

I happily and prayerfully dedicate to Swami Ramakrishnanandaji Maharaj this book on Revered Swami Tapasyananda Maharaj, an illustrious monk of the Ramakrishna Order, who was the seventh president of Sri Ramakrishna Math, Chennai, and one of the vice-presidents of the Ramakrishna Math and Mission.

There were a few occasions when I had had the opportunity to meet Revered Tapasyananda Maharaj. I met him first in 1957 or 1958 at our Delhi Ashrama when he had been invited by Revered Ranganathananda Maharaj to speak in a public meeting connected with annual birthday celebrations of Sri Ramakrishna held in our Ashrama. He stayed in our monastic guest house and would be always busy either with proofreading the publications of Sri Ramakrishna Math, Chennai or with studying some serious literature. He always carried with him a small Oxford dictionary! One day I proposed to take him around Delhi for sightseeing, if he so wished. He summarily rejected the idea saying, 'I don't have any interest in it.' He was too busy with the books except for the few minutes he would spare for his food!

I met him 5 or 6 times at Belur Math during 1961-62 when I was at the Probationers' Training Centre. He would have come to attend the four-monthly Trustees' meetings. He would "hello" when I offered pranams to him.

My next meeting with him was at Chennai (then called Madras) on the eve of his public lecture on Swami Vivekananda in 1972. He became suddenly ill, perhaps affected by flu. He kindly requested me to speak in his place. I felt his enthusiastic encouragement and blessings on youngsters like me.

Revered Tapasyananda Maharaj served as the president of Sri Ramakrishna Math, Chennai for 20 years. His influence on both monastic and lay and his contributions to this Math, especially its publication wing, has been immense.

On this sacred occasion of Swami Ramakrishnanandaji's Jayanti, I invoke abundant blessings of Bhagavan Sri Ramakrishna, Holy Mother Sri Sarada Devi, Swami Vivekananda and Swami Ramakrishnananda on all those who have shared their interesting and instructive reminiscences of Revered Maharaj and have thereby enabled innumerable spiritual aspirants for generations to come to derive guidance and inspiration from him and to assimilate the ideals he stood for.

Swami Gautamananda

4 August 2013

(Swami Gautamananda)
Adhyaksha
Sri Ramakrishna Math, Chennai

PHONES PBX : (033)
2654-1144 2654-5700
2654-1180 2654-5701
2654-5391 2654-5702
2654-9581 2654-5703
2654-9681 2654-8494
FAX : 033-2654-4071
E-Mail : president@rkmpresident.org
office@rkmpresident.org

RAMAKRISHNA MATH
P.O. BELUR MATH,
DIST. HOWRAH
WEST BENGAL : 711 202
INDIA

Sri Ramakrishna Sharanam

MESSAGE

June 10, 2013

I knew Revered Swami Tapasyanandaji Maharaj since nineteen forties. Revered Maharaj was an erudite scholar and lived up to the ideas and ideals of Ramakrishna Sangha. He was blessed with Sannyasa Diksha by Swami Shivanandaji (Mahapurush) Maharaj and had also received blessings from many other direct disciples. He lived very simple and austere life and served the Sangha with his multi talents. When he became Guru, he blessed many devotees with mantra Diksha. Revered Maharaj exemplified the teachings of Sri Ramakrishna, Holy Mother Sri Sarada Devi and Swami Vivekananda through his inspiring life.

I am happy to know that Ramakrishna Math, Chennai is going to bring out a commemorative book containing life and reminiscences of Revered Maharaj. I hope and pray that devotees, monks and brahmacharins will get inspiration by reading the book. I congratulate all who are behind this great effort and convey my affectionate blessings to them.

My earnest prayer to Bhagavan Sri Ramakrishna, Holy Mother Sri Sarada Devi and Swami Vivekananda for the success of the book!

(Swami Atmasthananda)
President
Ramakrishna Math & Ramakrishna Mission

Swami Gautamanananda
Sri Ramakrishna Math
Mylapore, Chennai - 600 004

Phone PBX :
(033) 2654-1144 / 1180
(033) 2654-9581 / 9681
FAX : (033) 2654-4346
Email : rkmhq@vsnl.com
Website : www.belurmath.org

RAMAKRISHNA MATH &
RAMAKRISHNAMISSION
(The Headquarters)
P.O. BELUR MATH, DIST. HOWRAH
WEST BENGAL : 711202
INDIA

July 1, 2013

Dear Gautamanandaji,

I am in receipt of your letter of 20th June 2013 regarding your planning to bring out a book on Swami Tapasyanandaji Maharaj.

I hardly have any reminiscences about him, for I never had an occasion to come in close contact with him. However, long before I joined the Order, o found his name mentioned in a book. It is mentioned there: "The Swami Tapasyananda here was a man of obvious integrity..." and "One element of this truth was the value of integrity. The yellow-robed monk by me had integrity.... Did he not owe it to his religion?" [In the Path of Mahatma Gandhi by George Catlin, Macdonald & Co. (Publishers) Ltd., London, 1948, pages 75 and 77].

Whenever I went to Chennai Ramakrishna Math, I found him working on a manuscript. Even whenever he came to Belur Math, he used to carry with him the books which he was working upon. He hardly wasted any time. An exemplary life indeed! Once a journalist asked him about his bio-data. Swami Tapasyanandaji replied, 'I am a humble servant of Sri Ramakrishna'.

I am sure that the book you are planning to bring out on him will be of interest to our devotees.

With best wishes and namaskar,

Yours affectionately,

(Swami Smarananda)
Vice-President

Swami Gautamanandaji
Ramakrishna Math
Mylapore, Chennai 600004

Section I

Biographical Profile

Swami Tapasyananda Maharaj in Madras Math garden

Part A: Life Sketches

Swami Tapasyananda
A Biographical Sketch

Swami Tyagananda

'I have no bio-data. My only introduction is that I am a servant of Sri Ramakrishna'—this is what Swami Tapasyananda Maharaj wrote in 1986, not long after he was elected a vice-president of the Ramakrishna Order. He was responding to a request for his bio-data prior to his visit to Port Blair, a remote part of India which is cut off from the mainland. In a postscript to the letter he added, 'I am enclosing a catalogue of books published by our Math.'

This short reply provides a good window to the life and personality of Swami Tapasyananda Maharaj and we get a glimpse into the dominant characteristics of his life: humility, self-effacement and an extraordinary missionary zeal in propagating the message of Sri Ramakrishna, Holy Mother, and Swami Vivekananda through literature.

Early Days (1904–1926)

Known in his pre-monastic days as K. P. Balakrishnan Menon, Tapasyananda Maharaj was born in 1904 in an aristocratic family of Ottapalam in Kerala. When he was only two, he lost his father, K. P. Achutha Menon. Balakrishnan had his early education at Calicut. His first acquaintance with the name and teachings of Sri Ramakrishna occurred

House where Tapasyananda Maharaj was born (not existing)

when he was studying in a lower secondary class. His mother Parukutti Amma spent a long time daily reading religious books in Malayalam. Browsing through some of those books, Balakrishnan learned about Sri Ramakrishna and Swami Vivekananda. He was so impressed by what he read that he felt like reading more and more about these divine personages.

Serious in temperament, Balakrishnan was a studious child. He loved to read, discuss and argue. Once he had a big argument with a school friend. The bone of contention was whether God could be seen. His friend maintained that it was impossible to see God, but Balakrishnan was fully convinced that God could be seen. He successfully refuted every argument of his friend and at last cited the example of Sri Ramakrishna as an illustration to prove his point.

He became closely acquainted with the Ramakrishna-Vivekananda tradition after a couple of years when the family went to stay in a new house which happened to be the residence of a devotee of Sri Ramakrishna. This devotee had already received initiation (*mantra diksa*) from Swami Brahmananda Maharaj and had also visited Belur Math. In his house, the photos of Sri Ramakrishna and Holy Mother were worshipped daily in the shrine. Balakrishnan was deeply influenced by this devotee's family. Soon a similar shrine of Sri Ramakrishna was set up in Balakrishnan's own home as well. His mother, who was already devoted to Sri Ramakrishna, now spent longer hours praying and worshipping in the family shrine.

It was during this time that an incident took place which Balakrishnan described later as "a landmark in my life". He saw for the first time Swami Nirmalananda Maharaj (Tulasi Maharaj), who had met Sri Ramakrishna, received his blessings, and moved closely with his direct disciples including Swami Vivekananda. Tulasi Maharaj was the head of the Order's centre in Bangalore, but he used to spend several months every year in Kerala. He would visit different places, meet devotees and inspire them to lead a spiritual life along the lines shown by Sri Ramakrishna.

Tulasi Maharaj had already established a centre of the Order's work at Trivandrum, started the Malayalam magazine *Prabuddha Keralam*, and arranged the visit of Swami Brahmananda to Kerala in 1916. Whenever Tulasi Maharaj would visit Calicut, he would stay in the house of Balakrishnan's friend. This was how Balakrishnan got an opportunity to come in close contact with Tulasi

Maharaj, whose holy company had a great influence on Balakrishnan's mind. Years later, he said:

> The impression that Tulasi Maharaj made on my adolescent mind was tremendous. I found in him a striking and startling contrast to the ochre-robed mendicants who wander on the streets. He had an athletic frame, a tender and yet sonorous voice, an excellent command of simple, clear and well-articulated English, and an astonishing capacity to give ready and crushing replies to mischievous questions. I found him more than a match for the self-accredited intelligentsia of the locality consisting of lawyers, officers, teachers etc., who could take only a contemptuous view of a *sannyasin* till then. To this inherent worth of Tulasi Maharaj was added the halo of association with Sri Ramakrishna and Swamiji [Swami Vivekananda].

Balan, Parukkutty Amma, Appu

At the age of 15 or 16, when Balakrishnan was studying in the final year of his high school, he began to read Swami Vivekananda's books and also the magazine *Prabuddha Bharata*. The four-volume edition of the *Life of Swami Vivekananda* by his Eastern and Western disciples had a profound influence on him. It evoked in his mind a passionate admiration for Sri Ramakrishna and Swamiji. All of his other interests were drowned in the ocean of love for Sri Ramakrishna which now flooded his heart. His acquaintance with the Ramakrishna-Vivekananda literature, his close association with Tulasi Maharaj, and the continual inspiration and guidance he received from his own mother had made him ready to meet the great soul who was to be his guru.

Two of Sri Ramakrishna's illustrious disciples, Swami Brahmananda Maharaj and Swami Shivananda Maharaj (Mahapurush Maharaj) came to Madras in 1921 to inaugurate the new building of the Ramakrishna Mission Students' Home.

A few devotees from Calicut, including Balakrishnan's mother, had been waiting patiently for just this opportunity. Now, after a long wait, they would be able to receive initiation from Swami Brahmananda Maharaj. There was one hurdle, though. How would they communicate with Maharaj? These devotees spoke Malayalam, which Maharaj neither spoke nor understood. So they decided to take Balakrishnan along with them to act as the interpreter.

When they reached Madras, they received a cordial welcome from Swami Sharvananda Maharaj, president of Sri Ramakrishna Math in Madras (known popularly as Madras Math). Balakrishnan was deeply impressed by his first *darsan* of Swami Brahmananda Maharaj, who was the president of the Ramakrishna Order. Swami Brahmananda Maharaj was sitting on an easy chair with a hookah by his side. His face was calm and solemn, his eyes indrawn even when wide open. He did not speak much in that first meeting but gave them a few words of advice. Next they were ushered into the presence of Mahapurush Maharaj, who was then the vice-president of the Order. He was staying in what later became for many years the Holy Mother's shrine at Madras Math. Presently the room is to the right of the first floor prayer hall in the "Old Temple". In the early days it was a living room[1].

Balakrishnan found Mahapurush Maharaj strikingly different from Swami Brahmananda Maharaj. As against the forbiddingly solemn and elevating presence of Brahmananda Maharaj, he found in Mahapurush Maharaj a more human yet transcendentally glorious figure, endowed with an easily approachable personality. In later years, this is how Swami Tapasyananda Maharaj described him:

> Mahapurush Maharaj's face was wreathed in a gracious smile and his head nodded in an act of kind approval when we were introduced to him. He was in the pink of health. His face with somewhat high cheek-bones and elongated eyes gave it a slight Mongolian touch. It glowed with a reddish tinge and sense of carefree cheerfulness and universal benevolence.

Balakrishnan and those with him felt completely relaxed in the presence of Mahapurush Maharaj, who told them that repeating God's name with faith and devotion was in itself a potent means for spiritual development.

After meeting these two great monks, Balakrishnan and the devotees from Calicut went to see the new building of the Students' Home. Before returning to the guesthouse, they again came to the Math. Balakrishnan went inside to inform Tulasi Maharaj that they would be coming the next day. As Balakrishnan entered the Math gate, he saw

1. It was in this room the photos of Holy Mother, Swamis Vivekananda, Brahmananda, Ramakrishnananda were kept and worshipped.

an impressive scene. Swami Brahmananda Maharaj was standing with Mahapurush Maharaj and Tulasi Maharaj on his either side. It was an extraordinary sight to see these three spiritual giants together; it remained vivid in his memory all through his life.

Balakrishnan's mother and the other devotees from Calicut received [spiritual] initiation from Swami Brahmananda Maharaj. Balakrishnan's help was not necessary, as Brahmachari Gopal (who later became Swami Siddheswarananda) knew both English and Malayalam and he acted as the interpreter. Before leaving Madras, Balakrishnan's mother prayed to Maharaj that one of her

Tapasyananda Maharaj in his college days in Madras

sons should become a monk. Her prayer was evidently granted and bowing down at the feet of Maharaj, she joyfully took leave of him.

Balakrishnan returned to Calicut with his mother and the rest of the party. But a month or two later he came to Madras again for higher studies and joined the Presidency College. This gave him an opportunity to keep alive his contact with Madras Math. Raja Maharaj and Mahapurush Maharaj were still in Madras. Swami Sharvananda Maharaj had arranged for an elaborate puja[1] of Mother Durga in image. Sri Ramakrishna's nephew Ramlal—familiar to the readers of *The Gospel of Sri Ramakrishna*—was also present during the puja. The celebration was a grand success and attracted huge crowds. Swami Akhilananda, then a brahmachari, did the puja and Swami Sharvananda was the *tantradharak*. Balakrishnan attended the puja and had *prasad* on all the days. He saw Mahapurush Maharaj sitting daily before the Mother's image and reading the Chandi. This must have left a deep impression on Balakrishnan's mind, for he made this habit a part of his own life. Chanting passages from the Chandi became from then on an important ingredient of his daily devotions.

In April 1922, Swami Brahmananda attained *mahasamadhi* and the responsibility of guiding the Order fell on the shoulders of Mahapurush Maharaj. Soon after he became the president of the Order, Mahapurush Maharaj made a short trip to Madras and Balakrishnan was able to meet him again. It was during Mahapurush Maharaj's

---

1. Last four days (*sasti* to *dasami*) of *Navaratri*, Mother Durga is worshipped in Bengal. Following that tradition, puja was conducted in Madras Math also.

next visit, in December 1924, that Balakrishnan received [spiritual] initiation from him in the shrine of Madras Math. The day fixed for [spiritual] initiation happened to be Mahapurush Maharaj's birthday, which made the event even more memorable. Balakrishnan's younger brother, Achutha, who was also studying in Madras, received [spiritual] initiation on the same day.

The ceremony was short but impressive. The fervour with which Mahapurush Maharaj did *arati* to Sri Ramakrishna before giving [spiritual] initiation deeply impressed Balakrishnan. After the [spiritual] initiation, he prostrated at Mahapurush Maharaj's feet. The venerable and gracious figure of Mahapurush Maharaj, with hands uplifted in a mood of prayer and blessing, left a permanent imprint on his mind. Mahapurush Maharaj told him, 'Repeat the mantra regularly and you will find that *jnana* (knowledge), *bhakti* (devotion), *vairagya* (detachment) will automatically develop in you.'

Madras (1926–1940)

The following year, in 1925, Balakrishnan completed his M.A. In 1926 he joined the Order at the Students' Home. Two years later, Mahapurush Maharaj initiated Balakrishnan into the vows of brahmacharya and gave him a new name: Purnachaitanya. During this period, Balakrishnan received a letter from his mother complaining that he was neither seeing her often nor writing to her regularly. In reply, he wrote to her an inspiring letter[1].

Subsequently Balakrishnan was transferred from the Students' Home to the Math, which is the Order's Math

1. Letter no. 10, p 92.

branch in Mylapore, the same neighborhood in which the Students' Home is located. This Math is one of the oldest branches of the Order and was started in 1897 by Swami Ramakrishnananda, an eminent disciple of Sri Ramakrishna.

Around this time, a representative of the Maharaja of Mysore came to visit the Math and meet Mahapurush Maharaj. The evening *arati* was just over and he was sitting with Mahapurush Maharaj in the big hall. Balakrishnan was standing nearby. He heard Mahapurush Maharaj telling the gentleman, 'A man may be very wealthy and earn a big salary. But of what use is it ultimately? Death comes and swallows everything. The body is, after all, a *roga-mandira* (an abode of ailments).'

Another day, Balakrishnan approached Mahapurush Maharaj with some doubts on spiritual matters, especially meditation. He requested Mahapurush Maharaj to explain the meaning of the mantra he had given Balakrishnan at the time of [spiritual] initiation. Mahapurush Maharaj graciously explained it in a few simple words. Balakrishnan's next question was about certain psychological implications of meditation. In reply Mahapurush Maharaj spoke a few words and then stopped abruptly saying, 'You will get more light on these matters when you proceed with your *sadhana*.'

Years later, as a senior monk of the Order, Swami Tapasyananda Maharaj said:

> I do not know how much light I have got in the course of all these years, but I have learned that mind is a developing faculty. Ideas that seem significant at

Sri Ramakrishna Temple, Belur Math

one time cease to be so when more maturity comes. A genuine trust in the guidance of the inner Spirit is much more enlightening than the kind of trust people have in stereotyped forms and dogmatic assumptions. All the great teachers convey their lessons more through suggestions than lectures, putting more reliance on the reactive than the receptive role of the mind.

Maharaj followed the same pattern when he trained the monks and novices under his care. He would seldom give definitive answers to the questions raised in the after-dinner classes at Madras Math. It was certainly disappointing not to get a clear-cut answer to a clear-cut question. But with the passing of days, the monks understood that this was being done intentionally to make the questioner think on his own and reach the answer with his own effort. After all, what we get by our own effort becomes ours for all time; what is received from others can be lost unless it is made one's own through deep reflection. This was just one of the several ways Maharaj followed to train the monks of the Order. But we are getting ahead of our story.

Balakrishnan, now Br. Purnachaitanya, visited Belur Math in 1932. He received the *sannyasa* vows from his guru on the auspicious occasion of Sri Ramakrishna's birthday. He was given the name Tapasyananda, literally, "one who enjoys the bliss resulting from spiritual austerity". As he had received his *mantra diksa, brahmacharya diksa,* as well as *sannyasa diksa* from Mahapurush Maharaj, he used to say with great satisfaction that he was a disciple of Mahapurush Maharaj "in the fullest sense of the term".

Back in Madras, he continued with his work as the editor of *The Vedanta Kesari,* which he had taken over some months earlier as Br. Purnachaitanya. The editorials which Tapasyananda Maharaj wrote were thought-provoking and scholarly. In fact, the love for studies of spiritual subjects, which was present in him in seed-form from childhood, sprouted and flowered during this period of his life.

Swami Tapasyananda Maharaj also spent some months at the Mysore Study Circle[1], where advanced classes on Vedanta and other philosophies were held for a few, selected monks of the Order. This was a great opportunity and he made the best use of it. He was an admirer of Acharya Sankara. But he equally revered other Acharyas. Indeed, he considered every one of them great in their own way. It was this conviction of his that made him

1. Classes for monks of the Ramakrishna Order before the present Training Centre System was introduced.

study the lives and teachings of other Acharyas as well. The notes he made and the insights he arrived at, produced, years later, the scholarly book *Bhakti Schools of Vedanta*, which makes a systematic study of the lives and philosophies of Ramanuja, Madhva, Nimbarka, Vallabha, and Chaitanya. This was practically the last book he wrote.

Entrance to the Ramakrishna Mission Hospital, Sasthamangalam

Though he appreciated the intellectual flights of the Advaita philosophy, it was to Ramanuja's Visistadvaita that he was more drawn. This was understandable for, despite his scholarly and somewhat stern exterior, there pulsated within him a tender, devotional heart. His love for Visistadvaita was well-known in the Order. He never missed any opportunity to show the greatness of Ramanuja's philosophy and firmly defended it if anyone dared to make light of it in his presence.

Trivandrum (1940-1971)

Eight years later, in 1940, a new phase in Tapasyananda Maharaj's life started. The authorities of the Order wanted him to proceed to Trivandrum to take charge of the Ashrama there. The foundation stone of the Ashrama was laid by Swami Brahmananda Maharaj on 9 December 1916. Thereafter, the Ashrama activities were guided and developed by Tulasi Maharaj. Situated on top of the hill at Nettayam, the terraced building, solidly and elegantly built in granite, is a standing testimony to the grandeur of conception and dynamic spirit of Tulasi Maharaj.

Sometime in 1937, Tulasi Maharaj conceived the idea of starting some charitable activities for the poor living in that region. A plot of land with a decrepit building at Sasthamangalam was purchased and a small dispensary was started in the porch of the building. Tulasi Maharaj passed away in April 1938. The people who were managing the dispensary at Sasthamangalam made a fervent appeal to Belur Math to send a monk to guide the activities there. The three decades of remarkable development of the work that took place under the guidance of Tapasyananda Maharaj showed that the choice made by the Order's authorities was perfect. The austere habits of this young, hard-working swami were well-known to the authorities. So the letter sent to the management of the Ashrama specifically mentioned that the swami who was being sent was careless about his own comforts, so it would be the duty of the local devotees to look after him well.

After taking charge of the work in Trivandrum, Tapasyananda Maharaj slowly and systematically developed the medical activities of the dispensary. Adjacent plots of land were gradually purchased and new buildings constructed. A maternity ward was started in 1944 and the dispensary was converted into a hospital. Its first operation theatre was opened in 1948. A psychiatric wing was started in 1952 and a nursing school in 1962. The hospital celebrated its silver jubilee in 1965-66. To mark the occasion, a plan was drawn up to build a four storey building as an annexe, housing 100 beds, mainly for women and children, as also another operation theatre.

A separate building for the maternity ward, housing 16 beds, was constructed in 1967. By the time Tapasyananda Maharaj left Trivandrum in June 1971, a remarkable transformation had taken place in the Ashrama. In the place of a small piece of land with the old shed that existed at the time Maharaj took over in 1940, there were now several buildings spread over 1.56 hectares of land. The hospital had grown enormously–it now had an out-patient department, in-patient wards with 200 beds, well-equipped operation theatres, and many other departments. Due to rising costs of medicines and doctors' fees, the Sasthamangalam hospital became—and continues to be—the one place the poor could find the best medical attention without having to pay through their nose.

The growth of the institution from a tiny seed to a giant banyan tree is no doubt impressive. But how many people know the amount of sacrifice, self-denial, dedication, and faith that worked silently, watering and protecting the tender, growing plant? Everyone can see and appreciate a beautiful garden. But how many remember the hard labour of the gardener? Those who have seen Tapasyananda Maharaj in the early days at Trivandrum can never forget his tiny room in a thatched shed which served the purpose of his office in daytime and his living room at night. There was in it practically no furniture worth the name, except two benches which would be joined to form his bed at night.

Maharaj's food in Trivandrum was very simple; often only unripe papaya would be cooked for curry. Everything had to be measured to the last grain, for funds were scarce. His mother began sending a small allowance for his personal use, so that he could have at least the minimum nourishment necessary to maintain his health. He did not reject his mother's offer but used it silently to what he felt was more important. Taking just a token amount from it for his own use, he spent the rest of it for work among the socially deprived class in those days. He helped them in various ways. He made arrangements for their education and recruited, after due training, their daughters as nurses in the hospital. This improved the living condition of the those people there.

In November 1965, Tapasyananda Maharaj was elected a Trustee of the Ramakrishna Math and a member of the Governing Body of the Ramakrishna Mission. This additional responsibility required his visits to Order's headquarters at Belur Math at least thrice a year to attend the meetings of the Trustees. On his way to and from Calcutta he would stop at Madras, visit some big hospitals there, study their workings, and use the experience gained for improving the hospital at Trivandrum. He had acquired over the years a remarkable mastery over not only the administration of medical facilities but also over the science of medicine as well. His intellectual hunger and curiosity were inexhaustible. He would often be in the operation theatre, carefully observing a surgery in progress. Or one would find him at times in the laboratory, learning the use of the different equipments.

Alongside the Ashrama's medical activities, the religious and spiritual activities too were developed after Tapasyananda Maharaj came to Trivandrum. A shrine and prayer-hall came up in the hospital complex, and became a sort of extension of the Ashrama at Nettayam. In fact, as time passed, Sasthamangalam Ashrama became the hub of activities, and Nettayam Ashrama was made a sub-centre.

From 1952 onwards, Tapasyananda Maharaj regularly conducted *Gita* classes for devotees. He often visited the Divine Mother's temple in Kanyakumari, which held a special attraction for him. He was invited to many places to speak on spiritual topics. He was not an orator in the conventional sense of the term. But he spoke with conviction that can come only after deep thinking and experience. What impressed his audience was the originality of his approach in dealing with any subject. He had little patience with lecturers who went on rambling without having anything specific or worthwhile to say. He called such speeches a "*lathi* charge". His explanation for coining the term was simple. What do people do when police resort to lathi charge to control the crowd? They run away. Similarly, when a speaker begins to talk nonsense with no inclination to stop anytime soon, people in the audience begin to run away. And so, he would smile and say, 'I call it a *lathi* charge.'

The students of a Christian seminary in Trivandrum visited the Ashrama often, held discussions with Maharaj, and had their doubts clarified. His scholarship, integrity, simplicity, and spirituality won for him the respect and regard of one and all. Along with preaching work he continued his personal study of scriptures and prepared extensive notes which came in handy when his literary activities resumed after his return to Madras Math.

During the three decades that Tapasyananda Maharaj guided the activities of the Ashrama, he built brick by brick a grand edifice through his dedicated and painstaking effort.

The work of further expansion undertaken by his successors was rendered comparatively easy by the dynamism he generated and by the solid and sound state in which he left the Ashrama.

Madras Again (1971–1991)

In 1971, the call came. Tapasyananda Maharaj was asked to take charge of Madras Math, the centre where he had already spent more than ten years of his early monastic life. He was reluctant to leave Trivandrum. He was happy with the work there and did not feel inclined to start afresh in a new place. Madras, of course, was not really new to him, but he was then already 67 and felt it too late to take on fresh challenges. Transferring him from Trivandrum to Madras at that age was, he used to say, like "uprooting a fully grown tree and wanting it to take roots elsewhere". Initially he resisted, but he couldn't say no when he heard that Swami Vireswarananda Maharaj (Prabhu Maharaj), who was then president of the Order, had himself made the suggestion. Tapasyananda Maharaj had the greatest regard for Prabhu Maharaj and like a true soldier, he obeyed.

Thirty years earlier he had left Madras as a young monk—spirited, dynamic and confident. Now he returned, old in age, but with redoubled spirit, dynamism and confidence. This time he brought with him greater maturity born of experience. It didn't take him long to assess the needs and priorities of the Math. He first focused his attention on the publication department, which soon underwent a dramatic expansion. He noticed that while the Ramakrishna-Vivekananda literature in English was vast, there were very few books in Tamil and Telugu. He encouraged Swami Tanmayananda Maharaj to take up the Tamil translation of *The Gospel of Sri Ramakrishna*. The complete translation in three volumes was released in 1983-84. The first edition was sold out in record time. Many other books in Tamil and Telugu were brought out by the Math. He also supported the efforts of Swami Kamalatmananda to popularize the Tamil journal *Sri Ramakrishna Vijayam*, whose circulation rose from barely 2,000 to nearly 90,000 (now it has crossed 1,70,000) and an estimated readership of almost half a million people in Tamil Nadu and elsewhere. The journal now has the highest circulation among Tamil religious periodicals.

After coming to Madras, Tapasyananda Maharaj resumed his literary work which had practically stopped after his departure for Trivandrum in 1940. One of his first major projects was the translation of *Srimad Bhagavatam*, which he completed in 1976. Whenever he would sit at his table for translation he would be oblivious of the surroundings. His mind would be so absorbed that nothing could perturb it. Lightning struck a coconut tree in the Math one evening. The tree caught fire and everyone rushed there. When a swami reported the matter to Tapasyananda Maharaj, he coolly looked up, told the swami to call the fire brigade and resumed writing. The *Bhagavata* translation, available in four volumes, is one of his major contributions to the Order's literature. In subsequent years he translated many other important scriptures. Seeing that people had little patience and time to read big books, he wrote short biographies of Sri Ramakrishna, Holy Mother and Swami Vivekananda. These books became very popular.

Years earlier he had written a bigger biography of Holy Mother [perhaps in 1939 or 1940], the first one in English, which remains a favourite to this day. Another thing he noticed was that while many devotees had read booklets on and by Swami Vivekananda, very few of them had cared to study his entire *Complete Works* for lack of time or patience. So he came up with the brilliant idea of condensing and retelling in his own words the contents of those inspiring volumes. Three such books were published and are found very beneficial by sincere students of Swamiji's message.

Whenever new entrants came to join the Math as monastics, Maharaj interviewed them thoroughly. He was very particular that they have a healthy mind in a healthy body. Everyone was expected to do physical exercises daily. Once there was a theft at the Math. He suggested that it would be good if all the Math residents learnt Silambam (stick-wielding) which would be helpful for not only self-defence but also in times of theft. Sticks were purchased and the training began with full enthusiasm. After a few days, of course, everything cooled down. Maharaj probably knew this would happen. Nevertheless, he wanted the young brahmacharins to have a taste of martial arts.

But physical culture was not to take precedence over mental culture. So everyone was also expected to devote a few hours daily to serious study. Sanskrit scholars were engaged to train the novices in Sanskrit and scriptural study. Arrangements were made to help those who were weak in English. Maharaj was very keen that all possess a good knowledge of the English language. 'Butler-English won't take you anywhere,' he used to say. He probably had Indian butlers in mind! Occasional lectures were also organized on such varied subjects as physics, chemistry and medicine. The after-dinner reading class, presided over by Maharaj himself, was the grand finale of the day. There were lively discussions and roaring laughter during these gatherings.

The preaching activities of the Math were also expanded. Classes and discourses for devotees were organized even on week days and young monastics were encouraged to give classes. This served a dual purpose: it made religious teaching available to visitors throughout the week and simultaneously, it became a training exercise for young monks, who later became successful teachers of Vedanta. Maharaj also encouraged the founding of many centres which, though not officially affiliated to the Ramakrishna Math or Mission, are run on the Ramakrishna-Vivekananda ideology. He deputed monks to visit such centres spread all over Tamil Nadu for preaching work. It was primarily due to his efforts that one such centre in Madurai was formally affiliated to the Order.

Swami Tapasyananda Maharaj was easily accessible to all devotees. Anyone could walk into his office without any formalities and meet him. Devotees, even strangers, came to him with a variety of problems. He counseled them, encouraged them, and helped them get over their worries. Everyone returned with a new hope and a new strength after meeting him. He could come down to the level of the people he was talking to and lift them up. The suggestions he gave were very practical. He knew it was difficult for many to get over their problems through higher and subtler methods. They needed to "do" something. For instance, one day a young man came to him saying that he lacked courage and was always anxious and afraid of the future. Maharaj asked him to read Swami Vivekananda's books and advised him to visit regularly the Hanuman temple which was nearby and pray to Hanuman for strength. This benefited the young man immensely.

A devotee wrote to Maharaj that he wanted to bore a well and could Maharaj please suggest a date when the boring should start. The matter could have been dismissed by asking the devotee to consult an almanac or to meet an astrologer. But Maharaj gave a more reasonable solution. Why should you depend on an almanac when you have the freedom and the right to approach God directly? Can anything be stronger than faith and true devotion? Maharaj honoured conventions, but he refused to be a slave to them. His mind bubbled with ideas. So he wrote to the devotee that all the members of his family should take bath early in the morning and sit in a circle. In the centre of the circle they must place slips of paper with numbers from 1 to 31. With folded hands they should pray to God silently: 'O Lord, please guide us and help us find an auspicious date to begin this work.' Then they should meditate on God for a few minutes. The youngest member of the family, with eyes closed, should then pick up a slip and the work should be started on the date mentioned on the slip, with the firm conviction that the day was chosen by God Himself.

Maharaj loved children. Sometimes groups of children from nearby schools visited the Math. When they came to his office to pay their respects, he would give them sweets and candies, and tell them that they must do only four things: 'Pray well, study well, play well, and eat well.' Children from the nearby colony called Ramakrishnapuram visited the Math every week and he would talk to them and give them fruits and sweets.

In 1926, a Convention of the Ramakrishna Math and the Ramakrishna Mission was held in Belur Math to assess the work done until then and to plan for the future. Fifty-four years later, in 1980, a similar convention was organized in Belur Math, in which nearly 10,000 devotees from all over the world participated. Swami Tapasyananda Maharaj presided over one of the sessions at the Convention. His talk on "Practical Vedanta" was much appreciated by all the delegates.

When Maharaj visited Belur Math for a meeting of the Trustees in 1981, he fell ill there. He was taken to the Order's hospital, Seva Pratishthan, for treatment. A thorough medical examination there revealed that he had high blood sugar. The doctors prescribed strict diet regulations which Maharaj followed faithfully till the end.

At the hospital he had very little appetite. Besides, the Bengali preparations did not suit him. A swami from South India who was at that centre asked him if he would like to eat *idlis*. Maharaj's face lit up with joy and he said yes. It was difficult to get *idlis* in Kolkata. But a hotel was found where they were available and a few were immediately brought for him. He could, however, take only a half *idli*. When the swami asked him the reason, he said that the *idli* was not soft enough. Then the swami said, 'Don't worry, Maharaj, I shall myself prepare *idlis* for you.' From that day onwards, every day the swami himself collected all the ingredients and prepared nice, soft *idlis* for him. Maharaj was so happy and grateful for this "*idli* service" that he always looked on this swami with special affection. *Idlis* remained his favourite food all through life. He used to say that *idli* is most harmless. We do not know from where he got this information but he once said that *idlis* were first prepared during the reign of the great king Rajaraja Chola of 10th century CE.

In 1985, Swami Vireswarananda Maharaj, president of the Order, became seriously ill. Monks and devotees from all over India and even abroad flocked to Belur Math to meet him. When Tapasyananda Maharaj got the news, he too rushed there to meet him. Seeing Prabhu Maharaj's extremely weak condition, he said, 'Maharaj, we feel very sorry to see you like this.' Prabhu Maharaj smiled and told him, 'This is the way the body has to go!' What impressed Tapasyananda Maharaj most was that even in that condition, Prabhu Maharaj was extremely alert and fully conscious.

Returning to Madras, Tapasyananda Maharaj spoke with great feeling about this extraordinary feature of being able to keep the mind absolutely free and unaffected even when the body is afflicted by ailments and pain. He said, 'We have only read about the Cossipore days and the atmosphere in Sri Ramakrishna's room. When I was in Prabhu Maharaj's room in Belur Math, I was able to imagine how it must have been in Cossipore!' Tapasyananda Maharaj was reminded also about his own guru, Mahapurush Maharaj. He said:

> Even when Mahapurush Maharaj's health was broken down, he remained unaffected. A remarkable difference I noticed between Mahapurush Maharaj and an ordinary patient is that there was no depressing and melancholic atmosphere around his sickbed. His face remained always bright and cheerful in spite of a

sleepless nights due to asthmatic attack or high blood pressure. Mahapurush Maharaj's sickbed reminded me of his Great Master, Sri Ramakrishna, whose name he always repeated with tremendous faith and inspiration. Unless there was extreme detachment and absorption of the mind in God, how could his face remain bright and cheerful?

On 13 March 1985, Swami Vireswarananda Maharaj entered *mahasamadhi* with full consciousness. A pale of gloom descended upon all. He was succeeded by Swami Gambhirananda Maharaj as the president of the Order. Swami Tapasyananda Maharaj was elected a vice-president of the Order. Now a new type of responsibility fell on his shoulders, namely, to give spiritual initiation to earnest seekers of God. This naturally entailed an increased load of correspondence. Maharaj very patiently replied to the letters he received from the devotees and his disciples.

Once a disciple, who is a nurse in a big hospital in Calcutta, sent Maharaj a dhoti as a gift. He wrote back thanking her for it. But he added that he did not need such costly gifts. He advised her not to exhaust her limited resources in this manner. 'Use your money intelligently and sparingly for things which are essential,' he wrote to her.

That was also the attitude he himself held. Thrift was inborn in him. Moreover, his early days in Trivandrum had taught him the value of money and its proper utilization. While he objected to reckless expenditure, he did not mind when the money was spent for essential things. This was clearly observed when he wholeheartedly supported the purchase of modern and expensive equipments for the Math's printing press and dispensary. The quality of the publications automatically improved because of this. The dispensary too underwent a phenomenal growth during his time.

Maharaj was very "work conscious". Whoever went to meet him had to face in one form or other the question, 'How is your work going on?' Those who have lived with him for long feel that this was the way he made the visitor aware of the importance of systematic, goal-oriented work for success in life, spiritual or secular. Both laziness and aimless activity are harmful. Through his life of relentless work for the Order, Maharaj set an example not only to the monks of the Order but also to lay devotees and showed from his life the tremendously uplifting power of intense, dedicated and purposeful activity. When any such activity is backed by devotion to God and a true spirit of surrender at His feet, it can no more be distinguished from what is popularly called "spiritual practice".

In this connection, the profound dimension he gave to the concept of *guruseva* is worth noting. He said:

> The service of the spiritual teacher and living with him are considered the most important part of the spiritual discipline according to the Indian tradition. The *Gita* (18.67) goes to the extent of saying that spiritual teaching is not to be imparted to one who has not undergone this discipline of serving the teacher—*na ca aśuśrūṣave vācyam*. In the tradition of the Ramakrishna Order, there are certain spiritual conceptions that have led to a modification and extension of this great and wise rule sanctioned by age-old practice in India. Swami Vivekananda said that the Order he founded represented the physical body of Sri Ramakrishna, who is the real

Teacher of the Order, irrespective of the personality of the individual teachers through whom he functions. It is the Guru-seva of this wider conception that he expects his followers to perform as a part of their sadhana. In pursuance of this ideology, the monks of our Order get very little opportunity to stay with their individual teachers. They are sent to the far-flung centres of the Order to do all forms of work, physical and mental, with a sense of responsibility, detachment and dedication. It is this conception of Guru-seva that gives a special significance to the training in the Ramakrishna Order.

Swami Tapasyananda Maharaj's life was very disciplined. He maintained a strict routine of prayer, meditation, study, and work. It was inspiring to see him in his room, seated on the meditation-seat, hands folded near his chest, repeating with fervour in a deep, throbbing voice some of the devotional hymns to Sri Ramakrishna and other deities. He laid much stress on the daily chanting of such hymns, and to help sincere seekers, he translated a number of them and brought them together in a book

Kuala Lumpur, Malaysia, 1985

In Singapore

titled *Stotranjali*. His work at the office, correspondence, etc were very methodical and systematic. He was punctual in everything and did not like to see any time being wasted. He scolded his attendants if they were late for their allotted duties by even a few minutes. He wanted them to learn the value of time and the importance of punctuality.

Maharaj visited Singapore and Malaysia twice. He was much impressed by the cleanliness of Singapore and spoke highly about it after he returned to India. The lectures he delivered and the interviews he gave there left a deep impression on the minds of all. In India, he was invited to many places. Everywhere he went, he charmed and inspired the devotees by his scholarship, love, simplicity, austerity, and practicality. After becoming a vice-president of the Order, he visited Trivandrum twice—in March 1988 and August 1989. On the former occasion he spoke at a public meeting at the Vivekananda Institute, and on the latter, he gave a talk at the Ashrama. During both the visits, he gave initiation to several devotees. His friends, admirers and devotees from Trivandrum, where he had lived for thirty years, thronged eagerly to meet him.

On 19 February 1991, in the course of his usual evening walk in the verandah outside his room, he lost his balance and fell down. The cause: a sudden drop in his blood sugar. He was rushed to the Vijaya Health Centre with bruises on his face, upper lip and chin. On 25 February, he was discharged. This was the visible beginning of a gradual deterioration in his health. He had become much weak. So he decided to work in his own room and receive visitors there, rather than at the office which is a little away. Besides shouldering his responsibilities as the head of the Math, he continued to read proofs, correct manuscripts, and attend to correspondence with the help of his attendants.

In June, his health deteriorated further and he had to be hospitalized again. He was taken to the Vijaya Health Centre on 27 June and was discharged on 18 July. The specialists advised at least a month's bed rest for full recovery. He was being attended upon round-the-clock by the monks of the Math as also by some of his lay disciples. Besides, a number of doctors visited regularly, monitoring the progress. His health seemed to improve for a while, but on 31 August there was a setback: he had three attacks of heart failure. On 6 September he was admitted in the BSS Hospital, close to Madras Math, and was being treated under reputed specialists. He had difficulty in breathing on several days. After a detailed examination, the doctors confirmed the earlier diagnosis of TB. They said that the disease was silently spreading for past several years but could not be identified due to lack of symptoms. Now the symptoms were manifesting, but by this time considerable damage to the lungs had already taken place.

In spite of endless medical tests, medicines and injections, Maharaj remained characteristically unconcerned about the state of his health. His strong will-power and fearlessness became more prominent as the end neared. He used to say often that death is a natural process and there is nothing to be afraid about it. So he remained supremely detached, even when those around him were frantically trying to stop the gradual deterioration of his condition. As the news about his serious condition spread, monks and devotees from far and near came to see him. He made kind enquiries about all of them. He also asked for the details of some of the activities of the Ashramas from where the monks came. It was obvious that he knew that the end was near. About a month before his passing, he called his secretary, Swami Sukritananda, and asked him to write to all those who had registered their names for initiation to contact Belur Math. He gave away all the offerings that devotees had made.

On 24 September night, Maharaj slept very little. He was continually talking about bhakti and in particular, was explaining the meaning of the following verse from the *Bhagavata* (7.5.23):

श्रवणं कीर्तनं विष्णोः स्मरणं पादसेवनम् ।
अर्चनं वन्दनं दास्यं सख्यमात्मनिवेदनम् ।।

śravaṇaṃ kīrtanaṃ viṣṇoḥ smaraṇaṃ pādasevanam |
arcanaṃ vandanaṃ dāsyaṃ sakhyamātmanivedanam ||

> [The nine marks of devotion are] listening to the stories of the Lord, singing His glories, constant remembrance of the all-pervading Lord, serving Him in His devotees, ritualistic worship, constantly saluting the Lord, doing all work for His sake, friendship with the Lord, and complete self-surrender.

The following morning Maharaj went into a coma around 11.00. The last words he uttered were: 'I want peace, I want peace. Put me to bed. I want to sleep.'

On 28 September, at 5.30 a.m., he had breathing difficulty. As a last resort, the doctors decided to put him on a ventilator. There was a glimmer of hope in the initial stage when the report of blood-gas analysis indicated improvement. But as hours passed, he had frequent convulsions. On 1 October, the pulse became feeble and the blood pressure began to fall. On Thursday, 3 October 1991 at 6.32 p.m., when the evening *arati* to Sri Ramakrishna was in progress at the Math, Swami Tapasyananda Maharaj entered *mahasamadhi*. There was a remarkable glow of peace and fulfillment on his face. As the news spread and was also flashed on TV and broadcast on radio, streams of devotees, friends and disciples began to pour in at the Math. The body was kept in the Library building for *darsan*. There was continuous chanting from scriptures and devotional singing till 1.00 p.m. the next day, when the body was taken in a procession for the final rites.

A fortnight before, Maharaj had called a brahmachari and asked him, 'Are you singing *Ramnam* regularly on *Ekadasi* days?' He had also said to another monk, 'See that *Ramnam* is conducted at the Math regularly on every *Ekadasi*.' And it was on the following *Ekadasi-tithi*—which began on 3 October at 12.42 pm—that he chose to give up the body.

Truly spiritual people don't die. They leave behind a living memory of their great life. It continues to strengthen the weak, cheer the depressed, and inspire the seekers of God. Tapasyananda Maharaj wrote this in a letter to a devotee: 'All the great ones of the past have gone away. Giving up of the body at the end of their karma is for them only a release from the body-bound life of the earth into the infinite freedom and bliss of the Divine Life. So no one should take it in a spirit of depression or sorrow.' The correct way to honour the memory of this great monk of the Ramakrishna Order is to make an effort to imbibe into our own lives his qualities of dedication, service, and devotion.

Swami Tapasyananda Maharaj's Family Profile

Smt. Indira Krishnakumar[1]

Father : ***Sri Achutha Menon***
(1880-1906 A.D)

Achutha in Malayalam was derived from the Sanskrit word "Achyuta" (Imperishable). He belonged to Pannangat Tharavad (Family) in Cheruppulasseri, 17 km north of Ottappalam town of the present Palakkad District.

Maharaj's Father

Mother : ***Smt. Parukkutty Amma***
(1888-1971 A.D)

"Paru" is the colloquial Malayalam version of "Parvati". It is a common practice in Kerala to attach the word 'Kutty' (meaning 'child' or 'small') to male and female names to express affection for them. She hailed from Kizhakkepaat Palat Tharavad (Family) in Varod, 5 or 6 km from Ottappalam town. Both Cheruppulasseri and Varod belonged to the erstwhile Valluvanad Taluk (of Malabar), culturally, historically and linguistically very prestigious in terms of the Malayali ethos.

1. She is grand-daughter of Maharaj's aunt (mother's sister).

She was short and fair and after her husband's demise, wore very plain, fully white clothes, and was devoid of *bindi*, collyrium and jewelry. Like most of the women of Kerala of those times, her earlobes were also pierced and made fit for wearing huge chunky, golden 'thoda', a heavy kind of ear ornament. But having been widowed at an early age, she had to abstain from wearing it. Her face was unusually benign and expressive of her life-long penance. Her lips and tongue always moved as she used to do japa as "upamshu".

Brother: ***Sri K P Achutha Menon (1906-1984 A.D)***

Late Panangat Achutha Menon, father of Balakrishnan died in May or June of 1906 at the age of twenty six when Balakrishnan was two years and his mother eighteen years. When Parukkutti Amma became a widow, she was expecting her second child. The boy who was born after his father's demise was named as Achuthan, after his father. That is how Maharaj's younger brother came to be called K.P. Achutha Menon.

He studied intermediate in Wesley College, Madras, from 1923 to 1925. Thereafter he completed B.E. Civil Engineering in Bangalore Engineering College. Then he worked as an apprentice in Burma Mines, Tata Steel in Jamshedpur etc. This was followed by two years of study in the Indian Institute of Science, Bangalore. Thereafter, he joined the Water Works Department of Travancore State and retired as a Superintendent Engineer in the Government of Kerala in 1961.

During the period 1923-25, he, along with his brother Balakrishnan (who was then studying in Presidency College) would regularly attend Swami Saswatananda

Maharaj's classes on Sri Ramakrishna Leela Prasangha held on every Sunday in Madras Math.

On 23.12.1924, he was initiated by Mahapurush Maharaj [Swami Shivananda Maharaj] at Madras Math. Mahapurush Maharaj was ready to bestow on him the monastic vows after his studies, if he so wanted. But he entered into family life by marrying Sri Kumari Amma[1], daughter of Late Sri M.R. Narayana Pillai, a great devotee of Sri Ramakrishna and a disciple of Swami Brahmananda. Sri Achutha Menon's nick name was Appu. Sometimes, he would be formally called Appu Menon. He was a person of great integrity and was highly respected for his uncompromising adherence to principles and probity in personal and official life. His demise was earlier to Maharaj's.

His only son, Sri Udayanan[2] (also called Unni), born on 15 October 1946, studied in Ramakrishna Mission's High School at Puranattukara, Trichur (staying in the school hostel) for 8 years. He received *mantra diksa* from Swami Purushottamananda Maharaj of Vasistha Guha in 1961. He did his B.Com and worked as a manager in Vyasa Vidya Peeth, Palaghat. His wife, Smt. Prema, is a disciple of Swami Vireswarananda Maharaj. Sri Udayanan with his wife is now living in Sri Ramakrishna Nagar.

Ancestry:

Sri Panangat Achutha Menon's father's mother, that is, Maharaj's great grandmother, was a very pious lady. In her advanced years, she set out for Kasi (Varanasi) with her son,

---

1. Her reminiscences are published in this book (p 468).

2. He has helped in the preparation of this book by providing photos, diaries and other information.

that is, Maharaj's grandfather, and breathed her last at Kasi. For an elderly lady like her, belonging to the Nair community of Kerala in those times, her journey and stay at Kasi until the end was a singular act of courage and determination, considering the distance from Kerala to Kasi, the scanty transportation facilities, strain of the journey, her age and widowhood, the restriction posed on widows of those days, and the unfamiliarity of place and language. The travails of such a venture are beyond imagination. Sri K.P. Achutha Menon had made a note on 09.07.1979 in his diary for the information of his grandchildren (Sri Udayanan's children), Parvathi and Sarada. It says, '... Besides all this, you are the inheritors of another glory. My father's father's mother, in her old age, insisted on going to Kasi. This happened a hundred years ago. Those days, a journey to Kasi was very arduous. Her son who had great reverence and deep devotion towards his mother fulfilled her wish. Reaching Kasi, they had the darsan of Sri Kasi Viswanath and stayed there for a few days. When the question of returning came, she, being a staunch devotee, was unwilling to leave Kasi. The son was in a great dilemma as they had no relatives or friends in Kasi. The language too was different. He could not leave his beloved mother in those totally strange surroundings and return [alone].[1] He tried to prevail upon her repeatedly. All of no avail. He could not change the firm resolve of his heroic mother. Finally he made arrangements for her board and lodging for the rest of her life and returned home leaving her in Kasi. Among the Hindus, there is a belief that Sri Kasi Viswanath bestows 'mukti' on those

1. Probably it was around this time that his son, Panangat Achutha Menon, was born in Kerala. So he would have found himself in a difficult predicament on account of all these.

who breathe their last in Kasi. The meritorious great great grandmother of yours dedicated her life at the divine feet of Lord Viswanath and got herself merged therein. What firm and deep-rooted faith! The life of that heroic mother is a classic example of conquering death through surrender – surrender of everything at the feet of the Lord. Children, be proud that a portion of that courage and heroism is running in your veins.'[1]

History of Palat Tharavad :

Tharavad is a system of joint-family practiced by people of Kerala, especially Nairs and Thiyars. The relationships amongst *tharavads* were based on the matriarchal and marriage relationships. Each Nair *tharavad* had a unique name. As joint families grew and established independent settlements, the branches modified the names in such a way that even though they were distinct, the main *tharavad*'s names could be identified. In Nair communities, the *tharavad* name was identified through the mother's family.

The note in Sri K.P.A. Menon's diary says the following:

'In Kadathanad in north Malabar, there was a family called Palat. Before the conquest of Tippu Sultan, a branch of this Palat family, for some reasons, came down towards the South. One or two of them settled in Kozhikode (Calicut). Their descendants' group is now known as Chembil Palat. The rest of this branch settled around Mullemparambu Devi Temple near Chalisseri close to Kunnamkulam. Later they shifted to Chalavara, some ten

1. This is the translated version of the note originally written in Malayalam.

miles north west of Ottappalam. They built a good house there, worked hard, acquired property, constructed some temples and made generous donations for the pujas and temple rites. According to the custom of those days, they helped a namboodiri family also. Since they were educated according to the standards of the day and they were leading a moral and ethical life, the people of the place respected and loved this branch of the ancient Palat family that had taken roots in the new place Chalavara.'

A branch of this Palat family later moved from Chalavara to Varod. This happened in the latter half of the 19th Century. Such branches are called 'Thai Vazhi' meaning 'the mother's route' and referred to as 'Thavazi' in colloquial parlance.

Smt. Parukkutty Amma's mother's father (Maharaj's great grandfather) was Kizhakkepaat Rama Krishna Menon. He was known as Sub-judge Krishna Menon as he was the first Malayali to occupy that position in the judiciary during British governance. He married Palat Ammunni Amma. He was a great devotee of Devi Mookambika and was said to be the recipient of exceptional grace of the Goddess. He worked in Mangalore, Karnataka, and was deeply devoted to Mookambika at Kollur and served Her to his heart's content. He generously donated ornaments for the Deity and instituted funds for daily feeding of the brahmins at the temple. He passed away in 1897.

The world renowned painter Raja Ravi Varma is said to have visited Mookambika Temple in 1870 and while returning met Sub-judge Krishna Menon. Raja Ravi Varma had made a portrait of Sub – judge Krishna Menon, his wife Palat Ammunni Amma and three of their children.

Kizhakkepaat Palat Krishna Menon's Family: Art by Raja Ravi Varma

One of the children appearing in the portrait was Maharaj's maternal grandmother Kizhakkepaat Palat Lakshmi Amma.

In the Nair families, the lineage is traced through women of the family. A person is known by his mother's family name. The male members of the family had to use the family resources for the welfare of their sisters' children and other members of the *tharavad* rather than for their own children who anyway belonged to their mother's families and came under the care of their maternal uncles. Sub-judge Krishna Menon, having had his own income through the government job he held, had some personal wealth at his disposal. He had the unique distinction of setting up *tharavad* houses not only for his sisters but also for his own progeny. He was born in the Kizhakkepaat family of Kizhur, 12 km from Ottappalam. After he grew up, he moved with his sisters to a place called Sri Krishnapuram and set up a huge family house there. This thavazhi acquired the status of a *tharavad*. He made extensive arrangements for the worship of Devi in the house and set up a temple-like annex where meticulous ritualistic puja of the family deity, feeding of the brahmins and the poor were carried out regularly and perfectly. After he married Ammunni Amma of Palat at Chalavara and begot children, he built for them a splendid palatial house in the midst of lush green fields with picturesque beauty in Varod. This branch of the Palat family at Varod came to be known as Kizhakkepaat Palat. It was unusual for a *tharavad* to be identified with its male progenitor's family name. But such was the respect and influence Sub-judge Krishna Menon had. The first child to be born in this house at Varod was Parukkutty Amma, Maharaj's mother. She was the granddaughter of Sub-judge Krishna Menon (Lakshmi's [his daughter's] daughter).

Balakrishnan was born and spent his childhood in this house. It was for this reason that even though he should have actually belonged only to Palat Tharavad, he was identified with Kizhakkepaat Palat family and came to be known as Kizhakkepaat Palat Balakrishna Menon.

The *tharavad* house had elaborate arrangements for the worship of the Devi, Siva in form of a hunter, and other minor deities. Apart from the worship room in the main family house, there was a temple – like annex called '*matham*' – where Brahmin priests conducted the puja. Mullemparambil Devi was the family Deity. In the *matham*, there were eight or ten *salagramas, sivalinga* made of green coloured stone, and four *Valampuri*[1] conches. All these were

1. A conch with very rare reverse turning spirals.

procured by Sub-judge Krishna Menon from northern India. Besides, there were also the idols of Shanti Durga and Lord Ayyappa. Parukkutty Amma's devotion to these deities knew no bounds as is evident from the beautiful poems she had composed on them. No wonder young Balakrishnan too was steeped in devotion. His childhood games were imitation of pujas and rituals!

The *tharavad* properties were divided in the 1940s. The *tharavad* house went to the branch of Parukkutty Amma's sister Kunhi Lakshmi Amma and her descendants. Palat family got huge property of extensive lands. Smt. K.P. Parukkutty Amma, after the division of property, shifted to 'Tulasi Cottage' of Ottappalam. She lived there until she bought a house in Sri Ramakrishna Nagar in mid 1950s. This house was close to Ramakrishna Niranjan Ashram (founded by Swami Nirmalananda Maharaj) and the Sarada Ashram. This proximity to Sri Ramakrishna Ashram gave immense happiness and gratification to Parukkutty Amma. The house was named 'Sarada Mandiram'.

The prayer room in this house was like the shrines of Ramakrishna Ashramas. Along with the photos of Sri Ramakrishna, Sri Sarada Devi etc., a *Valampuri* conch obtained during the division of the property is also worshipped there even today. After her death, Sri Achutha Menon and his wife Smt. Kumari Amma continued the tradition with the same zeal. Today, their son, Sri Udayanan and daughter-in-law, Smt. Prema (a member of the Palat family and a disciple of Revered Swami Vireswarananda Maharaj), continue the tradition.

A Note on Swami Tapasyananda's Mother
(Smt. Parukkutty Amma)

Smt. Indira Krishnakumar

Born in January 1888 (on 8th Makara, 1063 by Malayalam Calendar)

Father: Vadakke Karimpatta Krishna Menon, an Advocate.

Mother: Kizhakkapat Palat Lakshmi Amma.

Maharaj's Mother

Smt. Parukkutty Amma lost both the parents in mid 1890s when she was seven or eight. Both the parents died in the same year. She got married to Sri Pannagat Achutha Menon in 1902 when she was 14. Their first child Balakrishnan, later Swami Tapasyananda Maharaj, was born in 1904. From the time her husband died in 1906, to the time her elder son Balakrishnan became a Brahmachari in 1928, she had undergone great sufferings. The first ten years after her husband's demise was a period of intense mental agony. Her son, Sri Achutha Menon records: 'My mother was born into a rich and reputed Nair family. But she lost both her parents in the same year when she was seven or eight. She got married at the age of 14 and destined, so to say, to become a widow at the age of 18. The onus of upbringing the two children fell on her young shoulders. The severe calamities that befell her were a bolt from the blue. She had absolutely no money at her disposal personally. She had great mental strength and firm faith in God. Still her mind was scorching in the heat of the sorrows. She could not find joy in anything. The only solace came from the infantile play and pranks of her tender children...

'Until she was 27 years old, days were passed without any mental peace. At this point of time, she first met Sri Tulasi Maharaj [Swami Nirmalananda Maharaj] and through his association, Rakhal Maharaj [Swami Brahmananda Maharaj] and Mahapurush Maharaj [Swami Shivananda Maharaj]. She had the good fortune to touch their holy feet. She also received *mantra diksa* from Rakhal Maharaj.'

Relief came to her around 1915. From the year 1915, great opportunities to meet the stalwart disciples of Bhagavan Sri Ramakrishna came her way. She was fortunate enough to meet Raja Maharaj, Mahapurush Maharaj and Tulasi Maharaj during this time. Further she had the precious opportunity to receive *mantra diksa* from Raja Maharaj in 1921. Also, her young sons got initiation from Mahapurush Maharaj in the year 1924. These fortunate developments were rich compensation for her otherwise gloomy life.

Although young and in bereavement continuously, she was keen to read and contemplate on Ramakrishna literature. She was ardently wishing to meet someone who had been associated with Sri Guru Maharaj. At this juncture, she went to Calicut with her sons to live under the care of her brother, Palat Krishna Menon, an Advocate, who was at that time practising law at Calicut. He was living there with his family. She went there to give good education to her children. They studied in the Zamorin's High School, Calicut from 1915 to 1919. The school is close to the famous Mahadeva Temple of Tali.

They were living in a rented house in Chalapuram in Calicut between the post-office and Achuthan Girls' High School. This was close to the Zamorin's High School where her children Balan (Balakrishnan) and Appu (Achuthan) studied. The rented house was owned by Sri Kozhippurath Appu Menon, an advocate. Smt. Appu Menon was a staunch devotee and disciple of a Raja Maharaj and a relative, a close friend, and coeval of Smt. Parukkutty Amma. Their children and Parukkutty Amma's children Balan and Appu were schoolmates. So Balan and Appu could move freely in their house. Their house was close to the house where Smt. Parukkutty Amma was living. It was in their house that she first had the *darsan* of Swami Nirmalananda Maharaj.

Sri Achutha Menon, Smt. Parukkutty Amma's second son, has recorded the details of their meeting with Swami Nirmalananda Maharaj as below:

'........ For me, my affectionate mother was everything to me on this earth. Since my father died before I was born, I had no opportunity to meet him. Till her end, my mother nurtured and protected me. Bestowing love, chastising and reprimanding, she reared and nourished me. She gave me all that was necessary for me to grow in this world. Among all the things that shaped me, the greatest was her flawless life. Steadfast adherence to the Chosen Ideal, selflessness and firm, unshaken faith in God were her special traits. She alone made our lives spiritually rich. I still remember I must have been nine or ten years old and my brother eleven or twelve. My mother, brother and I were living in my uncle's home in Calicut. One night, after my uncle and his children had gone upstairs to bed, my mother approached us and said, 'Kids, please take this. This is the leftover of what had been offered to Maharaj [Swami Nirmalananda Maharaj]. This is *prasad* of a great soul.' She unfolded a leaf-packet containing some food. It was the impact of this event that made my brother, then Balan or Balakrishnan, become the president of the SRK Ashrama of Mylapore, Madras, today. Yes, it is only because of the merit of her thinking that my brother and I had the good fortune to make entry into what can only be described as 'Sri Ramakrishna Bhakta Mahamandala'. My mother is my '*pratyaksha daivam*'. If I am to take birth again, my prayer is that I should be born to her only. The debt we owe to our parents, particularly to our mother, can never be repaid…'[1]

Sri Achutha Menon recalls in a note he made in 1973 when he was 67 years old that when his mother brought home the *prasad* as narrated above, both Balan and Appu were about to slip into a slumber. Time was past 9 p.m. The mother came, lantern in one hand and *prasad* in the other and woke them up. 'Children, this is *mahaprasad* of a Mahapurush.' He recalled that they ate *prasad* with much gusto. But, according to him, it was later that the potency and possibility of the divine blessing that lay hidden in that moment was realised. In retrospect, it is clear that she was waking them up to their spiritual awareness, shedding light

1. Sri Achutha Menon recorded this in Malayalam in 1978, i.e., seven years after his mother's demise and six years before his own demise.

on the path they had to tread and giving them sustenance for their forward journey. The wakeup call, the lamp and the *prasad* had greater significance than what met the eye.

Sri Achutha Menon's notes continue: 'Those were days when my mother, afflicted by various woes of *prarabdha* was living with a burning heart, not knowing what peace of mind meant. She was yearning to see a disciple of Sri Ramakrishna and was intensely praying for it to occur at least once in her joyless life. Not a day passed without that prayer. Those were days when young women were not expected to step out of their homes, except under the care of their parents, husbands or grown-up sons. So she was not very hopeful of this wish ever materialising.'

However, who can ever understand or predict the sportive plan of the Lord whose compassion for His devotees is infinite! Is it not extremely surprising that when this devotee was longing for such an opportunity, God sent one of His disciples to the very next house to where she was living most unexpectedly? And the lady of that house was Smt. Parukkutty Amma's best friend. She had invited her (the latter) to join the *satsang*. Next day, the children, Balan and Appu, went to meet and pay obeisance to Tulasi Maharaj. First, they had a purificatory dip in the pond within the compound; Maharaj was sitting on an easy-chair and conversing with someone. The young boys went to him and prostrated themselves before him. He greeted them with a smile and asked them a few things about them. He placed his hands on their shaven heads, gave them sugar candies to eat and talked to them for some time. That was how that meeting went off. After that, till Maharaj left Calicut, they would daily go there to pay respects. From that time onwards, Sri Achutha Menon gratefully acknowledges, there was a change in their lives. In his diary, he has recorded the following:

'...we touched the divine feet of Maharaj and became recipients of his blessings. From that day, we got linked to the Ramakrishna family. Day by day, that tie became stronger and stronger.

'Now I feel, that was the greatest and richest inheritance that we got in life. Is it possible for a mother to earn greater riches and pass on the same for her children?... That Balan, who was a child then, is today the president of Sri Ramakrishna Math, Madras. Under the name of Swami Tapasyananda, he is serving as a humble servant of Bhagavan. Balakrishnan, that lad who was modest in nature, laconic in speech, and confined to Palat Tharavad of Kerala, is today a main speaker and scholar of the Ramakrishna Order. He is today known as a recluse occupying a place of love and admiration, accepted by one and all, sannyasis and devotees.'

From the letters of those times, it appears that Smt. Parukkutty Amma used to go to Palat Tharavad at Varode leaving her children at Calicut in her brother's house. The children continued to study in Zamorin's till 1919.

Smt. Parukkutty Amma was the first child to be born in the new *tharavad* house of Kizhakkapat Palat, a 'Thaivazhi', i.e. branch of the ancient Palat House. She had one elder sister, three younger sisters, and a brother who was elder to her. True to the position of the first born in the new set-up, she was the first one to get associated with the Ramakrishna Order. She even exerted an influence over her maternal grandmother, Smt. Ammunni Amma, to bring her in close association with the Ramakrishna Order. It was Smt. Parukkutty Amma, who was motherless, who tended and took care of her old maternal grandmother till her end. Twice in Ottapalam town, Tulasi Maharaj was given a reception in a public place, viz., the Kamalalaya printing press. At least once this was hosted by Smt. Ammunni Amma, all under the influence of her grandchild, Smt. Parukkutty Amma. Kamalalaya Printing Press was owned and managed by Sri Kulakunath Raman Menon, who was Smt. Parukkutty Amma's sister's husband. He later took sannyas with the monastic name, Swami Amalananda. Smt. Parukkutty Amma's total devotion to Swami Nirmalananda Maharaj must have certainly created an impact on him. The credit of bringing a large number of her relatives under the "Sri Ramakrishna Umbrella" belongs to her.

After Smt. Parukkutty Amma met Swami Nirmalananda Maharaj, she established contact with Belur Math. She used to send parcels of 'Kali adakka', processed arecanuts to Belur Math. This was a customary gift among aristocratic families of Kerala. The letter she received from Belur Math, Raja Maharaj, Mahapurushji, Swami Saradanandaji Maharaj, etc. from 1918 to 1925 show how keen she was to send gifts to Belur Math. In one way or the other, she wanted to keep the channel of grace from Belur Math open and to be a rich recipient of letters and acknowledgements from the disciples of Sri Ramakrishna which had their holy touch.

Smt. Parukkutty Amma's longing to see Sri Sarada Devi, the Holy Mother, knew no bounds. Her correspondence with Swami Nirmalananda Maharaj and Swami Purushothamananda Maharaj of Vasistha Guha on this subject speaks volumes of this. She expressed her desire to meet Holy Mother, despite the great restrictions placed on her movements by the social customs which were heavily tilted against widows of those times. But in spite of all that, she was all set to go to West Bengal in 1920. But Mother's illness took a serious turn and strict restrictions were placed on visitors. In June 1920, Tulasi Maharaj wrote to her from Bangalore Math and advised her to wait as visiting the Holy Mother was severely restricted. Smt. Parukkutty Amma waited. But it was too late. God had willed it otherwise. The Holy Mother breathed her last on 20 July 1920. On receiving the news of Holy Mother attaining *mahasamadhi*, the grief and sense of loss she felt was indescribable.

And with this, her desire to take [spiritual] initiation from Raja Maharaj, the spiritual son of the Master, grew intense. When she learnt in 1921 that some people from Kerala had gone to Madras and received spiritual initiation from Raja Maharaj, she could wait no longer. This time her wish was fulfilled. Some of her relatives were going to Madras from Calicut in Mangalore-Madras Mail. Along with them she too travelled to Madras. She and her son, Appu, boarded the train at Ottapalam. She was able to visit the Math at Mylapore quite a few times. And her long-cherished dream of getting spiritual initiation was fulfilled. Receiving *mantra diksa* from Raja Maharaj, one could not have asked for anything more. Contented, she returned to Kerala. Sri Achuthan Menon, her son, who was also present in the team, has given a graphic description of that memorable occasion when they first met Raja Maharaj. That day, Tulasi

Maharaj was also present in Madras Math. Tulasi Maharaj asked them to go to the Shrine and wait after returning. Saying that he would ascertain Raja Maharaj's wish, Tulasi Maharaj went into the inner quarters of the Math. After sometime, they were ushered into an inner room, into the august presence of Revered Swami Brahmananda Maharaj. She recalled later: 'Rakhal Maharaj, held in great reverence by world conquering Swami Vivekananda, that spiritual son gifted to Sri Ramakrishna Deva by Mother Kali, was sitting on an easy chair. Maharaj was doing japa with eyes closed. He seemed to be unaware of what was going on around. Sri Tulasi Maharaj stood silently on one side like Mahavir, the best and best of bhaktas before Sri Rama Deva. Tulasi Maharaj, after sometime whispered something in Bengali into Raja Maharaj's ears. Must have been about our arrival. After sometime Maharaj, with a lot of effort, opened the eyes a bit and saw everyone. All of us prostrated before him. The women in the group sat down on the floor. The monks spoke to each other. Maharaj asked my mother and others to open their palms and show. Maharaj was frequently saying, 'Accha! Accha!' It looked as though an infant had been woken up from its sleep. All of us felt that Maharaj had taken a lot of effort to drag his mind from a higher plane to the normal surroundings. When Maharaj opened his eyes to look around, it was as though he had just come down from a far-away world. After indulging in conversation, for a while he would again shut his eyes, forgetful of everything around. Not even a shadow of show or forced response crossed that calm and solemn face. Maharaj agreed to give them spiritual initiation. A date for that was fixed. That meeting would have lasted for a short spell of fifteen to thirty minutes. But it was unforgettable. If it is difficult for worldly people like us to detach our minds from the surroundings, it was more difficult for Maharaj to take away his mind from the realm where his consciousness was wandering and bring it down to the level of the world we know of.'

During this trip, Smt. Parukkutty Amma got a lot of time to sit at the holy feet of Mahapurush Maharaj also. About the impact of the great blessing his mother had in receiving *mantra diksa* from Raja Maharaj, and receiving benedictions from Mahapurush Maharaj and Sri Tulasi Maharaj, Sri Achutha Menon writes:

'My mother's heart which was parched with sorrow became calm because of this contact with the three great souls who were the disciples of Sri Ramakrishna Deva, the Supreme among Incarnations, the *Avataravaristha*. This can be likened only to the transformation of the Kadamba tree on the banks of River Yamuna which had dried and gone dead under the impact of the poison of serpent Kalia and which revived and gave rise to sprouts when Bhagavan Sri Krishna's feet fell on it.'

Her friends and well-wishers instantly recognised the sudden and happy turn in her destiny. Some people congratulated her even long after the event. As for the family members, even the children of the fourth generation recall this with pride even today.

In her letter dt. 4th Dec., 1925, Smt. Kalyani Narayana Menon (wife of Sri P.N. Menon, chief Judge of the Chief Court of the Govt. of Cochin and daughter of Sri O. Chandu Menon, the famous writer and author of the path-breaking Malayalam novel "Indu Lekha") who was a well-wisher of her wrote to Smt. Parukkutty Amma: 'Extremely happy to note that you got the *darsan* of Swami Brahmananda and that you are the recipient of the *upadesa* of that great soul. God gave you worldly sorrows. But in the inward life, He has taken you to a very high position. For this, one should be the subject of the infinite grace of the Lord of the universe. That is what makes me very happy.'

This was an apt description. For Smt. Parukkutty Amma, it was a sudden transition from the depth of despair to the heights of bliss, from deep depression to the acme of joy.

In April 1922, she got a letter from Sri Kulakunnath Sankara Menon, later Swami Amalananda, dt. 11-4-1922, Tuesday, which announced the sad demise of her guru, Raja Maharaj. To quote from that letter, 'Yesterday, at 9 p.m., Sri Maharaj attained *mahasamadhi*. Perhaps this news has reached you. Needless to say how many people have been immersed in grief.'

When Holy Mother, Sri Sarada Devi, attained *mahasamadhi*, Smt. Parukkutty Amma was inconsolable. But now she had the solace that she has luminous memories of that great soul, the spiritual son of Sri Guru Maharaj. She had the *mantra* that Raja Maharaj gave. And God had bestowed on her the perseverance, will and devotion to hold on to it without a moment's respite. She used to do japa so constantly that in her later life her lips used to move incessantly. The habit became deep-rooted that japa was as natural to her as breathing.

Now what remained was the fulfilment of the prayer that she had made when she bowed down before Raja

Maharaj, that she be able to dedicate one of her sons at the feet and service of Sri Guru Maharaj. Soon the decks got cleared for this. Both her sons got spiritual initiation from Mahapurush Maharaj on 23-12-1924. The rest is a part of the hallowed life-story of Swami Tapasyananda Maharaj. The lesser known aspect is that Sri Achutha Menon, her second son was *'rishitulya'* [equivalent to a rishi]. His honesty, simplicity, adherence to scruples, surrender before god – everything showed that he was a true son of Smt. Parukkutty Amma, and a true brother of his Balettan whom he adored. In their conduct, Smt. Parukkutty Amma's sons exceeded her expectations.

In 1928, along with her son Balan, she went on a pilgrimage. About this trip, Sri Achutha Menon wrote as follows:

'... After some days my mother was able to go on a pilgrimage, accompanied by her son Balan, to holy places like Belur Math, Kasi, Gaya, Puri and Rameswaram. She had the good fortune and mental courage to dedicate her son at the feet of Swami Shivananda Maharaj. How many mothers, who have reared their children, expecting several worldly gains, have the good fortune to offer their beloved sons at the feet of the guru and pray with an overflowing heart, 'Kindly lead him to *sannyasa ashram*'! My mother lived, spending most of her time in the prayer room, in japa and meditation. Until her last, she had the full faith that, come what may, God is there to give shelter always. Financially her position improved. She was able to give large donations to religious activities. When I think of how we had so much of good fortune, I am reminded of what happened one night, 65 years ago. How strong and pure was the potency that lay hidden in the blessings that came to us in the shape of that *prasad*! How sacred, how divine!'[1]

Smt. Parukkutty Amma kept up the blessed association with Swami Nirmalananda Maharaj till her end. Sri Ramakrishna Niranjan Ashram at Palapuram (this locality is now known as Sri Ramakrishna Nagar, served by Sri Ramakrishna Nagar Post Office), Ottapalam, was founded by Swami Nirmalananda Maharaj. He consecrated and opened this Ashrama on 10 December 1926. Somebody gifted him this land for this purpose. And he started the construction with Rs.1000/- from Smt. Parukkutty Amma, Rs.500/- from Swami Amalananda and another Rs.500/- from Sri Ramakrishna Ashrama, Quilandy. She was a great source of support for the Namboodri women of the area suffering from certain social customs. Aristocratic Nair families of those days had large pieces of lands in their possession. The female members had a share for themselves and their children. They also got gold and jewellery by way of inheritance. But seldom did cash flow into their hands unless they had supportive husbands, brothers or uncles.

Although Smt. Parukkutty Amma had financial problems when her sons were growing up, she never wanted them to be mere bread-winners. She was contributing munificently to good causes. With the partition of the joint family i.e. Palat Tharawad, in the age of fourteen, she shifted from Varode to Ottapalam town. The name of the house she lived was called 'Tulasi Cottage'. Later, in 1950s, she bought a property in Sri Ramakrishna Nagar, near Niranjan Ashram. The house was named 'Sarada Mandiram'. She

1. Recorded by Sri Achutha Menon on 22 November 1980.

was keen to live near Niranjan Ashram and Sarada Ashram of Palappuram. In this house 'Sarada Mandiram', she lived till she breathed her last on 9 May 1971. Her life was one of long sadhana. Her house was like an Ashram.

Her end came at 11 p.m. on 9 May 1971. Thus came to an end a life of *tapasya*. No, a life of *tapasya* can never end. The vibrations it releases will always remain creating and promoting cosmic welfare.

Her last journey was to the banks of Nila where Swami Nirmalananda Maharaj was cremated. She was also consigned to flames on the bank of the same river, at a spot close to Swami Nirmalananda Maharaj's *samadhisthal*.

Condolences poured in. A large number of messages were received from sannyasins and householders. Many of them reiterated that she was an ideal mother who gave birth to a *tapasvi*. Many of them said that the sannyasi son sanctified her and her race. 'Kulam pavitram, Janani krithartha!' they said.

Both are true. Truer is the fact that the culture of our land, Bharata, is like an ever-flowing river. And occasionally in the flow appear beautiful lotus flowers. Here what we witness is the blossoming of two such beautiful, blemishless, impeccable flowers, one transmitting its beauty to the other and the latter adding to the hues of the former – the mother promoting and nurturing the son and the son sanctifying the mother and her clan, and both of them remaining as shining models for posterity.

A Note on Swami Tapasyananda's Brother
(Sri K.P. Achutha Menon)

Smt. Indira Krishnakumar

Sri Achutha Menon received spiritual initiation from Mahapurush Maharaj, Swami Shivananda Maharaj, along with his brother on 23.12.1924 at Madras Math.

While studying in Bangalore, Sri Achutha Menon was put up in the YMCA at Bangalore. Every Sunday, he would go to Ramakrishna Ashram, Bangalore. He would return only at dusk or after dinner. Thus he had opportunities to go to the Ashram frequently. Sri Menon writes, 'When I went to the Ashram at Basavanagudi on 29.10.1926, I found Mahapurush Maharaj and Tulasi Maharaj engaged in conversation. I prostrated myself before both the monks. The Ashram was conducting Kali Puja on 30.10.1926. That day also I went to the Ashram and partook of the *prasad* at noon along with the other devotees.

'04.11.1926 was Deepavali. I went to the Ashram in the morning itself. Swami Siddeshwarananda [Maharaj] was also present. (He later established an ashram in France and attained *mahasamadhi* there). Some other devotees also had come to the Ashram that day. Mahapurush Maharaj was talking with them many things about Sri Guru Maharaj. He told, "Bhagavan was living in a state of Supreme Bhava, reciting God's name day and night. We three disciples were living together with Bhagavan. We used to be given lots of good food at noon. At night, only light food was given. From among the articles of food received for noon, Sri Guru Maharaj himself would pick up and keep apart the items for night. He used to keep a watch over all our activities. At 3 'o' clock in the morning one could listen to Bhagavan singing hymns, brimming over with devotion, in an extremely sweet way. We also would participate in the *nama japa*. At daybreak, we would take bath. Thereafter, also *nama japa* and meditation only. What is the inner meaning of his words and actions, we did not understand at that time. It is only now, much later, that we realize the truth in that.

"The 'Leela' of the Mother of the Universe is indescribable. You will have the good fortune to see her most wonderful sportive ways in future. Some devotees wrote in the newspapers that an Avatar Purusha has been born. Hearing that Sri Guru Maharaj said, 'What all is written in the newspapers! These things should not be written now. The people who are immersed in gold and lust will not understand the truth of this. Let this body disappear. The Mother's wonderful *leela* will manifest. Let the pot of nectar that is this body shatter and let the nectar in it spread all around. Most wonderful will be the results.' We could not understand the truth of this at that time. Look, Sri Ramakrishna Ashram is rising up in America, nearly twenty thousand miles from here. Their customs, food, ways of living, are all different from ours. People there generally take us as black skinned and poor and dislike us for that. But today they are ready to sacrifice everything, nay, even their lives, for the sake of Sri Guru Maharaj and the institution. From America two lady devotees came to Calcutta two years ago. When Sri Guru Maharaj's name fell on their ears, their eyes shed tears. What devotion! Sitting on the banks of the Punya Theertha, River Ganga, they received 'Mantropadesha' from Swami Saradananda. We did not realize the greatness of Sri Guru Maharaj. Our position can be likened to that of Arjuna. Arjuna said, 'Oh Bhagavan Krishna, like a friend I played, laughed, slept, talked and reverted to your company. Those days, I did not even for once think of your highly elevated position from the point of view of soul or your glory. But now, in the middle of this terrible battlefield Kurukshetra, in the midst of hordes of over-bearing, arrogant elephants trumpeting in a terrifying manner, lakhs and lakhs of niggling horses charging and approaching like huge waves of the sea, great warriors wielding divine weapons and countless agitated soldiers, ready and impatient to die and kill, you have removed the veil of maya and shown your real form, Viswaroopa to me.' Today we are not seeing Bhagavan's erstwhile form. Today we are seeing his Viswaroopa. Today people of different castes, religions, countries and races unitedly work for Sri Guru Maharaj, forgetting all their differences, with brotherly love.

"Two days before the *mahasamadhi,* Swami Vivekananda said, 'Before long this body will disappear, but I will continue to work for several centuries. I cannot sit quiet. This work will continue. Nobody can stop or put hurdles in the flow of that power.'

"How many times had Swami Vivekanandaji put Sri Guru Maharaj to test! Still Swamiji could not believe that he was an avatar. Swamiji went to the room when Sri Guru Maharaj was lying, ailing and extremely weak, two days before his *mahasamadhi*. Even at that time this doubt was lurking in his mind. Because of the severity of the illness, Sri Ramakrishna Deva had not even talked for the previous four or five days. The body was skin and bones. The cancer in the throat had become dangerously acute. Suddenly Bhagavan's face was lit up. 'What, even now you do not understand my true aspect, isn't it? Who was born just as Rama and then as Krishna, that is me, myself,' Sri Guru Maharaj said this looking at the face of Swamiji. When he heard this, Swamiji became inebriated with Ananda. He sang and danced in joy. It was Ananda thandava.

"Both sannyasis and householders should live with the awareness that they are Sri Guru Maharaj's servants. Do not hate people of other religions. Help others to the extent possible. Let each raise through his own faith." All these words were uttered by Mahapurushji Maharaj.

'I returned to the hostel after 5 p.m., Sunday, the 7th November 1926. Went to the Ashram after breakfast. Prostrated before Mahapurushji Maharaj and Tulasi Maharaj. After sometime some devotees came there. One of them asked Mahapurushji Maharaj how he happened to meet and receive the blessings of Gurudev. He replied like this, "I was living in Punjab for quite some time. I was living there in a room along with a person who was a few years older than me. We lived there together, engaged in puja and bhajan. We used to discuss matters relating to God. I used to very often ask him about *Samadhi*. He would say that he did not know anything about *Samadhi* and that only a person living in Dakshineswar had full knowledge about *Samadhi*. From that time I started intensely wishing to see the Mahatma who was living in Dakshineswar. But I did not know how to get to that place. I lost my peace of mind as I was not able to get any clear knowledge about the truth of *Samadhi*.

"Later I happened to return to Calcutta. I was living close to the house of Sri Ramachandra Dutta. One day I got information that Sri Ramakrishna Deva had come to Dutta's house. I went there to meet him. I found him seated in a fairly large room, surrounded by several devotees. Remaining merged in a rare state of bhava. He was explaining to them the state of *Samadhi*. Listening to this, I was overjoyed. What exactly was the subject about which I had been yearning for and to receive instructions about, that very thing was the subject of discussion! I had been restless over this for a long time and that was the subject he was talking about. This was how my first meeting with Sri Guru Maharaj took place.

"Another day a friend of mine who was staying near Dakshineswar invited me to his house. Accordingly, I went there. From there, both of us went to Dakshineswar to pay respects to Sri Guru Maharaj. Bhagavan asked me about many spiritual matters. Sri Guru Maharaj told me, 'Today you may stay here. There is no use coming once in a while. So come here often.' Since I could not for certain reason halt there that day I went back to my friend's place at night. Later, one night I stayed on with Sri Guru Maharaj. After that, I went to Dakshineswar frequently. Infinite was his love. When we are there, we had no thought of father, mother, wife or children. Our minds longed for nothing when we were in that presence. There was no occasion for me to indulge in any kind of arguments. But Swamiji (Swami Vivekananda) would always argue with him. Sri Guru Maharaj would tell, 'Why are you worried thinking over these things now? When the appropriate time comes,

Mother Herself will bestow on you all experiences. You will necessarily have to believe that day.' Then Swamiji would reply, 'Alright, let Mother show me. Then only I will believe.' Sometimes in an instant, Swamiji's doubts will be cleared. In this way, we lived there with him several months, peace and joy over flowing. We never knew that he was an avatar."'

Mahapurush Maharaj stayed in Bangalore Ashram for a few more days and returned. During this stay of Mahapurush Maharaj in 1926 at Bangalore Ashram, Sri Menon was able to witness certain things which remained indelible in his mind. To quote his own words:

'One morning, Mahapurushji Maharaj was sitting on a chair outside. As was the custom in monasteries, Tulasi Maharaj came and prostrated before him. Then saying 'Jai Sri Guru Maharaj', Mahapurushji Maharaj stood up and embraced Tulasi Maharaj in the true Bengali style. That scene! It was like the merger of two oceans! How divine was the affectionate relationship between them who were gurubhais!

'One morning, I was going on a cycle to the Ashram. Mahapurushji [Maharaj], with a cap on his head and walking stick in the hand, was walking along the street outside the Ashram. Some street urchins had gathered around Swamiji [Mahapurush Maharaj]. Maharaj was talking to them something in Hindi, bending over them. The same kids were also speaking to him some things in their own dialect. They were laughing aloud. Maharaj took something from his pocket and distributed it among the children. I watched this rare leela from a distance. I was dumbfounded. The children, who would not have been more than eight or ten, had the satisfaction of having got a friend of equal age. Maharaj who was over seventy was, like a child, cutting jokes with them and laughing. This rare disposition can be found only in people who can see everything permeated with God.

'When we prostrated before Mahapurushji Maharaj, he had a charming way of tilting his head to one side and exchanging pleasantries with eyes half open and smiling. Wonderful, extremely wonderful, was the sweetness of that glance. Normally the ravages of old age will make a face look terrible. But the faces of great souls look attractive in all conditions.'[1]

On 09.07.1979, Guru Purnima day, Sri Menon recorded this: 'Because of previous merit (Poorva Punya) and the blessing of my beloved mother, I was able to get mantropadesh from Swami Shivananda [Maharaj]. I had the opportunity to meet great souls like Sri Swami Brahmananda [Maharaj], Swami Shivananda[Maharaj], Swami Nirmalananda [Maharaj], Swami Akhandananda [Maharaj] and all disciples of Sri Ramakrishna Deva, the yugaavatarpurusha. One night when I was studying in Bangalore, I was returning to my hostel after taking *prasad* from the ashram. I went to pay respects to Swami Shivananda [Maharaj]. I wished to request Maharaj to bless me, placing his sacred hands on my head. But hesitating to request thus, I only prostrated before him. Wonder of wonders! Knowing my desire, he kept both his hands on my head and said, "Let Sri Guru Maharaj bless you." What wonder! What grace!'

---

1. Written by Sri Menon on 15.02.1964, Sri Ramakrishna's Tithipuja day.

During the time of Durga Puja, Sri Menon had gone to Belur Math. He said later, 'Swami Apurvananda [Maharaj] took me to Mahapurush [Maharaj]. He was sitting on a cot with eyes shut and doing japa. Maharaj's mind and attention were all fixed in another world. Swami Apurvananda [Maharaj] said something two or three times in Bengali into Maharaj's ears. Then he half opened his eyes. He asked about mother and brother. He told me that I should go to Bhagavan's shrine and take *prasad* before I returned. Saying this he slipped into the former mood. He was nearly eighty years. His health was deteriorating. But his mind remained fixed on the Lotus feet of Sri Guru Maharaj. How calm was the face!'

The last *darsan* Sri Menon had of Mahapurush Maharaj was in 1932. He went to Belur Math when his brother Balettan, by then Brahmachari Purnachaitanya, reached there for conferment of sannyas. That was in March 1932. About this, Sri Menon wrote:

'After a few days, I got a letter from my brother sent from Belur Math. The gist of the letter was that brother had gone to Belur Math to receive sannyas and if possible I should take leave and stay in Belur Math for two days. Accordingly, I went to Belur Math and stayed there for two days. There I met Swami Tyagishananda[Maharaj] (founder of Thrissur Vilangan Ashram) and Swami Nishreyesananda [Maharaj] . They also got sannyas during this time.

'I went and prostrated before Mahapurush Maharaj. Because of old age and bad health, he was confined to bed. He was doing japa with eyes shut. Totally inward looking, he was unaware of what was going on around. Swami

Apurvananda [Maharaj] whispered to him something in Bengali for some time. When Maharaj opened his eyes, Swami Apurvananda [Maharaj] repeated, "Achuthan, Achuthan". Again Maharaj returned to the meditative mood. After some time with a smile Maharaj said, "Now I remember you, Achuthan. Hope your mother is fine. Stay here for two days. Didn't you see your brother?" What loving words! What merciful glance! What guileless, affectionate smile! A face that was lit up with infinite peace! I stayed there for two days. Before returning, I went to Mahapurush [Maharaj], touched his feet and took leave. I did not know that it was the final farewell. I wonder whether that great personage, who is now merged in yoganidra is today remembering me who is immersed in prarabdha. My firm faith that he is!'[1]

1. Sri Achutha Menon wrote about this last meeting in 1978.

Part B: Letters to His Family

Letters

A note

The letters of Swami Brahmananda Maharaj, Swami Shivananda Maharaj, Swami Saradananda Maharaj, Swami Nirmalananda Maharaj and Swami Vireswarananda Maharaj to Swami Tapasyananda Maharaj's family have been transcribed from the diaries of 1976 and 1978 used as notebooks by late K P Achutha Menon (1906 – 1984), the younger brother of Swami Tapasyananda Maharaj. He had himself copied the original letters by hand, maybe six years before his death. On the fly leaves of the diaries, late Sri Menon had written "true copies of letters".

....

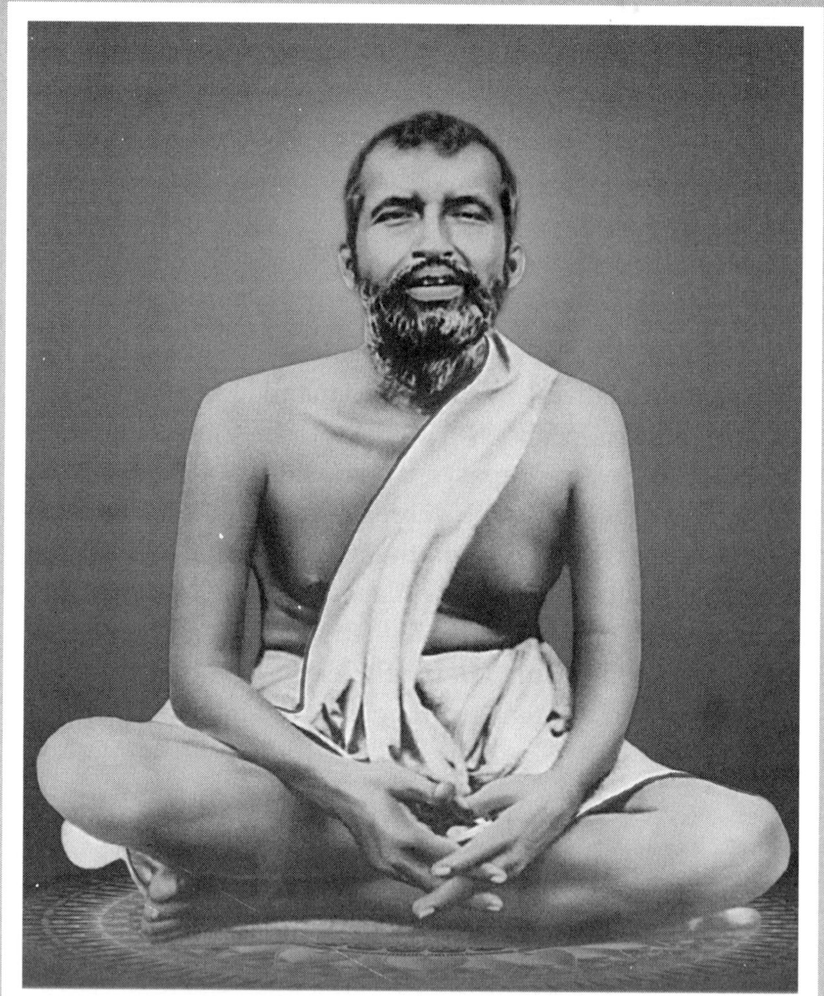

Bhagavan Sri Ramakrishna

Letters of Direct Disciples of Sri Ramakrishna to Swami Tapasyananda Maharaj's family members

Swami Brahmananda

1

To
K.P Parukutty amma
Palat House
Varode – Ottapalam

57 Ramkanta Bose ST
Bagbazar – Calcutta
30th Aug 19

Dear mother,

Yesterday I received your registered cover enclosed with a receipt of a parcel containing beetle-nuts[1]. I received

1. In Kerala, there is the practice of processing betel nut in such a manner that it would last for a long time. This is an industry in itself. The

the parcel, and am much pleased to have them in good condition. Those nuts are very useful and liked not only by me but by everyone, for it is very seldom in this province.

Holy mother is staying at Her own village at present & doing well there.

By the grace of the Lord I am doing well now. Hope you too are going on well with your health & spirit.

With my blessings

Yours in the Lord
Brahmananda

2

To
K.P Parukutty amma
Palat House
Varode – Ottapalam

Sri Ramakrishna Math
Bhubaneswar
DT Puri 8-9-20

Dear Mrs. Parukuti

I am very pleased to receive your parcel of betel-nuts. Now-a-days I am staying here as a new math of Guru maharaj is under construction.

---

product is called 'Kali Adakka'. Gifting this special product, particularly to those in other states was a normal practice in the aristocratic families in those days. Even today packets of banana chips and 'kali adakka' are considered to be befitting gifts during festivals like *Onam* & *Vishu*. The Swami's mother used to send these things to Belur Math as her humble offering.

I am very glad to know that you are doing well. With my love and blessings

Yours sincerely
Brahmananda

Swami Shivananda

3

The Ramakrishna Math
Belur P.O. – Howrah
22-2-25

My dear Achutha Menon

Received your card. I have reached here on 19th Feb. Now I am alright. Hoping you are doing well. My best wishes & affectionate love to your & your brother Balakrishnan.

Yours very affectionately
Shivananda

4

Sri Ramakrishna Math
Belur P.O. – Howrah
15-8-1925

My dear Achutha

Your affectionate card reached me duly. I am glad that you all saw Tulsi Maharaj on his way to Trivandrum. Yes, by the grace of Guru maharaj I am doing tolerably well. Hope you will pass your examination successfully. Convey my love & blessings to Kunchi Ram & all the members of your family. All the Sanyasins of the math are sending their love & blessings to you. With best wishes for success & affectionate love for you

Yours very affectionately
Shivananda.

5

Ramakrishna Mission
Belur P.O. – Howrah Dist
5-10-1925

My dear Parukutty Amma

My love & blessings of Bijoya to you & to all other Bhaktas of that place. The Puja of Sri Sri Durga mayee has passed on with much peace & joy at this place. Many Bhaktas assembled here on that occasion & about 6000 took Prasad during the three days of the Puja.

Your parcel containing Banana arecanuts & other things reached here safe. I think I have already informed you of it. However, the contents were in good condition & were offered to the Holy Mother during the Navarathri days.

I am glad to hear that your son appu has appeared in the intermediate examination this year.

My health is almost alright now & all other sadhus are enjoying good health here.

Know my best wishes & blessings I hope Tulsi maharajee has come to your place by this time & you are hearing of Guru Maharajee from Him.

Very affectionately yours
Sivananda[1].

The delay in acknowledging the receipt of the parcel is due to the wrong address the letter being returned from the Dead letter office, for which I regret very much I send this note again.

6

Ramakrishna Mission
Belur P.O. – Howrah Dist
18-12-1925

Sri Guru Saranam

My dear Achutha Menon

Glad to hear of you & your relatives and of Katyayani and her mother. My health is going on so so. The old rheumatism & cold are not yet off, rather with the coming of the winter, they are taking a little more stronger form. I am sorry to hear of your illness and hope by the grace of Guru Maharaj you are to your former health by this time.

---

1. Mahapurush Maharaj had signed this particular letter as 'Sivananda'.

Everything is going on alright now. The birthday ceremony of our Holy Mother and of myself are celebrated here with the blessings of Guru Maharaj with much pomp & anandam. In both occasions hundreds of Bhaktas assembled and took the Prasad of Guru Maharaj with joy & reverence.

Hope you are all now doing right by the grace of Guru maharaj. Have faith in him & he will surely take you out of all the difficulties which may beset you in your life of struggle.

With blessings, affection & good wishes,

Yours very affly
Shivananda.

P.S.: Give my blessings to Katyayani and her mother & Kunchiram.

7

Ramakrishna Math - Belur –
Howrah – Bengal 19-3-26

My dear K.P. Achutha Menon,

Infinitely glad to receive your very affectionate letter of the 14th March & to know that you are all doing well. Yes Tulsi Maharaj is in East Bengal now.

We are all doing tolerably well. My best wishes to & affectionate love to yourself & your good mother.

Yours very affly.,
Shivananda.

8

Sri Ramakrishna Math
Belur – Howrah
4th July 1925

My dear Achuthan,

I am very glad to hear from you after so long a time.

Don't be sorry for failure in passing the examination, but try the next chance.

Yes, I am at headquarters now. Glad you are all doing well & having good rains. We are not having good rains in West Bengal now. We are badly in need of it. By the will of Sri Guru maharaj I am doing fairly well & so all others of the Math.

With best wishes and affectionate love for you, your mother, sisters and all the members of the house.

Yours very affly.,
Shivananda.

P.S.: keep me informed at times.

9

Sri Ramakrishna Ashram
P.O. Khar. Bombay
27-1-27

My dear Achuthan

Very glad to receive your post card. I am pleased to know that through the grace of Sri Guru maharaj, you are keeping well. May he in his infinite mercy grand your Bhakti, Jnanam, love and purity.

I am also keeping well. Hope the Birthday celebration of Swamiji was performed at the Ashram grandly.

With my love, blessings & sincere good wishes to you,

Affly. Ever yours.
Shivananda.

10

Sri Ramakrishna Math
P.O. Belur Math
11-7-27

My dear Achuthan,

Very glad to receive your post card after a long time & to know that you have successfully passed through your 1st years course. May Sri Guru maharaj bless you with purity, bhakti. Know Sri Guru maharaj was purity incarnate so always pray to him to keep you pure also.

I am doing well through his grace. May this find you to be so. We are also having heavy showers here. With my love, blessings & good wishes.

Affly ever yours
Shivananda.

11

Ramakrishna Advaita Ashram
Lakola – Benaras City
30-11-27

My dear Achuthan

Very very glad to receive your letters. I am here now and intend to stay the whole of December next. I am through his grace well.

Hope this will find you well. May your bhakti and Jnanam increase through his grace. I am glad to know that your mother is doing well. Give her my blessings. Nirmalananda is now at Rangoon.

With my love, blessings & good wishes

Affly ever yours
Shivananda.

❋

12

Sri Ramakrishna Math
P.O. Belur Math
18-3-28

My dear Achuthan

I am pleased to get your letter. Your brother with mother was here during the birth day anniversary of Sri Guru maharaj and stayed with us for some days. From here they left for Benares. Balakrishnan was initiated with Brahmacharya through his grace and he is now known as Purna Chaitanya. You will also be initiated into if you wish to join the order after finishing your course and your mother permits.

I am doing well. Hope you have fared well in your examination. You did well to go to the ashram and partaking of Prasadam on your birthday. May Lord bless you. With my affectionate love, blessings & good wishes.

affly ever yours
Shivananda

❋

Swami Saradananda

To
K.P Parukutty amma
Palat House
Varode – Ottapalam

Sri Ramakrishna Math
Belur P.O. – Howrah DT
16-4-20

Dear madam

I request to inform you that as I do not know the dialect prevalent in your part of the country (viz. Malayalam) I could not decipher your letter. If you can find someone to write (what you want of me) in English, I shall try to serve you to the best of my ability.

With my blessings

Yours in the Lord
Saradananda

Letters of Swami Nirmalananda Maharaj

(written to Swami Tapasyananda Maharaj's mother and brother)

Swami Nirmalananda

1[1]

K.P. Parukkuty Amma
Palat House
Varode-Ottapalam

Bull Temple Road
Bangalore City
1920

Sri

Received your letter. Sri Sarada Mani Devi is extremely ill now. None is permitted to see. Even Sannyasins do not

1. This is the translation of a letter that Tulasi Maharaj had got written in June 1920 to Smt. K.P. Parukkutty Amma in Malayalam. Maharaj was not conversant with Malayalam. This was written by someone who knew Malayalam

have the opportunity to meet. So if you go to Calcutta now you will have no facility to meet Sri Sarada Mani Devi or get initiation. If you go to Calcutta now you can go to Belur Math, visit Dakshineswar and meet Sreemad Brahmananda Swamiji at Jagannatham. Presume that I need not accompany you merely for this. It would suffice if you take Bhakta or Kuntirama Menon. By the end of this month (in June) I am going to Calcutta. Immediately on reaching there I shall enquire about the health status of Sri Sarada Mani Devi. If there is enough abatement in the sickness so that you get an opportunity to meet, you will immediately be informed. It is felt, it would be better if you wait until you get that letter.

If you are keen to go to Calcutta at present itself I am willing to travel to Calcutta. But you will only be able to meet Sreemad Brahmananda Swamiji and visit Dakshineswar; you will not be able to meet Sri Sarada Mani at all. What you decide to do, considering all this, should be informed.

With affectionate āshīrvāda
Nirmalananda

2

Belur Math
28-12-24

My dear appu

Both your & your brother's post cards [were] brought by the same mail to me a few days back. I was very glad to receive them & to learn that both of you were blessed with initiation on Tuesday the 23rd of this month by Sri

Mahapurushji Maharaj. May you both be spiritually enlightened by the grace of Sri Guru Maharaj and lead a holy & pure life is what I sincerely pray for. I could not write a separate card to you brothers & as such you can show this to him. I am very glad to know that your mother, Sreemathi Ammunni Ammal and others of your house are doing well & are going on a trip to Rameshwaram. Convey to them all & to Balakrishnan my affectionate blessings. When you visit again the Mylapore Math after receiving this, convey my Sastanga pranams to Sri Mahapurushji. Hoping this will find you in health & spirits. With ever so much love & kind blessings

Very affectionately yours,
Swami Nirmalananda

A Letter of Swami Vireswarananda Maharaj to His Brother

Swami Vireswarananda

Ramakrishna Math
P.O. Belur Math – Howrah
June 25 – 1971

Dear Sri Menon,

I was very much shocked to hear about the passing away of your mother. Though death is certain of every mortal yet the separation of a near & dear one is always painful. But your mother was a devotee of Sri Guru Maharaj & He has graciously given shelter to her at HIS lotus feet for ever; this is our consolation. May her soul rest in peace at the lotus feet of Sri Guru Maharaj is my earnest prayer to Him. With Best wishes,

Yours in the Lord,
Vireswarananda
(President of the S.R.K. Mission)

At Trivandrum

Letters of Swami Tapasyananda Maharaj to his family members

1

Triplicane
17th July 1921

To
K.P. Ammunni Amma[1]
Palat House
P.O. Chunangad – Ottapalam.

Hope both the letters I sent earlier have been received. My stay is in the hostel now. There are two more Malayalis in my room. The food and the like are simply grand. The practice here is to bring the afternoon tea to the school.

I am about to buy the books and start studying. It is only one week since I joined the school[2].

To grandma yours Balan

---

1. Ammunni Amma was the grandmother of his mother Parukkutty Amma. That is, she was Maharaj's great grandmother. Parukkutty Amma's mother was no more by the time Maharaj was born. 'Muthassi' in Malayalam refers to both grandmother and great grandmother. This letter was meant for both his great grandmother and grandmother.

2. Maharaj is referring to his educational institution as 'school', instead of college by force of habit. Actually he had joined for the intermediate. During those days, the intermediate course was for 2 years; so were the B.A and M.A courses. So after the school, one had to study for 6 years to complete post-graduation. But in those days, 2 years' of B.A and 2 years' of M.A courses were abridged into a 3 year B.A Hons. course in Madras University. Bright students got admission to the Hons. course which was equivalent to B.A and M.A together. Since Maharaj completed the B.A Hons. course in Presidency College, it would mean that he was in Presidency College from 1921 to 1926.

When 'Prabuddha Bharatam' is received Komu Master should be asked to forward it to the following address[1].

K.P. Balakrishna Menon – Presidency College Hostel – Triplicane, Madras.

To mother yours Balan. Please convey my tidings to all.

2

Triplicane
4/1922

To
K P Parukkutty Amma[2]
Palat House – Varode
Ottapalam.

Hope the letter I sent a few days ago has been received. Everything fine here.

Yesterday I had been to the Ashram. I asked Gopala Brahmachari[3] about Maharajji's Samadhi. What is available

---

1. Maharaj was only 17 years at this point of time. He was already a subscriber to the *Prabuddha Bharata.*

2. The recipient of this letter Smt. Parukkutty Amma was Maharaj's mother and a disciple of Swami Brahmananda. She had come to know about the *mahasamadhi* in the first fortnight of April 1922 and perhaps she had written to Maharaj asking for more information. It was likely that she was herself a reader of *Prabuddha Keralam*. The *mahasamadhi* took place within a year of the her *mantra diksa*. Her collection of poems, which never found the light of the day, includes some touching lines in heavily Sanskritized Malayalam by way of Gurusmriti.

3. Gopala Brahmachari is none other than Revered Swami Siddheswarananda Maharaj.

in 'Prabuddha Keralam' is the only thing found by way of his last words. But it is heard that, apart from what is there in Prabudha Keralam, Maharajji said that his disciples need not fear of anything and that Maharajji would be with them always. When Gopala Brahmachari went to meet him, Maharajji asked about all of you. Gopala Brahmachari was by his side at the time of Mahasamadhi.

A few days ago Swami Turiyanandaji attained Mahasamadhi.

Nothing more. To Amma Yours Balan.

3

Thursday
R.K.M. Student's Home
23-12-26

To
Srimati K P Parukkutty Amma
Palat House.

No letter from Amma since I came away from there. Nothing heard on the opening of the Ashram[1]. Who is the Swamiji now residing in the Ashram?

Mahapurushji and others left here for Bombay on Sunday.

1. The reference to the opening of the 'Ashram' is to the founding of Ramakrishna Niranjan Ashrama by Tulasi Maharaj at Palappuram, Ottapalam. The consecration was on 10 December 1926. Today, the place is known as Sri Ramakrishna Nagar and is served by Sri Ramakrishna Nagar Post Office.

Has Appu[1] come home for the Christmas? Sad to learn that Gopi[2] did not get selection. Malathy[3]'s weight has now come up to 108 pounds. Hope you have letter from Valiyamma[4] giving all the news.

To Amma, Yours Balan.

4

Mylapore
20/1/27

To
K.P.A. Menon
Y.M.C.A. Buildings
Bangalore City.

Got your letter. So all news to hand. There came a letter recently from Amma.

Malathy is much better now. Her weight has now gone upto 112 lbs. She has started walking a bit.

---

1. Maharaj's younger brother, Sri K.P. Achutha Menon.
2. Maharaj's cousin.
3. Maharaj's cousin. She was very sick even from a tender age. He had a lot of concern for her. In many families, maternal cousins were considered as one's own brothers and sisters, not only because of the blood relationships, but also due to staying together in the joint-family system. Maharaj had a lot of concern for the studies, career and health of his brother and cousins. But in the entire archives of his letters, he had never evinced any interest in their marriage, parenthood, acquisition of property, etc. To those who had an inclination to hear, he would talk about spiritual progress. This cousin of his died at a young age.
4. Maharaj's aunt – elder sister of his mother.

Valiyachan[1] had gone to his home town. He has now come back.

My health is fine.

To Appu, K.P.B. Menon.

5

R.S. Home – Mylapore[2]
20-7-27

To
K.P.A. Menon[3]
Y.M.C.A. Building
Bangalore City.

Got your letter. The swelling on my leg is almost completely subsided. I had taken a medicine which is showing considerable effect. I am taking an English medicine now. That will be continued for a week.

I may not be going home except for Navarathri. Nothing else.

Yours,
K.P.B. Menon[4].

1. Maharaj's uncle – husband of the elder sister of his mother.

2. Maharaj was serving at Ramkrishna Mission Students' Home continuously from the time he passed out of the college till he became a Brahmachari. Seldom did he take a break even to go home. Long before he became a Brahmachari of the Ramakrishna Ashrama formally, he had in fact become a part of it.

3. K.P.A. Menon, also called Appu, was Maharaj's younger brother

4. This is the last letter traced as of now in which Maharaj had signed in his pre-monastic name.

6

R.K.M. Students' Home – Mylapore.
24-3-1928 – Friday[1]

To
K.P. Parukkutty Amma
Palat House - Ottapalam.

Hope you reached there safe. I reached here safe. Trust that 'Kala Bhairava Preethi'[2] etc. are over satisfactorily.

– for mother's information.

Purnachaitanyan[3]

Kindly convey the tidings to all.

7

R.K.M. Students' Home
Mylapore – Madras
8-5-28

To
K.P. Parukkutty Amma
Palat House - Ottapalam.

Sri

Received mother's letter. I am fine.

1. Written perhaps less than a fortnight after the parting at Trichinopoly.

2. Perhaps 'Kala Bhairava Preethi' was the rites performed at Rameswaram.

3. This is the first letter Maharaj signed as Purnachaitanya. Maharaj used to sign as 'Purnachaitanyan' whenever he signed in Malayalam. Similarly, Maharaj would sign as 'Tapasyanandan' whenever he signed in Malayalam. While signing in English, it was always Tapasyananda.

Now a new photo of Mahapurushji is available. A side-view of his, sitting bare-bodied on a chair. This was taken from the verandah upstairs at Belur Math. It has come out very well. I have not come across a picture which is better than this. If you want I can write to Calcutta and get it. The price is Rs.2/-. If others need it kindly let me know how many are needed. The money may also be sent. Kindly do this at the earliest.

To mother,

Purnachaithanyan

8

2.7.28, Friday

To
K.P.A. Menon
YMCA – Bangalore City

Sri

Got your letter. I am fine. I am still at the Home. I am working in the Industrial School here.

Glad to know that you have passed. There will perhaps be some competitive exams in the Railway Dept. etc. Wouldn't it be advisable to collect information on the same and compete? Nothing else in particular.

To Appu,

Purnachaithanyan

P.S.: Got the things sent through Kuttan.

9

R.K.M. Students' Home
Mylapore – 8.11.28
Thursday

To
K.P.Parukkutty Amma
Palat House
Varode
Ottapalam

Sri

Received your letter. Trust the problem with the hand is not too much. Hope all are fine there.

I am fine. We are getting good rains here this year. The climate is very good.

Nirmalananda Swami came here. It was mentioned in your letter that he must have felt certain things in his mind. Why take it that way? Is this what you have figured about him, knowing him for so long! Such a large-hearted person like Swamiji would not have such thoughts. I do not count one of Guru Maharajji's disciples apart from another. All of them alike have His own power.

It is learnt that Nambiathiri took sannyas and received the name Agamananda Swami. Kindly convey my namaskar to him.

For Amma's information

Purnachaithanyan

10

Ramakrishna Mission Students' Home
Mylapore, Madras
3.12.28

Sri

Received your letter. In it you say, not only do you not find me coming, but even a letter from me you do not find. Let me say a couple of words regarding this. I do not think anybody will object if I am to come there and stay for four or five days. But I did not come because of another consideration. You had written that you felt very uneasy when we changed trains at Trichinopoly. On that occasion I also felt likewise. But I did not say anything. It is natural for both of us to feel like that when we have to separate after spending a few days together. Is it proper for such feelings to arise in the life I have chosen? You also may feel — is it good?

Another thing must be mentioned. 'I do not have the good fortune to live with my children. No one else has children who do not love their mother'—when I find you writing like this, a doubt arises whether you do not fully approve of my joining the Ashrama. The greatest blessing a man can get is to be born in the family of those who are genuinely devoted to the Lord. This is indeed very rare. Does not the Gita proclaim—

अथवा योगिनामेव कुले भवति धीमताम् ।
एतद्धि दुर्लभतरं लोके जन्म यदीदृशम् ।।[1]

---

1. *athavā yogināmeva kule bhavati dhīmatām |*
etaddhi durlabha-taraṃ loke janma yadīdṛśam ||
[Or he is re-born in a family of men full of wisdom and spirituality. Re-birth under such conditions is passing hard to get in this world.]

I consider that I have this good fortune because I have been born as your son. It is not an ordinary good luck for a person to become a sadhu with the full approval of his mother. This has not been possible so easily even for Avataras like Sri Sankaracharya and Sri Chaitanya Deva. Such blessing by the mother will confer eternal benediction on an individual. I beg I may be granted that blessing. It was you who first instilled spirituality in me. That is my conviction. I crave for your blessing that I may progress on this path.

I am not boasting. For a mother it is a greater good fortune if her children are virtuous than if they live close to her.. I do not think that I and Appu have caused you any grief in this regard. It is the supreme dharma of a Hindu woman to bring up a son in a manner that equips him to become a sadhu, to encourage him to adopt that life, and to offer to the Lord whole-heartedly a most beloved object. This is a great sacrifice. Those who do this are certain to receive God's grace. You have fulfilled this dharma. It behooves you to attain full gratification by wiping away the natural mental agony in this venture through fortitude and remembrance of the Lord.

Many of the monks here say it is a great thing that I have been able to adopt this life with the consent of my mother. One swami told me that Nirmalananda Swamiji had said so to them in Bengali when he visited this place. 'She has given with full heart her son to the Lord. Here is a woman of extraordinary devotion.'

You should give up excessive attachment to your children. How else can you think of the Lord? All of us have obtained a great good fortune by His grace. The company of the disciples of Sri Ramakrishna Deva and their blessings are not something ordinary. We can speak of them in the same way in which Uddhava spoke of the Gopikas of Vrindaban:

नायं श्रियोऽङ्ग उ नितान्तरतेः प्रसादः
स्वर्योषितां नलिनगन्धरुचां कुतोऽन्याः ।
रासोत्सवेऽस्य भुजदण्डगृहीतकण्ठलब्धाशिषां
य उदगाद् व्रजवल्लवीनाम् ।।

आसामहो चरणरेणुजुषामहं स्यां
वृन्दावने किमपि गुल्मलतौषधीनाम् ।
या दुस्त्यजं स्वजनमार्यपथं च हित्वा
भेजुर्मुकुन्दपदवीं श्रुतिभिर्विमृग्याम् ।।

[*nāyaṃ śriyo'ṅga u nitāntarateḥ prasādaḥ*
svaryoṣitāṃ nalinagandharucāṃ kuto'nyāḥ |
rāsotsave'sya bhujadaṇḍagṛhītakaṇṭhalabdhāśiṣāṃ
ya udagād vrajavallavīnām ||
āsāmaho caraṇareṇujuṣāmahaṃ syāṃ
vṛndāvane kimapi gulmalatauṣadhīnām |
yā dustyajaṃ svajanamāryapathaṃ ca hitvā
bhejurmukundapadavīṃ śrutibhirvimṛgyām ||]

'Neither Sri Devi nor the goddesses in heaven have the good fortune of the Gopikas who experienced the touch of the Lord's limbs in the Rasotsava. No need to speak of others. These women have abandoned relatives, which are difficult to give up, as also family pride, and even the Svadharma extolled in the scriptures, in order to take sole refuge in the Lord. May I be born as a creeper or a pebble in Vrindaban so that I may be sanctified by the dust of their feet.' [*Bhagavata,* 10.47.60-61]

The glory of the disciples of Sri Ramakrishna Deva is in no way less. Just as in Sri Krishnavatara the Gopikas excelled even the austere sages because of the contact with the Lord's body, so too the eminent sannyasins like Swami Vivekananda stand sanctified through intimacy with Sri Ramakrishna Deva and by receiving his unqualified love. Excelling Uddhava, you have not only taken in this birth the dust of the holy feet of Sri Maharaj, who was the leader of the Lord's disciples, but also received his hearty blessings. You must not waste such a birth by thinking of trifles like children. Constantly remember the Lord — He is our only refuge. You have all the facilities in this regard. You have no obstacles that stand in the way of spiritual life. There is no occasion for you to grieve about money-matters or about your children except that they live at a distance from you. And as far as I am concerned, you have no cause at all for anxiety. What supports me in this life is that Divine Energy which is the sole support of creatures before birth and which again supports them after death. We must cultivate peace of mind, believing that pleasure and pain, disease and death, are but factors directed by the Lord for our welfare. So please do not worry about what may happen to me. Instead think of the Lord always.

Even we who have adopted the sadhu-life do not get the facilities that you have for sadhana. After attending to household duties for a few hours you can spend all the rest of the time in study, japa and meditation. It goes without saying that the bliss one gets from such practice far exceeds the pleasure obtainable through proximity to one's children.

Life is short; days are passing away one after another. Should we not try our utmost to concentrate the mind on the Lord before the body falls a prey to illnesses? If this is not done, what can be the result but sorrow?

I have not written all this to instruct you in any way. These things you know much better than I do. I have but indicated. I am only saying that you must deeply ponder on all this whenever thoughts about your children and allied matters arise in your mind.

Not that, in view of all this, I will not come to see you. Only you should not worry about it. It is only one year after I met you last. Is it not enough to learn that I am keeping well? I shall see you some time. The monks in the Ashrama also have mothers and relations. But it is not the custom for them to go and meet their mothers often. You have written that you may come here to see me. That is not at all necessary. When you feel that urge, please let me know and I shall come there to see you.

I have no illness now. The Chyavana-prasa has not been particularly beneficial. May be the mode of preparation counts.

I learn that Nirmalananda Swamiji has come to Ottapalam after inaugurating the Salem Ashrama. Trust you have met him. Nothing else in particular. I am not in the habit of writing such long letters. But here I have written all manner of mad things. I am only reporting. You can read, and laugh or enjoy.

Purnachaitanyan

PS: After writing this letter I understand that you have gone to Calicut or elsewhere. It was Gopi who wrote.

He says you will return after a month. Hence my delay in sending this letter. Meanwhile Nirmalananda Swamiji had come here. He has gone to Burma. He will return only after a tour of North India. He told me that he met you and that you enquired about me. I have not so far got the hymn that Abhedananda Swamiji has composed on Sri Ramakrishna Deva. A swami here has promised to order for a book containing all his stotras. Meanwhile I am enclosing herewith a hymn he has composed on Holy Mother, so that it may reach you before Mother's birthday. In exchange, please send me your song 'Ramakrishna Deva Tava.' Though I cannot sing, I am much attracted by that song.

11

R.K.Students' Home
Mylapore – Madras
29.3.1929

To
K.P.Parukkutty Amma
Palat House - Ottapalam

Sri

Received your letter. I am fine. Went through Valiamma's letter. Please ask her not to worry so much.

Appu had sent me a letter a few days ago. Here it is getting very warm. I have decided to move from the Home to the Math by the end of this year. The orders for the brass vessel have not yet been placed. Nothing else in particular.

For mother's information,

Purnachaithanyan

12

Sri Ramakrishna Math
Mylapore
Madras
2-4-1929

To
K.P. Parukkutty Amma
Palat House
Ottapalam

Sri

Received your post-card. I am still at Madras. I have not gone to Ooty. But I will be shifting to the Ashramam this month. But Ramaswami Iyengar says I may go after Swami Yatiswaranandaji comes. Swamiji is in Calcutta now. So I have not shifted to the Math fully. The practice is to come here at 8 A.M., do the work that I ought to do and then return in the evening (The work is to assist for *The Vedanta Kesari*).

I would request you to send me two or three books. Adhyatma Ramayanam, Harinama Kirtanam – available at Kamalalaya Press..., the first part of Bhagavatam with commentary (translated by Gopalan Nair and costing Re1/-). These may be sent to the Math by book post.

Purnachaithanyan

13

S.R.K.Math
Mylapore, 7-9-1930

To
K.P.A. Menon
Y.M.C.A. Bangalore City

Sri

No news from you after you left. Hope the hand is fully cured.

Read in the Hindu that Swamiji has created a Trust Board for all the ashramas under him. You can learn more about it if you ask the Malayali Swamis of the Ashrama. Who are all the trustees? Has the trust deed been registered? Where has it been registered? If you are able to collect information, please pass it on to me. I request you for a reply.

To Appu,

Purnachaithanyan

14

S.R.K.Math
Mylapore – Madras
11.3.30

Sri

Amma, your letter to hand.

Though not Guruswamy, I was examined by one of the best doctors of Madras. I have absolutely no problem now. I used to visit the doctor once a week. There is nothing to worry about, in his opinion too. The body gets tired only if there is more than usual physical activity. Again, I am much better than before. The doctor has asked me to stop all medicines. He says that there will be no problem if the activity is restricted to appropriate levels. I am taking an iron/ferrous essence for warding off tedium which is not anyway much. I have no difficulty in attending to the daily chores or walking for two or three miles. Instead of doing other exercise I am walking along the beach for one or two miles. That is the only difference. Do not please mistake that I am laid up. I think, even earlier, my heart was not particularly sturdy. And to change it completely will be difficult. That need not be reckoned as sickness. All that needs to be done is to avoid excessive strain. To ward off tedium I am taking milk in the morning and evening. Amma, if you think I am unwell and worry over that it will be totally out of place. No point in my going over or staying there. Gradually I will be as before. I wrote to you about this since there was a contextual mention of my going to the north, not because it is something serious. I repeatedly say that there is nothing for you, Amma, to worry about.

For your information,

Purnachaithanyan

15

S.R.K.Math
Mylapore, 26-6-31

To
K.P.A.Menon
Palat House

Sri

Received your letter. Glad to know that you have passed. Hope you will come to the Ashram when come to Madras.

May be it rains heavily there. Here it was very warm, all these days. Yesterday it rained a bit.

I am fine. Please show this letter to mother.

Poornachaithanya[1]

16

S.R.K.Math
Mylapore – Madras
2-8-1931

To
K.P. Parukkutty Amma,
Palat House – Ottapalam.

Sri

Received your letter. It was on Monday that Appu went back. It is not yet time to receive his letter.

I am not as bad as he wrote to you. He must have felt that I became lean because he has seen me after a long gap. No need at all to consult a doctor or start treatment. If at all necessary, will anyone go home leaving Madras for treatment? Anyway for mother's satisfaction I shall take "Chyavanaprasam". It is available here. I will be able to meet the cost from what Appu has handed over for train fare.

Regarding my coming over there, what I said was that, as done before, I shall come after Durga Puja i.e. after October. Here the responsibility of running a magazine fully rests with me. It will be difficult to leave it and rush

1. This is the only letter in available archives where Maharaj (as a brahmachari) had signed in English. He had used the spelling here as 'Poorna' and not 'Purna'.

home just like that. The trip can be made only after finishing one month's work in advance. I can come when the month begins and will have to return before the 15th. After the 15th the printed matter will start coming out. At that point of time to clear the same of mistakes, I have to be here. I shall try to come by the beginning of October.

Please do not worry unnecessarily, thinking that I am sick. I am fine. Getting lean, fat and so on may happen from time to time. No serious note is to be taken of that.

Glad to learn that your hand is better now. I shall let you know before I come.

For mother's information,

Purnachaithanyan

17

S.R.K.Math
Mylapore – Madras
17.8.31

To
K.P.A.Menon
Vivekananda Society
Jamshedpur
BIHAR

Sri

Got both the letters. Replying late. Generally mustard oil does not suit the southerners. It is better to shift residence before the stomach develops ailments.

Take special care about diet and pure air. Pure air will be required particularly after spending long spells in workshops without ventilation. So also, like that Swami from here said, be extremely careful while mixing with acquaintances who are drunkards and debauchers.

Some kind of an intellectual work is essential. Otherwise the workshop atmosphere will kill the intellectual side of man. It will be good to read books, over and above what had been studied in the College, general books on Engineering, up-to-date writings etc. It may not be good to forget the theoretical portions of professional studies just as it is not nice to forget what is studied in literature. It will become handy later. It is essential that you read on these subjects or Swamiji's works. Swamiji's works may be available in the Society. Do not give up the contact with the Vivekananda Society.

It is also easy to learn Hindi while living in these regions. It is a highly useful language. If you write to Madras Hindi Prachar Sabha, Triplicane, you will get the book Hindi-English Self Instructor. It is a very good book. It costs only one rupee. It will be helpful for learning the correct language.

Nothing else in particular.

Purnachaithanyan.

18

S.R.K.Nagar
Madras – 11-12-1931

Sri

Today I reached here. The trip was pleasant. Got ample space for lying down. It rained throughout, while on the way, in fact upto Madras, just as it was raining there when I started. There are fairly good rains in Madras also.

Everyone here liked Appam and jaggery-coated chips. But in my rating it is not of first-class quality; only the next grade.

For Amma's information,

Purnachaithanyan

19

S.R.K.Math
Mylapore – Madras
2-3-32

To
K.P.A.Menon
G-4- No.19, Burma Mines
Tatanagar - Jamshedpur

Sri

I am leaving for Calcutta today. Mahapurushji has given his consent for me to go there for receiving Sannyasa. It is for that I am going there. Though I will be passing close to Jamshedpur I may not be able to come there. Main reason is my reluctance to travel.

I had gone to the home town two months ago to meet mother. Stayed there for about a fortnight.

Hope you are fine. Nothing else in particular.

To Appu,

Purnachaithanyan

20

R.K.Math, Howrah
Calcutta
20-3-32

To
K.P.A.Menon
G4 – No.19, Burma Mines
Tatanagar

Sri

Received your card. Mahapurushji asked about you and mother. Though it is difficult for him to remember names or faces of people, once the memory comes he is able to recall important things about them.

I got Sannyas on the Jayanthi of guru Maharaj. Tapasyananda is the monastic name.

I will be staying here till the month-end. Will you not get two or three days' holidays for Easter? Thus, will it not be possible to come during that time even if you do not get leave? When you come you can stay here.

I am fine. Nothing more in particular.

To Appu

Tapasyanandan

P.S. Come, only if it is not bothersome. In case you are coming and you need it, I shall come to the station if you give information in advance.

21

S R K Math, Mylapore
Madras
12-4-32

To
K.P.Parukkutty Amma
Varode
Ottapalam

Sri

Received the letter you sent a few days back. I reached back on Sunday the 10th. I did not write till now as I thought I would write after return.

My monastic name is Tapasyananda. Stayed at Belur for about five weeks. I had written to Appu asking him to go there. He arrived and stayed there for three days.

Mahapurushji is very ill. He can neither walk nor get up without help. He has to sit or lie down on the cot all the time. He is suffering from breathlessness, fever, sleeplessness, BP [Blood Pressure] or one or the other. At times he is fit. And sometime most unexpectedly the sickness aggravates. It seems his body still has to fulfill a certain purpose. Perhaps Swamiji is alive for that purpose and that alone.

Swamiji cannot recognize some people though seen earlier. But when one or two details are registered in the memory, then he is able to recall connected people and things of the past one by one. When I was presented before Swamiji in an effectual manner, he was able to recall you and Appu. He remembers you very clearly. He asked after you several times. When I go to meet Swamiji, if other Swamis are present he would tell them,

"I knew his mother. She is a great devotee...' etc. Though he is physically sick, he is inwardly happy and enthusiastic. He cuts jokes and laughs heartily. He has one or two pleasing words for each and everyone who approaches him...

For your information, Amma,

Tapasyanandan

22

S.R.K.Ashrama
Mysore
14-12-32

To
K.P.Parukkutty Amma
Palat House
Ottapalam

Sri

Received your letter. I am fine. Though the medicines sent have not had any mentionable effect, my health is better after reaching here.

Now it is cold season here. Not extreme cold. Salubrious climate. It seems Swami Agamananda, Swami Arjavananda, Swami Adrijananda have reached Belur Math. Nothing else in particular.

For mother's information.

Tapasyanandan

23

S.R.K.Math
Mylapore, 2-8-1933

To
K.P.Parukkutty Amma
Palat House
Varode – Ottapalam

Sri

Got the letter and medicines sent by you. There is actually no need for the medicines. It is true that I was a little weak during the time Appu and Gopi came. After that I started taking a special soup. Now the physique is much better. Since I continue to take that I can start the medicines you sent only after some time.

Mahapurushji is much better now. The faculty of speech has failed. In the rest of the matters he is as he was in the past. So there is hope that Maharaj will live on for some more time. Quite for some time now he has not been able to walk or recognize people. It seems in this age such conditions cannot be expected to reverse.

You have mentioned that I should go over there now. What is the benefit of that? Just now only Gopi and others have returned from here and given you my news. Amma, why spend ten or fifteen rupees in these hard times? I shall come some other time.

The heat in Madras has abated. We get rains occasionally. Hope you are getting plentiful rains.

Amma, this is for your information.

Tapasyanandan

24

S.R.K. Math
Mylapore – Madras
16-5-1935

To
K.P.Parukkutty Amma
Palat House - Ottapalam

Sri

Received your letter. Got the powder. It is taken mixed in ghee. What you have sent will last for a long time.

You need not send this from there in future. It can be arranged for here. It is noticed that to send that pack of powder one one-rupee stamp has to be used. With that amount a greater quantity of powder can be got ready here.

Though it is rather hot, there is good sea-breeze. So the heat is not felt so much. Next month will be warmer.

Amma, this is for your information.

Tapasyanandan

25

S.R.K. Math
Mylapore, Madras
14-11-1936

My dear appu,

Very glad to receive your letter and to know that you have got an appointment in the Water Works Department of the Travancore State. Rs. 100/- as the starting pay is not a bad beginning. In a poor country like India no one need expect higher scales of salary. As you say

Alleppey is a bad place. I think Elephantasis is very common there. I would ask you to make use of the mosquito curtain a regular habit. All diseases carried by mosquito can be avoided by it.

As far the picture of Mahapurushji, I have got information you want. In fact I delayed in sending you a reply because I had to get the necessary information from Calcutta. We do not have the picture here. You may write to The Manager – Advaita Ashrama, 4 – Wellington Lane – Calcutta giving the description of the position as follows. Swami Sivananda – bare body – seated on a chair sitting in the verandha of the Math facing the Ganges. Piece with mount Rs. 12.

I am informed that mounted photo costs 12 Rs. And unmounted 10 Rs. You may write for whichever you want.

Yours affectionately,
Tapasyananda

26

To
K.P.A. Menon
Section Officer
Water Works-Alleppey

S.R.K. Math
Mylapore, Madras
10-4-1939

My dear appu,

Glad to receive your letter a few days back. I returned from my North Indian pilgrimage about a month and a half ago. My chief purpose in going was to collect material for a book on the Holy Mother which our Math will be publishing shortly. I went via Bombay stopping at Panderpari & Puna on the way. From Bombay I went to Agra stopping at Nasik for two days. Then Mathura, Brindavan, Delhi, Haridwar, Hrishikesh, Ayodhya & Benares are the other places visited. I went also to Kamarpukur & Jayarambati. As it was winter, the whole journey was very enjoyable. Of course it was very cold, but I like cold & it agrees with my system very well.

I am glad to hear of your pilgrimage to Sabarimalai. Of course I have heard about the place as it is famous all through Malabar.

I have all idea to go to Ottapalam sometimes hence. Mother has been pressing me, I should say pestering me with request to go over there. I am extremely unwilling to go; only consideration for her repeated request forces me to go. I shall be going to Ooty sometime hence in order to do some similar writing work & I propose to go to Ottapalam either on my way to that place or on my return.

Regarding small picture, photos of about 1 inch square of Swamiji's, Holy Mother & Guru Maharaj are available. They cost 1 anna each, they can be had by writing to The Manager of our Math at the address given in this letter head. If only a few pictures are required the cost may be sent in the form of postal stamps & they will send the pictures enclosing these in an ordinary letter.

With Love

Yours affectionately,
Tapasyananda

27

To
K.P.A. Menon
Section Officer
Water Works-Alleppey

S.R.K. Math
Mylapore
Madras
12-1-1940

My dear appu,

Received your kind letter. Glad to know you have recovered your health and are fit to undertake the pilgrimage to Sabarimalai.

Yes, I heard everything about the union effected between Belur Math and the disciples of Tulsi Maharaj. We are all glad about it & I am sure it will in the long run result in good to the work in Kerala.

I had been to Ottapalam about three months back & stayed there for about a week. As far as I can see there is no chance of my going to Trivandrum at present. If however I go I shall inform you.

I am in quite good health. My heart trouble was cured long ago. The leg too does not give any trouble now. With love & best wishes.

Yours affectionately,
Tapasyananda

28

To
K.P.A. Menon
Section Officer
Water Works-Alleppey

S.R.K. Math
Mylapore, Madras
13-1-1940

My dear appu,

You might have received my last letter. Since then the headquarters have all of a sudden sent me a letter asking me to proceed to Trivandurm to take charge of the work there. I am extremely unwilling to go, yet I have to do as they have instructed me. I am asked to be there by the 25th but I may not be able to do that as I have some commitments here. In any way I shall be in Trivandrum sometime hence & there may be a chance of my meeting you one of these days.

With love

Yours affectionately,
Tapasyananda

29

Prabudha Keralam Office
Trivandrum
22-1-41

Sri

Amma, got the letter you sent a few days back. I got malaria attacks now and then. The last instance was two weeks ago. I have taken nearly 10 quinine injections. If the fever recurs, I may have to take more injections. Significant results may not arise by switching over to ayurveda. For eliminating malaria completely from the blood, there is no alternative to quinine. That despite several shots there has been no complete cure shows that this is a virulent kind of attack. It is doubtful whether the disease can be eliminated through ayurvedic treatment. So it is proposed to continue with the allopathic system until its practitioners rule out the possibility of cure. Promoting cure is by way of intake food that builds up the body, change of place etc. How much of all that is practical in the present circumstances is a big question.

Amma, this is for your information,

Tapasyanandan

PS The letter enclosed may be sent to Ottapalam Ashramam.

30

Prabudha Keralam Office
Trivandrum
31.10.119[1] (7/1944)

Sri

Received the letter sent a few days back. I did not write earlier as there was nothing in particular to be conveyed.

1. The dt.31.10.119 is perhaps of Malayalam calendar. The English calendar is 825 years ahead of the Malayalam era. The current year, 2013, is 1188 by the Malayalam calendar. In Kerala, there is a practice of indicating the year by the last 3 digits. So, the year 119 is actually the year 1119.

Since people from here come there frequently I presume that they would convey news. I am fine. Totally free from malaria now.

The letter speaks about carrying the spiritual burden. Except God no one can carry the spiritual burden of another. Peace of mind will be attained only by remembering that God and seeking refuge in Him. Sankaracharya Swami in Sivananda Lahari [verse 35] says:

yogakṣema-dhuraṃdharasya sakalaḥśreyaḥ pradodyogino
dṛṣṭādṛṣṭa-matopadeśa-kṛtino bāhyāntara-vyāpinaḥ |
sarvajñasya dayākarasya bhavataḥ kiṃ veditavyaṃ mayā
śaṃbho tvaṃ paramāntaraṃga iti me citte smarāmyanvaham || [1]

What exactly is meant by taking refuge in God in this sense? I happened to read in this issue of Prabuddha Bharata what Swami Turiyanandaji had said about this:

"Taking refuge in Him means just this: to try to be content, however He may place you, viewing it as good, to merge one's will in the will of God, and to practice equanimity in happiness and misery, gain and loss, etc. That is to say, one can rightly take refuge in Him only when one

---

1. योगक्षेम–धुरंधरस्य सकलःश्रेयः प्रदोद्योगिनो
दृष्टादृष्ट–मतोपदेश–कृतिनो बाह्यान्तर–व्यापिनः ।
सर्वज्ञस्य दयाकरस्य भवतः किं वेदितव्यं मया
शंभो त्वं परमान्तरंग इति मे चित्ते स्मराम्यन्वहम् ॥ 35 ॥

What am I to petition unto Thee who bearest the responsibility for both the present and the future welfare of beings; who art ready to confer all good (on devotees); who art the perfect revealer of all religions existing and yet to exist; and who art all-knowing and all-merciful? Always do I think of Thee in my mind as my dearest and nearest.

becomes free. Before that it is the Yoga of practice. Perfect resignation of self to God is liberation. If one is honest in the practise of this attitude, it is sure to come some day through His grace."

I need not tell you anything about this Mother, this is something on which you know better than me.

Appu had written me a letter a few days ago. I did not respond until now, not knowing what to write. It is not in the least proper for me to speak to Sir C.P, on matters like this. First of all it will not fetch any result. Secondly my acquaintance with him is only in connection with the matters of the Mission. If one starts out like others to promote personal matters, it is below one's dignity. And it will cause hindrance not only in this matter, but in other cases too[1].

To get good remuneration one should move out. One should be efficient; so also one should be able to create in others an impression of one's capability. Nothing comes out of goodness alone.

Hope it is raining well there.

Mother, this is for your information.

Tapasyanandan

1. Below this letter, Maharaj's brother, Sri K.P.A. Menon, had made the following note: 'Balettan's aim was to adhere to Sannyasa dharma absolutely. He never bowed before power and pelf. Neither did he refrain from respecting people without money or position. Even householders (grihastashramis) should not accept money or other kind of help for personal benefit. And as for Sannyasins, this is to be totally avoided. One of the foremost qualities our mother had was this. The son inherited this.'

31

S.R.K.Ashram
Trivandrum
18.5.47

K.P. Parukkutty Amma
Tulsi Cottage
Ottapalam

Om

Amma, received the letter you sent a few days ago. I am not writing frequently because there is nothing here in particular. Also because you receive news about me through the letters sent from the doctor's house. Got the money you sent. Even if you do not find my signature on the money order receipt, kindly take it that the money is received here.

I went to Madras for a week to meet Swami Siddheswaranandaji and to stay with him for a few days since I had to be in Trivandrum for an urgent matter. I returned here straight. Swami Siddheswaranandaji stayed in Calcutta for quite sometime. He will return to France after Gurudev's festival.

I am fine. Hope you too are fine now.

Nothing else. Amma, this is for your information,

Tapasyananda

32

To
K.P.A. Menon
Executive Engineer
Water Works
Trichur

S.R.K. Ashrama
Trivandrum
19-1-58

My dear appu,

Received your card of 17th instant. It is quite good that a partition is decided upon. I do not know what type of a power of attorney I am to give for this. In order that it may be precise & in the correct form, it is better that you get one drafted by some advocate there. The advantage is that it may be done in consultation with you & others concerned. The draft may be sent to me & I shall execute it.

I would like to add one thing more. In this partition I do not want to have anything set apart in my name. The whole thing will go to you or if you do not like to settle it that way you may leave it to mother to dispose it off as she likes. Both of you may do as you please in consultation with each other. Let not anything be set apart in my name. Along with power of attorney & partition I shall execute whatever document is required for the purpose. It may be done now or afterwards accordingly as advocates advise you. Hope to hear from you soon.

Yours affectionately,
Tapasyananda

33

To
K.P.A. Menon
Sarada Mandiram
S.R.K. Nagar
Ottapalam - 3

S.R.K. Ashrama
Charitable Hospital
19-1-1964

My dear appu,

Received your letter of 16th instant about the state of mother's health. When I came to Trichur about a month back, I was informed her health was quite good. It is strange that in one month there has been such a marked decline. Whether there is albumin formation in the urine should also be seen. Heart condition has also got to be observed. Even for young & healthy people some kind of swoons take place to some temporary condition. Age is against her in this case & these symptoms have to be viewed seriously.

If she thinks of seeing me I shall go over there one of these days; just now I am held up here by the problems connected with land acquisition which make my presence here absolutely necessary. Towards the middle of February, I have to go to Nagpur and Calcutta. I shall try to be there either before my departure or at the time of my return.

I do hope it will not take a serious turn.

Then again if your doctor thinks that intensive treatment will restore her & if she is fit to travel you can bring her over here for treatment. But in the case of a very old person there is justification for this only in case there is a fair chance of recovery & there is need to give relief from great pain. For if the worst happens at this distance the difficulties will be immense besides the consideration that in place of relief or cure we will be inflicting injury & discomfort to the patient. Merely rushing a patient in panic is no good. These questions may be decided in the light of common sense considerations & the advice of the doctor.

Finally, it is one's Prarabdha that decides one's lease of life & if one passes away smoothly at a mature age God be praised. After all she has lived her life well & whatever awaits is only a more glorious chapter.

Yours affectionately,
Tapasyananda.

34

S.R.K.Ashrama
Trivandrum, 15-3-64

To
K.P.Parukkutty Amma
Sarada Mandiram
S.R.K.Nagar, Ottapalam

Amma, learnt that you were not well a few days back and that you are okay now after treatment. I had gone to Belur Math by the middle of February and come back on the 11th of this month. I thought of coming that way and meeting you. But because there is much work here, this being the year-end, I had to come back directly from Madras. I shall come to meet you sometime later.

Appu had come here two days back. He conveyed all news about you. He said that you refuse to take insulin injections. Insulin injection is the best remedy. Going about without treatment is running a great risk of developing boils and ulcers. On the other hand, in taking injections, you have to put up with only a pain as slight as an ant-bite once a day. Instead would you like to be troubled by ulcers and sores?

It is better to take regular treatment consisting of injections or tablets under the advice of a doctor. Injection should not be avoided merely because of the pain. That gives only the slightest of pain.

I shall come sometime later.

Amma, to you for information.

Tapasyanandan

35

Swami Tapasyananda
S.R.K.Ashrama Hospital
Trivandrum – 9-5-1965

Om

Most beloved mother,

In accordance with your instruction, Vasu has sent me a draft for Rs.500/- two three days back. The other day when I came there you happened to talk about it. At that time I had said that there is no need for this as here my needs will somehow be met and that such money can better be used for you. That you have still sent it is expressive of the sense of duty towards the children which is natural to a mother.

Since you have sent it I have no alternative to accepting it. But I will not use it for my personal needs. The sums of money you used to send from time to time are with me, remaining unused[1]. With what you have sent now I am starting a relief fund for the workers of the hospital. It is something dear to my heart and I am setting apart the amount you sent for this purpose. Coincidentally, the amount of Rs.600/- left by Swami Srikantanandaji in the postal Savings Bank has also been received. That also is being added to this fund. Thus let me inform you that the money sent by you is used for starting a fund which will be of benefit to the staff.

Vasu has written that your health is okay now. How about the eyesight? Hope days are spent peacefully.

Kindly hand over the enclosed letter to Vasu. I do not know his address and hence doing like this.

For Amma's information.

Tapasyanandan

---

1. Below this letter, Maharaj's brother, Sri K.P.A. Menon, had made the following note: 'Balettan [elder brother Balan] did not use for his personal purpose the money that mother sent him. He never cared for any luxury. He would spend money only on bare essentials. He stayed in Sasthamangalam Ashramam for 30 years. During these days he used to go for a walk every evening. He used to tell the Swami-in-charge of cash to keep a 25 ps. coin on the table lest it might be needed in the event of a bus-ride on return. The Swami did accordingly. But Balettan would bring back the coin daily and keep it in its own place. This drama went on for 30 years. In matters of money, our mother was also of the same nature.'

36[1]

S.R.K. Ashrama Hospital
Trivandrum, 18-12-70

My dear appu,

As informed earlier, I shall be arriving there at Palapuram by the morning train. I shall be going to Trichur next morning.

Yours affectionately,
Tapasyananda.

37

S.R.K. Ashrama Hospital
Trivandrum, 2-4-71

My dear appu,

Received your card. By the same post, I got the Registered letter mentioned by you. As directed by you I am enclosing it herewith.

I hope mother is carrying on as usual.

Our president Maharaj is coming to Kalady to lay the foundation of the Kalady Temple. I may attend the function.

I hope you are all doing well.

Yours affectionately,
Tapasyananda.

---

1. Sri K.P.A Menon had made a note in his diary which reads as follows: 'This was the last time Balettan [elder brother Balan] came home to see mother. This time, and once just before this, when Balettan was going back after visiting home, mother took the water of the sacred Ganga from the hands of Balettan and drank it. This moved the heart of the sannyasi son.'

38[1]

To
K.P.A. Menon
S.R.K. Nagar, Ottapalam

S.R.K. Ashrama Hospital
13-5-71

My dear appu,

I hope you have received by this time my wire in reply to yours, concerning the sad demise of our mother. From your card of the 10th which I received after the wire I could understand that she must have passed away peacefully. She lived an exemplary life of devotion and by the Lord's grace must have given her illumination & put her on the path of higher spiritual evolution. There is nothing to grieve when a good soul is released from a disabled body.

When I wired to you, I thought I shall go over there soon. But now I have changed my mind due to health & the situation here arising from my imminent departure to Madras. I was having some flue & it has left me weak & coughing. And after all she has passed away & what is the good of coming now. Hope to meet you sometime after.

I believe the 16th day falls on the 26th. Whatever else you may do on that day please make some offering to Sri Ramakrishna at the Ashrama. I shall do the same here. Sometime after I shall take a bit of the relics to be put in the Ganges.

Yours affectionately,
Tapasyananda.

1. This was the first letter Maharaj wrote after his mother's demise. Although in the last sentence Maharaj mentions his intention to carry the relics, he never did that.

39

S.R.K. Math
Mylapore, 16-8-73

My dear appu,

Received your letter of the 14th instant. In chalking out your programme, you have to remember that you are carrying the relics of mother for immersion in Triveni. Now it is not proper to carry about the relics of a dead person to all these Ashramas especially where there are shrines attached to living quarters. You have to remember that you have this limitation. You will therefore have to delink this immersion affair from your tour programme.

It is for this reason that I suggest that you should stop in as few places as possible between Madras & Allahabad. Even Brindavan case be omitted or one case go straight to Brindavan & then to Triveni, Banares, Gaya & Calcutta. After spending the Durga Puja time there you can either go to Delhi direct from there or visit Bhuvaneswar & from there go to Delhi. From Delhi your case go in whatever direction you like. This will no doubt involve some extra journey from Calcutta or Bhuvaneswar back to Delhi. But this is something that cannot be avoided under the circumstances. In your programme also this return journey was involved to some extent.

I would however request you to remember two or three points. Journey with too many breaks is very difficult these days because of the difficulties of railway reservation. For 1st class 20 days & 3rd class 10 days advance booking is required. How are you going to arrange this with so many stoppages on the way? Next you have to be very sure that at your age you can stand this continuous knocking about for two months with changing food, shake in the train & sleepless nights, if reservation is not got. You must think twice before you decide about it.

My advice is that you delink your present journey from your trip to Delhi, Brindavan for the time being. You can go to Triveni, Banares, Gaya etc., & finish the rites & go to Calcutta for Durga Puja visit Bhuvaneswar & Puri & return.

Next season you can go on a trip to Delhi & other places & that time you can visit Brindavan also. Brindavan is close to Delhi. You can do the trip leisurely.

Gopalaswamy has prepared for you a tour programme from 15th September which enable to you to reach Calcutta before the 2nd October, the Shashti day. The Pooja begins only that day. There is nothing special earlier, beyond reading Devimahatmya in the shrine. After the pooja you can come to the city, see different places & visit Jayarambati & Kamarpukur etc. Your case travel leisurely to Bhuvaneswar etc. In about a month or a little more you can finish this trip. Or if you prefer to go to Delhi from Bhuvaneswar you can do so. Direct reservation from there to Delhi without touching Calcutta can be made.

You please decide which of these two alternatives you decide upon… [You] can think over the matter over again & instruct about the reservation of ticket immediately.

Early decision is required also because we shall have to write to different centres sufficiently early on providing accommodation. Especially for Belur Math I shall have to write sufficiently early as their guest house will be crowded during Druga Pooja. So please send an early reply.

Yours affectionately,
Tapasyananda.

P.S. If my proposed route is accepted you need not start earlier than 10th. You can arrive here any time before that. On confirmation we shall take ticket for the 10th as the starting date.

40

23rd May 1975

Mrs. Indira Krishnakumar[1]
C/O Sri K. P. S. Menon,
'Viswasanthi'
P.O. Sri Ramakrishna Nagar,
Ottapalam-3
KERALA

Dear Indira,

Received your letter of 21st May. Glad to know that you have a girl baby. I pray to the Lord that your expectations of her as conveyed in your letter, come true by His grace. Dominance of spiritual aspiration is the only way to make life purposeful.

I am glad to know also that you have been selected for the Indian Postal Service. I hope by the Lord's grace you will have the strength to bear successfully the responsibilities of both a house-wife and an officer of an All India Service.

May the Lord bless you and your child.

Yours in the Lord,
(Swami Tapasyananda)

1. Maharaj's niece

Letters of Swami Tapasyananda Maharaj's Mother

1[1]

Belur Math
22-2-28

To
K P A Menon
Y.M.C.A. Bangalore City.

Hope you got the letter I sent before leaving. While on our way from Madras, we stopped at Jagannatham[2] and Bhubaneswar and reached Calcutta[3] yesterday. Came to the Math at 2 p.m. Mahapurushji asked us to stay in the guesthouse yesterday. Today we are shifting to a place close by. You must write to me in the following address[4]. It is long since I got a letter from you. Tomorrow Balan is receiving Brahmacharya[5].

T V Narayana Iyer
Kerala Mutt, Hanuman Ghat
Benares City.

---

1. This letter was undoubtedly written by the Swami's mother, even though she had not signed.

2. 'Jagannatham' is the abode of Lord Jagannath in Puri, Orissa.

3. From Kerala Smt. Parukkuty Amma traveled to Calcutta via Madras. On this most memorable trip, the Swami had accompanied her.

4. She wanted her second son Achuthan Menon to send a reply to the Kerala Math, Benaras as she was planning to return to Kerala via Benaras. At this time, Sri Achutha Menon was doing BE at Bangalore

5. From this letter it is clear that the Swami got Brahmacharya on 23 February 1928 and that his mother was there in Belur Math at that time.

2

Prayaga
12-3-1928

To K P A Menon
Y.M.C.A.
Bangalore City.

Glad to get your letter. While proceeding from Madras stayed for two days each at Jagannatham and Bhubaneswar. Stayed at Calcutta for eight days and nine days at Kashi. At Belur the stay was near the Math. Prasadam for both the meals. Witnessed the Tithi celebrations[1]. Maha (Mahapurushji) made enquiries about you. In Kashi also, the stay was close to the Seva Ashram. And for board, prasadam itself. A house was given for comfortable stay. Met Swamiji (Tulasi Maharaj) at Kashi. Performed Gaya-shraaddha. Tonight we are leaving for Madras after sending the Ganga (jal)[2] straight to Ottapalam. We will go to Rameswaram[3] and then return home. We met Vijnanananda Swamiji here.

To Appu, Amma.

---

1. Sri Ramakrishna's birthday celebrations.

2. Ganga water must have been sent by parcel post to Ottapalam.

3. Perhaps the Swami, who was Purnachaitanya now, travelled to Madras in the same train. This is probable because the Swami had written in his letter dt. 3-12-1928 to his mother, '...You had written that you felt very uneasy when we changed trains at Trichinopoly. On that occasion I also felt likewise....' Perhaps from Trichinopoly, the Swami changed train to go to Madras and his mother proceeded to Rameswaram, because there could have been no other occasion for them to travel together after the *Brahmacharya Diksa*.

Swami Tapasyanandaji Maharaj

Part C: Glimpses

In Trivandrum-A Few Glimpses

Smt. Lalita Menon[1]

In the following pages, a humble attempt has been made to assess the deep bond that had been forged between Swami Tapasyananda Maharaj and the people of Trivandrum. This journey into the past was made possible by meeting a handful of people who had known Maharaj and had moved closely with him from the time he arrived in Trivandrum in 1940 till he left for Madras thirty years later.

Granite temple, Nettayam Ashrama

Swami Tapasyananda Maharaj came to Trivandrum when he was thirty-six years old. The Nettayam Ashrama with a beautiful granite temple on top of a hill in the suburb of the city was established by then. In accordance to the motto '*Sivajnane Jeeverseva*[2]', a small dispensary was started in Sasthamangalam in 1937.

1. She is a long standing devotee of Sri Ramakrishna.
2. Seeing God in living beings and serving them.

An Artist's sketch of Maharaj

Dr. Raman Thampi, who was the chief medical officer of the Travancore Government and the Physician to the Palace and Honorary Physician to the Resident, on his retirement, decided to help in the development of the dispensary. One devotee, Sri N. Raman Nair, the son of Sri M.R. Narayana Pillai, a district judge, and Sri Padmanabha Thampi who were connected with some of the earliest of Ramakrishna Maths in Travancore, fondly remember the doctor who would come to the dispensary with his coat pocket filled with medicines meant to be freely distributed after the diagnosis.

This eminent doctor was the brother of Sri Padmanabhan Thampi who will be ever be remembered as the moving spirit behind the Ramakrishna movement in Travancore. The doctor's younger son, Col. R.T.M. Nair, who is now in his nineties and leading a peaceful retired life shared some of his memories which will be mentioned at a later stage. The doctor's elder son was the legendary Dr. R. Kesavan Nair who worked tirelessly for the hospital and was a household name in Trivandrum.

There was another Dr. Kesavan Nair known as Kesavan Nair Jr., who too had devoted his entire working life to the hospital and had seen the hospital grow from strength to strength. He had mentioned in his personal notes about the opening of the hospital. It is worth remembering here that he had developed a very warm personal relationship with Swami Tapasyananda Maharaj who arrived in 1940 when the dispensary had not yet become a hospital. The Doctor's children remember the depth of the regard and affection that each had for the other.

Maharaj spent thirty years in Trivandrum and was instrumental in developing the small dispensary into a full-fledged hospital. In this endeavour, he was ably assisted by a dedicated band of doctors, nurses and volunteers. Maharaj himself worked tirelessly from his modest room which served as his office during the day and bedroom at night with two benches kept together with a sheet on it forming a bed. Those who had seen him those days vouched for his austere life. The utter simplicity innate in his nature, his deep devotion to Sri Ramakrishna, and the sincerity with which he conducted Thakur's [Sri Ramakrishna's] work attracted devotees from all walks of life.

Maharaj's simplicity charmed and impressed those who came into contact with him. His clothes were simple, food Spartan. Before he had come to Trivandrum, the management there had been warned that Maharaj who was being deputed here was careless about his own comforts and it would be the duty of the local devotees to look after him. This instruction was followed with the utmost sincerity by the devotees of Trivandrum who spared no efforts to serve him. There are a few left today who had had the good fortune of knowing him and they were more than willing to share their precious memories of him. They could not but be struck by the Maharaj's unmistakable spiritual aura. The qualities of head and heart that he evinced in his dealings with everyone were only an extension of his spirituality and total commitment to service.

Side view of the Hospital, Sasthamangalam

Building the hospital was a major concern of Maharaj and he spared no effort to achieve this goal. There was to be no wastage of money or material. Every donation however small was gratefully accepted and every rupee was to be accounted. His personal needs were practically none. A devotee who had sent Maharaj a new dhoti was reprimanded by saying that the amount could have been spent more profitably. Sister Jagadeeswari Amma, who served in the hospital for over four decades, had worked with Maharaj only for four years; that was long enough for her to see how Maharaj functioned. He could not tolerate waste of any kind. In the early days of the hospital when there were no disposable needles available, the nursing staff was encouraged to use each needle with care, sharpen it on a special stone when necessary and keep it clean and sterile by boiling. When a high pressure steaming machine was bought from Palghat, Maharaj carefully studied the intricacies of its working and learnt to operate it himself. Then he taught the skill to others and warned them not to make any careless mistakes. This was mentioned by Mr. Krishnan whose association with the Math began as early as 1938 when he was a young boy. He met Maharaj in 1946 and continued to serve the Math in various capacities till the seventies.

Mr. Krishnan had another story to tell concerning Maharaj which is educative as well as a bit amusing. This story too deals with the thriftiness of Maharaj. Maharaj had a theory that nothing was to be thrown away for seven years however useless it might seem to be. He had a pair of old slippers which could no longer be used, but had not been thrown away. One day an old machine working on pedals in the operation theatre needed a bush urgently. Maharaj wondered whether the piece of rubber needed could be taken from his old slippers. The mechanic, Sri Aliyar, said it was possible and used a part of Maharaj's old footwear for the job. The machine functioned well and Maharaj beamed with delight!

Buying new dhotis for himself was unheard of. The old one was mended again and again till it was threadbare.

Quite close to the Nettayam Ashrama lives Thankamma leading a contented retired life ever maintaining that all her wellbeing after years of poverty was a blessing from the thrifty but kind Swami who often came to her tailoring shop to have his dhoti mended. Maharaj helped her with her tailoring unit and she prospered.

Maharaj did not believe in spending money on himself. 'I cannot waste what is Bhagavan's,' was his simple explanation. Sri T.V. Padmanabhan Nair who too is leading a retired life after many years of working with Maharaj mentioned this.

Maharaj used to walk to Nettayam and back - a distance of twelve kilometers. Even if the manager swami insisted on giving him the bus fare, the money would remain in Maharaj's pocket to be given to someone in need.

Sri Prabhakaran Nair has an interesting story to tell, regarding the meticulous way in which Maharaj functioned, however small may be the work at hand. When a building was being constructed as part of developing the hospital, bricks would be brought to the site in bullock carts - a consignment of 1000 bricks in three carts each time. Maharaj would inspect each brick carefully to make sure that it was well-baked. Those that looked a bit defective were kept aside. Later they were immersed in water. Those bricks that were found to be absorbing the water too quickly were not to be used. They were kept aside, counted carefully and returned. No loss was incurred.

Sister Jagadeeswari Amma remembers how, before boilers were introduced, water used to be heated by burning dry leaves and hot water was available for all. She mentions how Maharaj would be present in the operation theatre wearing a mask. She says that there is hardly anything in the medical science that he did not know. Such care taken in the smallest of details and the meticulous way in which the administration was managed helped the hospital grow rapidly. The above mentioned Sister remembers how Maharaj insisted that everyone, irrespective of his background and financial position, should get the same treatment.

That there was to be no preferential treatment for anyone was shown by an incident related by Sri Raman Nair. Sri Nair's sister who had been married to Maharaj's pre-monastic younger brother had to have an operation in the Sasthamangalam Hospital. She was treated with the same meticulous care and attention that every other patient got, not more, not less. Sri Nair laughed when he said that even the porridge that the patient took had to be paid for.

Maharaj was a strict taskmaster and disciplinarian. He would tolerate no slipshod work or dishonesty. He kept a watchful eye on the stores and if a lapse was noted it was severely dealt with. Sri Padmanabhan Nair remembers how a member of the staff caught for theft was dismissed promptly. Punctuality and promptitude were part of his nature.

Sister Jagadeeswari Amma insists that the strict discipline and prompt corrections were accepted without any resentment because they were always justified and behind the strict demeanour, one could not but be conscious of a compassionate heart. She adds that Maharaj took regular rounds and made sure that there was no neglect anywhere. She remembers that his motto was that a patient's satisfaction was the Hospital's prosperity. The staff and all the workers felt that they belonged to the same big family. For Onam, she remembers, there would be *sadya* (feast) for three days and Maharaj participated in it all along with the others. The hard-working staff got a lot of consideration from him. He used to insist that those on duty the whole night should get adequate rest before returning to duty. Sri Krishnan, a long-time staff member of the hospital, also remembers this humane quality of Maharaj.

Several eminent doctors in Trivandrum considered it a privilege to work with Maharaj in the hospital. Among them were Dr. R. Kesavan Nair, the son of Dr. Raman Thampi the pioneer, Dr. K.N. Pillai, Dr. Ponamma, Dr. K. Kesavan Nair and Dr. Sivarajan, to mention a few. Today, the hospital flourishes in the heart of the city with special facilities with over forty doctors and fifty nursing staff attending to the needs of the growing number of patients. A prestigious nursing-school also started functioning in Maharaj's time.

All those who had known him in the early days mention especially how Maharaj encouraged those who wanted to study – both boys and girls. Sri Krishnan remembers how Maharaj personally helped his sister with grammar lessons and later on saw to it that she was trained as a nurse. There were many other girls who became nurses under his guidance. Some of them were sent to the special nursing school attached to Seva Pratishthan in Calcutta for higher training. Sister Jagadeeswari Amma remembers that the girls who had to travel all the way to Calcutta were taken and brought back escorted by a responsible and an elderly person. Often Maharaj going to Belur Math on official work would himself be the escort.

Sri Padmanabhan Nair, now leading a retired life after working closely with Maharaj for several decades, has memories of Maharaj going back to 1945. As a young 16-year old, he had met Maharaj and remained with him till Maharaj left for Madras. He worked in the Mission till his retirement, in various capacities – as cook, compounder, a teacher of Hindi and *bhajans*. He remembers gratefully that it was Maharaj who had sent him to study Hindi at Dakshin Bharat Hindi Prachar Sabha. This stood him in good stead in the later years. Maharaj's approach was practical. He did his best to have a child educated and sufficiently qualified to find a job and earn his or her livelihood. Sri Padmanabhan Nair's sister was one such who was benefitted by Maharaj's timely help.

Innumerable are the people who were educated thus, whose intellectual growth was nurtured and who were guided along proper lines to lead full lives. They maintain that even the material prosperity they enjoy now is because of Maharaj's blessings.

In spite of the work in and for the hospital kept increasing, Maharaj found time to help the so-called outcastes in Kanjiranpara near Trivandrum. He encouraged several children there to study and improve their living conditions. Sri Padmanabhan Nair maintains that Maharaj ignored the disapproving attitude of some members of the higher castes regarding his association with the [so-called] outcastes.

Both Sister Jagadeeswari Amma and Sri Padmanabhan Nair mentioned that Maharaj was an adept in counseling and guiding young people. The Sister recalls that when she was getting married, Maharaj gave her some sound advice and useful tips to make her marriage a success. She said that she felt as though she was being advised by her own mother.

Maharaj had forged several friendships during his stay here. Some charming incidents are remembered by Colonel R.T.Madhavan Nair (Retd.), the younger brother of Dr. R.Kesavan Nair who is gratefully remembered by the public of Trivandrum for his work in the R.K.Mission hospital. Dr. Nair and Col. Nair are the sons of Dr. Raman Thampi, the earliest father figure in the R.K.Mission dispensary. Col. Nair mentioned about how the great doctor and his wife, Smt. Chellamma Pilla, welcomed Maharaj affectionately to their house. Maharaj used to walk over to their house in the evenings and over a cup of tea, discuss matters relating to the hospital. When he left, Maharaj took that day's copy of the Indian Express, which had already been read by the household, to be read it the next day while he rested in the afternoon. The paper was returned that evening. The routine continued day after day, the borrowing and the returning of the newspaper.

Sometimes the doctor felt that Maharaj was not taking enough food nor taking enough care of his health. Smt. Thampi used to cook some food and take it to the Ashrama and persuade the reluctant Swami to consume it. Another lady who used to do the same was Smt. Parukkutty Amma, the daughter of Sri Padmanabhan Thampi. Maharaj was ever content with simple food. Like Malayalis all over the world, he was fond of payasam [kheer] made of large ripe bananas.

Maharaj maintained excellent relations with everyone. This was not done with any special effort. He was just himself, a self-denying renunciate, working to the best of his ability for the great Order to which he belonged. So anyone coming into contact with him could not but respect him. The Dewan of Travancore, Sir C.P. Ramaswamy Iyer, was one such. It was he who opened the OP Wing of the hospital in 1943. In 1948, the In-patients ward was opened by Lady Mountbatten. In 1952, the Rajapramukh opened the Devaswam Ward. In 1970, the Annex building was opened by the tenth president of the Math and Mission, Swami Vireswarananda Maharaj.

Shrine Hall (side view), Sasthamangalam

People who had known him intimately talk eloquently about Swami Tapasyananda Maharaj's compassion. They all had first-hand experience of the tenderness that lay concealed behind a stern exterior. Mr. Krishnan remembers that Maharaj was once walking in front of the shrine in a deep contemplative mood. Seeing Krishnan he simply said, 'None of you are strangers. This yard is the Lord's playground.' Years later, when Maharaj was in Madras, Sri Krishnan and his family went to meet him. While they were waiting outside his room, Maharaj was told that there were some visitors to see him. They were then ushered into his room. The moment Maharaj set eyes on them he beamed and declared, 'These are not visitors at all!' On occasional meetings like this Maharaj would not only welcome his old friends warmly but would never fail to enquire after his old co-workers and associates in Trivandrum.

Even in the middle of a busy schedule revolving round the hospital, Maharaj's spiritual ministry was never to take a second place. He used to take scriptural classes twice a week. Sri Krishnan also remembers that periodically a few Christian priests used to come and engage in a deep discussion with him on spiritual matters. He would conduct the puja in the shrine and the way he would recite the *Sri Lalita Sahasranama* is well remembered. *Devi Mahatmyam* was his favourite and he daily read it with the text presented to him several years ago by his mother Palat Parukkutty Amma who was a deeply religious person herself.

In 1971, Swami Tapasyananda Maharaj who had been the anchor of the Trivandrum centre of the Ramakrishna Mission was requested to take charge of Madras Math. Several appeals went to the headquarters that Maharaj should be allowed to remain in Trivandrum as he had become an integral part of the Trivandrum, loved and respected by a large number of people. But Maharaj's *karmabhoomi* for the next twenty years had been decided and he created a great void when he left Trivandrum.

But Maharaj did return to Trivandrum periodically afterwards. Whenever he came there he was greeted with great affection and Maharaj responded warmly. As the vice-president of the Ramakrishna Math and Mission, he gave *mantra diksa* to many there. All his disciples revere him. Most of them are engaged in following the grand path of service shown by Maharaj. Apart from them, there are a few others – just a handful of them – now in their eighties and nineties who affectionately remember Maharaj, a young dedicated sannyasin, who arrived in Trivandrum in the early 1940s and won their hearts. They feel it a privilege to have served him. They cherish precious memories of him. Because of their willingness and cooperation, these memoirs could be compiled and written.

Sources

1. Sri Krishnan, now 83 years old, was introduced to the Nettayam Ashrama at the age of eight. He worked with Swami Tapasyananda Maharaj till Maharaj left for Madras. He continued working for the hospital till he retired. He and his family continue their close association with the Math. The booklet brought out by Madras Math after Maharaj's *mahasamadhi* was beautifully translated into Malayalam by Prof. Sulochana Nair at his instance.

2. Sri N. Raman Nair, now in his late eighties, maintains a youthful enthusiasm especially with matters concerning Thakur [Sri Ramakrishna]. His father, Sri M.R. Narayana Pillai, a district judge, along with Sri Padmanabhan Thampi was responsible for the setting up of some of the earliest Ramakrishna Ashramas in Travancore in the first decades of the 20^{th}Century. Sri Raman Nair retired as Headmaster of a well-known school in Trivandrum. His guidance during the Ramakrishna Bhakta Sammelanam was invaluable.

3. Sri T.V.Padmanabhan Nair, in his eighties now, had met Maharaj when he was 16 years old and worked at the hospital in various capacities and has been greatly influenced by Maharaj.

4. Sister Jagadeeswari Amma, retired Head nurse of the hospital.

5. Col. R.T.M. Nair (Retd.), in early nineties now, is the younger son of the great pioneer, Dr. Raman Thampi and the younger brother of Dr. R. Kesavan Nair whose selfless work for the hospital will ever be remembered by the grateful people of Trivandrum. Col. Nair formerly of the Army Dental Corps is leading a retired life in Trivandrum.

6. Personal notes kept by Dr. K. Kesavan Nair.

Section II

Reminiscences by Monastics

Old Temple, Madras Math

Srimat Swami Tapasyanandaji Maharaj

that a committed monastic member can have holidays in his spiritual practices or ask for retirement after serving Sri Guru Maharaj for a fixed number of years.

I always found him productively occupied. I have seen him at Madras Math and also at Belur Math, which he visited for attending Trustees' Meeting, and at other places. Everywhere he was occupied with reading books or writing or correcting manuscripts or discussing scriptures with other monks. His solemn countenance, wearing a grave expression, suggested that he was always mentally busy with something higher. Yet, he could be light-hearted as well. I learnt from other monks that when he was the president of Madras Math, he would regularly attend the night class (the customary post-dinner gathering of all monastics where they read from a book and also exchange sundry information) and take part in all discussion. He would entertain the monks with his stories, comments and observations. His deliberations were often interspersed with jokes and subtle humour.

His life was simplicity itself. There was hardly anything in his living room which catered to more than his bare necessities. When I went to see him in his office at Trivandrum, I was astonished to see him sitting on a carpet on the floor, with a desk in front of him—as one finds in traditional temples or old shops. This was the office of the administrator, supervising a hospital with 100 beds, having specialities like psychiatric division and diagnostic facilities!

The evening prayers at Trivandrum centre were held in the same room, a part of which was used for office of the Swami in-charge. There were few monastic hands to assist him in supervising the hospital work. Evidently, he himself was doing the major work. I was impressed to note that while doing all his works, he maintained a strict punctuality in letter and spirit.

At Trivandrum, besides the hospital centre, there is a retreat centre at Nettayam, located on a hillock, about six kilometres away from the hospital. The foundation stone for the Nettayam centre was laid in 1916 by no less a person than by Srimat Swami Brahmananda Maharaj himself. I am not sure if Swami Tapasyananda Maharaj would visit it for any retreat—work itself was worship for him.

During his days at the hospital centre at Trivandrum, he hardly found time to pursue the literary interests for which he is well-known. Prior to going to Trivandrum, he was editor of *The Vedanta Kesari*, the spiritual and cultural monthly in English, brought out from Sri Ramakrishna Math at Madras. But after spending about thirty years at

Front View, Nettayam Ashrama

the hospital centre at Trivandrum, when he returned to Madras, he restarted his literary pursuits! At Madras, he would spend seven to eight hours daily, in reading and writing. He wrote and translated (from Sanskrit to English) several books. His writings have the sparkle of an illumining thinking, presented in his own distinctive writing style.

Just as language and thought are inseparable, so also was Revered Swami Tapasyananda Maharaj's life and his philosophical thoughts remained inseparable. They functioned in unison. This integration of thought and action was visible in his holy person and character. Though he had strong determination, what was more remarkable was his spontaneous love which sweetened his thoughts and manners. Perhaps, that is why he could get things done smoothly.

Let me cite an illustration. Holy Mother Sri Sarada Devi's conversation-teachings are available in Bengali in two volumes. Titled *Sri Sri Mayer Katha,* a part of this book had been translated into English (*The Gospel of the Holy Mother*) and published many years ago. Revered Swami Tapasyananda Maharaj wanted me to translate the remaining part of the book. I was rather apprehensive whether I was competent to handle this abstruse material, so I humbly declined to do it—as many as four times! But he would not leave and finally prevailed upon me and I had to translate the remaining portion into English. It was a pleasant and blessed opportunity. After the book was published, it was well received by all. I wrote to him, expressing my gratitude for his kindness.

In the early 1990s, it was diagnosed that he was diabetic and the doctors prescribed a rigid diet for him. As expected,

Revered Maharaj followed it sincerely. He was already fond of simple *idli*. Hereafter it became his principal food in the breakfast, noon meal as well as for the night meal! He used to tell that *idli* was an 'innocent dish' suitable for all; it does no harm to anyone. Once he disclosed to me *idli*'s historical background: it was the product of the creative genius of Rajaraja Chola, the tenth century emperor of Chola dynasty. I had not known this earlier.

Before closing my modest recollection, let me recall the salient features of his unique personality. His life was a spontaneous harmony of prayer, meditation, studies and serving the Master and His cause. We get a glimpse of his idea from his annotation of the *Gita*'s verse 67 of chapter 18 (published by Madras Math). Swami Tapasyananda Maharaj writes, 'A person who does not practice austere living, who has no genuine devotion to God and no true spirit of service is not entitled to the legacy of the teachings of the *Gita*. Moreover these teachings of the *Gita* need to be internalized and finally put into practice through one's thoughts, words and deeds.'

Revered Swami Tapasyananda Maharaj himself exemplified this verse. I offer my salutations at his feet.

2

A Saga of Hard Work and Dedication

Swami Amitabhananda[1]

I went for the first time to Ramakrishna Ashrama, Trivandrum at the end of November 1950 with Revered Agamananda Maharaj, the founder-president of Sri Ramakrishna Advaita Ashrama, Kalady. We met two monks there who were sitting on the verandah of a small tiled building. While Revered Agamananda Maharaj began to converse with one of the monks, I went to the prayer hall at the western end of the same building. After visiting the prayer hall, I asked Revered Agamananda Maharaj about the Hospital, and he, standing on the verandah on the eastern side, pointed out to a tiled building across a narrow lane and said that that it was the hospital. The Malayalam monthly magazine, *Prabuddha Keralam* was published from the Trivandrum Ashrama in those days and another magazine *Amrita-Vani* from Kalady. Revered Agamananda Maharaj talked with a monk there about transferring the *Prabuddha Keralam* to Kalady and merging the subscribers of both the magazines. (Subsequently, the publication of *Amrita Vani* was stopped and *Prabuddha Keralam* was published from Kalady.)

---

1. He is a senior monk of the Order who was closely associated with Revered Tapasyananda Maharaj.

In May 1951, Sri Ramakrishna Ashrama, Kalady was celebrating Sri Sankara Jayanti with appropriate meetings and cultural programmes lasting for many days. I was a student-volunteer for the celebrations. In one of the sessions, I was enthralled to hear through the loud speaker a forceful and eloquent speech given in a deep and solemn voice. When I looked at the stage, I recognized the speaker as the monk I had met at Trivandrum Ashrama – Swami Tapasyananda Maharaj.

After finishing my schooling and with the blessing of Revered Swami Agamananda Maharaj and other monks in Kalady Ashrama, I formally joined Madras Math in August 1952. Within a month of my joining the Math, Durga Puja in an image was celebrated on a grand scale at the Math after a gap of 31 years. Many monks, including Swamis Tapasyananda Maharaj, Yatiswarananda Maharaj, Agamananda Maharaj and Adidevananda Maharaj attended the puja.

During my stay at Madras Math from 1952 to 1962, Swami Tapasyananda Maharaj visited Madras three or four times *en route* to Belur Math to attend the monks' conferences. During such visits, Revered Kailasananda Maharaj would invite Revered Tapasyananda Maharaj to speak on some Sundays. His speeches were appreciated by one and all who heard him. A Director of a reputed educational institute commented later, 'What a marvellous English Swami Tapasyananda Maharaj has!' His capacity to take up an idea and develop it into a full lecture was really wonderful.

Although the food served at Belur Math was normally plain and simple, there would be sumptuous feasts, with a variety of dishes, during the conferences. In one of the night classes at Madras Math, Revered Maharaj himself mentioned that he had expressed his reservations about holding such feasts in the Belur Math. Then one swami there had pointed out that these feasts were like what pillars were to a building and that although the food was plain on ordinary days, these occasional feasts helped in maintaining the health of the body. Saying this, Revered Maharaj chuckled, adding that he had been immediately convinced with the argument.

I was in Belur Math from the end of 1962 to the middle of 1970. During that period, Revered Tapasyananda Maharaj would come there, first to attend the half-yearly Advisory Committee meetings, and later, from the end of 1965, when he became a Trustee of the Order, for the four-monthly Trustees' meetings. At the meetings, Revered Maharaj would express his views without fear or favour.

I was assigned the task of receiving him at the Howrah Railway Station and also see him off on his return journey. Revered Maharaj seldom travelled by air. While conversing with us once, he asserted that he would not spend a single paisa from the Hospital funds for any luxurious travel.

At Belur Math, I would go to his room whenever I found time and conversed with him freely. A few other monastics would also be with me on such occasions.

During his visits to Calcutta, Maharaj would reserve one of the evenings to go to the Seva Prathishthan Hospital in order to study the procedures practiced there and to explore the possibility of adopting them in the Sasthamangalam Hospital. Moreover, he would want to meet Sister Kalyani, the matron in Seva Pratishthan for a long time, and inform her devoted mother Smt. Parukkutty Amma (who visited Trivandrum Ashrama regularly) about her well-being. Smt. Parukkutty Amma was the daughter of Sri Padmanabhan Tampi (elder brother of Dr. Taman Tampi) the Police Supdt. of Travancore who later took sannyasa and assumed the name Parananda. Both the brothers and their whole family were ardent devotees and active supporters of the Ramakrishna Ashramas in Kerala.

During those days, the present nursing school of the Sasthamangalam hospital was not there. Only ANM [Auxiliary Nurse Midwife] training used to be imparted. Some students who qualified in this were sent for the courses offered at Seva Prathishtan. During his visits, Maharaj would enquire about the progress of the nurses from Trivandrum in their courses. Maharaj would go by car to the hospital with Swami Dayananda Maharaj, stay there overnight, and return the next morning.

Revered Maharaj brought me to Trivandrum Ashrama in June 1970 to work with him. I stayed with him for a year (till June 1971) and could observe him closely. The old Dispensary building (present prayer-cum-lecture hall) was Revered Maharaj's office and living room. He would sit on a chair with a table in front having some books and files. Behind his chair was a wall-bookcase with a few, but serious books which he would read or consult when he had leisure. I would sit next to him at a table with a type-writer.

A very small room behind the office building served as his bathroom and toilet. How he managed to take bath in such a small bathroom is unimaginable. We have heard that he would walk four miles up and down Nettayam in 1940 until his stay at the dispensary was arranged.

Revered Maharaj would punctually join us at 7.00 a.m. for breakfast, which usually consisted of only *idlis*, which he felt was the safest food. We would sit on wooden planks while taking food. Revered Maharaj began to sit on an armed chair (over which a wooden plank was placed) ever since he developed problem in his right foot. He did not allow himself even the luxury of using a table and a chair. Such was his austerity. He never cared for his own comfort.

Revered Maharaj himself did a simple puja in the shrine using two incense sticks, a few basil leaves, some water, and flowers if available. He would burn one incense stick in front of Holy Mother's photo in the prayer hall and conducted the puja by chanting *Sri Lalita Sahasranama*, for which he had a special liking. A few coconut *laddus* were also occasionally offered and distributed to children of Sisu-bhavan, run by Sarada Sangha, when they visited the prayer hall. When prayer hall was added to the original building, Revered Swami Madhavananda Maharaj, the then General Secretary of the Ramakrishna Math and Mission, had sent a hand-written letter to Revered Tapasyananda Maharaj with the instruction that since it would be difficult to maintain the ceremonial purity in a hospital centre, no ritualistic puja with elaborate offerings need to be conducted. The letter was framed and hung in the prayer hall to answer any inquisitive queries about the absence of ritualistic puja in the Ashrama.

In the evenings, Revered Maharaj would walk in the courtyard in front of his office. Either Swami Golokananda or myself would do the evening *arati*. Revered Maharaj would sit on a bench on the eastern side of the verandah and attend the *arati*. Thereafter till 8.00 p.m., he would meditate sitting there.

Maharaj would daily go around the hospital and enquire about the welfare of the patients, observe major surgeries so minutely that he could offer his suggestions to the surgeons. Most of the land where the hospital buildings stand was acquired during his tenure. He also added many new buildings to the hospital during his tenure.

Revered Maharaj was no doubt very frugal in his habits. He would preserve used envelopes to reuse them while sending lettering by hand within the city. Sri Madhavan Pillai, the office peon, would go by bicycle and deliver the letters in the city. But when it came to purchasing equipments for the hospital, he would select the best. He knew the names of each and every part of the equipments used. A doctor once admitted to me that even though he knew how to use the equipments, he was not conversant with the names of every part. But Revered Maharaj knew, having gone through the books with illustrations. Sometimes, he would go and see the working of similar equipments in other hospitals before placing a Purchase Order. He would negotiate with the dealer regarding some concession in the price, but once the deal was confirmed, he was prompt in paying the promised amount.

Revered Maharaj did not have much love for flower gardens. He preferred cash-crops like coconut, plantains, tapioca etc. He himself would supervise the manuring of coconut trees or the planting of tapioca.

Revered Maharaj would conduct weekly classes in English in the Ashrama prayer hall and a monthly retreat at Nettyam Ashrama. He regularly gave discourses in and around Trivandrum and also participated in the inter-religious discussions conducted in the city. Later, he rebuilt a bigger kitchen and dining hall at Nettayam Ashrama.

While leaving for Belur Math for attending monks' conferences, we would suggest him to avail the hospital van to reach the railway station. But he was unyielding. He would go only by bus. The office peon would carry his only bag on a cycle to the railway station. He would tell the person working in the canteen to get a few bananas that would ripen at different times of his three-day train journey.

One morning, I found Revered Maharaj very quietly sitting in his office. That was unusual for him. Usually, he would either be drafting letters, reading books, or engaging himself in giving instructions to the doctors and workers. But that day's unusual behaviour of Revered Maharaj surprised me. On enquiry, I came to know that a telegram had come that morning communicating the demise of his mother. A few days earlier, he had gone to Ottappalam to see her. She was a pious lady, actively involved in the activities of Ottappalam Ashrama. The legacy of the Palat family – her home – was rich and well known and had had produced many heroes like Palat Koman, whose exploits are sung in ballads (Vadakkanpattu) even today, famous citizens like Sir C. Sankaran Nair – former President of the Indian National Congress and later Executive Committee member of the Viceroy and one of the founders of the Justice Party of Madras, Sir K.P. S. Menon, who was a diplomat and Ambassador to Russia etc., and Lt. Gen. Candeth, if I remember rightly, who was Indian Army Commander in-charge of the liberation of Goa from Portuguese rule in 1961 and G.O.C. Western Command during the Indo-Pakistan War in 1965.

Revered Swami Vireswarananda Maharaj, the then president of the Ramakrishna Order, Revered Swami Kailasananda Maharaj, president of Madras Math, and many other monks came to Trivandrum one or two days before the inauguration of Vivekananda Rock Memorial at Kanyakumari. We, a party of 30 monks and devotees, then left for Kanyakumari. At Kerala House in Kanyakumari, in order to make Revered Kailasananda Maharaj's stay more comfortable, Revered Swami Tapasyananda Maharaj was ready to give up his own bed and to sleep over a mat on the floor! Such was the self-effacing and self-sacrificing spirit of Revered Maharaj.

The next morning at 4.00, we, along with Swami Chidbhavananda Maharaj of Ramakrishna Tapovanam, Swami Chinmayananda Maharaj of Chinmaya Mission and a few others from Bombay were taken to the Rock by boat. Revered Vireswarananda Maharaj dedicated the Statue by performing *arati* and garlanding it.

At 9.00 a.m., there was a public meeting on the mainland, presided over by Sri V.V. Giri, president of India. Revered Vireswarananda Maharaj, the then Chief Minister of Tamil Nadu, Sri M. Karunanidhi, Prof. V. Raghavan and a few others spoke during the august occasion.

A few weeks before the inauguration, some letters to the Editor, *The Hindu*, were published insisting on the erection of a statue of late Raja Bhaskara Sethupati of Ramnad on the rock along with that of Swami Vivekananda, claiming that the late Raja was solely responsible for Swamiji going to Chicago to the attend the Parliament of Religions in 1882.

This inaccurate claim irritated all those who were well-versed with Swamiji's biography. Swami Tapasyananda Maharaj wrote strongly against the proposed move (which was also published in *The Hindu*) and urged other prominent citizens to write similar letters to the newspapers. Subsequently, the proposal of Raja's statue was abandoned and the inaugural function went off smoothly.

Two or three days after the inauguration of Vivekananda Rock Memorial, an Annexe building to the hospital at Sasthamangalam, Trivandrum, was also inaugurated by Revered Swami Vireswarananda Maharaj. Revered Tapasyananda Maharaj had worked hard to collect donations from public and funds from Government of India for the completion of the building. Revered Maharaj heaved a sigh of relief after the building was dedicated to the service of the needy.

With Bhuteshananda Maharaj in Madras Math, 1989

Revered Swami Bhuteshananda Maharaj, the then Asst. Secretary of the Ramakrishna Mission, came on a visit to Trivandrum en route to Kanyakumari. Revered

Tapasyananda Maharaj had reserved a seat in a bus for Revered Bhuteshananda Maharaj. But somehow we could intervene and arrange an exclusive vehicle for Revered Bhuteshananda Maharaj to travel.

Once, the Kerala Government wanted to levy tax on our hospital. We had till then enjoyed tax-exemption as it was a charitable hospital, with more than one-third patients being given free treatment. Revered Maharaj vigorously pleaded for the continuance of tax-exemption since all the funds were utilized only for the benefit of the patients, unlike the corporate managements where the surplus income would be shared among the board members or share-holders. Revered Maharaj's pleadings had the desired effect.

Revered Maharaj was particular that admission to the Auxillary Nurse Midwife course be done strictly as per the rules and regulations. He never yielded to any kind of pressure, wherever it came from.

When Revered Swami Kailasananda Maharaj became one of the vice-presidents of the Order, the authorities in Belur Math proposed that Revered Tapasyananda Maharaj take charge of Madras Math in order to ensure the continuance of strict traditions established by Swami Ramakrishnananda Maharaj (Sasi Maharaj). Hearing the news about the impending transfer of Revered Maharaj, some prominent citizens of Trivandrum wrote to the General Secretary [of Ramakrishna Mission] pleading with him to refrain from transferring Revered Maharaj from Trivandrum at that juncture. The Government of Kerala had promulgated an ordinance prohibiting doctors and surgeons in Government service from serving in private hospitals. The Ashrama Hospital mainly depended on surgeons and specialists from Government hospitals. So the Ashrama needed to address this issue. Moreover, new surgeons were to be appointed to make the newly inaugurated annexe building fully functional. Citing these as the reasons for their plea, these prominent citizens of Trivandrum requested the headquarters to reconsider the decision. However, the authorities gave Revered Maharaj six months to address these issues and then to proceed towards Madras.

After Revered Maharaj left for Madras, I too took a transfer to Kalady Ashram. I had several other occasions to meet Revered Maharaj at Madras, Kalady and other places.

Revered Maharaj had come to Kalady for the temple dedication ceremony in April 1976 and to speak in one of the sessions during the celebrations. I took him to the Ashrama's old guest house where arrangements were made for his stay. When I wanted to change the old bed sheet and pillow cover and put new ones for Revered Maharaj, he forbade me to use a new set for his sake. Such was his simplicity.

People in Trivandrum still lovingly and reverentially cherish his memories. He had had a soft corner for the poor and would save every paisa to serve them without caring for his own comforts.

It would do us good, both individually and nationally, if we remember the ideals set before us by great souls like Revered Swami Tapasyananda Maharaj.

3

Houses for the Homeless

Swami Samagrananda[1]

It was in 1960 that I met Swami Tapasyananda Maharaj for the first time in our centre at Sasthamagalam in Trivandrum. He received me warmly and was very cordial and kind. He was staying in a room adjacent to the shrine. There was a wooden cot in the room. During the day, the bed was rolled up and he would spread the bed only when he wanted to lie down. By the side of the cot were a wooden chair and a table. He would always sit straight on the chair, either reading books or instructing his assistants or allotting duties to the workers.

Whenever I went to Trivandrum or Kanyakumari, I used to meet Tapasyananda Maharaj and spend some time with him. He had a regular routine. Whenever he was in the Ashrama, he would never miss his early morning japa and meditation and he himself would do a simple puja to Sri Ramakrishna. In the evenings too, he would take his food only after his japa and meditation. He was leading a simple and austere life. He was a great and an able administrator. All the activities of the Ashrama went on smoothly, as though by his mere presence. Everybody loved and respected him because of his monastic qualities.

---

1. He is a senior monk of the Ramakrishna Order who knew Revered Tapasyananda Maharaj for many years.

After some years Tapasyananda Maharaj took charge of Madras Math. In 1978, Madras Math started flood relief work in Trichirapally (Trichy) district. I was then staying in Ramakrishna Mission Vidyalaya, Coimbatore. Swami Kirtidananda was the Secretary of the flood relief and I was called in for the relief work. We visited the flood-affected areas in Trichy and distributed food, clothes, vessels and other necessary household articles. In the village

At Ramakrishna Mission Students' Home, Madras

of Vembanoor, two colonies were completely washed away. We built two colonies each having twenty-six houses and a shrine. The colony named Sri Ramakrishna Sarada Puram was inaugurated by the then governor Sri Bhimsen Sachar. The second colony named Vivekananda Puram was inaugurated by the Chief of Southern Army, Sri Mahadevan, who was an alumnus of Ramakrishna Mission Students' Home. Swami Tapasyananda Maharaj attended the inauguration of the second colony. He was immensely happy to see the houses built for the homeless so tidy and strong. Usually he used to be very grave, but on that day I found him exceedingly happy. While I was standing near him, he happily enquired me about the relief work and was watching the celebrations joyfully.

Once I went to Ramakrishna Ashrama, Ottapalam and visited Swami Tapasyanada Maharaj's parental home. At that time his mother was living there. It was a great privilege for me to take food from her who was initiated by Swami Brahmananda Maharaj himself.

Swami Tapasyananda Maharaj was a great scholar in Sanskrit and in scriptures. As all of us know, he had written several books and has translated a few of our scriptures. Conversing with him was always a learning process since we could gather so much knowledge about the scriptures and the teachings of the Holy trio.

We have to learn simplicity, austerity and steadfast devotion to the Holy Trio from his life and imbibe his habit of regular spiritual practice.

4

A Monk, Saint and Yogi!

Swami Tanmayananda[1]

The monks of the southern centres travelling to Belur Math and other places in the North would invariably pass through Madras. So we at Madras Math had the opportunity to meet many monks, have their holy company, interact with them and personally serve them. We also could meet some great monks. Their personalities and appealing conversations would be inspiring, elevating and instructive. Most of them would talk to us in the night class after dinner. We would put questions and they would gladly clear our doubts. Most interesting would be their reminiscences of their gurus and other senior monks. They would also narrate how they came in contact with Sri Ramakrishna's message and the Order and what made them to finally join the Order. All these narrations would be interesting and illuminating and greatly helped us in our formative period to increase our devotion to Sri Ramakrishna, Mother and Swamiji and the Order.

Particularly from Kerala, there would be a good number of Swamis visiting the Math. They were all great scholars and spiritually advanced, and their very presence

1. He was the manager of Madras Math for some years during Revered Maharaj's tenure as the president.

With Tanmayananda Maharaj, Coimbatore Vidyalaya

would be inspiring and elevating. Interacting with them would be such a great spiritual feast that we would be filled to the brim with their inspiring words.

I had the opportunity to meet Revered Swami Tapasyananda Maharaj for the first time at Madras Math in the year 1956 when I had just joined. He came from Trivandrum, perhaps on his way to Belur Math. He stayed for two or three days at Madras Math.

He was simple in all aspects, his clothing, his mannerisms, talks and movements but at the same time had great scholarship and a deeply spiritual personality. Initially, I could not understand the depth of his spirituality. I was attracted by his simple and plain life and easy availability.

In those days, at Madras Math, there was acute shortage of accommodation due to less number of rooms. The temple of Sri Ramakrishna was the centre of our life and activities; there were partitions in both the wings of the building in the first floor overlooking the prayer hall. Monastics would be hustled together in the halls and rooms situated on the northern and southern sides. There would be seven or eight monks living on each wing. Being a junior, I occupied a small space in the southern wing.

In the mornings, before breakfast, I would chant daily for fifteen to twenty minutes. One day I was chanting the *Brahmananda Valli* of the *Taittriya Upanisad*, where the *Rishi* expresses his experience through the words Ha, U, Ha, U, Ha… I did not know that Revered Maharaj was staying in the next room. He quickly came out, sat behind me and began to chant with me in a loud and sonorous voice. I was simply startled. As I was a beginner, my pronunciation and chanting was a little faulty, but he chanted beautifully and explained afterwards how wonderful was the experience of the *rishi* who expressed through those words his realization of God. I did not remember now Maharaj's exact words and explanations. I was not able to grasp the inner meaning at that time but his expressions and the way he explained gave me some inkling about the idea of the Absolute. I was simply wonder struck at his simplicity and deep scholarship, and above all, such a great monk sitting with me and chanting! This created a lasting impression in my mind and lifted him to a great height in my estimation.

Subsequent meetings drew me close to him and I would be waiting for his subsequent arrival from Trivandrum. I had such a confidence in him that I would discuss many of my personal problems with him and get his guidance. In the initial stage (1956 to 1960), his guidance and advice helped me to grow in the right direction. One great trait of the Swami was, he would never thrust any idea on others but only would present before them with a sympathetic and analytical approach. He taught us more by his example than precepts.

I was interested to know more about his spiritual life and his life in the Order in general. Swami Swahananda Maharaj, a great admirer of Revered Maharaj, would tell me all about his spiritual life and his contributions to the Order - his dedication, scholarship and power of writing and speaking.

Swami Tapasyananda Maharaj was a monk, a saint and a yogi of a very high order. By nature, he was a *bhakta*. He was also a voracious reader and an extraordinary intellectual and scholar, with a keen sense of observation, right from the beginning of his monastic life, which fully manifested later when he was the president of Madras Math. In his early days, he was so much involved in studying that other monks would jokingly call him a 'book worm'. Such a scholarly person reduced his scholastic interests and plunged into *seva dharma* when he was sent to Trivandrum. He, as a great karma yogi, developed the hospital there and later the publication department and other activities at Madras Math. Karma yogi in him shone brightly as an example for others to see and emulate.

He was a great thinker. Whatever subject came to his notice, he would think deeply on it and make a wonderful comment which would demonstrate his deep and precise understanding of the subject in all its aspects.

As soon as I started coming to Madras Math in 1954, the first book I purchased and read thoroughly was his book on the Holy Mother. That being the centenary year of the Mother, this book was in good demand. The book, written in a scholarly fashion, vividly describes the devotion and love of the Holy Mother. The chapter *Cult and Culture* is dealt with in a clear and masterly way. I could understand

Sitting (Left to Right): Tapasyananda, Somananda. Standing (Left to Right): 2. Tanmayananda, 3. Atmaghanananda, 4. Bhaktikamananda, 5. Sukritananda (as a brahmachari) Coimbatore Vidyalaya, Perianayakanpalayam, 1988.

its great significance only after several years when I was more mature.

Whenever he would come to Madras Math from Trivandrum, he would make it a point to visit one big hospital in the city and study it closely in all its aspects. He would go incognito and freely move about in the hospital spending a long time in observing everything – toilets, kitchen, food, medicine administration, wards, beds etc. When the concerned people in the administration were eventually informed about his visit and came forward to help him, he would tell them, 'I have seen thoroughly whatever I wanted to and I could not have done so if I had approached for your help and guidance.' Such is his dedication to the work at hand. When he was managing the hospital, he wanted to get all information that was needed for its efficient functioning and to have a grip over the administration.

When Swami Tapasyananda Maharaj became the president of Madras Math, I was serving in the Vivekananda College, Madras. I was very happy to see him back in Madras and he too was happy to see me there. For four years, I had his holy company till I left the College for Belur Math. I would come to Math almost daily in the evenings and walk with him near the library. While conversing, he would tell many interesting things. He would freely crack jokes and have a lot of fun. He would take keen interest in everything connected with our nation and with our Order.

When Maharaj took charge of Madras Math, he told us that he would be actively working and would not be passive in his dealings or as a mere witness. He found that the condition of the Tamil magazine *Sri Ramakrishna Vijayam* was in a bad shape. The scholarly swami looking after the work was very old. He wanted to change the editor and also to increase the circulation. He could not immediately get a monk well versed in Tamil to take the responsibility of the magazine. He requested me to be the editor temporarily till an appropriate swami was identified. I, out of respect for him, accepted his request even though I had heavy responsibilities at the Vivekananda College and its hostel and the in-charge swami of the College opposed this proposal. Of course, I had to prepare only the editorial and Sri R. Ramakrishnan, a great devotee of the Math, took care of the rest of the work. This arrangement went on for nearly a year till a swami was deputed to take full charge of the magazine.

Maharaj brought me from Calcutta to Madras Math in April 1978 to be its manager. It was a great opportunity for me to be in his holy company and serve him. I was with him for seven years (till 1985). He wanted me to attend to two important and challenging works immediately. The first and most urgent was to make arrangements for shifting the National Primary School from its earlier location to its current premises as the old and dilapidated building was unsuitable for the running of the School. It had the sanctity and the blessings of Sasi Maharaj [Swami Ramakrishnananda], who started the school, but it was risky to keep children under a shaky and weak roof. Maharaj had visited the school earlier and noticed the horrible condition of the building. Then and there he decided to shift the School at the earliest opportunity.

Immediately we swung into action, and though it seemed initially impossible, it became possible through the grace of Sri Ramakrishna as also Maharaj's directions and blessings and we got another piece of land in the same locality (Mint in North Madras). He laid the foundation and the building came up in record time of six months and the School was shifted. Since Maharaj did not want to spend Math money on this project, every paisa was collected from public donations, sale of coupons and many other means. Once the School was shifted, Maharaj let a sigh of relief. His sincere wish was fulfilled, though it still seems like a dream to me.

The other task was the publication of the Tamil and Telugu translations of *The Gospel of Sri Ramakrishna*. Actually this task had been started in 1972 immediately after Maharaj took over as president of Madras Math. He was very unhappy when he found that the book was not fully translated and the available material was scrappy and the language was tough and academic. So he had summoned me from Vivekananda College where I was then serving and gently admonished me for not publishing this important book even though I hailed from Tamil Nadu. I pleaded my inability but he would not hear of it. In a way, he compelled me to take up the task immediately. I could not disobey his command. As a result, along with my duties in the college and hostel, I took up the task as a challenge and depended on Sri Ramakrishna for guidance and strength. Meanwhile, I was transferred to Calcutta in 1974. But I continued the work there and completed the manuscript. So when I came back to Madras, I picked up the thread and along with my managerial duties I plunged into this task with the blessings of Maharaj. In 1980, the first volume was released by Swami Vireswarananda Maharaj, the then president of the Order, and the other volumes in the succeeding years.

Maharaj's daily routine was very interesting. He would attend the *mangalarati* at 5 a.m. (later he could not attend due to his age and swollen legs). Then he would do japa, meditation and chanting of the *strotras* till 7 a.m. and would come to the dining hall for breakfast (later he would have his breakfast in the verandah adjacent to his room). While taking his breakfast, he would keenly observe everything making a rapid survey of the situation. He would watch everything, but would not comment on anything and when occasions arose, he would stimulate fun, jokes and laughter. I like to cite one incident here. In the kitchen, there was a helper who was a little foolish and behaved like a simpleton. We used to call him 'Aandi', meaning a semi-lunatic. His talks and mannerism would make us, including Maharaj, laugh. Maharaj would remark, 'We pay him for his work in the kitchen but he freely entertains us in the dining hall!'

At 9 a.m., Maharaj would come with a walking stick to the prayer hall and stand before the temple and pray for some time. After saluting the Master, he would slowly proceed towards the office. He would enter through the Book Stall and monitor the proper display of the books. He would then enter into his own office after passing through the manager's office. As Madras was usually hot, he would come to the office without any upper garment except for a small towel on his shoulder.

From 9 a.m. to 11.30 a.m., Maharaj would sit in his office and start reading proofs or preparing fresh manuscripts. Many visitors would come to meet him. He would be very brief in his talks and dispose them off quickly. He would not waste even a single moment in idle talk or by simply sitting.

Maharaj would then come to the dining hall for lunch (later he would take lunch in the hall adjacent to his room). After lunch, he would start reading the newspaper and that was his rest. By 2 p.m. he would go to office to attend to his regular work of proofreading, manuscript preparation and also correspondence. He would be absorbed totally in work and very thoughtful about whatever he would undertake.

Maharaj would have his tea in the office at 3.30 p.m. and slowly move to his room by 4.30 or 5.00 p.m. Anybody can enter his room at any time and he was easily accessible. He would take a walk in the terrace adjacent to his room. In the earlier days, he would walk near the library and we also would join him. At the time of evening *arati,* he would be in his room doing japa and meditation.

After dinner, there would be a class for a short while. Maharaj would crack jokes and there would be lot of fun and roaring laughter. Maharaj will not laugh much, but made others laugh and he would simply enjoy watching it. We could see the lighter part of Maharaj with his child-like simplicity.

His general health was not good, particularly in later years though he had full control over his body. We had seen him often having some trouble in the throat. But he would not complain much. He believed in homeopathy. He would say, 'On ordinary days, homeopathy, and if the house is on fire [meaning serious illness], then allopathy.'

His love for Sri Ramakrishna, Holy Mother, and Swamiji and dedication to the Order was unique. He was true to the great dictum 'poverty, chastity and obedience'. His respect for elders and obedience and dedication to the *Sangha* was unique. We had seen how much respect he would show to Revered Swami Vireswarananda Maharaj whenever he came to Madras Math. For the sake of his comfortable stay during his visit to Madras Math, Maharaj would vacate his own room.

He was very particular about the health of the *bramacharis* and their proper and regular diet suitable for monastic life. He would insist that they do regular exercise daily and be careful about their health. He himself would have watchful eye on their performance.

He always disliked luxury and exuberance. Of course, he will not force others to follow his example. Usually, monastics would be attracted by his simple life and automatically follow him as far as possible.

Once at the Math in the early 1980's there was a proposal to fix an Air-Conditioner for a VIP Swami. He vehemently opposed and ultimately the proposal was dropped since Maharaj did not like to break traditions to suit our fancies. The Swami had to move to T. Nagar Ashrama where such facilities were available.

Maharaj thought that the use of a car was a luxury that would invariably lead to misuse and bring trouble through the vagaries of the drivers. The previous car donated by a devotee was disposed off for similar reasons. His idea was to manage by travelling by public bus, autos and taxies. Waste of time in these modes of transport and other hardships were unknown to him. When we pointed out the advantages of having a car and the amount of money we would save, he agreed for getting back the sold car but on one condition that money spent must be through the donations and not taken from the Math. The point to be noted is that he was not rigid in his views and when he found a person who understood the value of money and was ready to take the required responsibility, he would readily change his opinion and give him freedom. It was his strong view that unless one collects money, they cannot understand the value of it. He felt that nobody should spend the Math money carelessly without having any sense of its value. Maharaj completely practised one of the most fundamental principles of monastic life.

Maharaj was not at all conscious of his position, status etc. He was simple and unassuming. Once he was to meet a dentist at T. Nagar. When he came to know that a brahmachari was planning to go that way on a scooter, he requested him to take him along on the scooter. We were all surprised at this and raised our objections. Maharaj immediately dropped the idea but like a child argued with us, 'What is wrong in going on a scooter? He anyway was about to go that way and if I had gone with him, we could have saved the money for the petrol which we are now spending by going by car.' He had made the issue so simple not being aware that he was the president of the Math and a Trustee of the Ramakrishna Order and his traveling on a scooter will draw the attention of many. He was actually living in another world of spiritual values and not of worldly values.

There was an incident showing his childlike nature and innocence. Once I brought a famous neurologist to examine him. Maharaj would take his tea at 3.30 p.m. in his office. As usual, he was waiting for his tea and it had just arrived and I also entered the room with the doctor. He requested the doctor to wait till he finished tea. I intervened and told Maharaj, 'Tea and snacks for all of us have been arranged. Doctor also will have his tea with you.' He laughed and said in his characteristic way, 'Please excuse me. See how intelligent is my manager swami. He has arranged everything.' The doctor was pleased by his simplicity and childlike behaviour. He had a hearty laugh and appreciated his innocence and frankness.

Taking advantage of his simplicity, many people would bring to his notice irrelevant issues and false complaints. Revered Maharaj would believe them at the face value, but when he would come to know the truth later, he would get enraged at the person who tricked him and would take him to task.

His correspondence would always be interesting. He would put his ideas in a brief yet powerful language, sometimes using even strong words to drive home the points he wanted to say.

Maharaj was very bold and frank in his talks and statements. His words were straight to the point. He would not mince words. Once a talented young swami became very arrogant and proud and would not care for anybody.

At Sarada Vidyalaya, T. Nagar, Madras

Maharaj would jokingly say, 'Look here! You know what he is like! A fine nutritious and tasty dish but salted twice. As a result, neither you can eat nor you have the mind to throw away such a fine dish.' In his talks and dealings, he would exhibit high degree of spiritual wisdom. It was always a pleasure to talk to him and seek his mature counsel.

Unfortunately, seeing his simple appearance and dealings, many would not realize his high spiritual attainments.

He was the president of various committees of the Mission—Students. Home, Vivekananda College and schools at T. Nagar. In the meetings, usually he would observe silence and avoided speaking or making any comments but closely watch the proceedings. But in the Sarada Vidyalaya (girls' institution) committee, he would take active part in the discussions. The reason was that Sarada Vidyalaya was under his direct management but in other committees, though he was the president, there were other monks to take care of the management. Of course, if any of those monks approached him with their problems and sought guidance, he readily would give his valuable advice.

He would seldom go out of the Math unless there was any work connected with the Math. He was involved constantly in the activities of the Math - strengthening and developing different fields of activity – and was also involved in reading and writing.

He would go to Belur Math three times a year to attend the Trustees' meeting. He would carry with him a big bundle of manuscript for correction on board and use the time properly while travelling by train which would be almost 24 hours. He would carry 3-4 packets of *idlis* as his meal on the way. With *idlis,* he would manage his trip. At Belur Math, during his stay, many monastic members would gather in his room after dinner to hear him speak on many interesting topics. He would be at his best enjoying the company of the brahmacharis.

On every birthday of the Holy Trio, there would be a talk in English and Tamil after the evening *arati.* Every talk of Maharaj would reflect some original thinking. And that would also express his deep love for the Holy Trio. No two talks of his would have the same approach. He would present his scholarly interpretations in a forceful and yet clear language.

He did not believe in simply giving *prasad* (food) to the devotees. They would eat and throw away the leaf and forget about it. It would only be a temporary emotion and would not create any lasting value at all. But if they have book as *prasad* they would read and it would be real *prasad* for the mind and the intellect. He felt that it would be a better *prasad* than mere food *prasad*, though that too had its value for the devotees. So he would purchase books, including those he authored, paying the full price with his *pranami* money and gift them to the devotees whom he felt were genuinely interested and would in turn gift copies of the books to others as he had done.

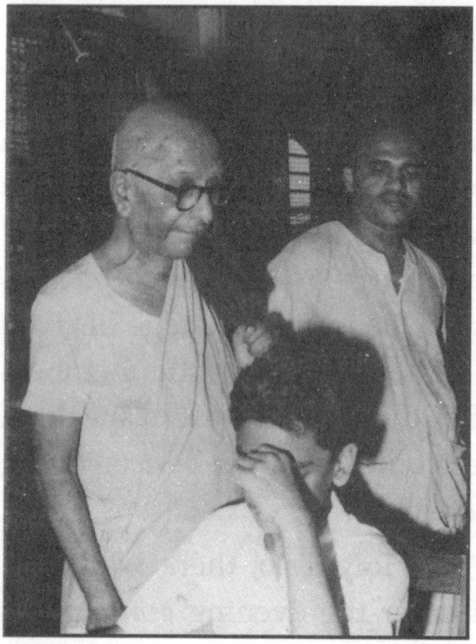

He was very much interested in the health and welfare of the children. Whenever he met children, he would invariably find out whether they got nutritious food and enough care and attention.

Maharaj was very affectionate and loving towards the poor workers – servants, gardeners, sweepers, and other unskilled staff. On

Ayudha Puja, the ninth day of the Navaratri festival, it is customary in southern India to worship all the implements and equipments. When the gardeners and servants would perform the ritual in their own characteristic way, he would show keen interest in that and witness it joyfully. He would accept the *prasad* given by them and also would give them some money. He would appreciate those workers who had *nista* and *sraddha* in these rituals. He would say that these people would get the grace of the Lord first and get liberated quickly. One gardener would come with the Vaishnavaite religious marks on his forehead. Maharaj would be very happy to see such devoted workers and would appreciate them for their sincere religious faith.

Sometime in the beginning of 1979, Dr. Raji Asrani, who stayed in the United States of America, came with her brother to donate a huge amount to the Math dispensary in memory of her sister who had died in a road accident. Her whole family was associated with the Math in the earlier days and so it was her sentiment that the donation should be given only to the Math dispensary. But Revered Maharaj did not agree for further expansion of the dispensary due to space and other constraints. She became angry and would argue with Maharaj. When she worked as a volunteer in the dispensary for a month, she would meet Maharaj almost daily. Maharaj, in course of his conversations, convinced her about the reasons for not expanding the dispensary. Eventually she became very devoted to Maharaj and contributed nearly 1 crore rupees to the Math in the subsequent years. With that money, the old and dilapidated buildings opposite to the Math were renovated. In 1980, Maharaj arranged for her spiritual initiation from Revered Swami Vireswarananda Maharaj during the temple consecration of Hyderabad Math. As a special case, Swami Vireswarananda Maharaj spiritually initiated her on the day of consecration itself because she had to leave the very next day for the United States. She was very grateful to Maharaj for all his help.

Maharaj was responsible for the affiliation of the Madurai Ashrama. Dr. Shanmugam, a disciple of Swami Virajananda Maharaj, and his friends started a *seva samiti* in the early 1970s and nurtured it with great care and devotion. He vigorously and persistently tried for affiliating it to Ramakrishna Mission from 1980s. He sought Revered Maharaj's help and met him at Madras Math repeatedly, many times in a month. Maharaj forcefully took up the issue at the Trustees' meeting at Belur Math and guided the process at every stage till the affiliation was completed.

It was Revered Maharaj who developed the publication section of Madras Math. Of the many books published, the most important was his English translation of the *Srimad Bhagavatam* in four volumes running to more than 2000 pages. It is a monumental work which was close to his heart. This scholarly work was well received all over the world. Maharaj was a great *bhakta* and so this book continues to be of great interest to the world of devotion. But in the beginning, he was a bit worried about the huge cost involved in the publication. He did not like to spend the Math's money and wanted the cost to be met through donations. Two monks went to Malaysia and Singapore for raising funds and with their contributions we could manage the publication cost. Maharaj heaved a great sigh of relief when he found that the publication cost was made good. With a peaceful heart, he plunged into the work and completed it in record time.

Revered Maharaj lived a detached life but he was attached to the work of the Lord at hand. It requires a greater skill, discriminating power and spiritual strength. Although he was physically living in this world, he was mentally living on a higher spiritual plane. He was full of love, affection and concern for others. In 1985, after an operation, there was a set back to my heath and I had to suffer for a prolonged period - for months together. I was shifted to Calcutta and it took a year for me to completely recover. Maharaj was upset and found fault with the surgeon for his negligence. For a long time he would narrate this sad tale to everyone who came to meet him.

After becoming the vice-president in 1985, he gave *diksa* in Cossipore Garden for the first time. During that time, I was at the Institute of Culture, Golpark, Calcutta, and so I was able to go over to Cossipore on that day. After the *diksa* ceremony, he was in a jovial mood and told me, 'This is my debut show. I was a little afraid.'

During his last days when he was undergoing treatment at Vijaya Hospital, I came from Coimbatore to see him. Meanwhile I heard that he was repeatedly asking the other monks to call the 'Coimbatore Swami'. When I entered his room in the hospital, like a helpless child, he repeatedly told me, 'Please take me away from the hospital to the Math. These people will not help me. I don't believe them. Take me back.' He was very weak and his health was in a bad condition. The doctors were treating him with all attention. In such a situation I was much embarrassed to see him insisting me to take him back to the Math. I tried to console him and left the room. The doctors, seeing his desperate condition, discharged him from the hospital.

After a few months, he was again hospitalized in a private clinic near the Math and after a few days, he passed away one evening. His body was brought to Madras Math and kept in the library building. We found a wonderful glow and smile radiating on his face.

Smell of holiness!

Swami Tapasyananda Maharaj once found some monks who were keen to maintain their "inner" cleanliness by neglecting their external cleanliness to the extent of their bodies emanating an obnoxious smell. Maharaj humorously called it "Smell of holiness!"

—***Swami Nityakamananda***

(An initiated disciple of Revered Maharaj)

5

As I Know Him

Swami Harshananda[1]

Swami Vivekananda once remarked that it is Jnana (knowledge, scholarship) and tapas (austerity) that contribute to the well-being of any monastic Order.

And, Swami Tapasyananda Maharaj, as his very name indicated (one who gets bliss in austerity) was typical example of this ideal.

It was perhaps in March 1956 that I first saw him at this Math [Ramakrishna Math, Bangalore] when he had come on invitation from Revered Yatiswarananda Maharaj, to speak at our Annual Celebrations. All of us were impressed by his simplicity and informal behavior.

I still remember vividly the one remark that Revered Yatiswarananda Maharaj made about him before his arrival: 'A top intellect, he is stuck up in that hospital centre [Trivandrum]!'

However we have to admit that it is his tapas aspect that got finally manifested during his long stay at the Trivandrum hospital centre. Absolutely simple personal life

1. He is a senior monk of the Order who knew Revered Maharaj for many years.

and hard work to build up the institution characterized his stay there.

Once the hospital centre grow up well and got stabilized, the Lord thought that he should be shifted to a monastic centre more congenial to the utilization of his other aspect viz. Jnana! He took over as the president of the Sri Ramakrishna Math at Madras.

During his long stint as the head of this prestigious institution he brought out a number of books mostly on the Hindu scriptures and allied subjects.

It was during this period (perhaps in May 1976) that I had spent two weeks at the Madras centre. At that time I was translating the book *Sri Ramakrishna Karnamritam* of Ottur Balabhatta, in Kannada since Tapasyananda Maharaj already translated it in to English, that book helped me greatly.

Chidghananandaji, Prameyanandaji, Vireswaranandaji, Tapasyanandaji, Uddhavanandaji, 1976

It was during these two weeks that I could get a glimpse into his personality, especially the human side. What struck me was the depth of his knowledge of our Vedanta scriptures and the clarity of expression.

A few years later, I had invited him to be a speaker at the temple inauguration of our Ulsoor Ashrama (1990).

He had invited me once to address the students of the youth convention held at Madras Math. I was surprised to see that he listened to my talk and even appreciated it! To say the least, I felt embarrassed.

When I sent a copy of my book *Hindu Gods and Goddesses* to him, he was kind enough to send some additional material to be incorporated in the introductory part of the book. I did it in the next edition.

This short account of his personality will be incomplete if we do not admire the extraordinary wonderful work – *The Bhagavatam* with English translation – done by him. Apart from a very correct and graceful translation, it contains a scholarly introduction and brief commentary of each section. It remains as a monumental work in the list of Hindu scriptures of the modern generation.

During his final illness, I had gone to see him in the hospital. Since he was in the I.C. Unit and unconscious I returned extremely sad.

In his demise, our Order lost one more link with the earlier generation of Jnana and Tapas.

6

He Who Saw Inaction in Actions

Swami Raghaveshananda[1]

I was familiar with the name 'Swami Tapasyananda' when I joined Sri Ramakrishna Math, Madras, as a novice in 1965. The first book on Sri Sarada Devi I had read was the book written by him. His charming English and the appropriate words he had used to express the various moods of Sri Sarada Devi had mesmerized me. That is probably the best biography of Sri Sarada Devi available till date. I was very eager to meet him and pay my humble respects. He was head of the Trivandrum Centre when I joined the Order. The hospital there is his brain-child. When he took charge of Trivandrum Centre in 1935, all that existed in the place of the present structure was a small shed with a board displaying the

At Madras Math

1. He was the manager of Madras Math for many years and had spent 20 years with Revered Maharaj during his tenure as the president.

phrase: "Charitable Hospital". Over a period of 34 years, he expanded this rudimentary structure into a big hospital centre of the Mission in South India.

After one year of my joining Madras Math, I was told that Revered Swami Tapasyananda Maharaj would be visiting Madras for purchasing medical equipment and that I should accompany him in the shopping. After reaching Madras, he called me at about 10 a.m. and said that I should be ready at sharp 2 p.m. His grim face and authoritative manner frightened me a little. I stood near the car ten minutes before 2 p.m. and he arrived sharp at 2 p.m. He was glad that I was waiting instead of making him wait. We went to the South India Surgical, a famous medical equipment store. The owner was well known to Maharaj and he cordially received him. After talking to him for a few minutes, he rushed to fetch the instruments. Maharaj selected the surgical instruments – meticulously testing each one in a surgeon like manner. He told the owner that some of the instruments in his shop were not of standard quality and would not last long. The owner just smiled and said that the government hospitals did not bother too much about quality.

I was wondering how Maharaj knew about the quality standards of surgical instruments. On our way back to the Math, I posed this question to him. He just smiled and said, 'Nothing but personal interest. I usually stand around with the doctors in the operation theatre, wearing sterilized clothes and observing every operation; moreover, I spend some time in studying medical books; I further gained knowledge by having medical conversations with doctors. We buy medical equipments with the donations collected from the public. So I personally select the instruments in order to put the public money to best use.'

During his visit to Madras, he used to walk on the terrace for about an hour every day. He kept up this habit practically till the end of his life. Once in a while, I used to interrupt his walk and casually put some questions to him. He would ask me to walk along while he answered. One day I asked him how he could find time to write the biography of Sri Sarada Devi, in the midst of his busy schedule of Hospital work. He exclaimed: 'Time? Everyone has plenty of time. To say *no time* is an excuse not to do the work. If you have the requisite desire, you will find time for everything.' I could see that this was very true with respect to his life. In the later years, I found that he never complained that he had no time for any work.

In 1971, the authorities at Belur Math decided to transfer him from Trivandrum to Madras Math as its head. He was most probably 67 years of age when this proposal was made to him, he strongly opposed saying that he was too old to take up fresh challenges. To substantiate his stand he gave the following reasons:

I am quite aged. I have spent most of my life in Kerala and that too in a Hospital centre. The present suggestion would be just like transplanting a grown-up coconut tree from Trivandrum to Madras. It might not survive and even if it survives, it may not bear fruits.

Being a Keralite, I do not know a single word of Tamil and it would be difficult to learn that language at this age.

I have spent most of my time working in a Hospital centre and it would be difficult to manage one of the big publication centres of the Order.

Then, he added, 'I suggest that a young and dynamic person who knows Tamil should be made in-charge of Madras Centre.' But the authorities insisted and convinced him that he is the only competent person at that moment. They also reminded him that he came with the advantage of having worked as the editor of *The Vedanta Kesari*, an English journal of the Order, brought out from Madras during his early monastic years. Having no choice, he reluctantly accepted the responsibility.

At that time I was in the Training Centre at Belur Math. I was about to complete the training and return to Madras Math. Even though I felt sad that I would no longer be in the company of Revered Swami Kailasananda Maharaj [the previous head of Madras Math], under whom I had joined and spent three years, I was at the same time excited that I would have the privilege of having the company of Revered Tapasyananda Maharaj. I never had dreamt that I shall live with him for 20 long years till the end of his life. At Belur Math, he called me that night and gave me a surprising update. He asked me to tell in detail about the different departments at Madras Math. He was asking very minute details about which I was quite unaware. I was surprised to know that his mind had already shifted from Trivandrum to Madras. He had detached himself from the big hospital of Trivandrum which he had built from scratch over the years and had set his mind to the further development of Madras Math. It was nearly 3 a.m. when our conversation ended. Within a few months, he took charge of Madras Math in 1971 and remained there till the end of his life.

At Madras Math, his routine was exemplary for any monastic. He would be up at 4 a.m. and would work till he went to bed at 11 p.m., except for an hour's nap in the afternoon. As long as his health permitted to squat on the floor, he would attend the *mangalarati* at 5 a.m. and would check if all the monastics were present. He also would attend the vesper service in the evening as long as his health permitted. When his health failed and he was unable to squat on the ground, he would sit for his prayers in his room. He was concerned about the spiritual practice of the other monastic members also. The following incident illustrates this.

He was to go to Belur Math once in four months to attend the Trustees' meeting. In those days, there was only one train –the Howrah mail - which used to reach at 4.30 a.m. on his return journey. He instructed that nobody should go to receive him, before 6.30 a.m. He preferred to stay on the platform till 6.30 a.m. The first time, I had gone there at 4.30 a.m. Seeing me there, he chided me for missing my spiritual practices and going to the station to receive him. He insisted that no monastic should go out of the ashram before 6.00 a.m. At last, the arrangement was made that the driver alone would go to pick him up at 4.30 a.m.

He also would not attend any public meeting beyond 6.30 p.m. His life was very disciplined. He maintained a strict routine of prayer and meditation. He would excuse himself and retire to his room for prayers. He laid more stress on prayer along with meditation. He would not mind if he is disturbed for any urgent work. Sometimes I had to disturb him. But it was a sight to see him in his room, seated on the meditation seat, hands folded near his chest repeating with fervor in a deep, throbbing voice some of the devotional hymns to Sri Ramakrishna and other deities.

He laid much stress on the daily chanting of such hymns. He also translated a number of them for the benefit of sincere seekers. They have been brought out in a book form titled *Stotranjali.* He maintained this routine till the end of his life.

One day, after a few days of his arrival, he asked for a slate and a piece of chalk in order to learn Tamil - unfortunately this attempt went in vain as he was too old to learn a new language. He made a personal enquiry regarding the books published from Madras Math. He was pained to learn that the major works on Sri Ramakrishna like *The Gospel of Sri Ramakrishna* and *Sri Ramakrishna, The Great Master* were not translated into Tamil. He immediately called Swami Tanmayananda, the then manager and asked him to take up the translation. He gladly accepted the responsibility. He really worked very hard for more than a year. When the book was published, Maharaj felt great joy and congratulated the Swami. His encouragement made Swami Tanmayananda bring out many more books in Tamil. He also encouraged Swami Kamalatmananda, who was only a novice at that time to improve the standard of Tamil magazine, *Sri Ramakrishna Vijayam.* Under his encouragement and support the Swami worked very hard and within a decade improved the standard and raised the circulation to about 90,000 copies. Even now, it has the highest circulation of 1, 70, 000 among Tamil religious periodicals.

To the unobservant eye, Maharaj used to appear as miserly, but those who knew him closely, understood and appreciated this characteristic economizing quality of his.

The following incident throws some light on it. There was a devotee-friend by name Sankaralinga Nadar. He knew Maharaj from the Trivandrum days. He used to come regularly every Sunday to meet Maharaj and spend some time with him. He also used to donate liberally to the Math. Nadar told me on many occasions that I should not hesitate to ask money for Maharaj's personal expenses. But those occasions never arose because Maharaj never spent any money on himself.

One day, Nadar was in Maharaj's office. Just then, Maharaj's new book had been published. I went to his office and gave a copy to Maharaj. Showing it to the devotee, he remarked, 'See, they have published one more book'. The devotee respectfully received it and requested Maharaj to autograph it but Maharaj replied, 'No, no, I have no right to present this to anybody. I am only a caretaker of the property of Sri Ramakrishna and not the owner. If you want a copy for yourself, you may have to buy it from the sales section and then I will sign on it.' I was embarrassed. I wondered why a book of Rs.20 could not be given free to a donor and that too by the president of the Math. But look at Maharaj's humility – he never was the owner but only a care taker. The devotee purchased the book afterwards. A day or two later, he wrote a letter saying that now he was convinced that every paisa donated to the Math is being utilized properly for the particular cause - something that is to be found only in the Ramakrishna Ashramas.

I saw Maharaj as the living embodiment of Lord Krishna's diktat: '*Karmani Akarma Yah pasyet*' [He who sees inaction in actions].

The following two incidents unravel my perceptions:

Incident 1: Revered Maharaj was simultaneously interested in and non-attached to all the activities of the Math. He took personal interest in gardening, especially in tending coconut trees. He not only instructed the swami in-charge about the amount of manure and water; but also used to supervise whether the gardeners were following his instructions. Even though he sparingly used water for himself, he instructed to irrigate the gardens with plenty of water. He would keep an account in his diary on how many coconuts each tree would produce annually. We were under the impression that he was unduly attached to the coconut trees. One evening, a lightning struck a coconut tree in the Math premises. And the tree caught fire and naturally many passers-by gathered to watch this unusual incident. I went to Maharaj's room to report the event and note his reaction. But his reaction stunned me. He was absorbed in his studies; he coolly looked up and said, 'Call the fire brigade and put off the fire.' He resumed his studies. Neither the loss nor the unusual incident had any effect on him.

Incident 2: Revered Maharaj was fond of reading English Newspapers; he used to read the papers from the very first to the last page. After breakfast, he would take two newspapers with him and read them, standing on the verandah in front of his room. We were all under the impression that he was addicted to newspapers. One morning, there were sensational reports about a politician's assassination. I mentioned it to him during breakfast. That day, he did not carry the newspaper with him, I thought he had forgotten and took it to his room. But he calmly responded that he was not interested in sensational news. I was amazed at the detachment that he was capable of. Many days later, he remarked during the night class, 'I wish that every one of you would read the newspaper regularly so that you can improve your English, I have benefited a lot from it.' It made us understand that he read newspapers regularly, not to get entangled in political affairs, but to gain knowledge about the nuances of language usage.

Revered Maharaj had deep affection and concern for monastics of Madras Math. He used to make fun of our English as "Butler-English". One of my fellow trainees had a good grasp of the language and Maharaj nick-named him "Shakespeare". Even when he chided or corrected us, we could feel the concern and affection in his words. The after-dinner reading class for the monastics, presided over by Maharaj was the grand finale of the day. There were lively discussions and roaring laughter during these night classes.

Among the philosophies, he was oriented more towards Visistadvaita than Advaita. Not that he did not appreciate the Advaita of Sankara, in fact he translated Sankara Digvijaya [The biography of Sankaracharya] from Sanskrit to English, but he felt that people were too biased towards Sankara to the exclusion of the study of other philosophies. Whenever we referred to Vedanta, we invariably meant "Sankara's Advaita". It would displease him. He would comment, 'Vedanta does not mean Advaita alone, *bhakti* schools of thought are also Vedantic.' In fact this idea was so deep-rooted in his mind; he wrote a classical book titled *Bhakti Schools of Vedanta*. It is a masterpiece which depicts

Tapasyanandaji (sitting), Ranganathanandaji (standing)
Ramakrishna Math, Hyderabad, 1988

the lives and philosophies of different Vedantic teachers like Ramanuja, Madhva, Nimbarka etc.

Once one of my assistants – Swami Jnanadananda (now President of Hyderabad Math) and I, had gone to Bangalore for a book exhibition, where we had taken a stall. Returning after 10 days, Maharaj made a detailed enquiry of the book sales. He was keen to know about the books which got sold. We spent nearly two hours in giving the detail. Just at the end, I said that there was a great demand for the translation of *Srimad Bhagavatam* in English, along with the original Sanskrit *slokas*. There was no such book available then in the market. We felt that it would be a valuable addition to our publications if Maharaj could take up that work. He brushed aside my ideas and said he was too old to do that kind of work - he was 75 years then. Swami Jnanadananda added that it would definitely be well received and also the public expects such books from the Ramakrishna Mission. After hearing this, Maharaj said that he would think it over.

After a week, he called us and said that if he took up that work, it might take two years to complete. We said, 'Time is of no significance Maharaj, but we are concerned about your health.' He didn't reply but his mind was already set on it. Next day, he called me and asked to fetch a supply of good quantity one-sided paper (he never used fresh white paper for his work. He always used to write on one-sided paper lest Sri Ramakrishna's money was wasted). I gave him a bundle of one sided-paper. He summoned me again for a slate and chalks. I wondered what he would do with it but his answer was astonishing, he said, 'Many times, the translation is not accurate, why waste paper? If I have a slate, I can erase, and then rewrite it on the paper.' He actually did so. The work was progressing slowly. He used to continue the work in his office also. If he had visitors, he would pause and talk to them and resume after they left. Sometimes, school children would visit him. He would entertain them also without any annoyance. He could admirably switch between the spiritual and mundane, with much ease!

After a few days, he called me and said, 'Look, the progress of the work is very slow as I am not finding enough time, so I think I should get up by 3 a.m. in the morning and translate till 5 a.m., after which I can attend to my spiritual practices'.

I did not like that idea. I felt, at his age, he should have enough rest, but he insisted saying that he would make an attempt and if the body doesn't cooperate he would stop exerting too much. Since I knew his nature, I felt it would be futile to argue further. After a month or so, he called me and said, 'The electricity department has imposed 'pay as per slabs' on power usage. The user has to pay double the amount per unit for the units that exceeded the allocated quota. This worried him so much - he did not want to use electricity unnecessarily. I was momentarily happy when I thought that at least now Maharaj would be forced to take rest. But I had a surprise in store. He asked me to get a lantern in the light of which he would work in the early hours of the morning. I protested strongly to his new venture saying that it would tell on his eyes. But he said that he was habituated to use the lantern since there was no electricity at home in his school days. I had to oblige. Just imagine the scene. An elderly monk, sitting at a table, with big books and with a lantern! All for the sake of Sri Ramakrishna's work. Fortunately this ordeal ended soon since the restriction was withdrawn.

The process of his translation was remarkable. First, he would write on the slate, and then it would be written on the one-side paper. The typist would type the manuscript which he would carefully go through. Then the manuscript would be given to C.S. Ramakrishnan, a scholarly devotee, to cross check. He would make his corrections and sit with Maharaj. Maharaj would accept the corrections if he was convinced that the corrections would make the writing better. Sometimes the discussion would go on for hours, after consultations with the dictionary. The manuscript would be re-typed. Once again, Maharaj would go through it. After he completed the translation, he called me and handed over the big bundle of the manuscript with a childlike joy on his face. He heaved a sigh of relief when the work was completed.

But what happened next was more interesting and reveals Maharaj's non-attachment. He called Swami Jnanadananda and asked him to make an estimation of costs to print the book. After a day or two, he gave him the estimate. It had come up to Rs.2 lakhs (in those days) – to bring out the book elegantly in four volumes. Revered Maharaj considered that amount to be too huge. He called me and said, 'It is futile to spend so much of Sri Ramakrishna's money on this work.' He asked me to pack it properly and keep it aside. It was unbearable for us because we had seen him work so hard for two years! We tried our best to convince him that it would not be a waste and that we would recover the money once the books were sold. We put forth our best arguments. But he was adamant. At last, we suggested that we would make a pre-publication offer and raise the Rs.2 lakhs necessary for printing that book. Very reluctantly, he agreed. In fact, he visited Singapore and Malaysia and gave discourses on *Srimad Bhagavatam* which also helped us to raise some funds. His attitude proved how egoless and detached he was.

In 1985, he was made a vice-president of the Ramakrishna Order. Once again, he was adamant in not accepting the position. We all had to plead for days on end to convince him to accept.

Before his demise, he suffered for more than a year with different ailments. It started with diabetes. As soon as it was detected, he avoided sweets and asked his assistant to serve tea without sugar. Probably he never again tasted sugar in his life. But it was no issue at all for him. He was against getting admitted to hospitals, however seriously ill he was. Once, we had requested our elders at Belur

Math to send a senior swami to convince him – later, he was admitted to the Railway hospital which had a good cardiology department in those days. Dr. Kurian, a famous Cardiologist, looked after him. He was very reluctant to stay in the Hospital. After a couple days of his admission when the surgeon came on rounds and put the casual question, 'How are you Swamiji?' Promptly came the reply, 'The moment you discharge me, I shall be perfectly alright.' We were all taken aback.

It was in the month of May and the heat was severe. The doctor suggested that an air- conditioned room should be provided for him at the Math. We knew very well that it would be impossible to convince him. However, we requested a devotee to broach the subject with Maharaj. Maharaj was unwell at that time. The devotee went to him and with folded hands made the following suggestion. 'Maharaj, I have a new air conditioner at my home which is yet to be installed. I very much wish and consider it a blessing if you use it for a month or two till you recover from your illness.' Even in his illness his reply was an eye opener, which could be expected only from a saint. He said, 'My dear friend, just walk behind our Ashrama where you find people living in slums. Among them there are people who are more aged than me. Can you provide air conditioner to all of them? To be frank, I am a sannyasin and a beggar. Sri Ramakrishna, out of compassion, has provided a room, a cot, a fan and what not. I am quite happy with whatever Sri Ramakrishna has provided.' The devotee returned with tears in his eyes admiring his renunciation.

Ten days before his demise, he had enquired when the next *Ekadasi* would be. We were surprised since he hardly observed such occasions. His secretary mentioned the date; later it was revealed that he had selected that date to depart from this world. In spite of so many bodily ailments, his mind was dwelling on higher thoughts. He was continuously talking to the monastic attendants about *Bhakti* and the ways to achieve it. He explained to them in particular the nine methods of *Bhakti* quoting the following verse from the *Bhagavatam* (7.5.23):

श्रवणं कीर्तनं विष्णोः स्मरणं पादसेवनम् ।
अर्चनं वन्दनं दास्यं सख्यमात्मनिवेदनम् ।। २३ ।।

śravaṇaṃ kīrtanaṃ viṣṇoḥ smaraṇaṃ pādasevanam |
arcanaṃ vandanaṃ dāsyaṃ sakhyamātmanivedanam ||

On 3 October 1991, at 6.30 p.m., when the evening *arati* of Sri Ramakrishna was in progress, to be followed by the singing of *Ramnam*, he entered *mahasamadhi*. There was a remarkable glow of peace and fulfillment on his countenance. In fact just before he passed away, the last words he uttered were, 'I want peace, I want peace.' He did attain peace – of course, he also had brought peace to many aspirants who had come in contact with him.

Revered Swami Tapasyananda Maharaj ever remains in my memory as an epitome of an ideal monk to be emulated in my life.

7

The Greatest Sacrifice

Swami Golokananda[1]

Many outstanding monks of the Ramakrishna Order have hailed from Kerala. Swamis Tyagishananda Maharaj, Siddheswarananda Maharaj, Agamananda Maharaj, Nishreyasananda Maharaj and Vimalananda Maharaj are well known all over India. Swami Ranganathananda Maharaj had the distinction of being known and admired by the entire world in his life time. Swami Ambananda Maharaj was a disciple of the Holy Mother, the only Swami to have had that blessing from Kerala. Swami Purushottamananda Maharaj was a disciple of Swami Brahmananda, who worked incessantly for building up the Ramakrishna Movement in Kerala. He later retired to the Himalayas and attracted a great following, especially in North India. The work of Swami Iswarananda Maharaj was confined to the Thrissur centre in Kerala, though in his younger days, he had worked in Madras Math also. Swami Tapasyananda Maharaj also had worked in Madras in his younger days but later took charge of the Trivandrum Ashrama. In the last phase of his austere and holy life, he was once again in Madras and became one of the vice-

1. He is a senior monk of the Order who was with Revered Maharaj for 12 years.

presidents of the Ramakrishna Math and Mission. I had the privilege of staying with Swami Tapasyananda Maharaj for twelve years.

Revered Tapasyananda Maharaj was born in the small town of Ottappalam, about thirty kilometers from Palakkad. As a student of Presidency College, Madras, Balakrishnan (later Swami Tapasyananda Maharaj) would frequent the Math at Mylapore, especially during the visits of the direct disciples of Sri Ramakrishna.

On one occasion, the sight of three great sannyasins, Swamis Brahmananda Maharaj, Shivananda Maharaj, and Nirmalanada Maharaj standing and talking together impressed him so deeply that later he described the trio as three stars that had descended from the heavens. In 1924, he was initiated by Swami Shivananda Maharaj.

Balakrishnan obtained his post graduate degree in 1925 and in that very year joined the Ramakrishna Math at Madras and was ordained into sannyasa in 1932 by Swami Shivananda Maharaj.

For eight years, Maharaj edited *The Vedanta Kesari* and in 1940 was sent to take charge of the Ramakrishna Ashrama, Trivandrum, which he served for three decades, and built a big hospital at Sasthamangalam, which was only a small dispensary in the beginning. Swami Yatiswarananda Maharaj used to visit Trivandrum every year during his time. He was very fond of Tapasyananda Maharaj and used to lovingly call him by his premonastic name, Balakrishna. Yatiswarananda Maharaj used to travel by car from Coimbatore to Trichur and Ottappalam was on the way. Once he stopped at Ottappalam to call on Tapasyananda Maharaj's aged mother.

When Tapasyananda Maharaj was asked to take charge of the Math at Madras, I was at Trivandrum. The headquarters wanted to send me to Ceylon; but Maharaj wanted me at Madras, because I had joined there as a brahmachari and lived there for twelve years and was therefore familiar with the place. The headquarters complied and I served Madras Math for nine years until I was transferred to Trivandrum to take charge of the centre. Maharaj's work in Kerala, especially his service to the 'Sick Narayanas' through the Ramakrishna Ashrama Hospital, had created a lofty image of the Order in the minds of the people.

This was Maharaj's second tenure in Madras Math. This second tenure in his mature years, in the spiritually surcharged atmosphere of the Math, rich with the memories of its holy associations with Swami Ramakrishnananda Maharaj, Swami Brahmananda Maharaj, and Swami Shivananda Maharaj, lifted his whole personality to loftier heights. At Madras, Maharaj seemed to get back his true elements.

Madras Math is second in importance only to the Belur Math. Madras Math had always maintained orthodoxy in the rituals and an intellectual temper, inherited from no less a person than Swami Ramakrishnananda himself. It is known that Swami Ramakrishnananda Maharaj, then as Sasi, threw away the Persian book he was studying when he discovered that he did not hear the call of his Master as he was absorbed in reading the book. Swami Tapasyananda Maharaj used to cite this incident and say that it was the greatest sacrifice an intellectual can make. Coming to Madras, Swami Ramakrishnananda Maharaj resumed his studies because here his Master demanded a different kind of service. He even started brushing up his English to communicate with the intelligentsia of the South. This had a parallel in Tapasyananda Maharaj's life. Although Maharaj was always a student and involved himself in studies with mighty tomes of books on his office table even while being in the Hospital at Trivandrum, it was in his second tenure at Madras, in his advanced years, that his intellectual life flourished and yielded an abundant harvest. It was also during this period that he became the vice-president of the Order.

Under Tapasyananda Maharaj's care, the publication department of Madras Math grew by leaps and bounds. The

In front of the dining hall, Madras Math, 1978,
Sitting below (Left to Right): 2. Tattvamayananda, 4. Ajaratmananda; (sitting) Kailasanandaji, Tapasyanandaji, Prasantananda (kneeling); (standing first row) 2. Jnanadananda, 4. Tattvarupananda, 5. Kamalatmananda; (standing second row) 1. Vibhudananda, 2. Gabhirananda, 3. Tanmayananda, 5. Golokananda

Math acquired its own press which considerably improved the quality of publication at a lesser cost. The printer who was engaged earlier to do the printing work had grown casual and often ignored the proof corrections made at the Math. One of the books he translated was so entrenched with printer's devil that it was adversely commented upon in a review. In almost apologetic terms, Tapasyananda Maharaj had to explain to the reviewer how in spite of his meticulous proof corrections, the printer had failed to execute them while printing.

Maharaj enriched Madras Math publications by bringing out new editions of important books like *Sri Ramakrishna, The Great Master,* all of which he carefully revised. He had painstakingly recast longwinded sentences in the earlier edition of the book for greater readability and easy comprehension. He again revised the language of Swami Adidevananda's translation of Sri Ramanuja's commentary on the *Gita.* He republished D.S. Sarma's *A primer of Hinduism* to which he added a brilliant introduction. Incidentally Professor D.S. Sarma was Maharaj's warden at the Presidency College's Hostel.

During this period, Maharaj seemed to be keen on attracting the modernized Hindus to the Puranas and the Bhakti tradition. He translated the *Narayaneeyam, Adhyatma Ramayana and* the *Sundara Kandam* of *Valmiki Ramayana.* To crown it all, he brought out an English translation of The *Bhagavata Purana* with a comprehensive and incisively analytical introduction which explained with deep insight all the aspects that usually baffle a modern reader—its strange geography, cosmology and superhuman history.

Maharaj's most valuable work was *The Bhakti Schools of Vedanta* which is a masterly study of the dualist and qualified dualist interpretations of Vedanta. Apart from these, he has contributed to both *The Vedanta Kesari* and *Prabuddha Bharata* innumerable articles, each one of which carries the stamp of his erudition, independent thinking, and spiritual insight. He was editor of *The Vedanta Kesari* way back in the 1930s and some of his editorials on the teachings of Sri Ramakrishna and the introduction he wrote to a Sanskrit epic on the Master's life, were compiled into a slim volume under the title *Sri Ramakrishna's Thoughts in a Vedantic Perspective* and published by Madras Math after his passing away. His translation and exposition of the *Gita* is a masterpiece. Apart from these, Maharaj was keen on interpreting lives and teachings of the Master, the Holy Mother and Swamiji and in drawing the attention of thoughtful people to the significance of their great lives. It was under his encouragement that *The Gospel of Sri Ramakrishna* and *The Gospel of the Holy Mother* were translated into Tamil. He authored the first biography of the Holy Mother in English. He later added a chapter or two expounding the concept of the Motherhood of God. He condensed the major works of Swami Vivekananda for the benefit of serious readers. There was significant increase in the circulation of the magazines published by Madras Math during his tenure.

At a meeting Maharaj had convened to discuss about the problems related to printing and publishing, the younger monks impressed upon him that one of the major handicaps was the Math not having its own printing press. Maharaj then turned towards the young monk in charge of printing if he was ready to give him an assurance that he would continue with the assignment for the next five years.The young monk had a technical background and understood machines. He gladly agreed and Maharaj readily consented.

Swami Tapasyananda Maharaj was an ascetic by nature. His frugal habits are legendary in both the centres he worked. True to his name, he found bliss in austerity, *tapas*. He abhorred wastage of any sort, whether it was money, food or water. He took to task any one wasting food during *prasad* distribution even if he were a respectable devotee.

It was inspiring to see Maharaj doing japa and meditation; he never relaxed his routine. He was a reluctant traveller, preferring to stay where he was posted and to devotedly carry out the responsibilities laid upon him, but as a vice-president, he had to travel all over India blessing many devotees with spiritual initiation.

Maharaj was keen about educating and training young novices. He saw to it that regular classes were held for brahmacharis on scriptures and Sanskrit. He was fond of the English language and was well read in western literature in general and western philosophy and Christian theology in particular. He wanted young monks to be proficient in the English language.

I feel it a privilege to have lived and worked with this great monk for twelve years, six years in Trivandrum and six years in Madras.

8

God's Full-Time Worker

Swami Kamalatmananda[1]

The Saga Begins:

Perhaps it was in 1968 or 1969 Swami Tapasyananda Maharaj visited Madras Math on his way to Belur Math to attend the Trustees' meeting. I had just joined Madras Math then, and as a novice, I was unaware that Maharaj was a highly respected monk, that he was the president of Trivandrum Ashrama, and that he was one of the Trustees of the Ramakrishna Math and Mission. Unaware of all these, one day, when he was sitting behind the 'Old Temple', I casually sat by his side and freely asked him several questions about spiritual practices. And he too freely replied to all my questions without giving any indication that he was someone important. If I had known about him, I would have never dared to converse with him sitting on the same pedestal! But what struck me then was his simple and unassuming nature that betrayed not even an inkling of his position and accomplishments.

Years later, a similar incident happened that demonstrated his unassuming nature. Just within two or

1. He was a brahmachari in Madras Math when Revered Maharaj took charge as the president. He served as the editor of *Sri Ramakrishna Vijayam* for many years.

three days of Maharaj taking charge as the head of Madras Math, he called me to his room. When I entered his room, sitting on a chair, he was writing something at the table. Seeing me enter, he got up from the chair, made me sit on it, and he himself sat on his cot nearby.

Coming to know of my affinity to Lord Shiva, especially my devotion to Lord Vishwanatha in Kashi, Maharaj once gave me a *rudraksha mala* which he had had with him for a number of years.

I normally consumed less food than others. Concerned, Maharaj persuaded me to eat more quantity of food, whatever I liked, and even instructed the monk who was then the kitchen in-charge to give me two glasses of milk at night instead of one.

His Food:

Maharaj would usually take his lunch around 1 p.m. By that time, the food would have become cold. But he never bothered about that. He would eat whatever he got and never craved for tasty food. He would never say the food tasted good or bad. Although there would be several dishes prepared on festival days, he would eat only his regular simple food. He was not interested in feasting.

Coffee, measuring to three-fourths of a glass, was generally given to the inmates of the Math. To Maharaj too, without asking him how much coffee he wanted, I would give him coffee measuring to only three-fourths of a glass. It went on like this for 4 or 5 months. Once, a senior monk from Kerala noticed me giving Maharaj only that much quantity of coffee. He then told me, 'In Trivandrum, Maharaj would have two glasses of coffee during his breakfast. You too try to give him that quantity here.' As advised, from the next day onwards, I gave two glasses of coffee to Maharaj. He too quietly began to take that much coffee.What surprised me was that when I gave him less coffee, he did not comment on it or demand more. When I gave him more coffee, even then he did not comment or express delight. He was completely equipoised.

Usually Maharaj took two slices of bread and milk for dinner at night. I was in-charge of the kitchen and Maharaj had taken charge of the Math just a month earlier. I was then not very diligent in providing him his course of meal. It so happened that on two or three occasions, there was no bread to serve him; I served him *rotis* instead. But he never made a fuss about it and accepted what was offered in the normal course.

Maharaj, I have heard, used to cook in Madras Math as a brahmachari. He was adept in cooking. Later, as a president of Madras Math, he would at times instruct the cook regarding the spices to be added in the dishes. After breakfast, I would dress vegetables. Maharaj would sometimes stand by my side and guide me. He would say, 'Vegetables must boil well. Less salt must be used. Keep salt separately for those who require more salt in the food.' He was very particular that the vegetables were boiled well.

While Maharaj was at Trivandrum, he would halt at Madras Math *en route* to Belur Math to participate in the Trustees' meeting. On those occasions, he would carry curd rice for his train journey. He would tell the kitchen in-charge of Madras Math, 'Please keep separately rice, boiled and cooled milk, and a small quantity of curd for mixing.' He himself would mix these things and pack it for the journey.

Years later, even after assuming charge of Madras Math, he continued this practice whenever he set on a train journey.

His Attire:

I have several times seen Maharaj wearing a torn vest. He would use a torn *dhoti* as a towel, and when it could no longer be used as a towel, he would use it as a foot mat!

When he came to Madras, he was wearing a pair of leather footwear. We were not sure when he purchased it. He would time and again repair that footwear and reuse them. A monk who knew him for several years later told me, 'He [Maharaj] has used that footwear for 16 years...'

His Health:

If Revered Maharaj had any ailment, he would use homeopathy medicine. Dr. Umapathy and his son, Dr. Ramakrishnan, would provide him homeopathic treatment.

He would not talk much. A spiritual silence would always prevail on his face. Even while assailed by ailments, Revered Maharaj would never express any discomfort. He always had the mentality of bearing the difficulties.

Once in 1972 or 1973, he had spells of severe headache. At those times, he would just sit on an easy chair without any proper sleep at nights. Every now and then at stipulated hours, he would take a spoonful of homeopathy medicine. He used to bear the ailment and pain without disclosing it to anyone. We could come to know of this only when the homeopathy doctor, Sri Umapathy, informed us. He had tremendous forbearance (*titiksa*) of his afflictions. But when he saw others' sufferings, he would do all that he could. I have heard that at Trivandrum hospital, Revered Maharaj would himself give medicines to the patients, sometimes even in the nights, forgoing his rest.

His Gardening:

When Maharaj took charge of Madras Math, I was also taking care of the garden. Maharaj took interest in gardening and advised me to plant a lot (more than a hundred) of coconut plant saplings. The trees later yielded plenty of coconuts. He also instructed me to plant Casuarinas saplings in a plot opposite to the library, to plant tapioca, pumpkin etc. in the backyard of the Math. The Casuarinas trees near the 'old temple' were all planted under the guidance of Maharaj. He ensured that greens and vegetables were grown in a planned and systematic manner. He would also instruct how to prepare manure pits.

His Devotions:

Revered Maharaj would perform japa with a *japamala*. Before breakfast, for about an hour, he would recite *Sri Narayaneeyam, Sri Lalita Sahasranama Stotra* etc. During those recitations, he would keep the book in his left hand and make gestures with the right hand as though he was speaking to God. It left an indelible impression on all those who had seen that.

In the old temple, relics of Sri Ramakrishna were earlier kept under his photo. On birthdays of Sri Ramakrishna, Maharaj would devotedly take the relics out and give it to Pujari Maharaj for worshipping it. Again, after the puja, he would devotedly place it back. Similarly, on birthdays of Holy Mother, Maharaj would devotedly take her relics kept in the drawer of the decorated wooden seat, give it to Pujari Maharaj to worship it, and place it back. But in spite of his devotion, he never encouraged elaborate and ostentatious puja.

Sri Madhusudhana Saraswathi, one of the prominent *Acharyas* of Advaita had used a phrase '*Krishna Bhakti Atisundaram*' in one of his verses. Reciting this verse, Maharaj once expressed his great appreciation of this Advaitin's great devotion to Sri Krishna.

His Reverence for Senior Monks:

Swami Tapasyananda highly revered Swami Saradeshananda Maharaj (Gopesh Maharaj) who was Holy Mother's disciple. Once Gopesh Maharaj visited some places in South India including Trivandrum. I have heard that when Revered Tapasyananda Maharaj came to know about his visit to Trivandrum, he was disappointed and told, 'Alas! Gopesh Maharaj did not visit our centre at Trivandrum!'

Revered Swami Vireswarananda Maharaj fell critically ill in his last days. All hopes of recovery were belied. Hearing this news, Revered Tapasyananda Maharaj rushed to Belur Math. He would usually travel by train. But anxious to meet Revered Vireswarananda Maharaj, he flew to Calcutta. When he returned to Madras after visiting Revered Vireswarananda Maharaj, he then said, 'Our scriptures say that soul and body are different. The Great Master had said in Cossipore, "Let body take care of its disease, but mind, stay at the feet of Kali." What the scriptures and the Great Master said, we could witness in Prabhu Maharaj.'

His Humour:

A branch of Ramakrishna Mission at Purulia, Bihar, was organizing the consecration ceremony of their newly constructed temple. One of the brahmacharis in Madras Math intensely desired to visit Kasi. Hesitating to request Maharaj for his permission, the brahmachari told him, 'I shall attend *Kumbabhisekam* [consecration ceremony] at Purulia and return to Madras via Kasi.' But Maharaj's sharp intellect quickly saw through the proposal. Amused, he humorously commented, 'He wants to go to Kasi. His intention to go to the consecration ceremony at Purulia is just a drama, mere smoke screen!'

His Monastic Training:

Maharaj was a strict disciplinarian when it came to spiritual practices. He wanted every monastic member of the Math to participate in the *mangalarati* in the shrine at 5 a.m. without fail. He had instructed Swami Chidghanananda Maharaj, the then manager, to note the names of those who missed attending the *mangalarati* more than once or twice in a month. He would then call them and take them to task.

To the newly joined brahmacharis, Maharaj would say, 'You are not students who are studying in a college and staying in a hostel. You have come here with lofty ideals to lead the life of a monk. So, early in the morning, you should practice japa and meditation. Those who do not sincerely practice this routine should not later complain...The monks of the Ramakrishna Math are not "part-time workers". They are God's "full-time" workers! A monk's life is not like the career of an advocate or a doctor!'

Once, Maharaj noticed a brahmachari watching the 'white-washing' of the kitchen done by the labourers. To him, he said, 'We do not want supervisors, we want workers.' He wanted everyone in the Math to be always involved in some creative or constructive work.

In the beginning of 1972 or 1973, there was a big fire accident in Mylapore. Br. Radhakrishna (later Swami Atmaramananda) went to Revered Maharaj and told him that we must initiate relief work. Revered Maharaj replied, 'Doing relief work is a good thing. But for doing that we do not have enough man power. If you can take full responsibility and carry out the relief work, go ahead.' Since Br. Radhakrishna was ready to take the responsibility, Revered Maharaj encouraged him and gave him freedom to unstintingly use the Math's money spent on relief work. Br. Radhakrishna distributed food, vessels, clothes, mats etc. to those who were affected by the fire accident. As he did not know Tamil, he would take me along with him.

But he did not encourage workaholism. To a monk who was always working hard on the assignments entrusted to him, Maharaj said, 'At nights, lights are always burning in your room. I do not know when you retire to bed. You are young now. But by the way you work hard and strain your body you would definitely spoil your health at a later stage. The work you are doing now was done before you came and will be done after you leave. So, under the pretext of doing Math's work, don't spoil your health.'

Quite often, Maharaj would emphasize that monastics should keep their bodies fit and healthy by a good amount of physical exercises. He encouraged young monastics to play badminton. He would say, 'Walking is meant for old people, the rest should do vigorous exercises.'

Some of us would use the books in the Bookstall for reference and return it to the Bookstall after using it. Maharaj discouraged us in doing so pointing out that once we had used the book, it would no longer be a 'new' book for the customers.

A brahmachari of the Math was intimate with a famous writer and storyteller of Madras. Almost daily the writer would come to the Math and spend more than two hours conversing with that brahmachari. It went on like this for nearly five months. Then Maharaj calling the brahmachari said, 'Do you want Sri Ramakrishna or that writer? You can decide for yourself. If you want the writer, you can go with him. If you want Sri Ramakrishna, cut off the relationship with the writer. You cannot have both at the same time. Decide what you want.' Thereafter, the brahmachari ceased interacting with that writer.

Once, Revered Maharaj said that Swami Vivekananda had given a variety of teachings. To follow all his teachings would be difficult for any person. His teachings were meant for the entire humanity. The Ramakrishna Math has taken only his teachings on sannyasa.'

A monk in-charge of the dispensary once enquired Maharaj, 'In connection with the work of the dispensary, I am forced into situations where I have to interact with women. In these situations, I do not know what is right. Please guide me.' Maharaj replied, 'You cannot avoid talking to women for the sake of work. But you should restrict your interaction only to the extent the work demands. You must always be aware of this. And do not have any personal talks with them.'

Regarding *guruseva*, Maharaj would say, 'Don't think by being with the guru and doing him service is alone *guruseva*. Serving the Math is serving guru.' I had seen him have firm conviction in this and follow it in his own life.

When I wanted to visit Kanyakumari before going to the Training Centre at Belur Math, Maharaj did not permit me then. After the training, I wanted to return to Madras Math after visiting Kasi. He did not permit me saying, 'In future, you will get a lot of opportunities to visit Kasi.' Only after my sannyasa, did he allow me to visit Kasi. I had been disappointed with him for not allowing me to visit Kanyakumari or Kasi. But it was later I understood that he wanted me to have a more stable mind before I undertook such pilgrimages.

Regarding monastics travelling to various places, he would say, 'If the organization demands, you should go, otherwise simply going (wandering) here and there is not good.' He himself never undertook any pilgrimage. I think he never even visited the Kapaliswar Temple which was so near to the Math! Although he would visit Belur Math to attend the meetings there, he never visited Dakshineswar, Kamarpukur or Jayarambati.

But when monks of Madras Math wanted to visit the famous Muruga temple in Tiruttani and stay there for three days begging their food and sleeping wherever they could, Revered Maharaj readily gave them permission saying that, 'Scriptures say that the food we get through begging is very pure. Bring to me a small quantity of the food got by such begging.' He happily consumed the food we got through begging.

Revered Maharaj never would thrust his views on others. For instance, Maharaj would expect the brahmacharis whom he sent to Belur Math for training to return to Madras Math. But if anyone, for any reason, wanted to be posted elsewhere, he would readily respect their wish and would not insist them to return to Madras Math.

Sometimes, some devotees invite the monks to their homes for a meal. And the monks so invited would also oblige the devotees on several occasions. Maharaj once said, 'Left to myself, I do not like the monks going to the houses of devotees just because they have been invited. But that is my personal opinion. But this custom is still prevalent. I cannot stop this practice, nor do I wish to…' The subtle message perhaps in this observation was that he expected the monks to be very discreet and selective in this matter. Maharaj, however, was also particular that no one should hurt the devotees visiting the Math. Once he said, 'To hurt the feelings of the devotees coming to the Math is *Bhaagavata Apacaara*.'

A lecturer of a University wanted to join Madras Math. To him, Maharaj said, 'Do not resign your job right away. Take leave for a few months and stay in the Math. Thereby you would get a taste of real monastic life. Thereafter, if you still wish to lead a monastic life, you can join the Math.' The lecturer followed his advice and finally joined the Math. Revered Maharaj gave similar advice to a young man from Karnataka. He too followed Revered Maharaj's advice and later joined the Math.

To join the Order as a brahmachari, there are some basic qualifications such as education, age, etc. There are some aspirants who could not join the Math for these reasons. At their request, Maharaj would often write recommendation letter stating that 'Sir, so and so is a deserving candidate to be initiated into sannyasa and you can very well give *sannyasa diksa* to him.' And he would send it either to Ramakrishna Ashrama at Ottapalam in Kerala or to Vivekananda Ashrama at Vellimalai in Tirunelveli district.

Once, a brahmachari asked Maharaj whether spiritual progress would accrue by being a monastic member at the Math. Maharaj firmly and categorically replied, 'All the monastics at the Math are definitely and without any doubt making spiritual progress.'

His Intellectual Training:

Revered Maharaj was an original thinker. He never indulged in any loose talks. We have never seen him indulging in self-praise and with an air of superiority. Maharaj always approached everything with a rational mind. Sentimental approach was unknown to him.

Referring to the high intellectual capacity of Maharaj, Revered Swami Yatiswarananda Maharaj is supposed to have commented, 'God normally keeps the brain in the head of a person, but for Swami Tapasyananda, He had kept the brain all over his body – from head to toe.'

Maharaj felt that brahmacharins must be trained in lecturing. I happened to be the first to deliver a 'lecture' on a particular day. But that day, I could not speak at all. I spoke in a very low tone. 'Speak loudly,' he instructed. 'I do not have the habit of speaking,' I said in my usual pitch. 'There you see,' he at once said, 'now you are speaking loudly!'

After I completed the training at the Training Centre, Belur, Maharaj told me to conduct weekly classes in Madras Math. At that time, I was only 29 years old. I felt I had not sufficiently gained proficiency in the scriptures to handle classes. Besides, I had my own apprehensions in lecturing in public. But Maharaj said, 'The reason why I am asking you to give classes is that you would study deeply, which otherwise you may not. It is to persuade you to study I am asking you to handle classes.' Further, he convinced me that by delivering lectures outside the Math, I would be gaining invaluable experience. I had heard that Maharaj had even suggested that examinations be conducted in the Probationers' Training Centre, Belur Math, to ensure serious study of the subjects taught there.

Once I told him, 'Maharaj, I am not able to offer any new idea. I am repeating the same thing.' To that he replied, 'Spiritual books try to provide certain ideas and impress upon us from different angles. In spiritual life, some ideas have to be repeated time and again. Only then it would make the necessary impact on our lives.'

Once, I was to give a talk on Hinduism. Revered Maharaj called me and said, 'Hinduism does not talk only about moksa. It gives due important to everything–Dharma, Artha, Kama and Moksa. Ensure that you highlight this point in your talk on Hinduism.'

In 1976, after undertaking certain medical tests in Madras, Swami Chidbhavananda of Thirupparitturai Ashrama came to Madras Math to meet Maharaj. Along with him, there were two other monks of his Order and Dr. C. Subramaniam (the then Governor of Maharashtra). I had started writing articles in the newspapers then. Revered Tapasyananda Maharaj introduced me to them with words: "He is a budding writer". Swami Chidbhavananda responded to this by saying, 'Our Ramakrishna Movement needs many monks who are excellent speakers and writers.'

Sri Varagur Kalyana Sundara Saastri was a great scholar well versed in Sanskrit and Vedanta. He used to give classes on *Vishnu Sahasranamam* at Madras Math once a month. Right from 1960, he had been giving *Upanishad* classes to the brahmacharis of the Math twice a week. After Maharaj came, the medium of these classes became Sanskrit and Maharaj himself would attend these classes. Once, Sri Sastri had gone to Belur Math. Incidentally, Maharaj also was then in Belur Math. At his request, Sri Sastri gave a talk on *Mundaka Upanishad* for the monastic members of Belur Math.

Maharaj always encouraged Sanskrit study. He once arranged Sanskrit classes for the devotees. The teachers too were paid a good remuneration. The attendance was high initially, but came down in the course of months and finally stopped completely.

Maharaj once said, there are many source books, researched books and articles on Sri Ramakrishna, Holy Mother Sri Sarada Devi, Swami Vivekananda and Sri Ramakrishna's direct disciples that for a person to read and assimilate all of this in a University, it would become a 'ten year course'!

Referring to people who wanted to write articles and books, but do not turn out to be good writers, Maharaj said, 'It is not sufficient for a person to be just well-read. It is not necessary that they would become good writers just because they have wide reading. After writing something, they should show it to an accomplished writer and seek corrections. He should then read the corrected version carefully. And then he should write again on his own. By doing like this many times, he would know how to write.'

Once, Maharaj said that it would be a big loss if the monks of the Math ignored their mother tongue.

His Talks:

Once, while giving talks at the Math, Maharaj talked about Divine Incarnations mentioning the following: 'Presume that there was a king or an emperor who wanted to meet a person in the slums. Being an emperor, he need not go to that slum to meet that person. He does not gain anything out of it. Yet, due to love for that person, he himself goes to the slum, meets the poor man and showers his love on him. Like this emperor, God too, out of love for man, incarnates as a human being in this world and uplifts humanity.'

In another lecture he said, 'Why did not Lord Narayana, instead of incarnating himself as Rama, sit in *Vaikuntam* itself and wish that Ravana should die? Why Sita had to suffer so much? God manifests himself as a human being, lives with others like a human being, and shows humanity the right path.'

Once, Maharaj said, 'In a big city, a cloth or toothpaste comes up for sale. To impress the product upon the people, repeated and extensive advertisements are given through the newspapers, magazines, television channels and wall posters. Similarly, Sri Ramakrishna through his various teachings has impressed upon the minds of the people that God really exists.'

Maharaj would say that Sri Ramakrishna was '*ativarnashrami*', that is, one who had transcended the limitations of *varna* and *ashrama*.

Sometimes, he would tell funny things in his classes. Once, he mentioned that in olden days, learned pundits would praise and extol the virtues of kings. Expecting monetary rewards from them, they would even flatter them with words, which in truth, were nonsense. As an example, he quoted, '*Dvaja Sthambam Mahacharyam, Ennakku Kittanampanam!*'[1]

On special days, Maharaj would lecture in English and I, in Tamil. Speaking on the occasion of the *Buddha Poornima,* Maharaj commented, 'After Buddha, it was Swami Vivekananda who brought about a system where everyone, without any caste considerations, could become a *sannyasi.* Hence, in this respect Swami Vivekananda can be hailed as the spiritual heir of Bhagavan Buddha!'

Once, during an interaction session, a lady raised a question, 'In Hinduism, there is no such thing as women renouncing the world and living as nuns. Hinduism does not encourage women to become nuns. This is being supported by traditional maths. But Swami Vivekananda wanted to establish a nunnery. Is he not antagonist to Hindu ideals?' Maharaj replied, 'What Swami Vivekananda preached is the real ideal of Hinduism. What he preached was the real Hinduism. Swami Vivekananda was not antagonist to Hinduism. He was, in fact, the protector of it.'

In a programme held at Madras Math, a lot of devotees had come from different places. In his lecture, Maharaj said, 'Devotees of Sri Ramakrishna, wherever they are, must create a forum in the name of Sri Ramakrishna.' A

---

1. It means 'Flag Post, Great teachers, I should get money!' This phrase has no meaning except that they want money.

devotee from Sivakasi was impressed with what Maharaj said. He went back and established a *Ramakrishna – Swami Vivekananda Peravai* which is functioning even now catering to the spiritual and social welfare of people.

Once, Maharaj visited Sanskrit College, Madras to deliver a lecture on the topic *Krishnasthu Bhagavan Svayam.* In that lecture, he pointed out that the topic which in itself is an important statement is the *mahavakya* for the devotees of Sri Krishna.

Maharaj went to Singapore and Malaysia and gave lectures. Some of the *pranami* he received there was used for the publication of his translation of *Srimad Bhagavatam.* He sent some amount to Calicut Ashrama, which had meager financial resources.

With Kamalatmananda (standing), Port Blair, Andaman on 17.2.1986

Once I accompanied Maharaj to the Andaman. There Maharaj gave a talk in English at the Kali Temple. Then, we went to an education centre managed by Vivekananda Kendra. There Maharaj spoke in English and I spoke in Tamil. At Andaman, there is one famous temple of Lord Muruga. There when he spoke in English, he mentioned the importance of prayer to Lord Muruga. He then said, 'When I was young, my mother took me to Palani Temple and asked me to take *Kavadi.*'

His Interactions:

Revered Maharaj would normally converse in English with everybody. Only to those who knew only Tamil, he would attempt to speak in Tamil. He would also try to speak in Tamil with workers of the Math.

Sri Villivakam Krishnamachari was a great scholar attached to Sri Ahobila Math. He met me once regarding *Sri Ramakrishna Vijayam*. I then introduced him to Maharaj. Sri Villivakam Krishnamachari can fluently speak in Sanskrit and can only understand (not speak) English. Maharaj could speak fluently in English and can only understand (not speak) Sanskrit. So when they met, Sri Villivakam Krishnamachari spoke in Sanskrit and Revered Maharaj in English! Sri Villivakam Krishnamachari later became a pontiff of Sri Ahobila Math.

Justice Ismail, was earlier working as a lecturer in Vivekananda College, Madras. He had read several books published by Madras Math. He especially liked Anna Subramaniam's translations of the *Upanishads*. He would participate in various functions of the Math and had given talks on Sri Ramakrishna and Swami Vivekananda. He had admiration for Hinduism. Further, he had established

Kamban Kazhagam in Madras. Knowing this background, Maharaj would call him as "Ismail Sastri".

Sri Giridhari Prasad was one of the eminent spiritual speakers in Tamil Nadu. When he visited Maharaj once, I was present then. Maharaj appreciated him by saying, 'You are spreading the gospel of devotion.'

Sri Kannadasan was a popular poet in Tamil Nadu. On my request, he visited the Math. I introduced him to Maharaj and they discussed various matters for half an hour and also had noon-*prasad* that day.

His Appreciations:

Sri Avinasilingam had established the Vidyalaya [now called Ramakrishna Mission Vidyalaya] at Coimbatore. He had written his autobiography called *The Sacred Touch*. It was published by Bharathiya Vidya Bhavan. That book depicts the simple and selfless devotion of Sri Avinasilingam. Maharaj once commented, 'Vidyalaya is the manifestation of the devotion of Avinasilingam for Thakur [Sri Ramakrishna].'

Sri Pe. Su. Mani, a renowned Tamil writer, wrote a book called *Tamil Nadu and Sri Ramakrishna Movement* in 1990. Maharaj wrote a preface for that book. One of the sentences was: 'It is interesting to watch a tiny seed sprout and grow into a huge banyan tree whose spreading branches afford shadow and shelter to countless beings.' He referred to the Math and Mission in such glorifying words.

His Literary Activities:

During 1974-75, I was in the Training Centre, Belur Math. An article written by Maharaj on *Srimad Bhagavatam* was then published in *The Vedanta Kesari*. One of my *Acharyas* in the Training Centre praised the articles saying, '*Srimad Bhagavatam* is a very testing treatise even for learned scholars. And Swami Tapasyanandaji has written on it in a very scholarly manner.' When later Revered Maharaj came to Belur Math, I told him about this feedback. When he heard this, he quietly said, 'Forty years of work has gone behind that article.'

Maharaj, as a brahmachari, had compiled and edited a book called *Sayings of Sri Ramakrishna*. The book was later translated in to Tamil and Telugu, perhaps to other Indian languages as well.

Maharaj had gone once to have *darsan* of Sri Ramana Maharishi and wrote an article about this visit in *The Vedanta Kesari*.

Once I asked Revered Maharaj, 'Have you gone to Kasi, Prayag and other holy places?' He replied, 'During 1930, I wrote the life history of Holy Mother. To write the book, I had gone to Kasi and Prayag for collecting information. At that time, I met Swami Vijnanananda Maharaj. In Kasi, I met Sarala Devi [later president of Sarada Math as Bharatiprana].' It was purely for the sake of writing the book that he had visited those places. He never visited them again.

Sri Mahendranath Gupta (M.), the author of the book, *Sri Sri Ramakrishna Kathamrita* [*The Gospel of Sri Ramakrishna* in Bengali], translated a portion of the book into English and published it as *The Gospel of Sri Ramakrishna – Part I.* Revered Tapasyananda Maharaj wanted to reprint it and publish it as *The Condensed Gospel of Sri Ramakrishna*. The book at the subsidized price was released on 1 January 1978. More than one lakh copies of that book was sold.

The *Condensed Gospel of Sri Ramakrishna* had been translated into Tamil by Swami Paramatmananda Maharaj and was published by Madras Math under the title, *Sri Ramakrishnarin Mozhiamudam*. But Revered Maharaj was very particular that the entire *The Gospel of Sri Ramakrishna* should be translated into Tamil and published by Madras Math. Due to his efforts, the Tamil translation was published as *Sri Ramakrishnarin Amudha Mozhigal*.

Revered Swami Vireswarananda Maharaj visited Madras during his South Indian tour. We arranged for the release of *Sri Ramakrishnarin Amudha Mozhigal* by Revered Vireswarananda Maharaj. While introducing him, Revered Tapasyananda Maharaj said, 'Prabhu Maharaj is Holy Mother's disciple. When Swami Sarvananda Maharaj was the head of Madras Math, he was a brahmachari here. Later he was also the General Secretary of the Ramakrishna Math and Mission…' While mentioning that Revered Vireswarananda Maharaj had authored several books, Revered Tapasyananda Maharaj said that he was telling all this just for formality and remarked, 'Prabhu Maharaj does not require any of these praises. He has crossed all these and gone to such a height.'

Sri N. Mahalingam, Chairman of Sakthi Sugars, was one of the prominent industrialists in Tamil Nadu. He was associated with Madras Math right from his student days. He was also interested in Tamil literature and Saiva literature. He requested Revered Maharaj to publish the English translations of *Periyapuram* and *Thirumandiram* considering the importance of these two books. Revered Maharaj immediately recognized their importance and arranged for the publication of these books.

Referring to the book *Sri Ramakrishna for Children,* Revered Maharaj pointed out this being a book for the children, it should not have the picture of Sri Ramakrishna trying to cut his throat for the sake of getting the vision of Kali.

Maharaj once said, 'Our Math has published many books on Advaita Vedanta. One book should also come out on Bhakti Sampradaya and the Bhakti Schools of Vedanta. As desired, he himself later wrote a book titled *Bhakti Schools of Vedanta.*

Sri Ramakrishna Vijayam:

When I was the editor of *Sri Ramakrishna Vijayam,* the circulation had increased from 1100 to 10000. Once, when Revered Swami Vireswarananda Maharaj visited Madras Math, I was called to his room. When I went there, Revered Tapasyananda Maharaj pointing towards me said, 'He is the current editor of the magazine. Now the circulation has gone up to 10,000. So I had called him to introduce him to you.' Revered Vireswarananda Maharaj gave a sweet smile and blessed me through it! I even now vividly remember it.

To a person who was unfairly comparing *Sri Ramakrishna Vijayam* with other magazines, Revered Maharaj retorted that in spite of several handicaps, he [referring to me] was running the magazine and therefore such comparison were unwarranted and prejudiced. Maharaj was ever ready to defend me!

I wanted to publish in *Sri Ramakrishna Vijayam* the Tamil translation of a chapter on *Bhagavad Gita* written by Maharaj for *The Cultural Heritage of India*. When I requested for his permission, he said, 'I wrote that article many years ago. I feel that if it is published in the present-day context, it will have greater acceptance. If you think you can make use of it for your magazine, you are quite welcome to do so.'

A prominent person would write articles on *Periyapuranam* in *Sri Ramakrishna Vijayam* continuously for 14 years. I had felt that the contents and expression of the articles were not up to the mark. So when I took charge of the magazine as its editor, I stopped publishing the subsequent articles. However, this was not to the liking of that author and he wrote a letter to Revered Maharaj requesting him to arrange for its resumption. When Revered Maharaj called me and enquired, I gave the reasons. I also wrote a letter to him apologizing for any misgivings that might have crept due to this. But I did not resume publishing subsequent articles. But what struck me in this episode was the complete freedom Revered Maharaj gave in to my decision. He just expressed his opinion, but did not insist or force me to do anything contrary to my own stand.

In 1990, Revered Maharaj had written an article in *The Vedanta Kesari* titled *The Myth about St. Thomas*. He told me that the Tamil version of that article should appear in *Sri Ramakrishna Vijayam* too. Accordingly, a translated version of that article under the title *Saint Thomas Patriya Kattukathai* was published in the August issue of that year. This article caused a sensation among the readers in Tamil

Nadu. Appreciating the article, Revered Maharaj received hundreds of letters from the readers of *Vijayam*.

When I was the editor of *Sri Ramakrishna Vijayam*, the Holy Mother's disciple Swami Apurvananda was in-charge of the Varanasi Centre. He would tell me, 'Sri Ramakrishna's grace through Swami Tapasyananda has made you an Editor.'

Night Class Treats:

Revered Maharaj believed that the night classes should not consist of only passive reading of the book and would therefore encourage discussions. All the monastics must come for the night classes on time. If anyone came late, he would get annoyed.

Once Swami Tapasyananda made an interesting observation and illustrated it by way of a story: 'A man was working in a house for many years. He was loyal and of good character and was very much liked by the master of the house. The master reposed great faith in the man's words and opinions. Without consulting him, he would never do anything. One day, out of great love he had for him, the master held his hands and made him sit on his chair. The servant was shy. In spite of his hesitation, the master persuaded him to sit on his chair. He said, 'Do sit on my chair. After all you and I are the same and there is no difference between us.' Expressing his opinion on this story, Revered Maharaj said, 'The master should say that he and his servant are the same, instead you should not say that you are equal to the master like someone who advocates the Advaita philosophy without attaining the required maturity proclaiming that he and his Master are same!'

Once Maharaj said, 'This whole world resembles the holy feet of the Lord! Here, serving the people and other living beings amounts to our serving the holy feet of the Lord!'

Once during the night classes when he was referring about Sri Ramakrishna, he opened up his two arms and said, 'God's gracious energy led to the birth to Sri Ramakrishna.'

Once, Revered Maharaj said that both in *The Gospel of Sri Ramakrishna* and *Sri Ramakrishna, the Great Master,* elements of both the Eastern philosophy and Western philosophy are either directly or indirectly ingrained.

Once in a night class, he mentioned that the general public had full confidence that the donations given to the Ramakrishna Mission for relief work would be spent properly. And to that extent, the Mission had earned the trust of the people. But he was also of the opinion that Ramakrishna Mission is basically a preaching organization.

A book titled *The Gift Unopened: A New American Revolution* was published in America. The author, Eleanor Stark, comments that Swami Vivekananda gifted a great spiritual treasure to the Americans which came to them unexpectedly and that Americans could enrich their life by utilizing the gift. Referring to the author's comment, Revered Maharaj said that the "unopened gift" was not only for the Americans but for Indians also.

In one of the night classes, a senior monk expressed his opinion that Math should focus on only spiritual practices and not so much on activities, social welfare schemes, etc. Referring to this in the next night class, Maharaj emphatically said that although spiritual practices are important, activities, social welfare schemes etc. were also equally important. I got a glimpse of what both of them were driving at.

Once during a night class, a question arose, 'Whether the stories in the *puranas* had really taken place or are they only imaginations?' Revered Maharaj dealt with this issue at length and expressed several opinions. The one I remember now is, 'The stories in the *puranas* have the potentiality to create bhakti in the minds of people.'

In a night class, Maharaj said that in Christianity, it is mentioned that 'Hell' is a place where a man goes permanently for his misdeeds on this earth, whereas, 'Hell', according to Hindus, is a place where man is 'purified'.

'Jesus Christ was one day walking along the sea shore when a devotee approached him and asked him, "Lord, how can one attain God? "Jesus directly walked into the sea with the enquirer and immersed him in the water. After a short time, he released him, and raising him by the arm, asked him, "How did you feel?" The devotee replied, "I felt as though my last moment had come - the condition was desperate." Upon this, Jesus said, "you shall see the Father when your heart pants for Him as it has panted for a breath of air just now."'[1] In the night class, a discussion arose about the above passage where the

1. Sayings of Sri Ramakrishna, no. 624, p 166, published by Sri Ramakrishna Math, Chennai.

name of Jesus Christ is mentioned whereas this incident is not mentioned in the Bible! Revered Maharaj explained, 'There were 4 or 5 versions of the Bible earlier. But the Church kept only one version which it approved and banned all the other versions. When Sri Ramakrishna was alive, two or three versions of the Bible were in circulation. This story of Jesus Christ told by Sri Ramakrishna is in one of those versions.'

His Spiritual Instructions:

Once Maharaj commented, 'Our ancestors, by reciting *slokas* in the morning, and doing *parayana* of *stotras* started their day in an auspicious manner. But today the only *stotras* and *slokas* that the modern generation read are the newspapers! As a result of this, we commence our activities for the day with a confused mind, instead of a composed mind.'

A young girl took *mantra diksa* from Maharaj. To her, Maharaj instructed, 'Memorize fully the *Srimad Bhagavad Gita*. That will be useful throughout your life.'

On 14 February 1986, Maharaj went to Andaman. I too accompanied him. I then had the opportunity of serving him food, washing his clothes and arranging for spiritual initiation etc. An Engineer, who had hearing and speech disability, was one of the candidates for spiritual initiation. Maharaj made him sit with him in his room and wrote down all that that needed to be instructed during initiation. Revered Maharaj patiently spent nearly an hour and a half with him and ensured that he understood all that was communicated.

His distinguishing quality:

Ever since Revered Maharaj came to Madras Math in 1971 till his demise, I had the opportunity of living with him. I noticed one important quality in him. He had spent 30 years in Trivandrum and had practically built every inch of the hospital, experiencing several inconveniences, struggling to cross several hurdles. But not even once did he ever mention about Trivandrum centre to us in Madras Math, lest it may (even indirectly) indicate any self-praise. I feel this detachment was the most distinguishing quality of Revered Maharaj.

Conviction and Clarity[1]

Once, Swami Tapasyananda Maharaj, who had been the editor of *The Vedanta Kesari* 15 years earlier, was visiting us [at Madras Math] from Trivandrum. As the current editor of *The Vedanta Kesari*, I asked him that if he were writing now, how his writing would be different from what he had written earlier. His reply was, 'In conviction and clearness.'

1. *My Days in Madras Math*, Swami Swahananda, *The Vedanta Kesari*, December, 1997, p 558

9

Will I Return Safely?

Swami Virupakshananda[1]

Revered Maharaj was a very austere monk. He was a learned scholar and had independently translated several scriptures on bhakti. His masterpiece, according to many scholars, is his massive introduction to *Srimad Bhagavatam*.

Once we both went to Belur Math. At Belur Math, the Swami-in-charge of the Advaita Ashrama, Calcutta, invited us for lunch. Accepting his invitation, we went for the lunch. Revered Maharaj praised the great and efficient work done by the Swami-in-charge of the Advaita Ashrama. At lunch, many tasty dishes were served and one of them was a sweet called *Rajbhog*. Revered Maharaj did not relish sweets and therefore did not consume *Rajbhog*.

In earlier days, he did not travel by air. He took his simple food in a tiffin carrier during his train journey and would relish eating it.

Maharaj strongly discouraged indiscipline in the Math. If anyone was not punctual in attending to his work, Maharaj would reprimand him and remind him about the sanctity of life and work. And he would insist on implicit obedience.

---

1. He is a senior monk of the Order who knew Revered Maharaj for many years.

Virupakshanandaji, Vireswaranandaji, Tapasyanandaji, Office Block Inauguration, Chengalpet, 1983

When Maharaj fell ill, he was admitted to a nearby hospital. Once I went to see him in the hospital when his condition was quite serious. I went and touched his feet. He asked me a strange question, 'Will I return to the Math safely?' I was quite dumbfounded at this question. I knew that his health was deteriorating. I simply replied that we were praying to the Lord that he may safely return to the Math. However, four days after this incident, Revered Maharaj passed away in the hospital.

With his passing away, the Order lost a very learned and spirited monk. His strict behaviour with people was ideal. He would never gossip. I was very much attracted to him because of these qualities.

10

Personification of Moderation

Swami Jnanadananda[1]

I joined the Ramakrishna Math, Madras in 1972. It was my good fortune that Revered Swami Tapasyananda Maharaj was the president of Madras Math at that time.

Several times I have been recollecting the sweet memories of my association with the great and noble soul called Swami Tapasyananda and they fill my heart and soul with such joy and blessedness that words are inadequate to convey these wonderful feelings.

I have had innumerable opportunities to be very closely associated with Revered Maharaj. For almost five years, I stayed near about his room in the Math. I was amazed to watch him vigorously follow a strict routine. He used to lead an exceptionally austere life that greatly befitted his name *Tapasyananda*. His life was full of *tapas*. He was very regular in his spiritual practices, doing his japa and meditation every morning and evening without fail. I had seen him in the shrine attending the morning *mangalarati* day after day. Not even a single day would he miss the morning *arati*, whether ill or well, in rain or shine.

---

1. He joined Madras Math in 1972 as the first brahmachari under Revered Maharaj and was in his company for 2 decades. He was later the manager of Madras Math for many years.

An Ideal monk

Purity, Poverty and Perseverance - these are the important characteristics of an ideal monk. I found in him all these qualities in abundance.

His renunciation was remarkable. He would wear very simple clothes. He kept his needs to the bare minimum - like soap, tooth paste, a few dhotis and shirts – and these articles were supplied from the common stores of the Math. He always washed his own clothes; used minimal water for bathing. Even in his advanced age, he chose to travel only by train.

When Revered Maharaj became the Vice-President of the Ramakrishna Order, he began to give *mantra diksa* to the deserving devotees. He used to get money as *pranami* (offering) from these disciples as well as from the devotees in general. All the money that he received would be given away then and there as donation to the fund for the poor. He never used to keep any money separately for his personal use. A person of exemplary renunciation!

Revered Maharaj led a very simple and incredibly austere life. I have seen him carrying a small leather bag as his travel kit. This leather bag might have been with him for more than fifteen years. It had worn out due to constant wear and tear. When I noticed this I told him, 'Maharaj! This leather bag is in very bad shape. It is torn in one or two places. Can I get a new bag for you?' His reply was, 'We should not waste anything. This bag can be used for some more years. You take it to a shop, get it repaired and bring it back. This is sufficient for me.' He had imposed it on himself the ideal of 'poverty' voluntarily and practiced it cheerfully with contentment.

An Ideal Karma Yogi

Revered Maharaj's quality of perseverance was very evident when he was at work. He was very meticulous in attending to his duties. He was very punctual and systematic. He would reach his office right in time, to the minute, and meet the visitors. He would himself carry his books with him to the office. When there were no visitors, he would zealously peruse through those books.

Revered Maharaj was a man of few words. I noticed that whenever visitors came, he would speak to them cordially, but would dispose them off as early as possible. Then immediately he would be immersed in studying or writing books.

His command over English was extraordinary. He has written the authoritative book, *Life of Sri Sarada Devi* and a few booklets like *Life and Teachings of Sri Ramakrishna, Sarada Devi: Life & Teachings,* and *Swami Vivekananda: Life & Legacy*. He has also translated *Srimad Bhagavatam* (four volumes), *Bhakti Ratnavali* and other theological books. *Sankara Digvijayam,* depicting the life of Sri Sankaracharya, is a masterpiece.

He could use any amount of paper for his work. But he was so thrifty in such matters that he always preferred one-side-blank papers (the other side already used) to prepare the manuscript of his books. He would first make a draft, and then go on rewriting and revising them until he was satisfied with the manuscript. He would then send the manuscript for typing, and after it was typed, again on one-side-blank papers, he would painstakingly go through the typed script twice or thrice, correcting the errors. Then it would go to the press for printing.

But his meticulousness would not end there. When the 'proof' came from the printing press, he would go through them twice or thrice again to make sure that all the mistakes were rectified. Many a time, he used to call and assign me the duty of proofreading. He lovingly taught me how to go through the proof and to make corrections thoroughly. In this way, he kept track at every stage so that the book could be published with perfection. Such was the persevering zeal of a karma yogi I have observed in Revered Maharaj.

Training new brahmacharis

Being a strict disciplinarian, he used to keep a close watch on all the new brahmacharis who joined under him. He would call all the brahmacharis once a month and make detailed enquiries as to what book he was reading, whether he was attending the morning *mangalarati* and evening *aratrikam*, doing regular physical exercise etc. Maharaj would guide the brahmacharis individually regarding the books they must read, insisting them to dedicate at least two hours every day for studying the scriptures. He advised us to make notes while going through the scriptures. I distinctly remember how he used to encourage me to memorize some verses from the *Bhagavad Gita*. He also specifically advised me to study the Telugu literature since my mother tongue was Telugu and also to write articles now and then for the Telugu magazine, *Sri Ramakrishna Prabha*. I used to derive lot of inspiration and joy from his spiritual guidance.

He never accepted much service from other monks or brahmacharis. He himself used to take care of his personal needs. While travelling, he would carry very less luggage, which he himself would pack. Once I offered to pack his luggage. He smiled and said, 'Oh! You want to help me in packing my things! You may help me here. But who will help me while travelling in the train? You won't be with me in the train to help me. So, I always do things myself.'

Guiding the monastic members

I found that Revered Maharaj was a constant source of inspiration for all the monastic members under him. Whenever we had any problem, we used to approach him and present the problem before him without any hesitation. With his experience and insight, he would give right solutions to our problems. He would lovingly correct us when we went wrong and saw to it that we followed the right path. He was always approachable and amicable. Revered Maharaj was a highly motivated soul, and he would greatly motivate others as well.

Whenever I think of Revered Maharaj, the following verse of the *Bhagavad Gita* (6:17) comes to my mind:

युक्ताहारविहारस्य युक्तचेष्टस्य कर्मसु ।
युक्तस्वप्नावबोधस्य योगो भवति दुःखहा ।।

yuktāhāravihārasya yuktaceṣṭasya karmasu |
yuktasvapnāvabodhasya yogo bhavati duḥkhahā ||

[(A yogi practices) Moderation in food, movements, activities, in his sleep and waking state; this moderation in everything removes misery in life.]

I found Revered Maharaj to be the personification of this verse. He was very moderate in eating - he took only as much as he needed to maintain a healthy body. He ate at fixed hours and never ate anything at other times. His sleeping habits also were very disciplined. He would go to bed in time and would wake up in time. He used to be very precise in these aspects. He was also judicious while interacting with people of different types. I have tried to inculcate these qualities in my own life as I have accepted Revered Maharaj as my role model.

From the day I joined the Math under him in 1972, till today, I have always held him in high esteem and considered him as my guardian angel in every respect. I consider myself very fortunate to come under his ever-loving and ever-guiding umbrella.

All glory to Bhagavan Sri Ramakrishna, Holy Mother Sri Sarada Devi and Swamiji.

11

Respecting Others

Swami Veetamohananda[1]

I knew Revered Swami Tapasyananda Maharaj since we met in 1961. He used to come every year to Madras Math on his way to the Belur Math. I used to arrange his train tickets from Madras to Calcutta. Revered Maharaj would be very simple and friendly.

It was in 1971 that Revered Maharaj became the president of Madras Math. I was then a newly ordained monk. Revered Maharaj used to be quite cordial and sympathetic with me. I used to stay in the room next to his. We used to exchange views on different subjects quite often.

The entire management of Madras Math took a different turn when Revered Maharaj took charge of it. He deputed two managerial functionaries to run the Math in a dynamic way. This arrangement produced a remarkable improvement in all spheres. The monastic traditions were strengthened and everyday life was made more intense. Every monastic had the freedom to study Sanskrit, scriptures, music and other subjects of interest. The celebrations were oriented towards spiritual deepening

---

1. He was with Revered Maharaj for some time in Madras Math.

and upliftment. His classes and discourses were of great interest for deep thinkers.

Revered Maharaj was an ideal for the simplicity of a real monk. He was very regular in his practices of meditation. He enjoyed being alone in his room during general prayer and meditation hours.

Revered Maharaj was a keen observer and would give the right direction whenever and wherever needed. He appreciated the silent and serene nature of the spiritual aspirants. He would not hesitate or be afraid to say anything that was right or true for the benefit of spiritual seekers. He was quite open to all sincere seekers.

The study of the scriptures was most important to him. The different publications accredited to him were the results of his deep study and deep reflections. His self-sacrifice and love for the ideals which he demonstrated in his own life are the great ideals before all of us too. He wished that everyone practiced these great ideals. Capable monks were asked to conduct classes on scriptures every evening to inspire others.

Revered Maharaj respected everybody's need and temperament. He asked me to take up puja which requires regularity and sincerity. He appreciated the way I applied myself for the worship in the shrine. He was very regular in his coming to the shrine and being absorbed during the hours of worship. He would encourage me in devotional singing in the shrine. Anything done usefully gave him immense joy.

Revered Maharaj expressed his happiness when I was asked to go to Kalady, Kerala, to perform the worship of

Sri Ramakrishna in the newly built temple. He also told me that different types of activities ennoble our personalities.

Revered Maharaj was all encouragement when I was shifted to Mysore to work in the Institute of Moral and Spiritual Education. Later, when I visited him with the students of the Institute, he welcomed us all with his whole heart and soul. He spent the available time with us discussing about various activities, study of subjects, etc.

I could not meet him before I left for France due to various official obligations. I felt immensely sad when I heard of his departure from this world and deeply regretted for not having met him. Let us all try to imbibe the true ideal of Revered Swami Tapasyananda Maharaj.

12

What's in a Name? Perhaps a Lot

Swami Tyagananda[1]

Among my earliest memories of Swami Tapasyananda Maharaj is this little incident that occurred in 1980. Maharaj had come from Madras to Belur Math for the Order's tri-annual Trustees' meeting. I was studying at the monastic training centre and some of us brahmacharins had gathered in Maharaj's room. The topic of monastic names came up and Maharaj said that every monk got the name that was a perfect fit for his personality. Referring to Swami Ranganathananda Maharaj (who was staying next to his room), Tapasyananda said, 'Look at his name. "Ranganatha" means the master of the dais, a name perfectly suited for an extraordinary orator and carrier of the Great Master's message.' The "Great Master" was Maharaj's favourite way of referring to Sri Ramakrishna.

I think Maharaj didn't anticipate where his explanation would lead his young listeners. One of us said, 'Maharaj, your name is perfectly suited too for your dedicated and austere life.' Maharaj backtracked immediately, waving his hands frantically with, 'Oh no, no, no. In my case, the name simply reminds me of the ideal I should be striving

1. He was with Maharaj in Madras Math for eight years. He was the editor of *The Vedanta Kesari* for several years.

for.' We smiled and he smiled too. Three years later I was in Madras under Maharaj's care and had the privilege to see him at close quarters for eight years, that is, until 1991, when he entered *mahasamadhi*. Today I can say with absolute certainty that no name other than "Tapasyananda" could have suited his personality better.

Obviously I did not analyze his personality when I was in Madras. Nor did I do it later. I was in Madras for 15 years and now it is almost 15 years since I left it. This provides sufficient space, even geographically, for me to be able to look at my Madras experience objectively and examine the lessons it taught me. The biggest and brightest source of my training in Madras was—no surprise here!—Swami Tapasyananda Maharaj. I learned many lessons

Sitting below (Left to Right) Jnanaswarupananda & Sukritananda; Sitting (Left to Right) 1. Deshikatmananda, 2. Jnanadananda, 3. Kamalatmananda, 4. Tapasyanandaji, 5. Raghaveshananda, 7. Tyagananda (last); Standing (Left to Right) 1. Ajaratmananda, 3. Vishveshananda, 6. Kapalishananda, 7. Vyomatitananda

from him and my memories of him continue to be a source of inspiration.

Among the first things that come to mind is Maharaj's punctuality. Years of discipline had created for him a daily routine which he seldom violated. The time he woke up, bathed, went to the shrine and then to his office, the time for his meals and evening walk, the hours spent in meeting visitors, answering letters, reading and writing were all fixed. No time was wasted and that partially explains his enormous literary output. He did not spare himself where work was concerned. When he was not meeting with visitors, he was translating texts in his office. He carried his books and papers everywhere, even to Belur Math for the Trustees' meetings three times a year. Because he was focused on work—the "Great Master's work," as he called it—he expected the monastics in his centre to also work hard and with single-minded dedication. Anyone, monastic or lay, who showed signs of inertia or ineptitude in work, received a scolding.

We didn't have any fans in the dining hall and it really got uncomfortably hot, especially during summer. We couldn't complain, because Maharaj himself sat with us in the same hall and he was twice as old as most of us in the Math. I was told that Maharaj didn't want fans in there because he felt that it might make us sit longer in the dining hall, which would lead to our eating more than we needed to, which in turn would make us sluggish and sleepy, affecting our post-lunch duties. That was how the absence of fans in the dining hall and the importance of work were related. A little farfetched perhaps, but there is no denying that there was some truth to it. But most of us were young and our energy levels were high, so we spent a long time in the dining hall anyway, exchanging stories and jokes, and often discussing and arguing over philosophical issues. Maharaj did not mind this kind of healthy exchange between his young monastics, so he seldom objected to our extended dining hall breaks. We made sure, though, that the duties we were entrusted with did not suffer.

But our life in Madras Math did not revolve around simply work, work and more work. There was plenty of play too. During the time I was in Madras, we had a badminton court in the inner courtyard between the 'Old Temple' and the dining hall. Maharaj would walk up and down the corridor in late afternoons and the rest of us would play badminton. There was a lot of laughter. We were a noisy bunch. He rarely stopped to see us play but he kept a vigilant eye on who played and who didn't. He expected everyone to play because he believed that it would provide us good exercise. I had been briefed about this by a monastic brother when I first arrived in Madras in 1983. When I didn't show up to play for a few days, Maharaj called me as I walked into the courtyard one day. He said, 'Well, I don't see you playing.' Rather than give an explanation for my absence (I had hurt my knees while playing some days earlier), I told him what I was doing instead: 'I take regular exercise in my room, Maharaj.' He nodded approvingly and said, 'Oh, then it is all right.'

I can never forget Maharaj's loving concern for me. Soon after I arrived in Madras, he told me, 'You are not accustomed to our (meaning, South Indian) food. If you need any special dish to be prepared for you, let me know. I shall instruct the *bhandari* (the brahmachari who was the kitchen-manager) accordingly.' I told him, 'Maharaj, I am doing fine.' Every fortnight or so, he continued to ask how I was adjusting and to offer special food for me. Every time he did so, I politely declined. After about three or four months, he concluded that I was doing all right and he stopped asking. Because he was known for his frugal and austere ways, many find it difficult to believe he would make such a generous offer to a young brahmachari. Those of us who lived with him know that behind his stern demeanor lurked a loving, compassionate heart.

When Maharaj contracted chicken-pox in 1985, he was sequestered in a guest room on the upper level of the dispensary building. Since I too lived in an adjacent room, this gave me more opportunities to serve him and spend longer hours with him. He was 81 then, and the pox was particularly hard on his aging body. The skin rash covered most of his body, including his head, and it was painful for us to see, and obviously it must have been considerably more painful for him to endure. During a month or more that it took for him to recover fully, we were privileged to see his stoic acceptance of the pain and amazing adaptability to a changed routine. He maintained his composure in spite of the physical suffering and spent as much time as possible reading and writing, although his weakened body forced him to spend long hours in bed.

Maharaj seemed to have mellowed during that period and we dared one day to ask him to tell us about his childhood. To our great amusement, he told us that he was quite naughty as a child and mentioned some of the pranks he and his friends played in school, one of which was layering the teacher's chair with glue! By the time he recovered and it was time to return to his own room, he looked different since he had not shaved for about a month. His bearded face made him look like an emperor and we begged him to let us photograph him, but he seemed reluctant, so we did not press further. I wish we had. That would have been a rare picture!

Maharaj was not too reluctant, though, when we requested him one day to cook for us. He had told us some days earlier that, when he was at the Vedanta Study Circle in Mysore in the 1930s, he occasionally cooked for other brother monks. We were tempted to test his cooking skill and to our great joy he agreed to our request. He gave instructions to the *bhandari* about the provisions needed etc., and one evening he marched into the kitchen and cooked a delicious curry which we all enjoyed to our hearts' content.

A few months after my *sannyasa*, sometime in late October of 1986, Maharaj called me to his office and told me that he *wanted* me to be the editor of *The Vedanta Kesari*, a move that took me completely off guard. I was until then assisting Sri C. S. Ramakrishnan, a long-time devotee, who was ably editing the journal for many years. Everything was going so well that there seemed to be no perceivable reason for a change. Anyway, Maharaj seemed determined about this appointment, so I agreed without much resistance.

My resistance came a few days later. Maharaj called me and asked me to go to a place near Madras to give a lecture. He said that the devotee group there had requested for a swami to give a retreat. I politely declined and told him, 'Maharaj, you have asked me to be the editor. This work will need my full attention. I want to do the best I can, and I won't be able to do so if my time and energy get divided like this.' I said that I would be happy to lecture at the Math whenever needed, but I don't want to travel outside for lectures. Maharaj responded with the familiar shaking of his head and hands, 'No, no, no. You must do it. There are so many invitations and we don't have many speakers here. This is a part of your work. You've got to do it.' I persisted and more or less repeated what I had said. I was polite but firm: 'Maharaj, please I cannot do this. I want to concentrate on study and writing in order to do justice to the responsibility you have given me.' Once again, he insisted that I go to Ranipet and lecture, and once again I pleaded with him not to force me to do so.

It must have gone back and forth like this for about ten minutes, or at least it felt like that. It almost looked like we both were trying to wear each other down. It was a test of perseverance. Finally, he paused, there was silence, I looked at him wondering what was coming next and, to my great relief, I saw him smiling. He had a very sweet smile. He said softly, 'I know, I know, I know.' He paused. More silence followed. I waited. Maharaj continued, his voice gentle and soft, like a mother singing lullaby to her baby: 'I understand what you are saying. I too was editor of *The Vedanta Kesari* many years ago. The work does need total dedication and concentration. Very good then. You need not go. I won't ask you to travel outside to lecture.' I was grateful and thrilled beyond words. Maharaj kept his word. He never asked me to travel outside again.

When I returned to my room, I kept asking myself, did I do the right thing by saying no? Shouldn't I have obeyed his command without resistance? There is little doubt that it would have made Maharaj happy if I had agreed to go out and lecture. But I am also certain that he was happier to see how I was approaching my newly entrusted responsibility as editor, never mind if it involved my saying no to him. So was this an act of obedience or disobedience? I don't know. All I know is that Maharaj appreciated what in less charitable terms can be called my stubbornness, which strengthens my belief that he was probably testing my resolve when he kept insisting that I go out and lecture. I like to believe that I passed the test.

As head of Madras Math, Maharaj was technically the editor of *The Vedanta Kesari*, but he really saw every issue only after it was published. In those days, the real editor was officially known as joint editor. This practice was discontinued in the early 1990s, when the head of the publication centre became the managing editor and the real editor became, well, the 'editor'. Most readers did not know this fine distinction. So it was not unusual for Maharaj to receive letters appreciating a particular editorial or the quality of the journal. He would occasionally call me to his office and show such letters to me and say, 'These people direct their praise and appreciation toward me, but I don't even see the magazine until it is printed!' and we both would have a good laugh.

Maharaj was a model of humility. He was working on the lives and philosophies of Vedanta philosophers that came after Sankara, such as Ramanuja, Madhva, Vallabhacharya and others. He would pass on the manuscript to me after finishing the section on each philosopher with a casual remark, 'Well, well, here is something for you if you find it suitable for publication.' There was no affectation, no pretension, no false modesty. Just plain and simple humility. It was embarrassing for me to hear him say that. 'Maharaj, it is a great blessing to have your articles in the journal,' I used to tell him. His brilliant research was later published as the book *Bhakti Schools of Vedanta*. This was one of the few books that Maharaj wrote. Most of his literary efforts were directed toward translating ancient Sanskrit texts into English and making them easily accessible to a general reader. His four-volume translation of *Srimad Bhagavata* remains a masterpiece, as are his translations of *Vishnu Sahasra-Nama, Lalita Sahasra-Nama, Bhakti Ratnavali, Narayaneeyam, Adhyatma Ramayana, Sundara Kandam*, and the *Bhagavad Gita*. When Maharaj would be at his desk working on some translation, he would be so absorbed into his writing as to be oblivious of his surroundings.

This was even more so when Maharaj was meditating. I found this out quite accidentally. The librarian would leave the newspapers on a table outside Maharaj's room on the first floor of the monks' quarters after the library closed in the evening. One evening I was looking for a piece of news reported in the papers and went to the porch outside Maharaj's room to look for the newspaper. It was quite dark, Maharaj was in the room but his door was wide open. The mosquito net was drawn and I saw Maharaj sitting cross legged on his bed, his hands folded, and chanting a Sanskrit hymn to Sri Ramakrishna in his deep, sonorous voice. His fervour was palpable and the chanting was unbelievably sweet and moving. I sat on the steps outside and listened. It made such a deep impression on my mind that for several days I went outside his room around the same time and sat on the same spot to listen to him chanting. The whole place seemed charged with power.

Our after-dinner gatherings of monastics were most lively. In those days we were reading Swami Saradananda's *Sri Ramakrishna The Great Master*. One of us was the designated reader and the rest of us listened. Sometimes during the reading, but more often at the end of it, Maharaj would raise a point and encourage a debate. Or he would ask a question and we were expected to share our views. Some days a vigorous discussion would follow. Almost always there would be some wisecrack and ripples of laughter would ensue. The gathering had a strange mix of seriousness and light heartedness, and we learnt so much without even realizing that we were being taught. When we had visiting monks from other centres, they would be invited to address the novices and the younger monks.

The importance of study was always emphasized. Maharaj also arranged for our scriptural study under Sri Kalyanasundara Sastrigal, a renowned Vedanta scholar who was trained from childhood in a Vedic school. His knowledge of English did not extend beyond a few words and some amongst us did not know Tamil. So we had the blessed privilege to study with him in Sanskrit for twelve long years. This became possible only due to the encouragement and permission of Maharaj and we all remain grateful to him for that unique opportunity.

Maharaj had a reputation in the Order for frugality. His needs were few and his room and his office always had the minimalist look. His wardrobe was small and his clothes simple. His towel used to be so tattered that it often had holes in it, but Maharaj would refuse to throw it away. 'It's doing its job, so why do I need a new one?' he would ask. Only when he went to Belur Math for the meetings would we have the chance to take away the old towel from his room and replace it with a new one. When he returned to Madras and noticed the change, he had to be told a white lie, 'Maharaj, we couldn't find your towel, so we had to replace it.' I suspect that Maharaj saw through the game, but he kept quiet.

The office assistant who typed Maharaj's letters was on vacation once. Maharaj wanted an urgent letter to be typed and I offered to do it for him. After typing the letter I took it to his office. Since the letter was to be mailed with several enclosures, I used a paper clip to keep all the documents together. Maharaj thought I'd hand over the letter and leave, but I didn't. I stood there waiting for Maharaj to read the letter and sign it, so I could then hand it over to the despatch department for mailing. After reading the letter, Maharaj signed it and yet he wouldn't hand it over to me. He sat there silently. He looked up at me, then he looked at the papers again, and stared blankly at the wall in front of him. I still did not leave the room. When Maharaj realized that I wouldn't leave until I got the signed letter from him, he looked at me again and winked—he winked!—and asked, 'Do we really need to use this paper clip?' I realized why he asked me that question and promptly answered, 'No, Maharaj. We don't really need it.' He then removed the clip, carefully folded the letter and the accompanying documents and put them in an envelope. As he gave the packet to me for mailing, he said, 'My principle is not to waste anything. All these papers are in the envelope and there is no way they are going to be separated. So using a paper clip would be a waste.' I nodded in agreement.

This incident might make us feel that the idea of frugality was taken too far, but not if we put it into context. Maharaj, and other monks of his generation, joined the monastery in the early decades of the last century, when the Order was small and its financial resources extremely limited. Living as frugally as possible was not a matter of choice but a necessity. A testimony to what Maharaj accomplished about 70 years ago with extremely slender resources is the Order's hospital centre at Trivandrum. We were told by elderly monks how Maharaj's office there with a simple table and chair doubled up at night as his bedroom. His bed was a cloth draped over two slender benches which were used during daytime by patients waiting to be examined by the doctors. His food was always simple, even when he later returned as head of Madras Math in the last twenty years of his life.

Frugal as Maharaj was in his personal life, he did not pinch pennies when it was needed for the "Great Master's work". When the idea of starting a printing press in Madras Math was first mooted, Maharaj was reluctant. During a discussion when it was pointed out that having our own press would not only expedite the publishing of our books and journals but also bring down the cost, Maharaj was convinced that the press would be a good investment and help spread Sri Ramakrishna's message. Starting a press involved major expenses and the project received Maharaj's enthusiastic blessing. Madras Math had been a publication centre almost from its inception. But it was during Maharaj's time that its publication department had an unprecedented spurt of growth both in quality and quantity. Today Madras Math is the largest publication centre of the Ramakrishna Order. Maharaj's contribution to its success is enormous.

Those who lived and worked with Maharaj soon learnt how to pitch new projects to him to elicit his permission. They tried to show him how the new project would improve quality and help in the work of the Order. In spite of his predominantly scholastic temperament, Maharaj had a shrewd and practical mindset when dealing with financial and administrative matters. He listened attentively and took his decisions only after careful deliberation.

When I look back at my days in Madras, I can see before my mind's eye Maharaj walking with a stick to the shrine—he was almost 80 when I went to Madras— going up the steps slowly, and then to his office. He sat on a simple wooden chair with a straight back. His face was calm and he had an aura of peace around him. When he laughed, the joy seemed to emanate from his whole being. Maharaj's simplicity, discipline, dedication and, above all, his love and compassion have left a permanent imprint on my heart. Through the infinite grace of Sri Ramakrishna and Holy Mother, I hope to make a sincere effort to live up to those ideals in the remaining part of my life.

13

Study Seriously and Think Deeply

Swami Amareshananda[1]

I, along with my friend who was a disciple of Revered Yatiswarananda Maharaj, was on a pilgrimage to Varanasi, Gaya etc. We heard the news on radio at Bolpur railway station about the demise of Revered Yatiswarananda Maharaj on 27 January 1966. We then left for Belur Math.

After staying in Belur Math for five days, we continued our journey via Bhubaneshwar, Puri and southern pilgrim centres and reached Sasthamangalam Hospital Centre, Trivandrum in the last week of February.

We met Revered Swami Tapasyananda Maharaj who was sitting on a wooden armless chair on the verandah of an old tiled building and offered our *pranams* to him. He enquired about our purpose of visit. On hearing from us, he directed us to board a bus and proceed to Kanyakumari to reach there before nightfall. We reached Kanyakumari at night and stayed close to the sea as we were particular about watching sunrise and sunset.

We watched the sunrise the next morning and after bath, we visited the Kanyakumari Temple. We spent some

1. He is a senior monk of the Order who knew Revered Maharaj for many years.

time in the temple whose environs were calm even though there were many people. We visited the Vivekananda Rock (at that time, there was no Memorial) by boat and meditated there. After watching sunset, we returned to Trivandrum.

Next morning, we were served *appalam* during the breakfast. Revered Maharaj explained the process of pounding rice and black dal together with a wooden rod. He also mentioned that patients in the hospital were served *idlis* and coffee/tea for breakfast. The hospital had 40 beds. After visiting Nettayam, we left Trivandrum.

Since March 1970, I was in Belur Math and would meet Revered Tapasyananda Maharaj whenever he came there and would attend on him. In those days, one had to travel two days and three nights to reach Howrah from Trivandrum by train. He would write early to book his return tickets – 'First Class, Lower Berth and Not on Wheels'. Whenever he came, he would carry with him writing materials – a slate and white chalk. When we would enquire about it, he would say, 'Why should we waste stationery?'

He added a new chapter 'Holy Mother as a Revelation of Divinity of Motherhood of God' to his book, *Holy Mother Sri Sarada Devi* published earlier. He spoke about this chapter in the Probationers' Training Centre, Belur Math.

Whenever Revered Maharaj came to Belur Math for the four-monthly Trustees meeting, he used to carry few clothes and stay in Belur Math itself. In the evening of the second day of the meeting, he would go to Seva Pratishthan, a hospital centre in Calcutta, with Revered Dayananda and Gahanananda, in order to observe the work going on there and to meet the nurses known to him who were undergoing training, stay overnight there, and return next morning for the meeting.

He liked *idlis* to be served for his breakfast. He would remark, '*Idlis* are not harmful and easy to digest and easy to prepare and carry while travelling.'

He used to talk freely with the probationers and impressed upon them the habit of serious study and deep thinking on the topics read. He encouraged the brahmacharis to ask questions. He would regularly walk for some time in the evenings on the verandah of the Library block.

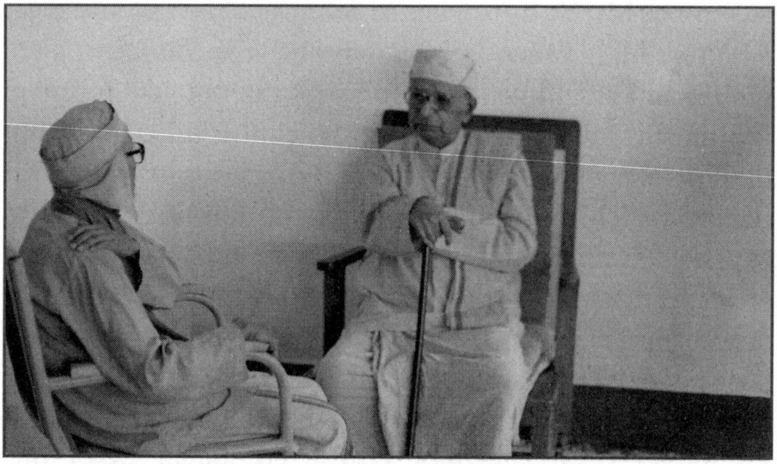

Revered Maharaj translated the *Srimad Bhagavata Maha Purana* – twelve cantos with Prologue and Epilogue – into English in four volumes. He used to write on the slate and make corrections. Only on being satisfied would he transcribe it onto a paper. He would always be found engaged in reading or writing.

On the day of his departure, he would ask me to keep his stainless steel vessels and bottles ready. Then he would instruct me that at noon, before the food was served, I put the rice into the steel vessels, cool it, and add water (he would point out the level). And the boiled vegetables were to be put into the bottles keeping onion separately. He would also ask me to collect bananas and one loaf of bread. He usually avoided eating food prepared outside the Math. He used to take *idlis* and tea only at Bhadrak railway station when the train used to reach there those days at seven in the morning.

At Madras, he was very regular in attending prayer and night reading class (lasting for half-an-hour). He would correct wrong pronunciations of the reader. He normally did not go out of the Math in the evenings except when there were Managing Committee meetings of Vivekananda College, Students' Home or Sarada Vidyalaya of which he was the president.

He belonged to the old generation who believed in living an ideal life than merely talking about it.

14

An Embodiment of *tapasya*

Swami Yatatmananda[1]

First Impressions

Revered Swami Tapasyananda Maharaj was an embodiment of *tapasya* or austerity. It was a name befitting his personality. He was given this name by his Guru, Swami Shivananda Maharaj, a direct disciple of Sri Ramakrishna and the second president of the Ramakrishna Order.

I first met Revered Maharaj in Belur Math when I was a brahmachari in the Training Centre. I had the good fortune of attending on Revered Swami Ranganathananda Maharaj who used to stay next to Revered Maharaj's room at Belur Math. Whenever both the monks came to attend the Trustees Meeting, they used to stay in the adjacent rooms. And I had the opportunity to have their *darsan* and observe them.

As I was serving Revered Swami Ranganathananda Maharaj, I had to go to his room quite often. During my visits, I also observed certain things about Revered Maharaj. I observed that he himself used to wash his clothes and dry them. He was very meticulous in his daily routine. From Madras, he would bring with him print-outs of the books

1. He was with Revered Maharaj in Madras Math for many years.

under preparation and proof-read them. In order to help him carry on this work, a table lamp used to be arranged in his Belur Math room. He was very regular in his evening walks. He would always make inquiries about what brahmacharis were studying in the Training Centre. I have seen Prabhakar Maharaj (now Swami Atmapriyananda) engaging Maharaj in serious discussions on philosophical topics.

Yatatmananda, Tapasyanandaji

His Daily Routine

When I was posted to Madras Math, there I observed Revered Maharaj regularly attending the morning *mangalarati* in the 'Old Temple'. He was very particular that all other monastic brothers should also attend the *mangalarati*. He used to inquire about this in the night class. Manager Maharaj had instructed me to maintain an attendance register for it and show the same to Revered Maharaj. He would say that the Math is not a hostel or a boarding house but a monastery with a chapel; not just a temple but a monastic chapel.

He would daily chant various *stotras* and *suktas* before breakfast. After his bath, he would visit the shrine to pay his obeisance to Sri Ramakrishna and then go to his office. He would not turn back while walking.

He was very particular that devotees who had back pain should not bend to offer *pranam*. He was sensitive to their physical well-being. He also felt that there need not be any show of devotion. Prof. C.S. Ramakrishnan, a former editor of *The Vedanta Kesari* and a close devotee for decades, once humorously called his inability to bend due to knee pain as 'unbending devotion' and we enjoyed this phrase very much.

When he would go to office, he would humorously remark that devotees should not 'waylay' him. In case someone offered *pranam* from behind, he would tell them that he had no eyes on his back to see them. While in the office, he had his own method of correspondence. He would write his letters in a diary kept separately for this purpose. Then the typist would type the letter without any carbon copy. That diary itself would serve as the office copy of that letter.

Training the Monastics

Revered Maharaj used to say that monastic aspirants intending to join the Order should not resign from their jobs immediately. They should wait for a month or two after joining, find out if they can adjust to the monastic life and routine and then resign the job and join the Math formally. He would tell them in advance to bring with them simple bedding, especially a mosquito curtain, as the Math resources were meagre. Maharaj himself had to face much difficulty for want of a mosquito curtain, he was concerned that others should not suffer like him. Maharaj would carefully observe the aspirants for a few years before officially filling up their formal application to join the Order.

Many brahmacharis joined the Order during his time. Two staff members of the Math wanted to join the Order and he encouraged them to join in Madras Math itself. He told, 'If there is any opposition from your house you should overcome it from here itself by facing them boldly and not by going away to faraway places.'

Maharaj encouraged monastics in playing badminton to maintain good health and arranged for a badminton court behind the 'Old Temple'. When some people objected to it, he shifted the court behind the monastic quarters and ensured that the playing continued. He would say that one should spend time to play and to do exercises rather than fall sick and spend money to buy medicines!

He wanted the formally ordained brahmacharis to take weekly classes in the Math. He insisted that it was necessary to maintain the habit of study, self-learning, etc. He would say that one had to study and prepare well in order to take classes. By giving some lectures no one would become a *jagadguru*; only the perceptions would become clearer.

His Classes

The night classes (the customary night gathering of monks after supper) would be very interesting. After reading, he would ask the brahmacharis to restate it in their own words—in the way they have understood. He would tell us how a reader should critically look at an idea. The classes were very lively.

Once he was down with chickenpox and was shifted to the guest room above the dispensary so that others may not get infected. In spite of this isolation, 'durbar' [as the night classes were called] continued every night, with Maharaj sitting inside his room and other monastics on the terrace outside the room.

On Sunday mornings, in his office, he would take classes for close devotees on *The Gospel of Sri Ramakrishna.*

His Intellectual Aspect

As president of Madras Math, he encouraged translations of many books into Tamil. Many new titles were published in Tamil during his time. His book *'Sri Ramakrishna—an Interpretative Study'* gives a detailed explanation of 'Bhava Mukha' state of Sri Ramakrishna. His article in the souvenir published on the occasion of consecration of a new temple at Ramakrishna Math, Kalady, Kerala, was truly revealing. He gave a new outlook to the definition of 'Pravriti' and 'Nivriti' in the light of Ramakrishna-Vivekananda ideology.

Revered Maharaj would give special talks on Jayanthis of the Holy Trinity. I still remember his talk on Holy Mother. He said that in the present circumstances, it is difficult to perform Yaga or Yajna as in olden days; it is also difficult to do Yantra puja (unless you know Sanskrit, etc). We can reap the same fruit by worshipping and praying to Holy Mother in a simple manner. Her fame is growing like the fabled fish which sought refuge at the feet of a *rishi*. She comes down to all like an elephant bending down, folding its legs to allow even the children to climb on to it.

His Personality and Work

Revered Maharaj started the printing press at Madras Math. There were some objections for the printing press

Ramakrishna Mission Ashrama, T.Nagar

to be located right at the entrance of the Math. The press apparently made a lot of noise, and seemed to disturb the silent and spiritual atmosphere of the Math. When the matter was taken to him, he simply brushed it aside by saying that it was not a business activity but an instrument in spreading the message of Sri Ramakrishna and people do not seem to understand its great significance.

He had made a rule that no waste paper should be thrown away in the dustbin in the shrine. All papers, including used wrappers, should be brought to the book despatch section and kept there for waste-paper sale later.

Swami Uddhavananda of T. Nagar Ashrama in Madras would often organize various programmes. He would always offer the first copy of the invitation to Sri Ramakrishna in Madras Math shrine. Revered Maharaj, amused at the innumerable programmes organized by Swami Uddhavananda, would teasingly call him as Utsavananda! (one who finds joy in organizing celebrations)

His Regard and Concern for Monks

He had great regard for Revered Swami Saradeshananda Maharaj, a disciple of the Holy Mother. He took interest in publishing Revered Saradesananda's reminiscences of Sri Sarada Devi—*Mother as I saw Her*. He greatly appreciated the book.

Revered Maharaj earnestly requested Revered Swami Bhuteshananda Maharaj to translate and write books. He said that as Revered Maharaj was a great and deep scholar, his knowledge should be persevered for posterity.

He would ask Swami Ranganathananda Maharaj to take care of his health and not to overburden himself with too many travel programmes. Swami Ranganathananda Maharaj was a good speaker, travelling all over the world. Swami Tapasyananda Maharaj was a good writer and known to the world through his thoughtful writings. He would jokingly tell there are two types of body constitution—one is Subrahmanya type of constitution [suitable to go around the world] and another is Ganesa type of constitution [meant to stay put at one place].

As the Vice-president of the Order

It was Revered Swami Vireswarananda Maharaj, the then president of the Order, who requested Swami Tapasyananda Maharaj to take charge of Madras Math as its president. Though he was not in favour of leaving Trivandrum because of his fairly advanced age, yet he obeyed. His apprehension was how could an 'old trunk of a tree' (refering to himself) be transplanted to another soil to sprout again and thrive. Yet he not only adjusted himself to the new place and carried on the regular activities of the Math, but also instilled a great vigour into the Madras Math.

He was initially much reluctant to take the post of vice-president, but once he took it up, he diligently discharged the duties of that post. In earlier days, he did not want any brahmachari to be exclusively posted to assist him. However, he would take one swami or brahmachari with him sometimes.

He would himself give the application forms for the *mantra diksa*. He would interview the candidates with various questions on the life and teachings of the Holy Trio. One of his favourite questions was: 'Who was Totapuri?' He would give *mantra diksa* in the present 'Old Temple'.

Last Days

In his final days, Revered Maharaj, despite his unwillingness, was admitted to BSS Hospital, Mandaveli, in Madras. Shortly after he was admitted in the hospital, he went into deep coma (he was administered morphine).

On the very next day of his admission to the hospital, I had gone to see him around 6.00 a.m. Seeing me, he enquired how many new members had joined the library and how much was the book sales the previous day. He was filled with the thought of the activities of the Math and the mission of the Great Master.

Maharaj passed away on an *Ekadasi*. Hearing that a great *mahatma* had passed away, there was a big crowd of people from the local Mandaveli area as it was considered very auspicious to have a glimpse of his mortal remains. Many people thronged the Math on this occasion, even those who had never visited the Math earlier, just to get a glimpse of his mortal remains. His mortal remains were consigned to flames in the Mylapore crematorium.

I had the privilege of living with him which was training and education in itself. He was a great source of inspiration. He always held that institution was more important than any individual and principles were greater than any person. His life was an embodiment of austerity, scholarship, tenderness and spiritual practices of a very high order.

15

An Intellectual of Rare Type

Swami Amritananda[1]

Revered Maharaj was an intellectual of a rare type. His understanding of the spiritual import of the scriptures was something remarkable, which perhaps even a well-trained scholar would find it difficult to grasp. It was even more so regarding the Ramakrishna-Vivekananda ideology.

There came a time when he had to take a quick decision regarding the expansion of the publication activities of Madras Math. Not only did he take the right decision, but also plunged into bringing out many valuable publications, solely depending on his own resources. Maharaj brought out simple and clear translations of books like *Adhyatma Ramayana*, besides bringing out lucid translations of voluminous and philosophical works like *Srimad Bhagavatam*. Judged by any standard, his work on *Srimad Bhagavatam* is excellent.

Once, when I was watching him translate the *Srimad Bhagavatam*, he suddenly turned to me and asked, 'How do you like it?' I spontaneously replied, 'It is highly lucid.' Hearing that, he was immensely pleased.

Srimad Bhagavatam is a text difficult to understand and much more difficult to translate it into simple English.

1. He is a senior monk of the Order who had close contact with Revered Maharaj, especially when he was the Secretary of Ramakrishna Mission Vivekananda College, Madras.

Some of its philosophical thoughts are abstruse, language elliptical, and idiom untranslatable. With the successful translation of this text, a good reputation of the Math publications was guaranteed.

There are many articles written by Revered Maharaj throughout his long life which vouch for his intellectual acumen. In 1985 or so, he wrote an article explaining the term *Bhava mukha* in *The Vedanta Kesari*. As far as my knowledge goes, none had attempted to explain this term before Revered Maharaj did. In explaining the term *Bhava mukha,* Revered Maharaj uses the illustrations given by Sri Ramakrishna. Revered Maharaj clearly explains various terms such as *jnana, vijnana, chit, chit-sakti,* images of *chit, parinama, vivarta, avatara vada* and the whole essay is an intellectual feast.[1]

1. This essay is now a part of Swami Tapasyananda's booklet, *Sri Ramakrishna: His Life and Teachings.*

16

My Intellectual Mentor

Swami Atmapriyananda[1]

"Yo Brahmanam Vidadhati Purvam..."

यो ब्रह्माणं विदधाति पूर्वं यो वै वेदांश्च प्रहिणोति तस्मै ।
तं ह देवमात्मबुद्धिप्रकाशम् मुमुक्षुर्वै शरणमहम् प्रपद्ये ।।

yo brahmāṇaṃ vidadhāti pūrvaṃ
yo vai vedāṃśca prahiṇoti tasmai |
taṃ ha devamātmabuddhiprakāśam
mumukṣurvai śaraṇamaham prapadye ||

'He who in the beginning created Brahma and delivered the Vedas to Him, in that Deva (the Shining, Divine Being) do I, the seeker of liberation, take refuge.' (Svetasvara Upanishad, 6.18)

निष्कलं निष्क्रियं शान्तं निरवद्यं निरञ्जनम् ।
अमृतस्य परं सेतुं दग्धेन्धनमिवानलम् ।।

niṣkalaṃ niṣkriyaṃ śāntaṃ niravadyaṃ nirañjanam |
amṛtasya paraṃ setuṃ dagdhendhanamivānalam ||

'[That Divine Being is] without parts (that is, is Indivisible Whole), actionless, tranquil, blemishless, unattached, the Supreme bridge to Immortality, and

1. He was closely associated with Revered Maharaj from his student days. He is currently the Vice-chancellor, Vivekananda University, Belur.

like the fire that has consumed its fuel.' (Svetasvara Upanishad, 6.19)

असतो मा सद्गमय तमसो मा
ज्योतिर्गमय मृत्योर्मा अमृतं गमय ।।

asato mā sadgamaya tamaso mā
jyotirgamaya mṛtyormā amṛtaṃ gamaya ||

'Om, lead me from the unreal to the Real; lead me from darkness [of ignorance] to Light [of Divine Knowledge], lead me from death to Immortality.' (Brihadaranyaka Upanishad, 1.3.28)

The serene and sonorous tone of the chanting of the above mantras by Swami Tapasyananda Maharaj of revered memory is still ringing in my ears and reverberating in my heart. Having listened to these remarkably elevating verses for years on end and internalizing them unconsciously, I now find myself prefacing most of my talks on spiritual topics, particularly the *Upanishads,* with the above mantras, chanting them with the same rhythm and style as he used to chant and as they entered my psyche more than four decades ago in the holy ambience of Madras Math sanctified by the touch of spiritual stalwarts among the direct monastic disciples of Sri Ramakrishna, Swamis Ramakrishnananda Maharaj, Brahmananda Maharaj, Shivananda Maharaj etc.

Two types of spiritual teachers— the 'grape'-type and 'coconut'-type

Sanskrit literature has a famous verse that describes the characteristics of the two types of persons usually found among literary geniuses. This little known verse is quoted by *Acharya* Krishnamohana Sastri in his *Lakshmi-vyakhya* on *Sahityadarpana*. (Ref.468 of Chowkhamba Sanskrit Sansthan Edition). We give below the original verse as quoted by Krishnamohana Sastri and provide a simple English rendering:

अर्थगम्भीरिमापाकः स द्वेधा कविसम्मतः ।
द्राक्षापाको नारिकेलपाकश्च प्रस्फुटान्तरौ ।।
द्राक्षापाकः स कथितो बहिरन्तःस्फुरद्रसः ।
स नारिकेलपाकः स्यादन्तर्गूढरसोदयः ।।

arthagambhīrimāpākaḥ sa dvedhā kavisammataḥ |
drākṣāpāko nārikelapākaśca prasphuṭāntarau ||
drākṣāpākaḥ sa kathito bahirantaḥsphuradrasaḥ |
sa nārikelapākaḥ syādantargūḍharasodayaḥ ||

'Men of standing [in the literary sphere] say that the maturity [of wisdom]—also meaning tasteful delicacy—of poets is of two types. "The manifest difference between these two is like that between the delicacy of the grapes and that of the coconut. In the case of the grapes, the juice gets visibly expressed, bursting forth within and without, while in the case of the coconut, the rising of the taste is hidden within." '

These two types have always existed in all the spheres of higher wisdom and more so in the spiritual realm. In the Ramakrishna tradition, Swami Premananda Maharaj and Swami Brahmananda Maharaj were two glorious examples of these two types, the former's overflowing love visible and transparent like the grape, while the latter's deep feelings often unfathomable and difficult to comprehend on superficial observation, like the coconut. In recent times, we have noticed these two types in Swami Bhuteshananda Maharaj and Swami Tapasyananda Maharaj. The grape-type of tangible, visible and overflowing spiritual love and the coconut-type of deep, not easily fathomable, soul-stirring, profoundly transforming spiritual solicitude and somewhat mystical love, has been running parallel in the Ramakrishna tradition and the harmonious and beautiful blend of these two strands, forming its majestic multi-coloured mosaic, is its great spiritual glory.

Nirguna Bhakti and 'intellectual love of God'

Two types of Bhakti or love of God are often recognized in the devotional literature: one, the devotion to *Saguna Brahman,* whose chief-most manifestation is as the *Avatar,* the Divine Incarnation, 'Word made flesh' in the Christian tradition, in which the devotee either does not recognize or is not particularly concerned about the impersonal (*nirguna*) aspect of God. Two, the impersonal devotion (*nirguna bhakti*) that awakens in the mind of illumined souls belonging to the category of *Ishwarakotis* or *Avataras* (Godlike souls or Incarnations of God) like Sri Chaitanya Mahaprabhu, Sri Ramakrishna, etc., where in supreme devotion (*parabhakti*) overwhelms the mind after attainment of spiritual illumination or God realization.

Swami Tapasyananda Maharaj's views in this regard and his consistent insistence on the second type of devotion, *parabhakti,* in his interpretation of the scriptures, particularly, the *Bhagavad Gita,* are his invaluable contributions to the spiritual tradition of the Ramakrishna Order.

Temperamentally, Maharaj was himself a devotee par excellence, but his devotion was of the type that he himself used to call, following Spinoza, 'intellectual love of God'. Having seen him, lived and interacted with him rather closely for nearly two decades, that too during the stages of my own spiritual formation, I have tried to critically understand his own moods and attitudes, his inclination and proclivity in spiritual matters, his main intellectual and emotional thrust. I can vouch to his being an ecstatic lover of God, his devotion based on Ramanuja's *prapatti marga,* the path of absolute surrender to God. Although he was highly rational in his approach, open to debate and discussion, always practising, even in matters of religion and spirituality, the basic scientific principles like suspension of judgment, investigation with an open mind, he was quite firm and uncompromising when it came to accepting Sri Ramakrishna as the highest Divine Manifestation of Godhead and practising unflinching, prayerful, surrendering devotion through *kainkarya* or service to his Universal Manifestation in all beings as taught by Swami Vivekananda, as well as in his special manifestation through his likeness or photograph wherever he is invoked and worshipped with faith and devotion, as taught and practised by Swami Ramakrishnananda and Holy Mother Sri Sarada Devi.

Two types of monks are usually seen in Ramakrishna Order: one type emphasizing the Vivekananda way of worshipping Sri Ramakrishna in all being through selfless service and another type extolling the shrine room worship and dedicating one's life to 'sitting near' (*upasana*) him in the temple or the shrine, chanting and singing his glories, repeating his holy Name or mantra, etc. It is interesting to observe, and the present author has had the blessed opportunity to observe so many such instances in his more than four decades of spiritual grooming in Ramakrishna Order, that those trained and taught by the direct disciples of Sri Ramakrishna, had a unique and wonderful way of harmoniously combining, happily blending the Vivekananda emphasized type of worshipping the *Virat* or *Viswarupa* Ramakrishna manifesting through and dwelling in all beings and creatures through selfless, dedicated service of all possible types, with the Ramakrishnananda and Sarada Devi emphasized type of worshipping the palpable Presence of Ramakrishna in the shrine room and the temple where his likeness, photograph or image, is invoked, worshipped and *atmavat seva* (service as one's own Self) is performed with devotion and surrender to the *Arcavatara* (the Presence of God in the image, the manifested Spiritual Presence in the shrine room or the temple). In fact, there is no contradiction or opposition between these two ways, they complement, supplement and fulfil each other, and the practise of both run parallel as a living illustration of Swami Vivekananda's dictum *atmano mokshartham jagaddhitaya cha*, 'for one's own spiritual emancipation and for the welfare of all beings', is the holistic and all-comprehensive spiritual path shown by Sri Ramakrishna.

At the feet of Swami Tapasyananda Maharaj, we could learn this harmoniously blended ideal and practice through his precept and practice. Most of the time he would be absorbed in studying and translating the various holy scriptures from Sanskrit to English, with critical notes and a masterly introduction, and maintained a serious spiritual and intellectual mood.

On one occasion, there was a serious legal issue involving the interpretation of some points of law as applied to our educational institutions in Madras. The

Inauguration of Sri Ramakrishna Educational Trust, Madras

matter was referred to Maharaj who was the president of Madras Math and ex-officio president of the Managing Committees of the various educational institutions in Madras. We observed with wonder and admiration how Maharaj could turn his attention with perfect ease from the flights of spirituality embedded in the scriptural passages which he was translating at that time to the so-called mundane law books and began avidly studying these books with equal interest. He suspended his translation work for a few days, devoted his entire time to studying and understanding the implications of the law as applicable in the case of our institutions, quickly wrote down a brilliant 'thesis' on what needs to be done in the situation as guide notes for our lawyers. Having finished this task, he again plunged into his translation work with equal enthusiasm. We could thus see demonstrated in his work the attitude of worshipful surrender to Sri Ramakrishna and his Cause, work and worship going hand in hand without any conflict or contradiction.

Cult and Culture in Ramakrishna tradition; Swami Tapasyananda Maharaj's elevation as a Vice-president of the Order

Swami Tapasyananda Maharaj was fond of talking about two strands or streams in the Ramakrishna tradition as indicated above. One was the 'Cult' and the other 'Culture'. As is well known, he was the first person who authored an authentic biography of Holy Mother Sri Sarada Devi as early as 1940, hardly two decades after Holy Mother entered into *mahasamadhi*. Not much material was available at that time, that too in English. Maharaj wrote this biography not merely as a narrative of Holy Mother's life story, but as a philosophical and spiritual interpretation of Holy Mother's unostentatious but extraordinary life unknown to public gaze. The chapter on 'Holy Mother's revelation as the Motherhood of God' and another on 'Her message' are masterpieces in spiritual literature, replete flashes of new insights. Maharaj, as is well known, had an unusual gift of felicity of expression and a rare capacity to couch some of the abstruse spiritual and philosophical ideas in pithy phrases and aphoristic sentences. For example, talking of Holy Mother Sarada Devi's inability to see others' faults, he writes: 'The Holy Mother had a constitutional disinclination to see the faults of others.'

He once explained to us that Swami Saradananda Maharaj's *Sri Sri Ramakrishna Lilaprasanga* (translated into

English originally as *Sri Ramakrishna the Great Master* by Swami Jagadananda Maharaj and re-translated later on as *Sri Ramakrishna and His Divine Play* by Swami Chetanananda Maharaj) was not a mere biography, a historical or even a religious account of Sri Ramakrishna's life. What was it then? He answered this question by the following meaningful expression: 'It is a treatise on the psychology of an Incarnation of God'. Discussing Sri Ramakrishna's philosophy, he would talk with great passion and joy about the concepts of *bhavamukha* and *vijnana,* pointing out that these are unique to Sri Ramakrishna. In this connection, he would point out that the commentators' on the *Gita,* the great *Acharyas,* had interpreted the term *vijnana* in the *Gita* rather differently and that is not exactly what Sri Ramakrishna meant. He would often say that these unique contribution of Sri Ramakrishna to Vedantic thought, born of his direct realization and spiritual experience may not always be considered 'logical' in the accepted sense of this term. But they are not illogical either even from philosophical point of view. They are supra-logical which could be termed 'alogical' because they are born of his mystic experience. Sri Ramakrishna's philosophy therefore could be called 'alogical mysticism'. What a unique way of expression and how wonderfully appropriate! His definition of God was also unique. He would say: 'God is that Supreme Being in Whom all contradictions meet and lose their 'contradictoriness'!' These are certain gems of expressions that I have had the blessed fortune of cherishing in my memory over the years and they have remained for me subjects of reverential contemplation for decades.

Regarding 'cult' and 'culture' in Ramakrishna tradition, he writes in his biography of the Holy Mother that the 'culture' aspect is of universal appeal and is meant for all of humankind—it is this aspect of Swami Vivekananda propagated and preached from the world pulpit. Although Swami Vivekananda was aware of the 'cult' aspect of Sri Ramakrishna, he chose not to emphasize it as a universal doctrine. He initiated this 'cult' of Ramakrishna with the *Yugavatar*, the Incarnation of the Age, Sri Ramakrishna, as the centre of all devotion and worship, leaving people to understand and appreciate him in any light according to their understanding, but be seriously devoted to preaching Sri Ramakrishna's universal principles which had a timeless appeal. Swami Vivekananda was apprehensive that the cult of Ramakrishna could degenerate into a sect with all the dogmatic and fanatical overtones of a sect, but he wanted this movement to retain the intensity of a sect minus the fanaticism of a sect with its sectarian, dogmatic and fanatical underpinnings. He said we could solve this problem by having what he called a 'non-sectarian sect', with all the advantages of a sect and eliminating its disadvantages. This 'cult' aspect of Ramakrishna was nurtured and given a universal shape by Holy Mother Sri Sarada Devi and Swami Ramakrishnananda Maharaj (Sasi Maharaj). In fact, Swami Ramakrishnananda Maharaj once said (as reported by Sister Devamata in her book *Days in an Indian Monastery*): 'You see, Sri Ramakrishna gave a huge, universal message to Swamiji (Swami Vivekananda). To me, he gave a "small" message which he did not give even to Swamiji.' What is that "small message"? We may easily guess what that "small message" could be: it is the worship of Sri Ramakrishna, the *Yugavatar*, the Incarnation of the Age, the symbol of Divinity in the modern age.

Although not given to or fond of elaborate ritualism, Maharaj was nonetheless deeply devoted to Ramakrishna worship as initiated and shown by Swami Ramakrishnananda Maharaj. In fact, he was extremely particular that all the details in regard to the worship be meticulously followed, although he always emphasized the spirit of *atmavat seva* or *kainkarya* (devoted service as one's own Self) to the Incarnate Deity rather than mechanical observances. It was Swami Tapasyananda Maharaj's daily practice to rhythmically and sonorously chant the Sanskrit *stotras* or hymns composed by Swami Vivekananda, Swami Abhedananda, Pramadadas Mitra and several others on Sri Ramakrishana, Holy Mother Sarada Devi, Swami Vivekananda. Young devotees, student-volunteers like us who used to frequent Madras Math and render service in the worship room (*Thakur ghar*) used to eagerly wait to silently listen to Swami Tapasyananda Maharaj's chanting of these hymns, unobserved, so that he may not get disturbed in his devotional mood. Absorbed in divine thought, he would be chanting these hymns with such fervour that we could palpably feel his innermost soul pouring forth in torrential devotion quietly and unostentatiously. This aspect of Maharaj was rarely visible even to intimate devotees for he always kept this surrendering devotional aspect of his nature carefully hidden from others. This made him truly humble —even as a vice-president of the Ramakrishna Order, he always behaved as a humble servant of all. The story of his elevation as vice-president may be recalled in this context. Swami Gahanananda Maharaj, the then Assistant Secretary of Ramakrishna Math and Ramakrishna Mission at the headquarters of Belur Math called Swami Tapasyananda Maharaj over telephone and humbly requested him to take

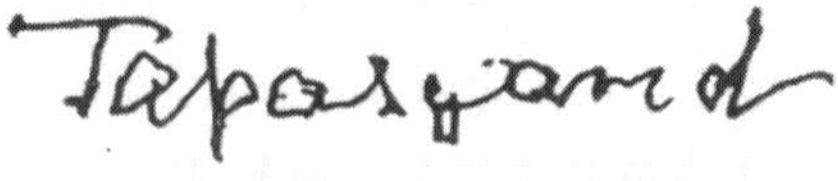

(Swami Tapasyananda)
Vice President
Ramakrishna Math & Ramakrishna Mission

Belur Math

up the mantle of spiritual ministration as a vice-president. Swami Tapasyananda Maharaj was quite reluctant, but Swami Gahananda Maharaj persuaded him to agree. He was elected a vice-president and the venue of the first initiation (*mantra diksa*) was fixed as the Kashipur, the sacred place where Sri Ramakrishna entered *mahasamadhi*. I was particularly close to Swami Tapasyananda Maharaj and would take liberties with him, sometimes even cutting innocent jokes at his expense! He was at Belur Math staying at the small room just behind the main temple of Sri Ramakrishna, and some of us, brahmacharins, were having fun with him. I told him, 'Maharaj, how wonderful that Sri Guru Maharaj is now using you to be his instrument to spread his name and awaken the spiritual consciousness of people!' He was also answering in a lighter vein: 'You see, I have been dressed up in the green room, tomorrow I have to dance, it is my *arangetram*!" referring to the preparations he had had to undergo to be trained in some of the technicalities of giving *mantra diksa* under the expert advice of Swami Bhuteshananda Maharaj who was then a senior vice-president. *Arangetram* in Tamil means the first performance of a dancer who, after completing the dance training and lessons, will, for the first time appear on the stage. He was comparing his first *diksa* (spiritual initiation) session to this first stage appearance! He then added with a twinkle in his eyes and a smile on his lips: 'You see, I am a disciple of Swami Bhuteshananda, who has given me training in this assignment!' It may not be out of place to mention at this point that Swami Tapasyananda Maharaj held Swami Bhuteshananda Maharaj in very great esteem and reverence. He was all admiration for Swami Bhuteshananda Maharaj's philosophical depth of thought, originality of approach and unusual clarity and lucidity of expression. When Swami Tapasyananda Maharaj was talking in such a light-hearted vein, suddenly there was a change of expression in his face and he became intensely serious. With moist eyes, he said in a choked voice: 'You see, they (meaning the Trustees) are forcing me to do this (to give spiritual initiation, *mantra diksa*). What do I know? But I can only take consolation in Holy Mother's words that the broom-stick itself may be dirty, but it can be used to clean otherssss!" (He had the habit of lingering on to the 's' that occurred at the end of a word!). All of us listening to him were greatly stuck by his sense of humility, spirit of surrender and felt blessed in having seen the inner world of this senior monk, a disciple of Mahapurush Swami Shivananda Maharaj, overwhelmed by such a wonderful sense of surrender and helplessness that nothing can be accomplished by a human being without the grace of God. Swami Tapasyananda Maharaj himself often told me about one important step in Ramanuja's scheme of ultimate surrender or *prapatti*, namely, *karpanya*, a feeling of utter helplessness that we have no power to save ourselves without the Lord's grace. This is followed by the next step, namely, faith or conviction that the Lord will certainly save us: *raksisyati iti viswaasah.*

His austerity was proverbial. He was extremely frugal in his habits and would not brook extravagant spending on the part of any of the monastic members under his care. Many would mistake his frugality as stinginess, read miserliness and ungenerousness in his over-cautious spending habits and lack of effusiveness in entertaining guests and visitors! So much so, when he once invited me fervently to visit Madras Math (after I had come away to Belur Math as a brahmachari), several of my friends among the monks made fun saying that this was perhaps the first time in Maharaj's long innings as the head of a centre to have invited somebody with such fervour and feeling! His love was so subtle and restrained—just the contrast of what we normally see in worldly affection even among monastic brothers, effusive or demonstrative—that one could understand the depth of his feeling and genuine spiritual concern only when one could penetrate into the thick shell of his seriousness. We would do well to remember the grape-type and coconut-type of enlightened human beings described at the very beginning of this narrative.

We would watch with wonder how he would himself carry, being the senior monk and the head of such an important centre, a Trustee and fairly advanced in age being in his late sixties, his water pot filled with drinking water to his room (in the first floor) from the kitchen after dinner. An old tattered towel would only cover the upper part of his body except when he would meet visitors in his office and his food habits were exceptionally simple. Extravagance in anything—be it food, speech, expenses, socializing—was so alien to this nature that he used to himself practise and insist on others practising the *Gita* dictum *uktahara viharasya ukta cheshtasya karmasu*, etc., that is moderation in food, habits and movements, efforts, and so on.

He also would be very particular about following the Ashrama routine—prayer services both in the morning and evening, meditation in the shrine, work schedule, classes, eating together in the dining hall, etc. He would keep a meticulous watch on monastic members not attending the dining hall during routine meal and breakfast time, enquire about their absence, chide and advise them that following a routine and participating in the community life of the Ashrama are *sine qua non* for spiritual growth, pointing out that Swamiji himself made these strict rules for our spiritual benefit and it behoves us to follow them with *sraddha*.

When he would travel to Belur Math for the four-monthly meetings of the Trustees, he always preferred to take a railway train rather than travel by air. When asked, he would say with a smile: 'You see, my time is not that precious; I take my books and keep reading or translating for which I get plenty of time in the train.' When he became old and had difficulty in walking, Swami Vireswarananda Maharaj, for whom Swami Tapasyananda Maharaj had the greatest respect, lovingly implored him to agree to travel by air saying that after all it was the headquarters at Belur Math that was paying the cost of air fare. Swami Tapasyananda Maharaj's reaction was interesting. He said, 'Maharaj, it is not a question of who is paying the fare. The question is whether it is necessary at all!' Swami Vireswarananda Maharaj would not so easily let the matter go and finally Swami Tapasyananda Maharaj had to yield. But then he would not take any assistant with him. Even when he was the vice-president of the Order, he would not take his secretary swami or any other monastic assistant with him while travelling to Belur Math by flight. As I was so free with him, would behave like a little kid imploring a loving dad, I once told him forcefully that it was improper that he travelled without any monastic companion to help and assist him. Suryanarayana Maharaj (later Swami Sukritananda) was providing Swami Tapasyananda Maharaj all the secretarial and other assistance that he needed and I powerfully pleaded that Suryanarayana Maharaj should accompany him while he travelled, for there was a risk of his falling down due to imbalance and lack of steadiness in walk. Swami Tapasyananda Maharaj smiled and commented with his ready wit: 'What will that fellow (that was his way of affectionately calling his close monastic brothers) do? He cannot hold me *before I fall*! After all, I am an old man, and somebody will come to my help.' That was Swami Tapasyananda Maharaj, the unassuming, austere, simple and frugal in spending from what he called Sri Ramakrishna's resources.

His dedication to the *Sangha-rupi* Sri Ramakrishna (that is, Sri Ramakrishna in the form of the Ramakrishna *Sangha* or Order) was total. It is a great saga in the Ramakrishna *Sangha*'s history how Swami Vireswarananda Maharaj, the then president, moved the two stalwarts, Swami Kailasananda Maharaj and Swami Tapasyananda Maharaj from their respective seats in Madras and Trivandrum respectively after they had settled down, each in his own position, for more than two decades! We were young volunteers, college students, and could understand nothing of the significance of these changes. We watched with dismay how Swami Kailasananda Maharaj, quite reluctant to move away from Madras where he spent almost quarter of a century as the monastic head, openly expressed his unhappiness at the prospect of moving to Belur Math and starting a totally new chapter in his life at a fairly advanced age. Although we were not eye witnesses to Swami Tapasyananda Maharaj's reaction at the prospect of leaving Trivandrum and taking charge of Madras Math as the head, we have heard that he also was not quite happy about the change. But the beauty of both these great monks, both of them disciples of Mahapurush Swami Shivananda Maharaj, devotedly obeyed the command of the *Sanghaguru*, the president of the Order, Swami Vireswarananda Maharaj. This is a lesson for us, the relatively younger monks. With my own childishly 'audacious' frankness that Swami Tapasyananda Maharaj's kindness had granted me to indulge in, I once asked him after he had settled down as an author, translator and administrator at Madras Math, about how he came to accept the change of centre from Trivandrum to Madras. With great feeling of respect, bordering on worship, and in an intensely emotional tone, Maharaj said: 'You see, Prabhu Maharaj (as Swami Vireswarananda Maharaj was affectionately called) *compellingly persuaded me* and I couldn't bring myself to saying no!' I was amazed at his feeling as well as his most appropriate choice of words and expression!

Some of his other prominent traits: austere, frugal, unassuming, seriously witty, self-effacing

It has been mentioned above that the most fundamental trait of Swami Tapasyananda Maharaj character was *prapatti* or self-surrender. This manifested as much in his sense of utter devotion to Sri Ramakrishna as the Supreme Manifestation of the Divine as in his dedication to the Ramakrishna *Sangha* (Order) that he served with unswerving devotion for decades on end. The saga of his dedication to the *Sangha*, looking upon it as the veritable manifestation in gross form of Sri Ramakrishna himself as Swamiji taught, is a model for emulation for all of us. He also would say that wherever one is posted by the authorities of the *Sangha* should be considered as the place wherefrom Sri Ramakrishna has graciously chosen to accept our service. 'Stay put' with self-effacement and self-sacrifice as the key practices—this was the constant refrain of his advice to the younger monks. He always quoted the example of Swami Ramakrishnananda Maharaj (Sasi Maharaj) who, being chided by his divine Master (Guru) that too much absorption in studies to the neglect of *guruseva* (service to the Guru) would harm his devotion (*bhakti*), threw away all his books into the Ganga. Swami Tapasyananda Maharaj added that for a person of Sasi Maharaj's intellectual calibre, to abandon studies and intellectual pursuit for the sake of devotional service is infinitely more difficult than for a worldly person to give up wealth and riches! That's not all. Having abandoned all his intellectual pursuit for the sake of devotional service at the command of his Master Sri Ramakrishna, Sasi Maharaj once again took up his studies seriously at the command of Swami Vivekananda in whom he saw his own Guru manifested and playing in a different form. This, Swami Tapasyananda Maharaj would emphasize, was a supreme example of self-sacrifice and self-surrender—not operating through one's own egoistic impulses even in the matter of sadhana.

We have the well-known parable of Sri Ramakrishna about two persons—spiritual seekers or sadhakas—wanting to know from Narayana (God) through Narada, the great devotee of God, how many lives they needed to wait before God would grant them liberation. Narada enquired of Narayana about the fate of these two sincere aspirants and on coming back from the Abode of God (Vaikuntha), he told the first person that he needed to wait for just four lives before he could get *mukti* or liberation. The aspirant got greatly dejected and cried, 'O, God would make me wait for *four more* lives before liberating me!' He started weeping. Narada told the second person, 'You see, you need to wait much much longer. Do you see this tamarind tree with innumerable small leaves? You would have to go through as many lives as there are leaves on this tree, that is, you have to be born repeatedly millions of times and only thereafter you would be granted salvation.' This person became overwhelmed with the thought of the mercy of God, that He would grant this poor soul, underserving and wretched that he was, liberation after millions of lives! How great is His grace and mercy!' He danced and cried for sheer joy at the thought of God's infinite, unconditional grace. A divine voice told him, 'My child, you are liberated this very moment.' Swami Vivekananda quotes this at the end of his Raja Yoga exposition. Swamiji interprets this by saying that you should have such infinite patience to be able to access the Kingdom of God and for God's grace to descend upon you.

Once I asked Swami Tapasyananda Maharaj about what he thought was the significance of this story. He said with great feeling, 'You see, the first fellow thought that he *deserved* liberation, and was therefore not liberated quickly. The second fellow knew and realized that he did not deserve God's grace, but God, in His infinite grace, was unconditionally showering His grace even upon him, His humble devotee! This very thought liberated him because his ego vanished in a trice. Even in matters of sadhana, the egoistic feeling that 'I am a great sadhaka', 'I am a holy man' etc., is the greatest obstacle to spiritual advancement. Sadhana should be non-egocentric, but God-centric. One should feel spiritually strong in His strength and not on the strength of one's own ego. Sri Ramakrishna often gave the example of Hanuman, Mahavira, the great devotee of Sri Ramachandra, who felt possessed of extraordinary power and strength because Rama's power and strength were flowing through him.

Swami Tapasyananda Maharaj very often told us that the greatest and the worst form of ego is the egoistic feeling that 'I am a holy man', 'I am a great sadhaka'!

Ramanuja's perspective in Swami Tapasyananda Maharaj's philosophical thought reinforcing his Ramakrishna-Vivekananda thought structure

One unique characteristic of Swami Tapasyananda Maharaj was his absorption in philosophical thought almost the whole day. We could rarely see him read or discuss matters that did not have a bearing on philosophical matters. He did not discuss philosophy for intellectual pleasure nor for the sake of preaching. Rather, it had become a second nature with him to be absorbed in some subtle thought world which to him was often Ramanuja's philosophical perspective, juxtaposed with and reinforcing his well thought out, well-reasoned Ramakrishna-Vivekananda thought structure. His sheer originality of thought and the precise philosophical expression thereof were a delight for the listener and I had the blessed privileged to listen to these expositions containing deep insight, day after day, year after year. What little I know in matters philosophical I owe to him, my chief mentor in this regard, along with a few others, like Swami Satswarupananda Maharaj, Swami Bhuteshananda Maharaj, Swami Bhajanananda Maharaj, to name a few. I used to hang upon his word with bated breath and would almost commit to memory his favourite expressions and phrases!

Swami Tapasyananda Maharaj was one of the very few scholar-monks of our Order who had spent enormous amount of time deeply thinking about Sri Ramakrishna's philosophy, particularly the concepts of *bhavamukha* and *vijnana,* although he did not write any separate book on this subject. I often would persuade him to write a monograph on this subject, but he seemed to be always hesitant in undertaking such a task, feeling that his understanding was pretty little and incomplete. However, he has left quite a few articles and write-ups that embody his thoughts on this subject. These form part of at least two of his books: one, *Bhakti Schools of Vedanta,* one of his masterpieces, and two, *A Short Biography of Sri Ramakrishna,* which he wrote within months of his taking charge as the president of Madras Math. He wrote three short biographies of Sri Ramakrishna, Sri Sarada Devi and Swami Vivekananda, each of them bearing testimony not only to his scholarship, but his gift of clear and precise expression.

Just as the write-up on the *bhavamukha* concept is his unique contribution in the Ramakrishna biography, so are his writings on the *Legacy* of Swami Vivekananda forming the second part of his short biography of Swamiji, particularly the section on *Swamiji's contributions to Vedantic Thought* wherein he has analysed, point by point, the unique contributions made by Swamiji to Vedanta in the modern age of science and reason. Inspired by his ideas, I myself wrote a small piece on Ramakrishna's philosophy in the light of Einstein's theory of relativity and showed it to Maharaj. I was just a brahmachari, a spiritual novice, but the kind of liberty that he allowed me in my interactions and discussions with him out of his kindness and love for me always bring tears to my eyes. He not only had unqualified praise for this piece of writing of mine, but sought my 'permission' to include it in his book *Bhakti Schools of Vedanta* as an Appendix. He himself wrote another Appendix, elaborating the idea of *bhavamukha* that I had just touched upon without any elaboration in my own paper. Even now I feel proud and humbled (if such an oxymoron is acceptable!) when I see my own little paper, written when my thought processes had not attained the kind of clarity that was a *sine qua non* for attempting to write on Sri Ramakrishna's philosophy, appearing side by side in this book with his own brilliant paper on *Bhavamukha*. I sincerely believe that Maharaj is the pioneer in carrying forward the trend of thought on the subject of Sri Ramakrishna's philosophy based on the concepts of *bhavamukha* and *vijnana*, a work that was initiated by Swami Saradananda Maharaj in his magnum opus, *Sri Sri Ramakrishna Lilaprasanga*, although the latter does not talk of *vijnana*. Interestingly, the *Lilaprasanga* does not speak of the *vijnana* idea that Sri Ramakrishna emphasizes and mentions times without number in the *Kathamrita* (*The Gospel of Sri Ramakrishna*), while the *Kathamrita* does not mention the idea of *bhavamukha* (except perhaps on one occasion). It is to Swami Tapasyananda Maharaj's eternal credit that he has juxtaposed these two ideas together and shown their identity of content.

Swami Tapasyananda Maharaj wrote to me once, 'whenever you find a senior monk of our Order, enter into conversation with him on matters philosophical and relating to Ramakrishna-Vivekananda thought and try to learn from him. If you keep away, they also will keep quiet and loss will be yours. There will be none in the Order to spoon-feed you.' Maharaj would be waiting for me eagerly for philosophical discussions and to share his knowledge on innumerable subtle matters of philosophy. As a college and University student in Madras I would rush to him often, whenever I found the time, for discussions during his routine evening stroll in the gardens at the Math. Later on, when I joined the Order as a brahmachari at Saradapitha, an educational complex near Belur Math, I would constantly hang around his room whenever he would visit Belur Math for the periodical meetings of the Trustees. On all these occasions, his eagerness to share his knowledge and wisdom (for which unfortunately there were not many takers!) was remarkably touching—he was never tired of hours of discussions, now on Ramanuja's *visistadvaita* vis-ā-vis Chaitanya's *achintya bhedaabheda*, now on Nagarjuna's *sunyavada* and the subtle doctrine of *pratitya-samutpada*, now on Sri Ramakrishna's *vijnanavada* and the significance of *bhavamukha*, now on the interpretations of some of the verses of the *Bhagavad Gita* in the light of Shankara, Ramanuja and Madhusudana's commentaries, and many many other topics of endless variety. Imagine such a variety of discussions whose benefits came to me, unworthy as I am, uninterrupted for nearly twenty years! What a blessing and special grace of Sri Ramakrishna that I was the recipient of such a storehouse of wisdom, although my limited capacity could take pretty little. But then the indelible impressions of these interactions are the thought-bank and a storehouse of rich ideas carefully preserved in my unconscious mind wherefrom I draw inspiration to 'lead kindly light' in my spiritual journey.

Bhagavad Gita verses that Swami Tapasyananda Maharaj was often fond of quoting and interpreting

I had the blessed privilege of attending Swami Tapasyananda Maharaj's Sunday classes on the *Bhagavad Gita* right from the days when I was a college student. What a luminous mind he had and what remarkable insights we received from his interpretations! Over the years, when my own understanding and maturity grew, his explanations and interpretations became more and more meaningful and vivid for me, powerful enough to transform my understanding and continuously recast and remould my world-view. When I first heard his interpretation of the verse *evam pravartitam chakram...* (*Gita* 3.16) as the cosmic cycle embodying the fundamental law of sacrifice (*yajna*) which is the basis of all creation: *sahayajnah prajah sritva...* (*Gita* 3.10), positioned in the modern context, a new world of meaning and relevance opened up in my mental horizon.

The listeners in Swami Tapasyananda Maharaj's classes would be struck with the profundity of his thought and exposition, juxtaposed with his deep devotional fervour. As he was not much of an orator who could move audiences, his class audience always used to be quite small.

When he would explain the following verse in the *Gita*: *brahmano hi pratisthaham*… (14.27), contrasting the pure Advaitic position of Sri Shankara with that of the Bhakti school, particularly of Sri Chaitanya, his face will be aglow with joy and excitement at the very utterance of terms like: *tanubha* (the effulgence of the embodied *Saguna Brahman*), *ghanibhuta prakasha eva suryamandalam tadvat* (quoting from Sridhara Swami's commentary on this verse), 'just as the solar orb or the solar sphere is nothing but condensed light'. These insights made our young minds get seriously interested in the study of the *Gita* and develop the habit of discovering the inner significance of some of these verses in the light of the rare insights that Maharaj provided.

He was also very fond of discussing the exegetics of the *Gita* from the point of view modern Western scholars, often throwing up some revolutionary thoughts like, 'Some Western scholars think that the *Gita*, at least some verses in the *Gita*, are post-Buddhistic, for phrases that have a suffix of *–bhuya* or *–bhuta* after Brahman (for example, *Brahmabhuta, Brahmabhuya,* etc.) are scarcely found in any of the pure Vedantic texts and certainly not in any of the *Upanishadic* texts', 'the phrase *nirvana* used often in the *Gita* seems to have been borrowed from the Buddhist parlance, for this word is conspicuously absent in Vedantic texts and the *Upanishads* do not use the word *nirvana* at all'.

The comments and notes that Swami Tapasyananda Maharaj has given in his translation of the *Bhagavad Gita*—the book published under the title *Bhagavad Gita, the Scripture of Mankind*—are his invaluable gifts to the world of spiritual literature with special reference to the *Gita* literature. The added significance of these notes are that, one, they are so refreshingly original, two, they are highly rational, appealing to reason especially in the modern age of scepticism and questioning, three, they reveal the relevance of the ancient wisdom to the changing social and religious thoughts. For example, his explanation of the concept of *svadharma* delinking it from the *varnashrama* (the traditional Hindu view of castes and stations in life) framework is such a welcome insight that provides a new modern meaning of this ancient idea often spoken of in the *Gita* in the old setting. His elaborate discussion and delineation of the concept of *Avatara* (Divine Incarnation) both from the point of Hindu spirituality as well as the Christian theology, with practical implications in our daily spiritual practice, is a sheer delight to study and reflect upon. The Ramakrishna-Vivekananda perspective percolates, interpenetrates and informs all the elaborations and discussions and this adds new meaning in the modern world of scientific spirituality and demonstrates that these deliberations are not for intellectual pleasure or scholastic satisfaction, but are deeply grounded in practice of spiritual wisdom for individual awakening as well as collective good.

He would conduct monthly spiritual retreats at Madras Math—a project that he initiated—called *antaryoga* and would spend a few hours answering questions. Later on, he patiently wrote down these answers and published them for the benefit of larger audiences in the monthly journal, *The Vedanta Kesari*. The collection of all these answers has been published as a book titled *Spiritual Quest* by Madras Math and I personally feel that this book is a priceless possession, to be read and re-read, contemplated and analysed, assimilated and lived, by every serious spiritual sadhaka and a thinker on spiritual matters. Its importance in clarifying so many spiritual and philosophical concepts in the modern context can hardly be overemphasized.

Swami Tapasyananda Maharaj's great love for study and for acquisition of knowledge

Swami Tapasyananda Maharaj often would say that love for study and cultivation of a passion for knowledge are as important for spiritual progress as meditation, japa and other traditional practices. Knowledge acquired for elevation of mind, clarity of thought and understanding of the scriptures is a great asset for spiritual aspirant, particularly for a monk. He always would highlight the concept of a scholar-monk and illustrate this concept from the Mahayana Buddhistic tradition of extraordinary examples like Nagarjuna, Dharmakeerti, Vasabandhu etc. Nalanda Viswavidyalaya, the great monastic University that drew scholars from all parts of the world, was a pride of Indian spiritual wisdom where knowledge was cultivated, teaching and research attained the finest peaks, and cutting edge research manuals were published. History reports that when this seat of learning was destroyed by the vandalism of the invaders, its library, comprising the rarest collection of most valuable research material and other precious manuscripts, burnt for full six months! Many of these rare books were saved by the Buddhist scholar-monks who transporting them to Tibet, translated them into Tibetan and preserved them carefully. Some of these, particularly by Sri Nagarjuna, have since been re-translated into Sanskrit and published. Maharaj would emphasize that a deep study of Sri Nagarjuna's philosophy in particular and Buddhistic philosophical literature in general, is essential for understanding Advaita Vedanta of Sri Shankara, which again is essential for understanding the other Bhakti Schools of Vedanta like those of Sri Ramanuja, Sri Madhva, Sri Nimbarka, Sri Vallabha, Sri Chaitanya and so on.

I had the privilege of questioning him and learning from him so much about the Buddhistic philosophy as well as Vedanta in many of its forms and facets. Day after day, year after year, hours together he would expound to me the various aspects of these philosophies, always positioning them in the fabric of Ramakrishna-Vivekananda philosophical thought. I recall these memorable hours with tears of gratitude for the great fortune that providence (*prarabdha karma* as we call it in Hindu parlance) bestowed upon me in providing such a golden chance to listen to the profound words of wisdom from such a great scholar-monk like him. What little I know of these various aspects of philosophy I owe, in no small measure, to Maharaj and his unbounded kindness in pouring his heart out to this foolish little boy, who was nonetheless so eager to listen and to absorb.

While on the topic of his great love for the cultivation of knowledge, for higher studies, etc., an interesting anecdote comes to mind. I was in the first year of the Brahmacharins' Training Centre at Belur Math at that time. As usual, whenever Swami Tapasyananda Maharaj would come to Belur Math for the periodical Trustees' meetings, I would spend most of my spare time with him discussing philosophical subjects, questioning and learning. He also would wait for me eagerly. Once another Brahmachari, a monastic brother and a close friend of mine, asked Maharaj in my presence, apparently with some pique: 'Maharaj, why is he (meaning me) so special to you? You spend so much time with him and always keep enquiring when he would come to meet you! Why, we are also here!' At this Maharaj felt amused and said with a smile on his lips: 'You see, he is one fellow with whom I can discuss things of philosophical import!' He was so eager to share his knowledge and wisdom with the youngsters and often felt sad that, alas, there were few takers!'

During the Trustees' meetings, Swami Tapasyananda Maharaj and Swami Bhuteshananda Maharaj often would stay in adjacent rooms. While Swami Bhuteshananda Maharaj's room would be crowded with people who would be asking for stories and jokes, there would great fun and laughter, Swami Tapasyananda Maharaj hardly had any visitor with him, the poor me being one lone visitor eagerly listening to his expositions of Ramanuja's philosophy vis-ā-vis Madhva's or Chaitanya's and their intimate relationship with Ramakrishna-Vivekananda philosophy! I would also often go to Swami Bhuteshananda Maharaj when he was almost alone and freely put philosophical questions of all verities. With infinite patience he would explain and expound, provide rare insights and elevate the mind to a high level of comprehension. I often remember those golden days in the formation of my own philosophical thought and feel so greatly blessed!

Now, coming back to the interesting anecdote I was beginning to narrate: As has been repeatedly mentioned, I was so free with Swami Tapasyananda Maharaj who gave me great indulgence to say or ask anything, however stupid! He was asking me about the classes in the Training Centre, what were the subjects being taught, and so on.

With Bhuteshananndaji at the President Maharaj's Qtrs, Belur Math, 1989

He asked me specifically: 'How are the classes?' I replied, rather foolishly but frankly, 'Absolutely boring, Maharaj.' He was rather taken aback at this blunt and brusque reply and quipped, 'Why, why, why, why,...' (This was Swami Tapasyananda Maharaj's habit of talking when he was excited about something: he would repeat the word several times! For example, whenever he would see me at Belur Math after several months, he would be so excited with affection that he would often repeat, 'Well, well, well, well, ...' expressing his joy and greeting!) Then I told him what I felt, that in the Training Centre, there must be adequate scope for learning three things thoroughly, one, Sanskrit grammar, particularly, Panini's grammar, two, Vedanta based on the original commentaries on the *Upanishads* by Shankara, and three, Ramakrishna-Vivekananda literature in philosophical and spiritual perspective rather than as a simple narrative. He became quite agitated and serious. In the afternoon session of the Trustees' meeting, he made a powerful plea to start an advanced course in the Training

Centre giving special emphasis on the aspects that I had told him about.

Maharaj took the whole thing so seriously that he saw to it that an advanced course was started at the Training Centre for those interested and serious about advanced study. This advanced course is still being run at the Training Centre. He was also seriously mooting the idea of adding one more year to the Training Centre for those brahmacharins who were eager and capable of receiving more advanced knowledge. He, along with Swami Ranganathananda Maharaj, got a full-fledged scheme prepared for this additional one year.

Freedom to question, interact and argue—the lessons I learnt through this process

If it were not for great monks like Swami Tapasyananda Maharaj in the initial stages of my spiritual life and later Swami Smaranananda Maharaj, presently a senior vice-president of the Ramakrishna Math and Ramakrishna Mission, I would have felt stifled in my intellectual and spiritual growth, for having been brought up in a tradition of scientific enquiry from my infancy, I was given to question and argue, sometimes, although not too often, endlessly, but all the time with *sraddha,* faith and respect. I began my monastic life under the loving care of Swami Smaranananda Maharaj at Saradapitha, an educational complex closest to Belur Math, and the kind of freedom I enjoyed to express my views frankly, to question, to interact and to argue, is something I would always remember with intense gratitude. He would watch with loving admiration and patiently respond when I would endlessly argue philosophical issues with him. This training to question, interact and learn through dialogue in an atmosphere of freedom of thought and expression was imparted to me by Swami Tapasyananda Maharaj long before I formally joined the Ramakrishna Order of monks at Saradapitha under Swami Smaranananda Maharaj later. I never felt the difference in age or seniority while discussing philosophical and spiritual matters with either Swami Tapasyananda Maharaj or later with Swami Smaranananda Maharaj. What were the lessons I learnt? It was at the feet of very senior disciples of the Holy Mother Sri Sarada Devi and of the direct disciples of Sri Ramakrishna, like Swami Vireswarananda Maharaj, my own guru, Swami Satswarupananda Maharaj, Swami Kailasananda Maharaj, Swami Tapasyananda Maharaj, my spiritual and intellectual mentors, that I had the blessed privilege of learning the alphabets of spiritual life, to form a firm and deep intellectual and philosophical framework, and to groom my spiritual infancy into the Ramakrishna mould.

So complete was the surrender to Sri Ramakrishna that I could see in these monks that I could unconsciously learn my first spiritual lesson that the attitude of self-surrender and self-effacement, of self-abandonment and ego-obliteration, of offering one's all in loving service to Sri Ramakrishna, was the acme and essence of spiritual life. That Sri Ramakrishna was the Presiding Deity (*Adhithatri Devata*) of the Ashrama and surrender to him through loving service was the greatest spiritual sadhana ingrained and inculcated in me at every step by these great monks. I learnt that it is Sri Ramakrishna, and he alone, is the Head, the Presiding Deity, the Supreme Refuge, the Lord and the Witness of all that is happening in the Ashrama—we may recall Swami Shivananda Maharaj, Mahapurush

Maharaj's words, quoting from the *Gita* (9.18): 'Gatirbharta, prabussakshi, nivasashsharanam, suhrid...' I was taught that reporting to Sri Ramakrishna in a mood of absolute self-surrender every one of your thoughts, your actions, your feelings, your emotions, your plans, your predilections, even your fanciful prejudices, in fact, your everything at all times and in all situations, was the highest kind of sadhana. This lesson has got indelibly imprinted on my mind. When I walk down the memory lane along the corridor of time nearly four decades and relive my life as a newly come teenager student-devotee to the Ashrama, I can feel the thrill of the imprint of this lesson on my immature, adolescent mind at that time and realize how the lessons learnt then through the precepts and examples of these great monks have shaped my spiritual and intellectual life and sustained it for more than four decades—that Sri Ramakrishna is the Presiding Deity, he is the Lord and the Witness, he is the Supreme Refuge: *Gatirbharta prabhussakshi...*

Manmana bhava madbhakto madyaji mam namaskuru...

The *Gita sloka* (verse) beginning *Manmana bhava madbhakto madyaji mam namaskuru...* is extremely important for at least two reasons: one, the first line of this verse quoted above occurs twice in the *Gita*, at the end of the ninth chapter (9.34), and again at the end of the eighteenth and the very last chapter (18.65) which is considered by all the commentator-*Acharyas* as the essence and summary of the entire *Gita*; and two, Bhagavan Sri Krishna says that this and the verse following it in the eighteenth chapter are the greatest spiritual and mystical secrets in the *Gita* among all the esoteric and secret doctrines in the world of the Spirit—

sarva-guhyatamam. Hence the supreme importance of the two *Gita* verses: 18.65 and 18.66. The simple meaning of the above quoted line uttered by Bhagavan is as follows: *Have your mind and heart absorbed in Me, be devoted to Me, worship (or sacrifice for) Me, bow down (or surrender) to Me.*

I have witnessed the practise of Bhagavan's exhortation *mam namaskuru* by Swami Vireswarananda Maharaj, Swami Kailasananda Maharaj, Swami Tapasyanananda Maharaj, and several other disciples of Sri Ramakrishna's direct disciples that I began to understand the importance and beauty of this simple sadhana. Although the intensity of Swami Tapasyananda Maharaj's devotion was rarely visible from outside, we would watch with joy and amazement, how he would get deeply moved with devotional fervour while discussing devotional topics. His was more of an impersonal love without any visible external manifestation.

Blessed are such lives that are soaked in Ramakrishna Consciousness, whose souls are absorbed in divine thought, whose egos are completely erased in the overwhelming devotion to the Divine in the form of Ramakrishna Manifestation. Blessed are we who, at the formative period of spiritual life, during spiritually immature adolescent age just in the teens, had the privilege of witnessing such wonderfully elevating lives and of being groomed by such personalities who had no other concern but the spiritual welfare of all those who came in contact with them. These memories, cherished in the recesses of my innermost being for more than four decades, when stirred up to the surface consciousness, spur me on to more intense spiritual struggles and convince me that absolute erasing of one's puny ego in Divine Consciousness, self-abandonment and self-surrender, *prapatti,* is the one sure and simple way to the ultimate goal of God realization. Whenever Swami Tapasyananda Maharaj's serene face, beaming with devotion, lights up the mind of a poor struggling soul like me, I can only hear with moist eyes and grateful heart his grave voice resonating in my heart: '*Yo brahmanam vidadhati purvam yo vai vedansca prahinoti tasmai...*' A new wave of spiritual enthusiasm then sweeps my consciousness and the spirit is fired with tremendous power and confidence. May the unconditioned grace of such souls who come to elevate and inspire, to transmit a living and vibrant tradition of spirituality, and to pour their hearts out in blissful abandon at the feet of the Divine Manifestation in Sri Ramakrishna, be our sheet anchor in our journey in the unchartered sea of spiritual life amidst gales and tempests of temptations, whales and sharks of the senses, is our only prayer to our Beloved God, the most gracious, all merciful Sri Ramakrishna!

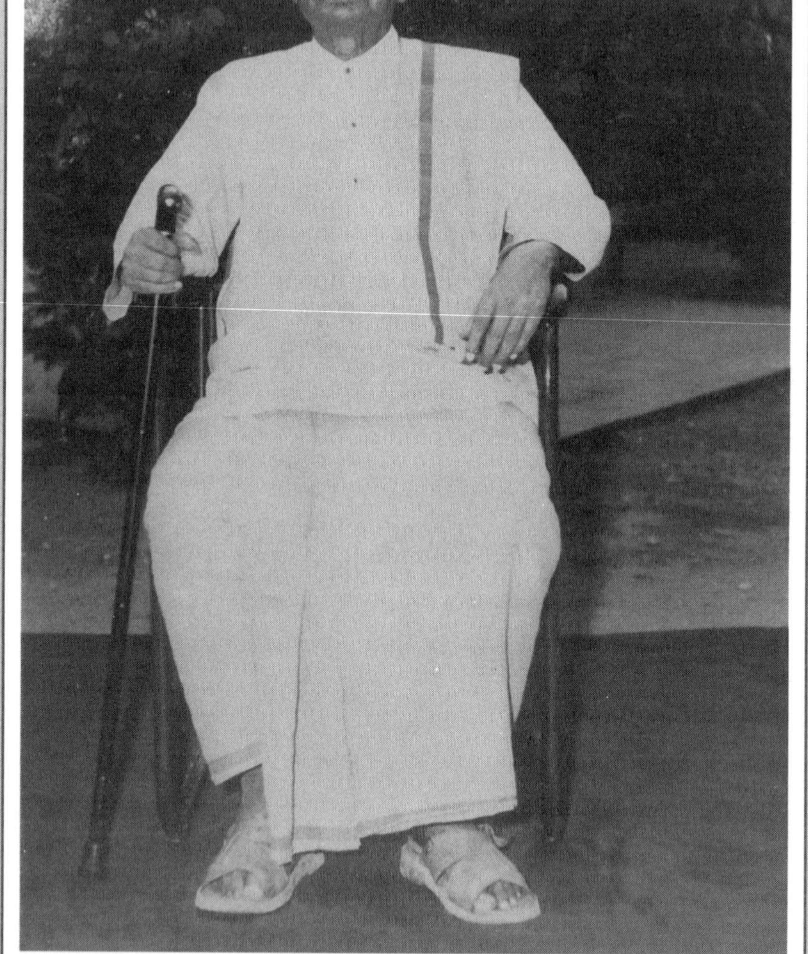

In Madras Math

17

A Channel of Sri Ramakrishna's Grace

Swami Sukhatmananda[1]

The life of Revered Swami Tapasyananda Maharaj is the saga of a great illumined soul who became a wonderful channel for Sri Ramakrishna's grace to flow. Even during his college days, he had the rare privilege of coming into contact with Revered Swami Brahmananda Maharaj and Swami Shivananda Maharaj, the illustrious disciples of Bhagavan Sri Ramakrishna. True to his name, Revered Swami Tapasyananda Maharaj was an exemplar in austerity, self-discipline, dedication, service and devotion—noble virtues that have enriched the tradition of monasticism. In addition, he was a scholar of great eminence leaving behind vast religious publications. Yet he led a most simple and unassuming life.

Revered Maharaj was one among many intellectual and spiritual stalwarts of the Order who commanded utmost reverence and respect. To contemplate on some of the memorable qualities of late Revered Maharaj is highly rewarding.

---

1. He is a senior monk of the Order who was closely associated with Revered Maharaj, especially when he was in Ramakrishna Mission Vivekananda College, Madras.

Although coming from an aristocratic family of Cochin, his life was built around the ideals of *tyaga* [renunciation] and *seva* [service] right from his early days. He was very frugal in his habits. It is said, during his college days at Madras when he lived with his brother in the same hostel, he used to save as much as possible the money he received from his family for meeting his personal expenses at the college and hostel while his brother could never meet his two ends together. When he later took to monastic life, his tendency to be frugal only helped him to appreciate the importance of practicing poverty—a mandatory vow for a monk.

His tendency to be frugal also helped him in handling various problems which one encounters in the monastic community life. He believed in the self-sustaining principle of any work undertaken. To recall an incident, though apparently very trivial, is of much significance. When he was at Trivandrum as In-charge of the Hospital, he got a refrigerator with lot of effort during those difficult days. And to make good for the money spent on it, he came up with a proposal of selling ice-creams to children who visited the Hospital, offering to collect the daily sale proceeds himself. Such frugality sometimes comes to one's rescue while facing a crisis. For instance, during water crisis in Madras during 1973, he would advice everyone to take bath with a few mugs of water instead of buckets full. Someone humorously referred to this as 'gamcha-bath' (wetting the towel and wiping the body).

In July 1978, Revered Maharaj had been invited to release a film on 'B.P Telemetry' and 'Man, the maker of Destiny' (directed by Hrishikesh Mukherjee) at a meeting of the Association of Surgeons of India (IMA) at Chepauk in Madras. But he could not attend the meeting for some reason. However, it was very inspiring for me to hear at the meeting about Maharaj's contribution in transforming a humble dispensary into a full-fledged Hospital at Trivandrum and his great capacity in managing that institution.

Revered Maharaj's simplicity in dress, food habits and life-style reflecting a highly self-disciplined person was simply astounding. He would come in the mornings and in the afternoons exactly at fixed time and sit in his small office for hours poring over the literary works related to Ramakrishna-Vivekananda-Vedanta.

He very much insisted on physical fitness of the young novices, as he himself kept good health throughout, encouraging them to do exercises and yogasanas, and he even set up a shuttle badminton court at the Math for the monastics to play. In the evenings, one could see him walking daily for an hour or so either in the narrow verandah below his room or on the terrace.

Even from his days as a novice, he was well known for tremendous intellectual discipline. That he authored a book on Holy Mother in the late thirties, when not so much material on Holy Mother was available, indicates his enormous intellectual labour and an attitude of research.

His intellectual hunger was something amazing. It was at his office that Sri Kalyansundara Sastrigal's Vedanta classes would be held twice a week in the afternoons with some five to six junior monks attending the classes. Sri Sastrigal, a great scholar honoured with the title '*Bhashya Bhavajna*' [one who could grasp the essence of the commentaries], was well known for his scholastic attainments in teaching Vedanta to the public for more than six decades. Revered Maharaj would sit through the class very attentively, ready with his pen and paper.

Whenever Swami Vimalananda Maharaj, another great scholarly-monk of the Order, would visit Madras, he too would attend those classes and ask intricate questions to Sri Sastrigal with a twinkle in his eyes to make the classes more interesting and enlightening. Sri Sastrigal too was very enthusiastic to teach Vedanta to the monastics at the Math and did so for more than 40 years. Sri Sastrigal would consider it a greater honour to receive a gift of a *dhoti* and a *chaddar* from Swami Tapasyananda Maharaj than all the scholarly honours he had received elsewhere.

Sitting (Left to Right): Vimalanandaji, Kailasanandaji, Tapasyanandaji in Trivandrum

A deep thinker that Revered Maharaj was, his lectures were very scholarly and insightful. I remember we once attended a seminar in Theosophical Society, Adyar, on the 'Theory of Creation'. Various speakers from different religions presented their theories. Revered Maharaj spoke on the Sankhya System which was a master-piece presentation and interpretation.

As the head of Sri Ramakrishna Math, Madras, he was the president of the Managing Committees of various institutions of the Mission. He would especially make it a point to attend the meetings of the Vivekananda College. His love for this Institution of Higher Learning was very keen. He showed great interest in its growth and development. He, as the president of Sri Ramakrishna Math, Madras, would every year inaugurate the 'Religion Classes' at the beginning of the academic year, a tradition of the college ever since its inception. Everyone at the college would eagerly await his talk which was considered as an important annual event.

Though a scholar of such a great repute, one could see in Revered Maharaj an eternal seeker eager to learn whatever he could from his seniors. Whenever the president of the Order would visit Madras, there would be interactions with Revered Maharaj every night after food. During those interactions, questions or topics for informal discussion would be initiated invariably by Tapasyananda Maharaj and such sessions would generally last for an hour and a half. It was at his insistence only that Revered Swami Vireswarananda Maharaj talked of his old days at Madras Math and about Holy Mother which are recorded in the *Glimpses of the past*.

It was a wonderful experience for the brahmacharins of the Training Centre, Belur Math, to meet and hear him talk informally on spiritual practices and scriptural studies. He had a wonderful capacity to guide those who came to him with doubts and answer their questions to their satisfaction. He was not given to instruct much, rather people learnt more from his life.

During the classes and lectures, he would stimulate the thinking of the listeners by his scholarly and deeply analytical discussions on the topics he dealt with. Flashes of insight and deep understanding would come out effortlessly.

The glory of Sri Ramakrishna as an Incarnation was not a mere intellectual conviction for him; it transformed fully into devotion. On the birthday celebrations of the Holy Trio and the direct disciples at Madras Math, one could see him fully in devotional mood, especially when he would hand over the relics of Sri Ramakrishna for puja and take it back after the puja.

Such was the personality of Revered Maharaj. From him, we can learn great lessons for developing our lives. Those of us who saw him lead a completely intellectual and spiritual life feel really blessed. However brief might have been our association with him, it has been helping us in our struggle to overcome our weaknesses and to become better in this very life.

18

What Is Rest?

Swami Kapalisananda[1]

Swami Tapasyananda Maharaj was very austere, but people mistook that to be miserliness. He had a rough and stern exterior but was very soft and considerate at heart. He was very empathetic, especially to the hard working monks, labourers and casual workers. He took lot of pains to look after their welfare and that of their families.

Revered Maharaj spoke little and lived more. His approach was simple and direct. He was a harmonious combination of Karma, Jnana and Bhakti.

Regarding handling of dilemma in one's spiritual life, Maharaj would tell me, 'Look here, it is necessary to have some discrimination. There is a simple and practical way to resolve any dilemma; whenever you are going to take up anything, ask yourself three questions: 1. Is it necessary? 2. Is it spiritually useful to me or anybody else? 3. Is it useful to this holy organization? Then automatically you can arrive at a correct conclusion and proceed forward.'

Usually in the morning hours, Revered Maharaj would sit in his office. In the evenings, he would stay in his room itself and attend to his duties. Sometimes Maharaj would be

1. He joined in Madras Math under Revered Maharaj in 1978.

very serious about matters that appeared petty to us. But later we found a lot of meaning in that. For example, he used to scold if the water leaked from the tap or from broken pipe. 'See, each drop of water is money. You fellows do not understand how much we pay for the electricity.' But the same person was ready to spend any amount of money to upgrade the medical equipments or machines if that meant improving the service activities of the Math.

Once a funny incident took place. As I have mentioned, Maharaj was always particular about using less water. So he would never allow water to be sprayed on lawns and waste groves. During hot summer, we once watered the lawns and plants in the night so that he may not notice it. But it so happened that he noticed it the next morning when he was going to his office. He angrily asked, 'Hey, why did you water these dirty plants?' I simply said, 'Maharaj, it might have rained last night.' Like a child, he simply nodded and went away. Later he enquired someone whether it rained the previous night. When he replied in negative, Maharaj understood my prank and said laughingly, 'See, that fellow simply fooled me!' Like a child he would tell this to everyone and have fun over it.

Maharaj was good at retorting. Sometimes it was jovial, sometimes thought provoking. Once, a man came to Maharaj after a serious lecture and said, 'Maharaj, last night you had come in my dream and had told me something. Kindly tell me that.' Maharaj calmly retorted, 'Sir, tonight you can try again; I shall come in your dream and tell that.'

In those days, there were only a few monastic members. So we had to work in two or three departments. Naturally we became tired. When we had leisure, we would manage to take some rest. But we would always have our Sanskrit classes at 1 p.m. So on many days, many monastics would absent themselves from the class. Maharaj would scold us saying, 'You must know how to manage your time. Taking rest does not mean you go to sleep. **Switching from one work to another work is rest.** See the birds when they fly, they move from one tree to another tree. In the same way, we also should take rest by switching from one work to another.'

19

A Fatherly Figure

Swami Kamalananda[1]

I joined the Order in Bangalore in 1969 and was sent to New Delhi in March 1970. On the way, I halted at Madras Math when Revered Swami Kailasananda Maharaj was the president.

During my stay in New Delhi, I heard about Revered Tapasyananda Maharaj's transfer from Trivandrum to Madras. Although it was my initial days in the Order, after coming in contact with many monks, I understood that any person who stays too long in a place finds it difficult to leave that place. Revered Maharaj had stayed in Trivandrum not only for a long period but had spared no pains in developing the hospital giving his personal attention to all the minute details, including equipments et al. I came to know that Revered Maharaj had taken this transfer without showing any attachment to the centre and left with his few belongings to take charge of Madras Math. Then I started imagining what a great soul he must be, who can move without any attachment from one place to another.

---

1. He is a senior monk of the Order who was in contact with Revered Maharaj since 1978. He was later the manager of Advaita Ashrama, Calcutta for some years.

Ramakrishna Mission Students' Home, Madras, 1921

Although I was in Belur Math during 1974-77, I do not remember to have met Revered Maharaj even though he might have come there for the Trustees' meetings etc. It was only in 1978, when I was posted to Students' Home, Madras, I had an opportunity of coming in contact with him. During my stay at the Students' Home, I would visit Madras Math on special days and once in a fortnight.

Whenever I met him I found him busy in literary work or if it was in the evening, he will be walking near the dining hall. He used to make kind enquiries about my personal life and also about the Students' Home. I had found in him a fatherly figure.

Later in 1981, I was posted to Advaita Ashram, Calcutta, and I was its manager between 1985 and 1990. During this period, an incident happened which proved the statement *'saadhuder raag joler uprar daag'* that is, the anger of the monk is [only] like a mark on the water.

In 1987, it was felt that some decisions needed to be taken regarding the type of books to be published by Advaita Ashrama and Madras Math. Incidentally, that was the year when Revered Maharaj had just assumed the office of the vice-president of the Order. I had submitted my proposal to the headquarters. The matter was discussed in the Trustees' meeting. However, Revered Maharaj was not in favour of my proposal and was therefore unhappy with me.

Next day in the morning, I went to Belur Math from Advaita Ashrama to meet Revered Maharaj. On seeing me he sternly asked, 'Are you that manager, who gave such a proposal?' His voice sounded with a tinge of anger. But before he could proceed further, I simply fell at his feet and said, 'Maharaj, you are the vice-president of the whole Order and what is Advaita Ashrama or Madras Math for you!' Immediately he told himself 'Yes, I am the Vice-President of the whole Order.' Then, after getting his blessings, I requested him to visit Advaita Ashrama to which he readily agreed and asked me to fix a date. He was gracious to visit the Advaita Ashrama and spend a couple of hours and blessed us all. Is it not true that a monk's anger is momentary?

My next meeting with him was in 1991 when I was doing rehabilitation work in Andhra Pradesh. One day Revered Atmasthananda Maharaj, the then Asst. Secretary, told me over phone that Revered Maharaj's health was in a very bad condition and it would be good if I go immediately to Madras to have his *darsan*. On the very same day, I left Rajahmundry and reached Madras. Revered Maharaj was in the hospital on a ventilator. It was a sad sight to see. That was my last *darsan* of Revered Maharaj.

20

Develop Free Thinking & Independent View

Swami Tattwamayananda[1]

I got acquainted with Swami Tapasyananda Maharaj when I was a brahmachari for about two years after I joined Madras Math. But that period was remarkable, because, in spite of its brevity, it left an indelible impression on me and exerted a profound influence on my monastic life.

I first heard about Revered Maharaj when I was a college student from one of his old friends, the late Sri Ottur Unni Nambudiripad, the author of several poetical works in Sanskrit on devotional themes, including *Sri Ramakrishna Karnamritam,* a poetical hymn on Sri Ramakrishna's life and teachings.

I joined Madras Math in August 1978 at a relatively young age. Almost all the monastic members there were elder to me. The Math premises, especially the 'Old Temple', associated with memories of the direct disciples of Sri Ramakrishna, provided a serene atmosphere, isolating us from the disturbances of the city traffic outside.

In those days, at Madras Math, newly joined brahmacharis were generally asked to render some service

1. He was a brahmachari at Madras Math under Revered Maharaj for a short period. He had contact with Revered Maharaj even while he was serving in other centres.

in the temple, shrine, kitchen, library etc. I was initially given the duty of assisting the Pujari Maharaj in the temple – cleaning the shrine room and the steps outside, preparing the offerings etc. Once a week, I had to go to the market at Parry's Corner for purchasing various items for the temple. Occasionally, I had to do some proofreading and also go to the library to assist the Swami in-charge there. I was totally inexperienced in all these duties and often ran into difficulties. On all these occasions, Revered Maharaj graciously helped me with proper instructions and advice.

Revered Maharaj gave both responsibility and freedom to the juniors. He would always strike that fine balance between giving unlimited freedom and it's opposite - tyrannical control - in training the brahmacharins who joined under him. After giving them duties, he would watch, guide and help them. He could instantly discover the talents and potentialities of the new brahmacharins and he would take every care to encourage and help them to develop those skills so that they could serve the Order more effectively. Although he greatly admired dynamism and efficiency in work, he never approved restlessness and workaholism at the cost of spiritual practices. He insisted that all those who had newly joined should be regular in attending *Mangalarati*, meditation, japa etc. But he never spoke in a soft diplomatic tone. He was always direct and unsparing. As years passed, we realized that Revered Maharaj had an eye on all our activities and was doing everything necessary for our spiritual welfare.

Although endowed with an intellectual bent of mind, Revered Maharaj was essentially a devotee at heart, with a strong inclination, according to many of his admirers, towards the Ramanuja school of Vedanta. But surprisingly, even the junior monks could openly express different views and he would enjoy debating with them on philosophical topics. One had the freedom even to disagree with some of his views on philosophy or religious doctrines. He was always ready to encourage free thinking and forming of independent views on such subjects. He was especially careful to encourage brahmacharins and junior monks to develop a regular habit of studying scriptures and whenever he found any special talent or academic interest among them he would enthusiastically encourage them to develop those skills.

He never wasted even a minute. Even while wholly absorbed in his administrative responsibilities, he engaged himself with characteristic zeal and enthusiasm in literary work, translating classics like *Narayaneeyam, Bhagavata Purana* etc. and writing independent works like the *Bhakti Schools of Vedanta,* thereby doing a valuable service to the English-knowing world. He also encouraged the junior monks in the Math to take up literary work and continue their regular scriptural studies as an important part of their daily routine.

As a writer, Revered Maharaj seemed to belong to that group of traditional and conservative archetypal scholars who follow their literary pursuit with fervent single-mindedness concentrating on the classical tradition. But he was traditional without being orthodox, modern without being shallow and superficial.

It is said that, while going for monthly collections in Trivandrum, one of the brother monks slipped a four-*anna* coin into his pocket, in case he would need to return by bus in the evening because of exhaustion. But, as it happened, he never used that coin as he did not want to spend even such a meagre amount for his own comfort!

Occasionally some people felt that Revered Maharaj was a bit miserly in spending money. But he was practicing rigorous austerity only in his own personal life. He himself led an extremely austere life; but he was generous and accommodative in granting whatever the younger generation of monks required. He was always tenderly, considerate towards others and never compelled other monastics to practice extreme austerity. He made great demands from those working under him, but he also treated them with affection and sympathy. In him the task-master and the mentor were interwoven. He was a living embodiment of that age-old dictum in spiritual life—'strict with ourselves and sympathetic towards others'.

There may be many who are overwhelmed by the scholarly achievements of Revered Maharaj and fail to see the monk in him. But behind the translator and the scholar, one could always see him as the intense devotee and the matchless practitioner of Karma Yoga. Madras and Trivandrum centres acknowledge their debt to his tenacity and hard work. Even while working hard with superhuman tenacity for building up the hospital in Trivandrum, he led the inner life of a contemplative with a perfect understanding of the problems of poor people and of members and staff of the Ashram and the hospital.

I stayed in Madras Math for nearly two years before getting transferred to the Trichur branch of the Order. Of course, even in later years, when I was at the Training Cenre, Belur Math, and in the Advaita Ashrama, Calcutta, I would

meet Revered Maharaj and converse with him whenever he came to Belur Math.

Swami Tapasyananda Maharaj was a supreme example of detachment. He was completely detached from anything associated with worldly honour, name and fame etc. Above all, he was the embodiment of the last and most difficult type of detachment – detachment from himself. His personal humility, self-effacement, doctrinal conservatism with regard to the fundamental principles of monasticism, sense of obedience to the seniors in the monastic hierarchy, deep commitment to the task of training his juniors, especially the brahmacharins who joined under him - all these made him an unforgettable ideal, even for those like me who were with him for a brief period.

His stern and austere life, natural simplicity, deep interest in not only the traditional scriptures and philosophical systems, both Eastern and Western, but also in subjects like history and literature – all these presented before us a very high monastic ideal.

21

Light of Knowledge

Swami Vimalatmananda[1]

I first met Revered Swami Tapasyananda Maharaj at Belur Math when he had come for the Trustees' meeting, Heads' and Monks' Conferences in October 1974. Before that I had only heard about him. Revered Maharaj was a scholar in devotional literature. Although I did not come in close contact with him, but I had watched him at close quarters whenever he came to Belur Math.

Revered Maharaj was simple by nature. His dress was very ordinary. He was very meticulous in spiritual practices and wanted all the monks and brahmacharis also to be equally meticulous. He was a monk with strict discipline. He never idled away his time. Whenever I went to his room (he would stay in the Trustees' building) in Belur Math, I saw him either reading a book or writing something. Revered Maharaj would give talks to the brahmacharis of the Training Centre whenever he visited Belur Math. Although his talks were very scholarly, he would speak from his heart. He never deviated from the subject.

Revered Maharaj was very particular in maintaining the tradition of Ramakrishna Order. He was very careful in

1. He is a member of Governing Body and Board of Trustees of Ramakrishna Math and Mission.

spending money. He used to tell us that devotees' money is hard-earned money, and therefore we had to spend it carefully. He would never tolerate any careless wastage of things.

Revered Maharaj was well-versed in scriptures and I was charmed to read the articles he authored which were published in *The Vedanta Kesari* magazine. His book on Swami Ramakrishnananda Maharaj (*Swami Ramakrishnananda: The Apostle of Sri Ramakrishna to the South*) fulfilled our great expectation. He was the pioneer to do research on Swami Ramakrishnananda Maharaj who was instrumental in spreading the message of Sri Ramakrishna in South India. Revered Maharaj's translation of the *Bhagavatam* is simple, wonderful and lucid. It created wide interest among the English knowing people. His other books are also excellent.

When Revered Maharaj was elected as a vice-president of the Ramakrishna Order, we saw some changes in him. He became very kind to all, very affectionate to the devotees, and blessed everyone who sought it. Revered Maharaj's life was absorbed in the thoughts of Bhagavan Sri Ramakrishna, Holy Mother Sri Sarada Devi and Swamiji. He received the blessings of Swami Shivananda Maharaj, his Guru, and a few other direct disciples of Sri Ramakrishna. He got the light of knowledge from them and handed it over to others who came in contact with him. That light, which illumined his exemplary life as a monk for 65 years, came to an end in 1991. But his legacy lingers even now.

22

A Time and Place for Every Emotion

Swami Sukritananda[1]

On 20 February 1979, I reached Madras Math with an intention of joining the Order. I however had no letter of introduction from any of the monks of the Ramakrishna Math in the town I hailed from. I was informed that the president of Madras Math, Revered Swami Tapasyananda Maharaj, was not in station and would return only after a week.

First Meeting

After his return, I met Revered Maharaj at his room on the first floor. He looked grave and enquired why I intended to join the Order. In reply, I said I wanted to become a monk to realize God. I had already been introduced to the life and teaching of Sri Ramakrishna and to other literature of the Ramakrishna Order. Revered Maharaj asked me whether I had brought with me a mosquito curtain! I replied that I had.

At His Service

During my initial days in the Math, I was assigned the duty of assisting in the Cash Department. Thereafter, I was

1. He was the personal secretary of Revered Maharaj for 6 years. He joined at Madras Math under Revered Maharaj in 1979.

At Ramakrishna Mission Students' Home, Madras, 1990
Sukritananda (standing behind), Veetabhayananda

instructed to serve in Sri Ramakrishna's shrine stores and also serve Revered Maharaj. Thus I got a grand opportunity to watch this sagely monk from close quarters and benefit by his holy company. But he would hardly allow others to do anything for him. He would himself wash his clothes. He would however allow me to dye his clothes once a week.

Two years later, I was instructed to serve in the kitchen as its in-charge. In that capacity, I had to oversee the food arrangements of Revered Maharaj. He would not demand anything special for him. He would take whatever was prepared for all. He would normally eat less and avoid oily dishes and sweets. He expected me to just keep the food on the table and not wait on him.

Even after a year of my joining the Math, Revered Maharaj had not filled my pre-probationer's membership form which had to be sent to Belur Math. As a novice, I had my own exaggerated worries regarding my crossing the prescribed age limit. No one was admitted into the Order when their age crossed the prescribed limit. Troubled with anxiety, I broached to Revered Maharaj the subject of filling the pre-probationer's form. Revered Maharaj observed my nervousness and told me not to be bothered about less important things and to remain focused in serving Sri Ramakrishna. His spiritual counsel relieved me of my worry in a moment. Within three months, he sent my pre-probationer membership form to Belur Math.

His Living Room

He lived for 14 years in a small room with minimum furniture – cot, table, chair and a stool for keeping books. He used to keep some books on the shelf. After becoming the vice-president of Ramakrishna Math and Mission, he attached the adjacent room too with that of the existing one.

His Daily Routine

When Revered Maharaj enjoyed good health, he never missed attending the *mangalarati*. He would keenly observe whether all the other monastics also attended it.

I heard from elderly monks that in the later part of 1975, he woke up at 3.00 a.m. to go through the proofs of his English translation of *Srimad Bhagavatam*. Once when I requested him to take some classes for brahmacharins on spiritual topics, he replied that he wanted to complete the translation of *Bhagavatam* before taking up any other task.

Maharaj would usually rise at 4:30 a.m. After ablutions, he would sit for meditation till 6:00 a.m. At the end of meditation, with great devotion, he would chant the following *slokas*.

भक्तहार्दतमो भेदी दिव्यज्योति स्वरूपिणे ।
प्रपन्न त्राण दीक्षाय रामकृष्णाय ॐ नमः ।।

bhaktahārdatamo bhedī divyajyoti svarūpiṇe |
prapanna trāṇa dīkṣāya rāmakṛṣṇāya Om namaḥ ||

O Thou who art the shatterer of the darkness of ignorance in the heart of devotees!

O Thou who art the light Divine!

O Thou who art vowed to give protection to all the ones who surrender!

O Thou who hast come as Ramakrishna!

O salutation to Thee Om!

नमो नमो वाङ्मनसादि भूमये नमो नमो वाङ्मनसैक भूमये ।
नमो नमोऽनन्त महाविभूतये नमो नमोऽनन्त दयैकसिन्धवे ।।

namo namo vāṅamanasādi bhūmaye
namo namo vāṅamanasaika bhūmaye |
namo namo'nanta mahāvibhūtaye
namo namo'nanta dayaikasindhave ||

I Salute Thee again and again who transcends the ken of both speech and mind!

I Salute Thee again and again who art the sole support of all that can be denoted by mind and speech!

I Salute Thee again and again who art possessed of infinite Divine powers!

I Salute Thee again and again who art the one ocean of all that is known as grace!

न धर्मनिष्ठोऽस्मि न चात्मवेदी न भक्तिमांस्त्वचरणारविन्दे ।
अकिञ्चनोऽनन्य गतिश्शरण्य त्वत्पादमूलं शरणं प्रपद्ये ।।

na dharmaniṣṭho'smi na cātmavedī
na bhaktimāṃstvacaraṇāravinde |
akiñcano'nanya gatiśśaraṇya
tvatpādamūlaṃ śaraṇaṃ prapadye ||

Neither am I established in the practice of Dharma,

Nor in the knowledge that "I am the Atman"!

I am not also endowed with devotion to Thy lotus feet,

O Bestower of refuge! Destitute as I am of all virtues and powers,

I have no shelter except Thee!

He would have his breakfast at 7.00 a.m. and bathe at 7.30 a.m., followed invariably by the study of scriptures till 9.00 a.m. At 9.30 a.m., before beginning his day at his office, he would visit the shrine to offer prayers.

He was very prompt in replying to letters. He was very particular to attend to the work at hand without any delay. Anybody would freely meet him during the office hours. He always had time to meet people and patiently listen to their problems. He would refuse no one citing that he was too busy to attend to them. If there were no visitors, he would continue his work or study. Around noon, he would return for noon-*prasad*.

After lunch, he would glance through the newspaper for half-an-hour and take a short nap. At 2.30 p.m., he would be usually engaged in literary work. If any non-local visitors sought to meet him then, he would meet them in the verandah outside his living room. At 3.30 p.m., he would have a cup of tea with a couple of cream cracker cookies.

At 5.30 p.m., he would walk for an hour. At 6.30 p.m., he would sit for meditation. Between 7.30 to 8.30 p.m., he would read scriptures. He would take his supper-*prasad* at 8.30 p.m. He would then attend the night class – the closing session of the day. Before 10.30 p.m., he would retire for the day.

He was so punctual and thorough going in everything that one could set the clock by watching his movements.

Night Classes

In every Ramakrishna Ashrama, as part of the monastic routine, the inmates assemble after dinner for what is called the 'night-class'. Apart from some reading from Ramakrishna-Vivekananda literature, it also provides an opportunity for the monastics to meet and have some lighter moments before retiring for the day. Revered Maharaj never missed the night class. He would encourage novices to raise questions on any topic and clarify their doubts. His presence and utterances would make the gathering very lively. Hearing my reading in the class, he once commented that my voice was 'musical'.

Once in a night class, someone narrated the following joke: A person went to a shop looking for tissue paper. Unfortunately the shop didn't have it. The shopkeeper, however, unwilling to lose the customer asked him innocently whether sandpaper would serve his purpose. Everyone burst into laughter. Revered Maharaj too laughed, much amused thinking of what might have happened to the customer!

Tapasyananda Maharaj attending a lecture

On another day, Revered Maharaj humorously called the avid speakers who were reluctant to leave the mike as *lathi chargers*. He then asked us whether we knew the meaning of *lathi charge*. And he himself explained: 'During riot, police do *lathi charge* at the crowd. People then run away from spot. Likewise the speakers also perform their *lathi charge*. But sadly in this case, the listeners cannot run away!'

Once he asked the brahmacharis whether they knew what was 'butler English'. He then elaborated. 'A tamil speaking servant was serving in an Englishman's house. The servant gave the following description of cat to his master: '*nalukalu* [four legs] sir, *oruvalu* [one tail] sir, *mew mew* sir.' Those present convulsed in laughter.

The classes would go on for 45 minutes like a mart of joy. Maharaj would be in his elements during that time. He would exhibit a keen sense of humour. This humour, coming from an otherwise serious and seemingly reserved person, demonstrated the fullness in his personality.

His Personality

Revered Maharaj was austere to the core. His name befitted his character. He was *'anvartha namadheya'*. He would never permit others to wash his clothes. He himself had daily washed his clothes till he was 77 years old! He diligently denied himself all forms of external comforts and luxuries. Even in his later years, when his health deteriorated, he would not allow installation of geyser in his bathroom. Every morning at 8.30 a.m., a jug of hot water would be kept for his bath. He would mix a small amount of it with cool water and have his bath.

There was water scarcity in Madras. He would be very economical in using water, be it for bathing, washing or laundry. After washing his clothes, he would flush the commode with the remaining water and not just throw it away.

Revered Maharaj was particular that no electricity should be wasted. If he found electric lights burning in daytime, he would ensure they are switched off immediately. He would also ensure that the light and fan was switched off while closing his office.

Revered Maharaj was very sensitive to human feelings and was very careful in his expressions, lest any inadvertent utterance hurt others. Revered Maharaj would also tolerate the mistakes of the monastic and try his best to correct them. Even when he found any monastic member committing some gross mistake, he would reprimand them not more than using the words, 'fool' or 'stupid'. Once while attending on him, an attendant advertently broke a table clock. Revered Maharaj neither got upset nor made any harsh comments. At that moment, a senior monk came there. Pointing to the attendant, Revered Maharaj just said, 'He has managed to break the clock!' On another occasion, while I was washing his dentures, it slipped from my hand and fell and broke. I was afraid that he would scold me. But he did not utter a word nor even refer to it later. He just got a new set from the dentist.

Revered Maharaj was not only concerned about the health and well-being of monastics, but would also keep a close watch on the health of the supporting staff of the Math. If anyone had not turned up for work, he would enquire about his health, and if he was found to be sick and required hospitalization, Revered Maharaj would immediately instruct Manager Maharaj or the Bhandari Maharaj to take the necessary action.

When his health was in good condition, Revered Maharaj would dine in the dining hall along with the other monastics. That gave him an opportunity to observe the food habits of the novices and he guided them accordingly.

Monks generally love to experience the joy of visiting holy places. But with Revered Maharaj, his pilgrimages were only the annual visits to Belur Math for administrative purposes. His soul had self-contentment; seeking neither pleasure nor happiness outside. He was always in the realm of joy.

Revered Maharaj had an innocent fancy for funny comparisons. This would make his listeners convulse in laughter. He liked *idlis* for breakfast. But if they were big, he would call them *Bhimanna idlis*! If people laughed awkwardly, he would equate them to yawning buffalos! When brahmacharis used more water, he would refer to them as unruly elephants in the pools!

Revered Maharaj would always converse in English unless visitors from Kerala wished to converse with him in Malayalam. In my presence, however, he would always converse in English. He was very particular in speaking the language known to all those who heard him. He was in the habit of reading *National Geographic* – a popular American monthly magazine. According to him, the English in that magazine was "crisp".

In 1981, Revered Maharaj visited Belur Math to attend the Trustees' meeting. There he fell sick and was admitted in Seva Pratishthan. He was found to be affected by diabetes. He had difficulty in walking and a walking stick became his constant companion. When he returned to Madras Math, he humorously told the other monks that a sugar factory was discovered in him!

Revered Maharaj neither received nor made phone calls for personal matters. Perhaps Revered Maharaj knew Swami Asheshananda Maharaj's (a disciple of Holy Mother) saying that 'God vision and television never go together'. Once, in 1988, during the Heads' conference in Belur Math, arrangements were made to screen a documentary in which Revered Mahapurush Maharaj, who was his own guru, is seen taking a stroll in the Belur math grounds. Revered Maharaj was invited to watch the documentary. But in adherence to the wisdom inherited from that worthy disciple of Holy mother, he refused to participate in the gathering. In fact, he had never watched the television in his life.

Revered Maharaj's sagacious and loving personality won the hearts of all. His seniors had heartfelt love for him.

His suggestions and recommendations were honoured without any second thought.

Training young novices

Revered Maharaj would instruct novices to read *Life of Sri Ramakrishna*, which had a foreword by Mahatma Gandhi; lives of Holy Mother and Swami Vivekananda; *The Gospel of Sri Ramakrishna* by Mahendranath Gupta in English. He would also insist they daily read the editorials of *The Hindu* newspaper in order to acquire proficiency in English.

In the evenings, Revered Maharaj would do brisk walking on the terrace of the dining hall. He would insist that the novices do some physical exercise in his presence. He would take initiative in teaching us preliminary warm-up exercises. After the preliminaries, we had to jog for half-an-hour in front of his watchful eyes. So there was no question of missing the regime, even though it was difficult for some of us who had never even stepped into a playground! Later when the shuttle badminton court was laid, he would observe whether all brahmacharis participated in the game.

Advice to Monastics

Revered Maharaj would usually give the following advice to monastics:

We are servants of Sri Ramakrishna and also His children. The ashrama belongs to Sri Ramakrishna.

Monastics should not build up friendship with lady-devotees. If they come for sake of work, they would be attended to only for that purpose and no further.

One should preserve and imbibe the sanctity of the temple. Worship of Sri Ramakrishna should be done with utmost care. The fruits to be offered to Sri Ramakrishna must be carefully washed before dressing them. Particularly, grapes must be soaked in water for half-an-hour before offering.

I never asked any questions to Revered Maharaj regarding spiritual life, nor did he instruct me specially. But watching him from close quarters, it appeared to me as though he was instructing me through everything he did. It seemed as though that he was inspiring me to imbibe the spirit behind every action of his.

Intellectual Service

Revered Maharaj was a deep thinker, impressive speaker and a prolific writer. He authored a few books and translated scriptures in Sanskrit like *Srimad Bhagavatam, Adhyatma Ramayanam, Sundara Kandam, Bhakti Ratnavali,* and *Narayaneeyam*. In his later years, when his health was not good, he could not sit on the chair for long. He would then ask us to place a small desk on his table and use it for his translation work or for correspondence, all the while standing. He would write the draft of his letters in a diary and would have them type-written.

May the study of Sundara Kanda enable you to cultivate devotion like that of Hanuman.

Tapasyananda
13-11-84

It is a common practise of devotees to offer some money to Revered Maharaj. He would use that money to purchase Ramakrishna-Vivekananda literature and freely distribute them among youngsters who would happily receive them from him as his *prasad*.

Revered Maharaj would be invited to deliver his benedictory address in various institutions, especially educational. On those occasions, Revered Maharaj would use simple English in his address. He would advise the young listeners: 'We must have four wells – Eat well, Play well, Study well, Pray well.' Saying this, he would explain each of them in detail.

In March 1983, Revered Maharaj suggested to me to take up the editorship of the Telugu magazine, *Sri Ramakrishna Prabha*. But for some reasons I could not then take up that responsibility. But after the *mahasamadhi* of Revered Maharaj, the assignment was again given to me. With Revered Maharaj's grace and blessings, I could work for the magazine for 14 years!

Maharaj encouraged monks and ordained brahmacharis to give classes in the Math. With his encouragement, I gave some classes on *Vivekachudamani* in 1987.

Becoming Vice-president

In March 1985, a phone call came from one of the Assistant Secretaries at the headquarters and requested Revered Maharaj to accept the chair of Spiritual Ministration. Since long, Revered Maharaj had stopped answering phone calls due to the difficulty he faced in listening to muffled voices over the receiver. The then manager, Swami Raghaveshananda Maharaj, communicated to Revered Maharaj this request of the headquarters. Revered Maharaj like a small child shaking his hands expressed his refusal to play the role of guru by saying "no, no, no"! Finally, however, he had to yield to the plea of the Trustees.

When Revered Maharaj was appointed as the vice-president, I was at that time in the Training Centre in Belur Math. Revered Maharaj requested the headquarters to send me back to Madras Math after the training. I could feel his love though he would never directly express it. When I was posted back to Madras Math, Revered Maharaj graciously accepted me as his personal secretary. I would then accompany Revered Maharaj to his office in the mornings. He would call me his assistant even though he never depended on anyone for his personal matters. Later, when he underwent a surgery, someone had to constantly attend on him.

My role as his assistant was limited even though it was to my full time duty. Revered Maharaj therefore deputed me to work in other departments part-time. According to the need of the hour, I was assigned duties in Library or in printing press or in dispensary. This was an important lesson for me – never to idle away the time.

Revered Maharaj allowed me to attend the classes on *prasthana traya* conducted in Sanskrit for monastics in the Math.

Brahmasri V Kalyanasundara Sastry, a reputed scholar in Nyaya, Advaita Vedanta and Vyakarana, and a lecturer in Sanskrit, Vivekananda College, Madras, would come to Madras Math for giving classes to the monastic members. Revered Maharaj himself would attend his classes for the pleasure of listening to Vedanta from a scholar of traditional upbringing.

Spiritual Ministration

After Revered Maharaj became a vice-president, he had to visit many centres of the Order to spiritually initiate the devotees. Revered Maharaj would travel by air. He would make arrangements for my travel by train. It is customary for the devotees seeking initiation to bring dhotis, fruits, money as offerings to the guru. Revered Maharaj would graciously accept these, but leave them behind with the in-charge of the centre (to be used by the monastics of that centre) – a demonstration of Sri Ramakrishna's teaching, both in letter and in spirit, that monks should not accumulate things.

Whenever Revered Maharaj visited Bangalore Ashrama, he would take me with him by flight. After I was fully ordained as a monk, I always travelled with him by flight.

In July 1988, Revered Maharaj visited Belur Math to attend the Trustees' meeting. Swami Mumukshananda Maharaj, head of Rajkot Ashrama, invited Revered Maharaj to visit Rajkot. I happened to be there in the room when Revered Maharaj was invited. Pointing towards me, Revered Maharaj replied, 'He is serving me so much. I am not doing anything for him. If you can show him around Rajkot and arrange for his *darsan* of Dwaraka and Somnath, then I'll come to Rajkot.' That was his extraordinary love and concern.

Affiliating Madurai Math

Ramakrishna Mandiram in Madurai was a religious establishment run by a group of devotees of Sri Ramakrishna.

Dr. Shanmugam, a prominent member of the *Mandiram* suddenly fell ill suffering from a heart ailment. He felt that the *Mandiram* should be affiliated to Ramakrishna Math and Mission to serve a larger purpose. He approached Revered Maharaj several times for getting the *Mandiram* affiliated. But the headquarters was not very keen on the affiliation. Once, when Revered Maharaj was hospitalized in Madras, the then General Secretary of the Ramakrishna Math and Mission visited him at the hospital. Revered Maharaj fervently appealed to him for affiliating the Madurai *Mandiram*. Due to Revered Maharaj's earnestness, the headquarters finally decided to affiliate the *Mandiram*.

Last Days

After Revered Maharaj took the great responsibilities of spiritual ministration, his body suffered from ailments like hypoglycaemia (reduced levels of blood sugar) due to which he would lose balance while walking. Somebody had to attend on him constantly. Once, with a touch of humour, he told me, 'What can be done? You cannot protect me from falling.' And it exactly happened that way. When I once just turned to meet a brahmachari for a minute, he had by then fainted and had fallen down.

Although he needed assistance in the nights, he rejected all my entreaties to permit me to stay in his room at night. In spite of his resistance, I would sneak into his room after he had retired to bed and sleep over a mat on the floor. It so happened once that when he woke up in the middle of the night to answer the calls of nature, he lost his balance even before he stepped down the cot and was about to fall. I then quickly held him from falling.

Working till the End

During Revered Maharaj's visit to Ulsoor Ashrama, Bangalore, in February 1991 in connection with the temple consecration, Swami Dayatmananda Maharaj casually asked Revered Maharaj, 'Maharaj, when are you going to retire?' Revered Maharaj replied, 'Well, they say I don't have retirement!' After uttering these words, he became grave and said, 'What for retirement? We have to do the Great Master's work till we give up our body!' And he did work for the 'Great Master' till the last moment of his life.

All through his life, he demonstrated the path of devotion and surrender to Sri Ramakrishna. In fact, He was a *jnani*, a *bhakta* and a *karmayogi* in one.

Revered Maharaj was always a source of inspiration and enlightenment for all those who met him. Whatever little I have learnt in my life is only through his grace! May he ever protect us is my prayer to him!

23

Can You Do It?

Swami Tattwarupananda[1]

I met Revered Tapasyananda Maharaj when I joined Sri Ramakrishna Math, Madras in October 1973. As he was a man of few words, he made brief enquiries about my health, education etc. He instructed me to study the book, *Life of Sri Ramakrishna,* which had a foreword by Mahatma Gandhi and make a summary of each page. He would then peruse through it. This, he said, would instil in us a habit of writing and retain in our memory the subject we have read. He insisted that we learn Sanskrit. A Sanskrit teacher would come every afternoon to teach us. Maharaj himself would attend the scriptural classes held in Sanskrit medium for monastics.

Maharaj would be very particular about the daily routine like attending *mangalarati,* japa, meditation, physical exercises and evening *aratrikam.* He would encourage only 30 to 45 minutes rest in the afternoons. He would insist on either physical exercise or gardening in the evenings before *aratrikam.* According to him, the evening *aratrikam* was very important because during that time, we honour the 'Great Master' and offer the fruits of our daily work at his feet. He would encourage us to sing if we had the talent. He would

1. He joined under Revered Maharaj in Madras Math in 1973.

recommend moderate eating to avoid affecting our studies and spiritual practices. Along with studies and japa, he would expect everyone to diligently and attentively work in their respective departments and ensure that the work is efficiently and perfectly done. He would say that the in-charge in the Bookstall had to properly display the books, enthusiastically explain about the books to the customer and guide them to select the book they want. He would encourage the reading of newspapers (to improve English - in vocabulary and style of writing). After others had finished reading the newspapers, he would read them for some length of time. He would appreciate and encourage any swami attempting to write books, articles etc. We have never seen him speak loudly or order us to do any work. He would rather politely ask, 'Are you free?', 'Is it possible to do this work?' or 'Can you do it?' and only then give him that work.

Austerity was reflected in every action of Maharaj's. His clothes would be simple. Occasionally he would wear a shirt; at other times, he would just cover his upper torso with a towel. He would take only simple food. Even while travelling by train, he would take only *idli* packets. It was instructive to see him use soap and soap powder sparingly while washing clothes, sharpen the shaving blades with a tumbler and reuse them, use the worn out dhotis as bedspreads! He would say that it was more meaningful to spend money in printing more books at concessional rates rather than in constructing buildings with brick and mortar. That way, the message of Sri Ramakrishna can spread.

Maharaj would say that life in the Order is to serve Sri Ramakrishna. He wanted every monk to dedicate

himself completely to Sri Ramakrishna's service and also pursue spiritual practices and studies. In fact, some aspects of the prescribed routine in the Training Centre at Belur Math were his suggestions.

Maharaj would be amused to read long titles of the speakers, like '*Sakalagunakalasampanna shiromani vidvatakhiladisha* etc.' printed in some invitations. We too would participate in the amusement.

In the night class for the monastics, he would explain the intricacies of various philosophical thoughts, emphasizing more on Visistadvaita. There were some objections from certain quarters in society to his book on *Sankara Digvijayam*, but he tenaciously explained the authenticity of his arguments. His opinion was that a lot of arguments can be raised in favour of any (even contradictory) stand-points. Sometimes the night classes would extend more than an hour if any topic required further explanations.

Although he was known to be a strict disciplinarian, it was a good experience for all who could associate themselves with him.

24

One Who Found Bliss in Austerity

Swami Asutoshananda[1]

The Beginning

Sometimes we rush to the railway station, only to find that the train had already left. These are not isolated experiences in our lives. It could happen in spiritual life too. All along we would have had the opportunity of staying with a holy saint, but before we begin to realize his greatness, he would have left the world. Most of the times, while we were in his company, we might have been busy noting his imperfections. But Time makes us realize what a great person he was and what a golden opportunity we have had to live with him! As we advance in age and gain experience, we begin to understand his life in all its glory. This has been the experience of many who have had the fortune of living with Swami Tapasyananda Maharaj.

After my studies, I spent some time in the Himalayas, and in 1982 I came to join Sri Ramakrishna Math, Madras. But I had no letter of introduction. I met Maharaj in his office and after enquiring about a few sundry things, he told me, 'I do not have much faith in the wandering style of the Himalayan life. Those who are habituated to a wandering

1. He joined Madras Math under Revered Maharaj and was with him for 9 years. He is currently the manager of Chennai Math.

life cannot settle down in one place and work. Life at the Ramakrishna Math is different from the Himalayan lifestyle and it requires a certain temperament to stay here. Therefore, it is difficult to admit you straightaway. However, you can stay here – food and accommodation will be provided to you; but other things like clothes etc. can be given only after a year.' Then with a stern voice, he told me, 'Stay here for a couple of years, carry out the duties assigned to you and prove yourself. Afterwards, I shall think about admitting you as a member of the Order.' Further, he asked me, 'Do you accept Sri Ramakrishna as an incarnation of God?' I replied, 'Yes.' 'Then all right,' he said and allowed me to stay in the Math.

As promised, he recommended for my admission into the Order only after two years. Although he had said that he would provide me clothes only after a year, after a week, he however gave me a set of clothes and all the other things I needed. Thus began my life in the Math under Revered Maharaj.

I was initially baffled at his stern dealings and appearance that gave me an impression that he was not a person who could be approached easily. But as days passed, he endeared me with his love, especially when he found that I had some interest in studies; it was one of his noble characteristics to encourage anyone in studies because he himself was one of the greatest thinkers and scholars of the Order.

Lighter Moments

After my joining, the brahmacharin who had been personally serving Revered Maharaj left for Belur Math [in

1982] to be ordained into *sannyasa* vows and I was given the opportunity to serve Revered Maharaj. When I was serving him - it was nothing more than doing two simple jobs—to carry a jug of hot water from the kitchen in the morning for his bath and to rinse his clothes. An austere monk that he was, he had very few personal needs, and even those few, he did not like others to perform for him.

Revered Maharaj used to mix hot water brought from the kitchen with a bucket of cold water and then bathe. One day the water from the kitchen was hotter than usual. So, after keeping the hot water in the bathroom I told him, 'Maharaj, today the water is very hot. Please take care.' On hearing that, he immediately went inside the bathroom and had a look at the jug containing the hot water. He then called me and said, 'It is not enough to simply possess a brain, you have to use it.' At first, I could not understand what he meant. I thought I was intelligent enough to have told him beforehand that the water was hotter than usual. But he explained: 'If the water was very hot, you could have brought lesser quantity so that I could have mixed it with the usual quantity of cold water. Now, I have to waste some hot water.' I understood that to be intelligent was not that easy!

The bath towel of Revered Maharaj was literally 'holesome'—there were more holes than the cloth! One day I told him to discard it and get a new one. 'I use this only to wipe out the water from the body after bath. I am not going to wear it and go outside. It is perfectly useful as a towel. And that is more than enough,' was his curt reply. I understood that he did not want to talk about this any further!

In his office, Madras Math

Once I was having some pain in my eyes. Doctors, after examination, advised me to wear dark glasses for a few months. As a novice, I was shy to wear dark glasses in front of others. But I was hesitant to tell Maharaj about it. So I would wear the glasses when I was with Maharaj and would remove them at other times! Days passed thus. But one day somehow I was caught! Thereupon, he severely rebuked me saying, 'What is given to you is not a necklace that you wear and remove it at your convenience; it is a pair of glasses which is to be worn all the time. I do not want to see you any more without the glasses on.'

Revered Maharaj's advice to the students and the brahmacharis was– 'Eat well, study well, and play well'. It was compulsory for all brahmacharis to either play or jog for an hour in the evening. Monks and brahmacharis would play shuttle badminton in the open courtyard in front of the present dining hall. He would be walking on the verandah observing us. One of the brahmacharis, who was a bit fat, used to fall down frequently while playing. If Maharaj happened to see this, he would, along with us, laugh heartily. Sometimes we would laugh so much that he would comment, 'They laugh like Ravanas!'

The present Universal Temple was not there in those days. What is now called as the 'Old Temple' was the main temple then. Before vesper service in the evening, frankincense used to be burnt in the temple, for which burning charcoal was taken from the kitchen. The brahmachari, who had been assigned the duty of carrying it, would generally pass through the courtyard while Maharaj walked and we played. If there was any delay in that brahmachari coming there, he would humorously ask, 'What happened to that "smoke man", he is not to be seen?!'—incense powder when sprinkled over live charcoal produces thick smoke, and for Maharaj, one who produces smoke is a 'smoke man'!

Tapasyanandaji with Purushotmanandaji of Vasishta Guha, Hrishikesh

Once, it was arranged to take a photograph of Revered Maharaj. A brahmachari was supposed to be the photographer. We were not sure whether Maharaj would agree to be photographed; however, it was decided that Maharaj would be requested to be photographed when he returned from his office at lunch time. A chair was arranged in front of the current *The Vedanta Kesari* office. Revered Maharaj came out of his office around 12.30 p.m. When Manager Maharaj requested Revered Maharaj to be photographed, he reluctantly agreed. He came and sat on the chair. The brahmachari who was supposed to take the photograph took a lot of time adjusting the flower pots around Maharaj. Then he got busy with adjusting Maharaj's clothes. Time was ticking away. Maharaj felt hungry. At last, after all other things were set right, the brahmachari went near Maharaj and requested him, 'Maharaj, please bend your head a little. Only then we can have a good photograph of you!' Instantly Maharaj replied, 'If you delay any further, I need not bend my head consciously, it would droop automatically!' We all laughed heartily.[1]

Once, a play on Sri Ramakrishna was staged in the Math. Maharaj never watched plays. However, the photos taken of the play were shown to him. In the play, Totapuri, one of the teachers of Bhagavan Sri Ramakrishna, was portrayed as wearing only a loin cloth. Then thinking that it may look indecent, the loin cloth was covered with a small towel hanging in the front. Seeing that photo of "Totapuri", Maharaj asked, 'Who is this man with vertical towel?' Such hilarious comments and phrases of Maharaj are there for us to enjoy forever!

These are some of the cherished memories that come to my mind when I think of Maharaj!

Dewdrop-influence

Dewdrops fall gently—unseen and unheard. Nevertheless profound is their influence in making the flowers blossom. Such was the gentle and yet profound influence of Maharaj on all those who were fortunate to come in contact with him. It is difficult to say how many

---

1. The photograph printed on the cover page was taken on this occasion.

truly realized how privileged they were to be with him. But in retrospect, it is clear that he had left a lasting impression on each and every one of those who came in close contact with him.

Revered Swami Tapasyananda Maharaj was one of the greatest monks produced by the Ramakrishna Order. In this light, whenever I think of him, it is his renunciation that instantly comes to my mind. Being a monk of the highest order, the material world had no glamour for him; he found no pleasure in the so-called pleasures of the world. He gave no importance to food or clothes or any other thing. He did not show interest in music, drama, or any other recreational activities.

Even the all-renouncing monks would like to go on pilgrimages. Maharaj had no interest even in pilgrimages. Dakshineshwar is the Kashi and Brindavan for the devotees of Sri Ramakrishna. But Maharaj was not keen even in visiting these places. He would visit Belur Math thrice a year for the meeting of the Trustees. It takes just half an hour to reach Dakshineshwar from Belur Math. But he would not go. 'Maharaj, have you ever visited Dakshineswar?' he was once asked, and his answer was, 'Yes, probably some 40 or 45 years ago.' To the question, 'Have you been to Himalayas?' he curtly replied, 'Oh, no!' He strongly discouraged such questions.

It should not be misconstrued that he had no faith in pilgrimages. For him, the real pilgrimage was to go within; diligently do Sri Ramakrishna's work with a pure mind. And for these, he felt austerity to be the only way. That is why he found bliss in austerities – he had no interest in the material world, reduced his needs to bare minimum, and did not accept anything for himself from others.

Another striking quality I found in Revered Maharaj was his treating others with respect. When he wanted to meet even a novice, he would not command, 'Tell him to come.' Rather he would send such messages like 'meet me when you find time' to that novice.

Again, I had never heard him use a language that would hurt the feelings of others. When angry, at the most, he would scold, 'Useless fellows, you don't have brains.' But, we never felt hurt by these words. On the contrary, we would enjoy his scolding. Not only the monastics, even the employees and devotees had felt the same way.

He was very unassuming. He would usually come at 12.30 p.m. to the dining hall for lunch, and the other monastic members would have finished their meal by then. He would help himself with the food kept ready on his plate. He did not like anybody to wait on him. If any item like salt was missing on his plate, he would not call anyone. He himself would go to the kitchen shelf and help himself.

Maharaj never liked anyone serving him, in spite of the fact that he was a senior monk and the president of the Math. Once, he was laid down with high fever – we came to know of it only when the temperature rose to 102 °F – earlier to this, he was bathing, attending to his work, writing etc. as usual. While he was down with fever and was lying on his bed, he felt uncomfortable and tried to vomit on the floor. Incidentally I was present there and rushed to get a bowl. I held it near his mouth for him to vomit into. Unwilling to be served, Maharaj pushed me away with his hand and held the bowl himself! Although it was a small incident, it made a profound impression on my mind.

Maharaj did not like monks or devotees hovering around him for no reason. It was customary for the monastics to offer *pranams* to him whenever he left the Math or returned. Maharaj did not even like that. Sometimes he would humorously say, 'You have no study habit, no involvement in work. What to do? Well then! This old monk is going out. Come on, let us all go and offer *pranams* to him. Like this you waste your time.'

Similarly, Maharaj did not like any monastic member accompanying him to go to the railway station or airport to see him off or receive him. He used to say, 'Send the car. The driver will help me transport my luggage. That's all what is needed.'

In his earlier days, Maharaj would travel alone to Belur Math by train. After persistent requests from the General Secretary Maharaj and other authorities, he agreed to travel by air, that too without any escort. Due to swelling in the legs, he had difficulty in walking and bending. Although many felt that he should not travel alone in this condition, he preferred to travel alone.

During one such visit to Belur Math, one of the Assistant Secretaries broached again to him the topic on having an escort. As expected, Maharaj disapproved the proposal. When the Assistant Secretary Maharaj persisted, Maharaj in his characteristic style remarked, 'You want an escort to accompany me so that he would help me in case I fell down, right? Let me explain. I am an old man, more so a monk. If I fall down, some co-passenger will definitely come to my help. Things have not deteriorated to such an extent in India that nobody would render help to an old monk in times of emergency. So, there is no need to take a monk as my escort spending Rs.2,000/-. Let us assume a monk accompanies me. What best he can do? He cannot do anything before my falling down.' Saying so he laughed; others too laughed. After some months, because of repeated pleadings by many, he consented to take his secretary swami with him.

Simplicity was his ornament. As the Vice-President of the Ramakrishna Order, he had to travel a lot for spiritually initiating the devotees. To take care of his things, a monk was assigned as his secretary. Till then he had only a couple of *dhotis*, shirts and *chaddars*. He used Lifebuoy soap. He will use it till it dissolved to a tiny piece. He would not then throw it away. He would put it into a tin. Later he would join all the tiny pieces and use them again! Similarly, he would not throw away the shaving blade after it gets blunt; he would sharpen it and reuse it! He even had a stone for sharpening his blades!

Simplicity was natural to Maharaj. He had led a simple life even in his younger days, even though he was born in a royal family. His younger brother, Sri Achutha Menon would sometimes stay at Madras Math. In the initial days, Maharaj gave permission to his brother only for his stay at the Math. It is said that he would tell his brother to take food in a nearby hotel. When other monks had requested Maharaj to permit his brother to take *prasad* (food) in the Math, he had told, 'Math is meant for devotees. Even though he is my brother, he is not a devotee. It is appropriate that he dines outside.' However, after repeated requests, he finally relented and permitted his brother to take *prasad* in the Math.

We would interact with Maharaj's younger brother when he stayed in the Math. Once he mentioned about the simple living of Maharaj. 'Both of us studied in Madras Presidency College and stayed in the College hostel. From our home money was sent to both of us every month. My lot would have been spent even before the end of the month. But my brother (Maharaj) would write home, 'I still have some money with me. Do not send any more now. I will write when I need more.' Then a letter would come from my mother scolding me, 'Both of you are staying in the same hostel, studying in the same college. He still has money left. How come you have exhausted all the money?'

Maharaj's mother would send a fixed amount every month to Maharaj. Those days he was the president of the Trivandrum Ashrama. As it was sent to him by his mother, he would take Re.1/-for himself and spend the rest on the poor living nearby the Ashram.

Maharaj disliked elaborate rituals and preferred them to be performed in a simple manner. In 1988, he had gone to Belur Math. A devotee there had gifted two costly sarees to decorate Holy Mother's photo. One of the sarees was given to Revered Maharaj for adorning Holy Mother's photo in Madras Math. While receiving the saree, Maharaj remarked, 'Somehow, I do not relish the idea of decorating the photo of Holy Mother with such a costly saree. We know that she liked to wear simple sarees in her lifetime. Anyway, since you are giving, I shall take.'

On another occasion, a few days before he left for Belur Math, the silver idol of Krishna and some silver vessels were stolen from Swami Brahmananda Maharaj's temple in Belur Math. Maharaj, on hearing about it, commented,

'We invited thieves by keeping silver items. After they have stolen, we lament. I do not think Sri Guru Maharaj has exhorted us to worship with such costly items. He would gladly accept a simple puja.'

Maharaj was unruffled in all circumstances. The bodily afflictions seemed to have no impact on him. Once, he was admitted to (perhaps) Vijaya Hospital for an operation in the urinary tract. He was administered anesthesia. In spite of all efforts, the operation was not successful. The monks and doctors were hesitant to inform Revered Maharaj about this. But Revered Maharaj must have guessed the situation after coming out of the anesthesia. He simply asked, 'Oh, the operation was unsuccessful?' And made light of the whole thing.

For Maharaj, time was precious. In spite of high administrative responsibilities of the Math, he continued his literary work. He would not waste time in talking to people unnecessarily. Even at the office, he would be immersed in his literary work. Some employees, volunteers and devotees were in the habit of offering *pranams* to him daily. He would repeatedly forbid them from doing so. Sometimes, after their *pranams,* he would enquire, 'What is the matter?' Generally, they would reply, 'To have your *darsan,* Maharaj.' He would simply retort, '*Darsan* is over, you may leave now.' He was very conscious of not wasting in gossip.

The literary work of Maharaj generally involved translating scriptures in Sanskrit into English. His original works are only very few like *Holy Mother Sri Sarada Devi,* the first authentic life of Mother in English and

Bhakti Schools of Vedanta, a unique work of its kind. His translations include – *Srimad Bhagavatam, Adhyatma Ramayanam, Sundara Kandam, Narayaneeyam, Bhakti Ratnavali, Stotra Ratna, Arati and Ramnam.* When someone asked him why is he doing more of translation work, he would say with all humility, 'What new thing can we write! Our great saints have already left enough spiritual treasures. Is it not a good fortune to translate these and make them available for a wider public? Is not this work a spiritual practice in itself?' Such was the humility and large heartedness of Maharaj, who was one of the greatest and most learned monks of the Ramakrishna Order! Even as a brahmachari, he was the editor of *The Vedanta Kesari,* one of the English periodicals of the Ramakrishna Order published from Madras Math. His editorials stand testimony to the depth of his knowledge!

Revered Swami Gahanananda Maharaj, the then Assistant Secretary and later the 14th President of the Ramakrishna Order, took keen interest in compiling the editorials of Revered Maharaj on Sri Ramakrishna and publishing them as a book. He had talked to Maharaj regarding this on several occasions. But Maharaj never approved the proposal. He would say, 'Those editorials were written in my early days. I have no interest in publishing them.' But Swami Gahanananda Maharaj did not give up; after the passing away of Revered Maharaj, he arranged for publishing it from Madras Math. The book is titled *Sri Ramakrishna's Thoughts on Man, World and God.* The book clearly reflects the depth and extensity of his knowledge.

The traits which made Maharaj stand apart were his devotion to and faith in Bhagavan Sri Ramakrishna. His life was totally dependent on Sri Ramakrishna. He usually referred to Sri Ramakrishna as the 'Great Master'. The way he would utter that word [Great Master] itself showed the depth of devotion and reverence he had for Sri Ramakrishna. Early morning at 4 a.m., he would sit on his cot and chant hymns on Sri Ramakrishna. Tears would trickle down his eyes and his voice would choke with emotional fervour.

In his later days, he was not able to prostrate on the ground or bend and offer his *pranams* to Sri Ramakrishna. However, he never failed to stand for a long time before Sri Ramakrishna in the temple on his way to the office at half past nine in the morning.

He had an unshakeable faith in the living presence of Sri Ramakrishna and in his saving grace under all circumstances. Once he had to go to a nearby place (perhaps Chengalpattu) by train. As usual, he went alone and did not take any escort. While he was leaving, the then Manager Maharaj requested Revered Maharaj to keep some money with him. To this Revered Maharaj replied, 'You people are taking me by car to the railway station and there too I will be received and taken to the destination, the travelling time is less than 2 hours, so what is the need for money?' When Manager Maharaj said, 'In case there is a delay and you have to eat something on the way...,' Maharaj was silent for a moment and said emotionally, 'Oh, I think we have forgotten the existence of Sri Guru Maharaj!' He had complete faith that Sri Guru Maharaj would take care of his needs at all times.

Traits like simplicity, austerity, purity which manifest in a person who has totally surrendered to the Lord were all natural in Revered Maharaj.

The End

One of the monks of our Order remarked, 'I consider it a rare privilege to contemplate on him and write on him, for, whatever I am today is nothing but his contribution!' Echoing that note and sentiment, I wish to conclude my reminiscences of Revered Maharaj.

Vedanta is the back-bone of Hindu Culture

Tapasyananda

13-11-84

25

His Humility

Swami Shantatmananda[1]

I came into contact with Revered Maharaj sometime in 1972. But the first significant interaction was in 1973 when I wanted Revered Maharaj's guidance regarding my spiritual initiation. I met him personally and discussed certain serious matters with him which had a great bearing on my life. Revered Maharaj helped me to subsequently get spiritually initiated by my guru. I continued to meet Revered Maharaj regularly till I joined the Holy Order at Bangalore in the beginning of 1977.

Within a short time I was transferred to Belur Math. It was during my stay of about 30 years in Belur Math that I met Revered Maharaj regularly whenever he came to the Math for the Trustees' meetings every four months. On most occasions, I went with Swami Atmapriyananda whom Revered Maharaj liked very much for his knowledge of the scriptures as well as of Ramakrishna-Vivekananda literature. Revered Maharaj would be overjoyed to see Swami Atmapriyananda (initially as a brahmachari and later as a fully ordained monk). I used to enjoy listening to

1. He was closely associated with Revered Maharaj from his student days.

Revered Maharaj's wonderful explanations of many intricate points in Indian Philosophy, particularly his explanations of the verses in the *Gita* correlating the commentaries Sri Sankara and Sri Ramanuja.

I, along with few others, met Revered Maharaj a few days after he had become one of the vice-presidents of the Order. We offered our *pranams* and told him that we were really happy that he had become one of the vice-presidents

and that he would soon be initiating the devotees into spiritual life. Immediately Revered Maharaj became grave and told us, 'I am reminded of the Holy Mother saying that the broomstick itself may be dirty, but it is used to clean dirty places.' We were simply dumbstruck at Revered Maharaj's humility and how he responded to his elevation to the post of vice-president.

Revered Maharaj had a unique way of guiding his disciples. A young man, an officer in the Indian Navy, who was spiritually initiated by Revered Maharaj, was in a dilemma about the future course of his life. He asked Revered Maharaj whether he should renounce the world or marry and become a householder. Without a moment's hesitation, Revered Maharaj advised him to select a good and healthy girl and marry her.

It was an elevating experience to meet Revered Maharaj and to be in his presence. His extraordinary simplicity and his deep interest in scriptural study were sources of great inspiration. Moreover, it was amazing to see how he would use every single minute in either reading or writing even amidst his busy schedule of meetings for which he would come thrice a year. Revered Maharaj used to take keen interest in other organizational matters such as finance, investments etc. My contact with Revered Maharaj for more than three decades gave me many opportunities to have detailed discussions on various topics with him. However, I am not able to recollect most of them.

26

Why Shirk From Responsibilities?

Swami Vyomatitananda[1]

During school days, probably when I was in 7th or 8th standard, I happened to read a book on Swami Vivekananda. Afterwards when I was in Pre-degree, equivalent to today's Higher Secondary, I read the third volume of the *Vivekananda Sahitya Sarvaswam* in Malayalam. When I was studying in my college, on a day when the college was on a strike, two classmates of mine and I visited Ramakrishna Math, Trichur. Afterwards, now and then, I would visit the Trichur Math. When I was working, I started thinking seriously about serving the cause of Swami Vivekananda. Once, when I expressed this idea to Revered Swami Mridananda Maharaj, he suggested me to join the Ramakrishna Order, and advised to join at its Madras centre. He asked me to send a letter addressed to the president, Sri Ramakrishna Math, Madras. I received a reply from Revered Swami Tapasyananda Maharaj.

As per the instructions of Revered Maharaj, I reached Madras Math in the night sometime during August 1984. Next morning, Revered Swami Tanmayananda Maharaj, the then Manager of Madras Math, took me to Revered

1. He joined Madras Math under Revered Maharaj and later served as in-charge of dispensary for several years.

Tapasyananda Maharaj's office and introduced me to Maharaj. Maharaj asked me why I chose Madras Math to join. I told it was Swami Mridananda Maharaj who suggested me to join Madras Math. Maharaj asked why Swami Mridananda asked me to join at Madras Math, to which I had no answer. On that day, I was wearing a jeans pant. Maharaj asked me why I was not wearing a dhoti. When I replied that I had brought only a lungi, a coloured dhoti, Maharaj expressed his displeasure and asked me to go to the market and purchase a white dhoti. Afterwards, he was pleased to see me wearing the dhoti. He then asked me about my personal details. When I told that I had come to the Math with one week's leave, he asked me to leave the Math after three days; he insisted that I should book my return journey ticket on that day itself. He further said if my intention to join the Math was really serious, I should take a long leave and stay in the Math, at least for a couple of months, before joining the Math. After staying in the Math for three days, I left.

On 4 January 1985, I finally joined Madras Math. Next morning, late Swami Desikatmananda Maharaj enquired about the smallpox marks on my face. I told him that I had suffered from both smallpox and chickenpox. He then took me to Revered Maharaj's room and told Maharaj that as I had already suffered from chickenpox, I could serve Maharaj. Maharaj readily agreed to this proposal. Then Swami Desikatmananda Maharaj informed me that Maharaj had contracted chickenpox. Thereafter, I began serving him.

I had absolutely no experience in serving others. But with his abundant patience he tolerated me and taught me how to serve a sick person. Just before getting chickenpox, he had suffered from a bout of diarrhea and lost all his physical strength when attacked with chickenpox. He had become so weak that one day he asked me to help him turn on to his side, as he was unable to turn himself. Although he was physically very weak, I would wonder at his clarity of thinking, orderly and methodical way of doing things.

From the beginning, I felt his special concern for me. I was serving him for nearly six months and not even once did he scold me. Instead of asking me to go for *mangalarati* and evening *aratrikam,* he asked me whether I know the timings of the *mangalarati* and evening *aratrikam.*

I had never handled a refrigerator before joining the Math. One day Maharaj asked me to bring prunes that had been sent by some foreign centre for dinner. The brahmachari in-charge of the kitchen asked me to take the bottle from the deep freezer. I told him that I had not handled a refrigerator before and so there was a chance of the bottle getting broken. But the kitchen in-charge asked me to pull out the bottle. I pulled the bottle and it fell on the floor and broke. The prunes, of course, could not be used. At dinner, Maharaj asked me about the prunes and I told him what had happened; he did not show any further interest in the prunes and never did he mention about it afterwards. When I cleaned the portable commode, he would see how I was doing it and would tell me how to wash it thoroughly with disinfectants. Like this, Maharaj would teach me many things.

After Maharaj recovered fully from chickenpox, for one year I worked in various departments of the Math. When Swami Desikatmananda Maharaj, who was looking after the Math Dispensary, wanted a transfer,

Maharaj asked me to look after the Dispensary. When I expressed my apprehension to shoulder such a huge responsibility, Maharaj did not listen to my objections and told emphatically 'I know you can do that work; why

In front of the Dispensary, Madras Math

are you shirking from responsibilities?' I had to yield to his persuasion. And I continued to work in Madras Math dispensary till the year 2009. I could serve in the dispensary for many years only through the grace of my guru, Revered Swami Tapasyananda Maharaj.

I had absolutely no idea about the work in the dispensary. Maharaj was instrumental in my learning the work. He, with abundant patience and understanding, would encourage me to take initiative, think independently and implement the decisions. After giving his approval, he never would ask me about the progress of the project or how it was being implemented. He had complete trust in me. Looking back now, I am surprised at the extent of his trust in me. During my six years of association with him, I got scolding from him only on one occasion for some administrative decisions. Even then, he listened to me when I explained and thereafter never did he mention about that incident.

Maharaj was particular that every monastic member does some physical exercise - either play badminton or do physical exercise, yogasanas etc. Monastic brothers would play shuttle badminton in the quadrangle between the temple (the present 'Old Temple') and the dining hall. Revered Maharaj would be walking on the verandah in front of the dining hall; he will walk from one end of the verandah to the other end, turn around, and stand for a minute, before resuming his walk in the opposite direction. Maharaj would observe those who were playing. While walking, Maharaj would never turn and look behind.

In those days we would have afternoon tea at 3.30 p.m. and dinner at 8.30 p.m. Nothing was provided in between. After playing badminton, the brothers would have some tea before attending *aratrikam*. Under the impression that Maharaj might not like us having tea at that time, we would run from the 'Old Temple' to the dining hall when Maharaj walked away from us! It is really amusing to recollect such small incidents!

While Maharaj had contracted chickenpox, he was staying above the Dispensary building. Swamis Tyagananda and Yatatmatananda, who were then brahmacharins, would go to his room and spend some 20 to 30 minutes with him after dinner. At that time, Maharaj would be in a very light mood. He would tell that the lizards gave him company during the day. He would observe the lizards moving on the walls and the ceiling of the room hunting small insects. I felt that he enjoyed spending his time in a light way for a short while.

At times, there would be some discussions during these quite informal gatherings. When he recovered from chicken pox, Br. Parthasarathy (now Swami Vishveshananda) and I would give him neem bath. I would prepare the water by keeping the water in the hot sun with some neem leaves in it and he would have his bath between 2 and 3 p.m. We would prepare a paste of neem leaves and used it as soap. He would enjoy these bathing sessions.

Maharaj was concerned about the health of the inmates of the Math. When I was in the Dispensary, he conveyed me to report to him about any inmate who was sick. Once when one brahmacharin was down with chickenpox, Revered Maharaj asked me to convey to that brahmacharin that due to his old age and difficulty in walking, he was not in a position to go to his room and therefore he had conveyed his enquiries about his health.

On another occasion, when one of the inmates had some cold and cough, I thought Maharaj need not be disturbed with such common problems. At that time he taught me that as the head of the Math, he must know the health of all the inmates and that it was my duty to inform him accordingly and not to inform him selectively. Whenever a monastic inmate was sick, he would ask me whether the doctor had advised him any special diet and if so, to inform the kitchen in-charge accordingly.

In general, everyone should come to the dining hall in time. Whenever someone was not able to come to the dining hall due to illness, food had to be served in the room, but immediately after the recovery, he should come to the dining hall. Again he was very particular that all should leave the dining hall immediately after the food; no gossip was allowed in the dining hall.

Maharaj would encourage me in adding new facilities in the Dispensary. In fact, he wanted development in all the departments of the Math. During his time the printing press – first offset press of Madras Math – and the generator were acquired. Ultrasound services, Physiotherapy, ECG, Pediatrics and rural medical work were added during his time. Whenever any new proposal regarding the Dispensary was submitted to him, his only question would be, 'Is it going to be of any use to the general public?', for the money donated by the devotees should be utilized fully for public welfare. He would enquire about the manufacturers from whom we purchased drugs for the Dispensary. He would further tell me that we should give quality medicines and patients should feel that even though the medicines were given free, they were of good quality.

When we purchased the first Ultrasound scanner, Maharaj was very anxious to have a qualified and experienced doctor to give quality reports to the patients. In this instance also, he clearly told me that no patient should feel that our reports are inaccurate or unreliable because our charges were low.

I was posted back to Madras Math after my training in Belur Math. When I returned, I saw Revered Maharaj's health had deteriorated completely. Within two or three months, much against his wishes, he was admitted into the Vijaya Health Centre. Revered Swami Atmasthananda Maharaj came to Madras for this purpose and got Maharaj admitted to the Vijaya Health Centre. He was in the hospital for almost 5 weeks. By then, his health improved and he came back to Madras Math. He stayed in the Math for nearly two months and afterwards he was admitted to the BSS Hospital. He was unconscious for seven days. He regained his consciousness and asked, 'Sukantho, How are you?' Sukantho was one of the *sevaks* Belur Math had sent in March 1991. This incident showed that there was no loss of memory, though he was unconscious for one week. When he was unconscious, we could see that his tongue was always moving as if he was doing japa constantly. After a few days, he breathed his last.

His face radiated a beautiful smile. I had not seen such a beautiful smile when he was alive. Whenever that smiling face comes to my mind, I feel that was the smile of contentment that he had attained his goal in life – he had had the vision of Sri Ramakrishna. Such expressions on the face of *bhaktas* who have attained *mahasamadhi* reassure us the presence of Sri Ramakrishna and is looking after the *Sangha*. Thus ended the life of an illustrious son of Sri Ramakrishna who dedicated his entire life as a *tapasya* in serving the living form of the Master - the Ramakrishna Order.

27

We Are Also Your Brothers

Swami Lokahitananda[1]

I had the opportunity of meeting and interacting with Swami Tapasyananda Maharaj a few times. I came to Madras to attend a symposium on tuberculosis and stayed at Madras Math from 15 December 1981 to 22 December 1981.

Revered Maharaj requested me to deliver a public lecture on Holy Mother on 20 December 1981 which happened to be a Sunday. As I was not used to public speaking, I was reluctant. However, persuaded by him I had to agree. I spoke on the life of Holy Mother. After the speech, Revered Maharaj expressed his appreciation but added that I should have also talked about some of the teachings of the Holy Mother. He was very keen on monastics seriously studying the scriptures and felt that they would not do so unless compelled to conduct classes for the public.

Once during my short stay at Madras Math, my sister came to meet me. Maharaj told her, 'We are also your brothers; you should come and meet us too!'

---

1. He is a senior monk of the Order who knew Revered Maharaj for many years.

I next met him in Trivandrum, probably in 1982, when he came and stayed for a few days there. Although he was not keeping good health, he cheerfully and enthusiastically met many devotees and humourously conversed with them.

Dr. T.D.G Pillai, who served as Honorary Physician in our Trivandrum Hospital for 26 years, told me once that he was attracted to Swami Tapasyananda Maharaj since he saw him going to various places with worn-out slippers.

I have heard that even while waiting for the train in the railway station he would be preparing drafts for his literary works.

Starting straight away as a Guru

Swami Tapasyananda Maharaj had a natural sense of humour, which he used to amuse the people who attended his classes. Once he told a story of a would-be disciple going to an ashrama and enquiring from the Guru about the respective duties of the Guru and the disciple. The Guru explained that the disciple should work hard like cleaning, cooking and other such manual work while the Guru would sit down and give advice and instructions to the disciple. Thereupon, the would-be disciple exclaimed: 'Okay then, I would like to straight away start as a Guru!'

—Swami Nityakamananda

28

Mother at Heart & Father in Dealings

Swami Jnanaswarupananda[1]

The Turning Point:

In 1983, I began to visit and do some service in Salem Ashrama under the loving guidance and care of Swami Vijnananda, who was the head. I also would attend his scriptural classes on Sundays.

It was in 1985 when we were busy preparing for the inauguration of the Sri Sarada Hall at the Salem Ashrama. Revered Swami Tapasyananda Maharaj was to come from Madras to inaugurate the Hall and also to give spiritual initiation to aspiring devotees. One day my friend suggested me to take spiritual initiation from Maharaj. I did not know what spiritual initiation was and he explained it to me. I took his suggestion seriously and prepared myself for getting spiritual initiation. On 14th of October, I was spiritually initiated in the newly inaugurated Sri Sarada Hall along with 36 devotees. This was the second occasion when Maharaj gave spiritual initiation; the first one was at Cossipore. The third occasion was at Madras Math itself.

---

1. He was initiated by Revered Maharaj and joined Madras Math in 1985 under him.

After receiving initiation, my mind got completely changed and I immediately decided to embrace monastic life. On Friday, 18th October, I met my guru and told him, 'I want to join the Order.' He told me, 'Yes. You can join at Madras.' He further asked, 'When are you coming?' I told him that I would reach Madras on the subsequent Monday.

As scheduled, I reached Madras at noon and waited there as the gates of the Math would be opened only by 4 p.m. On reaching Madras Math, I was taken to the dining hall for the evening tea. I saw a plate on the table carefully covered. Someone told me that Maharaj had instructed them to keep the food for me. I palpably felt his love and concern for me!

Maharaj's life was very simple. He used an old dhoti as his bed sheet and two or three folded dhotis as a pillow. As long as his health permitted, he never allowed anyone to wash his clothes.

Encouragement for Further Studies:

Maharaj always encouraged novices to study further so that they would be more useful in serving the Sangha. After completing my regular studies I was doing M.A in Tamil literature. Before joining Madras Math I had completed the first year of M.A. One day Maharaj called me and advised me to complete the M.A Course. He arranged for my fees and other things.

Maharaj's Food:

In 1989, I was serving in the kitchen and one of my assignments was to take the breakfast for Maharaj to his room [as his health did not permit him to come to the main dining hall]. Just five minutes before the bell rang for the breakfast, I would usually take his breakfast to his room. One day I reached his room one minute late. He was waiting as usual. Seeing me he asked, 'Why late by a minute?' I had no reply. He was very punctual in his routine.

Often while taking his food, he would tell some Malayalam root words and ask me the Tamil equivalent. By this comparison, he pointed out the similarities in these sister languages.

He once read in the newspaper that chillies and excess salt were harmful to health. Thereafter, he instructed me about the number of chillies and the quantity of salt to be used in the food.

Morning Exercise:

Maharaj would regularly walk on the verandah outside his room. One day he asked me whether I exercised. I told him that I did yogasanas regularly. He felt jogging would do me good and instructed me accordingly.

Admonition to a Friend:

Once, one of my college friends came to meet me. Since his wife was a student of the Sarada College at Salem,

I thought of taking him to Maharaj for his blessings. I asked him to make *pranam* to Maharaj. He did that reluctantly. Perhaps that was the first time he ever did *pranam* to a monk! Then Maharaj asked him, 'Have you read the *Bhagavad Gita*?' It was an unexpected question, and he replied, 'No, I haven't.' 'You are a Hindu, and you have not read the *Bhagavad Gita*?' Maharaj admonished him seriously. He instructed him to read the *Bhagavad Gita* regularly. My friend, like many people, was under the impression that *Bhagavad Gita* was to be read only after retirement!

Admonitions to Me:

I had the opportunity of personally serving Maharaj for about a year including a month's stay with him at the Vijaya Hospital. Suryanarayanan Maharaj and I used to give Ayurvedic oil massage to his feet. I was a novice in the art of massaging and his feet were very soft. So I had to be very careful while moving my fingers downwards. Sometimes unknowingly I would give more pressure with my fingers and that would cause him pain. Maharaj would then admonish me. But I took it as his blessing to improve myself because I knew that in his heart of hearts, he had only love and no grudge against me.

Maharaj's Steadfastness in Spiritual Practice:

Maharaj would sit on the chair and do japa and meditation. Then he would chant some hymns from his memory. Once, he was admitted to the Vijaya Hospital for some ailment. I was staying in the hospital and serving him for a month. Before the operation, when the doctors were to give him anaesthesia, he requested them to give only local anaesthesia so that he could carry on his japa.

Maharaj's Strong Will:

A young man was admitted near our ward for the similar ailment and was operated on at the same time. After the operation it took more than a week for the young man to get up from the bed and walk, whereas Maharaj insisted on walking just after the second day of the operation. That was his will power!

I too once had a minor operation. After the operation I was staying in the guest room. On his way to the office, he would visit me and enquire about my health. After a few days, before the bandage was removed, he told me, 'Now go and work in the shrine. Nothing will happen to you.' Although I felt a little uncomfortable, it proved to be more joyful than simply lying on the bed.

Two Brothers and a Sister at Puri:

For nearly one and a half years, I had the blessed opportunity to stay with my guru and serve him.

But I had to leave for Belur Math for the training. Before leaving, Amlan Maharaj and I went to offer our *pranams* to him and informed him about our proposal to visit Puri on the way to the Belur Math. He remarked, 'Oh, you are going to Puri. Go and see the two brothers and a sister there together.' With his blessings, we went to Puri and had *darshan* of Sri Krishna, his brother Balarama and his sister Subhadra - a strange combination of deities, not seen in other temples.

Our Seva to Maharaj at Belur Math:

Revered Maharaj would come to Belur Math for the Trustees' meetings. Being his disciples, Sridhar Maharaj and I were allowed to serve him during our free time. We had the opportunity to serve him food, wash his clothes, and accompany him during his evening walks. There were also discussions about scriptures, saints, and Ramakrishna-Vivekananda Literature. Maharaj was very fond of discussing *Bhavamukha* of Sri Ramakrishna. Swami Atmapriyananda was one of the visitors who would pose questions to Maharaj. We were amazed at Maharaj's depth of knowledge in different subjects. I had seen him incessantly read or write or translate books as much as his health allowed, resulting in 8 biographies, 6 in-depth studies on Ramakrishna-Vivekananda Literature and Bhakti Literature, and 17 translations. One remarkable thing is that he used to give us the entire *pranami* (money offered to him) he received from devotees during his stay at Belur Math. I found that at heart he was a mother, and in dealings he was a strict father!

Last meeting with Maharaj:

In 1991, when I was still in the Belur Math Training Centre, I heard the sad news that Maharaj was very ill. He was admitted in the Vijaya Hospital. I wanted to see him. I also came to know that Swami Gahanananda Maharaj, the then General Secretary, was going to Madras to visit him. When I sought permission to go to Madras and see my guru, he consented.

After reaching Madras Math, I went to see Maharaj in the hospital. He was unconscious. I spent some time there. It was in the evening and he was taken around in a wheel chair. I simply stood and saw him go past. A thought came to my mind: 'This is last time that I am seeing him.' With a heavy mind I returned, thinking that hereafter my life was not going to be the same. I would miss him forever.

Although he recovered a little, after a month, he again became very sick. On 3 October 1991, on *Ekadasi*, he passed away. After hearing the news, I was very much shocked and an unspeakable grief possessed my heart. I sat for a long time at the Training Centre Prayer Hall. With other disciples I took *havisanna* (boiled rice taken with ghee along with boiled vegetables) at Belur Math for 13 days, praying and remembering his inspiring life.

Years later, I visited his parental house at Ottapalam in Kerala from Coimbatore to pay my homage.

Inside the Dispensary, Madras Math

29

Observe and Join

Swami Satyajnanananda[1]

I was at Salem, my native place, and was employed in the Steel Authority of India Ltd. (SAIL) for a short period. Prior to that, I was at Madras, and though a bachelor, I was interested in religion and used to spend time in chanting and visiting temples. Although I was only casually reading the books of Swami Sivananda of Divine Life Society, it inspired me to lead a spiritual life. Strange as it may appear, I could not sleep or be comfortable at my home in Salem quite contrary to my Madras days! My serious introspection led me to our Salem Ashrama. It was in 1982 that I was advised to decide at once [whether to join the Order] as I was already 25 years old. And this took me to our Mylapore Math at Madras and in turn to Revered Swami Tapasyananda Maharaj. He advised me to take 'maximum leave' of my duties at SAIL, stay at the Mylapore Math, observe, and then decide about joining the Order. He was very particular that I should not repent later. Also, he suggested that I bring some money with me so that *en route* to the Training Centre at Belur Math, I may visit our Centres at Vishakapatnam, Vijayawada etc. But as my request for 'leave' was not granted, I resigned the job and joined the Order at Madras submitting myself totally to the guidance

---

1. He joined Madras Math under Revered Maharaj and stayed with him for many years.

of the Revered Maharaj. I was secure and confident in his fatherly stature and felt no tension or anxiety.

He was very particular about our physical exercise, running and playing games. Just behind the 'Old Temple', in front of the dining hall, many of us used to play badminton. He changed the venue lest the noise should disturb the devotees in the shrine. He insisted on everyone attending the *mangalarati* and the night class. He would invariably question us as to what we had understood in every session. On a Sivaratri night, I could not keep awake. Later when I told him that I had slept off, he did not reprimand me, though he himself had adhered to the discipline. He was a great scholar. By simple and austere living he inspired everyone to tread his path.

Tackling the frightened babies

On the day of *Vijaya Dashami*, babies would be brought to Swami Tapasyananda Maharaj for initiating them into the world of learning. The babies had to be made to write some letters on a sheaf of rice sitting on the lap of the Swami. But invariably, these babies would get frightened to leave their parent and sit on the lap of Maharaj. However, Maharaj would affectionately and smilingly play with the baby that it would accept him as its chum and cooperate to write!

—Swami Nityakamananda

30

Don't Just Read, But Study!

Swami Vimurtananda[1]

I had the blessed opportunity to spend four years with Revered Swami Tapasyananda Maharaj, of which I was fortunate to be his *sevak* and physically serve him for three years, from 1987 till March 1991.

His Orderliness

'*Sariramaadyam khalu dharma saadhanam* – the body is an instrument for practice of Dharma' say the scriptures. Revered Maharaj literally followed this dictum. Whether it was working, writing, lecturing, praying, bathing, exercising or resting etc., there was orderliness in whatever he did. He considered his body to be an instrument given to him for doing good work and therefore he paid every attention to keep the body fit and healthy.

He would diligently use water; he would bathe with 10 litres of water, use a litre or two of the remaining water to rinse his clothes, and would still use the remaining water for cleaning toilet!

In those days, I did not know how to use water diligently. I would lavishly use water and then receive his

1. He was initiated by Revered Maharaj. He joined Madras Math in 1987 under Revered Maharaj. He is currently serving as the editor of *Sri Ramakrishna Vijayam*.

All Left to Right (sitting below): 2. Satyajnanananda 4. Vireshananda 7. Sukritananda 9. Kumarananda 10. Kamalatmananda 12. Vimurtananda; Nityamuktananda (kneeling); Standing: 1. Nandananda 2. Jnanadananda 4. Raghaveshananda 5. Aparokshananda 7. Jnanaswarupananda 9. Kapalishananda; Standing behind: 2. Tyagananda 3. Asutoshananda

admonition! Revered Maharaj would then explain, 'We read in the Vedas – *aapo vai brahma* – water is Brahman. If we waste that Brahman, can we grow spiritually?' This question would make anyone thoughtful.

When I was serving Revered Maharaj, his age would have been above eighty. Walking was his only physical exercise. But daily after bath, he wanted us to wipe his body with a soft towel first and with a rough towel again applying some pressure; he felt that that would give sufficient exercise to his skin.

His Gardening

Revered Maharaj was an expert in gardening. Like everything else, he paid full attention to the details like what soil was suitable for which plant, how to maximize the yield, how to fully utilize the produce etc.

For example, he planted many coconut trees in Madras Math. When enquired why, he explained: 'It is not only for the coconuts, the leaves could be used for thatching the roofs, the hard portion of the leaves could be used for fencing, we would get tender coconuts, fully ripened coconuts and dried coconuts. Even the trunk of the tree can be used as a pillar! So every part of the tree is useful to us...'

One fine morning, it drizzled a bit and a cool breeze set in. Looking at the plants in the garden, Revered Maharaj exclaimed: 'Look, these are dancing with joy! Do you see?!' He had the sensitivity to understand the feelings of the plants.

With Children

Revered Maharaj always looked regal. It was impossible for those people whose minds were running amok to approach him. But children and students would really be free with him. His constant advice to the students who visited him would be: 'Work well, Eat well, Play well, Pray well, Sleep well.'

Sometimes when enthused, he would hold his steel walking stick drawn in front of his chest and suddenly fold it into three parts; then again straighten it back! He was very fond of entertaining the children this way!

We would visit the poor children in Ramakrishnapuram in Mylapore, Madras, and coach them in their academics in a building which was owned by the Math. The work was entrusted to me from 1987 for a few years. The classes were held on Saturdays. On Sundays, those children would visit the shrine in the Math, then cursorily visit the library, and then meet Revered Maharaj. He was fond of conversing with those children with his smattering of Tamil, which would be a scene to watch!

I left for the Training Centre at Belur Math in March 1991. While replying to one of my letters, Revered Maharaj once wrote, '...After you left, the children of Ramakrishnapuram do not come here regularly. Please write to them and ask them to regularly visit the Math as usual...'

Perhaps it was in 1989 a 12 year old American boy visited India travelling all alone. I do not remember who brought him to the Math. Revered Maharaj highly appreciated the boy's courage and conversed with him for half an hour.

His Training

Revered Maharaj showed exceptional care for monks and brahmacharis. He wanted all of them to be adept in scriptures. He would encourage those who were studying the scriptures and would admonish others to study. To those who were acquainted with scriptures, he would guide them further. He would encourage them to give lectures and write for magazines.

Once, I showed a few books to Revered Maharaj and asked, 'What shall I read, Maharaj?' Immediately came his reply, 'Don't read anything, but study.' He wanted us to deeply study, not casually read the books.

In my initial days at the Math, out of some enthusiasm, I wrote about Sri Sarada Devi's grace in English to the best of my understanding and showed it to Revered Maharaj. But Revered Maharaj was renowned for his proficiency in

English. So instantly I realized my folly in showing him my 'English article'! But he said, 'You have tried to write something. Good. You learn to write in Tamil.' It was the grace he showered on me that day that has enabled me to become an editor of the Tamil magazine of the Order.

Once Revered Maharaj said, 'Those who join the Math must learn puja, cooking, accounting and gardening. Then they would be able to perform well in any branch of our Order.'

In 1988, on the eve of Swami Vivekananda's birthday celebration (Tithi puja), Revered Maharaj summoned me. As usual, I ran to him 'like a gazelle' (as Revered Maharaj would refer to my running!). When I met him, Revered Maharaj enquired, 'Do you know how to perform special puja[1]?' 'I know to some extent.' I mumbled. 'Vinaykananda (Kamat Maharaj) said that you know to do special puja. Tomorrow you perform the special puja and *homa* for Swamiji [Swami Vivekananda],' was his command. I felt as though the earth was quaking under my feet and the sky falling on my head. I froze in shock and fear. I had studied the mantras of special puja to some extent, and I could have managed the puja to some extent with the help of *tantradharak* swami. But I had no know-how of homa and I tried to tell that to Revered Maharaj, though very feebly. Who had the courage to tell him boldly! I just stood there like a statue. I do not know what he made out of it. But he said, 'What is the use of standing in front of me? Go and make the arrangements for the puja.' I came out running not knowing what to do. I broke down before Kamat

1. An elaborate puja that is performed on the birthdays of the Holy Trio.

Maharaj and explained to him what had happened. But that Swami assured me, 'Why are you so confused when your guru's blessings are upon you in this way? I will assist you in everything during puja, don't worry.' In spite of his assurance, only I knew my apprehensions. At 7.00 p.m., I began to learn the mantras and by 11 p.m., I had gained some confidence.

Before the puja the next day, I took Revered Maharaj's blessings and then entered into the temple. Kamat Maharaj told me, 'Pray to Sri Ramakrishna thus: "Sri Guru Maharaj, please accept the puja performed by me."' During puja, I felt that I was only an instrument and all mantras came to my mind at the appropriate time. After the puja, I offered my *pranams* to Revered Maharaj. Revered Swami Veetabhayananda Maharaj, who was present there, told Revered Maharaj that 'he [referring to me] had done the puja very well'. Revered Maharaj replied, 'Yes. Initially he lacked confidence. But I forced him to do it.' What?! Did he force me? He showered his grace upon me! I went to Revered Maharaj after doing the *arati* to Sri Ramakrishna. He made funny gestures by moving his hands up and down and amusingly asked me, 'While doing *arati*, did your hands move like this?!'

Once, a 17-year old boy from Kerala came to join the Math. Revered Maharaj told him, 'You now study a course on Sanskrit in our Vivekananda College. Later, when we are sure of your committed decision to lead a monastic life, you can join the Math.' The boy gave several justifications. But Revered Maharaj's reply was decisive when he said, 'Now, at this stage, I cannot trust your monastic aspiration completely.' The boy studied and obtained his degree.

But as predicted by Revered Maharaj, he could not lead a monastic life and therefore left the Math.

His Personality

Revered Maharaj did not know what words like 'jolly mood', 'time pass', 'picnic', 'leisure', 'entertainment' etc. meant. Because of this, many thought him to be a 'dry sadhu'. Some people had some false notions that he preferred seclusion; he was unwilling to speak with others etc. In my initial days at the Math, I too was misled. But all those who had moved closely with him knew that all these notions were completely wrong. Not realizing his greatness earlier, I missed too many opportunities to freely interact with him.

In 1989, somehow the denture Revered Maharaj wore did not fit in properly. It produced some discomfort thereby obstructing his flow of thought. Once he asked me, 'How is my new denture?' Without much thought, I said, 'With this denture, you look very serious.' He gave a faint smile as he went slowly bending his head.

Many devotees would visit the Math to have Revered Maharaj's *darsan*. Instead of merely offering them *prasad*, Revered Maharaj would be keen to know about their lives, their career, their families, the books they read etc.

Having accustomed to being 'shown' love, Revered Maharaj's unexpressed love was new to us. Whether with monks, devotees, disciples or scholars, he was particular in providing them only what was really necessary for their welfare and development.

Once, Revered Swami Atmasthananda Maharaj came for the golden jubilee celebrations of Sarada Vidyalaya,

Madras. The secretary of the School, Sri Sivaraman, made grand arrangements for the celebrations. Revered Atmasthananda Maharaj was honoured with an ochre dhoti made of silk. On reaching the Math, he gave that cloth to Revered Tapasyananda Maharaj and requested him thus: 'Maharaj, please accept this silk dhoti. I make a fervent plea that you wear this when you initiate the devotees.' But Revered Maharaj, with much hesitation said, 'No Maharaj. I do not wear such clothes. You should forgive me.' But Revered Atmasthananda Maharaj did not relent so easily. He persisted. So Revered Tapasyananda Maharaj used the silk dhoti once during spiritual initiation, that too with much reluctance. As soon as the initiation was over, the first thing he did was to go to his room, remove the silk dhoti and wear his usual one.

When Revered Tapasyananda Maharaj once entered Sri Ramakrishna's temple in Belur Math, Pujari Maharaj gave him *arghya* to be offered to Sri Ramakrishna. But Revered Maharaj politely refused. When enquired why, Revered Maharaj said, 'What right do I have to offer this *arghya* to Sri Ramakrishna? Did I plant the trees which gave the *bilva* leaves and flowers? Somebody else had planted it. Did I at least do something for these plants to grow? Did I at least water these plants once? No. When I have not done any of these things, what right do I have to pluck and offer them to Sri Ramakrishna?'

His Inimitable Tribute

In 1988, the then president of the Ramakrishna Order, Revered Swami Gambhirananda Maharaj, attained *mahasamadhi*. Revered Tapasyananda Maharaj, in the memorial meeting, revealed his reverence and devotion to Revered Gambhirananda Maharaj. He said:

'In Hindu tradition, we call those who have written commentaries to the *prasthana traya* (*Upanishad, Gita* and *Brahmasutras*) as *acharyas*. Sri Sankaracharya, Sri Ramanujacharya and Sri Madhvacharya have written their commentaries. In our Ramakrishna tradition, Swami Gambhirananda Maharaj also has translated and written commentaries to the *prasthana traya*. Therefore, he is our *Acharya*, Guru.'

Last Days

One day, the blood pressure of Revered Maharaj dropped so drastically that he stumbled and fell down while walking. He was admitted to Vijaya Hospital, Madras, for treatment. Swami Sukritananda Maharaj, I, and a few others served him. Even in the hospital, he was busy proofreading the manuscript of the book, *Bhakti Schools of Vedanta*.

Most of the nurses in the hospital were from Kerala. Those nurses, who were Christians, began to interact freely with Revered Maharaj when they came to know that his mother-tongue was Malayalam. They shared their difficulties with him and got solace. It was nice to see the affection the nurses had for him and the concern he had for them.

It is very rare to see those who completely devote their life to help others grow physically, mentally and spiritually. It is only through God's grace that I could live with and serve such a great personality!

31

My Life Support

Swami Nishthatmananda[1]

'Hmm…' said Revered Swami Tapasyananda Maharaj when I offered my *sastanga pranams* to him. I stood before him with folded hands with a mixed feeling of joy and fear. It was joyful because it was my first private meeting with him, though on many occasions I had *darsan* of him from a distance. It was fearful because I did not know how to talk to a senior swami like him and was afraid about my language and conduct. Maharaj was seated facing west in his office. His office was in the extreme left room on the ground floor of the Holy Mother's Centenary Annexe building. For half a minute there was silence. I was waiting for Maharaj to ask me something. I was perspiring heavily. My voice was choked as I finally said, 'Maharaj, I just wanted to do *pranam* to you.''Ooof! Again! Wasting the time,' Maharaj said frowning at me. I was trying to say that I had come to do *pranams* to him and that it was over. But Maharaj misunderstood that I wanted to do *pranam* for a second time. Then I remembered his *sevak*, Swami Sukritananda Maharaj's instruction given before I entered Maharaj's room, that I should talk a bit loud as Maharaj was a little hard of hearing. I went close to him and shouted, 'Maharaj,

1. He was initiated by Revered Maharaj and joined Madras Math under him.

I have already offered my *pranams*.''Fool! Am I closing my eyes? I know that.' I suppressed my laughter lest I should get another scolding. I didn't know how to proceed further.

I gazed at him with an odd mixture of embarrassment, contrition and incomprehension. Then Sevak Maharaj entered in and told me, 'You tell clearly what you want to say.' I stared at him. This caused further anxiety to Revered Maharaj who said, 'That fellow is already confused and you are troubling him further.' Then Sevak Maharaj helped me in taking up the conversation further with Revered Maharaj by saying, 'Maharaj, he is Vijayaraghavan, working in a bank, in Madras itself.'Then turning towards me he asked, 'Which bank?' I replied, 'IOB'. He then said, 'Tell the full form of IOB.' I replied, 'Indian Overseas Bank.' Then Sevak Maharaj in turn told Revered Maharaj, 'He is working in Indian Overseas Bank and also studying in college?' Maharaj raised his head and looked at me, 'Studying in college also? How is it?' Then, when I was about to reply, Sevak Maharaj intervened and signalled me to keep quiet and himself told Revered Maharaj, 'Maharaj, he is studying in evening Law College.' I realized that Revered Maharaj became serious as he said, 'Hmm…That's good. Are you going to give up bank job and practice law?' I didn't have any ready answer for his question as I was studying in Madras Law College just for time pass and not with any serious motive. Understanding my difficulty Sevak Maharaj told to Maharaj, 'Maharaj, he has not decided. He is just studying.' Then Sevak Maharaj signalled me to move out but I hesitated as I felt that the conversation had ended abruptly. I wanted to offer my *pranams* once again before taking leave of Maharaj, but I was afraid that it would create unpleasantness again and therefore stepped back and waited outside the room.

After a few minutes, Sevak Maharaj came out of the room holding a few files in his left hand and an umbrella in his right hand with his back pushing one of the swing doors. When I rushed to pull the other swing door, Revered Maharaj came out. Seeing me Revered Maharaj told Sevak Maharaj, 'Tell him to take *prasad* and go.' Sevak Maharaj signalled to me to stay back and as I stood, he held the umbrella for Maharaj who started moving. Instead of waiting there, I too followed them. After entering into a courtyard, Sevak Maharaj told me to stop there and they proceeded further. They climbed the staircase that led to the first floor of the opposite building and entered a room in the extreme right corner. I felt extremely peaceful. My heart was filled with joy. After a while, Sevak Maharaj led me to the dining hall and arranged for my taking the *prasad*. To my surprise, it was a full meal. I thought *prasad* meant a cup of cooked items or fruits. It was a sumptuous meal and I felt very happy. This incident happened towards the end of 1986. Although initially there was fear and hesitation, later I derived inner strength, confidence, inspiration and peace.

I was 25 years then. Until then, I had never met anyone whose image brought me inexplicable mental strength and solace. Maharaj's question, 'Are you going to give up the bank job and practice law?' was lingering in my mind although I was not at all serious about my study of law. But the idea of giving up the bank job was sown in my mind. Attraction and attachment towards parents, job, close friends and other dear ones began to lose their hold on my mind and my heart was longing for Sunday mornings to have the *darsan* of Maharaj. My regular Sunday visits gave me an idea about Maharaj's office timings. I would arrive at the Math and stand by the prayer hall waiting for

Maharaj to pass by on his way to his office. Exactly by 9.30 a.m., Maharaj would come holding the walking stick in his right hand. His *sevak* would be accompanying him holding the umbrella for Maharaj. Seeing me, Maharaj would slow down his walk and say to Sevak Maharaj, 'Long fellow has come, he will do long *pranam*!' As I was tall, and would also stretch my hands while offering *sastanga pranams,* I would require nearly 9 feet of space before Maharaj.

Once while offering my *pranams,* my leg hit a flower pot and it tumbled down. With great fear, I hurriedly got up, put back the flower pot to its place, and turned again to touch Maharaj's feet. Thereupon Maharaj laughingly said to Sevak Maharaj, 'This fellow offers *pranams* to me with his head and long hands and to the flower pot with his legs!'

Maharaj would usually go and stand in front of the shrine for a few minutes and then move towards the Bookstall (present *The Vedanta Kesari* Editorial Office). I used to follow Maharaj. On many occasions, I had seen Maharaj enquiring about the release of some new books, giving instruction to the volunteer Sri Mahadevan, who was looking after the sales at the book stall to display such and such book and then enter into Manager Maharaj's office. I would stop following Maharaj and start seeing the books for some time in the book stall itself and then go to library or shrine.

On Saturday, 28 March 1987, Maharaj blessed me with *mantra diksa* in the 'Old Temple'. After the *diksa* was over, Sevak Maharaj led Maharaj to his quarters. Nearly half an hour was left for *prasad.* I sat for doing japa. No sooner did I sit, than a doubt arose in my mind about the pronunciation of the mantra. Then I decided to go to Maharaj immediately.

On the way, my mind got another doubt about the recitation of the Gayatri Mantra. Maharaj was sitting on a chair outside his room in the verandah without any upper garment. Maharaj seemed tired, but his face was serene. I did my usual long *pranam*. Maharaj looked graciously at me and enquired, 'How do you feel? You feel hungry?' 'No, Maharaj. No hunger at all. I feel extremely peaceful but have a doubt Maharaj about the pronunciation of the mantra.' Maharaj said, 'It is a very simple mantra. Then he pronounced the mantra slowly and I carefully listened to it. Maharaj then asked me, 'Is it clear now?' I nodded my head and again offered *pranam* to Maharaj. When I was coming down the staircase, I realized that I forgot to ask about the recitation of Gayatri Mantra. When I again climbed up the staircase and stood before Maharaj, I could guess from his facial expression that he was a bit annoyed. He rebuked, 'You will never leave me.' I bowed down my head as I stood in front of him and said, 'Maharaj, sorry for disturbing. Only one more question, please Maharaj.' 'Quick, quick, Maharaj will go inside for taking rest,' Sevak Maharaj hurried me. I asked Maharaj, 'Maharaj, Shall I stop reciting the Gayatri Mantra and do japa of your mantra only?' 'Ooof! Fool! It is not my mantra. Sri Ramakrishna's mantra it is. Don't stop the Gayatri Mantra. First do japa of Gayatri Mantra as you are doing now, and then follow what you were told today. Go and take *prasad*.' I bent down with folded hands and took leave of him.

Sometime in 1989, I told Maharaj that I felt no interest in life and that everything seemed mechanical and meaningless. Maharaj was then sitting in his room, writing at the table. I placed some fruits and a Threptin biscuit box over a chair kept near his table. These were my usual offerings to Maharaj. Initially, Maharaj was not happy that he should receive anything from me. But he condescended after my repeated requests. After offering *pranams*, I waited for a few seconds for Maharaj to withdraw his mind from his work. Maharaj's usual way of recognizing me was to say something like, 'Hmm…Oh! Long fellow!' Even today I cannot understand the mesmerizing power behind these words. The joy those few words gave me was exceptional.

Maharaj asked, 'Is everything alright?' I told, 'Maharaj, I do not feel any difference after getting *diksa*. I don't know where am I erring?' 'You see, *diksa* is a vow to hold onto the *Ishta* and His name. Once you take it, it becomes your duty to do it, whether you get any result or not. But results are not perceptible. In *Sri Ramakrishna, The Great Master*, you will come across a discussion on *Shambhavi diksa*. The guru and disciple both would not know what was happening, but somehow the power of association with the guru will bring transformation in the disciple. In Bhagavan Sri Ramakrishna's life, you come across many lay devotees coming in contact with him, who saw him from a distance or had casual talks with him. By Guru, I do not mean myself, it is Sri Ramakrishna whom we call Sri Guru Maharaj and we pass on His holy name to those who want to have it.' I said, 'Maharaj, I desire to join the Math.' 'Why? You are in a good position; getting good salary from the bank. What's difficulty over there?' I said, 'Maharaj, I wish to become a monk.' 'Don't be in a hurry. Many come like this and flee away without information. At best you can take 3 or 4 days leave from office, stay here, see whether food here suits you and all that,' he advised me. 'Maharaj, I need your blessings to become a monk,' I pleaded. 'See, these things depend on your own mental maturity and conviction. You know better what is in your mind than me. Tell Sankar [Swami Raghaveshananda] in the office before your coming. Bring sufficient clothing, a few books, and a mosquito net is a must. Don't forget to bring it. Inform your house about your stay here,' Maharaj advised. I didn't expect that so soon I would get an opportunity to stay in the ashram even though only temporarily and therefore I felt happy about it. But I could not understand the advice to bring a mosquito net.

'So you have come. Hmm... You can take *idlis* in the morning, boiled vegetables and curd in the noon and few *rotis* in the night. Keep your stomach light; you won't feel any difficulty in staying,' Maharaj said to me when I went to stay in the Math for four days. Mosquito net, *idlis*, boiled vegetables, *rotis* etc. – these things were a big revelation to me. The so-called spiritual life starts with these things. Then I remembered the teaching of Swami Vivekananda, 'If you really want to judge the character of a man, look not at his great performances. Every fool may become a hero at one time or another. Watch a man do his most common actions; those are indeed the things which will tell you the real character of a great man.'

Daily *darsan* of Maharaj, work in the shrine store, reading the books that I had brought with me, good food and sleep, attending evening prayer and doing japa – all these brought me a new life, a new birth so to say. Maharaj's silent and simple life spoke volumes to me. From then on, using the mosquito net had become my daily routine.

One day, before taking my breakfast, I went up to Maharaj's room to offer *pranams*. Maharaj was reading the newspaper in a standing posture facing the east. Over a table, a small desk was put and Maharaj was resting his arms over that desk while holding the newspaper. As I was already late for the breakfast due to some work in the shrine store, and I also had to dress vegetables in the kitchen after the breakfast, I wanted to offer my *pranams* then, for otherwise, I would miss the opportunity of offering *pranams* that day. So hurriedly I offered my *pranams* to Maharaj but accidentally, my hands touched Maharaj's legs. It was a terrible jerk to Maharaj, as he was deeply absorbed in reading the newspaper. He shouted, 'You fool! Do I have a third eye to see you coming and offering your nonsense *pranam*?' My whole body trembled and I began to perspire. I didn't have the guts to stand in front of him and quickly went down. It was a great lesson for me that we should not offer our *pranams* to anyone mechanically, without inviting the attention of the person concerned.

While taking leave of Maharaj after my short stay at the ashram, I enquired Maharaj, 'Maharaj, whether inside the Math or outside, how to lead the spiritual life?' 'You see, spiritual life is not a part time job. You should try to create a spiritual connection with each and every one you come across. Selfless gestures need not entirely be spiritual, though they may pave the way for that. Helping someone because it is nice to do is not all that matters, but do we see that person as divine? When we put aside our ego, then we will be able to forge spiritual connection with others,' Maharaj advised me.

On Tuesday, 27 February 1990, on the birthday of Sri Ramakrishna, I joined Sri Ramakrishna Math, Madras, aspiring to lead a monastic life. After having *darsan* of Sri Ramakrishna, I went to Maharaj's room and offered *sastanga pranams*. 'At last you have come. Sankar [Swami Raghaveshananda Maharaj] knows about your coming. He will help you getting accommodated. Be punctual for food,' Maharaj advised. Swami Raghaveshananda Maharaj, the then Manager Maharaj of Madras Math, instructed me to assist in Accounts also apart from the service at the temple and dining hall.

Almost all the novices invariably gained weight after they joined the ashram; but my physical structure remained the same. Hence with an intention to make me gain some weight, Maharaj advised me to jog on the roof of the kitchen block (at that time there was no other room on the first floor except Maharaj's room and one other room adjacent to it). The running should be done in front of him. That meant I should run for half an hour when Maharaj had his evening walk on the verandah. I have to run to become fat. There was one monastic brother who was fat and Maharaj wanted him to lose some weight. We both used to jog, one for gaining weight and another to lose!

Since my regular duties did not allow me to spend some time with Maharaj, I expressed my dissatisfaction to Sevak Maharaj. At that time, Swami Vimurtananda and Bipin Maharaj would massage Maharaj's legs every morning after breakfast. For some reason, Bipin Maharaj had to discontinue this service and Sevak Maharaj told me to take his place. So from then on, Swami Vimurtananda and I would massage Maharaj's legs. Usually Maharaj would recline on a easy chair and read the newspaper. He would stretch out the newspaper fully that he would not be able to see us. Since this type of work was new to me, after 6 or 7 minutes, I would get pain in my shoulders and therefore my pace of massaging would slow down, sometimes it would even stop. Finding that I was sitting idle or gossiping with Swami Vimurtananda, Maharaj would say, 'Hmm... What's happening?!' Then I would resume the massaging! Sometimes, Swami Vimurtananda would crack jokes and I would start laughing. Maharaj would suddenly put down the newspaper and look at us. But we would be massaging his legs like innocent boys! Maharaj would then resume his reading.

In the middle of 1991, due to Maharaj's ill health, there were some changes in his routine and we were not allowed to offer our *pranams* to him. Maharaj was admitted to Vijaya Hospital at Vadapalani and then shifted to B.S.S Hospital, Mandaveli. At both the places, I got some opportunity to attend on Maharaj.

After Maharaj's *mahasamadhi,* a brahmachari helped me to get Maharaj's footprints. A few days later, items used by Maharaj were distributed among his brahmacharis who were his disciples. I received Maharaj's table clock, pocket watch and a pen, always reminding me of my association with Maharaj.

Maharaj's life is a proof that the teachings of Bhagavan Sri Ramakrishna, Holy Mother Sarada Devi and Swami Vivekananda can be practiced even today. He is my life support. If I own an iota of spirituality, I owe it to his blessings and guidance.

32

No Thermometer to Measure Spiritual Progress!

Swami Ekagratananda[1]

I had the good fortune of meeting Swami Tapasyananda Maharaj in 1990. I was then 23 years old and a P.G. student in Madras. I was interested in *The Complete Works of Swami Vivekananda.* These books were available in my college library and I was reading them seriously. Noticing this, my friend told me that these books are published by Ramakrishna Math and that they have a branch in Mylapore. He added that monks lived there and the president was Swami Tapasyananda Maharaj. My friend advised me to go there and meet the President Swami.

I started going to Ramakrishna Math, Mylapore, on Saturday and Sunday evenings, read books in the library and also listened to spiritual discourses, but the President Swami's office remained closed every time. After some visits, I enquired and learnt that Revered Maharaj came to office only in the mornings. So I went the next Saturday morning (sometime in March 1990) and found Revered Maharaj seated alone in the office. I asked an elderly volunteer in the

1. He was initiated by Revered Maharaj and joined the Ramakrishna Order after Revered Maharaj's demise.

book stall (current *The Vedanta Kesari* Office) for permission to meet Maharaj. He told me that there was no need for permission; everyone was free to meet him.

I entered Maharaj's office and made *sastanga pranams*. He was writing something. He asked my name and what I was studying. I replied. He told that I will get a nice job with a good salary and stopped the conversation. 'I am busy,' he told. But I had gone there to ask him something. So I said, 'Shall I come some other time when you are free?' He replied, 'I will be busy like this always. If you want to tell me anything you tell it now.' I told him, 'I want to realize the Truth.' Maharaj had some hearing problem. He asked me to repeat. I did three times and the third time was at the top of my voice. Then only he understood. Immediately, he put his pen down and asked me to sit in a chair in front of his table. When I hesitated to sit in his presence he told, 'I am hard of hearing. Unless you sit at the same level, I cannot understand what you are telling.' So I sat on the chair. The conversation went on like this:

Maharaj: 'You say you want to realize the Truth. For that you require great yearning.' He further told, 'Yearning means with a '**Y**' in the beginning; not bank balance (earning).'

Me: 'I have.'

Maharaj: 'You say you have. But you should do the following things:

'Firstly, give up Cinema.

'Secondly, give up bad company. Bad company can pull the mind very low.

'Thirdly, come here occasionally.'

He continued:

You are initiated in the Gayatri mantra. Are you not? Do you repeat it daily?'

Me: 'Yes.'

Maharaj: 'You should repeat the Gayatri mantra a number of times daily with great devotion. Do you know the meaning of the Gayatri mantra?'

Me: 'No.'

Maharaj was surprised that I was taught the mantra alone and not its meaning. He explained the meaning briefly. He then got up, opened a shelf, took out three small books and presented them to me. They were *A Primer of Hinduism, Om, Gayatri & Sandhya* and a pocket size book on *Bhagavad Gita,* translated by Revered Swami Vireswarananda Maharaj. Much later, I came to know that he himself had translated the *Gita*; but he gave me Revered Swami Vireswarananda Maharaj's book.

I was much satisfied and happy with this meeting. I never expected that he would talk to a young student like me so freely. There was no fear in me, for he was friendly and kind. Since then, whenever I met Maharaj, I spoke to him freely as though I was talking to a close relative.

My mother and other family members were not pleased with my visits to the Math. Though they were devoted to God in general, they were afraid that if a person visited the Math, he may end up becoming a sannyasi. So, they strongly opposed my going to the Math. Luckily, I got a helpful hint from that month's issue of *The Vedanta Kesari*. In that a monk had mentioned how he solved a similar problem. On weekends he would leave home telling his mother that he was going to the College library, but he would go to the Math. After that he went to the College library also, so that truth was not compromised. I followed this idea; every Saturday morning I went to Math and from there to my College library. As I had to travel 1½ hours by bus from home to Math, I went there only once a week. I used every opportunity to meet and talk to Revered Maharaj for 5 to 10 minutes.

During my second visit, I carried a bag with me expecting that Maharaj would give me more books. But he didn't give any books that time. He asked me whether I was attending the evening *arati* in the temple. I replied in negative; I was only listening to the discourses whenever I went. Maharaj told me that I should attend the *arati* whenever I visited the Math; that was very important. He also asked me whether I was first visiting the shrine before coming to meet him. He was very particular that after entering the Math, we should directly go to the shrine. During my first visit, he had told me to do *Gayatri* japa. I asked him whether I should do *pranayama* also. He told that was not necessary, but if I was very much interested, then I may practise rhythmic breathing 3 times, without holding the breath. He warned that practising *pranayama* was not advisable for anyone and everyone, and may cause heart problems or nervous breakdown if the person was unfit.

During my third visit, he asked me what books I had read in Ramakrishna-Vivekananda literature. I told that I was reading *The Complete Works of Swami Vivekananda*, *The Gospel of Sri Ramakrishna* and *Sri Ramakrishna the Great Master*. Maharaj was satisfied and said, 'Yes. You should read these big books, not only the small ones.' In the meantime, somebody (may be a Math worker or a salesman) entered the room and started to talk about some office work. Maharaj scolded that person telling that he was talking something important with this boy (me) and that he should wait. Maharaj was particularly happy to know that I was reading *The Gospel of Sri Ramakrishna*. He once again presented me a book and said, 'This is *The Condensed Gospel of Sri Ramakrishna*, written by 'M.'[1] himself in English - not a translation. You should read this *Condensed Gospel* every day.' That book written by 'M.' in old but beautiful style of English gave me tremendous inspiration.

During these visits, I had a conversation with another swami who was giving discourses at the Math. He advised me to request Maharaj to give me *mantra diksa*. Until then I did not know that Revered Maharaj was a Vice-President of the Order or that he was giving *mantra diksa*. So, when I visited him next, I requested him for *mantra diksa*. But Maharaj didn't hear what I said even after I repeated; he thought I was introducing myself and replied, 'Yes, yes, I remember you. Sit down.' I then asked him how to practise brahmacharya. He gave me some advice regarding brahmacharya, and continued, 'Doing physical exercise is also necessary for the practise of brahmacharya. By looking at you, I feel you have never done any exercise in your life.' I confessed that he was correct. He then scolded me, 'That is a blunder which many young men commit nowadays. You should run daily and then do exercise for half an hour.'

Maharaj continued, 'If you practise brahmacharya and do your physical exercises, around 30 years of age would

1. 'M.' was the penname of Sri Mahendranath Gupta, the recorder of *The Gospel of Sri Ramakrishna*.

be the best time to marry.' I replied, 'I am not interested in married life, my only aim is God-realization.' Maharaj was happy and told, 'Oh! Then after you finish your studies come and join this Math and take to the life of sannyasa.' I was so happy; life of sannyasa attracted me from very young age but till then I did not know that one can join the Math and become a sannyasi. Maharaj then enquired whether I was spiritually initiated. When he learnt that I was not, he fixed a date then and there. Then he told me, 'You should read Swamiji's *Bhakti Yoga*. It is a small book only!'

Mantra diksa took place in the prayer hall upstairs (now 'Old Temple') after the Pujari Maharaj completed the daily puja in the shrine. Revered Maharaj entered the shrine and performed a small *arati*. He then came to the prayer hall (upstairs). Revered Maharaj spoke in English and read out some portions in Tamil. He said, 'Bhagavan Sri Ramakrishna is the actual Guru, we are only instruments.' He taught us to repeat the mantra as if we were calling God, the way we would call someone standing nearby. One of the candidates was a roadside flower vendor. Maharaj told her in Tamil, 'I will explain to you again later.' *Mantra diksa* was over within an hour. Revered Maharaj told, 'Some of you may be fasting. All of you go down and take breakfast. At noon, you will be served lunch *prasad*. After eating lunch *prasad* you can go home". After we finished breakfast, we were allowed to meet him individually and clarify our doubts. I had some questions but when my turn came, Maharaj told me that as I was a local boy I can meet him some other day, so that outstation candidates can get more time.

During the next visit, I asked my doubts, all of which he answered very patiently. I told him that I was not able to meditate on Sri Ramakrishna as seated in the heart. Maharaj replied that Sri Ramakrishna is really seated there, but at first it has to be imagined; in course of time it will become real. I told Maharaj that I felt sleepy when I sat for japa in early mornings. Maharaj told me that even if I felt sleepy I should not stop japa or go to bed. I should sprinkle water on my face, walk a little, sit again and continue the japa. I asked whether I can do japa while travelling in bus. He told yes, but that should be in addition to doing japa regularly at home and not at the cost of it. Once again he advised me to read Swamiji's *Bhakti Yoga*. When I asked him whether I have spiritually progressed, he gently retorted that there was no instrument like a thermometer to measure spiritual progress!

Once I asked him how to improve concentration during japa. He told, 'There are two ways. First is, along with every repetition of the mantra, you should think that you are offering a flower at God's feet. Or, follow the second way - listen to the mantra while repeating it silently.'

I saw him again in the evening of *Vijaya Dasami*, 1990, in the prayer hall. Many monastics were present. That was a wonderful occasion. At first the monastics chanted *santi mantras*. Then *Santi Jal* was sprinkled by Manager Maharaj. After this, devotees offered *pranams* to Revered Maharaj one by one and he gave sweet *prasad* to all. There were many devotees, but Maharaj noticed every regular visitor. When I met him after a few days, he told me that he noticed me during *Vijaya Dasami*.

I again saw him on Holy Mother's Jayanti. After evening *arati*, two senior monks gave enlightening discourses on Holy Mother. Next came Revered Maharaj's turn. He entered with a small book and told that as the two monks have already mentioned all important things, he will only read a little from that small book. He showed the book to the audience and informed them that the book was *Teachings of The Holy Mother* compiled by Revered Swami Vireswarananda Maharaj and that the book was for sale for a highly subsidised price. He read and explained wonderfully, interspersing it with some jokes also. I heard his short talk on Kalpataru Day also.

The next time I met Maharaj, he asked, 'What happened to your resolve to join the Math?' I told him that I had the intention, but my studies were not yet over and above all, my mother was strongly persuading me to go abroad after getting the PG degree. He asked me whether I have informed my parents about my intention to become a sannyasi. I replied in negative. Then he remarked, 'That will be the main problem. You have to first tell them your intention.' Next time when my mother enquired about my future plans, I let the matter out; I told her that I am going to become a sannyasi in Ramakrishna Math. It was a terrible blow to her.

All through my interactions with Revered Maharaj, I never had enquired about his health as he was always in a joyful mood. One day I went with my friend who was also a disciple of Maharaj. My friend asked him, 'How is your health, Maharaj?' Immediately Maharaj called a monk and told him with great amusement, 'Show them! Show them!' The monk opened a rack; it was full of medicines and the monk told us that Maharaj was taking all those medicines daily. Maharaj was too happy to show that. After that, pointing to me, Maharaj told my friend, 'You put some courage into his heart. He is not joining because he is afraid of his mother.'

My friend asked a question about *upasana*, 'Maharaj, you have asked us to meditate on Sri Ramakrishna in the heart. How to do that?' Maharaj replied, 'Heart means not this physical heart but the core of one's being. When I told you to put some courage into your friend's heart I did not mean his physical heart but something else. To meditate on Sri Ramakrishna in one's heart also has to be understood in the same way.' A wonderful explanation indeed!

On my next visit, I had a feeling that I have not done any *seva* to the Guru. As soon as I entered his room, he told me, even before I offered my *pranams*, 'Go and help him. He is cleaning.' A monk was tidying up his room and bed. I helped him a little and got a small opportunity to perform *guruseva*.

I got a job in an establishment in Pune and left Madras to join there in May 1991. Before that, I went to the Math to inform Maharaj. He made fun of me to a monk standing nearby, 'This boy told that he would join the Math after his studies. But he will not join the Math; instead he is going to join a job for a fat salary.' Maharaj expected that I would renounce home and become a monk, which I did next year. But Revered Maharaj attained *mahasamadhi* before that.

33

Everything is Brahman

Swami Vireshananda[1]

It was in the year 1989. I was then just 18 years old. I wanted to join the Ramakrishna Order. I was influenced by the wonderful lectures and melodious devotional *bhajans* of Swami Purushottamananda Maharaj of Bangalore Math and hence I approached him. He was kind enough to introduce me to Swami Chidananda Maharaj, the then President of Ramakrishna Ashrama, Bangalore. Immediately after my 12th Standard exams, I joined the Bangalore Math as a brahmacharin.

I had not yet received the *mantra diksa*. Swami Chidananda Maharaj decided to send three brahmacharins including me to Madras for receiving spiritual initiation from Revered Swami Tapasyananda Maharaj. I filled up the application form prescribed for spiritual initiation. In that form, a question was asked, 'Do you believe Sri Ramakrishna as an incarnation of God?' To this I wrote, 'I do not know whether Sri Ramakrishna is a God or not. But to me, definitely he is more than God.' The application forms were sent to Madras Math by Swami Chidananda Maharaj.

1. He joined Madras Math under Revered Maharaj and was initiated by him. He is currently serving as the editor of *Viveka Prabha*, Kannada monthly published from Ramakrishna Ashrama, Mysore.

In his office, Madras Math

After a few days, Swami Chidananda Maharaj informed me that Revered Swami Tapasyananda Maharaj had agreed to give us *mantra diksa*. He also told me that Revered Maharaj wanted me, just 18 years then, to pursue higher studies. Revered Maharaj had written that if I was willing, I might join B.A course in Sanskrit in Vivekananda College, Madras. Maharaj was also kind enough to allow me to stay at Madras Math as a student! When I was informed about this suggestion of Revered Maharaj, I was really thrilled beyond words! Revered Maharaj had not even met me yet. He was far away in Madras and I was in Bangalore. Yet, he had showered his grace upon me even before I came to know him personally. This is how the story of my blessed association with Revered Maharaj began. Indeed, it was Sri Ramakrishna's grace showered upon me through my future guru.

I went to Madras with other two brahmacharins for spiritual initiation. He personally interviewed me and solved many of the problems I was facing. I returned to Bangalore, collected the necessary documents, and went back to Madras to join the Vivekananda College.

As soon as I reached Madras, Revered Maharaj gave instructions pertaining to the books I had to study. Apart from Ramakrishna-Vivekananda literature, two important books he insisted me to read were the *Bhagavad Gita* and *Vivekachudamani*. He even presented me a copy of his own translation of the *Bhagavad Gita* with some benedictory words.

Revered Maharaj was closely observing my routine and gave valuable suggestions regarding my physical and spiritual well-being. He ordered me to exercise daily in his presence in the evening during his daily walk in front of his room. I was under Maharaj's personal scrutiny and guidance for about two and a half years before he gave up his body in October 1991.

Revered Maharaj was the very personification of austerity or *tapas* as his very name indicated. Though he was a senior monk, a vice-president of the Ramakrishna Order, he led a very simple life with few wants. He had no full-time secretary or attendant almost till the last days of his life.

Revered Maharaj was always studious by nature. He had immense capacity to study and write books for hours together. He would take rest only for a brief period during the day. He would attend to official duties during the morning and would devote whole afternoon for his literary activities. He was a great scholar both in English and Sanskrit, which is evident from his books, authored or translated.

Although Maharaj was serious by nature, he could often be very humorous. He was probably very fond of buffalos and would use the word 'buffalo' while scolding. Once, he imitated the walking style of a lean Brahmacharin comparing him with traditional artists who paint themselves like tigers and dance during festivals in Kerala.

Many a time, I used to be an irritant to Revered Maharaj, a strict disciplinarian, because of my boyish pranks. Once he found out that I was sluggish in my daily exercise. He shouted at me, 'You are a humbug.' I did not understand the word 'humbug'. In my adolescent innocence, I asked him what the meaning of the word 'humbug' was. He became angry and gestured me to get away from him.

In Madras, I often used to fall ill. Once I was diagnosed as having typhoid and was shifted to a separate room. After 3 or 4 days, I felt alright and returned to my original room, without taking permission from Revered Maharaj. He was annoyed and ordered me to write an apology letter. I wrote a short letter seeking his forgiveness. In that letter, I included a verse culled from *Stotraratna* of Yamunacharya, which Revered Maharaj himself had translated. In that verse the devotee begs the Lord for His benevolence. Revered Maharaj was very much pleased with the letter. Not only did he simply forget the whole episode, he also corrected the grammatical errors in that letter and returned it to me.

One day, he asked me whether I could write articles in Kannada, my mother-tongue. His interest in this regard was so much that he said he would get my writing examined by Swami Raghaveshananda Maharaj, the then manager of Madras Math, whose mother-tongue was also Kannada. I now strongly feel that Revered Maharaj had the intuition about my future as it is evident from the fact that, through his blessings, I am serving as the editor of the Kannada magazine of the Ramakrishna Order.

During those days, Vidvan Kalyanasundara Sastrigal, a great scholar was conducting classes on *Upanishads, Bhagavad Gita, Brahmasutras* and other allied works. Revered Maharaj encouraged me to attend those classes and would inquire about the classes regularly. Though he was fond of Ramanuja's *Visistadvaita,* he had great reverence for Sri Sankaracharya and his philosophy; it is evident from his lucid translation of *Sankara Digvijaya,* a traditional biography of Sri Sankara.

There was a great Dvaita scholar by name Sri Nagaraja Rao in Madras. He would often visit Revered Maharaj. Once, Revered Maharaj introduced me to that scholar saying, 'Though he hails from a Dvaita family, he will study Advaita in the future.' His prophetic words really came true.

Once, Revered Maharaj asked me to transliterate the verses of *Vivekachudamani* for a book to be published with translation of Swami Turiyananda Maharaj. He showed how to transliterate Devanagari text into Roman script with diacritical marks. During his last days, he had developed a distinct habit of identifying a person with some query. Whenever I went near him, he would always ask, 'Have you finished the transliteration work?'

Revered Maharaj was a great exponent of philosophy of Bhakti. In order to introduce me into the Bhakti doctrine, he gave me a book called *Bhakti Ratnavali,* a collection of verses from the *Bhagavata* and asked me to read the introduction written by him outlining the salient features of Bhakti. I took the book to my room and started reading but could not make head and tail out of it, as both the subject and the exposition were very intricate. After few days, Revered Maharaj enquired whether I had read the introduction. I humbly replied that the text was beyond my comprehension. He stared at me for few seconds and in his own characteristic style, ordered me to return the book which I promptly obeyed.

Revered Maharaj's benevolence and paternal love towards me is beyond any comparison. Senior Swamis would tell me that Revered Maharaj would often become impatient, if I did not turn up to have his *darshan* on any particular day. At the fag-end of his life, just before he became terminally ill, he would quite often call me and enquire about my well-being. He was very concerned and anxious about me till the end.

Although Revered Maharaj was very kind towards me, he would enforce the rules of the monastery very strictly. At the very outset of my coming to Madras, he told me curtly, 'You are only a student. You are not yet a brahmacharin. Yet, you have to follow the routine of the monastery.' When he found out that I did not attend morning *mangalarati* for a few days, he demanded an explanation and reprimanded me for the lapse. Also, Revered Maharaj was very keen that I should attend all the classes in the college. Whenever

I returned early from college, he would notice it and would demand an explanation.

Once, I was reading lying on the bed and fell asleep without switching off the light. As Maharaj's room was exactly in front of mine, he observed light glowing in my room sometime during late night. His attendant swami told him that I may be studying. Revered Maharaj with a hearty laugh remarked, 'No, no. He is sleeping.' Actually, I was in deep sleep at that time!

Once, Revered Maharaj suffered a fall during his daily walk. From that day onwards, his health slowly deteriorated. He was admitted to Vijaya Hospital and then to BSS hospital, near the Math. There he breathed his last. Just 3 or 4 days before his passing away, I went to visit him. The attendant swami had gone out of the room and I was alone with Maharaj. I could not follow all that Maharaj was uttering feebly. In spite of this, I could hear him say loudly and distinctly, "***Everything is Brahman***". He merged into that divine consciousness after a few days.

34

Switching Off The Mind!

Swami Namratananda[1]

My First Visit:

In September 1988, as we were seeking spiritual initiation, one of my high school friends, Ravichandran, took me and another friend of mine, Srinivasan to Revered Tapasyananda Maharaj. Since it was about noon, he had just closed the office and was about to leave for noon *prasad*. So he told us to visit him the next day.

Meeting Revered Maharaj:

Next day before noon, we went and had a long conversation with him. Ravi had already given books on Bhagavan Sri Ramakrishna, *Amudha Mozhigal* [Tamil version of *The Gospel of Sri Ramakrishna*] etc. for us to read and reply to Maharaj's questions. Some of Maharaj's questions which I remember now are:

Maharaj: 'Are you going to temple regularly?'

Me: 'Yes, I am going to Anjaneya shrine in Ekambareswarar Temple regularly.'

Maharaj: 'Where is God?'

1. He was initiated by Revered Maharaj and joined Madras Math under him.

Me: 'God is everywhere.'

Maharaj: 'Then why are you going to the temple?'

Me: 'God is everywhere, but His presence is more manifested in temples. As Sri Guru Maharaj told, "Although there is milk in cow's body, but we have to squeeze the udder to get milk." So, we have to go the temples.'

He asked me many such questions. I was bubbling with energy and answered them in my own way, with gestures and with whatever English I knew, using a few words in the vernacular and through signs (by moving my hands). I was not sure whether the answers were right. Srinivasan was silent all along, and since Ravi had been already spiritually initiated by Maharaj, he did not venture to intervene.

Ravi was tall and lean, while Srinivasan was short and lean. My physical frame was strong then. Maharaj brought *prasadi* books titled *A Primer of Hinduism*, and gave a copy each to me and Srinivasan. Then Maharaj kept his right hand on my left shoulder and said, 'He is a strong man.' I remarked, 'I do yogasanas regularly.' He replied, 'You must have started just two weeks ago.' It was exactly true.

Initiation:

Maharaj noted Sri Srinivasan's name and my name in his diary and instructed us to come on 26th November at 8 a.m. for spiritual initiation. We all made *sastanga pranams* at his holy feet and left.

When the spiritual initiation was over, the disciples were allowed to clarify their doubts. I took this opportunity to meet him personally. He was seated on a chair, with head covered with a cap, doing japa with *japamala* (which was in a small handbag).

Further Visits:

From then on, I would regularly visit him on Thursday mornings at the Math. He was easily approachable without any appointment or prior intimation. During those visits, I would offer some flowers and *tulsi* [Basil] leaves at his feet and make *sastanga pranams*. Maharaj, sitting erect would accept my offerings with a benign nod. Once, he accepted my offering standing.

I had many doubts in my mind. But in his presence, I would forget them in a wave of emotion. When I told him about it, he advised me to write them down and bring them to him.

I once expressed that I was unable to meditate, and even though my eyes were closed, many thoughts were arising in my mind. He told, 'See God with open eyes.' He advised me to read *Nalayira Divya Prabhandam* [4000 hymns of Alwars] and *Thiruvachakam* [a collection of poems and songs on Siva by Sri Manikkavachakar, one of the foremost saiva saints].

Child of God with Children:

When he was in good health, he regularly went for a walk around the Math. He would walk between his office and the library through the rear side of the dispensary. On a Sunday evening, I went to the Math to attend the *Gita* class of Swami Tyagananda Maharaj. I learnt from my friend that, on that very day, Revered Maharaj, while on his walk, noticed two young boys (maybe in the age group of 7 to 12) playing cricket behind the dispensary. The player in the saint found expression. He stood behind the batsman and he too held the bat. So both of them were holding the same bat, one was 7 years old and the other 85 years. The other boy bowled five balls wide. Maharaj then told him, 'Either put the ball to this (showing the bat) or to that (showing the stumps), and not here and there.' Oh! Bad luck! The sixth ball too went wide. 'Hopeless bowling,' he remarked and went away. In the meantime, a crowd had gathered to watch the game of God's Great Child! I was however not fortunate to watch the episode.

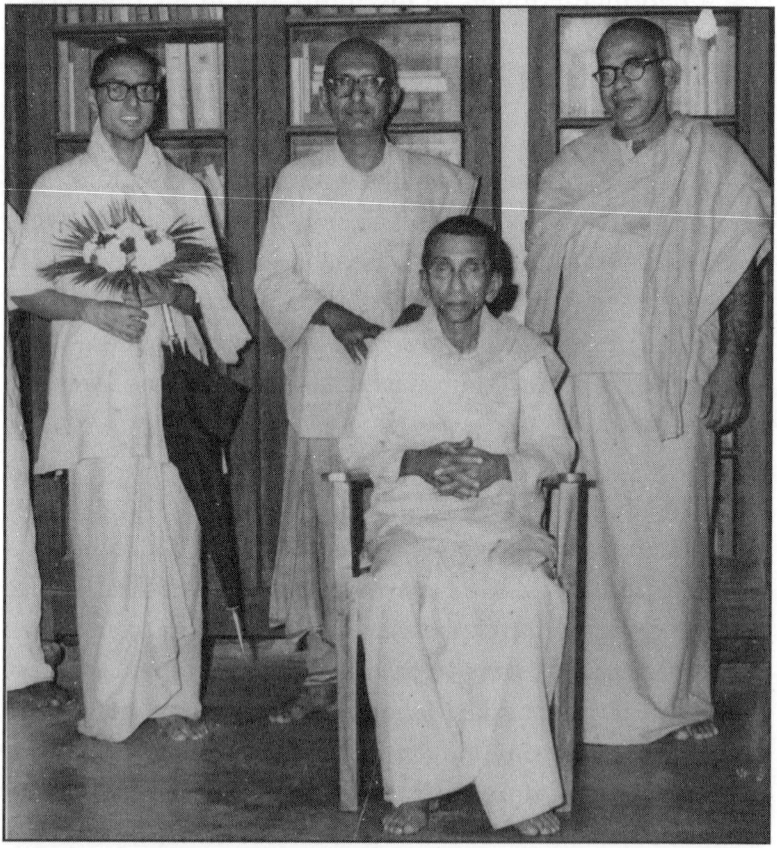

With Vireswarananda Maharaj at Trivandrum

Devotion to Holy Mother:

On one of the Jayantis of Holy Mother, I could sit near his feet in the prayer hall and listen to his lecture. He explained the meaning of a Sanskrit verse on Holy Mother in English. He had great devotion for Holy Mother. I have heard that he brought nothing from Trivandrum, except Holy Mother's photo and a picture of Om.

Although he was not a frequent traveller, he went to Varanasi exclusively in connection with his writing the book on Holy Mother.

Pure Love:

He was considerate to the poor and the illiterate. His affection to the poor children of Ramakrishnapuram and the Bala Mandir boys was well-known. He would distribute fruits and sweets offered to him by the devotees to these boys at weekends.

I have heard Swami Siddhinathananda Maharaj relating that when he had come to Madras Math and was suffering from severe back pain, Revered Maharaj himself applied oil and massaged his body, even though he was elder and senior to him [Swami Siddhinathananda Maharaj].

Although there were no external expressions of love from Maharaj, I felt deep within that his love for me was more than all the love of my family members put together, because it was pure and selfless to the highest degree. It is this love that helped me to break the worldly relationships and bondages.

Joining the Math:

On 18 August 1991, Sunday, I joined the Math. From the very next day, Swami Raghaveshananda Maharaj, the then Manager of the Math, gave me an opportunity to serve in the dispensary. I had the good opportunity of seeing Revered Tapasyananda Maharaj every day from close quarters.

One morning, Revered Maharaj was sitting outside the dining hall on a wheel chair. One of his *sevaks* took me to Maharaj and introduced me thus: 'He took spiritual initiation from you. He is joining the Math. Please give permission and bless him.' Revered Maharaj nodded his head in affirmation.

After a few days, Revered Swami Raghaveshananda Maharaj, on seeing me firm in my resolve to continue the monastic life took me to Revered Maharaj and informed me about my intention to join the Math. Revered Maharaj asked my name. After I told him my name, he asked, 'Where is your house?' I told him the locality. It was 8 kilometers from the Math. He exclaimed, 'Then you can run away very easily!' He then laughed, and the monks who were with him also laughed. He then said, 'Ah! Don't go from here.' I promised him that I would not go anywhere leaving the Math. And added, 'Maharaj, please bless me from the bottom of your heart.' I was the last person to join Madras Math as a brahmachari when Revered Maharaj was the president. I was very fortunate to receive his permission and blessings.

Last Days:

Maharaj was admitted to Vijaya Hospital in February 1991 due to sudden drop in blood sugar (his Tuberculosis had not yet been diagnosed). He returned to the Math within a week. In the month of June, he was readmitted and discharged in July. There was an announcement in the blackboard in the prayer hall requesting the devotees not to disturb Revered Maharaj and to co-operate so that there was speedy recovery of his health.

When Maharaj was bed-ridden at the Math, all the brahmacharis were attending on him in the night by turns. One of the brahmacharis thought he did not get any personal instruction from Maharaj. One night, while he was serving Maharaj, Maharaj told him, 'Ah! Speak the truth always. Don't tell lies. We left our hearth and home for the sake of Truth.'

Maharaj would many times address me as 'fool'. I once got annoyed and shared my misgivings with another brahmachari. He said, 'Really you are a fool, if your guru calls you a fool, will you lose anything?' Realizing my mistake, I again became very joyful.

Again in September (perhaps on 1st) 1991, Revered Maharaj was hospitalized in B.S.S. Hospital. The doctors announced that Maharaj had been attacked by tuberculosis. Almost three-quarters of the lungs had already been affected. This information, however, was not divulged to Maharaj.

I had the good fortune of preparing his special diet 11 times in a day and taking it to him and sometimes even feeding him. I would usually go by cycle to the hospital with food. I never stayed at night in the hospital because I had to prepare his diet from morning till night at 11 different times. I would, however, wash his dishes, clothes etc. I was always occupied with only one thought – that he should get well and live long with good health.

When I was serving him in the hospital, he would ask, 'Are you attending *Ramnam* regularly?' He instilled in my mind the importance of *Ramnam sankirtan*.

One afternoon I was with Swami Sukritananda Maharaj in the hospital. Revered Maharaj told him referring to me, 'He is a new brahmachari. Give him rest.'

Many monks and brahmacharis came from far and near to visit him. In spite of his own ill-health, Maharaj would be more concerned with the health and well-being of the visiting monastics.

Dr. Ayyappan of B.S.S. Hospital advised us to avoid creating any situation that would make Maharaj speak much. He did not even encourage us to sit or stand in front of Maharaj because that might prompt him to speak. He suggested that we sit in a corner and attend only important calls.

Maharaj did not want to be in the hospital, which he considered worse than death. He wanted to breathe his last in the Math. To many he told several times, 'Take me to Math.'

Maharaj eventually went into coma, and the doctors put him on a ventilator. Liquid food was administered through a tube. Two days before his *mahasamadhi*, Dr. Ayyappan told Raghaveshananda Maharaj: 'It is now a question of hours.'

On 3 October 1991, in the evening, Br. Sukanto, Br. Ramachandra and I were in Maharaj's room. Suddenly his pulse rate came down rapidly and he passed away at 6.32 p.m. on *Ekadasi.* I was on the right side of Maharaj, touching his right hand and right foot. The news reached the Math and was conveyed to others. Swami Sukritananda Maharaj came with an Ambulance to take Maharaj's mortal remains to the Math. I returned to the Math by cycle.

I have seen Maharaj facing several hardships with complete fearlessness. He would also bear patiently even excruciating pain. The nurses would inject him through a central nerve. He would neither cry nor shout. He would tolerate everything silently. When the nurses could not find a suitable nerve to inject saline water, they would try at different locations. But Maharaj would never utter anything. One of the nurses told me, 'In this condition, the body pain will be terrible. Any other person would have screamed in pain. But the Swami tolerates with patience.'

Once Swami Siddhinathananda Maharaj told me an incident, 'Revered Maharaj had developed sores on his body due to prolonged sitting. So he could not sleep. When I enquired on the next day whether he could manage to sleep, he told, "Of course, I could not sleep. I sat on an easy-chair and *switched off my mind.* Is that not enough?" "Switching off the mind? What a wonder! It means stopping the mental activity at will!" I exclaimed.'

For Revered Maharaj, the body was an instrument of God. So he strived to keep it fit and healthy and perform the Lord's work. But he had no attachment to his body. He underwent several physical suffering knowing it to be a part and parcel of life. He had no fear of death. He had totally surrendered to God; so his mind was not perturbed by physical pain, mental worry, or fear of death.

His mind never came down, because Sri Ramakrishna had filled him with the great qualities of devotion, peace, blessedness, purity, wisdom, straight-forwardness and kindness.

It was due to Sri Guru Maharaj's and Revered Maharaj's grace that I could get the rare opportunity of doing some *guru-seva*.

The Surgeon's Mouth is Watering

Swami Tapasyananda Maharaj would put his heart and soul into any task that he undertook, to the extent of mastering it to an amazing perfection. When he was building the hospital at Trivandrum, he would plunge deep into the theory and practice of surgeries. He became so thoroughly acquainted with the surgical instruments that no surgeon could hoodwink him assuming him to be an ignorant monk. So he ensured that the surgeons would neither buy the instruments for a high price nor buy extra ones when what was purchased earlier remained underutilized. However, he believed in purchasing the latest and most essential surgical instruments and would make the surgeon sit and select the items. When the Swami found that the surgeon was so excited seeing the catalogue and at the prospect of buying those instruments, he humorously expressed it as "The surgeon's mouth is watering!"

—Swami Nityakamananda

35

At My Guru's Feet

Swami Yadunathananda[1]

Joining the Math

On 1 January 1990, I could fulfill my long cherished dream of joining the holy Order. I was given the duty to assist the Pujari Maharaj in the shrine from the very first day.

I was fortunate to move closely with Revered Tapasyananda Maharaj, observe his purity, holiness, and discipline, at close quarters for over two years, which included my serving him in his last days.

After I joined the Math, I took to the habit of prostrating before Revered Maharaj thrice a day. Once, when I had offered *pranams* to him in his office, he looked at me and said that he had received a letter from my elder brother. Revered Maharaj informed me that my brother had written him questioning him why he had accepted me into the Math. And that he [Revered Maharaj] had brain-washed me, misdirected me, and did nothing to convince me to return home. Revered Maharaj handed the letter to me and

---

1. He was initiated by Revered Maharaj and joined Madras Math under him.

At Madras Math on 2-4-1976: Sitting: 1. Ekatmananda 2. Amoghananda 3. Abhayanandaji 4. Vireshwaranandaji 5. Tapasyanandaji 6. Nishkamanandaji 7.Chidghanananda Standing: 1st Row: 1. Uddhavananda 2. Swatmananda 3. Raghaveshananda 4. Sukhatmananda 5. Vitamohananda 6. Karunananda 7. Golokananda 8. Prameyananda 9. Amritananda 10. Gabhirananda Standing: 2nd Row: Brahmacharins 1. Rammohan 2. Umeshachaitanaya (Nandishwarananda) 3.Rameshwar (Tattwarupananda) 4. Niranjanachaitanya (Kamalatmananda) 5. Dayachaitanya (Durgananda) 6. Murarichaitanya (Jnanananda) 7. Vijay 8. Ananda (Anandarupananda), Ratnavelu, Achyutan (Deshikatmananda)

asked me to read it. I did not say anything. I just took the letter and was about to proceed towards my room when Revered Maharaj called me and asked me to reply to the letter stating that it was my own wish to join the Order and no one had forced me. He also told me to write that senior monks here wanted me to lead a life that I had voluntarily chosen.

He then paused for a moment and told something which made me understand him in greater depth. He told me that my brother had written in his letter that he [Revered Maharaj] would go to hell for accepting me into the Order. Revered Maharaj wanted me to reply to this stating that he [Revered Maharaj] was ready to go to hell for such a noble cause. I was just dumb-founded at his reply. It made me realize the indomitable love he had towards me. That moment was a turning point in my life in strengthening my reverence and love for Revered Maharaj.

I took the letter and drafted a reply. Before I could post my reply, my mother and brother came to the Math. The divine sight of Revered Maharaj must have transformed my brother also! Because, instead of arguing with Revered Maharaj, he quietly enquired about my well-being, took *prasad,* and left the Math in a very peaceful manner. My mother blessed me and left with the satisfaction that I was under the loving care and able supervision of Revered Maharaj.

Fruits of Serving

I was instructed by Pujari Maharaj that I should serve four pieces of apple, six pieces of orange and ten grapes to

Revered Maharaj at his lunch. I was given this instruction on the very second day of my joining the Math. Without realizing that Revered Maharaj took fixed pieces of fruits, I had served him a few extra pieces. On that day, Revered Maharaj ate his usual quantity and left the remaining pieces untouched. I again served extra pieces of fruits the next day. Revered Maharaj again took his usual quantity and left the remaining pieces untouched. But when I repeated it on the third day, Revered Maharaj took me to task. 'Who instructed you to serve?' he asked. 'Pujari Maharaj,' I replied. 'Did he not tell you the quantity you should serve?' he enquired. I nodded in reply. 'See, the first day you served me, I did not eat the extra fruits. The second day too I did not, hoping that you would understand. But today again, you have done the same thing without any understanding. Don't do it henceforth,' he advised.

This made me realize that he would not take one piece more than his regular intake on the pretext that they were offered to him or that they were tasty.

From the next day, I implicitly followed his instruction.

Every work is Sri Guru Maharaj's work:

On Tuesdays, the kitchen in-charge and I would go to the fruits and vegetable market to purchase fruits for the shrine and vegetables for the kitchen.

Once, when the kitchen in-charge was unwell, Revered Maharaj instructed me to go alone and purchase the fruits and vegetables. Since I was habituated to paying attention to the purchase of fruits, I decided to purchase the fruits first, and then the vegetables. But by the time I finished purchasing fruits, all the fresh vegetables had already been sold out. The cost too was higher than usual. Anyhow, I purchased whatever vegetables that were available and returned to the Math.

After offering my *pranams*, I informed Revered Maharaj that I had purchased both the fruits and the vegetables. Usually, he would ask two questions:

1. 'Did you get fresh fruits and vegetables?'
2. 'Were they comparatively cheap?'

He would also sometimes enquire about the cost of peas. He normally consumed 10 raw peas in the morning and he would become concerned if the prices of the peas increased, for he did not want to spend the Math funds unnecessarily.

On that day, when Revered Maharaj asked me whether I purchased fresh vegetables, I admitted that I could not because I had gone for the purchase of the fruits. Instantly came his reply like a thunderbolt, 'You fool! Do you think that shrine work alone is Sri Ramakrishna's work? Every field of work is His. Sri Ramakrishna is offered cooked food including vegetables and hundreds of people take that as *prasad* in the Math...When you knew the particular time when fresh vegetables would be available, why did you not purchase them first, and then the fruits?'

I was dumb-struck...

He then ordered me to procure fresh vegetables from elsewhere. I went to a nearby shop and managed to get some fresh vegetables. But the prices were naturally higher. My heart was beating faster when I thought how I would face Revered Maharaj. With racing heart beats, I stood before Revered Maharaj. But he quietly pointed out: 'See, because of you, the vehicle had to ply twice to the market, spending more money on fuel etc. Don't repeat this in the future...Every work is an offering to Sri Ramakrishna...Go and arrange the vegetables in the kitchen.'

Simple Living

One day Revered Maharaj asked me, 'How many sets of clothes do you have?'

I replied, '5 sets.'

He exclaimed in surprise, '5 sets! Oh, my God!'

He then asked, 'Why do you require 5 sets of clothes?'

I did not answer.

He then advised, 'Keep only two sets with you. As a monk, you should not accumulate anything. We are responsible and indeed answerable to every grain of food we take, therefore we have to be very careful even in small things.'

He himself set an example through his own simple and dedicated life. He never wasted anything nor had anything more than he really needed.

Exercise Regimen

As per the instruction of Revered Maharaj, there was a practice of recording the weight of everyone in the Math. Once, there was an increase of 5 kilograms of my weight within a month. When Revered Maharaj came to know of this, he exclaimed, 'What! Increased by 5 kilograms within a month? So you do nothing than eating and sleeping!' He called a senior swami and told him, 'Give him [referring to me] a half-trouser! Let him work along with the gardeners in the garden. He has gained 5 kilograms within a month!

I think he probably does not do anything!' The swami cackled at me and asked, 'Are you ready for the half-trouser?!' From then on, I became very cautious while eating...I restricted my food and reduced 3 kilograms the subsequent month.

Next month, I reported to Revered Maharaj that I had reduced my weight by 3 kilograms. He was happy to hear that, but was not completely satisfied. He said that being over-weight or bulky would create health problems, which in turn would affect both our day-to-day life and our spiritual life. He asked me whether I did any physical exercise. I told him that except for walking a few minutes, I did nothing. Then he instructed me to jog in the terrace along with another swami for 45 minutes. With help of a clock, he would daily check whether we jogged for 45 minutes! This regimen improved our mental alertness and in turn, our spiritual growth.

A Pinch of Salt!

Once, there was an article in *The Indian Express* about the negative impacts and side-effects of excessive salt consumption. Revered Maharaj read through the article and told a swami to paste it near the entrance of the dining hall so that everybody could read it.

One day, Revered Maharaj asked me whether I had read the article and reduced my salt consumption. Although I had read the article, I had not reduced my salt intake. When I told him, he became upset. He scolded me for not reducing my salt intake in spite of knowing its harmful effects. He then asked whether I took pickle too. I nodded in assent. He then instructed me, 'From now onwards, avoid taking pickle and salt with the curd rice. This would help you in maintaining good health and in your sadhana. Try to eat sattvic food and that would help you a great deal in your spiritual practices.'

Getting to Sleep!

Revered Maharaj would usually take tender coconut water around 11.30 a.m. After giving him the tender coconut water, I would wait for a few minutes as he would usually tell me something. One day, when I was about to leave after giving him the tender coconut water, he asked me, 'At what time do you go to sleep in the night?' I told him that I generally go to bed at 10.30 p.m. 'What time do you wake up?' he asked next. 'At 4.00 a.m.,' I replied. 'Henceforth, go to bed at 10.00 p.m. itself. You need to have at least 6 hours of sleep, if you have to get up at 4.00 a.m.,' he advised.

Although I was comfortable going to bed at 10.30 p.m., I tried to follow Revered Maharaj's advice. I followed it for some days and then felt it more comfortable to go to bed at 10.30 p.m., my old schedule. After a few days, Revered Maharaj asked me, 'Are you going to bed at 10.00 p.m.' 'No,' I nodded. 'What is the difficulty in going to bed early? If I had asked you to go to bed late, then it would have been difficult. Don't spoil your health. Do you think of Sri Ramakrishna before going to bed? Chant the following verse of the *Chandi* [V:23-25] a few times before going to sleep.' And he told the verse:

या देवी सर्वभूतेषु निद्रारूपेण संस्थिता ।
नमस्तस्यै, नमस्तस्यै, नमस्तस्यै नमो नमः ।। २३ –२३ ।।

yā devī sarvabhūteṣu nidrārūpeṇa saṃsthitā |
namastasyai, namastasyai, namastasyai namo namaḥ ||

I salute again and again the Divine Mother who abides in all beings in the form of sleep.

Switching on Lights!

Usually in the evening, the watchman of the Math would switch on the lights outside the shrine around 6.10 p.m. before the evening *arati*. One day, the Pujari Maharaj wanted me to switch on the lights before I attended the *arati* for three or four days as the watchman was on leave. That day, I had switched on the lights at 5.50 p.m. itself. Revered Maharaj had noticed it. The subsequent day too, I had again switched them on at 5.50 p.m. Noticing the same, Revered Maharaj could tolerate it no more and called me immediately. He asked whether I was instructed to switch on the lights so early. 'Pujari Maharaj told me to switch on the lights before going for the *arati*,' I replied. 'Then why did you switch them on so early? It is just 5.50 p.m. and the lights are usually switched on at 6.10 p.m. If there is an increase in next month's electricity, you would have to pay for it – for your carelessness,' he said. From the next day, I was careful, and fortunately there was no increase in the electricity bill! This incident only shows how minutely he took care of everything that happened in the Math!

A Piece of Paper

One day Revered Maharaj asked me to quote a few incidents in Sri Ramakrishna's life in English. I wrote some incidents on a piece of paper, using the full page on one side and only a quarter page on the other. I had struck off the rest of the page. I showed my writing to Revered Maharaj. He began to read and when he saw that I had struck off three-quarters of the second page, he became annoyed. 'How can you waste the Math's property like this? I can write your entire life history in this space. Never do this again,' he reprimanded me.

It was an eye-opener which made me realize that we have to handle even a small thing of the Math carefully.

Discovering the Cover

One day Revered Maharaj wanted my certificates. When I told him that I had given them at the Math Office, he wanted me to get them from the office. I got the certificates from the office and showed them to Revered Maharaj. After perusing through them, Revered Maharaj told me to return them to the office. I had brought the certificates in a cover and while leaving, I had forgotten to take the cover.

On the next day, when I had gone to Revered Maharaj to offer my *pranams,* he asked me whether I had left anything in his office the previous day. I thought for a while and replied in the negative. He then took out the cover and showed it to me. He had safely preserved it. He asked me how I could forget the cover. He said at least at the time of handing over the certificates in the office, I should have realized it. 'You are young and how can you forget such a small thing? If this is the case, then how can you perform the shrine work? Will you forget something there also? Don't repeat this. Be careful in whatever you do,' he said.

My English!

Revered Maharaj was very particular that the monastic members of the Math must be proficient in Sanskrit and English. So he made arrangements in the Math for these two subjects to be taught to us. There were three classes a week for each subject and Revered Maharaj was particular that we attend them without fail.

One day, as I was offering *pranams* to Revered Maharaj, he asked me whether I had been to the market that day. Instead of replying that I had been to the market the day before, I replied, 'Tomorrow, I went to the market.' 'Oh! If you stand here for a moment more, I too would forget the little English I know,' came his immediate reply. Meanwhile, a senior swami entered the room. Revered Maharaj narrated to him about my reply and instructed him to keep a close watch on whether the English classes were conducted properly and whether I attended them regularly.

Nasty Hit!

One day, when I went to offer my *pranams* to Revered Maharaj, he was writing something at his writing desk. When I offered *pranams,* I hit my head badly against the writing desk and Revered Maharaj's pen flew to the corner due to the jolt. My head was reeling in pain. I had expected that Revered Maharaj would show sympathy towards me. But he said, 'What are you doing there? The body is made of just flesh and blood. Go and fetch the pen.' I quietly took the pen, gave it to him, and left the room in disappointment.

After about an hour a senior swami came to my room as directed by Revered Maharaj to inquire about my injury and pain. He gave me an ointment and instructed me to apply it on my head at least for two days.

In the evening, when I met Revered Maharaj, he enquired about the pain and asked me to consult a doctor if the pain persisted. I conveyed to him that I had applied the ointment and found some relief. He advised me to apply the ointment for two days till the pain subsided completely.

In the meanwhile, he had related this incident to the other monks in the Math with a lot of concern. He had told them that my health was important. It was only when other monks who came to enquire about my pain related to this did I realize the depth of his concern which he never showed outwardly.

The Final Days

One evening, while going for his usual walk, Revered Maharaj lost balance when his walking stick got entangled in a desk and he fell down. As he fell, his spectacles broke and injured him badly. That was, unfortunately, the beginning of a series of illnesses he suffered thereafter. He had to be frequently hospitalized from then on, since his health was deteriorating more and more day by day.

Although he was physically unwell, he was very alert mentally and intellectually. He was always in good humour. Once, after a series of tests in the hospital, he was enquiring about the test results.

'How is my Blood Pressure?'

'Normal, Maharaj.'

'How is my sugar level?'

'Normal, Maharaj.'

'How is the ECG report?'

'Normal, Maharaj.'

'Oh! So everything is normal…Am I the one then who is abnormal?!'

Saying this, he burst into a hearty laugh.

Slowly, his health condition became worse. He was persuaded to use a water bed obtained for him from Singapore to lessen his pain and discomfort. Monastic brothers took turns to serve Revered Maharaj. My time for serving him was between 1.00 a.m. to 2.00 a.m. On medical grounds, the doctors had advised us not to give him water to drink as it would have an adverse impact on his health.

One day, there was a testing period for me while I was serving Revered Maharaj. While massaging his legs, I noticed that Revered Maharaj was struggling to convey something to me. When I went nearer, I could hear him very feebly say, 'water…water.' I did not know what to do. I stood confused. Should I give him the water he so desperately needed or should I follow the doctor's advice and avoid giving him water? Unable to bear his desperation, I gave him three spoons of water. After drinking it, Revered Maharaj gratefully looked at me and said, 'Thank You.' That touched my heart and I was really moved by his gesture.

Next morning, I confessed to Revered Maharaj's secretary swami that I had given him water the previous night. He, however, endorsed my action to my great relief. Although some others took me to task for giving him water, I was happy to recollect the satisfaction expressed on Revered Maharaj's face.

After some days, Revered Maharaj went into a coma. Before that, he had expressed his desire to be allowed to go into deep sleep. And on a *Ekadasi,* his heartbeat stopped at 6.32 p.m.

Bountiful Blessings

It was a great blessing to have been in the company of such a great soul who profoundly guided me in my spiritual life. His bountiful blessing would go a long way in strengthening and enhancing my spiritual life. I had always felt at home with him and was really fortunate to have served him.

At Trivandrum

36

A Unique Monk

A Monk[1]

I knew Revered Swami Tapasyananda Maharaj for nearly three decades, and lived with him in Madras for about two and half years.

Revered Maharaj would come to Madras Math every four or five years on his way to the Belur Math. When he became a Trustee in 1965, he would go thrice a year to Belur Math via Madras. Thus we had a good opportunity to meet and converse with him. He used to be free with us though brief in his conversation. His nature was always serious and prone to deep thinking.

He came to take charge of Madras Math in 1971. Some of the monastics who were intimate with him asked him, 'Maharaj, how do you feel coming here as the In-charge? He replied, 'An ascetic should not stay in a place for more than 3 days; I consider 33 years of stay at Trivandrum as 3 days stay and return to parental home.' He further said, 'It is not good for me to be the head of this institution here.' We asked the reason. He said, 'You see, I am advancing in age. This Math being second only to

1. He is a senior monk of the Order residing in one of the Kerala centres.

Belur Math, traditions have to be kept up, and there are a lot of activities - it requires a young, energetic and dynamic person to be the In-charge.

Gradually, he observed the routine of Madras Math. Earlier he was in a Hospital centre, whereas now he was in a Math centre, where many monks and brahmacharis live and a lot of devotees visit. Earlier, there used to be only Sunday classes. Realizing the need of the devotees, he arranged for daily classes an hour before the evening prayer. He improved various departments like dispensary, library, garden etc. But he mainly improved the publications including the three monthly magazines, *The Vedanta Kesari* in English, *Sri Ramakrishna Vijayam* in Tamil and the *Sri Ramakrishna Prabha* in Telugu [Now, the Telugu Magazine is being published by Ramakrishna Math, Hyderabad]. The circulation of the Tamil monthly was going down in number. So Maharaj was seeking for a young swami who could fit in as the editor.

He was requested to write some books, to which he replied he didn't like to write any book at random. Earlier he had written a book on Holy Mother's life and teachings, an authentic book, which is now quite popular. He was a great scholar in Sanskrit also. So the monks requested him to translate some scriptures. 'Yes, but many stalwart Swamis have translated *Upanishads, Gita, Brahmasutras, Prakarana Granthas* etc., so what else remains.' We reminded him that *Srimad Bhagavatam* could be translated. But it was a huge work which would take a long time, perhaps even two years to complete. He asked a printer about the cost of printing. He said for 3 or 4 medium sized volumes, it may cost seventy-five to eighty thousand rupees. Immediately he said, 'I don't have money.' Monks protested saying that Math can pay. He said, 'No, I used to ask other writers – normally, if they want to publish their books, they have to give money for printing.' Realizing Maharaj's predicament, some devotees of Singapore, Malaysia and Madras collected money for printing. Thus, slowly he began his translation work.

Regarding his health, one thing may be mentioned. He was prone to cold throughout the year. Always he used to wear a cap covering the head and throat just as Revered Vijnanananda Maharaj, a direct disciple of Bhagavan Sri Ramakrishna, would do. When he came to Madras, the monks suggested, 'Maharaj, you can take homeopathy medicine for your chronic cold and cough.' He replied laughingly that what he had to take was neither homeopathic nor allopathic but 'Umapathic' medicine! All began to laugh because there was a pun on the word - the doctor who prepared and gave him the medicine was Umapati Mudaliyar and Lord Siva was also Umapati.

After repeated requests, he finally agreed to take homeopathy medicines. He took them for 10 days. In the meantime, the doctor went away somewhere, giving instruction that no allopathic medicine should be taken in the interim period. A few days after taking homeopathy medicine, the cold began to aggravate, giving pain to the throat. He was unable to take food or sleep at night. Doctor too was not in Madras, and so we requested him to take allopathic medicine for the time being to get relief from the throat pain. But Maharaj was very disciplined; he didn't take allopathic medicines, lived only on milk and bread, sleeping for some time either sitting on chair or lying on the bed. This went on for 10 or 12 days. By then, the doctor returned and apologized for the trouble and prescribed the same medicine to be taken more frequently. In a few days, he became all right. After 3 to 4 weeks, he said that the treatment was really very effective. Thereafter, he was not affected by cold.

In the year 1985, he was made vice-president of the Order. So, he had to spiritually initiate and bless devotees in different parts of the country.

During his time, a number of private ashramas came up in Tamil Nadu. He was particular that people, especially among the middle class and the poor, should know about Sri Ramakrishna, Holy Mother and Swamiji. He would, out of the money people offered him, gift books on Sri Ramakrishna and Holy Mother to those who were too poor to purchase books. When he was questioned why he didn't use the Math's money for this purpose, he would tell, 'No, it shouldn't be given from Math; while I have money I can buy and give.'

Earlier he used to be strict and stern. After he began initiating devotees into spiritual life, his attitude became like that of a mother.

Mentioning the names of a few devotees, he would tell that if at all anyone would get salvation, it would be these people. Not those so-called monks or spiritual aspirants. When enquired about the reason, he would say, 'These people never think of time or health. Anytime they are ready to come to the Math and work continuously and also work outside without caring for anything, whereas some of our monks are particular about timing, food, japa, meditation etc.

Regarding linguistic expressions, he used to tell, 'To propagate the ideas of Sri Guru Maharaj and Swamiji, the language should be simple.'

Revered Maharaj had to suffer for nearly a month when he was hospitalized. He never expressed any difficulty, pain, or trouble to anybody. He was always smiling and enquiring about the Math activities. For the last ten days of his life, he was admitted in a nursing home near the Math to facilitate more monks and devotees to visit him.

What is surprising is that a great intellectual like Maharaj also proved himself to be a great *karmayogi* while at Trivandrum, converting a dispensary into a big hospital. After coming to Madras, he proved himself to be a great Bhakta and a Jnani by translating *Srimad Bhagavatam* and authoring several books and spiritually initiating devotees.

37

Does Rest Mean Sleep?

A Monk[1]

I was very fortunate to have the inspiration and guidance from Revered Swami Tapasyananda Maharaj for about one and half years before and another one and half years after the Training Centre (1976-78).

Revered Maharaj lived in a small room on the first floor of the dining hall of Madras Math and I was staying next to him in a bigger room. There was little deviation from his strict routine of sadhana and seva. Sometimes I would find him sitting on a wooden chair in the verandah with one or two small pillows to support his back and doing japa with mala in the night. In spite of having intense back pain, he never complained. Maharaj had great difficulty in squatting. But whenever he visited the room besides the shrine where the relics were kept, he would sit there squatting for hours.

Monastic Life:

While training the monastics, he would never impose but inspire. For example, once in the night class, Manager Maharaj complained to Maharaj that many brahmacharis were not attending the *mangalarati* in the mornings. We

1. He is a senior monk who was in Madras Math as a brahmachari during Revered Maharaj's tenure.

expected that Maharaj would get angry. But he simply smiled and said, 'In winter, it is pleasant to sleep a little more in the cool morning. But dear brothers (now gravely), there would be greater temptations in future. Beware!'

On another occasion, it was found that some brahmacharis overslept in the afternoons and were therefore late in attending to their duties. One brahmachari even ventured to tell Maharaj, perhaps in half-jest, that Swamiji [Swami Vivekananda] in his rules for the Math has mentioned about two hours rest in the afternoons. Maharaj calmly asked, 'Can you show me in any dictionary that *rest meant sleep*? By rest, Swamiji meant that you were free from duties to utilize the time for reading, washing clothes, etc. *He never meant* you should do *Kumbhakarna Upasana* and snore away your precious time.' All laughed and got the message.

Holy Mother Sri Sarada Devi

38

Connecting to Guruparampara

Pravrajika Atmadevaprana[1]

Swami Virupakshananda once told Revered Tapasyananda Maharaj that a girl known to him wanted to be spiritually initiated. But Maharaj replied him, 'Ask her to write to me why she wants to be initiated?'

Well, I didn't imagine asking for initiation will lead me to such a trouble. I sat in as many corners as possible in the prayer hall of Ramakrishna Mission, Chengalpattu asking myself the question and trying to answer it. At last I wrote, 'Revered Maharaj, please accept my humble *pranams*. As a girl of 23 years, I have lost all the hopes of leading a meaningful life in this society where women are meant to be child producing machines and nothing else. But Sri Sarada Devi's life as the Mother of all, and her gracious words gave me some courage to at least try to follow her footsteps. From *The Gospel of the Holy Mother*, I came to know that initiation from a Holy Guru provides physical purity and his blessings and guidance to perform spiritual practices is the first step meant for those who want to rise

1. She was initiated by Revered Maharaj and with his blessing joined Sri Sarada Math, Madras. She is currently serving in Ramakrishna Sarada Mission, Colombo, Sri Lanka.

Sitting: Vireswaranandaji, Tapasyanandaji,
Standing: 3. Tanmayananda 4. Virupakshananda
Office Block Inauguration, Chengalpet, 1983

spiritually. So I pray to you to bless me by accepting me as your holiness's disciple and guide me to perform spiritual practices.'

With a personal prayer to him, I ended the letter. Maharaj graciously consented to spiritually initiate me. As I have read in the reminiscences of Holy Mother how her disciples after initiation used to offer flowers at her holy feet, I also brought big lotuses for that purpose.

The 'Old Temple' at Sri Ramakrishna Math, Mylapore, which is surcharged with holy vibrations even today, is where I had the good fortune of being spiritually initiated by Srimat Swami Tapasyananda Maharaj. And during initiation, the Holy Mother's Shrine which was adjacent to the main Shrine was kept open and I was thrilled with the feeling that Holy Mother was witnessing everything and showering her grace. After the initiation, we were asked to offer *Guru daksina* consisting of garland, dhoti etc and bow down to him to receive his blessings; but no question of offering flowers.

I was feeling terrible and when we came down to take breakfast it was announced that those who wanted to meet Maharaj personally can go one by one. I was determined to fulfil my wish. I did not have any flowers then. And I did not know whom to ask. By Holy Mother's grace, the Pujari Maharaj, who did *arati* in the shrine, came that way. I at once ran to him and told him of my heartfelt desire and begged him for some flowers. He was in a dilemma and said, 'I don't think Maharaj likes these sentiments.' Anyhow he brought some flowers in a plastic bag, but he instructed me to be the last person in the queue. I stood in the queue praying to Holy Mother to grant my desire.

As I entered his room, I saw him seated behind the table and without saying anything I showed him the flowers.

He asked, 'What?'

I said, 'Flowers to offer at your feet'

To my surprise, he held both his palms together in a prayerful attitude and asked me to offer the flowers. I offered a small jasmine garland, two lotuses, and some hibiscus flowers and bowed down to him to my heart's content.

Then Maharaj asked me to take my seat. He asked me about my family background, educational qualifications etc. I conveyed to him my wish to remain unmarried and lead a monastic life. And also added, 'But my parents want me to marry and I have to disobey them.'

'No. They should not force you to marry,' he said.

'Can I join the Sarada Math?' I asked. I also added that Swami Virupakshananda Maharaj had told me that there is a women's Math of Ramakrishna Order where I can join.

'Yes you can. Here also boys come to join. But you youngsters are so easy going that though you people are earnest, you don't want to strive hard. That is the problem,' Maharaj commented.

With this comment, he kept quiet and I bowed down to him and went to the shrine to do japa as instructed. Pujari Maharaj, looking at me could make out that flower offering went off well.

Within two days, Maharaj wrote to Virupakshananda Maharaj about me, giving a suggestion that I could work in the School run by the Mission at Port Trust [at Mint?] and stay in the Ramakrishna Mission's women hostel, adjacent to Sri Sarada Math, which would help me to keep in touch with them. Virupakshananda Maharaj receiving the letter, at once exclaimed, 'See, your Guru is thinking about you! You think over the proposal and let me know.'

I said to him 'I don't think I can stay outside for I may have to face some difficulties from my relatives.'

At this remark of mine, Virupakshananda Maharaj at once turned and thundered at me, 'Jump into the Ramakrishna current. Let it take you where it wants'. After much prayer, I decided to join Sri Sarada Math at once and Virupakshananda Maharaj informed my Guru of my decision and he sent the details about me along with a request to Pravrajika Nirbhayaprana, president of Sri Sarada Math, Madras.

On *Ekadasi,* I left for Madras, first to go to Sri Ramakrishna Math, Mylapore, to get my Guru's blessings on my way to Sri Sarada Math. I expected him to be displeased with me for not following his suggestions and for having hurriedly taken this decision. He was in his office, busy with his writings. He looked up and I said to him, 'Maharaj, I am going to join Sri Sarada Math today, please bless me' and bowed down to him. He noticed that I had put on a white saree and had removed my jewels and said, 'good'.

'Maharaj, I want your guidance,' I requested humbly.

'Try to adjust,' he advised.

Saying these words, he resumed his writing. I was relieved to notice that he was not displeased with me. After joining Sri Sarada Math, Madras, I had the fortune of having his *darsan* a couple of times. After being there in Madras Centre for about 14 months, they decided to send me to the Sri Sarada Math's headquarters at Dakshineshwar. Maharaj was not well then and was not giving *darsan* to devotees. But before leaving for Calcutta, I went to Ramakrishna Math, Mylapore, and explaining my situation, humbly sent a request to Maharaj to bless me. He at once came out, seated in a wheel chair and was happy to learn that I was going to Dakshineshwar for the training. I did *sastanga pranams* and I somehow intuitively felt that I may not see him again for he looked so weak and shattered in health.

After nearly a month, I wrote him a letter from Dakshineshwar but unfortunately I could not get his reply for he had entered *mahasamadhi* too soon. When the news of his *mahasamadhi* reached me, I at once ran to Holy Mother's temple for solace. When Revered Pravrajika Dayaprana, (whom Holy Mother took in her lap as a child) vice-president of Sri Sarada Math saw me running to the temple, she at once sent words for me through a sannyasini and consoled me with her valuable advice. She said, 'Although you lost your Guru in a physical sense, you must always think about the *Guruparampara* – from the great Adi Sankaracharya, in his line Sri Totapuri, Sri Ramakrishna, his direct disciple Mahapurush Maharaj Swami Shivananda and his disciple your Guru. Just try to think how graciously your Guru connected you to this spiritual *Guruparampara* and try to follow his instructions'. I felt as if my Guru handed me over to this venerable nun who took a keen interest in guiding me after this incident.

In another disciple's life also, Maharaj's grace was a turning point. When on her way to another institution, she met Maharaj in Madras to receive his blessings and guidance to lead a noble life, Maharaj at once wrote a letter requesting Revered Pravrajika Dheeraprana, president of Sri Sarada Math, Thrissur, to accept her as a novice. And now she is a sannyasini of Sri Sarada Math. I came across another brahmacharini, a disciple of Maharaj who showed me a letter in English written by her to Maharaj which he had corrected with red ink and sent it back to her with the remark that her English was not that bad as she thought and if she tried she could improve it.

Even now whenever I am in difficulty, the gracious figure of my Guru accepting flowers in his palms in a prayerful attitude gives me immense strength and support.

My humble salutations to the *Guruparampara*!

39

Japa, Study and Service

Pravrajika Sarvahitaprana[1]

'Nobody is a stranger. Learn to make the whole world yours,' said the Holy Mother.

How many people are willing to empathize with others' sorrow without expecting anything in return? This divine quality can be found in abundance among the Direct Disciples of Sri Ramakrishna and the monks of the Order established by them. Maharaj, being a true follower of Holy Mother, was an epitome of kindness.

My mother would take us to many temples and pray for getting the association of a *Mahatma* who would guide us on the right path. Her sincere prayers did bear fruit. One day, by chance, she took us to Sri Ramakrishna Math at Mylapore. This was our first visit to the Temple located in the garden in a serene atmosphere, amidst the hustle and bustle of city life.

After paying respects to Sri Ramakrishna, we went to the office to have the *darsan* of the living representative of the Bhagavan. The Manager, Swami Raghaveshananda

1. She was initiated by Revered Maharaj in 1989 and had contact with him for 3 years. She is currently serving in Sarada Math, Bhuvaneswar, Orissa.

Maharaj, was in the office. My mother told him, 'We are coming from a faraway place. These are my daughter and son. Can we have the *darsan* of the President Swami? What payment has to be made for his *darsan*?'The Manager Maharaj, while informing us that we need not pay anything, pointed to a room marked as 'President' and sent us to have the *darsan*.

We went to the room and were dumbfounded to see Revered Tapasyananda Maharaj with a majestic smile. He gestured us to take our seats. We spent 10-15 minutes in the holy company of this great monk who treated us with utmost courtesy and love. The bell for the lunch rang. Revered Maharaj got up and called Manager Maharaj and told him, 'Sankar [Swami Raghaveshananda Maharaj's pre-monastic name], these are our own – arrange *prasad* for them.' What a kind and welcome expression! For the first time we came across a great person who considered ordinary people like us as his own. By the grace of Bhagavan Sri Ramakrishna, we became the recipient of the blessings of Revered Tapasyananda Maharaj forever.

Just as Mahendranath Gupta, like a peacock addicted to opium, would never fail to visit Sri Ramakrishna on holidays, we too, drawn by the deep love of Revered Tapasyananda Maharaj, never failed to visit Madras Math on holidays. We were fortunate to receive *mantra diksa* within a few months. We would long to listen to Maharaj. I was a small girl then. He used to guide me regarding how to do japa, what books to read and how to serve. He used to show his hand and patiently demonstrate the method of doing japa while counting. 'Do you read books? Then read this book, *A Primer of Hinduism*,' saying thus, he presented me the book that was kept on his table. Thereafter, I received many books from him.

Although many years have elapsed since Revered Maharaj attained *mahasamadhi,*I am able to experience the strength instilled by Maharaj. He had motivated me to do japa with full concentration, read good literature, and serve others. He revealed his greatness by accepting us as his own people.

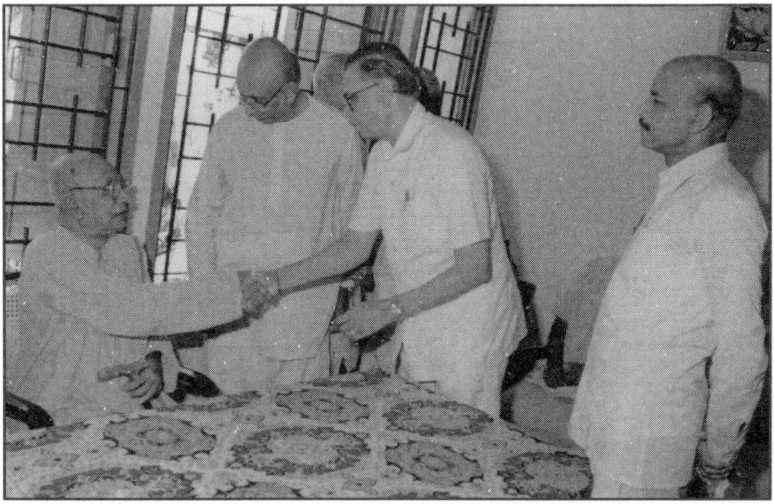

Salem Ashrama Temple Opening on 29-11-1968: Sitting: 1. Gahananandaji 2. Hiranmayanandaji 3. Adidevanandaji 4. Tapasyanandaji 5. Ishwaranandaji 6. Vireshwaranandaji 7. Sukhanandaji 8. Sambhavanandaji 9. Kailashanandaji 10. Chidbhavanandaji 11.Nishkamanandaji Standing: 1st Row: 1. Prameyanandaji 2. Somananda 4. Ananyananda 5. Sarvajnanandaji 6. Samprajnanandji 7. Ekatmananda 8. Golokananda 11. Mitrananda Standing: 2nd Row: Swamis 1. Jneyananda (Bharat), 2. Kirtitananda 3. Sakrananda 7. Chidrupananda 8. Devarupananda Standing: 3rd Row: 1. Sureshananda 2. Nandananda 4. Thathagatananda 6.Smaraharananda 9. Siddhatmananda? (Venkatakrishna, brother of Ananyananda). Standing: 4th Row: 1. Br Sridhar (Purandarananda) 3. Br. Madhavan (Bodhaswarupananda) 4. Haralal 5. Tridiveshananda 6. Siddhinathananda

Section III

Reminiscences by Lay Devotees

1

Become A Real Monk!

Smt. Kumari Amma[1]

Swami Tapasyananda, then as Balakrishnan, grew up in a joint-family system, called *tharavad,* in a place called Varode. Both his parents knew Sanskrit very well, and when his father had gone to Madras for pursuing higher studies, they would write to each other in Sanskrit. His father suddenly died of some disease which was rampant in those days. The young widow was disconsolate and spent most of her time in worship and *tapas* in the little puja room in the attic of her big three-storeyed house. But she was very meticulous in carrying out her daily duties.

When Balettan[2] (Balakrishnan, later Swami Tapasyananda) was about three years old, his mother took him to see his paternal grandfather. He saw the child and prophesized that the child would grow up to be a great *jnani*

---

1. Maharaj's younger brother's wife. She passed away in 1999. A few years earlier, she had shared her reminiscences of Maharaj to a devotee of the Math as she herself had seen him or heard about him from the elders in the family. The reminiscences published here are as recorded by that devotee.

2. The suffix 'ettan' means 'elder brother'. So Balettan meant either one's own elder brother Balan, or Balan, the elder brother of one's husband.

and *bhakta*. Balettan grew up to be an earnest and intelligent boy and was good at his studies.

Once, when Balettan was a boy of about 15 years old, the elders of the house gave him plenty of luscious mangoes to be distributed evenly among the children of the neighbourhood. So he sat down on the grass, told the children to form two queues on his either side and to come one by one. He noticed that some boys were taking the mangoes by breaking the queue. Despite his stern warnings, they persisted in doing this. So he calmly got up and threw the whole lot of mangoes into the ditch! Then, equally calm and unruffled, he walked away.

On another occasion, Balettan's mother brought him to my grandmother's house in Madras. My mother was a young girl then, but she told me that she remembered seeing him very lean and skinny. To fatten him a bit, my grandmother made him and his mother stay with her for some weeks.

The old *tharavad* house near Ottapalam was a huge three-storeyed building. Balettan would take his school books to the big verandah and get absorbed in his studies. This scholastic trend was prominent in him even as a young boy.

After passing out of high school with very high marks, Balettan was at crossroads about what he should be doing in future. At that time, his uncle (mother's brother) was a flourishing lawyer in Madras. So he suggested that the boy could stay with him in Madras and that he would meet all the college expenses of the boy.

While studying in college, Balettan would go frequently to Sri Ramakrishna Math. One day, the librarian noticing that the boy was an avid reader, gave him a book about Sri Ramakrishna to take it home and read. That one book changed his whole life.

Balettan completed his studies in Madras and passed the final exams with very high marks. He learnt of his uncle's intention to send him to England. His uncle wanted him to eventually appear for the I.C.S. exams (Indian Civil Services exams), get a job in India, and marry his daughter! So he told his uncle very politely not to spend any money on sending him to England, as he was aspiring to become a monk of the Ramakrishna Order.

Balettan's uncle was miffed at the boy's apparent selfishness and thought that his poor sister was losing her breadwinner! But the uncle was quite wrong. His mother (my mother-in-law) fully approved his decision to join the monastic Order of Sri Ramakrishna. She blessed him, and advised him to become a real *sanyasi* ("*Yathartha Sanyasi*" were the words she used).

When Balettan was a young probationer in Madras, my mother-in-law used to worry constantly about his health. He wrote a beautiful letter to her in Malayalam asking her not to be anxious about his health and that Sri Ramakrishna would take care of him. His total dedication and devotion came out in his letter to his mother[1].

When Balettan was in Madras Math, my mother-in-law and her sister went there and stayed with his uncle, who gave his carriage to them for freely visiting various places in the city. They went for some sight-seeing, but that was not their real intention of visiting Madras. They wanted to go to Sri Ramakrishna Math, offer *pranams* to Sri Ramakrishna

1. His letter dt. 3.12.28 is included in this book (letter no.10, p 92).

and see Balettan. When they reached the Math, the temple was closed. They asked if they could meet any of the monks. But they were told that as the noon meal was over, all had gone for rest.

Revered Swami Brahmananda Maharaj, who was on a visit to Madras then, heard them talking. He flung open his window (on the upper floor) and saw the two ladies below. He told his attendant to find out their problem. Coming to know of their wish, he told the attendant to seat the ladies in the hall and that he would be coming down in a moment. He also told the attendant to bring some fruit-*prasad* for the ladies. They were overwhelmed with joy, especially because they could offer their *pranams* to Revered Maharaj. My mother-in-law confessed later that after being in the mere presence of Swami Brahmananda Maharaj, all her sorrows left her heart.

While sitting at the feet of Revered Brahmananda Maharaj at the Math, my mother-in-law noticed how Revered Maharaj's mind was always soaring up into higher realms, and how he answered questions related to spiritual life from that high state of mind. If someone asked Maharaj any worldly questions – like when the son would get a job or the daughter would get married – she noticed that, though Maharaj never showed any annoyance, it was with great effort that he brought his mind down to normal plane from its natural lofty level in order to answer such questions. He was full of compassion and this quality was distinctly felt in his answers.

In Madras Math, Balettan was in the publication department[1], and that work was most conducive for him.

1. Maharaj was actually the editor of *The Vedanta Kesari.*

He could spend long hours studying, proof-reading and building up the nascent library. He would be in the library most of the time. He was not very interested in meeting people unless they wanted to talk about spiritual matters.

My husband had wanted to stay in the Math for a few days and prepare for his examinations. But Balettan did not let him stay, saying that he could study perfectly well in his own house. Many years later, however, my husband came and stayed a few days at the Math.

Balettan's mother lived to a ripe old age. One of her last wishes was to see him once more. When Balettan was informed, he went to see her over a week-end, staying in Ramakrishna Ashrama in Palapuram which was very close to his mother's house. Her eyesight was almost failing by then, but she very affectionately caressed his face and chin. She remarked very happily to me that at last her son (Balettan) seemed to have put on some weight.

A few days later, my mother-in-law passed away peacefully. As she passed away, there was a gentle smile on her face, as though confirming what she had told me earlier, that she was not afraid of death. She had added words to the effect that she was not afraid because she knew Sri Ramakrishna would take her to His *Loka* – the *Ramakrishna Loka*.

2

Inheriting a Glorious Heritage

Smt. Indira Krishnakumar[1]

'We parents do not mind you children taking to the holy orders, provided you do that with full conviction and commitment. If you can practice renunciation in the true sense and become a true sadhu like Balettan[2], you are free to embrace sannyasa,' were the words uttered by my mother, time and again, to me and my siblings, which has remained deeply etched in my mind since I was young.

Maharaj, in his pre-monastic life, was my father's first cousin. His mother Smt. Palat Parukkutti Amma and my father's mother Palat Nanikutty Amma were sisters. In the matriarchal setup of Nair families, maternal first cousins were considered almost as close as one's own siblings. Thus Balakrishnan was my father's elder brother. My father would call him Balettan. The respect and admiration

1. She received spiritual initiation from Revered Swami Vireswarananda Maharaj in 1972. She joined the Indian Postal Service in 1974 and retired as Member, Postal Service Board. She used to meet Maharaj at Madras Math now and then.

2. Maharaj's younger brother and cousins would address him as Balettan [elder brother Balan]. She too, as she herself says in her reminiscences, used to address Maharaj as Balettan imitating her parents. She should have actually addressed Maharaj as Balamama [Uncle Balan].

in which my parents held him is indescribable. My father had two younger brothers. They and their wives, that is, my uncles and aunts also spoke about Balettan with full reverence. The entire family was proud about the fact that Balettan renounced worldly life to join Ramakrishna Math and lived as a brilliant example and embodiment of the ideal of sacrifice and renunciation. If my mother could say that we, her children, could become sannyasis and sannyasinis if we were capable of living and renouncing like Balettan, it only showed how deeply the illustrious life of Balettan had shaped the psyche of the family. And aura of Balettan joining the Math was enhanced by the fact that his mother permitted him to do so with her whole-hearted approval. She was just sixteen when Balettan was born and became a widow at the age of eighteen. Balettan embraced sannyasa when he was twenty four years. He had however even earlier clearly declared his intention to join the Order. In the normal course, his mother, as a young widow, would have expected her son who had successfully completed his university education to be her support. She had undergone considerable difficulties to raise her children and give them good education. But with all that, she was only happy and proud to offer her elder son at the holy feet of Bhagavan Sri Ramakrishna. I have heard that when she had received spiritual initiation from Revered Brahmananda Maharaj in 1921, she had prayed to him that one of her sons may fully dedicate his life in the service of Sri Ramakrishna. In a way, unknowingly she had introduced a new ethos in the family – to deeply revere the institution of monasticism. Through her blessed association with Swami Nirmalananda Maharaj, several members of her family received *mantra diksa* and became the recipients of Sri Ramakrishna's grace.

My mother's father, Sri E.K. Ramavarma Raja, was the Valiya Raja of Kadathanad. He was a great devotee of Sri Guruvayoorappan and had great respect of sannyasa and sannyasis. He was proud to marry his daughter to a person whose father had become a sannyasi. In 1921, he was fortunate to receive spiritual initiation from Revered Brahmananda Maharaj in Madras. My paternal and maternal grandmothers and my father and his brothers were all disciples of Swami Nirmalananda Maharaj.

Sri Kulakunnath Sankara Menon, my paternal grandfather, after begetting three sons, that is, my father and his two younger brothers, became disciples of Swami Nirmalananda Maharaj and took sannyasa assuming the name Swami Amalananda in early 1930s when he was nearly forty. In 1984, he passed away at Sri Ramakrishna Ashrama, Puranattukura, Trichur. I have no words to adequately express his great efforts to expose me to Sri Ramakrishna's life and message.

Sri K.P. Sankaramenon, my father, was twelve years younger to Balettan. By the time my father was five years, Balettan had left for Madras to pursue his higher studies. So my father's remembrance of Balettan starts from the time Balettan used to come to their Palat House at Varod during college vacations. My father used to recall that Balettan, unlike the boys of his age, was more interested in god – related activities than mere gross and sensational games like football, 'head ball' (thalappanthu). The palatial house was surrounded by extensive grounds with ponds abounding in fish. Other boys loved hunting and fishing. But Balettan would not join them. He was content with praying and playing with images of gods. Imitation of puja was his favourite pastime. He never would romp around, shout, eat binges or indulge in mischievous pranks. He was studious, disciplined, reserved, decorous, and a man of few words and needs. Above all, he was an avid reader of religious literature and magazines like *Prabuddha Bharata*.

Sober and disciplined, Balettan would get irritated when other boys ran amuck and were indecorous. Once, at home, Balettan, as a young boy, was cutting juicy mangoes for the younger ones. Tempted by the fresh, luscious, and juicy pieces of mangoes, the boys started snatching them even while Balettan was cutting them. Initially, Balettan told them to be patient, assuring them that he would distribute the pieces to everyone after completing his task. But it fell on deaf ears. Then he warned them that he would not cut more mangoes if they continued to be undisciplined. Boys were boys and they paid no heed to him. When the menace grew, he just threw off the entire lot and simply walked away. That was Balettan!

I met Balettan for the first time, as far as I remember, in 1965, when he came to his mother's house 'Sarada Mandiram' in Sri Ramakrishna Nagar. I was 14 then. Considering the fact that he belonged to my father's generation I should have called him 'Balamama' [Uncle Balan]. But I got into the habit of referring to him as Balettan imitating my parents. When I reached his house with many other relatives, Balettan was sitting in the drawing room. It was difficult to miss his calm and serene bearing. When one after another prostrated before him, he sat with his hands clasped in a prayerful mood. It was evident from his expression that he felt that he was only a humble servant of Sri Ramakrishna. It was as though he was passing all our salutations to his Great Master.

After enquiring about our well-being, Balettan turned to us who were then students and advised us to study well, reading the lessons again and again. He asked us to tell about 'UNCTAD' and Rhodesia. That was a bolt from the blue. One was the United Nations Conference on Trade and Development and the other was a place in Africa. Beyond this, we were unable to say anything. Balettan was evidently dissatisfied with our level of awareness, or more precisely, ignorance.

UNCTAD had just been established in 1964, and for a developing country like India, it meant more in terms of the prospects and opportunities it promised. With the raging civil war, which later led to the Unilateral Declaration of Independence, Rhodesia had grabbed international attention at that time. It was unpardonable that we had not paid enough attention to these events. I felt embarrassed to realize that Balettan down rated our general knowledge. He seriously advised us to attentively read the newspapers and not just have a customary glance. My first meeting with him made such an impact on me that even today, nearly half a century later, I cannot think of Balettan without 'UNCTAD' and Rhodesia gushing into my mind.

Revered Swami Vireswarananda Maharaj, president of the Ramakrishna Order, was planning to visit Madras Math in August 1972. It was a long-cherished wish of my grandfather and Swami Amalananda Maharaj, that we, who belonged to the younger generation, took spiritual initiation from Revered Vireswarananda Maharaj. My father, who was serving in the Tamil Nadu Special Police, was posted at Avadi (in Madras) during those days. In accordance with my grandfather's wish, my father visited the Math in Mylapore, Madras, when Balettan was the president. On 22 July 1972, my father wrote to me giving the details about Revered Vireswarananda Maharaj's visit and that our spiritual initiation might be on the 4th or the 5th of August. My father made enquiries about the *guru daksina* to Balettan who said that there was no hard and fast rule about it. It may consist of flowers, fruits, clothes and cash as per the wish and capability of the aspirant.

My younger sister Valsala and I set out for Madras as soon as we received my father's letter at Ottapalam. My father took us to Madras Math on 4th of August. Details regarding our *ista devata,* how we saw Sri Ramakrishna etc. were collected from us. Early morning on 5 August 1972, without taking any food, we went again to the Math at Mylapore. Balettan asked us to sit in the prayer hall and be engaged in prayer. Several aspirants who had registered their names gathered there. Balettan was sixty eight years old at that time. I vividly remember his brisk gait and laconic speech, paying attention even to the minutest details. Some of the aspirants had brought several items as *guru daksina,* while some others had not brought anything. Balettan distributed the items in such a way that no one would approach his or her guru empty-handed. After receiving *mantra diksa* and partaking of the *prasad,* we departed. Thanks to Balettan's efficiency and administrative skills, the initiation took place smoothly.

One of my cousins, my father's youngest brother Sri Vasudeva Menon's daughter, Smt. Geetha Achuthankutty, recalls with gratification how she yearned to receive *mantra diksa* from Balettan and how her patient waiting proved to be fruitful. While her aunts and younger sister took spiritual initiation from one of the gurus of the Ramakrishna Order who visited Trichur Ashrama in 1980s, she withheld from getting initiated with a fond hope and a firm resolve to take the mantra only from Balamama. At that time, Balettan had not been authorized to initiate devotees. But in 1985, when he was authorized, Geetha went to Madras with her husband, mother and uncle (father's brother) Sri Ramakrishna Menon. Despite uncle's age, he was willing to accompany his niece to Madras because someone in the family was going to receive spiritual initiation from Balettan, for whom he had great respect and regard. After the initiation, Maharaj advised Geetha to chant at least ten *slokas* of the *Bhagavad Gita* and read a passage from *The Gospel of Sri Ramakrishna* as a daily practice.

In 1974, I was called for an interview after passing the written examinations of IAS and Allied Services Examination of 1973. As advised by my grandfather and father, I wrote to Revered Vireswrananda Maharaj and Balettan seeking their blessings. Both of them replied conveying their blessings. In his reply, Balettan also appreciated the clarity of thought and expression in my letter. He wrote reassuringly that clarity of communication coupled with hardwork and presence of mind should fetch good results in the interview. I was extremely happy to receive this letter, particularly after the 'UNCTAD and Rhodesia' incident a decade ago!

When the final results of the interview appeared in the newspapers on 3 June 1974, I was gratified to note that I was selected for one of the central services as a Class I officer. In mid-June, my husband, Sri Krishnakumar and I went to Madras *en route* to Raipur. While at Madras, we went to the Math at Mylapore and Balettan was pleased to know about the results of the Civil Services Examination.This time, he spoke at length about how the destination of people from Kerala intent on making money had shifted from Persia (now Iran) to Singapore and Malaysia to the Gulf recently. It seemed to me that Balettan was telling the youngsters like us to give some attention to the contemporary events and important national and international trends.

In 1975, a girl was born to me and I wrote to Balettan expressing my intense wish that Rema, my daughter[1], grow up as a child of Sri Ramakrishna and Sri Sarada Devi. Like before, he replied showering his blessings and benedictions.

In 1985, when I was posted to Tiruchirappally (Trichy) as the Director of Postal Services, I got several opportunities to visit Madras Math. During those visits, Balettan would talk to me more about spiritual practice and spiritual growth than anything else. On 15 August 1987, I went to the Math with the book *The Adventures in Religious Life* authored by Revered Swami Yatiswarananda Maharaj who was the guru of my mother and two of my aunts. I had bought the book from the Math five days earlier. Balettan autographed the book with the words "Spiritual endeavours alone make human life meaningful".

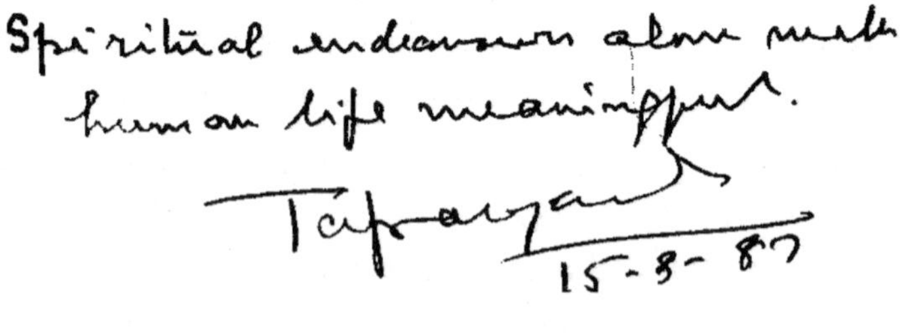

1. Her homage to Revered Maharaj is published in the Appendices of this book.

In the author's preface of this book, Swami Yatiswarananda Maharaj writes, 'Wishing to see me grow along intellectual and literary lines side by side with the spiritual, the Swami [Swami Brahmananda Maharaj] greatly encouraged me in my study of religion and allied literature.' Balettan also had this habit of insisting the youngsters to widen their mental and intellectual horizons in the realm of knowledge. But his ultimate message always was that spiritual endeavours alone make human life meaningful.

During one of these visits, I had lamented about lack of time to undertake some task. But Balettan said, 'First develop the habit of getting up at 3 a.m. in the morning. Then you would get a good head-start. If you prioritize your tasks and dedicate your time accordingly, you will never feel that there is lack of time. First practice this. Then see whether there is any room for complaining about "no time".'

Out of curiosity, I would ask people, who knew Maharaj as a monk, whether he was very stern. They would always say that he was strict with himself, but kind to others even though he always insisted on discipline. Several devotees would approach him with their personal problems and sorrows. He would not allow himself to be carried away in fleeting emotions, but would always analyze the situation discreetly and suggest practical solutions to them. His grave exterior gave the impression that he was impervious to all external impacts. But in his heart of hearts, he believed in concern, not sentimentalism.

In the beginning of 1990, I got the orders of transfer from Trichy to Calicut. Not long before this, I had gone to the Math. This must have been in the end of 1989. My husband's sister Smt. Thankam who had settled in Madras was keen to go to the Math this time. When we went there together, Balettan talked to us for some time and told us to partake noon-*prasad*. Normally Balettan would not extend this hospitality, particularly to people like us. For people like us, he always served only food for thought, which more than satisfied our hunger and appetite. But this time it was different. My sister-in-law who normally had reservations about taking food outside when her husband would be waiting for her to return home and serve him food, was also very receptive that day and warmed up to this invitation. I too was overjoyed. In bliss we partook *prasad* sitting in the abode of God. That was the last time I met Balettan. And perhaps that was the last time Smt. Thankam, my sister-in-law, had an opportunity to take *prasad* in a Ramakrishna Ashram. Today both Balettan and Smt. Thankam are not alive in a physical sense. In retrospect, I feel that there was a touch of conclusiveness about that occasion.

A year after I shifted to Calicut, in the second half of 1991, news reached me that Balettan was seriously ill. Balettan's younger brother, Sri K. P. Achutha Menon, whom we call Appumama, had passed away in 1984 at the Ramakrishna Ashrama Hospital, Sasthamangalam that Balettan had assiduously built up. On receipt of news of Balettan's illness, Appumama's son Udayanan, we call him Unniettan, went to Madras. Those were Balettan's last days. Soon after Unniettan returned from Madras, news of Balettan's *mahasamadhi* reached us.

When I met Unniettan in October 1991, I asked him about his last meeting with Balettan. Unniettan said that Balettan was extremely sick when he met him. He had asked Balettan,

'Balamama, do you recognize me?' At this Maharaj nodded his head as though to say yes. But Unniettan had wondered whether Balettan really recognized him. While this doubt was crossing his mind, Balettan mustered strength and said, 'Sankarankutty's daughter who is in the postal service.....' Balettan was asking about me. This assured Unniettan that Balamama had recognized him. When Unniettan narrated this incident, I felt I was the recipient of a great blessing. A great soul like Balettan had remembered me in his last days and was kind enough to ask about me.

Recently, I met Sri Damodaran Nair who works in Sri Ramakrishna Ashrama, Sasthamangalam, as a watchman and attendant. It would be interesting to learn how people who were engaged in manual labour under Balettan's supervision saw him. Sri Damodaran Nair would accompany his father to the Ashrama for work. He had the good fortune of working in the Ashrama from 1966 to 1971 when Balettan was the president. He was just a young boy of fifteen when he came. In 1967, the preparations for the inauguration of the psychiatric ward in the hospital were in progress. As the date of its inauguration was fixed, there was plenty of work that needed to be done – like leveling the ground in front of the building etc. Sri Damodaran had rendered considerable service which was highly appreciated by Balettan. Later when there was a requirement of a robust man in the Ashrama kitchen, Balettan called Sri Damodaran to join the kitchen. Sri Damodaran was then actually intending to join the canteen of LIC, Trivandrum, which promised him good pay. But when he learnt that Balettan wanted him at the Ashrama, without any second thought, he gladly took up the work in the Ashrama. Sri Damodaran was strong and sturdy and was more efficient in work, especially in heavy works like grinding the flour for *idlis* etc. Naturally there would be some rivalries and jealousies and some of the co-workers would complain to Balettan about him. Balettan would promptly call him and rebuke, 'Fool! How many times have I told you to be careful?' Those who complained would be happy to see the president giving his piece of mind to the 'troublesome' Damodaran. But after they left gratified thus, Balettan would tell, 'Don't worry. Do your work to the best of your ability.' Sri Damodaran says that 'fool' is the strongest word in Maharaj's vocabulary to convey his displeasure.

At nights, Balettan would sleep in the open verandah of the old dispensary and Sri Damodaran would also be lying down nearby in the nights. Being a youngster, Sri Damodaran loved going for movies. When the urge would fill him to the brim, he would seek Balettan's permission to absent himself for a few hours. Then Balettan would say, 'Damodaran, where is the need to go to a cinema? Whenever you visit the wards and the operation theatre, you witness smiles and tears, laughter and wailings pouring into your ears. Is it in any way different from what you get in a cinema? This life itself is like a cinema. What you get in a cinema is no different from what you see here.'

Sri Damodaran Nair nostalgically recalls with admiration, 'Maharaj had only one thing in his mind – institution, institution and institution all the way. He had no thought of himself. He would undergo any amount of hardship for the sake of the institution. Difficult to come across a person of lesser wants and needs…'

Innumerable are the occasions when I have introduced myself as Swami Tapasyananda Maharaj's niece to monastics and devotees. Each time I tell myself silently, 'Look, it is not enough to put forth this claim with self-importance. You have to live upto it. Do justice to the rich inheritance you have been fortunate to receive.' I am fortunate that, within the family, two sannyasis, Swami Amalananda Maharaj and Swami Tapasyananda Maharaj have been there to enrich our lives. They are like pole stars indicating the direction to be taken and lamp posts shedding light on the way!

3

Immortal Love

Dr. M.K. Mukherjee[1]

Prelude

Before I met Swami Tapasyananda Maharaj, under very interesting circumstances, I happened to come across his name in a book on the Holy Mother Sri Sarada Devi he had authored.

In 1965, I was posted to Bombay by the Government of India immediately after I was recruited for India's space programme. As if propelled by destiny, I had visited one of the famous bookstalls in Bombay and my eyes fell on the celebrated book, *Sri Sarada Devi The Holy Mother* by Swami Tapasyananda. Strangely, the very name of the author appealed to me and I began to deeply cogitate for some time the meaning behind the name until it went into my subconscious to surface again under another strange circumstance.

From Bombay I was deputed to France. At end of March 1966, I visited Ramakrishna Ashrama at Gretz near Paris. I met Swami Ritajananda Maharaj who exhorted me to visit

1. He was initiated by Revered Swami Vireswarananda Maharaj. He had very close contact with Revered Swami Tapasyananda Maharaj for 25 years. He is a very renowned scientist and had worked in ISRO. He currently stays at Ramakrishna Ashrama, Thiruvananthapuram.

the Trivandrum Centre of the Ramakrishna Mission after my return to India. After I returned to Bombay in 1966 in the month of April, I was posted to Thumba near Trivandrum a month later. As advised, I visited Ramakrishna Ashrama at Sasthamangalam on the eastern suburb of Trivandrum on 25 May 1966.

I had some difficulty in locating the Ashrama, and finally reached there late in the evening. Luckily, though the entrance to the Ashrama was dark, I could spot a young monk of the Ashrama (Swami Golokananda Maharaj) who informed me that Swami Tapasyananda Maharaj was meditating and would not be available till 8.00 p.m.When I told him that I may have to miss my supper if I returned too late, he helped me to find a place to finish my evening meal and wait for Swami Tapasyananda Maharaj.

First meeting with Swami Tapasyananda Maharaj

The meeting took place in the office cum living room of the President of the Ashrama, Swami Tapasyananda Maharaj. It was adjoining the shrine – as if Maharaj wanted to be as close as possible to Sri Ramakrishna. That he used the same room as his office and his bedroom revealed his austerity.

Maharaj had just then finished his evening prayer and was in a very serene mood. He gave a patient hearing to every word of mine and invited me to visit the ashrama again. After offering *pranams* to both the monks, I left for my place without knowing when I would get an opportunity to meet Swami Tapasyananda Maharaj again. Within a few days I returned to Bombay, and with a mysterious quirk of destiny, I came to Trivandrum again on 23 June 1966.

Second meeting with Swami Tapasyananda Maharaj:

I came by taxi to Sasthamangalam in the forenoon of a Sunday to meet Maharaj. I could witness his stern dealing with the taxi driver who tried to exploit and harass me. He suggested that I should report this to the authorities as a case of public harassment so that no one would be exploited in the future. I followed his advice and made the taxi driver to face the magistrate.

Little did I realise at that time that with Maharaj's sympathy for my struggles would help me to shift my residence so close to the Ashrama that I could reach the Ashrama by walking for a few minutes! Every time I met him, his affectionate smile would warm my soul with a feeling that I was with my father or mother. His deep affection might have been responsible for me to stay near the ashrama campus itself from 1967 to 1971, until he left Trivandrum Ashram to take care of Madras Math.

With Swami Tapasyananda Maharaj at Trivandrum:

The most significant aspect of Maharaj's life was his simplicity, austerity, deep devotion to Sri Ramakrishna's work done through the Ashrama and the charitable hospital. It was during his tenure that the hospital developed brick by brick, from a dispensary of modest facilities to a big hospital. Before his departure to Madras, he built another annexe to the main building to fulfil his dream of providing better facilities to the maternity ward. The ground floor was meant to be a "General Ward" for poor female patients and the first floor for the maternity ward. Earlier the mothers and their babies had to be accommodated in the main building whose tiled roof would leak during rainy season.

It took me some time to understand what the ashram was, the principles of monastic life and the ideals behind the charitable activities. Like a father training his son, Maharaj trained me to understand all these in course of time.

I took full liberty to enter Maharaj's office to discuss about some of my mundane (rather than the spiritual) problems. He too suggested brilliant solutions and relieved my tension and consoled me. It surprised me that he, as a monk, could understand the problems of a government employee in an entirely different working condition.

For instance, I complained to Maharaj that I could not return to the ashrama well in time due to the pressure of my work, and that sometimes I had to come too late in the night. I had expected, with a trembling heart, that he would order me to follow strictly the ashrama timings. But he spontaneously suggested me to keep the key of the ashrama gate so that I could enter whenever I returned!

A few months after I began to stay at the Ashrama, Swami Golokananda Maharaj, who had been participating in the *bhajans* in Madras Math for a long time, discovered that I liked to sing *bhajans*. However, in order to avoid disturbing others, we would practise singing when no one else was there. But in spite of being very careful, Maharaj came to know that we were practising songs, called us both to his office. Caught 'red-handed', we admitted the truth, saying in a kind of repentant voice, 'We like singing *bhajans* and other songs.' We were expecting some severe reprimand for doing something without the prior permission of the president of the Ashrama. But we were pleasantly surprised when he said, 'Alright, you may sing one hour during the evening prayer.' Our joy knew no bounds! Thus we began to sing in the evenings. But on some days, I could not reach the ashrama in time to sing in the evening prayer due to the pressure of my work. Once I was caught by Maharaj himself for stealthily entering the Ashrama gate a few minutes after the evening prayer began. I was trembling expecting again his admonishment, but he immediately understood my plight and urged me to rush to the prayer hall revealing to me that he liked our singing the soul-stirring songs! 'Go, go, sing, sing,' he said. He expressed a similar emotion when Swami Golokananda introduced *Ramnam* on *Ekadasi*.

I had to squat for an hour on the floor during the *Ramnam* even though I was not in the habit of sitting in that posture for a long time. Once, after the *Ramnam*, my hip-joints let a crackling sound as I got up. Although I somehow managed to walk out of the prayer hall and climb up the stairs to reach my room on the first floor, slowly, but surely, it began to pain around the hip-joints to such an extent that I had to consult the orthopaedic surgeon, Dr. Achyuta Menon, who examined me thoroughly and advised rest. Mean while, Maharaj came to know about my hip pain. I could understand the intensity of his affection and concern for me by the pain he himself suffered seeing me in that condition which made him to admonish me as a 'foolhardy fellow!'

Was Maharaj's sympathy only towards select individuals or was it for everyone? We would get the answers if we looked at the way Maharaj handled the staff members in the Trivandrum Hospital, which he had built from scratch, brick by brick, undergoing innumerable personal suffering in the process. In fact, the financial condition was so poor that he had to walk more than six kilometres from Nettayam Ashrama, where he was staying, to Sasthamangalam, where the hospital was located. Again, in the evening, he would walk back six kilometres to Nettayam Ashram. Perhaps that way he saved five paisa of the bus fare each time. But, in spite of this, he made every sincere effort to provide monetary help to the extent possible to the working and retired staff, particularly those

Interior view of Nettayam Ashrama

who were either at the lower middle class or the labourer class. Although the Ashrama itself was functioning on public charity, and therefore the finances were meagre, he would somehow try to find a way out to help the needy workers. The workers were aware of his sincere efforts, in spite of several constraints, and lovingly and gratefully regarded him as a fatherly figure. He too showered his love and affection because he saw them as the children of God.

I wish to conclude my reminiscences by describing some glimpses of Maharaj's personality which I observed during my stay with him at the Trivandrum Ashrama and occasional meetings I had with him at Madras Math.

His Personality:

Swami Tapasyananda Maharaj's appearance was so inspiring and radiated such pleasant warmth that I always felt at home in his presence. He never made me feel any time that I was a stranger in the monastery. He, in fact, through his smile and friendliness, gave me an impression that he was one of my best well-wishers, and that our relationship continued that way even after he left Trivandrum for Madras. In fact, it was so deep and emotional that it was very difficult to draw a line between his friendly attitude and parental care. An incident would illustrate this:

Once I was returning from Calcutta by flight to Trivandrum through Madras. I was requested to take an important parcel from Belur Math and deliver it at Madras Math since I had to stop a few hours at Madras before I boarded my flight to Trivandrum. I readily accepted this request because it would give me an opportunity to visit Madras Math and have the blessed *darsan* of Maharaj. Unfortunately, the flight from Calcutta reached Madras at such a time that I reached Madras Math around lunch-time. I just had enough time to hand over the article to Maharaj and rush back to the Madras Airport which was 17 kilometres from Madras Math so that I could board the flight to Trivandrum. To my utter surprise, Maharaj requested me to take lunch and then leave for the airport. I expressed my inability to take lunch there as I was in a hurry to return to the airport. With a painful expression, he muttered, 'Well, if you cannot take lunch here, then…' He said this with so much of feeling like a parent who would be pained to see the child leave home on a hungry stomach! But nevertheless I rushed for the airport, but all the while I was thinking about his deep feeling that I did not dine at the Math. While I was lucky to board the flight to Trivandrum, I felt unlucky that I could not comply with his request. But his deep parental affection remains vivid in my memory even today.

Sometime in the middle of 1991, I again visited Madras Math while returning from Calcutta. At that time, Maharaj was seriously ill and entry of visitors was restricted. However, to my pleasant surprise, one of his *sevaks*(helpers) who knew me personally took me to Maharaj who was then seated on the chair while the other monastic members were squatting on the floor in front of him. I also joined them and sat near Maharaj and listened to the conversation that was going on. I was however keenly watching Maharaj's face. I remembered the initial days of my acquaintance with him. I had once offered to purchase a higher class train ticket when he was planning to go Belur Math to attend monks' conference by the lowest class. But he flatly refused my offer, and I must confess, I was then a bit disappointed. But later when I understood him better, I was impressed with his simple and austere living.

Swami Tapasyananda Maharaj remains with me in the form of 'Immortal Love'.

4

Brothers of Distinction

Prof. V.S. Sharma[1]

Revered Swami Tapasyananda Maharaj was a distinguished monk of the Ramakrishna Order. I was fortunate to be introduced to him in 1956 by my respected teacher, late P. Seshadri Iyer, who was a staunch follower of Sri Ramakrishna and initiated by Revered Swami Nirmalananda Maharaj. Sri Seshadri Iyer was my father's teacher. After my father passed away, I became Sri Iyer's student. He taught me Vedanta, Sanskrit, Bengali and some other languages and also introduced me to the literature on Sri Ramakrishna and Swami Vivekananda.

When I joined the B.A course in Trivandrum, Sri Seshadri Iyer gave a letter introducing me to Swami Tapasyananda Maharaj. I went to the Ashrama in Sasthamangalam. It was a very humble establishment with three monks - Swamis Tapasyananda Maharaj, Siddhinathananda Maharaj and Maitrananda Maharaj.

I used to attend the classes on *Upanishads* by Swami Tapasyananda Maharaj on Sundays and classes on

1. He had contact with Revered Swami Tapasyananda Maharaj for 35 years. He is a former head, Malayalam Dept., and Dean, Kerala University and Mahatma Gandhi University, Kottayam. He currently resides in Thiruvananthapuram.

Srimad Bhagavatam by Swami Siddhinathananda Maharaj on Wednesdays. Both were very informative and enlightening. Swami Tapasyananda Maharaj would talk to me about various topics. For many years our relationship continued.

At Trivandrum

Maharaj had monthly discourses in Quilon, 50 miles away from Trivandrum. To catch a bus to Quilon, he would have to walk for three kilometres or more with a small bag and an umbrella. Many times I would accompany him from Sasthamangalam to Palayam Bus Stand. Those walks and talks were very beneficial for my mind and intellect.

After obtaining my M.A. Degree, I went for some job and returned to Trivandrum in 1962 or so as a Translator in the Government Secretariat, and after two years I joined the University as a teacher. Thus, I got more opportunities to be associated with the Ashrama and with Tapasyananda Maharaj.

One day Maharaj asked: 'Can you give a young Doctor to our hospital?' I replied, 'Yes, after six months.' My younger brother was studying a course on Medicine in Orissa. When the course was completed, as directed by Maharaj, my brother joined as Assistant RMO in the Ashram Hospital. He was given a room to stay, food, and other facilities.

Once Maharaj said, 'I am very happy to find two brothers of distinction are with us.' When I remember these words, my eyes become wet with tears.

My brother, who served the Ashrama Hospital for many years, undertook M.S. Course in Trivandrum Medical College and continued in the Ashram even after the completion of the course. He then worked as a Government Doctor for next 25 years. After taking voluntary retirement, he again joined Ashrama Hospital. After Maharaj left Trivandrum for Madras, he discontinued after some time.

When Maharaj left Trivandrum, all devotees were very sad. Under his guidance, a Vivekananda Centenary Memorial Institute came up in the city for which I was its Secretary for about 15 years. During my tenure, Maharaj's guidance and advice were very encouraging and useful for the running of the institution.

When Swami Tapasyananda Maharaj became the president of Madras Math, I had many opportunities to meet him there. When I visited Madras for the first time to attend a meeting in the University of Madras, I had taken accommodation in a lodge. When I met Maharaj, he lovingly and affectionately compelled me to stay in the Ashram whenever I came to Madras. I had many occasions to stay at Madras Math and meet Maharaj. We used to have many discussions regarding his publications. In one of his books, in the Introduction, he had mentioned my name and thanked me for providing some information to him. I was really surprised to see that and was grateful for his kind gesture.

I have pleasant memories of my association with Maharaj. He was a great intellectual, a man of sacrifice, a person of discipline, and he showed affection to all those who came to him. Being an ardent follower of Sri Ramakrishna, Holy Mother and Swami Vivekananda, well-versed in Indian mythology and philosophy, Maharaj was an inspiring personality, eminent teacher, guide and an excellent writer. Very rarely do we come across such persons. Even long after his demise, I still remember Maharaj's affection, encouragement and inspiration he gave me and my brother for a long period of time.

Sitting: Tanmayanandaji, Tapasyanandaji, Bhuteshanandaji, Veetabhayanandaji at Ramakrishna Mission Students' Home, Madras

5

Confluence of Three Rivers

Dr. T.G.K. Murty[1]

In everyone's life, there will be some turning points that would pave a new path for the rest of the life. For me, meeting Revered Tapasyananda Maharaj towards end of October 1969 at Ramakrishna Mission Hospital, Trivandrum, was such an occasion. Why so? When I look back, I distinctly remember during that period I was not much inclined towards going to temples or reading religious books, in spite of my upbringing in a religious family. It was likely that I was nourishing an idea that religious things are blind faiths and against the young and modern lifestyle.

At that time, we were three youngsters from Andhra Pradesh who joined the then Space Science Technology Centre (SSTC), presently called Indian Space Research Organization (ISRO). With an agnostic mind and being new to Trivandrum's culture and food habits, I was feeling a bit isolated and was aloof. Even in the organization which was just started, it had no full time activities. Having joined with a good academic back ground, I was in close contacts with

1. He was initiated by Revered Swami Bhuteshananda Maharaj in 1977. He had contact with Revered Swami Tapasyananda Maharaj for 13 years. He is an outstanding scientist and was with ISRO. He is currently working as Scientific Adviser, Department of Science and Technology, Government of India and resides in Bangalore.

a few higher ups in the organization. It was through my contact with Dr. M.K. Mukherjee, one of the then Directors of SSTC, that one day I visited the Ramakrishna Mission Hospital. I came to understand at that time that he used to live in Ramakrishna Mission - giving his assistance to the Ashram.

Dr. Mukherjee took me to the Ashrama and introduced me to Revered Tapasyananda Maharaj. It was evening 5 o' clock. Maharaj was standing in front of the small shrine adjoining the hospital. He asked my name and where I came from. I quietly replied that I was from Andhra Pradesh. To which he responded jocularly 'Oh!*gongura* and *aavakai*' [Two hot pickles, widely consumed in Andhra Pradesh]. I was surprised as my imagination about Swamis was different at that time. After a while, he suggested me to go to Nettayam Ashram at my convenience.

But on the very next day, something pulled me to Nettayam. When I visited that place with its calm and beautiful surroundings, the first feeling was very nice. This further accentuated when I met Maharaj there with his very kind words, 'Oh, you have come then. Come,come.' The Maharaj I saw at Sasthamangalam was totally different. That filled me with joy and I had the good fortune of spending the whole day there. The *Midas touch* of Maharaj on that particular day was the turning point that has made me what I am today, fully transformed and devoted to the monks of the Ramakrishna Order. Now I understand that such monks can transform the life of a person with a simple touch. This has imprinted on my mind so strongly that whenever I remember Maharaj, I feel a joy difficult to put in words.

When I recall my association with Revered Tapasyananda Maharaj, I find my contacts with him were sporadic but had left a permanent and cherishing imprint on my mind. To me, he is a confluence of three rivers, '*Trivenisangama*'. In him, I saw a great administrator, when he was at Trivandrum guiding the hospital as the president of Ramakrishna Mission, Trivandrum. When he became president of Sri Ramakrishna Math, Madras, I saw in him a great scholar and researcher translating *Bhagavatam*, an extraordinarily monumental work done by him. When he became the vice-president of the Ramakrishna Math and Mission, I found in him a benevolent mother.

1. Great administrator

During my stay at Trivandrum from 1969 to 1972, his influence and inspiration was so high that I would visit the Mission hospital every Sunday rendering my humble service as a volunteer. The work used to be related to the maintenance and upkeep of the medical instrumentation. On one occasion, Maharaj sat behind and asked me to demonstrate one of the calibrations to him. I was wondering why he was curious to see the calibration. During that time, the questions were so penetrating, and at one point of time he told very seriously, 'Voluntary service should not be taken casually but should be attended with utmost care.' He explained that these instruments are used by the doctors who are not familiar with their technical aspects but depend upon the results. He told that any compromise on the maintenance of the systems can lead to disaster to the poor and innocent patients. I have not done anything untoward but that laid foundations for the rest of my life in organizing the technical activities at my office too, since any negligence can result in failure of space borne systems. During that period, he used to appear as a serious monk with an eagle eye, and he used to emphasize the importance of attending to even the small works with utmost care and sincerity.

Some evenings, he would discuss about our space technology activities and one day he expressed his desire to visit SSTC. In January 1972, he visited SSTC and showed keen interest in understanding the then ongoing programmes through Dr. M.K. Mukherjee, Dr. S.C. Gupta, one other Director, and suggested that these activities should be useful for the common man. When I was in a dilemma whether to go abroad for higher studies or not, he advised me to go for a Ph.D., and in fact Maharaj put a word to Dr. Mukherjee in front of me that 'this boy will come back to serve your organization.' In those days, youngsters who went abroad rarely returned. But that assurance of Maharaj had such an impact on my mind that towards the end of 1976, I decided to return to India in spite of getting a lucrative job in Australia.

Just before going to Australia, I met Maharaj at Madras Math during the function organized to bid farewell to Revered Kailasananda Maharaj and welcome Revered Tapasyananda Maharaj as the president of Madras Math.

In November 1976, after completing Ph.D., I landed at Madras Airport and went straight to Sri Ramakrishna Math, Mylapore, to meet Revered Maharaj. The then Manager of the Math, Swami Tanmayananda Maharaj, asked me whether I knew Tapasyananda Maharaj earlier. I did not give a proper reply because I was feeling within that Maharaj would have forgotten me as I did not correspond with him for nearly five years. After waiting for a few minutes, Swami Tanmayananda Maharaj ushered me into Revered Tapasyananda Maharaj's room. The moment Maharaj saw me, he enquired with extraordinary love and affection expressed on his face, 'Oh Murthy, How are you? How did your Ph.D go? And how did you spend your time in Australia?' With these words, he transported me emotionally to another plane and tears started rolling down my cheeks. I had then a good opportunity to share my experiences with him. He then said, 'Glad you have come back. Now it is time to contribute in return and also go to our Trivandrum Hospital as often as possible.'

After a few minutes, he suggested, 'Why don't you take [spiritual] initiation? Revered Bhuteshananda Maharaj is coming [to Madras] in March 1977 and you too can come then to Madras Math.' Thus he had sown the idea in my mind that I should get spiritually initiated from the Ramakrishna Order. I felt very happy and came out jubilant only to get reprimanded from Swami Tanmayananda Maharaj who said, 'Murthy, why didn't you say that you know Maharaj earlier? In fact, I was short of introducing you to him but even before that Maharaj was so delighted to receive you.' I then explained to him about my earlier contact with Maharaj and my apprehension that he might not remember me after such a long gap. To which Tanmayananda Maharaj said, 'You know Revered Maharaj – he has got such a sharp memory; he can quote several references related to his work on the *Bhagavatam.*'

I went back to Trivandrum, but within a short time was transferred to Bangalore. I started going to Ramakrishna Ashrama, Basavangudi, and met Revered Adidevananda

Maharaj, the then president of Bangalore Ashram. Led by the circumstances, I had my spiritual initiation in Bangalore Ashrama itself instead of receiving initiation at Madras Math.

2. A scholar and researcher

Subsequently, during October 1977, I went to Madras Math with two things in my mind, first, to see Maharaj and second, to tell him that I could not come to Madras for spiritual initiation as originally suggested. This time I went straight and entered his room. He was seriously engrossed in writing, I later came to know, on *Bhagavatam*. While continuing to write, he lifted his head and looking towards me asked whether I went to the shrine before coming to his room? I kept silent and nodded my head giving some explanation. He became very serious and told me to go to the shrine first,spend a few minutes there, and return. I did so and returned to his room, this time with all his usual love, he said 'take *prasad* in the Math.'Then he said, 'Wherever and whenever in future you go to a Ramakrishna Math, first go to the shrine, even if you come across any monks on the way, offer *pranams* to them only after visiting the shrine.' This went so deep into my mind that during the last 35 years, with his blessings, I have not disregarded this advice. During this period, I found him totally different from what I have seen him at Trivandrum. He was a monk then fully engrossed in his literary work having a scholarly and academic approach to our *itihasas*. I found a great scholarly exposition penned by him in *Narayaneeyam* and *Bhagavatam*. I have not found such scholarly and professional approach even in the best scientific thesis.

During his visit to Bapatla in Andhra Pradesh, I got an opportunity of attending on him personally. It was on this occasion he came to Bapatla Saradapuri colony built by Ramakrishna Samithi led by B.S.R.Anjaneyulu,under the guidance of Ramakrishna Mission. At that time, I happened to feel free with him and ventured to ask him, 'Maharaj, the book on *Bhagavatam* translated by you is so scholarly and voluminous, who will read it?' That was at the breakfast time, he paused his eating and said with serious tone, 'It is for the posterity.' A little later, with some ease he said, 'Such a question had come from Swami Ranganathananda also.' Neither did I have the courage to ask him what the question was nor did he elaborate. But later I heard from others that one day Revered Ranganathananda Maharaj, after delivering a lecture at Madras, while passing by Revered Tapasyananda Maharaj's room remarked humourously, 'Write, write, who will read your abstract *puranas*!' Revered Tapasyananda Maharaj also seemed to have remarked, in an equally humourously way, 'Lecture, lecture, how many will understand and follow you!'

When I heard this, I realized the wonderful characteristics of these great personalities. Each one was distinguished in his own way and each one was committed to the upliftment of the people, knowing fully well the ground realities. This incident made a remarkable influence on my life. Irrespective of what we do, we have to do it sincerely, honestly, and with commitment, not worried about the end results. Then, our work would have its own impact. This is a great lesson I learnt.

Sri B.S.R. Anjaneyulu of Bapatla, Andhra Pradesh, related an interesting incident to me. He once travelled with

Revered Maharaj in a two-tier compartment with Maharaj occupying the upper berth. Maharaj usually preferred to travel by ordinary class like a common man. Sri Anjaneyulu, while getting down at his station, Bapatla, offered his *pranams* to Maharaj and requested Maharaj to bless him as he touched his head with Maharaj's feet. Maharaj, who was lying down, got up and came down. Bending his head, he requested Anjaneyulu, 'You have to bless me.' What humility! This only showed how great these monks were.

3. Benevolent Mother

In course of time, Revered Maharaj became the vice-president of the Ramakrishna Order. I was longing to see him in that chair for two reasons, one to express my happiness that he became the vice-president and secondly, I wanted to seek his blessings as I was going through a conflict in my mind. I went to Madras Math and expressed my wish to someone in the office that I want to meet Revered Tapasyananda Maharaj. They said that I can straight go to his room which was located on the first floor of the dining hall. I went upstairs hesitantly, the door was open, and he was lying on the bed. I gently knocked at the door and in response he asked me to come inside. After offering *pranams*, I sat on the floor as it was my

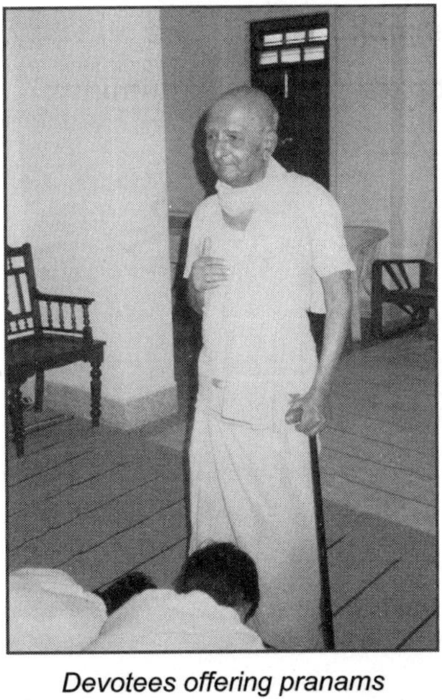

Devotees offering pranams

usual habit, but he insisted that I get up and sit on his bed by his side. Many strange feelings were going on and I could not resist obeying him for two reasons. Firstly, it was a great opportunity that he gave me and secondly, it was an order coming from the vice-president of the Ramakrishna Order. I had the good fortune of spending nearly 15 minutes which gave me a blessed feeling and he removed my conflict in the mind. During this period, I found in him an extraordinary motherly love and tenderness with a wonderfully serene face. He advised on a few things which I cherish in my bosom.

I could not meet him personally afterwards, but his words keep echoing in my ears. I saw the three great personality traits - committed administrator, scholarly vedantist, and a tender mother - all blended in him so beautifully that there was a *trivenisangamam*, a confluence of three rivers, in Revered Maharaj.

I bow down to that great personality with humility.

6

A Channel of Sri Ramakrishna's Grace

S.V. Unnikrishnan[1]

Swami Tapasyananda Maharaj was one of those rare persons who dedicated themselves heart and soul to the service of Sri Ramakrishna in the path shown by Swami Vivekananda. He was all that a monk should be, leading a very simple life and living in high realms of thought. I had the good fortune of having fairly intimate contact with him for about five years (1958 – 63) at Trivandrum.

Maharaj was then the head of Sri Ramakrishna Ashrama of Trivandrum, and lived at the city centre of the Ashrama where he had established, almost single-handedly, a great charitable hospital. The hospital, which started as a simple one-room dispensary, was by 1958, a complex of free wards and a few paying rooms. The free wards accommodated poor patients for whom everything was provided free – accommodation, food, treatment and medicines. The food given to them was the same as the food taken by the monks and some of the staff who took their meals in the Ashrama. There was a team of dedicated doctors, and several

1. He was initiated by Revered Swami Yatiswarananda Maharaj in 1960. He was associated with Revered Swami Tapasyananda Maharaj for 5 years. He worked in the Indian Audit and Accounts Service, and currently resides in Bangalore.

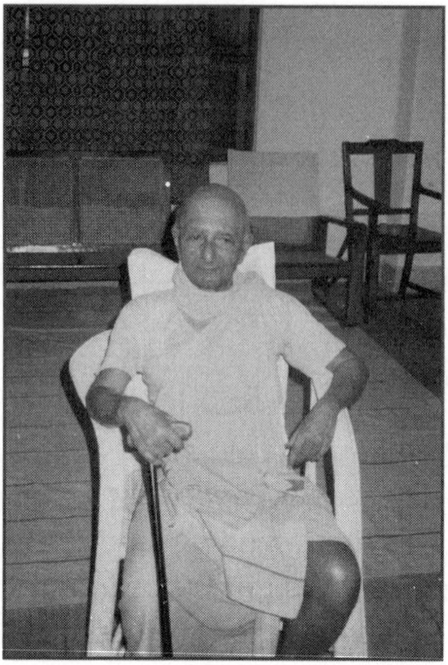

In his room, Madras Math

visiting doctors, some of whom were devotees of Sri Ramakrishna, such as the reputed senior surgeon Kesavan Nair and physician Kesavan Nair, who attended to both out-patients and in-patients. As the hospital grew in size, it became a multi-disciplinary institution with competent doctors and staff.

In 1963, the birth centenary year of Swami Vivekananda, a new large building was constructed in an adjacent plot of land. A Nursing school for training Anxiliary Nurses-Midwives was established later. There was a unique custom of holding evening prayers by the Nursing students which filled the hospital wards with a spiritual atmosphere. Tapasyananda Maharaj himself spent some time everyday in the wards; his very presence instilled discipline and efficiency in the staff. He also attended every operation conducted in the Hospital. There was another old monk, Swami Srikantananda Maharaj, who went around the wards in the evening and met every patient enquiring about his or her condition.

Swami Tapasyananda Maharaj was assisted by two monks, Siddhinathananda Maharaj, who was the manager of the Hospital, and Maitrananda Maharaj, who headed the pathological laboratory. Tapasyananda Maharaj's office room also served as his bedroom – a simple room, with a long bench and writing table on one side and a small table, with a typewriter on it, at the other. The adjacent small room served the same purpose for Swami Siddhinathananda Maharaj, while Swami Maitrananda Maharaj slept in the adjoining Prayer hall. Later an upper storey on the Dispensary building was constructed with enough rooms for the monks and visitors, but Tapasyananda Maharaj remained in his old room. He would wake up before 5 a.m. and, after ablutions, spend two hours in the shrine in meditation. Breakfast bell rang at 7 a.m.; for Tapasyananda Maharaj, breakfast, lunch and dinner all consisted of 2 *idlis* and a glass of tea each time. Maharaj used to take his bath after breakfast, pluck some flowers and do a simple puja of Sri Ramakrishna. There was no food offering in the shrine at the hospital. A brief spell of meditation would follow and then Maharaj would softly read a chapter of *Devi Mahatmyam*. The rest of the day was mostly spent in attending to the hospital affairs. When he was free in the evening, he would walk within the hospital premises for some time.

Sometime around 1960, Maharaj began to hold *Gita* classes in the evenings. A few ardent souls attended the class. Maharaj's talks were erudite and required close attention on the part of the audience. The *Gita* translation and commentary which he wrote later amply prove his scholarship and deep thinking. His elaborate notes on the use of the word "Brahma" and its derivatives show how deep a thinker and scholar he was. The time after dinner was spent in personal correspondence, which was not heavy, and from 9 p.m. to 11p.m., Maharaj would be engrossed in studies, mainly on scriptures. 'Man is a creature of ideas,' he would say and reading and reflection were essential to keep up the flow of ideas. In fact he would always appear to be engrossed in deep thinking. He would go to bed at 11 p.m., spreading a blanket and a sheet on the bench. His dress was most simple – a half sleeve shirt made of thick cotton drill and a double handloom dhoti.

Now some personal reminiscences. During the period 1958 – 63, I was working in the Accountant General's office at Trivandrum in a lower post. I was staying with some others in a rented house not far from the Ashram. I used to go frequently in the evenings to the Ashrama, spend some time with Swami Maitrananda Maharaj, attend the evening *arati* and return to my place. Swami Tapasyananda Maharaj would generally walk in the narrow open space in front of the office building. He had a stern appearance which was due to his scholarly bent of mind and meditative nature, and I had no courage to speak to him. Later I found that he was an extremely kind and affectionate person, especially towards devotees. Sometime during this period, I had to undergo a surgery to remove my tonsils. Knowing my financial condition, Maharaj had this surgery done free of charge. When I regained consciousness, Maitrananda Maharaj was sitting by my side. After a few months, one day Maharaj called me and said, 'Variyar (that was how he called me, by my community name), I find you are a serious person. When you come here, do not spend your time in idle talk. Meditate in the prayer hall for some time. We have a good collection of books in the Prayer Hall; take some book and read.' Thereafter I followed Maharaj's instructions.

In 1960, Swami Yatiswarananda Maharaj had come to the city for a few days stay. He stayed at the main Ashrama at Nettayam, about 6 km away from the city. On some days he would come to the city and talk to the group of devotees assembled there. Tapasyananda Maharaj himself took me to him and requested him to spiritually initiate me, as I felt too diffident to ask for *diksa*. It was readily agreed to; Swami Yatiswarananda Maharaj asked me to read the book, *Eternal Companion* containing the life and teachings of his guru, Swami Brahmananda Maharaj. Swami Tapasyananda Maharaj had great reverence for Swami Yatiswarananda Maharaj. A few days after initiation, Swami Tapasyananda Maharaj asked me how I was faring in the japa of the mantra. I said I was finding some difficulty in "internalizing" the mantra. Maharaj said japa would become natural and automatic with regular practice. This I found true and I could carry on with the japa almost throughout the day.

There were great expectations from me, especially after I graduated from the college, since I was the eldest among the six siblings of an average middle class family. I therefore wanted to appear for the Civil Services Examination, even though that examination was of a post-graduate level. Having a good academic record, this was not an insurmountable task, provided I could study well for the examination. The place where I stayed had hardly any facilities for undertaking any serious study. My first attempt did not succeed as I did not fare well in the interview, though I had cleared the written part of the test. I therefore wanted a more congenial atmosphere to study as it was my last chance to take the examination. The new upper floor of the dispensary building had some rooms unoccupied. I asked Swami Tapasyananda Maharaj for permission to stay in the Ashrama, though outsiders were not generally allowed to stay there for long periods. Maharaj consulted the other two monks and they endorsed my request. One evening, Maharaj called me when we were alone and asked, 'Variyar, what is the idea behind your request to stay in the Ashrama - is it to join the Mission or is it only for the purpose of preparing for the examination?' My family responsibilities always weighed heavily on my mind. I had also the ambition to prove myself that I could come up in life on my own merits. I explained these to Maharaj and his reaction was, 'It is very good that you told me. One should discharge one's family obligations. You can stay here. Occasionally, give me a little help in my correspondence.' I was overwhelmed by his sympathetic attitude. Once in a while, he would ask me to type a small letter, which I did though I had not learnt typewriting. Once he also gave me an article in English for translating it into Malayalam, which I did with the help of Swami Siddhinathananda Maharaj.

Staying in the Ashrama, I got a priceless opportunity to serve Bhagavan Sri Ramakrishna. The work of cleaning the shrine, removing dust from Thakur's large picture which was worshipped there, cleaning the puja vessels, collecting flowers, preparing sandal-wood paste etc. was being done by Swami Maitrananda Maharaj. At the instance of Swami Siddhinathananda Maharaj, I took up this work, the great value of which I realized only later.

After a year of staying in the Ashrama, I found myself successful in the Civil Services Examination. I got a job in Delhi to join the National Academy of Administration in July 1963. I did not have enough money to meet my expenses. One night, Maharaj called me and said, 'Variyar, you are going to a very cold place. You have to spend a good deal of money on warm clothes. You should also get a quilt to cover yourself when you sleep; the Delhi Ashrama will help you. Also get some ankle length tight underwear - that will keep you warm. Now, let me see whether I can help you. I have some money given to me for my talks on All India Radio, writing articles, etc. Let me see how much I have...' He opened the drawer of his writing table (it was never locked), and taking out an old leather purse, poured the contents on the table. There were many ten-rupee and five-rupee notes, all folded in the middle. Counting them, he found that it totaled to 450 rupees. He gave the whole amount to me and said, 'Keep this, you can return it at your convenience.' This was the monk who appeared so stern! I gratefully took the money; it helped me to tide over the initial expenses. Fortunately, the traders in Mussourie were willing to give us all the necessary woolen clothes on credit!

Maharaj was transferred to Madras as the head of that centre some years after I left the Trivandrum Ashrama. Regarding this transfer, he told me some time later, that it was like uprooting a big banyan tree and replanting it elsewhere, and that he was apprehensive whether it would strike roots there and thrive. As is shown by the prodigious work he did while he was in Madras, "the tree" not only struck strong roots but also produced many ever-lasting fruits. I lost touch with him till I was posted to Madras in 1981. I was working in a division of the main A.G.'s office, located in Mylapore, very near the Math. On many evenings, I would go to the Math and meet Maharaj. He always welcomed me most affectionately. His scholarship, command of English and Sanskrit and deep contemplative nature found full play at Madras. His classical work on the life and teachings of Sri Sarada Devi, a collaborative effort with Swami Nikhilananda Maharaj, had already been published in 1940. The biographical part was written by Tapasyananda, for which he travelled to Bengal and collected the material from original sources. This work remains unmatched in its classical style and presentation of the character and significance of Holy mother's life. Among his many works, the translations and explanatory comments of the *Srimad Bhagavatam, Narayaneeyam, Saundarya Lahari* and *Bhagavad Gita* stand out. Once he told me, 'I used to work for long hours daily on the translation of *Bhagavatam*. Sometimes the brain would get so tired; I would not be able to proceed with the work. Then I would just close my eyes and sit quiet without any thoughts for some time and would then feel refreshed. I would then take up the work again.'

Maharaj's translation of *Bhagavatam* is not just a literal translation, in which case it would have been very uninviting to read. It is a lucid translation, written in a pleasant style; whereas the idea in the original is too abstruse and difficult to understand, Maharaj has gone a step further and made the translation an explanatory statement. Thus, the reader does not feel stymied or perplexed at any stage. Sri C.S. Ramakrishnan, a great devotee of Sri Ramakrishna and a life-long associate of Madras Math and a former editor of *The Vedanta Kesari* was a collaborator of Maharaj in many of these works, especially, *Srimad Bhagavatam*. It was due to the enthusiasm of Maharaj and Sri C.S. Ramakrishnan that the material now appearing as Part I of Swami Yatiswarananda Maharaj's book, *How to seek God* was published serially in *The Vedanta Kesari.*

In the year 2000, I had written a comprehensive biography of the Holy mother in Malayalam, at the instance of Swami Sakrananda Maharaj, who was then the head of the Trichur centre. I sent a copy to Sri C.S. Ramakrishnan. His reply dated 12-2-2002 was significant. I am giving here some extracts from the same, as they have something about Tapasyananda Maharaj:

'It was Revered Tapasyananda Maharaj who drew me closer into the Holy Mother. My first collaboration with him was in drafting the chapter on the Motherhood of God which was added to his biography of the Mother. It was heaven working with him in all that he wrote, and you know how much he wrote, especially by way of translation of classic Sanskrit texts.

'Once while returning from Kerala to Madras, his train was held up at Jolarpet for 5 hours. Anybody would have got irritated, but he told me he was happy because he could go on with his reading and writing for 5 hours undisturbed.

'During a retreat at this Math, one of the participants wanted to know how the Sri Chakra is to be installed and worshipped. Tapasyananda Maharaj replied, 'Don't bother about Sri Chakra. Just keep a photo of Sri Sarada Devi before you. Offer a few flowers and meditate. That is the effective Sri Chakra puja.'

One could see Maharaj's ardent devotion to and faith in the Holy Mother in the last passage quoted above.

I had free access to Maharaj. A new edition of the *Upanishads,* with Swami Sharvananda Maharaj's commentary, was being published at that time. At the insistence of Maharaj, I wrote down the Sanskrit passages in Roman script. One evening, when I went to the Math, I was told that I cannot meet Maharaj at that time as he was taking his evening walk. I was about to leave when Maharaj called me from the terrace he was walking, 'Variyar, come up here. You can walk with me.' Whenever I visited the Math in the forenoon, Maharaj would ask me to take *prasad* (lunch) in the Math before returning home. I even now do not know whether I deserved such affection and sympathy from such a great soul like Maharaj.

My last and formal meeting with Maharaj at Madras was memorable. It gave me an insight into his practical and humanitarian nature. I had been subjected to frequent transfers to faraway places, which very badly affected our family life, my children's education, and my finances. I had completed 20 years of service and was eligible for voluntary retirement with a very moderate pension. I wanted to retire and live near the Math, rendering whatever service I could. I met Maharaj and put this proposition before him, seeking his advice. His response was, 'Variyar, don't retire now. You have two small children. You should give them the best education and see that they are well settled in life. You should also rise to the highest position available to the officers of your department.' And he added, 'Don't have any illusions about Ashram life.' I implicitly obeyed Maharaj's instructions and realized that a householder had to discharge his duties fully and at the same time pay attention to moral and spiritual life.

I left for Delhi after some days. I had some brief meetings with Maharaj when I passed through Madras and later, after he became one of the vice-presidents of the Mission, once at Bangalore. I was very sad to learn later that Maharaj was seriously ill and he had been affected by Tuberculosis. I wondered whether his extremely Spartan diet at Trivandrum had undermined his health.

For me, Maharaj was a wide channel through which Sri Ramakrishna's grace flowed into me and many earnest spiritual aspirants. Recently, I had translated his work on *Saundarya Lahari* and wondered at the way in which he had mastered the subject of Shakti worship and presented that system so lucidly. I regard my translation work as my humble tribute to him. For me, he would always be like my guru.

In his room, Madras Math

7

Faith Is Greater Than Reason!

Prof. M.C. Ramanarayanan[1]

I knew most of the monks of the Ramakrishna Mission in Kerala since childhood, and even enjoyed some acquaintance with them. When I met Swami Tapasyananda Maharaj for the first time, I was twenty three and had already done one year of teaching in the college. Unlike my relationship with other Swamis, there was a touch of formality and reserve between us. Sometimes, to my embarrassment, he consulted me on some matters in English usage, though on such occasions, I turned out to be the learner. He never asked anything about my personal details or about my family. He had not given me any spiritual instruction and on one occasion when I asked him something related to my practice, he gave a matter of fact answer which discouraged me from pursuing the subject further. But he always encouraged me to ask him on any other subject under the sun, and told me many things unasked. His words, whether in private conversation or

1. He was initiated by Revered Swami Yatiswarananda Maharaj in 1963. He was associated with Revered Swami Tapasyananda Maharaj for 25 years. He is a retired Professor of English, Ramakrishna Mission Vivekananda College, Chennai. He currently resides in Tiruvalla, Kerala and is in close touch with Ramakrishna Ashrama there.

Ramakrishna Mission Vivekananda College, Madras

lectures, put my otherwise wavering religious faith on a firm ground.

I had known Tapasyananda Maharaj's pre-monastic home long before I met him. His parental home was some thirty kilometers from my hometown, and situated next to Sri Ramakrishna Niranjanananda Ashrama. My father used to take us there for day long celebrations connected with the birthdays of Sri Ramakrishna, Holy Mother and Swamiji. Tapasyananda Maharaj's revered mother was Swami Brahmananda Maharaj's disciple. She used to keep Brahmananda Maharaj's *caranamrita* (the holy water with which the holy feet were washed)in a bottle which she gave us once. My father would fall prostrate at her feet to her embarrassment, because he stood a shade higher in the caste hierarchy.

There is an incident I have heard from Swami Siddhinathananda Maharaj that gives a glimpse of her personality. In her last days she often used to send word to her son that she wished to see him. At long last Maharaj consented to visit her. He sat at her bedside and when he was about to leave, the old lady asked him to give her some water.Although there were others nearby, she insisted that Maharaj himself should pour water into her mouth and then she told him that his last obligation to his mother had been fulfilled. Maharaj related this story to other Swamis and summed up his reaction thus, 'I was shocked'.

I have heard from sister-in-law of Maharaj that before he took orders, which he did with the blessing of his mother at a very young age, he had fulfilled yet another duty by taking her on a pilgrimage.

The only brother of Maharaj, Sri Achutha Menon, was also a man of lofty character. He was an engineer and had occupied many posts in government service and retired as chief engineer. When he was working in Trichur, he used to come home some days in the evening by a passenger train to the small station which was within the vicinity of his home. In those days of steam engines, burning coal from the engine furnace would fall on wooden sleepers of the railroad and burn and damage them. Before he entered his door, he would call his servant to fetch a bucket of water and a mug and see to it that the smoldering fires were doused.

Trivandrum Ashrama had [and even now has] a hospital centre at Sasthamangalam. It was a large hospital having a department for mental health also, a not-so-common feature in those days. Maharaj had built up the hospital with the help of Dr. Raman Thampi who was a disciple of Swami Brahmananda Maharaj. I have heard a story about Maharaj's ardent dedication to the hospital work from Swami Nityabodhananda Maharaj. In the early days of the nursing school, it was difficult to get proper textbooks at the elementary level accessible to girls with inadequate English education. Maharaj prepared a textbook himself and for this purpose observed the nursing during surgeries in the operation theater.

In 1965-66, I used to visit him almost daily. Maharaj lived in a sparsely furnished room. That was his office and living room. There was a cot with a mattress rolled up which he used at night. I visited him in the afternoons, usually after three, after the classes were over. It used to be at tea time. A large stainless steel tumbler of tea would be brought for him. He would order another glass for me too. That amused the other monks, who used to tease me saying I was the first to extract a little hospitality from him. That was mere banter, no doubt, but even that was uncharitable. Someone remarked a bit more seriously that his 'stinginess constricted his personality'.

Maharaj actually was committed to economy in the consumption and management of resources, whether of the Ashrama, the State or Nature at large. I have heard many stories about his 'miserliness'. He rarely travelled, but when he had to, he kept his expenses to the bare minimum. He either walked to the railway station or if he had to start late from the Ashrama Hospital, took a city bus. An attendant would go ahead with his bag on a bicycle and wait outside the station. He started travelling by air only in his old age.

At Madras, Maharaj was concerned about saving water. Once he told me in his own naïve way that one can take a proper bath, with two large mugs of water. This person who pinched and scraped from the Ashrama had absolutely no attachment to money. Sometime after he became the vice-president, one day as I was going to the shrine, I saw him coming from behind. He had a thick wad of currency notes in his right hand, and an umbrella in the left. From the way the notes were folded one might guess they were not counted. When I stopped to greet him he gave me the money, presumably money he had received as *pranami*, and asked me to put it into the collection box and walked away.

Maharaj had difficulty climbing steps because of a swelling in his leg (On one of the rare occasions when he spoke about himself, he said it was diagnosed at the Seva Prathisthan that it was not filarial). My impression is that he identified himself with larger collective entities like the institution of which he was a part, society, his country and humanity at large, but rarely with his biological self. I have seen him angry only when interests of any of these bodies were affected. He openly rebuked a visitor for wasting food at Madras Math. I have once received the full volley of his anger, that too in public, because he thought I had not acted in the interests of the institution. There was nothing personal about it.

Once, some gentlemen visited him at Madras Math. It was the season of cyclones in Madras. It was usual with the cyclones to build up threateningly off the Madras coast, oscillate from north to south unpredictably, putting the weather men of the city to breakfast on their own words every morning, and strike coastal Andhra, Orissa or Bengal expending all the pent up fury. That time also Madras was spared and the gentlemen in the course of the conversation remarked that the city was saved because the Acharya of their sect had performed a *Yajna,* a sacrifice. This provoked Maharaj and he sarcastically remarked that he must be a fine Acharya who deflected a visitation upon Tamil Nadu and allowed it to descend upon Andhra Pradesh.

Maharaj's parsimony was not confined to physical resources. He spared words and feelings alike. His writings and public speeches were devoid of personal anecdotes. He used no more than one illustration to make a point. His sister-in-law nursed a grievance that he did not fondle or show any special affection to her baby when she brought it to show him. He was like the proverbial coconut that cherished the tender and sweet flesh inside its hard shell. Once he said in a speech that people fritter away their emotions on worldly things that they are left with nothing to spare for God. Even now sometimes his earnest face, as he did simple *arati* at the Hospital shrine, often all alone, or in his old age standing at the steps of the hall below the 'Old Temple' in Madras Math on his way to his office in the morning, comes to my mind, all his tender feelings preserved inside his gruff exterior flowing in one uninterrupted stream to his Sri Ramakrishna.

Maharaj always sat erect in a straight backed wooden armchair. At the time I first saw him in Trivandrum, he was reading a voluminous Sanskrit book, most probably the complete works of Sankara, closely bound and its pages turning yellow. In those days all publications of Vedanta Centre, Hollywood were available in the university library and my introduction to Vedanta was through those books. I read them with great interest and formed my own ideas of Vedanta, however imperfectly understood. Maharaj also used to give me something or other to read. When I put a question to him, he would straighten himself, leaning back in his chair and his face would assume a grave expression. In the beginning I used to think he was displeased at the question, but he was actually giving me the full benefit of his attention.

My stay in Trivandrum lasted only for the duration of a short academic year. It was after six years, after many ups and downs in my life, that I was able to enjoy the privilege of listening to Tapasyananda Maharaj again. I had joined the Vivekananda College, Madras, as a tutor in English, and he had become the head of Madras Math. He had begun to hold classes and give discourses on important days. The classes did not last long, but the practice of discourses and answering questions during retreats continued, most of which I have heard. It must be added that Maharaj was not a popular speaker. He did not speak to an audience. He spoke to those among the gathering who cared to listen to him. I for one can vouch for it that those who took pains to listen to him were immensely rewarded. I shall try to summarize what I learnt from him. These ideas may be truisms to others but they had acted like powerful agents to bring about a sea change in my intellectual life.

Maharaj had a keen historical sense by which I mean a sense of continuity of ideas. He presented the teachings of the Master and Swamiji in the context of the continuing tradition of Hinduism. It was listening to Maharaj that I realized the import of T.S.Eliot's statement 'The historical sense involves a perception, not only of the pastness of the past but of its presence', which I had memorized for the examination years before. He emphasized the parallel between Veda Vyasa who consolidated and reinterpreted Vedanta preserving its multiplicity and all-inclusiveness, and Swami Vivekananda and Sri Ramakrishna who ages after, did the same. The truth of Vedanta, I realized is its continuity, its refusal to be falsified by time. Swami Vivekananda said that he taught the truth and the truth is as old as the hills, in retort to a criticism that he had said nothing new.

It was from Maharaj that I learned to appreciate the Puranas. Like all Hindus I have also been brought up on Puranic lore and temple worship and the many legends and myths connected with saints. When one goes through school and college these very stories seem ludicrous. One then relegates them to the realm of fairy tales. The geography, cosmology and history of the Puranas become mere fantasy and valueless to one's mind. I learnt from Maharaj that history is not the events that had happened and now can be chronologically determined but the reaction of the collective mind to those events. Historical events and personalities leave on the collective consciousness of the people impressions that influence their lives. Again puranic cosmology and geography are meant to help the devotee meditate upon the universe as the body of God and history as the play of the Lord. All these ideas are most lucidly discussed in Maharaj's masterly general introduction to his translation of that great *Bhagavata Purana*, in a section especially addressed to the man of modern education. Once this idea sank into my mind I began to see the genealogies and cosmologies of the epic as part of its sublime poetry. At this time, I had to teach portions of Milton's*Paradise Lost* in the college. For the first time in my life, I read with enjoyment and admiration, not only the prescribed portion, but the entire epic.

I believe that Maharaj's attempt to revive keen interest in Puranic literature is of great significance to India's Cultural Renaissance. Often, those acquainted with Swami Vivekananda's works superficially tend to emphasize the *Upanishads* at the cost of the Puranas. Hinduism proper, as distinguished from the universal religion of Vedanta, will lose its identity and uniqueness without the Puranic lore which makes it incarnate to its followers. Sri Ramakrishna spoke in the language of Puranas. He freely quoted the popular versions of the tales of Krishna and Rama obtaining in the rural theatre, the *Adhyatma Ramayana, Ramcharit Manas* and even local temple legends. He was not only the bridge to eternity, but also to the past and the future. Unless this rupture between the past and the present is repaired, and the continuity of tradition identified, the so called Indian renaissance will remain sadly incomplete. I am certain that Maharaj's translation of the *Bhagavatam* and also his *Bhakti Schools of Vedanta* will help Indian intelligentsia to enter the spirit of the Puranas.

I was in those days trying to read difficult texts on Vedanta and seeking elucidation from all sources. I had a colleague endowed with keen intelligence and was well read in western philosophy and had enough understanding of Vedanta acquired through translations. During a friendly discussion, he told me that the traditional analysis of the three states of waking, dream and dreamless sleep to establish the principle of an unchanging consciousness behind all experience was not flawless after all. The experience of restfulness in deep sleep cannot be proved by this reasoning. This experience is a result of the physical well-being one feels after a refreshing sleep. I do not know whether this is a valid reasoning and perhaps a cleverer person could have easily refuted my friend's argument, but it upset me. I had always thought that the analysis of the three states was the clinching argument of Vedanta. If this was unsound, I thought, the foundation of all religion was shaky. I went to Maharaj with this problem. I expected he would give me very strong arguments to reinforce my position. Instead he said he agreed with my friend. Then he talked to me for ten or fifteen minutes on the necessity of faith. He convinced me that faith is a greater faculty in man than reason. If animals are not capable of reason, neither are they capable of faith. If your country is under siege will you wait until you are convinced of the validity of your country's position before you take up arms? You do it in good faith. He spoke in this vein for sometime and once and for all cured me of my obsession. This is the greatest blessing I have received from him. I could later learn that all religious scriptures stress upon faith rather than reason.

Maharaj used to stress the importance of reading *The Gospel of Sri Ramakrishna*, *Sri Ramakrishna, The Great Master*, Holy Mother's life and the lives of the direct disciples and all related literature in his lectures and private conversations. Referring to Sri Ramakrishna's accepting Gurus and doing spiritual practices according to strict scriptural injunctions, in spite of His being a perfected soul and having no need for them, Maharaj would say that the Master was teaching us the necessity of absolute faith in the Teacher, the Deity and the Scripture. This is the traditional concept of *sraddha*. Maharaj in his commentary on the *Gita* had dealt with it at length. He often would refer to Sri Ramakrishna's vision of the unity of *Bhagavata, Bhakta* and *Bhagavan*. The three words cover all categories covered by religion, Man and God and God's revelation as scripture, the Sound-Brahman which is the same as the world. The devotee's meditation on the Self or on the Deity or studying the scriptures of the world in pursuit of truth, are essentially acts of faith, and how limited a role reason has in religion or in science!

Left to Right: 2. Tapasyanandaji 3. Bhuteshanandaji 4. Tanmayanandaji

8

Is This Not Food?

Smt. R. Gnanasundari[1]

Initially, we had contacts only with the monks of Trichur Ashrama and the nuns of Sarada Mandir. One day, Swami Sakrananda Maharaj asked us, 'Do you know Swami Tapasyananda Maharaj?' We replied, 'No, Maharaj.' He said, 'Revered Maharaj is near to your place, he is at Trivandrum. Please meet him.'

We went to meet Revered Maharaj after a few days. As soon as we entered the Ashram, Revered Maharaj told Swami Siddhinathananda Maharaj, 'Devotees of Swami Chidhbhavananda Maharaj have come.' Then, he asked us, 'Swami Chidbhavananda has come to Kollam. Do you know?' 'Yes, Maharaj, he stayed at our house.' I replied.

Swami Tapasyananda - austerity personified Swami, an apt name, a truly apt name. Simple living and high thinking! Once he enters the shrine in the morning, he would spend a lot of time there. Doctors would keep him informed in advance if he had to attend to any work before

1. She was associated with Swami Chidbhavananda Maharaj, Sri Ramakrishna Tapovanam, Tiruparathurai. She was known to Revered Swami Tapasyananda Maharaj for more than 25 years. She was conducting religious classes for children and women in Kollam. She currently resides in Tenkasi, Tirunelvel Dist. and conducts *satsangs*.

that. His breakfast and tea would be kept separately and he would eat the same after coming from the shrine (although it would have by then become cold).

He was the head of a big hospital. He did not even have a separate chair for him. All he wanted was a table, a bench and a few books. He would use the same bench during the day and the night. There was no separate room for him, no cot. Sitting on the bench, he wrote his books. Once we started visiting the Ashram frequently, he told us, 'Either write or call over phone before you come, so that I can come out of the shrine to meet you.'

We invited him to Kollam. He accepted our invitation and immediately fixed the date for his visit. When he visited Kollam, twenty devotees had assembled. Revered Maharaj was happy. He talked on general subject. He said, 'The devotees here are sincere. I will visit once a month and take class on *The Gospel of Sri Ramakrishna* in Malayalam.' A few devotees from Karnataka could not follow the classes in Malayalam. Acceding to their request, Revered Maharaj agreed to take class on *Katha Upanishad* in English from 4.00 p.m. to 5.00 p.m. and the class on *The Gospel* in Malayalam from 5.30 p.m. to 6.30 p.m. He would arrive before 3.30 p.m.

One day he arrived in the morning itself. He said, 'Henceforth, I will be coming in the mornings as I find it difficult to undertake train journey in this heat.'

A few children made the best use of Revered Maharaj's free time. He used to tell the children, 'Eat well, Play well, Pray well' and encourage them to read children's books. The children used to make him happy by singing songs from *Ramayana*.

Revered Maharaj was not at all particular about his food. Whatever was served he would eat. Once, there was a bottle of orange juice. Mistaking it for *rasam*, he poured it over rice. I requested him to leave it aside so that fresh rice and *rasam* could be served. Ignoring my plea, he questioned, 'Is this not food? Food, irrespective of its taste, should be consumed' and ate the rice mixed with juice.

The motor of the water pump was then running. He asked, 'What is that?' 'Water is being pumped up', I said. 'What will happen if it is switched off?' he asked. 'Water will not be pumped up,' I said. 'Will water remain at the same level,' he asked. 'No, once switched off, the water will come down.' He then said, 'Mind is also like that. Once the spiritual practices are stopped, the mind will come down to a lower level. With regular spiritual practice, we should not allow the mind to come down.'

Spiritual retreats were conducted at Nettayam Ashram and classes at Sastamangalam. Classes were in English as Revered Maharaj had just a working knowledge of Malayalam. He did not know literary Malayalam. Once, he gave a talk on the radio in literary Malayalam. When he came to Kollam, we asked, 'How could you talk in literary Malayalam?' He laughed and said, 'I told Siddhinathananda to write and I simply read.'

He was highly respected in Trivandrum. The entire city loved and respected Maharaj. Swami Sakrananda Maharaj narrated one incident. Once, a group of "Samelipuri Disciples" came to Sastamangalam Ashram and stayed there. On his return from Belur Math, he enquired about them. On being told that they were the disciples of Samelipuri, he told the ashrama people to drive the group out of the Ashram. As they left the Ashram, they were caught by the Police. The Police said, 'We were hesitating to enter the Swami's Ashram. To our good luck, the Swami had driven them out.'

When he was requested to go abroad, Revered Maharaj said, 'Please do not export me.' He used to say, 'This is my trench; unless two people push me out and two others pull me out, I will not get out of here.' But Revered Vireswarananda Maharaj took him away to Madras. 'I owe something to Madras Math; was it not there that I met my guru?' saying so, Maharaj took leave of us.

9

The Doctor Has Come For Injection!

Dr. M Rajamony[1]

It was during my final year MBBS at Thanjavur Medical College that I had the opportunity to meet and get acquainted with Revered Swami Tapasyananda Maharaj. It was a blessing and I relish my relationship with that great follower of Sri Ramakrishna.

My house was at Trivandrum and Maharaj wanted me to work in the Ramakrishna Mission Hospital at Trivandrum. By God's grace, I joined the hospital.

The hospital was vibrant with incidents related to Maharaj's effort and wisdom that laid the foundation for that great institution. Maharaj not only started the hospital but also was instrumental in training a group of people in carrying out Swami Vivekananda's ideas and ideals. The people he selected were from socio-economically underprivileged section. He gave them jobs at the hospital and trained them in Swami Vivekananda's method of Karma

---

1. He was initiated by Revered Swami Gambhirananda Maharaj in 1986. He was associated with Revered Swami Tapasyananda Maharaj for 7 years. He was with the Ramakrishna Ashram Hospital in Trivandrum from 1988 to 1995. He is presently an Anaesthesiologist in Kerala Government Health Service. He currently resides in Thiruvananthapuram.

Yoga. Over the years, these people not only improved their economic condition, but also developed great devotion towards Sri Ramakrishna. Their children too were better placed and they attributed their prosperity to Maharaj and the Math. Most of them got spiritually initiated and remained ardent devotees. I knew many of them personally and they have described how they have progressed economically and spiritually under the guidance of Maharaj. This was one of the methods Maharaj used to uplift the common people.

While managing the hospital, Maharaj would give attention to even minute details. He liked to enter the operation theatre and watch the surgeons perform the surgeries. The anaesthetist, surgeon and theatre staff respected his presence inside the theatre. They were astonished at the interest he showed towards surgery. He was familiar with every technique of the surgeon and whenever some medical professional came to him he used to mention those techniques. He was aware of the needs of the operation theatre and used to provide them even without asking.

Every renowned surgeon of those days considered it a privilege to work in the Ramakrishna Mission Hospital. And to get an appreciation from Maharaj was indeed a great reward for them.

Ramakrishna Mission Hospital, Trivandrum,was known for its Psychiatric Department since beginning and patients used to come from faraway places. I met one female patient who used to come for treatment. She had come for treatment with a six monthsold baby and Maharaj made a cradle for her child near the shrine. She used to say proudly that her child was caressed by Maharaj. Imagine the great monk fondling the child in the cradle!

In his room, Madras Math

Maharaj practiced simple living and avoided unnecessary expenditure. Devotees at Trivandrum remember him walking miles to avoid expenditure for the Math. Some have said laughingly that once a senior monk of the Order came to Sasthamangalam and he was asked to walk back to Nettayam Ashrama which was six kilometres away.

When Maharaj was ill at Madras Math, I incidentally happened to be there. I was asked to stay there till Maharaj became better. I felt honoured at the prospect of staying at the Math for some time.

As a doctor, I have come across patients with different attitudes. But Maharaj was entirely different. He never expressed any pain when assailed with bodily ailments. There was no expression of sorrow or despair on his face. He never complained about his bodily ailment. He never had the habit of talking about his difficulties. He was always calm and composed. All he wanted was to be left alone and not to be disturbed with different modalities of the treatment. Many devotees have been witness to this characteristic of Maharaj. To many of us, he was the living embodiment of Sri Ramakrishna's ideals.

During this period, there occurred an incident which demonstrated Maharaj's liberal attitude. One monk who left the Order had written his autobiography in Malayalam. An editorial was written about this book in one of the weeklies even before this autobiography was published as a series in that magazine. Even before its serialization, it had gained popularity because of the editorial. I read the first few chapters of the autobiography and when I told this to one of the monks in the Ashrama, he told me to stop reading that. He was of the opinion that the author was insulting the Math and Sri Guru Maharaj. During my stay in Madras Math, one of the brahmacharis, whose mother tongue was Malayalam, told me that Revered Tapasyananda Maharaj asked him to read that autobiography. I was astonished to hear that Revered Maharaj had recommended this book to a brahmachari who aspired to become a monk of the Order! But that was Revered Maharaj's liberality. He never lost patience when others were critical and abusive.

Maharaj, though known to be strict, was full of humour and fun. Even when he was ill, he was never bereft of humour. Some of the injections given were oily preparations and this caused a lot of pain for Maharaj. After his supper, the monastics used to assemble in his room. I would enter his room when it was time for injection. Seeing me, he would exclaim, 'The doctor has come for injection!' This would provoke wild laughter and I would be silent for some time. After a couple of minutes, he will agree to take the injection. Although he was reluctant to take injections and other medicines, he never wanted to disgrace the doctors.

My outlook towards Holy Mother was changed by Maharaj. He used to say that the *bhajans* depicting Holy Mother as Goddess with four hands and sitting on lion are not mere imaginations of a poet. In his opinion, Holy Mother was the embodiment of great strength and divinity and that behind the normal appearance of an ordinary human being, there lay infinite power and energy.

In his last days, he was admitted to a hospital near the Math. As a doctor, I can discern the smell and vibration in a patient's room. But the vibration in Maharaj's room was entirely different. It was never filled with pathos, as it was in the rooms of other patients. I could feel the vibration of peace and divinity in his room.

Maharaj went into coma during his last five days. On the previous night of his *mahasamadhi*, although he was in coma, his lips were moving and some sounds were muttered. To me, it seemed as if he was addressing an audience. I could discern certain words like Bhakti and a verse from *Bhagavatam*: '*Sravanam Kirtanam Vishno...*' Even at that stage it seemed his entire consciousness was at a higher level. There was silence in the room and a sense of thrill passed all over my body.

What made Swami Tapasyananda Maharaj unique? I used to ponder over this and then came to my mind the words of Swami Vivekananda,"It is love that pays and character that cleaves its way through the adamantine wall of difficulties".

10

Problems Are Universal

A Devotee[1]

By the time I was 15, I had lost the elders in my family. Opportunities for further studies were thus stifled and my life became like a rudderless boat, tossed about by ignorance on one hand and misinformation on the other.

In this situation, Sri Ramakrishna's benevolence beckoned me towards him. One day, when I was casually glancing through the newspapers at the cultural events in the city that day, I happened to see that there was a lecture on *Bhagavad Gita* by Swami Tapasyananda Maharaj at Sri Ramakrishna Mission Ashrama, Sasthamangalam, Trivandrum. I did not realize that time that my life was in for a great revolution. I went to the class just out of curiosity. I found this elderly monk's words elevating me so much that I began to go every week, Wednesday after Wednesday, like an iron scrap attracted to a powerful magnet. Such was the pull that, in those days of scanty transportation facilities, I would cycle or walk a distance of seven miles to reach the Ashrama in time for the class.

Swami Tapasyananda Maharaj's words were soft yet deep, clear yet subtle, and always to the point. He would sweep the minds of the audience with his supreme intellect,

1. He is a devotee of Ramakrishna Ashrama, Thiruvananthapuram.

and like a mother feeding her children, would feed us with the wisdom hidden in our ancient scriptures. He was at ease with physics as much as with metaphysics, quoting and referring to the works of scientists as much as to the works of ancient teachers. His analysis was both instructive and illuminating.

In the very first lecture I heard, Maharaj broke my flimsy ego-centric conceptions that my life alone was assailed with problems while the fact was that the problems were universal and spared none.

Years later, I saw him once speaking about the nine forms of devotion, and he dealt with *'atma nivedanam'* in great length that my mind went back to the first lecture I heard of him. Between those two events, Maharaj had dealt with the entire gamut of Vedanta in a way both the learned and lay could follow and totally obliterated the flimsy egoistic ideas in me through his spiritual guidance.

When I began to visit the Ashrama, Swami Golokananda Maharaj was also there in the Ashrama. An extraordinarily talented organizer, he would arrange symposia, special lecture series etc. Among these, one memorable event was a lecture series on *Bhagavad Gita*. In every symposium, Swami Tapasyananda Maharaj would chair the session, with two other speakers from different walks of life. Swami Tapasyananda Maharaj's opening and concluding remarks would be a life-time experience for any ardent student of philosophy.

Swami Tapasyananda Maharaj would always remind the spiritual aspirants to concentrate on the immediate goal in one's spiritual practices while keeping the ultimate aim of spiritual life in sight. He demonstrated this in practical

At Trivandrum

life, building the hospital brick by brick while keeping the larger picture in view.

After working thus for 30 years, Maharaj moved to Madras to continue his mission. He rendered the voluminous ancient scriptures into English even though he was more than 80 then. Prior to his departure from Trivandrum, the devotees gathered at Nettayam Ashrama to pay their respects to him. While bidding farewell, Maharaj humorously remarked, 'A sannyasin is supposed to stay in one place only for three days; in my life, one day has extended to one decade. Thus three days became three decades!'

Beneath the stern exterior, Maharaj was very kind and unassuming. The day he left Trivandrum for Madras, several devotees thronged the railway station to see him off. And when we all touched his feet while bidding farewell to him, there were no eyes that had no tears. That was the silent influence of this great monk.

11

His Life Is Precious[1]

Prof. C. S. Ramakrishnan[2]

In 1971 Swami Tapasyananda Maharaj took over as [the] president [of Sri Ramakrishna Math, Madras]. Earlier he had been warden of the Students' Home and then editor of *The Vedanta Kesari,* before he went away to develop the Trivandrum centre. After he became a Trustee of the Order, he used to come to Madras thrice a year on his way to Belur Math. I would accompany him to China Bazaar for purchasing articles for the Trivandrum hospital. In those days the hawkers used to spread their wares on the pavement and shout *'Onnara ana, rendra ana.'* All the exhibited articles were being offered for 1½ *anas* or 2 ½ *anas* as the case may be. Maharaj would carefully select items from the heaps, fill his two bags, and return to the Math with the joy of a student who has won a prize in a debate.

True to his name, Tapasyananda Maharaj was the embodiment of austerity. Once he fell ill with chickenpox.

1. Extracts from the article Down Memory Lane, *The Vedanta Kesari,* Dec. 1997, p 539-540.

2. He, popularly known as CSR, was closely associated with Chennai Math for 7 decades and with Revered Maharaj for 2 decades. He was initiated by Revered Swami Virajananda Maharaj and was the editor of The Vedanta Kesari from 1979 to 1986. He was actively involved in Chennai Math publications in so many ways. He passed away in 2008.

He had to use toilet paper. When the brahmachari attending on him gave him a good length of toilet paper, he frowned, tore off a small piece about four inches long, and said, that would do. But this frugality in his own case vanished when others were concerned. One of the boys doing kitchen work developed high fever which would not come down despite treatment by the Math dispensary doctors. Maharaj called me and asked me to get the boy admitted in a nursing home. I pointed out that nursing homes were rather costly. His reply was, 'The boy has been serving Sri Guru Maharaj. His life is precious. Don't worry about the cost.' The medical bill came to about Rs. 4,000. The president who would economize on toilet paper wouldn't mind a hefty expenditure on a worker.

Again, on a day when it was raining heavily I met him wearing a new raincoat. He asked me how much it cost. When I told him, he asked me to get 10 such raincoats for the brahmacharis. When I hesitated, he said, 'These careless fellows will walk about in the rain, catch a cold, and the Math work will suffer.'

A deep thinker and careful writer, he would be at the writing desk for 12 hours a day. His own literary output and diligent supervision made Madras Math the leading publication centre of the Order. His strong belief was that the message of Sri Ramakrishna, Holy Mother and Swamiji could reach the masses only through carefully edited literature. To deserving visitors he would present books, but he would pay for them out of the amounts he received as offering. Practically everything he wrote he would ask me to go through and correct wherever necessary. When I would protest, he would insist that four eyes were better than two.

C.S. Ramakrishnan behind Maharaj

He was fond of *Srimad Bhagavatam.* When I suggested that he should translate it into English, he demurred, saying it was such a big task that he might not live to complete it. I rejoined that on the contrary the Lord would not let him depart without finishing the sacred task. He agreed and the result is that his translation is considered the best even by reputed critics like Professor K. R. Srinivasa Iyengar, who praised it for its clarity and elegance. The fact is that Maharaj was very particular in choosing words. Every morning he would give me a list of Sanskrit words for which I was to find out the various shades of meaning. He would then choose the best term appropriate to the particular context…

When there was a phone call from Belur Math that the Trustees had chosen him to be a vice-president of the Order, he brushed aside the proposal. He did not want such formalities. But I recalled to him how he had found fault with a senior monk who refused to take up the headship of any centre as he was more interested in his literary work. The point impressed him. Devotion to the needs of the Order should take priority over all other personal considerations. He agreed to abide by the dictate of the headquarters.

12

A Purnakumbha of Knowledge

Dr.(Miss) M. Lakshmi Kumari[1]

स्वाध्याय वचनेमत्तो मितभाषी सभाजयी
तपोनिष्ठो निगूढोसि परमः पूतचित्तवान् ।
यस्यानन्दमयो भावः नन्दनन्दन वर्णने
पुनः पुनः स्मरामीशं तर्तुं संसार सागरम् ।।

svādhyāya vacane-matto mitabhāṣī sabhājayī
taponiṣṭho nigūḍhosi paramaḥ pūtacittavān |
yasyānandamayo bhāvaḥ nandanandana varṇane
punaḥ punaḥ smarāmīśaṃ tartuṃ saṃsāra sāgaram ||

[One, immersed in studies and preaching, of few words, victorious in scholarly circles, committed to supreme austerity, a hidden yogi, of purified intellect, who took delight in describing about Sri Krishna, him, the Lord, I remember again and again who is the cause of taking me beyond the ocean of worldliness.]

This simple *sloka* was written in adoration of Swami Tapasyananda Maharaj by late Pravrajika Shyama Prana

1. She was initiated by Revered Maharaj in 1989 and was in contact with Revered Maharaj for 20 years. She is a former president of Vivekananda Kendra, Kanyakumari. She is now Director, Vivekananda Kendra Vedic Vision Foundation, Kodungallur, Kerala.

Mataji of Sarada Math, Dakshineswar. It was passed on to me when Mataji heard that I had taken *diksa* from Revered Maharaj. Simple though the expressions are, they speak volumes of the personality of Revered Maharaj. Especially noteworthy was his great devotion to Lord Krishna out of which came his classic commentary on *Srimad Bhagavatam*. Equally significant are his commentaries on *Adhyatma Ramayana, Narayaneeyam, Saundarya Lahari* and others. What stood out in all these were his in-depth knowledge, practical approach and scientific explanations. Only a *purnakumbha* of knowledge and erudition could have achieved such spiritual and literary excellence.

About his childhood and other personal matters, he was very reluctant to speak. His meeting with Revered Nirmalananda Maharaj (Tulasi Maharaj) in his childhood was a turning point as it led to strengthening his devotion to Sri Ramakrishna. Even as a student in school, he started reading *The Complete Works of Swami Vivekananda* and the magazine, *Prabuddha Bharata*. He lost his father early in life, but his mother was a great devotee of Sri Ramakrishna and was a guidepost in his spiritual quests. It is said that Revered Maharaj's mother had prayed to Mahapurush Maharaj that one of her sons should become a monk of Ramakrishna Order! His visit to Madras, meeting Revered Swami Brahmananda Maharaj and Mahapurush Maharaj, were all part of the flow of his life that finally guided him to join the Math.

Revered Maharaj was a saint par excellence whose life was totally centered on Truth and at the same time dedicated to sharing it with the needy and the yearning. He was not a great orator, but his words had the power to go straight to the minds of listeners and leave their marks there. From

1942 to 1971, he was the president of Ramakrishna Ashrama, Trivandrum. Under his guidance, care and concern for the patients, the small health centre at the Ashrama expanded into a grand hospital of repute which is a landmark in Trivandrum today. It was during his Trivandrum days, that he made his name Tapasyananda truly meaningful. Extremely difficult and strenuous were the days when he struggled almost single handedly to build up the hospital. Indeed, it was the culmination of great *tapas*.

I was a worshipper of Swami Vivekananda from my childhood and others did not enter into my orbit at all, including Sri Ramakrishna. It was my surrender to Swami Vivekananda that caught the attention of Late Mananeeya Eknathji Ranade, way back in 1975, which was later instrumental in my leaving the sanctity and security of a governement job and move towards the unknown destiny that awaited me at Vivekananda Kendra, Kanyakurmari.

During my first visit to South Africa in 1987, I was the guest of the Ramakrishna Centre of South Africa, Durban. It was there that I watched and discovered with wonder the unfolding of Swami Shivapadananda's (president of the Centre) love and adoration for Sri Ramakrishna and how it worked wonders among the large number of devotees, predominantly of Indian origin. For them, Sri Ramakrishna was the Saviour, Lord and Master of their homes. Every home had a shrine for Sri Ramakrishna and Swami Shivapadananda Maharaj had initiated all of them, including children and installed in their minds the Great Master, Sri Ramakrishna. So when I was staying with him, he could immediately recognize the vacant throne in my shrine and he kept on insisting that I must take spiritual initiation from a great Swami and place Sri Ramakrishna as the Lord and Master in my heart. Slowly and steadily listening to the innumerable stories, anecdotes and miracles Sri Ramakrishna had worked among the devotees, my heart very naturally opened up to receive the Master at the earliest. But who was to be my guru? The only Swami of Ramakrishna Order with whom I was very close was Revered Swami Ranganathananda Maharaj. Naturally I thought of him as the right person to give me *diksa,* little knowing that the appointment of one's Guru takes place at a secretariat unknown to us, far far away somewhere in the cosmic realm. So it was in my case too.

When I broached the subject to Revered Swami Ranganathananda Maharaj, he was very happy but expressed his inability to spiritually initiate me as only president and vice-presidents were permitted to spiritually initiate the aspirants. He did not want me to postpone my decision and was kind enough to suggest the name of Revered Swami Tapasyananda Maharaj adding that he had a lot of affection for me. According to him, Swami Tapasyananda was the right person to guide me towards Sri Ramakrishna. I thought it over in my mind and said to myself that in it lies a message for me - that more *tapas* is needed from my side. It was on 28 January 1989 that I was initiated by Revered Swami Tapasyananda Maharaj at Sri Ramakrishna Math, Madras.

Usually the disciples would have some sense of fear in approaching their Gurus, but I did not feel anything like that and felt very close to him. Every time I went to Revered Maharaj, I would insist him to put his hand on my head and bless me, which he happily and smilingly did.

He used to address me as Vivekananda Rock Memorial, which for me hid many shades of meaning within. In a flash, it would bring to my mind the hard and dedicated work that had gone into its making. It would remind me that I am only an instrument in the Lord's hands just as Sri Ekanath was in creating this poetry in stone in the mid sea. It also pointed to the need of polishing me, from a rough and sharp edged stone into a smooth and blazing one. It used to bring tears to my eyes when I sensed Maharaj's message and blessings while addressing me thus.

When Vivekananda Kendra decided to create an exhibition as part of the commemoration of the centenary of Swami Vivekananda's *parivrajaka*(wandering) life, we invited Maharaj for the foundation stone laying ceremony. It was on 2 September 1989 that Maharaj laid the foundation for the Wandering Monk exhibition. It has now become a landmark at the tip of India.

On 1stSeptember, we, the life workers of Vivekananda Kendra, had a *satsang* with Revered Maharaj. Speaking on Swami Vivekananda, Maharaj described him as the *vibhuti* (glory) of Sri Ramakrishna. He added that Swami Vivekananda was like the epic *Mahabharata* from where everyone can get what they want. To know the truth of these words, one has only to go through *The Complete Works of Swami Vivekananda*.

When the seventh edition of *The Complete Works of Swami Vivekananda* was published, Maharaj, as vice-president, received one set of books for himself. He kept it with him for months and later when I went to meet him at Madras Math, he carefully took them out and gave to me with the inscription, written in his own hands - "*May the teaching of Swamiji establish you in spiritual strength*" dated 2.9.1989. He felt confident that I would make good use of it. Over the last one year,I indeed made good use of the volumes that would have pleased Maharaj very much. One effort was the compilation of 366 thoughts of Swami Vivekananda for daily reading in Malayalam at the request of DC publications, Kottayam. Following this, I have now compiled another set of Swamiji's incomparable thoughts under the name *Incredible India, Love India as Swamiji Loved Her* which has just now been published by Vivekananda Kendra Vedic Vision Foundation. I am sure Maharaj would have been very happy seeing it; I can feel the flow of his blessings.

My last visit to him was at the Vijaya Hospital during his last illness. He pointedly asked me about the preparations going on for the proposed *Bharata Parikrama* and ofcourse showered his blessings for the success of the *parikrama*.

It is very difficult to evaluate the role of one's guru in shaping one's life. So it was with me, more so because my contacts with my Guru were few and far. Firstly, I was at Kanyakumari as the head of Vivekananda Kendra, and Maharaj was at Madras heading the Sri Ramakrishna Math. Only while passing through Madras could I occasionally call on him and seek his blessings, which he poured on me in abundance invisibly helping me in my spiritual expansion and ascent. Not even a single day have I missed the japa of the mantra Maharaj gave me and naturally it is preceded by *pranams* to my *diksaguru* who ever remains the guiding star in my spiritual evolution.

13

Sri Guru Maharaj's Money

Sri Murali Krishnan[1]

Whenever sincere devotees needed any help in their spiritual and secular lives, the Guru appears and guides him. Swami Tapasyananda Maharaj was one such person who guided many devotees of Sri Ramakrishna.

I had the good fortune of visiting Madras Math along with my uncle, Sri C. S. Ramakrishnan, when Swami Tapasyananda Maharaj was there.

Maharaj lived a very simple life. At Trivandrum, he had never used a bed and would sleep only on a bare wooden bench in the nights. This habit continued even when he was in Madras Math.

Maharaj was very meticulous about the way Sri Guru Maharaj's money was spent and avoided luxury and wastage as far as possible. My uncle related to me about those occasions when Maharaj used to come to Madras from Trivandrum to purchase medicines for the hospital. On such occasions, my uncle used to go with him to Parrys' Corner by town bus for purchasing medicines at wholesale and therefore cheaper price. After purchasing, both of them used to carry bags full of medicines of all sorts. At those

1. He is a devotee of Chennai Math, actively involved in the activities of Math. He is currently residing in Trichy, Tamil Nadu.

times, Maharaj's face used to beam with joy and would happily remark to my uncle, 'We have saved Rs. 4/- of Sri Guru Maharaj's money!' That Maharaj was overjoyed at this and this was evident because the same statement was repeated many times on their way back to Madras Math.

When he had a boil in his hand, he used tissue paper torn into 4 or 8 pieces for cleaning the wound. My uncle used to request him to use the full sheet, but his reply would be, 'I cannot waste Sri Guru Maharaj's money.'

When Maharaj visited Trichy, he gave an extempore speech on Prahlada's *navavidha bhakti* (nine types of devotion) depicted in *Srimad Bhagavatam*.

One day, Maharaj was watching somebody cutting the trees as per his instruction. Then my uncle quoted a verse from *Jnanapana* (a hymn in Malayalam) of Poonthanam:

Kandu Kandangirikkum ***Janangale***
Kandillennu Varuthunnathum Bhavan

[You are the one, O Lord, who makes the **people** seen by all of us now to disappear from this world.]

And jokingly my uncle revised it as:

Kandu Kandangirikkum ***Marangale***
Kandillennu Varuthunnathum Bhavan

[You are the one, O Lord, who makes the **trees** seen by all of us now to disappear from this world.]

Immediately Maharaj enjoyed this joke and laughed heartily like a little child!

14

Dedicated service should be our motto

Prof. T. Indira[1]

यो न हृष्यति न द्वेष्टि न शोचति न काङ्क्षति
शुभाशुभपरित्यागी भक्तिमान् यः स मे प्रियः ।। १७ ।।

yo na hṛṣyati na dbeṣṭi na śocati na kāṅkṣati
śubhāśubhaparityāgī bhaktimān yaḥ sa me priyaḥ ||

(*Gita* 12:17)

He who is free from elation, anger, sorrow, and craving, who neither seeks the pleasant nor shuns the unpleasant —dear to Me is the man who is thus devoted.

Nothing can more aptly describe the qualities of head and heart of Revered Swami Tapasyananda Maharaj, as the above verse does.

Endowed with an independent, bold and decisive mind, and an indomitable will, Revered Tapasyananda Maharaj always commanded very great respect. Many monks who

1. She was initiated by Revered Swami Vireswarananda Maharaj in 1975. She was associated with Revered Swami Tapasyananda Maharaj for 18 years. She was a Head of the Dept., and P.G. Professor in English. She is very closely associated with the Math activities. She currently resides in Thanjavur and looks after the temple dedicated to the Holy Trio.

were associated with him for long years used to say with veneration that his life was a continuous meditation.

Absolutely unassuming and dedicated, Revered Maharaj was a constant source of strength and encouragement to the spiritual aspirants. He was simple, open-minded, affable and easily approachable. He would always insist upon hard work saying that there was an everlasting nobility and sacredness about sincere and dedicated work. He often used to say,'*Duty is devotion*' and '*Dedicated service should be our motto*'.

Elderly devotees in Trivandrum used to relate to me how Revered Maharaj tirelessly went about raising funds for the Sasthamangalam Hospital. He would walk long distances, go from door to door – at times he would get snubbed or insulted or they would grudgingly give one or two *annas* (of course, many gave willingly too). Like a true *sthithaprajna*, he would bear all these patiently, because it was for the Master!

The very mention of 'Madras Math Premises' and 'Madras Shrine' would throw Revered Maharaj to rapturous ecstasies. He would say, 'You must know how hallowed these premises are – sanctified by Holy Mother Herself and some of the direct disciples of the Master.' He would never allow anyone to loiter in the Math premises. 'Either sit in this Great Shrine or be in the library,' was his constant advice.

Leading a well-disciplined life himself, Revered Maharaj would always stress on a disciplined life, both in his lectures as well as in his private conversations. *Discipline, meditation* and *holy company* were his watchwords.

Once while giving a discourse on the 'Holy Mother and Her Divinity', Revered Maharaj narrated an interesting interaction he had had with Gopesh Maharaj, Revered Saradeshananda Maharaj, a disciple of the Holy Mother. Revered Tapasyananda Maharaj wanted to know from him if there was any special instance of the Holy Mother exuding her divinity, something apart from the well-known incidents where she revealed her divinity. It seems Revered Saradeshananda Maharaj closed his eyes and remained indrawn for a few seconds and said about *her eyes* (which were not of an ordinary human being) which speak volumes of not only her *motherliness* but her *divinity* as well – an unmistakable *divine spark*, soothing, comforting, consoling and elevating.

Revered Maharaj was deeply concerned about the deterioration of values and the disintegrating forces threatening the world which was already (and still is) on the brink of a disastrous chasm. He firmly believed that the ennobling, elevating, and saving grace comes from the Holy Trio; and a higher and nobler kind of humanity would evolve by following their footsteps. That was his remedy for the modern ills.

Revered Maharaj was a voracious reader and also wrote extensively. How many translations! How many works!He asked me to do proofreading for his translations. The first one was *Sri Ramakrishna Karnamritam* by Ottur Bala Bhatta, way back in 1974. 'You are a Professor of English. If you feel if any word is not apt, please feel free to change it,' he would say. But I refrained saying that his English was better than mine and moreover they were highly philosophical works – not merely literary. That was the one and only incident of my disobedience!

Once when *Narayaneeyam* was published, I purchased a copy and wanted Revered Maharaj's autograph. He asked me, 'Did you pay for it?' and he continued, 'The devotee at the Sales Section knows you and that you were doing the proofreading and he may have given it for free. You see, when I need a copy, I buy it. Only Revered Vireswarananda Maharaj gets a free copy. It's Sri Ramakrishna's money, you see…' Only after I showed him the cash receipt (which I had with me fortunately!) he complied with my request.

It was my special privilege to work on Revered Maharaj's translations. It continued for some of his other works as well – till I was transferred to Thanjavur in 1978. But whenever I visited Madras, he asked me to resume the work. If the publication wing in Madras Math had reached such great heights, it is mainly due to Revered Maharaj's tireless efforts. Because of his *tapas*, his guidance and his indefatigable work, the department is what it is today.

During Revered Maharaj's times there used to be monthly retreats in Madras Math. There were *bhajans*, reading from *The Gospel of Sri Ramakrishna*, his lectures on *Kapilopadesa* and his very interesting Question-Answer Sessions. All of a sudden, he decided to stop them much to our dismay. He said during retreats, there must be a very strict observance of silence and that he didn't approve of devotees sitting in groups and talking after noon-*prasad*! I organised a signature campaign requesting him to revive the monthly retreats assuring him of strict discipline. With his spectacles resting on the tips of his nose he looked at me and said, 'Well, we will think about it.' Soon after this incident, I got transferred to Thanjavur, and unfortunately, those monthly Retreats were never revived.

As some devotees think, Revered Maharaj was not against expansion or construction of a new big Temple. Even during his lifetime, some devotees were under the mistaken notion that he was not for changes. He had great respect for traditional customs and values, but he was essentially modern in outlook – modern in the true, strict sense of the term. In fact I asked him in 1989 whether he was not really in favour of Temple expansion etc. His reply was, 'No, well, the time is not yet ripe. It may take another 10 to 12 years. I will not live to see it.' How prophetic this utterance was, we realised in the year 2000 when the Universal Temple was consecrated.

We were indeed very fortunate to have come into contact with such a great soul. He was an ever-widening reservoir to draw inspiration from. We can say with Longfellow, '*Lives of great men, all remind us we can make our lives sublime*' and exclaim with Hamlet of Shakespeare, '*What a piece of work is Man! How noble in reason! How infinite in Faculty! … In form, in moving, how express and admirable! In action how like an Angel....*'

15

Remarkable Endurance

Dr. P. K. Baskar[1]

First Meeting:

I met Swami Tapasyananda Maharaj for the first time at the Ramakrishna Ashrama, Sasthamangalam, Trivandrum, where he was the head of the centre. I would stay there as a guest during my visits to Trivandrum Dental College as an Examiner. Following the custom, I would go to the head of the Ashrama and offer my *pranams*. I should confess that initially I did not have much interaction with Maharaj beyond offering *pranams*. As head of the institution, Maharaj was always preoccupied with managing the hospital as well as providing medicare to the needy. Running the hospital was the main activity of Trivandrum centre those days, so much so the math was small and the shrine smaller still.

I had the blessed opportunity of seeing Maharaj again in 1970 along with other senior monks - Revered Kailasananda Maharaj, Swami Chidbhavananda Maharaj and Swami

1. He was initiated by Revered Swami Yatiswarananda Maharaj in 1959. He was associated with Revered Swami Tapasyananda Maharaj for more than 20 years. He is an Emeritus Professor and Dental Surgeon. He currently resides in Chennai and is very closely associated with the Math activities.

Smaranananda Maharaj, during the inauguration of Swami Vivekananda Rock Memorial at Kanyakumari. Though I could not meet Maharaj personally, I took a photograph seated in the midst of many senior monks of our Order.

Working with Him:

I had the blessed privilege of serving Maharaj as a dentist for about 15 years. While being the head of Trivandrum Centre, Maharaj would visit Madras and I would accompany him many times to meet senior medical practitioners for guidance in matters relating to purchase of medical equipments for Trivandrum hospital. Maharaj would interact with those doctors at length and would ask them many questions relating to the utility of various medical equipments vis-ā-vis costs. He would go deep into the matter and weigh the pros and cons before deciding on purchases.

Maharaj became the president of Madras Math in 1971 after which I had the blessed privilege of meeting him more frequently and also serve as his dental surgeon. Besides this, on many occasions, Maharaj would also discuss with me matters that related to health and treatment of inmates of the Math and affairs of Madras Math dispensary, like setting up medical services, purchase of diagnostic equipments, medicines, lab management etc.

Treatment and Punctuality:

Maharaj with one brahmachari would visit my clinic for treatment which on an average may be three times a year. He would be very punctual that he would reach my clinic five to ten minutes before his appointed time and wait his turn at the waiting lounge just like any other person.

I found that not even once did he seek preference over others. Whenever he would come for treatment, he was very clear in his presentation of the symptoms and was extremely co-operative during the treatment. Although I would take utmost care in serving him he too would follow the instructions carefully and efficiently that would help the treatment process.

A Humorous Incident:

It was during one such visit that I would like to recall a very interesting and unforgettable utterance of Maharaj, which reflects his humour, wit and humility.

I would keep books and Math publications in the waiting hall instead of newspapers and magazines. One of my patients who would generally address small audiences on varied themes, while awaiting his turn in the lounge happened to read some portions of *Adhyatma Ramayana* translated by Maharaj and was noting down key passages. He happened to be a lay person and not a devotee of the Math. After treating Maharaj, I gently asked him if he would find some time to meet a patient of mine who was awaiting his turn in the lounge. Maharaj immediately agreed and I went out to bring in the gentleman to introduce him to Maharaj. When I told him that the translator of the book (*Adhyatma Ramayana*) he was engrossed in was verily inside the chamber, the patient became excited and was very keen to meet him. The patient then met Maharaj, paid his obeisance, took the blessings of Maharaj and then left the chamber. After the person left, Maharaj with a gentle smile said humorously that he was happy that at least one person was reading his book. I could not control my laughter and simply burst forth. I felt that Maharaj's humility and sense of wit was admirable. It is truly astounding that authorship of many scriptural and spiritual texts sat very lightly on Maharaj.

His Frugality:

Maharaj was generally very frugal and austere especially when it involved resources of the Math. He would seek an appointment to invariably coincide with the meeting he was to attend in Sarada Vidyalaya, T. Nagar (so that he did not come separately for this), till which time he would endure the pain and inconvenience, just to save the Math resources, however small it may be.

I would like to relate one such instance. Maharaj would invariably leave some message for me with Swami Raghaveshananda Maharaj, then manager of Math, at that time, that I should meet him before I leave the Math. On one such meeting with him he wanted to get treated for a painful tooth that he had been enduring for quite some time. Maharaj gently asked me if I was available for consultation at 4.30 pm on a particular day which was after a couple of days. I readily consented to be available on that day at that particular time. However, I was curious to know why Maharaj in spite of suffering a painful tooth which required immediate treatment was seeking an appointment on a later date. When I enquired Manager Swami about this, he smiled and explained to me that Maharaj had to go to Sarada Vidyalaya, T. Nagar on that day and since my clinic was situated near to it, Maharaj wanted to save the transportation expenses by combining the meeting with the consultation. As a devotee I felt that we have a great lesson to learn from this incident. Even though as a president of the Math he could have easily sought medical intervention earlier, Maharaj chose to endure pain and put up with great personal inconvenience just to save some material resources of the Math, however small it may be.

Much later, when he was on prolonged hospitalization, Maharaj, known for conserving the resources even at the cost of his personal inconvenience would always insist that the fan in his room be switched off to save electricity. However, we were worried about the possibility of his developing bed sores that we, without his knowledge, kept a small fan running under his bed to maintain good aeration.

Inauguration of Sri Viveka Institute of Dental Health:

4 March 1984 was a very blessed and unforgettable day in my life as a devotee of Sri Ramakrishna. It was on that day that Maharaj came over to inaugurate Sri Viveka Institute of Dental Health that was established to render dental service to the poor in rural areas. I had actually chosen that day as it happened to be the birthday (Tithi Puja day) of Bhagavan Sri Ramakrishna. It was indeed a touching experience for me to have Maharaj to inaugurate the Dental Institute (SVIDH), more so on a very special and auspicious day, when, as president, he normally would not condescend to leave the math premises on that day. It was a simple inauguration at 4 p.m. Maharaj cut the ribbon and remained at the premises for about an hour. The function was attended by a large number of my devotee-friends, relatives and officials. There however was no printed invitation, no rituals, in tune with his informal disposition.

Inside the Operation Theatre:

I was a Consultant in Vijaya Hospital, Madras, where Maharaj once had gone for his surgical treatment. I recollect an extraordinary experience of being with him sometime in the late 1980's in the operation theatre of Vijaya Hospital. Maharaj was admitted for a surgical procedure in Vijaya Hospital. The surgery lasted for an hour under spinal anesthesia. In these types of surgeries, the patient will be able to hear and be conscious of the various surgical processes undertaken, although the patient will not sense pain. Before being taken to the operation theatre, Maharaj gently asked me if I would be accompanying him into the operation theatre. I understood that Maharaj wanted my presence there and hence took the permission of the surgeon, put on the uniform meant for the operation theatre, and entered the theatre.

After administering the anesthesia, the surgeon was freely discussing with me the various types and difficulties he was encountering while performing the surgery. I was besides Maharaj and gently held his hand now and then. Maharaj, who was only under spinal anesthesia, was aware of the happenings around him. Even though the surgery took a little more than an hour, it was amazing that Maharaj was unruffled and kept calm, asking only three questions:

'Is the operation started?' – sometime during the initial stage of the surgery

'Am I co-operating?' – sometime when the surgery was in progress

'Is it over?' – towards the end, when the surgery was completed

It is even more astounding to note that his blood pressure remained the same, both at the beginning of the surgery and after the surgery, which was remarkable, particularly when he, as a patient, was conscious of what was happening around him during the surgery that lasted for a little more than an hour. This is a remarkable medical feat and inner endurance that I witnessed, which speaks volumes of his capacity to completely delink himself from the physical plane and transcend body consciousness.

A few days after the surgery, Maharaj wanted to know from the surgeon when he could get on his feet and start walking. When the surgeon gave his clearance, Maharaj started walking in his ward itself, even though it was a small area. He was one of those who believed in the benefits of walking as an exercise to stay active and healthy. During this period I visited him several times and had the blessed privilege to talk to him, especially regarding his health and well being.

Some days later, I returned from Singapore after attending a conference there. I had brought with me special surgical dressings for his use. When I went to see him the next day, he asked gently, 'I didn't see you yesterday' thereby meaning that I did not meet him for past some days. He was always very careful not to lay any personal demands on others. His gentle questions would only be suggestive and not intrusive.

His Deep Feeling for others:

My wife's brother was a disciple of Swami Yatiswaranda Maharaj. His parents too were devotees of Sri Ramakrishna and were initiated disciples of Swami Virajananda Maharaj, the 7th president of the Ramakrishna Order. When Sri Narendran passed away in his early 50's, Maharaj on coming to know about this, wanted to see me and my wife. My wife was very disturbed having lost her brother. Anyway, we decided to go to the Math to meet Maharaj.

When we went to meet him, he was very sympathetic to my wife's condition and spoke to her very affectionately. To quote Maharaj, 'Whatever we may tell to assuage you may not be enough to compensate the loss you have suffered. It is easy for us to say some consoling words but that is not going to diminish your grief. However, continue to pray to Holy Mother, Sri Guru Maharaj and Swamiji for strength and guidance.' After this meeting with Maharaj, my wife felt greatly relieved and was able to reconcile with the loss.

Guru Purnima Celebrations:

Devotees, spiritually initiated by various presidents and vice-presidents of our Order were celebrating their guru's birthdays with pomp and grandeur. These were becoming more person-centred than ideal-centred. Maharaj never approved of this tendency as he felt that these celebrations were not helpful in forging a common bond amongst the initiated devotees. He directed the devotees to pay their tributes to their gurus only on *Guru Purnima*. Maharaj held Veda Vyasa to be the *adi guru* [the first guru]. Sometime in 1970s, Maharaj, in one of his talks on *Guru Purnima,* openly dissuaded devotees from forming individual groups to celebrate their guru's birthday. He reminded them that Sri Ramakrishna was our ultimate guru and advised the devotees to visit the Math, participate in the worship of Sri Ramakrishna and do more japa to commemorate the occasion. This far-sighted advice of Maharaj acted as an integrative factor among the devotees.

16

Not A Wedding Invitation!

Smt. Malini Menon[1]

Serving as a volunteer in the dispensary of Sri Ramakrishna Math, Madras, in early 1980s gave me the blessed opportunity for regularly offering *pranams* to Revered Swami Tapasyananda Maharaj.

He would usually be engrossed in reading the proof of his magnum opus four-volume translation, with notes and commentary, of *Srimad Bhagavatam*. But however busy he may be, he would always put aside his work and accept my *pranams*.

One day, pointing to the junior monks, he said humourously that they wanted him, at such an advanced age of 79 years, to translate the *Srimad Bhagavatam*, and he wondered whether he would live long enough to complete this great undertaking. But immediately he also pointed out that it was not his work but the Lord's work.

When I came to settle down in Madras in 1978, I greatly desired to live somewhere within the vicinity of the Math. One morning Maharaj himself came with me to find

1. She was initiated by Revered Swami Ashokananda Maharaj in 1964. She was associated with Revered Swami Tapasyananda Maharaj for 10 years. She is a housewife currently residing in Chennai and is closely associated with the Math activities.

out whether I could board with an elderly lady living close to the Math. What kindness and consideration he showed through this gesture!

We had a black sheep in our family (known to Maharaj also), who, unfortunately, took to drinking. Though he was charming and intelligent, this habit ruined his career. Maharaj used to say about him, 'When the wine was in, the wits were out.' This expression aptly described his condition.

When I once went to meet him after the death of my close associate, he did not try to console me telling about the inevitability of joy and sorrow, loss and separation, in this temporal life etc. On the other hand, he just said a few words that instilled great faith and courage into me.

Once, his younger brother (of his *purvashram*) came from Kerala to stay for a few days in the Math. Maharaj greeted him cordially and talked for a little while with him; and then left his brother to the care of some young devotees and plunged into the work again.

On another occasion, a large group of devotees came to the Math. They had taken a big van from Kolkata, and came to South, visiting many centres of the Math and Mission on the way. Maharaj stood on the verandah, (just outside his office), and greeted them with folded hands. All of them wanted to offer *pranams,* but that would have taken too long. So the leader of the group selected a few among the group and asked them to offer *pranams*. Maharaj stood there, with a faint smile on his face, when this whole thing was going on. Later he remarked that the Bengalis were endowed with great devotion.

At Madras Math, 1989

Another time, some tourists from Australia came to the Math. They came to greet Maharaj. I remember an expression of pain on the Maharaj's face, because he could not understand a word of what was said – their English accent was so different from what he had been used to.

Once, on a *Kalpataru* Day, he sat on a chair on the verandah and many devotees came to him and offered *pranams*. He would now and then ask the devotees whether they knew the real significance of Sri Ramakrishna becoming a *Kalpataru,* and he himself would explain, very patiently and clearly, the great significance of this holy event.

On the night of Sivaratri, he came and sat with the monks on a mat spread on the floor, and his pain and suffering caused by sitting on the floor was evident. He had been having trouble folding his legs for quite some years and was also suffering from some problem in his back. However, he left all these physical difficulties behind when he was absorbed in his literary pursuits.

One day, I saw Maharaj standing on the little verandah outside his office with such a happy expression on his face while showing the first copy of the book *Invitation to Holy Company* which had just been released. Subsequently, whenever he saw anyone passing by, he would come out of his office to the little verandah in the front, and happily call them saying that he had an invitation for them! And, if I remember rightly, he would add humourously, 'Not a wedding invitation!' It was most heartening and uplifting for us to see him in such a joyful mood. Books, especially the Math publications, invariably put him into a very joyful mood!

17

My Siksa Guru

Dr. Y. Hariharan[1]

Perfect Jnani

It was in 1976, on Sri Ramakrishna's Jayanti, that I saw Maharaj. I was introduced to Maharaj by a friend. A novice to the Ramakrishna Order, I was awestruck at the simplicity and accommodative spirit of Maharaj as he received me with all warmth and love. Then followed a few words, a smile you can't easily notice, a blessing, and a gentle reminder that I should come to Math as frequently as possible in spite of my work place being 110 kms away from Madras! This is no myth or magic, yet, I was under the spell of his intellectual charm and even without my realizing it, Maharaj had become my *siksa guru*!

You cannot talk to Maharaj on any mundane matter - be it politics, personalities or any other topic. Any question on Holy Trio, direct disciples, history of the Order, or scriptures, Maharaj would be ready to answer or clarify. Impertinent questions of mine would be brushed aside

1. He was initiated by Revered Swami Vireswarananda Maharaj. He had contact with Revered Swami Tapasyananda Maharaj for more than 14 years. He is a retired Professor of Botany at CAH College and later at National College, Trichy. He is now actively involved in the activities of the Math.

silently and Maharaj would carry on with his reading or writing! Yes, Maharaj appeared to me as a perfect *jnani*.

Books are *prasad*

Once Maharaj asked me to get acquainted with the life of Sri Ramakrishna and asked me to get the book, *Life of Sri Ramakrishna*, immediately. I got a loan of ten rupees from my friend, went to the book stall (the present *The Vedanta Kesari* Editorial Office), purchased it and rushed to Maharaj's room. Saying 'Yes,' Maharaj wrote his blessings, 'May the study of Sri Ramakrishna`s life elevate you', signed it and gave it to me. Maharaj calls these books as real *prasad* and my receiving this *prasad* from him went on throughout his lifetime. He would insist every devotee to carry *prasad* of books whenever he or she comes to Math.

Maharaj and his writings

Impelled by my curiosity and eagerness to get an idea of what Maharaj was writing, I would quite often trouble him by asking details about what he is writing. Maharaj would never get angry; instead, he would briefly give an outline of the book, its importance, and its necessity for the devotee. Well, Maharaj once asked my opinion about the title of the book, *Invitation to Holy Company*. This book of reminiscences of direct disciples by Swami Jnanatmananda was no doubt an invitation. Other titles he showed were *Holy Mother as I saw Her* by Swami Saradeshananda and *In the lap of Himalayas* by Swami Akhandananda. These titles stimulate the reader to go through the books at once.

I had heard that Maharaj was confronted by a very young boy who had just finished his schooling to admit him into the Order. Having advised him to complete his degree and enter the Order, Maharaj wrote a classical piece on the Ramakrishna Order - the goal, ideals, procedure for joining it etc. - and this booklet [For the Enquirers about Ramakrishna Math and Ramakrishna Mission] even now is an authentic source of information, not only for the aspirant but also for the lay people.

Maharaj's companion volumes to *The Complete Works of Swami Vivekananda* also had a similar history. Every time I came to Madras, I would carry lot of doubts. Most of them were related to *The Complete Works of Swami Vivekananda.* Maybe Maharaj had several others like me seeking clarifications that one day he told me that he intended to write a companion series which would explain Swami Vivekananda's thought currents. Book on *Four Yogas* came out first, followed by *Nationalistic and Philosophical ideas of Swami Vivekananda.* Maharaj's lucid explanations were an elixir to us. Once a companion volume sees the light of the day, he will, on my next visit, promptly remind me to purchase it.

His critical appraisal regarding the period of Sri Sankaracharya is till date the most accurate analysis on the subject. Whenever I would excitedly go to him to convey my compliments for his writings, Maharaj would simply brush them aside and remind me of similar articles written by him or someone else in the earlier issues of *The Vedanta Kesari*!

The sage who lives in my heart

I vividly remember seeing Maharaj step out of his room, in rain or shine, holding an umbrella with his right hand and carrying a couple of books with his left hand held close to his chest. Punctually he would enter the President's office, salute the photographs of the previous presidents, and take his seat. He wore brown or orange coloured socks and moccasin footwear. Sitting comfortably facing west, he could watch anyone who stood outside the swing doors which were hinged at chest height.

The first one to get in to his office would be Prof C. S. Ramakrishnan, the then Editor of *The Vedanta Kesari*, who would discuss some matters with Maharaj speaking both in Malayalam and English. Swamis Chidghanananda, Tanmayananda and Raghaveshananda, who were successive managers of the Math during Maharaj's period, monitored the entry of visitors. The moment I stood outside his room, he would mildly say 'yes' and nod his head and I would see Maharaj, holding pen in his hand, looking at me through the edge of his spectacles.

Without any formality, appointments and such paraphernalia, this saint was in the reach of every devotee who came to the Math and I had the freedom to call on him either in his office or in his room.

Debating with Maharaj

One may wonder how I could hold heated discussions with such an eminent Swami and yet I had several occasions to provoke him and thereby drag him into lengthy discussions on critical topics. And yet Maharaj would never lose his calmness and serenity. He will allow me to put in my views and finally come down on my head with punching arguments. During these deliberations, he would neither raise the voice nor show any change in his facial expressions, and yet his words would be emphatic and assertive.

Maharaj's classes and lectures

In the late seventies, classes were held on all week days in the hall below the present 'Old Temple'. Maharaj took classes on *Sri Ramakrishna, the Great Master,* which would be held on first Mondays of every month at Swami Vivekananda auditorium at 5.30 p.m. and the entire hall would be packed with devotees.

I still remember Maharaj's talk at second convention of devotees at Belur Math in 1980, in which he reminded all that meditation should not be an invitation to sleep! I had the privilege of transcribing from the audio tapes Maharaj's talks given in Malaysia and Singapore.

With Jnanadananda, Kuala Lumpur, Malaysia, 1988

Friend, Philosopher and Guide

Maharaj blessed me to carry on the message of Holy Trio even to the remote villages and towns in the Vellore district. It was a coincidence and double blessing that my *diksa guru,* Revered Swami Vireswarananda Maharaj also had sent a letter to me to seek the guidance of Maharaj. But for Maharaj's vision, trust, support and guidance, I and several other devotees would have lost all enthusiasm. No doubt Maharaj's blessings have held us all together even today.

Conclusion

Although we have not seen the Holy Trio and the direct disciples face to face, everyone who came in contact with Swami Tapasyananda Maharaj could really get the blessings that helped them to feel the living presence of Sri Ramakrishna, Holy Mother, Swamiji and other direct disciples.

18

Whose Picture Is This?

Miss. K. Saraswathi[1]

A few months before taking over as the head of Madras Math, Revered Maharaj had come to Madras on a visit and took couple of classes on *Katha Upanishad*. Devotees were attracted by Maharaj's simplicity and courteous behaviour.

Initially, he would meet the devotees sitting behind the round table in the prayer hall. Even before he became the vice-president of the Order and started initiating the devotees into spiritual life, he would insist the devotees seeking spiritual initiation (from the visiting president/ vice-presidents of the Order) to read the book, *Life of Sri Ramakrishna,* which had the Foreword by Mahatma Gandhi.

The year he took charge as the president, the girls of Centenary School, Mint, visited the Math to receive his blessings for the Board Exam. Showing the picture of Sri Ramakrishna, Maharaj asked the girls, 'Whose picture is this?' The girls spontaneously replied, 'Lord Buddha.' It is

1. She was initiated by Revered Swami Vireswarananda Maharaj in 1966. She was associated with Revered Swami Tapasyananda Maharaj for 20 years. She is a retired teacher of Ramakrishna Math Vivekananda Centenary Girls' High School, Mint. She was closely associated with the activities of Madras Math for more than 5 decades. She currently resides in Ramakrishna Mission Home of Service, Varanasi.

In his office, Madras Math

difficult to imagine how Maharaj would have felt with this reply. He intimated the Secretary of the School to educate the students about the Math and its activities. If he found children engaged in gossip, he would advise them to read interesting books.

During his period, gardening work was undertaken in full swing. Plantain and coconut trees were planted. Vegetables were grown and the excess quantity was sold.

Those days, Swami Sankarananda's photo was hung on the pillar on the northern side of the prayer hall. Some devotees would garland the photo whenever they visited the Math. Revered Maharaj had the photo removed from there, lest a guru-cult would emerge out of their adoration!

Harikatha by renowned exponents and a meeting used to be organised from 2.30 p.m. to 4.30 p.m. on the first Sunday following the birthday celebrations of Holy Trio and Sasi Maharaj. A large number of women would attend the Harikatha programme. The hall would be jam-packed. After the Harikatha programme and before the meeting, most of the audience used to leave the hall. Maharaj felt it was a nuisance and discontinued the Harikatha programme. Usually, he was very particular that speakers should strictly restrict the talks to the allotted time.

Once when Maharaj was returning to Madras, there was disruption in train services due to accident and his train was inordinately delayed. But, at last, when he reached the Math, he appeared totally unaffected by the severe hardship he had suffered.

Even during illness, he would avoid visiting any hospital. But he passed away in B.S.S. Hospital. The first garland (of roses) to his body was offered by me and my late sister.

19

His Life was His Name

Sri S. Raghunandan[1]

As a humble pilgrim on the journey inwards, I had been blessed with the opportunity to come in contact with senior monks of the Ramakrishna Order. My associations with them have given me foretastes into the life sublime and have helped me learn valuable lessons in living. One such monk, who led an unbelievably simple life, embodying the ideals of austere living, was Revered Swami Tapasyananda Maharaj, with whom I was associated, serving him as a transcriber from February 1981 to October 1982.

Hailed as an exemplar of austere living (*tapasya*) and frugality in expending resources, both material and natural, Swami Tapasyananda Maharaj was a stellar exemplar and an ideal to behold. I was one of those privileged few to have received his grace and impersonal love. Sometimes when friends and well-wishers tell me that I am truly blessed, I am to humbly attribute that to the invasion of his grace

1. He was initiated by Revered Swami Vireswarananda Maharaj in 1984. He had occasional contact with Revered Swami Tapasyananda Maharaj for 10 years and was closely associated with him as his transcriber for 2 years. He served in various organizations including Indian Tourism Development Corporation. He has been closely associated with Chennai Math as a volunter for more than 3 decades. He currently stays in Chennai.

and mercy upon me. I would consider that these words of mine, frail as they may be, are undeserving to reminisce the hallowed memories associated with his name, and yet it is my priceless privilege to carry the treasure of wisdom and the flashes of brilliance that I partook of while in his service.

Visits to Sri Ramakrishna Math:

Sometime in 1971, when I was a class 8 student of P.S. High School, situated right across the Math, I strayed into the Math, if I may say so, with a couple of my classmates. It was one of those birthday celebrations [of the Holy Trio] when people would be sumptuously fed. I had a hearty meal that tasted heavenly. Since then almost every other day I would visit the Math. I would just go to the shrine, offer *pranams* and get back home. I began to like the math environs and the monks, who I felt were friendly.

Some days I would visit the library and spend time in the children's section. Maybe in 1972, for the first time I saw a group photo in which Swami Tapasyananda Maharaj was at the centre. Even as a boy, I seemed to have developed a vague reverence and liking for him, majestic and upright he stood out in those group photos. Little did I realize that I would one day have an opportunity to sit beside him as a transcriber!

I was regular in visiting the Math and rendering small service in the shrine stores. Many times in the early afternoons, I had seen Maharaj go to the bed room of Sri Ramakrishna besides the shrine of Holy Mother, Swamiji and Swami Brahmananda (in the present 'Old Temple'). The Pujari Maharaj then would signal us to speak in low tones. We would turn around to find Tapasyananda Maharaj getting into the shrine or coming down the few steps that led to the bed room of Sri Ramakrishna. He would stand in the inner sanctum before Sri Ramakrishna for some time and then gently walk down the stairs without calling anyone's attention.

A Life Time Opportunity:

Shankar Maharaj (now Swami Padmasthananda Maharaj), as a brahmachari, was assigned the task to transcribe as Swami Tapasyananda Maharaj dictated notes translating *Sundara Kandam* from the original *Valmiki Ramayana*. When Shankar Maharaj was transferred to the New Delhi branch, he was looking for a person who may be able to take over the work that he rendered to Maharaj. When he asked me of my inclination and availability, I readily agreed even though I had no idea as to what that work entailed. Although I had seen Tapasyananda Maharaj many times and occasionally made *pranams* to him I had not spoken to him before. I was however known to the manager (Swami Raghaveshananda Maharaj) for whom I had earlier typed manuscripts for some of the publications that he worked on.

I was ushered into Swami Tapasyananda Maharaj's living quarters and introduced to him. Maharaj accepted me readily and thus began my service to Maharaj as a transcriber from February 1981 to October 1982. I would visit Maharaj twice a week, sometimes thrice a week, for two hours; from 3 to 5 p.m. Maharaj gave me clear instructions on the first day itself that he was translating *Sundara Kandam* from the original *Valmiki Ramayana* verse by verse with annotations, and that as he dictated I was to write it down legibly in long hand in a note book sized diary which would then be typed by his assistant and brought back to him for corrections.

I applied myself to the task without difficulty and eagerly awaited my engagement with him week after week.

The Setting:

Maharaj's living room lay past a verandah on the first floor of the dining hall block. I would report to him well before the appointed time. On seeing me, he would gladly exclaim, 'Umh! You have come'. He would quickly set aside the work he was into then and immediately get ready for the task at hand. I would in the meantime draw a chair into his room from the verandah.

At Madras Math

His room was sparsely furnished - just a cot, a table which had a synthetic sheet cover on which he would keep volumes of books one upon the other and some blank diaries of previous years that he used to write the scripts for his works, a wooden chair with a pillow for back rest, a table lamp that he used during night study and another chair which I presume he used while he sat for meditation. On his table was an old case in which he meticulously kept his pens and pencils. We would begin our work at 3 p.m. and go on till about 5 p.m. Maharaj would dictate in chaste English as he translated verses from *Sundara Kandam* of the *Valmiki Ramayana*.

Those Glorious Days:

I was naturally attracted by his simple life, unwavering routine, and complete command over the language. I would sit in a chair just beside him sharing the same table, short of touching him. Maharaj would appear serious, but actually he would be lost in some deep thought. Occasionally he would refer to the voluminous books in Sanskrit or Malayalam kept on the table. I would keep pace with his dictation, lest I disturb his flow of thoughts. Maharaj's diction was flawless (no rephrasing or altering) and his intonation was very clear that I rarely had difficulty understanding his utterances. There were occasions, though rare, when Maharaj would keep a small desk atop his table and dictate standing looking into the yonder. I would feel very delicate to sit and write while he stood and dictated. Maharaj would soothe me saying, 'No! No! You sit and write'. Later I came to understand that he would do so to relieve his back pain.

Maharaj was in his mid 70's when I served him as a transcriber. He wore very simple clothes and would always sit erect. His face radiated peace and had an aura that was sublime. Never have I seen him sit in a relaxed posture, even though he had a pillow to rest his back. There were books neatly kept one over the other on the table. As he dictated, words would flow with astounding ease and spontaneity. There would be silence for a while when Maharaj would close his eyes or cogitate on the deeper meaning of some intricate verses. In those moments of stillness, I felt that I was beside a great *rishi* in a *gurukula* set in sylvan surroundings.

Many a time he would use expressions that were out of the ordinary. Whenever he made humorous remarks, (there were quite a few of them) I would have a hearty laugh but he would give away a gentle smile at the most. I remember one that he told on how people behaved on sensing seemingly small success while describing Hanuman's visit to the inner apartments in Ravana's palace. On seeing Mandodari, Hanuman thought he had discovered Sita and began to kiss his tail out of joy; clapped his hands and jumped from one pillar to another. On another occasion both of us had a good laugh at the description of *rakshasis* surrounding Sita in the *Ashoka Vana.*

Those days Suryanarayana Maharaj (now Swami Sukritananda Maharaj) would come up to Maharaj's room around 4 p.m., just before the bell rang for tea. He would wait outside near the threshold holding in his hands two biscuits and a cup of tea for Maharaj. In one other bowl would be two or three slices of cucumber, a couple of pieces of orange or sweet lime. That was all that Maharaj had at tea time. Many times Maharaj would be completely absorbed in his translation and dictation that he would not notice Suryanarayan Maharaj. When the bell rang, he would say to me, 'Go have your tea'. I would quickly go down to have tea and snacks and get back to Maharaj's room to continue the work. By 5 p.m., Maharaj would signal the end of work for the day by concluding the verse he was translating. He would accept my *pranams* with a benign nod and I would take leave. It was certainly an elevating experience to be in the closest presence of such an extraordinary monk.

Wholesome blessings:

When we completed the translation of *Sundara Kandam,* I, in my boyish exhilaration, pumped my fist in joy. Maharaj too was happy and gave a wide smile seeing my gesture. With grace abounding he said, 'A mere reading of *Sundara Kandam* confers on one great success, prosperity and happiness. You have taken part in the translation and you will get all these.' He further extolled the greatness of *Ramayana* and told that so long as rivers flow and the mountains stand, *Ramayana* will be a live text recited and revered by many all over the world. It was a moment of abundant joy for me and an experience that I always cherish and like to recall. Shortly after the completion of *Sundara Kandam* work, I landed on a good job with a public sector enterprise as an Assistant Manager and have been able to ride the rough tides in my life with the blessings that I received from Maharaj.

The Base Had Been Laid:

Maharaj seemed to have commended my effort and capacity to grasp the nuances of the language. When I suggested to him that I would be glad to undertake similar works, he readily agreed to utilize my service for translating *Adhyatma Ramayana*, another text with considerable literary beauty with a rich devotional exposition of the greatness of Sri Rama. I was able to associate in this work for about 10 or 12 chapters, when I received a call to join work in ITDC in New Delhi. I passed on the baton to Sri Subramaniam Swaminathan[1], my friend, who continued from where I left. The base which had been firmly laid by Maharaj for me subsequently paved way for me to serve as a volunteer in *The Vedanta Kesari*, reading proofs and copy editing articles under the guidance of the current editors. Whatever little language proficiency that I have had is a *biksa* (alms) that I

---

1. His reminiscences are included in this book (p 593).

received from Maharaj whose expressions of the language were lucid and artistic at the same time.

What I Observed In His Routine:

Maharaj's simplicity charmed and impressed anyone who came into contact with him. He wore simple clothes, had very minimal things to meet his needs, and his food was plain and Spartan. So concerned was he in conserving power that he would use only a table lamp of low wattage to light his room in the night. He was a minimalist when it came to use of resources. Punctuality was natural to him. Many times I had seen him walk to his office at about 9.30 a.m. clutching some books in one hand and holding an umbrella over him with the other. He had great love and reverence for Sri Guru Maharaj. He would stand in front of the prayer hall (now 'old temple') for some time looking intently at the photo of Sri Guru Maharaj in the shrine with love and reverence before walking towards his office on the ground floor of Holy Mother's centenary block. Anyone who beheld such moments would easily conclude that to Maharaj, Sri Ramakrishna was a living presence and so was the Holy Mother. Sometimes I would go to his office pushing gently the half swing door just to offer *pranams*. He would lift his head, spectacles resting on the bridge of his nose and would look over the frame in his characteristic style.

Maharaj would never miss his evening walk from 5.15 to 6 p.m. He would walk briskly either on the terrace of the dining hall or on the corridor in the forecourt of the dining hall, simultaneously keeping a watchful eye on the brahmacharis and monks who he insisted should exercise. Some would jog, while others would do sit ups and stretching exercises. There were others who played shuttle badminton. Clearly the health and well-being of the inmates were his prime concerns and physical fitness a *sine qua non* for mental alertness and spiritual growth.

His Easy Accessibility:

Another admirable quality that I observed in Maharaj was his easy approachability; any devotee can walk into his office without an appointment and could freely talk to him. I have seen many times school children visiting him. Without any prior information, they would get into his office, as if they were going to see an elder member of their family. He would entertain them without any annoyance, even as he was immersed in work.

Since he knew me, I would take the liberty to accompany him for a short while on his evening walks in the corridor at the forecourt of the dining hall. Normally Maharaj would walk in measured pace but he would walk briskly while walking to exercise. I would keep pace with him and freely engage him in conversation without being mindful that I was doing so with the vice-president of the Order. He would enquire about my work environs (I was working for hospitality services then). On one such occasion, he enquired about the menus, hygiene and food preparation in 5-star hotels. To my surprise he even remarked, 'I understand your chefs are the highest paid in hotel industry' and that 'getting good continental chefs is difficult'. It was truly astounding that he kept himself well informed on matters that others in his station of life would consider worldly. On yet another occasion, he enquired about Victoria Hostel, the condition in which it was and about the students staying in it. Maharaj fondly recalled his days in Victoria Hostel where he stayed as a post-graduate student of Presidency College, Madras. He also said that some of our senior monks like Swami Vireswarananda Maharaj (Prabhu Maharaj) were from Presidency College. On coming to know that I too had been a student of Presidency College for 5 years, he would curiously ask me many questions about the present day students, their conduct, and their life on the campus etc.

His readiness to oblige:

I received an interview call from a government enterprise in New Delhi. I had never been out of Madras. I somehow gathered courage and requested Maharaj to give me a letter of introduction and arrange for my stay in Delhi Ashrama. Without asking any further questions, he obliged me saying, 'Ask Manager Maharaj to write the letter.' Swami Tanmayananda Maharaj was the manager at that time. I was touched by his graciousness and my visit to Delhi Ashram was a pre-cursor to the many good things that were to unfold.

On yet another occasion, I was planning to visit Belur Math with few other devotees to participate in Sri Ramakrishna's 150th Birthday Celebrations on 1 March 1987, and to subsequently visit Kamarpukur and Jayarambati. An appointment was fixed with Tapasyananda Maharaj one day at 10.00 a.m. to request him to arrange for our stay in Belur Math. I, however, reached the Math only by 10.15 a.m. while the other devotees met Maharaj promptly at 10 a.m. I hesitantly went into Maharaj office, embarrassed as I was due to the delay, and informed him of my intended visit to Belur Math with the other devotees. Maharaj immediately accommodated my request and asked me to tell Swami Raghaveshananda Maharaj to include my name in the letter that he was to send to Belur Math. I was moved by his considerateness and felt greatly relieved that my long felt desire to visit Belur Math was nearing fulfillment.

Guru Purnima talks

On *Guru Purnima,* Maharaj would give a special talk after the evening *arati.* The atmosphere in the Math would be charged with spiritual fervour when Maharaj would describe the importance of *Guru Purnima* to the spiritual aspirants. I distinctly remember one such talk, perhaps given in 1981 or 1982, where Maharaj was taking a mild dig at those seeking name and fame, Maharaj said that Vyasa who wrote countless scriptural texts never appended his name to any of those and therefore he is revered as our *Adi Guru.* Sri Guru Maharaj, our chosen deity, was a modern day *rishi,* who like Vyasa, never sought to promote or publicize his efforts. Maharaj further stressed that although devotees may have received spiritual initiation from different gurus of our Order, ultimately it is loyalty to Sri Ramakrishna that should be held sacrosanct. He wanted spiritually initiated devotees to take off from their daily chores and spend the day in the Math chanting and reading scriptural texts.

Sunday Lectures and Monthly Retreats:

Sunday evenings between 5.30 and 6.30 p.m., Maharaj would give enlightening lectures on a chosen scriptural text in the hall above the library, perhaps till 1988. I had attended many of his Sunday talks, though not regularly. The atmosphere would be sublime; any listener would easily forget himself or herself and be immersed in divine mood even if it was for a short while.

The monthly retreats held during Maharaj's times, normally on the last Sunday of the month, would draw more devotees. These sessions would be anchored by Sri. C.S. Ramakrishnan. Maharaj would speak on a specific theme from 10.30 to 11.30 a.m. followed invariably by an interactive session that would be very lively, with Maharaj giving quick and appropriate responses. In his lectures, Maharaj would share deep insights on the lives and teachings of the Holy Trio. He would refer to Sri Ramakrishna as 'the Great Master'.

The Dew Effect:

In conclusion, I wish to say that even though Maharaj did not show any external expressions of affection, I could certainly feel his deep impersonal love. I had experienced his tenderness that lay concealed behind his apparently stern exterior. He did not preach or teach me anything in the conventional sense, but by his life, he made it plain to me that through austere living the rewards of inner joy and contentment are tangible. Maharaj's simplicity, austerity and love for language had left a deep impression in my mind and I strive to imbibe them in some measure even if only a little fraction. Maharaj had shown us the path - to live in harmony with Mother Nature and use minimal resources, a little self-discipline and commitment to the ideals of *tapasya*. His life demonstrated how these qualities would make a great transformation in our lives, like the gentle dew which blossom the fairest of flowers.

20

Spread Their Message

Smt. Sarada Mani[1]

My paternal family members were known to Revered Swami Tapasyananda Maharaj, even before he became the president of Madras Math. When he was the president of Trivandrum Ashrama at Sasthamangalam, he had stayed in my father's ancestral house at Kollam many times. My uncle, my father's sister's husband, who was the Chief Medical Officer of Trivandrum Palace was very close to Maharaj. My uncle used to visit the Sasthamangalam Hospital frequently. Maharaj would discuss about the affairs of the hospital with my uncle and would get his doubts in the medical field clarified. Maharaj also would get his advice regarding purchase of equipments and their operation.

My father introduced me to Maharaj, when he took charge as president of Madras Math. Although I have been visiting the Math from a young age, I had not interacted much with Maharaj because I not only had great respect for him but I was also afraid of him.

---

1. She was initiated by Revered Swami Vireswarananda Maharaj in 1973. She was associated with Revered Swami Tapasyananda Maharaj for 18 years. She is a retired teacher, Sarada Vidyalaya, T.Nagar and a devotee of the Math. She currently resides in Cuddalore.

With the blessings and help of Maharaj, I joined Sarada Vidyalaya as a teacher in the 1973. Before taking up the job, I went to seek the blessings of Maharaj, 'Try to spread the message of Sri Ramakrishna–Swami Vivekananda. Your teaching job will greatly help in this,' he said and blessed me.

After a few months, I went to meet Maharaj. He asked me whether I had taken *mantra diksa*. I replied in the negative. He said, 'Next month, Revered Swami Vireswarananda Maharaj is coming from Belur Math. You receive *diksa* from him after taking consent from your parents.' After taking the consent of my parents, I went to see Maharaj. I told him that I would take *diksa* from Maharaj. Immediately Maharaj asked, 'Have you read the *Life of Sri Ramakrishna*?' I could not answer. Suddenly, I remembered the book with a Foreword by Mahatma Gandhi. I mentioned about this to Maharaj. He was very happy and said, 'That is the best book. I recommend that book to everyone.' It is only because of the blessings of Maharaj that I received spiritual initiation.

A group of teachers from Sarada Vidyalaya wanted to visit Belur Math and other centres. Maharaj helped us to get accommodation in the Guest House of the Belur Math. Maharaj told us to meet him before our departure to the Belur Math. When we met him, he thoroughly briefed us about the places to be visited and their importance and how to preserve the sanctity of these places.

We were all eagerly looking forward for our departure. But on the day we were to leave, there was a tense situation in Madras because of the passing away of the then Chief Minister, Sri M.G. Ramachandran. Trains were cancelled. We could not leave that day. We felt very sad.

Maharaj and the Saraḍa Vidyalaya's Secretary, Sri Sivaraman, advised us to proceed the next day. Maharaj informed Belur Math over phone about the change in our programme. With the blessings of Maharaj we left the next day. My long felt desire got fulfilled with the grace of Maharaj.

Maharaj had helped not only me, but also my sister. My sister had to undergo a major surgery. She was terribly worried and met Maharaj and narrated about her health condition. Not only did Maharaj console her, but also advised her to undergo the surgery. He also advised her about the post-operative care. He also told her that he would pray for her health. My sister did not tell anyone then about her meeting with Maharaj. She underwent the operation with the mental strength she received from the advice of Maharaj.

After four days, when I went to meet Maharaj, I was surprised when he enquired about the surgery and the health of my sister. Afterwards when I enquired my sister, only then did she mention about her meeting with Maharaj. Maharaj always used to enquire about the welfare of our family. My husband used to seek the blessings of Maharaj before his pilgrimage to Sabarimala.

Although I now feel very happy to share my reminiscences of Maharaj, who helped me and played a great role in my spiritual life, I also feel sad that I did not make much use of the opportunity to seek more spiritual guidance from the great *tapasvi*.

21

Holiness Personified

Sri Subramanian Swaminathan[1]

I had the good fortune of serving Revered Tapasyananda Maharaj as a scribe for about two hours (between 3 and 5 p.m. with a break for about 15 minutes) every Sunday afternoon from November 1982 to February 1985. Revered Maharaj was then translating *Adhyatma Ramayana* into English, which was later published by Sri Ramakrishna Math, Madras, as a book. The blessed opportunity of taking down his dictation in long hand came about through a friend of mine by name Raghunandan who was earlier assisting Maharaj on a similar work. Sitting beside him in his room, I would take down his dictation verbatim which was then given for typing and proof correction.

When I visited Revered Maharaj at the appointed time in his living room on Sundays for taking the dictation, I would find him on the job immediately without wasting any time. Revered Maharaj used to sit in an upright posture always, having a pillow for resting his back against the chair. While the words were flowing like a stream; he now and then had a look at the original Sanskrit version kept by

1. He is a close devotee of Chennai Math. He was in contact with Revered Maharaj as his transcriber. He currently resides in Chennai.

his side, and sometimes took a pause looking meditatively into distant space. The *advaitic* concepts embedded in the version of *Ramayana* was thrilling, being translated by one who practiced it, and put into a beautiful form of classical English, of which Revered Maharaj was a master. As my English vocabulary was limited, I stumbled whenever a new word issued forth from his lips and when I would ask him to repeat for a second time I would sense a semi frown on his face, understandably from the disturbed thought flow. But all that disappeared the very next moment and Revered Maharaj would be his natural self, resuming his dictation in a calm and composed manner. When tea time arrived around 4 p.m., he would, without fail, send me to the dining hall where monks would assemble at that time to have tea.

It happened one day, while he was dictating, an erstwhile Brahmachari came to him and had a tearful pleading with him on some matter and for readmission into the Math. It was not clear to me as to what the matter was all about, but at the end Revered Maharaj asked him to have his meal before leaving, which I felt was an act of impersonal tenderness, even though he appeared firm while talking to him.

To me the Revered Maharaj was holiness personified. He always appeared deeply pensive and meditative, which rather imparted a serious look, but when he occasionally broke into a beatific divine smile on some matter of interaction, a childlike natural simplicity showed itself out. Revered Maharaj always evoked instant reverence and respect which subconsciously made one to keep a distance and desist from any worldly talk. I was one such who did not venture to ask him anything that concerned my personal life. Punctuality, discipline, captivating spiritual poise, and humane – these are the qualities that I saw in him.

After the translation work of *Adhyatma Ramayana* was completed, Revered Maharaj embarked on a project that related to condensed version of Swami Vivekananda's works which I believe was also released in book form. Though I was not associated in that work, I continued to visit him on Sundays for some time. Around early part of 1985, Revered Maharaj fell ill on sudden attack of chickenpox which unfortunately stopped my association with him.

I was a bachelor nearing 30 at that time and my only regret was that I never enquired about my personal matters - either mundane or spiritual. There I was sitting before a great *tapasvi* having got the rarest of rare opportunities to advance in spirituality, but I would have none of it, being used into metamorphosing my highly worldly-minded life into one that was utilitarian that bordered on spirituality. Whenever I recall my association and the time I spent sitting in the proximity of this great monk, I experience a current of joy and my association with him is perhaps the only green patch in my otherwise monotonous and stagnant life.

22

Practise Yoga

Ms. R. Nivedita[1]

As aptly named, Revered Maharaj was a *tapasvi*. He did reading and writing as *tapas*. Whenever I visited him, I would see him either reading or writting. There will be a slate and pencil on his table. He will write on the slate first - add, delete or correct - then write on the paper. He will use one-side blank sheet for writing. For this purpose, often he would get the sheets of old calendars cut to size and then use. It will be astonishing to see Maharaj not wasting anything.

The first time I met Revered Maharaj was in 1974. I had already received *mantra diksa* then. I felt that it would be nice to arrange *satsang* at our house. I told Maharaj, 'Please pay a visit to our house. We will arrange a *satsang*.' Maharaj rarely visited anybody's house. However, he acceded to my request. But, due to some unforeseen circumstances, we could not organize *satsang* then. But, by the grace of God, we got the opportunity in 1978.

---

1. She was initiated by Revered Swami Vireswarananda Maharaj in 1974. She was associated with Revered Swami Tapasyananda Maharaj for 17 years. She was working with All India Radio. She currently resides in Chennai and has been closely associated with the activities of the Math.

It was the day when we completed a *Mandala Parayanam* of *Sri Lalita Sahasranama* in our house. We invited Maharaj for the concluding session. I requested Maharaj, 'Swamiji, you had agreed to visit our house. Please visit us now on this auspicious occasion.'

Actually, I had invited Maharaj in the year 1974. When I had re-invited him, it was 1978. Pointing out this, he rejoined, 'What, you are worse than Kaikeyi. The promise I made when I was young, you want me to fulfil when I am old?!' Maharaj then burst into laughter and acceded to my request.

Finally, that auspicious day arrived. Swami Raghaveshananda Maharaj performed the Homa, Swami Jnanadananda Maharaj sang bhajan, Swami Desikatmananda Maharaj performed Arati, Swami Tanmayananda Maharaj and Swami Kamalatmananda Maharaj delivered talks in Tamil and Revered Maharaj delivered talk in English and blessed each and every devotee who had gathered in large numbers for the *satsang*. Seeing a large number of monks, Maharaj, while leaving, exclaimed, 'Oh, the whole Math is here!' in his own inimitable style.

I was under the impression that Revered Maharaj used to spend lot of time in meditation and japa only. Once I asked him whether he did *parayanam* (chanting of sacred texts). He answered, 'Yes, definitely. I do *parayanam* of *Sri Lalita Sahasranama, Sri Vishnu Sahasranama, Narayaneeyam* daily.'

One has to cross his office to go to the Library. He would watch the devotees going to the Library. On my return from

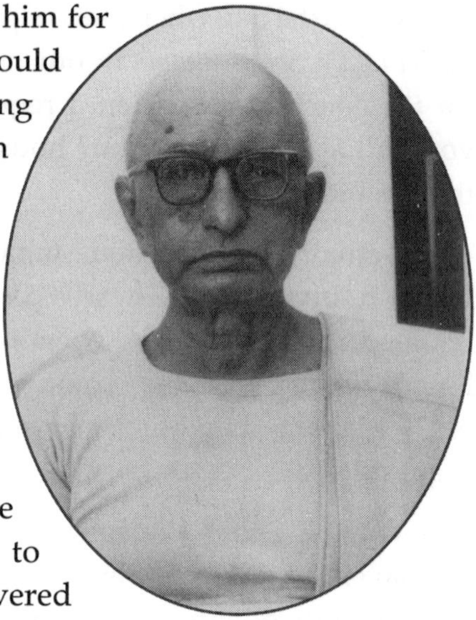

the Library, when I go to him for offering *pranams,* he would ask, 'I have been observing you taking old books from the Library, what are you reading?' Whenever I said, 'Reminiscences of Direct Disciples', he would feel very happy and say, 'very good' and would encourage me.

Once,a lay devotee had come to Madras to receive initiation from Revered Maharaj. He called me and said, 'Without even checking up with you, I have told her to stay in your house. Hope you will not mind.' He was really concerned about the comfort of the devotees.

Revered Maharaj used to provide lot of encouragement to the devotees and help them progress in their spiritual journey like a mother. He also used to guide them in their normal day-to-day life. He used to emphasise on physical exercises. He firmly believed on what Swamiji had said – 'Sound mind in a sound body'. He told me, 'If you were a boy, I myself would have taught you yoga. Practise yoga. It is very good for health.'

23

Simplicity Personified

Sri Bhaskar Roy[1]

I had the good fortune of coming in contact with the Ramakrishna Mission, New Delhi, during the early 1960's as a young boy and grew up amidst the loving care of the revered monks of the Delhi Ashram, then headed by Swami Swahananda Maharaj. Gradually, I became acquainted with the activities of the Order and became a lifelong student of the Ramakrishna Movement encouraged by the blessings and affection of my spiritual preceptor, Revered Swami Vireswarananda Maharaj for nineteen long years. Around the late 1960's, I heard about the special significance of Sri Ramakrishna Math, Madras, in the history of the Order and its then legendary head, Swami Kailasananda Maharaj, who, I was told, was at the helm of the Math since 1944.

As I was a subscriber of *The Vedanta Kesari*, I read in a particular issue in 1971 that Swami Kailasananda Maharaj had been transferred to Belur Math and had been replaced

1. He was initiated by Revered Swami Vireswarananda Maharaj in 1968. He was in contact with Revered Swami Tapasyananda Maharaj for 16 years. He served in Senior Managerial positions in TATA group. He has been closely associated with Ramakrishna Mission, Delhi and other centres for almost 5 decades. He is currently a full time volunteer of Ramakrishna Mission, New Delhi.

by Swami Tapasyananda Maharaj who was shifting from Trivandrum centre to Madras.

Swami Tapasyananda Maharaj, like Swami Kailasananda Maharaj, was also a disciple of Revered Mahapurush Maharaj (Swami Shivananda) and a Trustee of the Ramakrishna Math and Mission. We had heard that he was an extremely erudite scholar and an authoritative interpreter of the scriptures, which he wore rather lightly on his shoulders, and I soon became acquainted with his writings published in *The Vedanta Kesari* from time to time which included the translation of various scriptures and other topics of spiritual interest. His comprehensive work on the biography of the Holy Mother and the compilation of her conversations and teachings was already by then a land-mark volume in the corpus of Ramakrishna Vivekananda literature. I had also read with deep interest his reminiscences of his guru in *Shivananda Smriti Sangraha*, edited by Swami Apurvananda Maharaj, which also gave us an insight into his early life in the Ramakrishna Order.

Thanks to Swami Tapasyananda Maharaj's initiative, the teaching and preaching phases of the Math's activity expanded manifold and increasing number of devotees resorted to the Math as a result of this expansion. His organizational skills first came to fore with the extremely adept handling of the ten day long Platinum Jubilee celebrations of Madras Math which was held in August 1972 in the presence of Swami Vireswarananda Maharaj, the then president of the Ramakrishna Order. The special issue of *The Vedanta Kesari* brought out on this occasion and the issue of September 1972 bears ample testimony of the kind of celebration he organized and the galaxy of speakers, both monastic and lay, who took part in the function.

It was my great fortune to visit Madras Math along with my parents in May 1975 when I had the *darsan* of Swami Tapasyananda for the first time. I was then studying in the second year of my graduation course at the St. Stephen's College, Delhi. We were on a tour to various places of South India and Swami Vandanananda Maharaj, the then Secretary of Ramakrishna Mission, New Delhi, had very kindly given us a letter of introduction addressed to Swami Tapasyananda Maharaj to facilitate our boarding and lodging at Madras.

On a hot afternoon in May, we reached Madras after visiting Pondicherry. We reached the Math (in Mylapore) straight from Madras Egmore Railway Station and met Swami Tapasyananda Maharaj who was sitting in his small room in the old office building. His room had a half 'swing door' through which we entered and found him immersed in a sheaf of papers which he was perhaps proof-reading. He looked up and kindly received us with a gentle smile on his face. After offering our customary *pranams* to him, my father handed over Swami Vandanananda Maharaj's introductory letter to him which he read patiently and kept aside.

The first impression that we got of Swami Tapasyananda Maharaj was that of a great 'yogi' deeply immersed in *tapasya*! What a simple monk he was! The room which was, incidentally, marked as 'President' from outside, did not even have an electric fan, as far as I can recollect (or even if it was there, it was not used by him), and was sparsely furnished. But Maharaj was unperturbed even by the extremely stifling mid-summer Madras heat. He was bare-bodied with a crumpled *chaddar* wrapped carelessly around himself and his dhoti raised upto his ankles.

After the initial introduction, he smiled and told us that Madras Math did not have a Guest House for devotees but he would arrange suitable accommodation for us. He then called Swami Chidghanananda Maharaj (Ramamurthy Maharaj), the then Manager of Madras Math, and asked him to make suitable arrangements for our stay at the nearby Brindavan Lodge near the Math. 'But you must have noon and night *prasad* with us during your stay in Madras,' he insisted and we gladly agreed.

We told him that we had seen his huge picture framed in the Secretary's room of Sasthamangalam Ashrama at Trivandrum and his successor-Secretary, Swami Anantatmananda Maharaj's glowing praise about his tireless work in developing the hospital as one of the best in Kerala in those days. He only gently smiled hearing this.

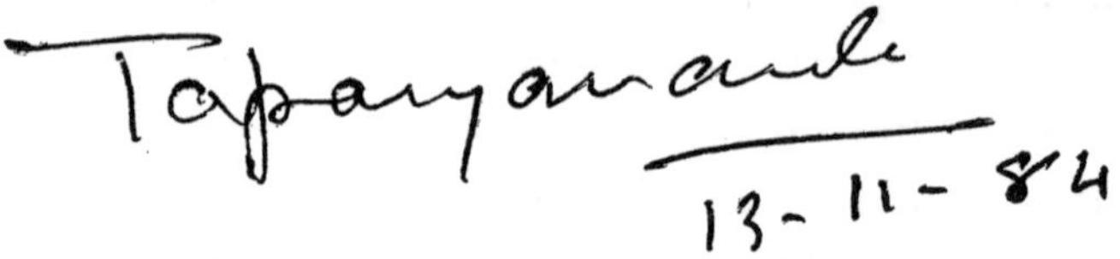

This was the sign of a real monk who remains unaffected by either praise or criticism and we saw it fully manifest in Swami Tapasyananda Maharaj.

Our seven day stay at Madras gave us an opportunity to watch Maharaj from close quarters. Every morning and evening we used to visit Maharaj to offer our humble salutations. Invariably, we would find him deeply engrossed in his literary work oblivious of the outer world. Sometimes he would not even notice our presence; so deeply he would be immersed in his writings. I later learnt that he was, at that time, translating the *Srimad Bhagavatam*.

Even while we had *prasad* in the dining hall, we would find him totally detached from the outside world. He would enter the dining room unnoticed, sit on the floor at his appointed place, have his meals without speaking a single word (not even bothering about what he ate), and leave the room as quietly as he had entered. The only piece of 'luxury' he indulged in was a small but rickety table in front of him on which he kept his plate and bowls. His diet was extremely simple which he ate patiently with a stainless steel spoon. Meals over, he would immediately get back to his office to continue his writing. He was indeed simplicity personified and even his foot-wear was of the cheapest variety available in the market. He spoke very little but whenever he did it was full of love and affection.

When my father incidentally told him that one of his grand-uncles was Swami Atmaprakashananda Maharaj (Priyanath Maharaj, a disciple of the Holy Mother and a 'wanted' revolutionary in his pre-monastic life, who later became a Trustee of the Order), Maharaj took off his spectacles, closed his eyes for a while and said, 'Oh, Mr. Roy, you have rekindled my old memories! I had the privilege to work with Priya Maharaj for a few years in the Malabar region almost forty years ago. What a loving swami he was.' This showed his utmost reverence for the senior monks of the Order and the respect he held for them even decades after they had left their mortal coil.

Maharaj succeeded in gathering around him a number of young as well as experienced monks and brahmacharins

Tapasyanandaji delivering a speech at the Students' Home, Madras, with Sri Anna Subramaniam and Raghaveshanandaji

who, under his firm but loving care, later turned out to be eminent monks shouldering onerous responsibilities of the Order. Maharaj encouraged and involved even lay devotees and scholars like Sri 'Anna' N. Subramanian, Sri R. Ramakrishnan, Sri C.S. Ramakrishnan, Dr. T.M.P. Mahadevan, Sri Giridhari Prasad, Justice M.M. Ismail and many others in the scholastic works of the Math, including *The Vedanta Kesari*.

It was Maharaj who introduced the scriptural and other classes throughout the week from Mondays through Sundays (in English and Tamil) and encouraged the monks and even brahmacharins to take these classes as preparation for their later responsibilities. During our stay, we participated in the day long 'Spiritual Retreat' held on a Sunday at the Swami Vivekananda Centenary Hall which was also newly introduced in Madras by Maharaj. For us too, it was a novel experience because Delhi centre did not have any such programme in those days.

Before leaving Madras for New Delhi we requested him to autograph a copy of the biography of Swami Ramakrishnananda he had authored to which he gladly agreed. The book *Swami Ramakrishnananda – The Apostle of Sri Ramakrishna to the South* is one of my prized possessions even today. Our few days in his holy company at Madras are etched forever in our minds and we consider it a rare privilege to have seen such an intense *yogi* from close quarters, even if it was for a short while.

I saw Swami Tapasyananda Maharaj next at the Convention of the Ramakrishna Math and Mission, held in Belur Math in December 1980. He delivered a wonderful presidential address one evening (on 24th December) in the session on 'Practical Vedanta' which had Swami Ranganathananda Maharaj, Swami Ananyananda Maharaj etc. as the other speakers. He also participated in the Christmas Eve programme the same evening.

I had to wait for another five years before I could meet Swami Tapasyananda Maharaj again in 1985 when he had just become one of the vice-presidents of the Ramakrishna Order. I had gone to Madras on official work and took some time off to visit the Math and have *darsan* of him. This time what struck me about Maharaj was that there was absolutely no change in his life-style and in his personal bearings even though he was now a vice-president of the Order. The same "fan-less" room, the same dress code, the same type of footwear, the same detachment in his outlook and the same pre-occupation with his writings on which he was deeply engrossed even then. He obviously could not remember me since my last visit was almost ten years ago but he very lovingly spoke a few words after reading the letter that I had brought from Revered Swami Niswananda Maharaj (Balakrishna or Baba Maharaj as he was more affectionately known), the then Acting-Secretary of Ramakrishna Mission, New Delhi. Even after this visit, I had the good fortune of having his holy *darsan* on a few more occasions till his passing away in 1991 during my official visits to Madras now and then.

Great monks like Swami Tapasyananda Maharaj exemplify the rare combination of the secular and the spiritual. While on the one hand, he was instrumental in establishing a huge hospital in Trivandrum and nurturing the centre for three decades, his next two decades at Madras saw him making one of the biggest contributions to the ever-growing corpus of Ramakrishna-Sarada Devi-Vivekananda and Scriptural Literature by dint of his exceptional scholarship and erudition. Although his spiritual ministry as vice-president lasting only for six years, he will always be remembered as the personification of simplicity and austerity: the twin qualities which he embodied, setting a glowing example for others to emulate.

My humble salutations to him.

24

Devote Fully To His Work

Smt. Kumari[1]

I was a volunteer in Madras Math's charitable dispensary. As a volunteer, I could get ample opportunities to offer *pranams* to Revered Tapasyananda Maharaj. He would usually be reading something. But whenever I went, he would invariably put down the book he was reading and greet me with a smile. He told me to always have *prasad* at the Math after the dispensary work. He also told me to meditate in the prayer hall till the bell for *prasad* rang. In the afternoons, I would serve in the Library. Thus I would happily spend the whole day in the holy precincts of the Math.

In 1976, when I first met Revered Maharaj after my husband passed away, as a way of consolation, he said that I should take it as the will of Sri Ramakrishna and devote myself more fully to His work. Perhaps these were the usual words, but coming from him, they had a very soothing and uplifting effect. Perhaps, it was with this in mind that Revered Maharaj suggested that I work in the Dispensary and the Library.

1. She is a devotee of Chennai Math.

Once, a medical firm from abroad – I think it was from Germany – sent some of its latest equipment for the dispensary of the Math. Revered Maharaj made a deep study of the new equipment so that he could guide the doctors and their assistants in using the new equipment in all possible ways.

Some tourists from Australia once came to the Math and paid their respects to Revered Maharaj. I happened to be there and noticed the extremely pained expression on his face because he could not understand anything of what they said in their Australian accent.

Although of a stern exterior, he was really very compassionate and helpful. I realized this personally. Wanting me to stay closer to the Math, he actually left his busy schedule one morning to look for a suitable accommodation for me!

25

Getting Initiated

Sri D. K. Mukherjee[1]

I had the privilege of receiving the affection and blessings of Revered Swami Tapasyananda Maharaj from 1976 till his *mahasamadhi.*

I was residing in Ranipet (120km from Madras) and was engaged in the manufacture of Epoxy resins. I would visit Madras Math quite often. It so happened that some cracks developed on the terrace and dome of now 'old temple' at Madras Math and water would seep into the shrine whenever it rained.

After some futile attempts of civil contractors to repair the terrace, the then manager, Swami Raghaveshananda Maharaj gave me an opportunity to explore the possibility of arresting the seepage with Epoxy resins manufactured by us. When the seepage was successfully arrested, Swami Tapasyananda Maharaj became very happy and was even more kind and affectionate towards me.

---

1. He was initiated by Revered Swami Visuddhananda Maharaj in 1957. He was associated with Revered Swami Tapasyananda Maharaj for 15 years. He is a renowned Engineer. He currently resides in Ranipet, Vellore Dist., Tamil Nadu.

After Maharaj became the vice-president, I met him one day and told him that the devotees of the southern region would then be able to get spiritually initiated easily. But Maharaj said, 'Nowadays it has become a fashion to have [spiritual] initiation. They neither study the literature on Sri Ramakrishna, Holy Mother and Swamiji nor do they practice meditation and japa [Immediately I do not think of giving initiation].' I then said, 'Maharaj, at the insistence of my mother, I was spiritually initiated by Revered Swami Vishuddhananda Maharaj when I was just 16 years old. Although I had been a volunteer in Bombay Math for some years, I had then not understood the significance of initiation. But today I feel that it would be better if I had been initiated even earlier!' Hearing this, Maharaj smiled a little.

After several days, I was informed by Swami Raghaveshananda Maharaj that Maharaj wanted to meet me. When I met him subsequently, I was surprised when he told me that he was going to spiritually initiate the devotees. He felt it necessary to inform about this to an insignificant person like me! It was certainly because of his love and affection.

A few days before he passed away, I visited him at the hospital where he was admitted. Like a child, he requested me to take him back to the Math since he did not like being in a hospital. I tried to convince him by saying that the doctors had decided to conduct a few tests in the next two or three days and thereafter he could return to the Math. Although he was not quite convinced, he kept quiet. This was my last meeting with Maharaj.

26

Limitless Love and Compassion

Ms. Harini Varma[1]

I was about 25 years old when I first visited the Sri Ramakrishna Math in Madras, sometime in the early 1980s. At that time, I really had no idea about spiritual life or the philosophy of the Ramakrishna Order. I remember being immediately taken by the peaceful, inspiring, and divine aura that seemed to pervade the green and beautiful premises. There was something about the atmosphere in the Math that just drew me in (I still do not know how to describe it even after thirty years), and I began visiting the Math now and then after that day.

A few months later, one afternoon, I was about to enter the shrine (which is today called the 'Old Temple') when I noticed an elderly swami walking towards the entrance of the Monks' Quarters. I walked towards him to offer my *pranams*, and the first thing I remember noticing was a calm and benevolent smile on his face. At that time, I did not even know how to address the monks at the Math. Was I to say "Maharaj"? Was I to say "Swamiji"? I had no clue. All I told him was, 'I am relatively new to the Math. It's

1. She was initiated by Revered Maharaj in 1986 and was associated with him for 11 years. She is Asst. Secretary, Sarada Vidyalaya, T.Nagar, Chennai and is closely associated with the activities of Chennai Math.

a very beautiful place with a wonderful atmosphere.' His reply was very short. 'Keep coming often,'he said, and went into the Quarters.

Later, I asked someone who was standing nearby about the Swami, and learnt that he was none other than Revered Swami Tapasyananda Maharaj, who was the president of the Math at that time. When I now think about that day, I realize how it had changed the course of my life in many ways. My association with Revered Maharaj and the Order since then has transformed my thought process from the mundane to the spiritual and noble. He later initiated me into spiritual life and into the deep ocean of the Ramakrishna Order through his immeasurable and limitless love, concern, and spiritual intuition. I still feel I did not deserve such profound love and care from the great Swami, but then, Sri Ramakrishna has his own unique ways of pulling people into his circle of love and spirituality.

Revered Maharaj had a deep understanding of the mental make-up and attitude of people. It so happened that the then Manager Maharaj of Madras Math asked me to talk to Ms Swatantra, daughter of Sri C Subramanian (Former Union Minister and a veteran statesman),about joining the Management Committee of the Ramakrishna Mission Schools in Madras. In the process, I introduced her to Revered Maharaj. Unexpectedly, he literally ordered me also to become a member of the Committee! I was completely taken aback, surprised and shocked! Here I was, a homemaker, with no professional experience or knowledge about the functioning of educational institutions. How was I to take up an engagement of this kind? However, Revered Maharaj had faith in me that I could do the needful and it was with this stimulus I took up the responsibility, and I daresay, the exposure and experience I have had over these years, discussing and sorting out various issues and problems that schools and students face, is something that has given me a new identity for sure.

So far, the major turning point in my life was the *mantra diksa* I received from Revered Maharaj in 1986. At that time, I was not fully into the rhythm of reading and appreciating spiritual books. One morning, Revered Maharaj asked me to apply for spiritual initiation that was scheduled to be given a month later. By that time, I was used to expect 'the unexpected' from Revered Maharaj, but still, this instruction was still a surprise for me considering that I had not yet read the biographies of the Holy Trinity, and I confessed about it to Revered Maharaj. He coolly remarked, 'That can be done later also. You should get initiated early.' When I subsequently mentioned this to a few others in the Math, they too were surprised, because Revered Maharaj was very particular about devotees studying the biographies before applying for spiritual initiation. I still wonder why this exception was made in my case. I haven't found the answer yet, but I am sure this is all Divine Grace and the blessings of my spiritual Guru.

I recall another interesting incident which reiterates his limitless love and compassion. Generally, after spiritual initiation, it is customary for the disciples to keep the pictures of the Holy Trio and the Guru in the worship room in their houses to perform japa and meditation. When I got a picture of Revered Maharaj and took it to him for blessings, he signed on the picture as well. Lo! All the other monastic members of the Math whom I know were surprised at this because, as they told me later, Revered Maharaj hardly signed on his own picture for the sake of the devotees. Needless to say, I was overjoyed and felt really blessed to hear this. It is no doubt his infinite grace and blessings are on me and my family.

As they say, to be born in the holy land of India is rare and the association of holy men like Revered Maharaj is rarer. I offer my humble *pranams* at his lotus feet and seek his blessings.

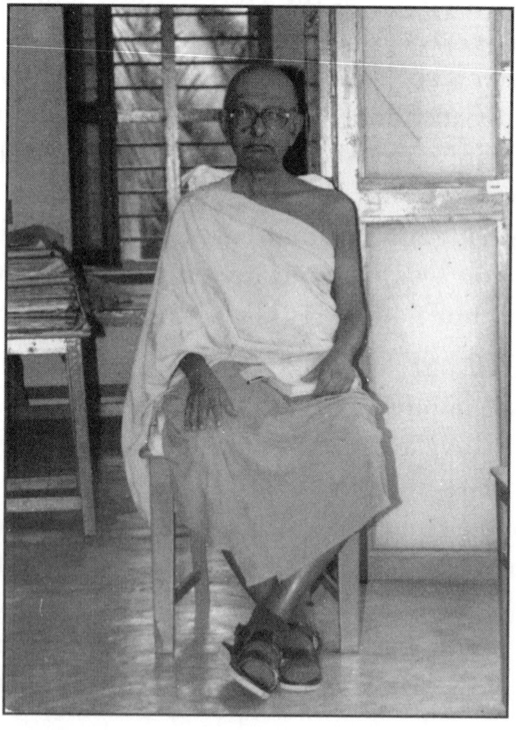

27

He Rocked the Cradle!

Sri R. R. Mukundan[1]

In the year 1950, when my father Sri R.Rajendran completed his school education, my grandfather sent him from Sivakasi to Kollam to work in the Timber shop of Sri Raja Sankaralingam.

Swami Chidbhavananda Maharaj and Swami Tapasyananda Maharaj would visit the house of Smt. Gnanasundari, wife of Sri Raja Sankaralingam, whom I and other children would affectionately address as 'Om Shakti Amma'.

My mother was not keeping well, in spite of several types of medical treatment. During the visit of Swami Tapasyananda Maharaj to Kollam for a spiritual retreat, Sri Raja Sankaralingam mentioned about my mother's health to him. Revered Maharaj advised to admit my mother in the Ashrama Hospital at Sasthamangalam.

From 1957 to 1965, my mother used to visit the Hospital for treatment. I shall recount what my mother shared with me.

---

1. He was initiated by Revered Swami Bhuteshananda Maharaj in 1982. He was associated with Revered Swami Tapasyananda Maharaj for 25 years. His parents are also initiated disciples. He currently resides in Kochi.

After attending to the hospital work, Revered Maharaj would write books till late night. There was no canteen facility at the time in the hospital. So, my mother was also served the same food that was prepared for Revered Maharaj. Revered Maharaj was very fond of ladies-finger *sambar*. So lunch will always include ladies-finger *sambar*. Even later, whenever ladies-finger *sambar* was served, my mother would be reminded of Revered Maharaj.

Around the year 1962, my mother was admitted to Sasthamangalam Hospital. I was then a 2-3 months old baby. The room in which my mother was accommodated was in between the office room and the rest room of Revered Maharaj. Revered Maharaj would visit my mother on his way from his office to the rest room. He would spend some time with my elder sister and elder brother and before leaving, for a few minutes,he would rock the cradle in which I was sleeping. It is because of such close association with Revered Maharaj that my entire family, wife and children remain the devotees of Sri Ramakrishna.

In the year 1968, my mother was admitted in a hospital at Madras. Hence, we also moved to Madras. In the year 1971, Revered Maharaj became the president of Madras Math. During the visit of Swami Vireswarananda to Madras, perhaps in 1972, my mother desired to receive spiritual initiation from him. My father was not in favour of it. But my mother was very keen on it. My father instructed my mother to seek the advice of Swami Tapasyananda Maharaj. Next morning, my parents and I went to Math at Mylapore, Madras. My father informed him of my mother's keen desire to receive spiritual initiation. Revered

Maharaj gave a patient hearing to my father. Revered Maharaj asked my mother, 'Who is Guru Maharaj?' Out of fear, my mother was silent. Then, she whispered something. My mother always had great respect for Maharaj. But she was somewhat afraid of him also.

Swami Chidghanananda Maharaj, who was watching all this, took my mother to his office and put the same question to her with ease, to which my mother answered *Avatara Purush,* an Incarnation of God. The Swami asked her a few more questions, to which my mother answered. The Swami took us back to the room of Revered Maharaj and told him, 'Jayammal knows about Sri Guru Maharaj thoroughly. 'Revered Maharaj smilingly informed her that she could receive initiation the very next day. She was advised to read more books on Sri Guru Maharaj. From the

Sitting in chair: 2. Veetasprhanandaji 3. Tapasyanandaji 4. Gananandaji, Kalady, May 1988

day she received initiation, till she breathed her last, she was a staunch devotee of Sri Ramakrishna. My mother always used to tell that we are the children of Swami Tapasyananda Maharaj and that she had lived on his grace.

Now, I shall recount my own reminiscences of Revered Maharaj.

We had moved from Madras to Kochi in the year 1982 for the sake of our father's business. In 1985, Revered Maharaj visited Kalady for a function. My parents, elder sister and I visited him. He was staying in the house of a devotee. The picture of Dr. Radhakrishnan, drawn by her grand-daughter, was shown to Revered Maharaj. He commented, 'Radhakrishnan's nose is not sharp'. I marvelled at his taste in the art of drawing.

I think it was on Swami Niranjanananda Jayanti. Revered Maharaj, other monks and brahmacharis were having their *prasad*. After *prasad*, a brahmachari belonging to Tamilnadu uttered "*Jai Sri Guru Maharaj*" and in the end he uttered "*Jai Sri Niranjanananda Maharaj Avarkalukku Jai*"[1]. All the Brahmacharis burst into laughter spontaneously. Revered Maharaj said with a tinge of anger, 'What is this? This is not a joke.' There was absolute silence. Brahmacharis felt sorry.

Because of the blessed association with Revered Maharaj, we could get the opportunity to receive the blessings of Revered Swami Vireswarananda Maharaj and

1. After *prasad*, on special days, slogans are uttered to hail the Holy Trio etc. Generally, the Hindi word 'ki' (for) is used. The brahmachari used the Tamil word 'avarkalukku' for 'ki'.

get initiation from Revered Swami Bhuteshananda Maharaj in the year 1982.

In the year 1988, after my marriage, we went to Madras and received the blessings of Revered Maharaj. That was our last meeting.

Reading Yoga

For many years, I had a habit of reading many books without any plan or purpose. But my guru, Revered Swami Tapasyananda Maharaj, taught me what to read and why to read and how to read. Right from my first meeting with him, he guided me (and a few others) in the study of the *Bhagavad Gita* and other sacred books, and his books were my staple diet for study and self-improvement.

He explained to me that neither self-aggrandisement, nor any worldly benefit, not even for a mere thirst for knowledge is the purpose of study. Its purpose was for spiritual development - to be freed from the hold of the body and realize one's kinship or unity with the Divine.

I gained a new insight into the significance of study. And instead of reading something for mere time pass, I began my 'Reading Yoga'.

— Smt. Sakthi Kirubhakaran

28

See God in All

Smt. Jamuna Kannan[1]

In the last week of January 1986 (or 1987), I told Swami Kamalatmananda Maharaj (then Editor of *Sri Ramakrishna Vijayam*) about my desire to receive spiritual initiation from the Ramakrishna Order. Maharaj told me that it would be better if my husband also had spiritual initiation. Next day around 10.00 a.m., Swami Kamalatmananda Maharaj introduced us to Revered Tapasyananda Maharaj and mentioned about our desire to receive spiritual initiation.

Revered Maharaj had a private talk with us. My husband and I received spiritual initiation on 8thFebruary.

Whenever I visited the Math, I used to offer *pranams* to Revered Maharaj and receive his blessings. Once, with a longing heart and a feeling of insecurity, I told Maharaj weeping, 'I want to have the *darsan* of God.' He told me to sit down. He then assumed the pose of the Lord with the protecting hands and said, 'God will not present Himself in front of you with four hands, wearing ornaments, adorned with a crown. If you really want to have the *darsan* of God,

1. She was initiated by Revered Maharaj in 1986 and was associated with him for 5 years. She is a house wife. She currently resides in Chennai and closely associated with the activities of Chennai Math.

you should see God in all. He looked out of the window and told, 'You should see God in all living beings including trees and plants. 'He told me to participate in all the programmes of the Math like discourses, *Ramnam* etc. Since then, I have been able to do my spiritual practice and to attend to my daily chores with peace of mind.

When my second son came on leave to Madras from Pune Army College, he was feeling very sorry that the atmosphere there was not congenial as some of his friends consume liquor, drugs etc. He wanted to receive spiritual initiation from Revered Maharaj. He met Revered Maharaj and a date was fixed for his spiritual initiation. But, on that day, he had to be present in the Army College and so left for Pune without getting spiritually initiated. Instead, my first son had spiritual initiation on that day.

My second son, who left for Pune after receiving the blessings of Revered Maharaj, informed us that he, along with his room-mate, visited the Pune Math in the afternoon, and that his mind became calm and inclined towards God. During his next visit to Madras, he received spiritual initiation from Revered Maharaj.

We palpably feel that Bhagavan Sri Ramakrishna, Holy Mother Sri Sarada Devi, Swami Vivekananda and Swami Tapasyananda Maharaj have been protecting us all the time. We offer our prostrations to them.

29

The Missing Cauliflower!

Sri M. Radhakrishnan[1]

One who removed my ignorance and gave me knowledge, I met him in 1984 for the first time and received spiritual initiation from him in the same year.

When I approached Maharaj for spiritual initiation, he asked me the reason. I replied that I was struggling to overcome the problems I was facing in life. When he learnt that I was from Kerala, he started speaking to me in Malayalam.

He asked me, 'Who was Sri Ramakrishna?' I replied that my mother had clearly told me that Sri Ramakrishna was an *avatara*. Revered Maharaj said, 'That has brought you here.' and gave me spiritual initiation.

He taught me the method of doing japa with *mala*. He said, 'Initially one may use *mala* for japa, subsequently mind itself will take the role of *mala*. 'He advised me, 'Do not tell lies. If you cannot tell the truth, keep quiet, do not talk anything.'

---

1. He was initiated by Revered Maharaj in 1984 and was associated with him for 18 years. He has retired after working in Private Sector. He is currently a volunteer of Chennai Math.

I had doubts. I asked Maharaj about going to Sabarimala, performance of *Pitru Karma* etc. Revered Maharaj said, 'You can do all these things. But always think of Sri Ramakrishna.'

I would meet Revered Maharaj in the evenings. One day he asked me questions about elephants – the quantity of food an elephant would consume, its weight etc.

When I casually asked Maharaj about the stick he was carrying, he humourously replied, 'It is used as a walking stick, it will also be useful to discipline people like you.'

Once, yield of cauliflower was very high in the Math garden. Next morning, a large quantity of the vegetable was missing. Turning towards me, he asked, 'Did you take away the cauliflower last night?' The Asst. General Secretary Maharaj was also there. Pointing at me he told Asst. General Secretary Maharaj, 'He is a cauliflower thief' and made fun of me. I took it as a blessing from Revered Maharaj.

Maharaj was a great Kali devotee. He was also a devotee of Lord Hanuman and Holy Mother. He wrote a book on the Life of Holy Mother in English.

Maharaj would say, 'One should do the work with calm mind, otherwise, even others will not be able to offer help to complete the work.'

During his last days, he presented a book, *Sri Krishna Karnamrutam* and a shawl to me.

I pray for the grace of my Guru to remain pure. I offer my humble *pranams* at the holy feet of my Revered Guru.

30

In Search of My Guru

Smt. Girija Devi[1]

I saw my guru, Revered Swami Tapasyananda Maharaj for the first time on 22 March 1989, the day of my long awaited spiritual initiation.

It was during 1973-74 that I started going to the Ramakrishna Ashram located in Basavanagudi, Bangalore, taking my son in my arms. Though I had great reverence for monks, I hesitated to approach them and talk to them. I was working in a state government office and generally went to the Ashram only on holidays. At that time, spirituality was a new subject to me. I did not know that the devotees can get spiritual initiation from the Ramakrishna Ashram; my impression was that the ashram was involved only in social service. After sometime, I had to stop visiting the ashram due to the objections raised by my family.

I was close to my mother's elder sister, who was associated with an ashram in Andhra Pradesh. She tried to persuade me to take a mantra from a brahmachari of that ashram. I was not impressed with this idea. However,

1. She was initiated by Revered Maharaj in 1989. She had been frequently corresponding with Revered Maharaj while she was residing in Bangalore and Mysore. After her retirement, she is residing in Ramakrishna Mission Home of Service, Varanasi.

I then understood the meaning of spiritual initiation. Thereafter, I started wishing that I had my own guru and an ashram I could claim to belong to in my own city! One of my colleagues visited the Ramakrishna Ashram regularly. From her I came to know that aspiring devotees can have their spiritual initiation from the Ramakrishna Ashram. I was surprised and thrilled. I was then working in Mysore. To fulfill my desire of having 'my own guru', I travelled several times from Mysore to Bangalore to visit the Ramakrishna Ashram. I started reading books on the Holy Trio. I prayed to Sri Ramakrishna sincerely to show me the right path. Finally, he gave me 'my own guru' on 22 March 1989. Along with many other devotees, I had my spiritual initiation from Revered Swami Tapasyananda Maharaj. After the initiation and the noon *prasad,* I went near my guru to take his photograph. When one of his attendants prevented me from taking the photo, my guru immediately intervened, 'Don't prevent her! Let her take, let her take.' I now worship this photo in my shrine.

I was full of doubts and questions. I started doing japa regularly as instructed by my guru expecting very quick *darsan* of Bhagavan Sri Ramakrishna! I wrote a letter to my guru to know when this would happen! He was so kind to give satisfying and assuring answers even to my foolish and silly questions. Whenever I think of all this, my heart is filled with joy and peace and my eyes shed tears. His letters always uplifted my spirits.

In his letter dated 15 June 1989, he consoled me like this, 'If you will have full faith in Sri Ramakrishna and in the mantra relating to Him, your spiritual progress is assured. But you have to remember that all your prayers are just like the cries of a baby for its mother. It is left to the mother to lift the child. The cry must be from the bottom of our heart and it must be constant without any sense of disappointment due to the delay in fulfillment. You would have read Sri Ramakrishna's parable of the angler, putting the angle and waiting for any length of time, as he knows that the fish is in the lake and will swallow the hook at some time or other. Spiritual realization is the result of God's grace. We cannot purchase it by our sadhana as it is a matter of grace. Yet regular performance of sadhana is necessary for enhancing the small flame of aspiration that one has got. With this attitude, we should perform our sadhana. Bhagavan Sri Krishna assures us that one who thinks of Him constantly all through his life, will have His grace and His vision at least at the end of one's life.'

I read the book, *Call of the Spirit*, published by Madras Math. Many doubts cropped up in my immature mind about using the rosary etc. I immediately wrote to my guru who replied, 'If one can repeat japa in mind continuously without break - that is the best way. But generally people won't be able to do that. Counting on the *mala* or the fingers is just the means for drawing back the wandering mind to your object of concentration. This process is called *pratyahara*. If this *pratyahara* is achieved, the mind gets fixed. But that is an achievement long way off for most people. So repetition with *mala* or fingers is helpful for all of us in our early stages. Even now, after repeating the mantra with *mala*, when the mind gets more or less concentrated thereby, you can do the japa purely in the mind.'

I reproduce below some of the clarifications given by my guru in his letters about performing worship of Sri

Ramakrishna, chanting *Sri Lalita Sahasranama* etc., as these may help other devotees also.

1. '*Lalita Sahasranama* is a *stotra* as distinguished from a mantra. A mantra has to be repeated in the mind or in a way inaudible to others. *Stotras* are to be chanted a little more loudly. It need not be very loud, as if meant for others outside to hear. That the *sahasranama* is *gopya* means only that it is very sacred. *Sahasranamas* of Vishnu, Devi, etc., are often chanted loudly by priests in temples for the devotees to hear. Devotees can chant them at any time, if they know them by heart, as you say, while cooking, preparing for puja etc. That is a very good way of thinking of the Divine at all times.

    "That these sacred mantras should not fall on those who are attending nature's calls etc.," is an objection that I cannot understand. In the first place, people attend to these things only in privacy and they are not likely to hear it. Secondly even if they do, you do not incur any sin. In olden days it used to be said that Vedic chanting should not be done in the hearing of anyone except the *brahmanas*. Now there are Vedic scholars ready to teach anyone but there are no students to hear or study. So all that I can say on this matter is that different people have different views on these matters, and these views change from age to age and from time to time. So no serious attention need be paid to the objections raised by the Devi *upasakas*.'

2. About seeing the form of *Ishta* during japa: 'Seeing the form or not is not very important. You should do the japa of the mantra with concentration and hear mentally the sound vibrations that the mantra represents. The

mantra is the Deity in sound form. Just as you see the form of the Deity with the eyes, you commune with Him through sound. Some who are very psychic see forms easily, others may not. What is important is devotion and self-surrender. With every japa one should surrender oneself to Him. This self-surrender is the highest form of worship. We realize Him fully – I do not use the words see or hear – when His grace is bestowed on us. Ultimately it is only divine grace and not our power that can lift us from *samsara*. Our prayer, meditation and other forms of spiritual practice are just like the cries of an animal that has fallen into a disused well. Its voice may be heard by someone above and he may help it to be lifted up. If the animal remains noiselessly in the well, it will have to remain there for all time. So we have to do our duties as offering to God, meditate, pray, etc. with an intense yearning for Him, and wait for His grace to lift us up.'

3. Regarding offering puja and *aratrikam* to Sri Ramakrishna: 'You can do *Aratrikam* even without a formal puja. But you have to be careful that when you are showing the lamp lighted with camphor etc., clothes and other inflammable materials on oneself or in the room do not catch fire. I mention this because it has actually happened in the private shrine room of some devotees elsewhere. As a token puja, an offering of some flowers is sufficient. Along with it, you can give a simple *naivedyam* of some sugar candy or fruits or coconut *laddus*. If cooked rice is ready, you can place this also before Him, and pray that He may purify it. But these need not be made into a regular practice. Such offerings

should be made before one has eaten any part of it. Even in our Ashramas, cooked rice is not offered everywhere. But you can do it if you get greater satisfaction by it than otherwise. The simplest way of offering is to think that when you are taking food, you are offering it to Him who dwells within you. If you look into the *Gita*, you will find: 'Based in the body of living beings, I manifest as the digestive Fire, Vaisvanara, and in combination with the vital energies known as Prana and Apana, digest the four kinds of food taken by them.' [15:14]. You will find it also stated: 'Whatever you do, whatever you eat, whatever you offer in sacrifice, whatever you give as charity, whatever austerity you perform – do that as offering unto Me.'[9:27]. So a devotee can derive the fullest satisfaction even by this form of offering.'

I did not know that college students were also given spiritual initiation. Under some mysterious and unexpected circumstances, my son, who was then a first year degree student, received spiritual initiation from my guru at Madras Math in August 1989. For next two years, my son stayed in Madras Math during his summer vacations. In his letter, welcoming my son to stay in the Math, my guru wrote, 'He will live here as one among us. But beware. He may catch our spirit by too close association.' Though this statement appears to be in jest, I am sure my guru had foreseen the future of my son. After completing his higher education, my son joined the Ramakrishna Order in 2003. I am told that he is the last disciple of my guru to join the Order.

For various reasons, I thought of taking voluntary retirement from the government service. I wrote to my guru about this more than once and each time he gave me very practical advice. He told me, 'Hasty steps like retiring from job etc., will not carry you far. If you read the life of Sri Ramakrishna and his sayings intelligently, all these matters will become much clearer.' Again in another letter he said, 'It is better you practice patience for some time. Patience is always to be practiced by all in all situations. The fortunes of people in life vary from time to time. We have to put up with it, accepting that they are all due to our karma. When our fortunes are low at one time, it may come up again after sometime like the spokes of a wheel. .... Make your decision after giving sufficient time for ideas to take firm shape in your mind.' I continued in my service. After retirement, I now receive a good pension and live in the Ramakrishna Mission's old age home in Kashi.

31

On Paramahamsa

Dr. P. Gangadharan[1]

I am the only son to my mother. Due to some reasons, I had to leave my native place. I requested one of my friends to send a false telegram – "Go to Madras immediately" – from the nearest post office. The very next day I had collected money from my mother for the journey and left for Madras. My uncle (father's younger brother) was working in a company in Madras and was staying with his family in Mylapore near Kapalaeeswarar Temple. I stayed with them.

One day, my uncle told me about Sri Ramakrishna Math. The very next day, I visited the Math at about 11.00 a.m. after visiting Kapaleeswarar Temple. My mind was filled with doubt and fear while entering into the gate. I saw an old man taking care of the footwear of the devotees. He showed me the way to enter. I saw a number of holy sannyasins in saffron dress and brahmacharis in white. It was the first time in my life I saw such people.

I did not know how to conduct myself in that holy place. Some enquired about me in English. But I could not

1. He was initiated by Revered Swami Vireswarananda Maharaj in 1977. He had contact with Revered Swami Tapasyananda Maharaj for about 15 years. He is a Homeopathic Consultant, practising in Elembachi, Kasargod Dist., Kerala.

understand what they asked. They showed me the way to the shrine and I went into the shrine, prayed, offered *pranams* and returned. Then I saw a monk (later I came to know he was Swami Golokananda Maharaj). He enquired about me and instructed me to meet the President Swami (Swami Tapasyananda Maharaj). I went straight into the room and offered *pranams*. Maharaj motioned me to sit through a facial gesture and enquired about me.

Maharaj : 'What are you doing?'

Myself : 'Writing stories for performance.'

Maharaj : 'What type of stories are you writing?'

Myself : 'Stories on Bhagat Singh, Sivaji and other revolutionaries.'

Maharaj : 'Why not on the life and teachings of Sri Ramakrishna Paramahamsa, Holy Mother Sarada Devi and Swami Vivekananda?'

Myself : 'Who will listen to stories of Swamiji? Keralities are more interested in the stories of revolutionaries than on Swamiji.'

Hearing this, Maharaj laughed.

Maharaj : 'Can you find any other revolutionary like Swami Vivekananda? Swamiji's words enter into the heart of the people like fire.'

Then the bell rang for *prasad.*

Maharaj got up and took me also for *prasad*. There, I saw monastic members sitting and reciting *slokas* from the *Bhagavad Gita*. Maharaj showed a place to sit. I was over-conscious of myself and thought everyone was watching me. I tried my best to adjust to this new situation.

After taking holy *prasad,* Maharaj took me to his room and blessed me and told me to come again. Swami Golokananda Maharaj was waiting outside with a smiling face. He said, 'You have got blessings from Swami Tapasyanandaji, you are very lucky.'

After that, I would daily attend the mangalarati at 5.00 a.m., evening *arati* and *bhajans* and began to involve myself in other activities of the Math.

Swami Tapasyananda Maharaj, even in his busy hours, would make me sit near him and speak to me about Sri Ramakrishna, Sarada Devi and Swami Vivekananda. Moreover, he gave me some holy books which were very difficult to procure. Maharaj introduced me to other devotees who visited him regularly. By that time, the seed of "Paramahamsa" had been sown in my mind.

I would sit in the Library, prepare the *rupa* and *bhava* for the stories, and then write poems and stories. Swami Golokananda Maharaj made arrangements for my writing. I would daily visit Swami Tapasyananda Maharaj with my writings, and he would make corrections wherever necessary.

On 17 September 1977 after attending *mangalarati,* I was overwhelmed with great joy. The Math was beautifully decorated. Swami Chidghanananda Maharaj (the manager) asked me, 'Are you also taking *mantra diksa* tomorrow?" I asked, 'What is *mantra diksa*?' I was informed about the arrival of Revered Swami Vireswarananda Maharaj, the president of the Order, for giving *mantra diksa* and that I should talk to Swami Tapasyananda Maharaj regarding this.

I entered into Maharaj's room.

Myself : 'Maharaj, *mantra diksa...*'

Maharaj : '*Mantra diksa*? Who told you? Go, not now...'

I came out of his room disappointed. Then, I met Manager Maharaj. He asked whether I had got the permission. I said Maharaj had declined. He then urged me to try once again. So I went into Maharaj's room again.

Maharaj : 'Why have you come again?'

Myself : 'Maharaj, I want *mantra diksa*.'

He smiled at me and agreed and told me to come in the morning and contact the office. I went to the office room and was given a list of items to be procured for *diksa*. I was not able to collect all the things in the list at that time. I again contacted Maharaj and expressed my inability to bring the items in the list. With full of love and affection, Maharaj told me to come in the morning after bath with flowers for 25 paise.

On the next day, that is, on 18 September 1977, I was astonished to note that arrangements for the items were already made for me. I was blessed to receive *diksa* from Swami Vireswarananda Maharaj. I consider it as a great fortune.

Under the guidance from Swami Tapasyananda Maharaj, I stayed for nearly a month in Ramakrishna Ashrama, Puranattukara, Trissur, and with the blessings of Revered Chakrananda Maharaj, on 10 June 1978, the story of "Paramahamsa" was performed with back ground music of Sri Lokanadhan and Prof. Balakrishnan. The programme came out to be a really excellent one.

Now, I am leading a very blissful life with my family with the blessings of Swami Tapasyananda Maharaj and spreading the messages of Guru Maharaj by conducting programmes in almost all Ramakrishna Ashrams and in other social organisations.

As I had mentioned earlier, it is only the grace of my guru that forced me to move to Madras,though by sending a false telegram through my friend. Our family too has been blessed by Swami Tapasyananda Maharaj.

32

A Soothing Tonic

Smt. Rukmani[1]

I am proud to be a disciple of the great Revered Tapasyananda Maharaj.

It was in 1984 that my husband and I visited the Sri Ramakrishna Math, Madras, to meet Maharaj. But we could not meet him at that time.

Two years later, in 1986, the sacred day came when I could meet Maharaj. It was after *arati*. A few devotees went beneath the jasmine *pandal* near the staircase room. I too followed them. I could notice Swami Tapasyananda Maharaj telling in a clear voice, 'hmm…a new face.' I was nervous and tried to turn around and leave. But he beckoned me and asked where from I came. When I replied, 'Aminjikarai', he said in a soothing tone, 'Why in this late hour from a faraway place? Come in the morning!' I told him that that was the time I was free, for I had four children, and had to prepare them for school in the mornings…From that moment, I felt happy that I had met a great soul. I always visited him whenever I came to the Math.

---

1. She was initiated by Revered Maharaj in 1987. She was closely associated with Revered Maharaj for 5 years. She currently resides in Chennai and has been actively involved in the activities of Chennai Math.

All along I was under the impression that monks would have long beard and hair! At home, I have seen such photos of Gurus and Siddhas. But to my surprise, the monks of the Math had their heads neatly shaven, most of them spoke good English, wore watches and Bata chappals!

Some of my friends, who were well acquainted with the Math, wanted me to get *diksa*. I was foolishly retorting, 'I must be told by Sri Guru Maharaj himself in my dreams.' However, one of them said that Maharaj was a *sishya* (disciple) of Mahapurush Maharaj [Swami Shivananda] and so I must get *mantra diksa*.

Maharaj was glad to know my intention and enquired why my husband did not get *diksa* and whether there were any barriers. I had already completed reading books like the *Amudha Mozhigal* [tamil translation of *The Gospel of Sri Ramakrishna*] and other books. In 1987, when *diksa* was given in the 'Old Temple', the instructions were given only in English. Maharaj with his utmost kindness remembered to assure me that I can later take it from him the Tamil translation of the instructions.

Following me, my whole family got spiritually initiated, inspired by Maharaj's kindness, dignified demeanour and his simple yet superb language. He talked less but would be very clear and forceful. One can feel great peace after having his *darsan*.

My visits to Math were joyful and I would return home refreshed even if it wasat midnight if that day I had the chance to pay my obeisance to my guru. Initially I could not ascertain the right time to have his *darsan*. But later I tried in the Math to be before 5.30 p.m. in the evenings so that I can have the *darsan* of my guru during his walk.

Once when my uncle had come to get spiritually initiated, an old lady in the hall also expressed her desire to get spiritual initiation. When I told her that she should have read the life histories of the Holy Trio – Sri Ramakrishna, Sarada Devi and Vivekananda, she was so unhappy because she was an illiterate. Later when I happened to tell this to Maharaj, he suggested that her grandchildren can read the books to her and thereby she can become qualified to get *diksa*. And following this advice, she subsequently got *diksa*.

Whenever I would buy fruits for Sri Guru Maharaj, I would also buy some for Revered Maharaj. Once he told me to bring some eatables prepared by me instead of purchasing them from the shops. It just opened a floodgate of happiness for me. From then on I would carry some homemade snacks for him and he would appreciate that, since it was made by one's own effort as an expression of devotion. He liked *idli* and *dahivada*. On Tamil New Year, *Poli,* a sweet prepared by me was offered to him. I little knew that he was diabetic and insisted that he take a little of it. Although that food did not suit him, he still accepted a little of it at the dinner, just to make me happy.

In those days discourses in the Math used to be only in English. I wanted some Tamil lectures too so that more people would be benefited. He jokingly said, 'However, you all want your children in English Medium School!'But my suggestion was subsequently carried forward and lectures in Tamil were arranged.

The special puja on Krishna Jayanti used to continue upto midnight. I had to leave by 9 p.m. to board a town bus. This was noted by Revered Maharaj; and I learnt from

The shrine room of a disciple of Maharaj, Madras, 1994

Swami Jnanadananda Maharaj later that Maharaj had made arrangements for the pujas to be concluded by 9.30 p.m. itself in the subsequent years. An important decision! His keen observation of devotees and his intention to make everyone - rich or poor, enjoy the puja was clear in this decision.

Likewise his observation of the devotees' regular presence in the Math was of highest order. Whenever I did not visit the Math for many days for some reason or the other, he would made enquires about me. His kind enquiries always made me feel that he cared for me.

His sense of humour waswell known in the Math. Once a small and short girl named Vasanthi had come from Dindigul. When she expressed her wish to get *diksa* (spiritual initiation), I took her to Maharaj. She was a veterinary doctor. Maharaj was surprised to hear that. 'An elephant is so big, but this small girl gives injection to that big animal!' he exclaimed and laughed like a child. He appeared so sweet and innocent.

He reminded me once to keep a watch on my relatives and check whether they did their japa, puja etc. regularly. At that time, he asked me whether I had read the *Bhagavad Gita*.

He always had great concern for the welfare of the devotees. Once I hurried to the Math after doing puja at home. He did not fail to advice that in my anxiety I should not do *arati* hastily and burn my fingers! He instructed me to plan my time and do things properly.

Once, my relative who met Maharaj was lamenting about his miseries. Maharaj detected my relative's weakness and advised him to avoid watching films. Others were surprised at this because no one had informed Maharaj about this earlier!

Temple Prayer Hall, Madras Math

In 1989, when Swami Bhuteshananda Maharaj visited Madras Math, there was a group photo session with Revered Maharaj and monastics. Thereafter, devotees were allowed for another group photo. I stood near Swami Tapasyananda along with my children, nephews and nieces. We have preserved that photo even to this day. On another occasion, Maharaj put his autograph on the back of Holy Mother's photo. He was happy to know that I had given a nice place for Holy Mother beside Sri Ramakrishna in my puja room.

When my in-laws wanted us to move to Kanchipuram, I refused to go because I wanted to be in Madras so that I could frequently visit Maharaj, my mentor and guru. His appearance was always awe inspiring. But I always felt like a child before him waiting for a motherly affection to be showered upon.

The Temple at Ulsoor Ashrama was to be consecrated. So Maharaj had gone there. I decided to visit my sister who stayed near Ulsoor Ashrama and also meet Maharaj in Bangalore. In the bus, I was almost in tears in anticipation of meeting him. I had taken my niece to visit Maharaj. The heavy crowd of many visitors and monks made us wait for a long time, but when we met Maharaj, he was so surprised but never failed to enquire about my family members, their welfare, education etc. in that brief time! Later I heard from my sister how he struggled to get into the car due to his failing health.

In 1990, it was the month of Karthigai Deepam. It was the turn of my elder brother to get *diksa* and it was the last time that Maharaj could give *diksa*. After the *diksa* procedures were over, I went to his room to pay my respects and obeisance. But my wheezing problem was severe and

I was gasping for breath. Even then I struggled to express my inability to do service in the Math. But I decided to ask the million dollar question, 'I want to see Sri Guru Maharaj (God)?' He said that one cannot see God unless the mirror (mind) is clean, that is, he meant that I had not yet attained to mature spiritual stage.

In the year 1991, my husband and I visited him at the Math. He told me how my husband was worried about my poor health. But as always, his one graceful look was enough for me to act as a soothing tonic for many days!

With Bhuteshanandaji in Madras Math garden

33

Thrice Blessed Meetings

Sri S. Suryamoorthy[1]

I would like to share my experiences that I had during three blessed meetings with Revered Tapasyananda Maharaj.

The First Meeting

My life took a positive turn when I entered the room of Revered Maharaj in December 1989, with a fond hope of receiving spiritual initiation from him. Revered Maharaj explained that *mantra diksa* was not an isolated event and that it was a culmination of our attempts to concentrate our mind which is tormented with various distractions. He explained the importance of studying my own religion thoroughly and presented the book, *A Primer of Hinduism* by Dr. Sarma. He also instructed me to study the *Bhagavad Gita*. He emphasized that getting a mantra was not everything, but laying a foundation and creating an environment for spiritual life was essential before receiving the mantra. He said that the mantra would only then nurture our spiritual growth. He told me that he would inform me about the date of spiritual initiation through a letter.

1. He was initiated by Revered Maharaj in 1990 and had contact with him for a year. He currently resides in Tiruppur, Coimbatore Dist., Tamil Nadu, and is working for a private enterprise.

The Second Meeting

I was studying textile technology in A.C. College of Technology, Madras. When I revealed to my friends my intention to get spiritually initiated they ridiculed me, more due to ignorance than anything else.

I was fortunate to receive a letter on 7 April 1990 that I can take spiritual initiation. My parents would have objected to my taking *mantra diksa*, for *diksa*, in those days, usually meant becoming a sannyasi. But luckily for me, they went away to our native place and I was free to come to the Math on that day.

I went there wearing trousers as I was not aware that I had to wear a *dhoti* for the initiation. When the volunteers there objected my entry, I was doubtful whether I would receive *mantra diksa* that day. But fortunately Revered Maharaj permitted me inside.

After the initiation, I had the blessed opportunity of getting his autograph on the book, *Vedanta – The Science of Freedom*. I did not know Sanskrit and so I could not pronounce the *bija mantra* correctly. I softly asked Revered Maharaj about it. He told me to speak a little louder. I did and he then corrected the pronunciation and also explained the meaning and significance of it.

The Third Meeting

Two or three months after receiving the mantra, I met him again to inform that I was not able to practise japa regularly and whether it should be done at specific times. He explained that early morning was ideal for the repetition of the mantra. He also presented me a book on the teachings of the Holy Mother and instructed me to read it regularly and that whatever doubts I had regarding japa, I could get the clarifications from that book.

These three meetings were one of the most important events in my life. Before the initiation, I was not clear about spiritual life; my mind was highly turbulent; and there was no way to control it. But after receiving the mantra, I realized that I had the best weapon to calm down my turbulent mind, though I had to struggle hard to use this weapon against a strongly resisting mind.

After 23 years, I realize day by day that more the repetition, clearer my mind becomes and more successful in eliminating the negative thoughts.

In Madras Math

34

Family Friend, Guide and Guru

Smt. Rani Rajendran[1]

One evening, as I was proceeding towards the temple in Madras Math, I met an elderly monk standing near the temple. I offered my *pranams* to him. 'Where are you coming from?' he enquired. I replied, and instinctively, I also added, 'I have no father or mother.' I did not know why I told him this. But all he said with a smile was, 'Go upstairs and salute [Sri Ramakrishna].' Perhaps what he meant was that I had Sri Ramakrishna and Sri Sarada Devi as my 'parents'.

I would daily visit the Math and meet Maharaj and offer my *pranams*. He too, always with a smile, direct me to the temple to offer my *pranams* [to Sri Ramakrishna]. I never enquired who he was. 'An elderly monk' was what I saw him as.

One day, while I was discussing about Sri Ramakrishna with Swami Kamalatmananda Maharaj, he said, 'Have you not received *mantra diksa* yet? Immediately meet the president swami, Revered Tapasyananda Maharaj.'

---

1. She was initiated by Revered Maharaj in 1990. She had contact with Revered Maharaj for 8 years. She currently resides in Chennai and is actively involved in the activities of Chennai Math.

I enquired where I could meet Revered Tapasyananda Maharaj and finally met him in his office. I was dumbstruck when I saw him, and soon I felt intensely happy. The elderly monk who ushered me daily to offer *pranams* to Sri Ramakrishna and Sri Sarada Devi was none other than the president of Madras Math!

'Have you not been [spiritually] initiated yet?' he asked with a smile. He himself filled the application form for me. But I could not go to the Math that day to receive *mantra diksa*. Two days later, I received a handwritten letter of his which said, 'Why did you not come for *mantra diksa*? You have missed a golden opportunity. Meet me at the earliest.'

I went to him and explained the reason for my inability to receive the *mantra diksa* that day. 'At least come on 27.10.1990 without fail,' he advised with concern. I had the fortune of receiving the *mantra diksa* and his invaluable blessings on that scheduled day.

Once, I had a quarrel with my husband. Agitated, I immediately went to Math and reported the matter to Revered Maharaj. He called my husband and advised, 'The cart can move along a path only if both the bullocks pull the cart in the same direction. Likewise the household too must be conducted in unison.'

This way, Revered Maharaj was a family friend, guide and guru, and I cherish his memories always in my heart.

35

No More Articles

Sri A. Venkataramani[1]

I had a great opportunity to work for Revered Swami Tapasyananda Maharaj for more than a decade. When I was working in EID Parry, I used to get holidays on Saturdays and Sundays. I used to visit the Math on those days to type various articles written by him. His writings were in a very simple language. Sri Ramachandran and I were very familiar with his style of writing and hence we were able to type his articles. Maharaj was very simple and very cost conscious. He will ask me to use only one-side blank papers for typing his articles. He also would tell me not to use the computer for typing his articles. I would type roughly 20 pages per day which would give him some sort of happiness that the typing of his articles were progressing well.

Maharaj will bring his manuscript to his office on Saturdays and Sundays and he would eagerly be waiting for me. If I didn't turn up at the Math on weekends, he would ask me why I had not come. I was very regular in going to the Math on weekends and missed only in cases of emergency. Several books written by Maharaj have been published by Madras Math. I am really happy that I too contributed for the publications through my service.

---

1. He was associated with Revered Maharaj for 15 years. He has retired from service in the Private Sector and has been a volunteer of Chennai Math. He was initiated by Revered Gitananda Maharaj in 2006.

Two decades ago, on Swami Vivekananda's birthdays (12th of January), garlanding of Swamiji's statue at the Marina Beach was done in a grand manner. All our schools, College, Hostel, Students' Home and the Math would send their big and heavy garlands for Swamiji's statue. School and College students would assemble near the statue. In those days, we had one long ladder to climb up to the statue. Swamiji's statue was cleaned with holy waters, and smeared with *vibhuti*, sandal paste and *kunkum* on the forehead. Garlands would be tied to a rope and would be pulled one by one. A devotee of the Math was doing all these and I used to help him. When Maharaj saw that devotee very shaky while climbing the ladder due to his age, he immediately said that devotee need not henceforth climb the ladder and that I should take charge of garlanding the statue. Due to Maharaj's instruction, I had the great opportunity of garlanding Swamiji's statue for a number of years.

Till his last, Maharaj continued writing articles. A day prior to his demise, I visited him in the hospital. At that time he told me that he will not be able to write any more articles in future. It seemed that he sensed his end. On the next day, in the evening, I saw on the television the flash news that Revered Swami Tapasyananda Maharaj passed away. I immediately rushed to the Math to pay my homage. His body was kept in the Library and the funeral procession started in the afternoon on the next day. Thousands of devotees took part in the procession. Sandal wood pieces were arranged over his body and tins of ghee were poured for the cremation.

36

Children of God

Smt. Lakshmi Subramanian[1]

One day Revered Tapasyananda Maharaj was coming down from the shrine. I was standing below. Revered Maharaj said, 'We are all children of God. We are all servants of God. Your son [who joined the Ramakrishna Order] works very sincerely.' I said, 'All due to your blessings.' I prostrated before him. He would call my granddaughter' chocolate devotee'. She would prostrate before Maharaj and he would bless her and give a chocolate.

One day I went to his room upstairs. He presented a book on the *Gita*. I offered my *pranams* and he blessed me. Whenever I visited the Math, I would go to his office and offer *pranams*. He would offer a seat to me.

We received a phone call informing us that Revered Maharaj has attained *mahasamadhi* in the hospital. My grand-daughter and I went to the Math at 8.00 p.m. In the

---

1. She was initiated by Revered Swami Vireswarananda Maharaj in 1972. She was in close contact with Revered Swami Tapasyananda Maharaj for 18 years. She was a house wife and very closely associated with the activities of the Math. Her son is a monk in Ramakrishna Order. Uttering the name of Holy Mother, she passed away peacefully on 7 February 2013.

Math, there was chanting of all the 18 Chapters of the *Gita* and Tamil scriptures along with other chantings.

Caranamrita and a garland worn by the Lord had come from Madhava Perumal Temple and were offered on the mortal remains of Revered Maharaj. We returned home at midnight. We again went to the Math at 6.00 a.m. next day. The mortal remains had been kept near the Temple and *arati* was shown to Sri Guru Maharaj. My grand-daughter and I went to the crematorium. There was a miracle. The sun was shining during cremation; after the cremation, there was a sudden downpour as if like a blessing from the heavens!

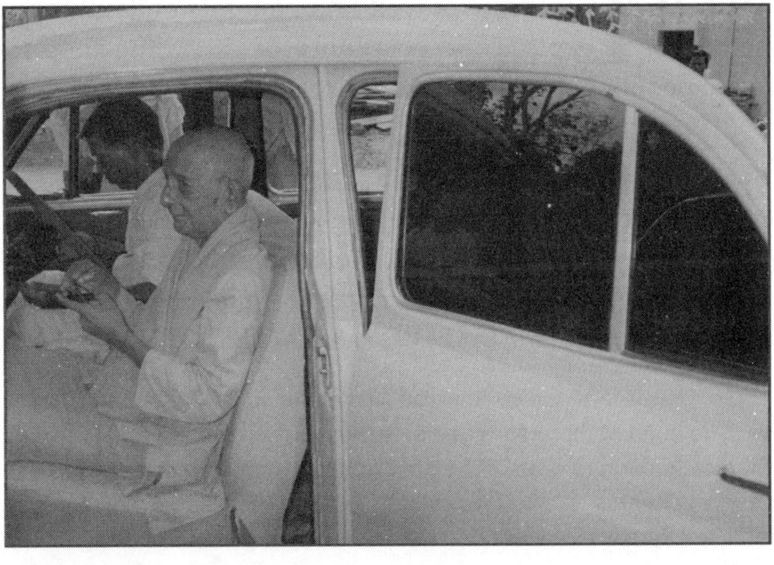

37

Service To The Afflicted

Sri R. Siva[1]

Noble souls have their own way to be like gentle dew that falls, unseen and unheard, yet making the fairest of the flowers to blossom. Swami Tapasyananda Maharaj was also like that, making our lives blossom!

It was decree of the Lord that I should become a Health Inspector in the field of Leprosy. During my initial days of service, especially in the slums, I was deeply moved by the pitiable condition of the people. I contacted Sri Ramakrishna Math, Madras, which was well-known for its philanthropic activities, to explore the possibility of extending help to these people.

On one blessed day, I had the opportunity of meeting Swami Tapasyananda Maharaj in his room. He had a majestic figure with a compelling spiritual power strongly emanating from him. After briefly introducing myself, I poured out the feelings of my heart to him. After patiently hearing me, Maharaj said, 'We monks cannot do everything

1. He was initiated by Revered Maharaj in 1989. He was in contact with Revered Maharaj for 3 years. He has retired from National Leprosy Eradication Programme of the Government. He is currently a volunteer of the Chennai Math, co-ordinating the rehabilitation of Leprosy Afflicted Persons.

as you desire. We have our own restrictions. But you can do it and we will support you.'

After giving thought over what Maharaj had said, I decided to serve the Leprosy Afflicted Persons (LAPs) rather than step into an entirely new field of service. With the approval of Maharaj, a new scheme was started for the Leprosy Afflicted Persons. Interestingly, Maharaj had already created a fund for the helping such people, much earlier to my meeting with him! It is said that Maharaj's mother would send him some money and Maharaj would save some of the money for the service of afflicted people. As the money kept on accumulating, he had been keenly awaiting for a person to handle this service activity.

The tiny plant planted by Maharaj has now grown and spread its branches to even Kanchipuram and Chengalpattu districts.

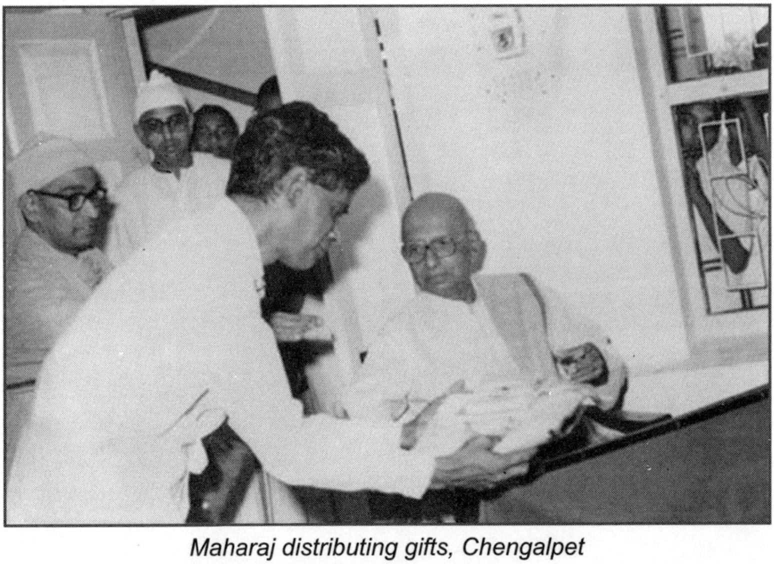

Maharaj distributing gifts, Chengalpet

Maharaj's unconditional love did not stop with this; he himself volunteered to give spiritual initiation to my wife and myself. He had remarked, 'You seemed to have a good spiritual background and you should take [spiritual] initiation.' It was in the early 1990s, on a blessed day, that both of us were spiritually initiated!

There was another such occasion which stood as testimony to Maharaj's unconditional love. When my wife and I requested Maharaj to perform *aksharabhyasam* for our three year old son and bless him, Maharaj readily agreed for that!

I can narrate several incidents about Maharaj, but end is inevitable. Adi Sankara in his famous *Saundarya Lahari* says, 'O Mother! Narrating your divine glory is just like lighting camphor in front of a radiant sun.' My reminiscences about Maharaj can also be viewed that way.

38

Our Godfather

Smt. M.L. Vanaja[1]

It was in the year 1988 and I was 32 years old. I was sunk deep in misery because I was destituted with two young children. I was deserted by my husband and relatives; and to add to my misery, I also lost my father, who was my only support . I was alone with no one to support. Many days I felt like putting an end to my life which I thought would put an end to my misery.

I held a small time job in Electricity Board, as meter reading assessor, going from door to door of the shops. One day I happened to see on a mill shelf a book titled, *Jnana Yoga*, with Swami Vivekananda's picture on the cover. I requested that flour mill owner to lend me the book so that I can read and get some solace. My worries seemed to die down after reading the book. I got inspired; it awakened in me the spirit to face any adversity in life than die out of fear!

The address of Sri Ramakrishna Math was printed on the book. I immediately wrote a letter to the Math. 'Can I come to the Math? Am I permitted?' To my great joy, in

1. She was initiated by Revered Maharaj in 1988 and was in contact with him for 3 years. She has retired from Tamil Nadu Electricity Board and is actively involved in the activities of Chennai Math. She currently resides in Chennai. Her daughter is a nun in Sarada Math.

just four days, I got a reply inviting me to the Math! My joy knew no bounds.

I came to the Math through the Book Stall. I informed a monk there about the purpose of my visit. He told me to visit the Shrine (now called Old Temple) and also to visit Kapaleeswarar temple as it was too early for the *Aratrikam*.

I did as I was told; I also bought some books and an issue of *Sri Ramakrishna Vijayam*; and I felt happiness and hope coursing through my nerves. My next few visits were not regular, but were nevertheless taking me closer to some purpose in life.

One day, I was directed by a monk in the Bookstall to meet the president, Revered Swami Tapasyananda Maharaj, and have his *darsan*. I with my two children went to see the "great mentor-to-be of my life". Something in me prompted to tell my daughter, 'Our life is going to have a turning point. We are blessed to see a great monk. We are no longer orphans; we have a father in the godlike person of Revered Maharaj.'To my surprise, Revered Maharaj listened with a smile to my 15-minute monologue! He was so kind and his face expressing grace and dignified benevolence gave me instant assurance of inexplicable peace.

Within days, I requested Revered Maharaj in person for *mantra diksa*! He sat silent for a few minutes. Then he asked me to come next Saturday and have my spiritual initiation. It was all like having a divine experience; no words are in my dictionary to describe the feelings regarding the *diksa*.

He was concerned whether I was doing my japa, meditation and prayer properly. Even if I answered in the negative, he would never chide or scold me but would just smile and bless while making me understand the importance of these disciplines.

Revered Maharaj considered me and my children are his own. An incident happened that illustrated this. Once, it was almost noon. Despite his old age, Revered Maharaj walked down several steps from his room with his walking stick. He wanted to make sure that my children and I had *prasad*. He entreatingly requested the manager, 'Can you please give them noon *prasad*? They are our own.' Manager Maharaj assured him that he would arrange for our food immediately and requested Revered Maharaj to take rest. Revered Maharaj was like a mother taking care of her children selflessly.

Revered Maharaj was concerned about our health and instructed swami in-charge of dispensary to do our periodical health check-ups and report to him. His concern was that we may neglect our health and hygiene because of my meagre income.

Revered Maharaj also advised me to save money for the future. He insisted on chastity, boldness and self-respect to be the prime qualities I should imbibe in my life. When I felt like leaving my job due to some problems, he discouraged me saying that I must learn to face the problems putting them in proper perspective. He said that running away like a coward is not necessary when one is honest.

On the very first day of our meeting Revered Maharaj, I had told my daughter that our lives would change. And it did happen. My daughter was so devoted to this Order that she got her *mantra diksa* at the tender age of eleven and today she is a nun in Sarada Math.

Revered Maharaj didn't want me to spend money to get a costly *mala* for my daughter after her *diksa*. So he told me to divide my *rudraksa mala* of 108 beads into two and give one half to my daughter and to count the beads twice for the japa.

Once I wanted to shift to another place for my own reasons, but he wouldn't agree. He got for me one of the houses belonging to the Math so that I can live safely. He thus gave us the greatest shelter. And it has helped me to really do more service in the Math.

Just before his departure to the hospital for a surgery, I, like a fool, without understanding the situation ran to him as usual to pay my obeisance to him. He was very kind to me even then. No sign of pain was seen on his face. He was such an austere and dignified person. He always showed utmost patience even while having pain.

Revered Maharaj was admitted in the Vijaya Hospital. Once when he was on the wheel-chair and breathing some fresh air outside,I went to see him. Just saw his eyes. And those eyes were blessing me!

In the last stages of Revered Maharaj's illness, he was in B.S.S. Hospital. There were no signs of movement. He was lying still! My friend and I visited him. We were standing near the door of the room in great grief. Suddenly, he turned towards us for a second. The eyes were beckoning us to come. But afterwards there was no sign of movement. Next day, on *Ekadasi,* he attained to the lotus feet of Ramakrishna Paramahamsa. His physical body was kept in the Library for devotees to pay homage.

Now, his physical presence may not be there. But he is our *Govardhanadhari*[1], always protecting like a Godfather.

1. An epithet of Sri Krishna, which means "one who holds up the Govardhana hill" in order to protect the people of Brindavan.

39

Humility and Self-Effacement

Sri R.B. Athreya[1]

Swami Tapasyananda Maharaj was undoubtedly one of the greatest monks who ornamented the Ramakrishna Order. It is interesting to note that he was associated with Sri Ramakrishna Math, Madras soon after he joined the Order in 1924 as a brahmachari, then after he was given sannyasa in 1932, and again for 20 years from 1971 to 1991 as president of Madras Math before he attained *mahasamadhi*. Thus, he was popular in Madras and there are hundreds of devotees who have been influenced by his spiritual personality and gentle teachings in South India in general and Madras in particular.

I must accede with humility that I was one of those privileged devotees to have been blessed with the opportunity of having had his grace and affection. This, I must acknowledge, was possible only because I happened to be the disciple of Brahmasri Anna Subramaniam who was

---

1. He was initiated by Brahmasri Anna Subramaniam into Sri Vidya. He had contact with Revered Swami Tapasyananda Maharaj for 5 years. He is a retired Executive of S.B.I. and a devotee of the Math. He was a member of the Managing Committee of the Mission Students' Home, Mylapore. He contributes articles to *Tattvaloka* and *The Vedanta Kesari*. He currently resides in Chennai.

With Sri Anna Subramaniam (wearing rudraksha mala)
Ramakrishna Mission Students' Home, Madras

very close to Maharaj and was associated with him in the publication of several of Maharaj's writings, particularly his commentary on *Saundarya Lahari*. Another notable feature of their relationship was that both of them were blessed with *mantra diksa* by Mahapurush Maharaj on the same day.

I had given up a lucrative assignment in the Middle East in 1985 when I was just 48 years old and returned to Madras to be with and be of service to my guru, Brahmasri Anna Subramaniam, who had initiated me into Sri Vidya and trained me in the procedures of related puja and rituals. To help my guru who was advanced in age, I took over the performance of all his pujas and also accompanied him in his visits to the Math and the Students' Home in Mylapore, and to any other place he desired to visit.

This was how I got introduced to Maharaj. Even in the first meeting, I could feel his spiritual strength and began developing a great respect for him. He also, out of infinite compassion, took a liking for me. He was particularly appreciative of the fact that I was taking care of Anna and attending to his needs. I was fortunate to be present on several occasions when Anna had met Maharaj to discuss various intricate points in our scriptures, including the *Upanishads* and the *Gita*, and the commentaries of our great Acharyas on them. As Anna, due to his old age, was short of hearing, I used to convey Maharaj's responses to Anna and Anna's responses to Maharaj. This simple act also impressed Maharaj very much.

One day I was thrilled to hear Maharaj tell Anna that he would very much like to use my services for the Math but for the fact that I was already serving Anna. As a compromise, he suggested Anna that I may be inducted as a member of the Managing Committee of the Students' Home. This was how I came to be formally associated with the Home, though I was already connected with it informally. Maharaj was also kind enough to pay a compliment to me in the presence of other monks of the Math that I was to Anna like what "M." (Mahendranath Gupta) was to Sri Guru Maharaj.

Maharaj impressed one and all by his qualities of head and heart, the most important of which was his great humility (*Vinayam*) and self-effacement (*amanithvam*), virtues highlighted in the thirteenth chapter of the *Bhagavad Gita*. I was witness to the demonstration of these qualities when he was exchanging views with Sri Anna on the commentary he was writing on *Saundarya Lahari*. Not only did he discuss with him at great length several portions of the work (even as he was writing it) with an open mind, but was highly receptive to the suggestions given

Shantatmananda, Sukritananda, Sri Athreya, Tapasyanandaji at the Staff Qtrs. Foundation Laying ceremony, Students' Home, Madras

by Anna. He succeeded in persuading Anna to write a foreword to that book and also graciously acknowledged his gratitude to Anna for his suggestions in his introduction to the book.

Another trait most people would have observed in Maharaj was his forthrightness and directness in communicating his views though at the same time he would be prepared to listen to other views and accommodate them to the extent he was convinced of the validity of such views. I can recall one instance when he had told Anna that he wondered why the book *Sandhya Vandanam* authored by Anna and published by Math, which according to him was rather elaborate for modern day householders, busy with their preoccupations, could not be abridged and simplified. When Anna replied that *Sandhya Vandanam* being a vedic ritual (*srauta karma*), it will not be appropriate to make any changes in the procedure or the text, Maharaj readily accepted this position.

One other quality of Maharaj which needs mention is his easy accessibility(*soulabyam*). Any devotee can walk into his office or room without appointment and was free to communicate with him.

I would like to end this small but heartfelt homage to the Revered Maharaj, who showered on me and my wife (whose role in my spiritual pursuit, Maharaj was kind enough to appreciate) his grace and kindness, by seeking his blessings for successful continuation of our spiritual journey.

1. Padmasthananda 2. Sukritananda 4.Tapasyanandaji 5. Aksharanandaji at Maharaj's office, Madras Math, in 1988 or 1989

40

God Is Watching Us

Smt. Hamsavathy Nithyanandam[1]

It was customary for Ooty Math to celebrate in a grand scale Sri Ramakrishna's birth anniversary as *Guru Puja*.

Once when we were residing in Ooty, Swami Tapasyananda Maharaj visited Ooty in 1988 and stayed at the Ooty Math for three days. During these three days, I and a few others were fortunate enough to prepare and serve him tea, breakfast, lunch and dinner.

Revered Maharaj gave a discourse on the occasion of *Guru Puja*. The people belonging to Baduga community of Ooty had come dancing all the way to the Guru Puja as an expression of their devotion. Referring to this in course of his discourse, he said, 'Expressing your emotions and dancing in front of God is only a step towards true devotion. It is much more essential that you must be able to realize God within yourself.'

On that day, a lady devotee offered *pranams* to Maharaj and sought his blessings. After doing so, she did not rise immediately. Only after Maharaj placed his palm on her

---

1. She was initiated by Revered Maharaj in 1985. She was in contact with Revered Maharaj for 5 years. She has been closely associated with Chennai and Madurai Maths. She currently resides in Madurai.

At Ramakrishna Mission Vidyalaya, Coimbatore, 1988

head did she rise. Revered Maharaj chuckled and said, 'This is not a place for sleeping.'

One another day, when we attended a night reading class, Revered Maharaj was discussing Vedanta. A devotee posed a question, 'Was Sri Ramakrishna an Advaitin or a Visishtadvaitin?' Maharaj replied, 'Sri Ramakrishna was one who was beyond and surpassed the principles of Advaita and Visistadvaita.' He further elaborated on *Nitya* and *Leela, Bhava Mukha* and *Vijnana*.

Revered Maharaj was ready to depart for Ramakrishna Mission Vidyalaya, Coimbatore from Ramakrishna Math, Ooty. At that time, some of us met him and sought his guidance to lead our spiritual lives. Maharaj gave us his blessings saying, 'God is all the time watching over us. Don't forget it.'

41

Sri Ramakrishna Bhagavata

Sri Rasipuram Ramabadran[1]

Revered Swami Tapasyananda Maharaj was born in the year 1904. My father was also born in the same year. For this reason, I have always considered Revered Maharaj as my spiritual godfather.

I received spiritual initiation (*mantra diksa*) from Revered Maharaj at Sri Ramakrishna Math, Madras on 29 March 1986.

The 150th Birth Anniversary of Sri Ramakrishna was celebrated in 1986. I served as a volunteer to collect donations from the public for the celebrations. Revered Maharaj was pleased with my service.

In 1988, my younger brother, Sri R.S. Mahadevan, wanted to receive spiritual initiation from Revered Maharaj. My brother suffered from many psychological problems. While Revered Maharaj consented to spiritually initiate him and accept him as his disciple, he also remarked that no one should expect that *mantra diksa* would miraculously cure his psychological problems.

---

1. He was initiated by Revered Maharaj in 1986 and had been in contact with Revered Maharaj for 7 years. He has retired from S.B.I. and currently resides in Chennai.

Publication of Sri Ramakrishna Bhagavatam

As a result of reading the Ramakrishna-Vivekananda literature for 25 years, I wrote the book *Sri Ramakrishna Bhagavata* and published it in 1989. The book compares Sri Ramakrishna and Sri Sarada Devi with 30 Hindu gods and goddesses. Revered Maharaj graciously wrote a foreword to my book. In those days, his health was not good. He could not sit, and therefore he would stand and attend to his daily works. Even in that condition, he patiently went through the manuscript of my book and wrote a foreword to it. This kind gesture of Revered Maharaj touched my heart. It remains an unforgettable event in my life.

In his foreword to my book, Revered Maharaj wrote: 'Sri Ramabadran's *Sri Ramakrishna Bhagavata* is an example of the production deriving inspiration from the personality of Sri Ramakrishna and his message. His knowledge of the Hindu *puranas* and *itihasas* on the one hand and of the life and teachings of Sri Ramakrishna on the other, have helped Ramabadran to find parallelisms in the Puranic lore for most of the incidents and sayings of Sri Ramakrishna. In an ingenious way, he has superimposed the two mutually and forward a nexus providing matter for deep thought. The book provides stimulating reading.'

In my book, I published a photograph of Revered Maharaj covering a page. But it was not printed well; it was too dark. I was shocked to see that. But to my great relief, Revered Maharaj did not mind it, nor was he angry over it. On the contrary, he praised the good printing of my book saying, 'You have got the book in the old-fashioned way, through manual typesetting. But the printing is very good and clear; it is better than even laser printing.'He ignored the bad printing of his own photograph and took into account the over-all good printing of my book.

Soon I had another stroke of good fortune. Revered Swami Ranganathananda Maharaj visited Madras just after I got my book printed. He was to deliver a speech at Madras Math on 6 September 1989 in the evening. Swami Raghaveshananda Maharaj requested him to release my book just before his lecture and he graciously agreed to it. Revered Ranganathananda Maharaj told me, 'Swami Tapasyananda himself has written a foreword to your book. What more can I say about it.' Then Revered Ranganathananda Maharaj read out Revered Tapasyananda Maharaj's foreword and released my book. It was another unforgettable event in my life!

Cutting the ribbon (Ice Factory)

42

A Scholar-Monk

Smt. Kshama Rangarajan[1]

Many people would highlight many qualities of Revered Swami Tapasyananda – his phenomenal scholarship, outstanding organizational ability, compassionate spiritual ministry etc. But when I think of him, the image that comes to my mind is of a scholar-monk sitting in his small room surrounded by books and papers and working on his latest book or translation– a picture of concentration. Knowing my interest in Philosophy, he was kind enough to speak on certain topics which indicated his profound thinking. With my limited capacity, I can now only recollect somewhat imperfectly some fragments of what he said.

Maharaj was quite emphatic about the tremendous import an incarnation had on the spiritual life of spiritual aspirants as well as on the world order. When I was a little sceptical about the idea of incarnation in general, he was quite displeased. He said that one must go beyond devious thinking to understand the mystery of an Incarnation. He

---

1. She was initiated by Revered Swami Vireswarananda Maharaj in 1974. She had contact with Revered Maharaj for 17 years. She is a home-maker and a freelance copy editor for *Book Review Journal, Education Dialogue* and *Encyclopaedia of Hinduism*. She is a devotee of Chennai Math. She currently resides in Chennai.

said, 'As the Great Master said, one must become simple to understand the Simple One.' In his writings and translations, he had emphasized that God incarnated to guide people by His life and teachings to bring about an inner transformation which would illumine their lives. And the Great Master, out of immense compassion for suffering humanity, kept his mind turned towards the world of phenomenon rather than soaring away and beyond to the Absolute. This feature of accepting the sufferings of the phenomenal world to uplift people was the essential significance of an Incarnation's divine mission.

When asked if he had seen the Holy Mother, Maharaj said he had not, nor did he regret for not seeing her, for one had to be adequately prepared for this profoundest encounter. I was taken aback for a moment by this blatant admission of one's unworthiness. If someone like him was unqualified to see the Mother of All, how could people like me aspire for her *darsan*. It was perhaps an oblique instruction that one must be evolved and prepared to derive any spiritual benefit from holy company. Otherwise, it would be like the parable of the Master about sinful people taking bath in the Ganges. They are temporarily absolved of their sins, only to get latched on to their sins as soon as they leave the holy river.

Once Maharaj mentioned that a certain gentleman had questioned him on the necessity to build temples for Sri Ramakrishna. In support of his argument that gentleman had quoted Swami Vivekananda who said to the effect that all temples should be closed down and man must be served and that service to the downtrodden was more important than ritualistic puja. Maharaj then said that he in turn showed to that gentleman another saying of Swami Vivekananda which emphasises temples of Sri Ramakrishna to be built – so that the Master's liberal ideals and lofty teachings could be disseminated to the whole of humanity. Maharaj then commented that he appreciated Swamiji [Swami Vivekananda] as a wonderful dialectician who could vigorously uphold contradictory opinions because each opinion had its relevance according to the context.

Usually, the shrines in Ramakrishna Ashramas would have Sri Ramakrishna's photo at the centre. I however happened to see a shrine where Holy Mother's photo was placed at the centre. When I mentioned this somewhat excitedly to Maharaj, he was surprisingly unmoved. After some thought, he just said that in the course of time, Sri Ramakrishna would reveal himself in myriad ways. I think he said that in his opinion, Sri Ramakrishna transcended personalities.

Once I told him that I was trying to study the *prasthanatraya* with Sri Sankaracharya's commentary with help of a Sanskrit scholar. Half teasingly, he asked me why I, belonging to a Sri Vaishnava family, was doing so being inclined towards monistic Vedanta.

More than two decades have passed since he attained *mahasamadhi*. I still cherish those precious moments I spent in his elevating presence.

43

My experiences during *Mantra diksa*

Sri A. R. K. Sarma[1]

I would like to share my experiences while receiving *mantra diksa* from Revered Swami Tapasyananda Maharaj in November 1988.

Hearing the name 'Tapasyananda' itself creates a feeling of veneration even in those who did not know him. His name 'Tapasyananda' fully justifies his countenance and stands as a testimony to the saying, 'Sun does not require a lamp to see him.' But those who did not really understand that his true happiness lay in doing *tapasya*, misunderstood him as non-amicable. I too misunderstood when I met him for the first time on the day of initiation. But my misunderstanding was dispelled after talking with him for a few minutes. I realized that he was surely amicable, but his serious way of responding to the queries created such an impression in many.

When I talked to him for the first time, I was a bit afraid by the deep expression of seriousness on his face, but this fear was dispelled immediately as I could instantly

1. He was initiated by Revered Maharaj in 1986 and had association of 5 years with him. He is Additional Vice-president in Tata Tele Services Ltd., Mumbai. He has close contact with many centres of the Math and Mission. He currently resides in Mumbai.

sense his kind heart and true concern for spiritual welfare of devotees.

After taking *mantra diksa,* I mentioned to him about some of my spiritual experiences I had had in the past. His face immediately became very serious on hearing it and asked, 'From whom have you taken initiation?' I was much perplexed with his serious face and replied, 'No. I have not taken *mantra diksa* from anyone earlier.' His expression immediately changed and he assumed an assuring and a benevolent look. I could gather my courage realizing his inner feelings and the true concern he had for a devotee even in the first meeting. I told him, 'Maharaj, my heart is more bent towards Holy Mother Sri Sarada Devi, but I have received Sri Ramakrishna mantra. Please grant me Sri Sarada Devi mantra also so that I can reach Sri Ramakrishna through Sri Sarada Devi.' But Maharaj retorted immediately, 'Why don't you try to reach Sri Sarada Devi through Sri Ramakrishna?' I found it very difficult to convince him, but I pleaded, 'Maharaj, it will be far easier for me to reach Sri Ramakrishna through Sri Sarada Devi rather than reaching Sri Sarada Devi through Sri Ramakrishna.' I was looking into his eyes with a great expectation that he would grant me Sri Sarada Devi mantra also. Revered Maharaj looked straight into my eyes, but this time there was no seriousness on his face and in its place was an inexpressible concern for a devotee. To my great surprise, he conceded to my request and immediately gave me Sri Sarada Devi mantra. I was astonished to see his ability to change his moods at will and quickly come down to the level of others with sympathetic outlook and shower blessings on them. I did japa of the names of Sri Ramakrishna as well as of Sri Sarada Devi.

My wife would often say that I was very persuasive and would grab things I wanted at every opportunity. She used to jokingly chide me that while my guru gave me one mantra (that of Sri Ramakrishna), I snatched the other mantra (that of Sri Sarada Devi) also from him. Whatever that may be, I am fortunate to have it from Revered Maharaj.

In Madras Math

44

Reach Home Quickly

Sri M.A. Ramachandran[1]

Maharaj would everyday go through the newspapers after tea in the evening. My wife used to deliver a particular newspaper every day in the evening for him to read. The newspaper was to be kept on a large table outside Maharaj's room.

She was so punctual in delivering the paper at 5 p.m. that Maharaj, who was an epitome of time management, used to call her the time-keeping lady.

Once, my wife had to visit Sarada Math with a few devotees. Prior to her leaving for Sarada Math, she had requested one of the monks to hand over the newspaper on time so that the routine would be unaffected. Unfortunately, the paper reached an hour late and Maharaj started enquiring others about her. When she had gone to deliver the newspaper the next day, Maharaj enquired her about her absence on the previous day as any head of the family would ask his family member with all concern. Maharaj's true concern and love for her, which she felt that day, has become deeply etched in our minds.

---

1. He was initiated by Revered Swami Bhuteshananda Maharaj in 1980. He had contact with Revered Swami Tapasyananda Maharaj for 30 years. He has retired from service from the Transport Corporation. He is a former volunteer of Chennai Math. He currently resides in Tiruvilwamala, Thrissur Dist., Kerala.

When Maharaj was ill and hospitalized at Vijaya Hospital, we had gone to visit him and enquired about his health. We travelled by the city bus and therefore reached late, almost towards the end of the visiting hours. We were however lucky to meet him and sit by his bed. Maharaj was wearing a mask to sustain his breathing. In spite of his struggling to breathe,he showed his compassion and love by enquiring about us and our visits to the Math. We were overwhelmed when he asked us to reach home quickly as it was getting dark and he didn't want us to go home late. We were in tears seeing his deep concern for us contrary to his usually stern behaviour. Maharaj's true love and compassion for us always had a soothing effect on our minds and has protected us all along.

This is an anecdote which we heard from Late Sri C.S. Ramakrishnan, who was a very close devotee and an ex-editor of *The Vedanta Kesari*: 'Maharaj was a very systematic person. One of his normal routine was to have a glass of water before he goes to his office. Once, it so happened that he was thirsty and drank the glass of water kept covered on his table. The habit took the better of Maharaj and he began to walk to his office. He reached his office and was surprised that it was closed. The manager's office nearby and the cash section adjacent to it (during those times) were all closed. Maharaj was a bit angry to see that people haven't been conscious of coming to the office on time. Finally, it required a monk to explain to him that he had walked into his office at 7 a.m. in the morning instead of 9 a.m. Maharaj then realized what had happened and had a good laugh with others.'

45

Humane Concern

Smt. Thoyajakshi Devendra[1]

In the late seventies, on behalf of "*Mangayar Mangalam*", a women's voluntary organization that rendered service to the less fortunate women of the society, I approached Swami Tanmayananda Maharaj, the then manager of Sri Ramakrishna Math, Madras, to seek permission to use their primary school premises at Mint, to meet our beneficiaries on every Saturday afternoon there.

Manager Maharaj introduced me to Revered Swami Tapasyananda Maharaj, then president of Sri Ramakrishna Math, Madras, and I put forth my request to him. Revered Maharaj gracefully granted our organization the required permission to use the school premises by the needy women of that locality.

After a few months, one fine morning late Sri Rajaram, a very sincere and dedicated life worker of Sri Ramakrishna Math, Madras, came home to inform me that President Swami desired to provide me an opportunity to serve the cause of Mission at Madras, and to meet him at the Math in this regard.

---

1. She had contact with Revered Maharaj for more than 15 years. She has retired from Central Government Service and is residing in Chennai. She is actively involved in the activities of Chennai Math.

I was very happy at the prospect and so went over to the Math to meet Maharaj. He, gentle and soft spoken, said with a kind smile that he would offer me an opportunity to serve the Mission as the Secretary of the Primary School at Mint and also as a member of the Managing Committee of Sarada Vidyalaya at T. Nagar, Madras, if I was willing to accept them. I humbly accepted Maharaj's offer but told him to exempt me from all the financial transactions of the school as its Secretary, especially from signing the bank cheques jointly or singly. I volunteered to take care of the educational activities of the school and discharge the administrative responsibilities.

Maharaj was not disturbed at my strange request. Rather, with a hearty laugh he said that I was the first person whom he had come across who was unwilling to involve myself in the financial transactions of the school but was very willing to take care of the educational aspect of it.

My memories of Maharaj are deeply soaked in reverential regard for him. My association with him was brief, but it had a profound impact on my thinking. I was much impressed by three distinct aspects of Maharaj's personality. His austere way of life, both in personal living and external transactions, befitted his very name 'Tapasyananda'. The small room he occupied as the Presidential chamber at Math was sparsely furnished. Along with his table, chair and a cupboard, there were two chairs opposite to his table and a bench. This was all he had in that room. When he was not transacting official duties or giving audience to the devotees he would either be reading or writing books.

At school meetings he chaired, only school activities would be discussed. Regarding the collection of donations, Maharaj would insist on receiving donations by way of cheques. He always advised members to avoid receiving cash from donors, because they may give their unaccounted money as donation. He was also very strict in instructing the Secretary to issue the receipts for money received with a duplicate copy for auditing, having Sri Ramakrishna as the witness to one's conscience.

Another aspect of Maharaj's personality was his perceptible humane concern for the devotees. When he offered me the supervision of the school at Mint, I was then a resident of Mylapore. It was a long way for me to reach the school from my house. He, with humane concern, offered to pay me an honorarium to meet my travel expenses. And he was very satisfied when I told him that my parents had taught me to serve spiritual organizations without receiving any monetary reimbursement for the service rendered as far as I could afford.

As I offered to take care of the educational activities at the school, Maharaj suggested that I should teach *Srimad Bhagavad Gita* to the students of Sarada Vidyalaya who were residing in the hostel at Mangayar Street and Sri Ramanuja's philosophy to the inmates of the working women's hostel at G.N. Chetty Road, T. Nagar. There was a rule then that all inmates of the working women's hostel should compulsorily attend the evening prayers at the prayer room. Later they attended my talks. These classes went on well for some time and the response from the participants was also good.

But after a while, the Secretary of the school felt that they should give due attention to the academics and so advised the children to be exempted from 'Gita class' if they had class test the following day. This was extended to the working women's hostel also. I felt their irregular attendance would affect the continuity of thought in learning the spiritual texts. But I remained silent. When Maharaj learnt about it, he told me, 'If people think their secular studies are more sacred than their spiritual awakening you need not exert yourself to go over to teach them.'

Whenever I visited the Math, Maharaj would give me audience and talk about the book he was writing in his scholarly tone. At times he would read out the passage he was writing and would ask for my comment. At times I felt elated when he would patiently listen to and ponder over my suggestion, however trivial.

He was gracious to give me permission to walk straight into his room to pay my respects if there was no one transacting official business with him.

Maharaj's simplicity, austerity, erudition and humane concern have left a deep impression on my mind and I strive to imbibe these qualities in me.

With reverence, I bow my head at the lotus feet of this great Maharaj.

46

It Is Not Your Fault

Sri S. Padmanabha Pillai[1]

I received *Navakshari mantra* initiation from Sri Anna Subramaniam in December, 1988 and was doing meditation and *Sri Lalita Sahasranama Archana.*

Revered Maharaj visited Ramakrishna Math, Madurai in August, 1989. As advised by Sri Anna, my wife and I received Sri Ramakrishna mantra initiation from Maharaj on 13 August 1989 at the Madurai Math. Maharaj spiritually initiated about 50 devotees that day.

Although Maharaj appeared physically weak, I was attracted by his calm and bright face, and sweet talk. He was not seated in a separate room. He sat among the devotees on an ordinary chair. No permission was required to go near him and offer *pranams* or talk to him. I was really surprised that without any difficulty I could have the *darsan* of a great and elderly saint who was the vice-president of a renowned worldwide organization.

1. He was initiated by Revered Maharaj in 1989. He was in contact with Revered Maharaj for 2 years. He has retired from service from the Social Welfare Department of the Government. He currently resides in Cholapuram, Kanyakumari Dist., Tamil Nadu

I was working as an Inspector in Social Welfare Department. Due to pressure of work, I had to skip japa and puja many times. I felt very sad and wrote a letter to Maharaj. To this Maharaj replied promptly, 'There are many people in your condition anxious to do puja and japa in a very intense manner every day. It is not your fault. So you incur no guilt by this failure.' His reply was really consoling and I started doing my spiritual practices more vigorously.

It is only because of my association with Maharaj that I could realise that God is very kind and easily accessible and my faith in God has become unshakeable. I consider this as a divine blessing.

Tapasyanandaji with Sri Prabhudas Patwari, Governor of Tamil Nadu

47

Help the Patient to Recover Soon

Ms. Mariamma[1]

I was a young trained nurse and lab technician when I sought for a placement in the Charitable Dispensary of Sri Ramakrishna Math, Madras, where I intended to serve the poor under the guidance of a person like Swami Tapasyananda Maharaj. I was actually referred to by some devotees to meet Maharaj. Accordingly I came and requested Maharaj. My interview is still fresh in my memory. I did not answer the questions in English, but in Malayalam. Maharaj found me good at work and more than that, he identified in me a spirit to zealously serve. I was coming from another state (Kerala) and was new to this place. But I found this environment so nice and safe and came down to settle here with my family immediately.

I am a Christian by faith. Therefore I had not taken any spiritual initiation from Maharaj. But he was more than a guiding spirit in my work, thought and action, even today. It was not the religious precepts, but the love and affection he showered on me and in improving my work that I felt like a worthy person respected in my place of stay and work.

---

1. She had contact with Revered Maharaj for 6 years. She is a staff in the Chennai Math Charitable Dispensary.

A little later, one more Christian lady, Mercy, joined as a technician and assisted me. The Swami would say, 'Mercy, oh! Your name should be the attitude you need to follow.'

The Swami had special love for the dispensary as he had earlier been managing a hospital in Trivandrum. Hence he took much care in suitable expansion of the facilities like better equipments for diagnosis etc. I should mention about building the paediatrics floor on the top of the small dispensary with the help of Dr. Indira. Today, the paediatrics department having dedicated doctors is a proof of his special love for infant care and health of poor children.

His advice still rings in my ears. 'It is not money making…when we order for tests, your dedication in work will help the patient recover soon...' He never liked to collect any money for any service rendered [at the dispensary]. He would say, 'Truth, honesty, and dedication should be the motto of our service in hospitals!'

I am proud to say that I am what I am today only because of him! He is my mentor in every aspect of my life. He is my guru in the real sense, even though I had no spiritual initiation from him. His advices to me were invitations to turn myself into a good soul and be service minded in a true sense. My friend Mercy too would endorse all these with tears of appreciation.

48

No One Is A Stranger!

Sri K.K. Venkatraman[1]

Vivekananda Kendra, Kanyakumari, is running English medium residential schools for the tribal children of Arunachal Pradesh, a North-Eastern State, since 1977. I was then involved in the administration of these schools. While in those days (1980s), there were higher secondary schools for boys; schools for the girls were only up to secondary level. Therefore, girls wishing to pursue higher education had to either join Government Schools in the State or join the schools in other states. The parents of the girls felt that Madras would be the ideal place for their wards to pursue their higher studies.

In 1990, the parents of a few girls of our first batch of students approached us for arranging admission for their wards in a school in Madras. We had close contact with Ramakrishna Mission Hospital at Itanagar, the capital of Arunachal Pradesh, and Swami Prathamananda Maharaj, the then Secretary, was known to us. When I approached him,

---

1. He was initiated by Revered Swami Ranganathananda Maharaj in 2000. He had met Revered Swami Tapasyananda Maharaj only once in 1990. He is a former Army Captain and was an Honorary Worker of Vivekananda Kendra, Kanyakumari. He is currently a volunteer in Chennai Math.

he advised me to write to Revered Swami Tapasyananda Maharaj.

As I was going to Kanyakumari for an official meeting, I thought it would be better to meet Revered Maharaj personally. I had not met him before. On my way to Kanyakumari, I visited Madras Math. I first met the then manager, Swami Raghaveshananda Maharaj. He was kind enough to arrange my meeting with Revered Swami Tapasyananda Maharaj. But he advised me to make it brief as Revered Maharaj was not keeping good health and I assured him that I would. When Manager Maharaj took me to Revered Maharaj and introduced me, Revered Maharaj offered me a seat and started enquiring in detail about the activities of Vivekananda Kendra in Arunachal Pradesh. Although I answered all his questions, I also felt that I might be misunderstood by others as wasting Revered Maharaj's time.

I then raised the topic of admitting our girls in the higher secondary section of Sarada Vidyalaya. Revered Maharaj said, 'You have come at the right time. Today at 4.00 p.m., we are having the Managing Committee Meeting of Sarada Vidyalaya at T.Nagar [in Madras]. You come there and present your case before the Committee.' I thanked Maharaj and sought his permission to leave. As I got up from the seat, he asked me, 'From where will you be coming to T. Nagar?' I replied, 'Mylapore - my parents stay here.' Then, Revered Maharaj told me, 'In that case, you can join me, but you have to return on your own.' I thanked him. As I was about to leave, Revered Maharaj asked, 'Where do your parents stay in Mylapore?' I answered, 'on Dr. Ranga Road.' Immediately, Revered Maharaj said, 'In that case you need not come to the Math. You wait at Dr. Ranga Road itself, you will be picked up on my way to T. Nagar.' I offered *pranams* and left.

Accordingly, I was picked up from a place nearby my house and we went to Sarada Vidyalaya. The members of the Managing Committee, who were waiting for the arrival of Revered Maharaj, were surprised to see a stranger (myself) alighting from the car with Revered Maharaj.

As we went into the meeting room, Revered Maharaj offered me a seat and introduced me to the members. He told me, 'Before we start our meeting, you present your case.' I presented the case and the Committee was unanimous in accepting my request for admitting our girls in Sarada Vidyalaya. Then Revered Maharaj told me, 'Your job is over, you can go.' I left after thanking Revered Maharaj and all the other members.

I was overjoyed and amazed by the genuine desire of Revered Maharaj to help deserving people. More than 20 years have since elapsed, but it is still green in my memory. When I met Revered Maharaj for the first time, little did I realise that it would be the last one too.

49

A New Face!

Ms. Premalata Naik[1]

It was perhaps during my second or third visit to the Math that I met Revered Swami Tapasyananda Maharaj. While I was coming from the temple (now the 'Old Temple'), Maharaj was going to his room from his office. When I approached him to do *pranam,* he remarked 'I am seeing a new face!' I was surprised to hear that because thousands of people came to the Math, and still he could identify a new comer!

One day I asked Maharaj whether women can go to work during the menses. Excitedly he replied, 'Why not? These things are put into your minds by your great grandmothers that "you shouldn't go to temples, should not do japa etc". It is just a biological function of the body. For that matter, men and women carry the waste material in the body and go to temples, do puja etc. Does anybody think about it? The mind should be pure and devoted to God. Did you get it?' I reverentially did *pranam* and took leave of him. From that day onwards my mind was freed from all superstitions and I felt that my heart had expanded.

---

1. She was in contact with Revered Maharaj for 6 years. She is a house wife and is currently residing in Mumbai.

Swami Vivekananda

50

Official Inaugurator of Vivekananda Vidyalayas

Sri B. Govindaraj[1]

Having been associated with the Vivekananda Rock Memorial at Kanyakumari since its inception in 1963, I had been in close contact with Sri Eknath Ranade and therefore had opportunities to frequently visit Sri Ramakrishna Math, Madras for consultations. It was the time when Vivekananda Educational Society was being founded. Initial hurdles were many and there were many anxious moments too. But Swami Tapasyananda Maharaj and Swami Amritananda Maharaj of RKM Vivekananda College, Madras, appreciated and welcomed the move and blessed and encouraged us.

North Madras, with its several industries and their employees, with the inflow of immigrants from Burma who were rehabilitated in these areas, was densely populated, fostering criminal and anti-social activities. It was felt that properly educating the younger generation of these areas should be our priority and therefore it was decided to start

1. He had contact with Revered Maharaj for 18 years. He had held senior positions in the Private Sector. He has been actively associated with the Vivekananda Kendra since its inception. He is a Founder Member and former secretary of Vivekananda Educational Society. He currently resides in Chennai.

one school in the name of Vivekananda Vidyalaya every year in different localities.

Swami Tapasyananda Maharaj visited these areas and inaugurated all our schools in the presence of Sri K.R. Sundaram Iyer and Justice Krishnaswamy Reddiyar. People in the locality always looked forward to the Swami's visit and assembled in large numbers. His holy presence, happy smile, greeting and blessing, enchanted the community and his address in simple language declaring the opening of the Vivekananda Vidyalaya made the local people rejoice with happiness. He talked with the newly appointed teachers for sometime and also gave *Aksharabhyasam* to the kindergarten children which made the parents very happy. He took pride in calling himself as the 'Official Inaugurator' of our Vivekananda Vidyalayas. With his benign blessings, each and every school started growing and became the hallmark bringing some respectability to the locality, and cultured families started settling in these localities thereby improving the socio-cultural texture of these localities.

Swami Raghaveshananda and Swami Kamalatmananda were in close touch with us and guided us at all times. We required no prior permission and could freely access Revered Tapasyananda Maharaj even in the inner quarters of the Math. He too was too willing to guide us at all times. 'Where are you going to establish the next school?' he would always ask with a smile. If it was around *prasad* (food) time, Revered Maharaj would not let us go without taking *prasad*.

He was always found to be a voracious reader, and his compilation, *The Nationalistic and Religious lectures of Swami Vivekananda,*with about 35 chapters, is a valued gift given to me.

I had the opportunity of being with him several times during his illness in his last days with a swell in my heart and tears in my eyes. His fond memories will always remain cherished by all those who have been associated with Vivekananda Educational Society.

Smallest man talks longest

Swami Tapasyananda Maharaj's lectures were brief and to the point. He would also expect other speakers delivering public lectures to speak briefly and to the point. However, on one occasion, when the Swami was presiding over a meeting, speaker after speaker went on lecturing and then came the turn of one short and innocent looking man. Maharaj happily expected that this short man would speak only a few words and that he could bring this rather long session to a close. But the man spoke for so long that Maharaj humorously remarked later, 'The smallest man, but longest talk!'

—Swami Nityakamananda

51

Mother will give you solace

A Devotee[1]

It was in 1986, when I was contemplating on getting *mantra diksa,* that I first heard about Revered Swami Tapasyananda Maharaj. As I had spent most of my life outside India, I was confused while deciding whether to have my spiritual initiation in the country where I was living or in India. After a lot of thinking, I took the decision to get initiated by Revered Maharaj in June 1988.After fixing the date for initiation with Manager Maharaj, I arrived at Madras a week earlier to meet and talk to Revered Swami Tapasyananda Maharaj.

Not familiar with the ways of the Math at that time,I was nervous when I waited to meet him for the first time. Soon I was ushered into his presence. I just stood in front of him totally taken in by his calm composure and serene look. I stood still for a while before I fell at his feet to seek his blessings.

After getting formally introduced by Manager Maharaj, he spoke to me at length on the Holy Trio and instructed me to read *The Gospel of Sri Ramakrishna* everyday. He answered

1. She was initiated by Revered Maharaj in 1986 and was associated with him for 6 years. She is a teacher and currently resides in Singapore.

patiently all my questions on spiritual initiation, meditation and practice of japa. Now on reflection, I feel that some of the questions I asked were just commonplace. Nevertheless,he answered them all without showing any sign of boredom.

What struck me in my first meeting with him was the simplicity and austerity in him. His dhoti and vest were faded and he wore a pair of flip flops that needed to be replaced. His office was sparsely furnished with minimal furniture. I noticed he had a stack of papers held together on a clip board. Later I learnt that he used those one-side blank papers to write letters. I learnt from the monastics at the Math that he was very thrifty and was very careful in the way he used things. He was equally vigilant about his surroundings and would not allow any wastage. What I saw in the ensuing days prior to my initiation left a deep impression on me. It changed my attitude towards life and taught me to question before I rushed to buy things that caught my fancy. Even today,before making a new purchase,I ask myself how often am I going to use it and do I really need it. It has helped me to develop discrimination and thriftiness.

26 June 1988 dawned bright and sunny as I entered the portals of the Math at 6.30a.m.There were four of us to be initiated on that day. On arrival, a volunteer directed us to the temple and told us to sit in the temple and wait for Maharaj.

It was in the present 'Old Temple'. Maharaj arrived at 7.00 a.m. We offered our *pranams* to the Holy Trio. Maharaj was seated at the left hand corner of the temple. All of us sat facing him. The air was electrifying. He began giving us instructions on the dos and don'ts as well as the steps in doing japa effectively. Then one by one we were initiated into our mantra and the instructions to follow in our daily practice. After offering our *Guru-daksina*,we came out of the temple around 9.00 a.m. After breakfast,we were instructed to spend our time in the temple. Maharaj was to meet us at 10.30 a.m. to clarify our doubts. I had never felt so much peace within myself. I was in an elated state of mind.

At 10.30 a.m.,Maharaj met us in the parlour next to his room. There he emphasised the importance of reading the scriptures daily and having a routine established for our spiritual life. He repeatedly told us that all we needed to do was to read *The Gospel of Sri Ramakrishna* and the *Bhagavad Gita* daily. He said we would find answers there to all the questions that may rise in our minds. Over the years, I can confidently say that what he told was very true.

I have not been a frequent visitor to India prior to 1988. But after my spiritual initiation, my trips to India became an annual or sometimes even a bi-annual affair. The time I spent with Maharaj taught me the value of time. Whenever I met him after the initial pleasantries, he would insist I come to the point and ask whatever questions I wanted to ask without beating around the bush. He was also very prompt and meticulous in the way he replied to my letters.

During one of my visits, I came to meet him with my friend. As both of us were educationists, Maharaj enquired us about the educational system in our country. During the course of conversation, we mentioned that our secondary school students used a set of books to study Hinduism. He requested us to send a set to him. After perusing the books, he recommended them to be used in the monastic Probationers' Training Centre as the basic texts on Hinduism for the trainees. Subsequently, he requested for a few more copies of the books for various Math libraries. Such was his interest in developing the minds and hearts of the trainees of the Math.

There were two instances when I was blessed with his compassion. He was intuitive and could sense the crisis I was passing through in my family in 1992. I conveyed to Manager Maharaj my desire to meet Revered Maharaj as soon as I arrived [at Madras]. Hearing this, Revered Maharaj must have sensed my desperation. He informed me, through Manager Maharaj, to come to the Math directly from the airport. Eventually, I arrived at Madras and reached the Math directly from the Airport at11 p.m. I was astonished to see him waiting for me in his office! I fell at his feet and broke down. He did not ask me anything. He told me that things do not work the way I would like to have it and whatever happened was the best thing to happen in the long run. He put his hand on my head and remained silent for a while. Then he bid me to go to my place of stay and come the next morning. Even though the problem remained unresolved, I felt better and went back nearly at midnight! I saw a father in Maharaj that day!

Next day, he told Manager Maharaj to ask me to meet him in the parlour next to his room as otherwise there would be a constant flow of visitors to offer *pranams* to him. He spent almost two hours listening to my problems and then advised me. He kept repeating, 'Hold on to His feet. Pray to Mother. She will give you solace.' He also advised me to accept whatever happens as His will as we do not know most of the time what is good for us. It was difficult to comprehend his line of thinking at that time. But Time has proved the soundness and correctness of his advice. How blessed I was to have a Guru who not only took care of my spiritual welfare, but also to console and comfort me in times of worldly problems and difficulties!

As a regular visitor to the Math, I had access to him without prior appointments. Sometimes, I would just sit in Maharaj's office from morning till lunch. Visitors would stream in to receive his blessings or seek his advice. Just sitting at his feet gave me vigour and spiritual impetus. But such occasions were less because his health began to deteriorate in February 1991. He was off and on to the hospital and even when he was in the Math, he remained in his room and we could only go and offer *pranams* to him. I visited him in June after I heard from Manager Maharaj that he seemed to be getting weaker. He was in the hospital at that time and Manager Maharaj took me to see him. As I entered the room, he recognized me and acknowledged my presence. I went up to him and again he touched my head and blessed me as I offered my *pranams*. That was the last time I met him.

On our way back, Manager Maharaj mentioned that as Maharaj could hardly get up from the bed, the doctors had recommended him to use water bed to prevent bed sores. On hearing the cost of the bed, Maharaj had forbidden him to purchase it. Returning home, we purchased the water bed in our place and flew to Madras to deliver it. Initially, he refused to use it. But after the doctors' advice, he used it for just one month before attaining *mahasamadhi* on 28 September 1991, just when the *Ramnam* was being sung at the Math, that day being *Ekadasi*!

A great soul -a compassionate and loving person - had left this world! When the news reached me,I was numb for some time. First thing that flashed through my mind was, 'How will I be able to go to Madras Math and not see him there?' It took a while for me to accept the reality. I called Manager Maharaj and spoke to him. He confirmed that the news was true. He told me not to grieve as Maharaj would never like that. He told me to sit in my shrine and sing the *Ramnam*. That, he said, would please my Guru.I did as he advised and felt much better after that.I was fortunate to receive the picture of Maharaj which was used for prayers at the Math on the thirteenth day. It is still in my shrine today!

When Maharaj was alive, I would spend as much time as possible in his holy presence whenever I came to India. But after his demise, finding that he was no more with us, a feeling of emptiness overwhelmed me. It was at this time a friend asked me if I had visited Maharaj's hometown, Ottapalam. It had never occurred to me earlier to visit this place! I was not sure how to get there or where to stay when I was there. So I got in touch with Revered Swami Kaivalyananda Maharaj of Kayankulam who suggested me to visit Ottapalam and that he would make all the necessary arrangements for my stay there.

When I visited Ottapalam the first time, I drove from Coimbatore and visited the Ottapalam Ashrama with some of my relatives. There Swami Kaivalyananda Maharaj arranged for my visit to Revered Maharaj's house. It was a typical village house. It was then occupied by his brother's family.I was shown some old photographs of the family taken on different occasions. I was then taken to their puja room. Many of the articles used by Maharaj were kept there. Spending some time in the shrine lifted my spirits to a great extent. While driving back, I decided to visit this place once again and stay at least for two days to enjoy the place better.

That opportunity came in 2010, when I attended the consecration of Sri Ramakrishna Temple at Kayamkulam with a friend of mine who was familiar with Kerala. We left for Ottapalam before the consecration to spend a day there. We were accommodated in the guest house next to the Ottapalam Ashrama. On the next morning, after attending the puja at the ashrama, I was again taken to my Guru's house. I met Maharaj's nephew there. He related whatever he had heard from his grandmother and father about Maharaj. He said Maharaj was very studious and pious and would never indulge in frivolous talk even as a youngster. They had some of the books he had read when he was in that house. I was happy being in that house, just trying to imagine the kind of life he must have led there.

The two visits to his hometown have left a deep impression on my mind. I often recall my visits there and imagine the things he must have done at home and the conversations he must have had with the family members. Memories of these visits and the time I had spent with my Guru help me in pursuing my spiritual life. For this, I am ever grateful to my Guru.

52

Study Again and Again

Sri K. Srikanth[1]

नमः सद्गुरुरूपाय दक्षिणामूर्तिरूपिणे ।
श्रीमत् तपस्यानन्दाय शिष्याणां हरिरूपिणे ।।

namaḥ sadguru-rūpāya dakṣiṇāmūrti-rūpiṇe |
śrīmat tapasyānandāya śiṣyāṇāṃ hari-rūpiṇe ||

[Salutation to Srimat Tapasyananda who is in the form of sadguru, in the form of Dakshinamurti, and in the form of Hari for his disciples.]

Even as a young boy, I had great reverence for Revered Swami Tapasyananda Maharaj. I would place fruits and sweets at his feet and pay obeisance to him. He once said: 'If you place them there, how can I eat them? You should place them on the table.' Thereafter, I would place the fruits and sweets on the table and offer *pranams*, and he would accept the same with a smile.

He once affectionately gave me the book *Sri Ramakrishna: Life and Sayings* which he had authored and told me to read it. After a few days, he asked me if I had

1. He was initiated by Revered Maharaj in 1989. He had contact with Revered Maharaj for 2 years. He is a Software Engineer and a volunteer of Chennai Math. He currently resides in Chennai.

read it. I replied that I had. He made me understand that the book was not for just reading once, but for studying again and again.

In 1984, he published his translation of the *Bhagavad Gita* (*Bhagavad Gita: The Scripture of Mankind*). Thereafter, he published many books in English and Sanskrit. Though he did not write in Tamil, he was aware of the books in that language. He was indeed a great scholar. During initiation, he offered to autograph two books selected by me. Although I was young then, I still selected Revered Maharaj's book on the *Bhagavad Gita*. As I received initiation, I also received my copy of the *Gita*. For me, the grace of the guru and *Bhagavad Gita* are inseparable.

Virupakshananda at the mike

53

Difficult To Get Devotion!

A Devotee[1]

I have been blessed to be associated with Madras Math when Revered Swami Tapasyananda Maharaj was its president.

Long before Maharaj accepted me as his disciple, he initiated me into the service of Thakur. On a Sunday morning, after my prayers in the shrine (now 'Old Temple'), I went to Manager Maharaj's office (now *Sri Ramakrishna Vijayam* office) to offer my *pranams* to him. Manager Maharaj was not there, but in the meanwhile, Revered Swami Tapasyananda Maharaj came there on his way to his office. Maharaj usually went to the shrine first, then to the book stall (now *The Vedanta Kesari* Office) and through Manager Maharaj's office went to his own office. One gentleman came there at that time and asked Maharaj for a recommendation letter regarding an admission to a school. Maharaj told him that he had drafted the letter[2] but his typist was on leave. I humbly

1. She was initiated by Revered Maharaj in 1989. She had contact with Revered Maharaj for 7 years. She currently resides in Chennai and renders honorary service in Ramakrishna Mission Matriculation Higher Secondary School, T. Nagar, Chennai, and is actively involved in the activities of Chennai Math.

2. It was Revered Maharaj practice to write all his letters in a diary.

offered to type the letter for him. Maharaj was happy that I knew typing and immediately took me to the typewriter in a room behind the office. He gave me the letter pad and his diary in which he had drafted the letter meant for the gentleman. I typed the letter and gave it to Maharaj for him to sign. Thus began my service to Sri Ramakrishna, and by His grace, is continuing even now.

One day, when I went to do *pranam* to Maharaj, I asked him to bless me that I may have devotion to the lotus feet of Thakur. Maharaj with his usual smile said, 'God will give moksa very easily but it is difficult to get devotion.'

On another day, I asked Maharaj what I should read daily and he advised, 'Read the 15th chapter of the *Bhagavad Gita*.'

Photo taken at Madras Math: (All Left to Right) Sitting : 1.Paramatmanandaji 2. Kailasanandaji 3. Siddheswaranandaji 4. Aseshanandaji 5. Chidbhavanandaji 6. Chinmatranandaji Standing (Middle Row): 1. Bodhaghananandaji 2. Muniswami Chettiar 3. Mridanandaji 4. Sthitatmanandaji 5. Sakranandaji 6. Vareshanandaji 7. Maitranandaji 8. Siddhinathanandaji 9. Tapasyanandaji 10. Nityabodhanandaji 11. Sarvajnanandaji Standing (Last Row): 1. Budhanandaji 2. Sandhyananda 4. Ritajanandaji 5. Br. Anandaraman (left), 6. Gitananda 7. C.S. Ramakrishnan 8. Sundananda

54

I Want Diksa!

Sri C. Saman[1]

On 26 January 1979, I came to Sri Ramakrishna Math, Madras with Swami Sarvajnananda Maharaj of Nattrampalli Ashrama. I was 12 years old.

After waiting for a while, we could meet Revered Swami Tapasyananda Maharaj. Seeing me, Revered Maharaj enquired about me. When Swami Sarvajnananda Maharaj informed him that he had brought me to work in the Math, Revered Maharaj asked, 'He seems to be too young. Will he be able to work?' Swami Sarvajnananda Maharaj briefed him about my condition. That was the first time I had *darsan* of my future guru.

I joined the Math for work. I would clean the dining hall, sweep courtyards etc. Everyone in the Math was educated. And I was not and so I felt a bit alone. 'I was in Nattrampalli Ashrama earlier. Even here, I am under the care of Sri Ramakrishna. He will certainly protect me,' I would think and console myself. As days passed, I was

1. He was initiated by Revered Maharaj in 1988. He was closely associated with Revered Maharaj for 12 years. He joined as a worker in Chennai Math in 1979 and served as Revered Maharaj's driver for 5 years. He continues to work in Chennai Math.

trained to cook. I also used to clean Revered Maharaj's room, bring him hot water etc.

Time passed. I began to feel an urge to get spiritually initiated by Revered Maharaj. 'Maharaj, please give me *mantra diksa,*' I pleaded. 'What are the books you have read?' he asked. 'I have read several booklets on Sri Guru Maharaj,' I told. 'You would have read some 'Thus spake' booklets. Can you be initiated on that count?' he remarked and dismissed my petition.

But I was determined to receive *diksa* from him. 'Maharaj, I want to receive *diksa,*' I would pester him while arranging for his bath etc. 'That can be thought about later. Attend to the work now,' would be his curt reply.

I would also request Swami Desikatmananda Maharaj to recommend for my initiation. Several days passed thus and one day he told me to be ready for spiritual initiation on the subsequent day. 'Am I so blessed?' I wondered happily. On the next day, 13 devotees, including me, received spiritual initiation from Revered Tapasyananda Maharaj. I wanted to ask him about the meaning of the mantra. But I was afraid. With the encouragement given by Swami Sukritananda Maharaj, I approached Revered Maharaj and learnt the meaning of the mantra.

One day, I had an uncontrollable urge to watch a film. After completing the tasks at hand, I went for a night show. When I returned, the gates of the Math were closed. I scaled the gates and entered the Math compound (in those days, the main gate, that is, the present 'old gate', could be seen from the verandha of Revered Maharaj's room and he had seen my adventure vividly). When I went to Revered

Maharaj's room the next day, he asked, 'Where did you go yesterday?' I did not realize that he had seen me scaling the gates last night. 'I did not go anywhere, Maharaj, I was in the Math only,' I bluffed. 'Did you not scale the gates last night at 12.30 p.m.?' he asked. 'It is not I, Maharaj. Perhaps it was Venkatesh[1]…,' I continued bluffing. 'From when did Venkatesh start wearing half-trousers?' was he next question. I was trapped. Sri Venkatesh never wore half-trousers! 'Alright, don't repeat this again, and don't bluff,' he said and went away. My conscience kept pricking me that I had bluffed to Revered Maharaj, who was not only the president of the Math, but also my guru. I thought when opportunity arose, I should confess my misdeed and beg pardon of him.

Revered Maharaj tutored me and corrected me in so many ways. For instance, once, I had left his soap without washing it after his bath. 'Wash it and dry it in the sun, we can use it for six months if you keep it dry,' he said, thus instructing me in thriftiness.

On another occasion, I had prepared and kept some *chappatis* [unleavened flatbread]. While eating them, he said, 'Why did you prepare such hard *chappatis*? Next time you prepare, let me know. I shall teach you how to prepare *chappatis*.' Next evening, after preparing the dough, I informed Maharaj who was then walking on the corridor outside dining hall. He came to the kitchen and patiently taught me how to divide the dough into equal portions and roll them out uniformly into nice circular shapes! Just as he

1. A respectable and elderly gentleman who was a volunteer in Accounts Sections. He used to work late in the night. He always wore dhoti.

had told, *chappatis* bulged while baking! Like this, he would teach me several tips in the art of cooking.

Revered Maharaj was not only my guru in my spiritual life, he was also a mentor in my day to day life. He taught me how to live. When I did the work well, he would heartily appreciate and encourage me.

With the permission of Revered Maharaj, I learnt to drive. When I had to drive the car to drop him at the Madras Central Railway Station, he said since I was inexperienced he would sit in the rear seat and observe how I drove. On reaching the railway station, he said, 'Not bad. But practise a little more.'

In 1988, I wished to go to Belur Math with Revered Maharaj. I expressed my desire to him. 'It would be expensive trip. Do you have so much money?' he asked. I said I would manage the money somehow. After some days, I, along with few others, got an opportunity to visit Belur Math with Revered Maharaj. With concern, he instructed me, 'You do not know the language here. Don't go anywhere without informing me.'He chalked out a plan for us to visit various places in Calcutta and Kamarpukur and Jayarambati. He called and informed the people there about our arrival. The moment we returned to Belur Math, we were told to meet Revered Maharaj immediately. We were told he had been very anxious that we should return safely and without any difficulty. When we met him, he was relieved and affectionately enquired, 'Did you visit all the places?'

One day, I made some mistake while working in his room. With some annoyance, Revered Maharaj asked,

'Why are you doing your work like this. Do you have any paruppu[1]?' Though I was then working in the kitchen, I still was confused why he wanted pulses at that time. But then it flashed in my mind that Revered Maharaj, who knew only a smattering of Tamil, wanted to say "poruppu"[2] and had instead told "paruppu". Realizing this, both of us had a hearty laugh.

I was once afflicted with Malaria and was tossing about on my bed with severe headache. Coming to know of my condition, Maharaj advised me to visit the hospital immediately. In spite of taking medicines, I found no relief. He then instructed Manager Maharaj to admit me in a hospital. When I was admitted in a private nursing home for a week, Revered Maharaj took lovingly care of me by arranging for my food in time and monitoring my improvement.

How fortunate I was to be taken care by Revered Maharaj in so many ways! I however do not understand why he showered so much of love on me. I am thrilled whenever I remember that he took care of me more than my mother! If at all there are any future births for me, I wish to spend them in serving monks like him.

When Revered Maharaj became critically ill, he was admitted to Vijaya Hospital. Some of us had gone to the hospital to visit him. I stood at his feet. Even in that critical condition, looking at me he enquired, 'How are you? How is your health?' I broke into tears.

---

1. Tamil word for pulses.
2. Tamil word for responsibility.

'Sukritananda is giving me medicines after medicines. Request him to allow me to relax a bit,' he said. After he regained his health, we took him to the Math. I felt happy and peaceful and resumed my duties. I thought how fortunate I was! How I wish those blessed days had continued!

The pain I experienced when he was admitted again to B.S.S. Hospital is indescribable. My marriage had been fixed then. I got his blessings. When he attained *mahasamadhi*, I was filled with pangs of separation from my venerable guru.

Today, I am living on the memories of Revered Maharaj. There is not a moment when I do not think about him. I ever pray for his blessings.

Tapasyanandaji sitting behind Vireswaranandaji, Madras Math, 1972

55

Our Only Refuge

A Devotee

Sometimes great and holy people make a deep influence in our lives with their kindness and compassion. Revered Swami Tapasyananda Maharaj was one such who influenced my life and whose words of advice still 'ring' in my ears, even though 27 years have elapsed.

In 1986, I suddenly lost my husband who died of a heart attack. As a young widow, I shifted to Madras with my daughter who was in her teens. I happened to meet Revered Swami Tapasyananda Maharaj whose doors were open for all. He felt aggrieved about my widowhood and would listen to my problems with patience and compassion.

One day, I broke into tears in Maharaj's office. But his compassionate words soothed my heavy heart. He told me not to feel sad and advised me to pray to, contemplate on and serve Sri Ramakrishna as he was our only refuge. He said this alone would give me some solace. He also advised me to visit the Math frequently. Could I have had any better advice? I got all my strength from Sri Ramakrishna to face the ravages of life. My sadness slowly turned into peace and joy. Even after so many years, I still 'cling' to his words of advice.

A thousand salutations to Maharaj who showed me the right path.

56

Embodiment of Human Values

Dr. Atmakur Ramanaiah[1]

I had the great privilege of serving Revered Tapasyananda Maharaj by cleaning his room and the place around it for the last two years of his life. Perhaps, it was due to the *punya* of my previous births that I had the blessed opportunity to serve him this way.

Whenever the image of Revered Maharaj appears in my mind, the following great verse of *Srimad Bhagavatam* flashes forth:

अथ मां सर्वभूतेषु भूतात्मानं कृतालयम् ।
अर्हयेद्दानमानाभ्यां मैत्र्याभिन्नेन चक्षुषा ।।

atha māṃ sarvabhūteṣu bhūtātmānaṃ kṛtālayam |
arhayeddānamānābhyāṃ maitryābhinnena cakṣuṣā ||

"Having converted all living beings into my dwellings, I live in them. Therefore all living entities are to be treated equally with charity, respect and friendship."

[*Srimad Bhagavatam* III. 29:27]

---

1. He was initiated by Revered Ranganathananda Maharaj in 1998. He has worked in Chennai Math in various capacities since Revered Maharaj's tenure. He has been conferred with a Ph.D degree from University of Madras for his research on *Humanism of Swami Vivekananda* in the Department of Telugu. He is currently working in the composing section of the Publication Department of Chennai Math.

These divine words were told by Sri Kapila Maharshi, who is supposed to be an incarnation of Sri Mahavishnu. The values like charity, respect for others, equality, and friendship are succinctly expressed in this verse.

Revered Maharaj diligently followed these four values. And that made his personality all the more glorious. This is not an exaggeration, but something I actually feel as true.

Perhaps it was in 1989 or 1990. I was living in a thatched hut in Santhome (a locality in Madras). It was in a fishermen's colony of about 500 huts near the beach. Once, during summer, the whole colony was reduced to ashes in a fire accident. The people who were living there got stranded having lost all that they had. Due to the fire accident, my hut too was reduced to ashes and I was left with nothing. Fortunately there were no casualties.

At that time, I had already begun to work in the Math in various capacities - as gardener, watchman and kitchen helper. Coming to know about this calamity, Gopal Maharaj (Swami Kapalishananda Maharaj) and Suryanarayana Maharaj (Swami Sukritananda Maharaj) enquired about my situation and advised me to seek help from Revered Tapasyananda Maharaj. Following their advice, I went to meet Revered Maharaj in his office (the present ITD Dept.). Initially, I felt very hesitant to enter inside and meet him. I had interacted with him only once earlier. So with much trepidation, I entered into his office. He was then immersed in perusing a book. After a few moments, he gradually turned his attention towards me. He gestured me to sit on a bench nearby. Too shy to sit, I joined my hands in *namaskar* pose and continued to stand. Looking at me kindly, Revered

Maharaj, through a gesture[1] enquired what brought me there. Without wasting his precious time, I told him briefly about the fire accident and that I had lost everything I had had. After listening to me, he again motioned me to sit. Realizing that it would be improper to disobey him now, I sat on the corner of the bench. He immediately called Sankar Maharaj (Swami Raghaveshananda Maharaj), who was the then manager of the Math, and told him to do the needful. On that occasion, I understood how to serve distressed people through Revered Maharaj's gestures. He demonstrated how to treat the needy with kindness and concern, without impugning their honour or self-respect. Revered Maharaj arranged for my accommodation and allowance for my sustenance. I was thus rehabilitated. It left an indelible impression on my mind seeing Revered Maharaj's readiness to help anyone in need without any discrimination. I understood how Revered Maharaj embodied the values of charity, respect, friendship and equality enumerated in the *Bhagavata* verse above.

It was very surprising that after meeting him, my mind which was agitated, confused, and disturbed till then, at once became calm and peaceful. The kindness with which he treated me then had overwhelmed me. Only when I came out of his office did I realize that the peace I experienced was due to his gracious and kind response to my treatment of me. Even now when I look at his photograph, I experience the same peace.

---

1. Revered Maharaj could not follow Tamil or Telugu and Sri Ramanaiah did not know English.

There were many occasions in my two year association with him that bore witness to these qualities.

Another incident that deeply impressed me was:

On the left side of what we now call the 'Old Temple' was a rectangular garden. A life size Sri Anjaneya statue was there in the middle of that garden, called the Hanuman Garden. As a gardener, it was my duty to keep the surroundings clean, especially on *Ekadasi*. One morning on a *Ekadasi*, at 9.30 a.m., I was absorbed in collecting the dry leaves and trimming the flower plants. I did not notice that Revered Maharaj was passing by that way. Revered had gently patted me on my back with his walking stick, but thinking that a leaf or twig had fallen on my back, I continued my trimming. Then I heard the soft voice of Swami Sukritananda Maharaj calling me 'Ramanaiah!' I immediately turned around and was dumbfounded to see Revered Maharaj standing there with Swami Sukritananda Maharaj holding an umbrella over him. Swami Sukritananda Maharaj mildly admonished me for not responding even though Revered Maharaj had tapped on my back twice.

Revered Maharaj gently smiled at me and said, 'We feel miserable when there is an injury to our hands or feet. These tender plants too must be wincing with pain when you are cutting them like that. Just think about it.' Gently reprimanding me thus, he moved on. Perhaps Revered Maharaj was following the injunction, '*Atmavat satatam pasyet*' ('treat everyone as your own self').

Another incident I now recall is about his simple living.

Revered Maharaj would use mugs with broken handles and buckets with broken rim in his bathroom. I tried to replace them with new ones, but Swami Sukritananda Maharaj dissuaded me saying that he himself had tried many times to replace them, but Revered Maharaj had never allowed him to. Revered Maharaj had told him not to waste money on new mugs and buckets. Revered Maharaj continued to those things till his *mahasamadhi*. Revered Maharaj did not want to spend even a little money for a few mugs and buckets, but when I was in distress, he did not mind spending money generously to help me! Acting according to the requirements of the situation was one of his great qualities.

Now let me relate my first meeting with Revered Maharaj.

I began to work in Madras Math in 1985. In the beginning, I was doing the work entrusted on me rather mechanically. Swami Nandananda Maharaj, who used to visit Madras Math often, advised me not to do the work mechanically, but to keenly observe what is happening around in the Math. I understood that being alert at work was like worship to Sri Ramakrishna and Holy Mother as declared by Swami Vivekananda. This motivated me to learn more about the lives and teachings of the Holy Trio. So I began to read the Telugu translations of booklets written by Revered Maharaj.

To clarify my doubts, I would usually go either to Swami Tyagananda Maharaj or to Swami Jnanadananda Maharaj. One day, with a sudden impulse, I went to Revered Maharaj to clarify my doubts regarding the battlefield of Kurukshetra.

I was in my garden dress. I was wearing an old dhoti and a vest torn at several places. On the whole, my attire was dirty. I was so foolish to present myself like this to a great person like Revered Maharaj. Feeling a bit shy, I stood before him. That was my very first interaction with Revered Maharaj.

As soon as I entered his office, Revered Maharaj's looked at me in a pleasing way. I felt tremendous joy within. I stood still after conveying my *namaskars*. Revered Maharaj motioned me to sit on the bench nearby. With some hesitation, I sat on that bench. He enquired about my problem through gestures. With great fear and hesitation, I put forth my two doubts:

1. How did the battlefield get the name 'Kurukshetra'?
2. Why is it called 'Dharmakshetra' when there had been so much of bloodshed?

Revered Maharaj, who was listening to my questions, now bent his head slightly forward, and with a sweet smile lighted on his face he began to explain: 'A king named Kuru acquired a huge piece of land in order to perform *yajnas* and *yagas* for the welfare of his subjects. That is how that place came to be called Kurukshetra. After him, during the time of the Kauravas and the Pandavas, Kauravas committed many unrighteous deeds against the Pandavas. In order to stop the practice of *adharma*, the battle between cousins had to take place on that piece of land in presence of the Lord himself. That is why it came to be called 'Dharmakshetra'...'

Revered Maharaj in this manner explained and cleared my doubts. Then with a sweet smile, he asked me whether my doubts have been clarified. With deep gratitude and satisfaction, I saluted him and took leave of him. I was astonished at the way he spoke to me, coming down to my level.

To conclude, I would like to say that one has to follow the example of Revered Maharaj if one has to live a pure and contented life; one has to give up ostentatiousness and pride and develop inner beauty. Even now, when I think or hear about Revered Maharaj, I would feel an inexplicable lightness and happiness within me.

Special Blessings

In Swami Tapasyananda Maharaj's last days, when he was admitted in the hospital, he sent word for me. He used to always refer me as 'lady in white sari' and not by my name. When I went there, he kept his right hand on my head. How long it prolonged like that, I did not know. Then he said, 'Right, you can come (meaning "You can go").' Later, I heard the news of his passing away. It was such a shock to me.

—Smt. Ambal Ramanathan

(A devotee of Chennai Math)

Inauguration of Shoba Ice Factory[1]

Our family has been devotees of Sri Ramakrishna Paramahamsa from the year 1966. In 1977, Swami Tapasyananda Maharaj blessed us by inaugurating our Shoba Ice Factory at Tambaram. On that day, many curious spectators were present to witness the opening ceremony by a swami. They waited in the scorching sun to have a glimpse of Maharaj. A few photos of Maharaj were also taken during that occasion. We were surprised at the number of technical questions asked by Maharaj about the factory. He became very enthused like a child when he saw the huge ice blocks weighing about 175 kilograms each.

On the whole, it was an unforgettable experience for us. Even after so many years, the memory is still fresh in our minds. We are ever grateful for his blessings.

With Chidghanandaji (standing first) at the Shobha Ice Factory Inaguration

1. Contributed by Smt. Uma Krishnamurthy on behalf of Sri H.G.V. Setty.

Appendices

Maharaj during spiritual initiation on 24-7-1985

Part A

Smt. Parukkutty Amma's gift of Poetry

Smt. Indira Krishnakumar

Smt. Parukkutty Amma had penned several poems. Her pen touched different subjects ranging from the mundane to the spiritual. It is a matter of great joy to go through her poems. She wrote in Malayalam, but in heavily Sanskritized diction.

As she had lost her parents in her early childhood and her husband in her teenage, she was obsessed with her concern for the health and longevity of her sons. She prayed intensely that she be permitted to see her sons alive as long as she lived. Since her beloved son, Balakrishnan, had embraced sannyasa at a very young age, she also ardently prayed to the Father and Mother of the universe that they bestow their grace on her sannyasi son so that he treads steadily forward in the path of renunciation and holds aloft the ideals of Vairagya.

Since her own marital life came to an abrupt end when she had just been married for four years, she was greatly concerned about the marital bliss of her younger sisters. She knew that rain or shine, man has to depend on God. She realized that for all real and imagined ills of humanity, grace from the superhuman power alone was the panacea. Petitioning God for His mercy and taking refuge at His feet-this alone was the way open to her or to anyone. She was fully aware that it was 'Maya' that was making her obsessed with such concerns for the worldly welfare of others. She knew that detachment is the ideal to strive for. All these she had penned in many of her poems in a touching manner.

Smt. Parukkutty Amma's lines on Sri Ramakrishna, Raja Maharaj, Tulasi Maharaj, *Kalpataru* day and such other spiritual topics are highly impressive and inspiring. It appears she was so full of poetry that she used this medium to convey greetings on weddings and birthdays, condolences on bereavement, advice on married life to newly-wedded couples and so on. She also had such erudite friends that they exchanged news and ideas with her in verse.

Puranic themes also figured in her poems. She was deeply influenced by the "Sandesha Kavya" style of poetry of the early 20th century Kerala.

The deft use of Sanskrit words and expressions show that she had a good grounding in Sanskrit. Some of the lines in her Malayalam poems happened to be fully couched in Sanskrit language though the script is Malayalam.

Some of Smt. Parukkutty Amma's Poems

1[1]

रामकृष्ण भगवन् नमो नमो पालयाशु करुणानिधे नमो ।
पाहि लोकजननी मदम्बिके मातृदेवि सततं नमो ।।

rāmakṛṣṇa bhagavan namo namo pālayāśu karuṇānidhe namo |
pāhi lokajananī madambike mātṛdevi satataṃ namo ||

1. Poem for making obeisance before Guru Maharaj and Holy Mother.

Salutation to Bhagavan Ramakrishna

Salutation, protect me quickly!

Salutation, O merciful One!

O my Mother, Mother of the universe, protect me!

Salutation ever, O Divine Mother!

2[1]

करवरघृतचापां दुष्टसंहारिणीं ताम्
कुवलयदलनेत्रां चारुमन्दस्मितास्यां
सुरुचिरकरभाषां शोणपाणिप्रवालाम्
सुरनुत चरणाब्जाम् नौमि दुर्गां हृदिस्थाम् ।

karavaraghṛtacāpāṃ duṣṭasaṃhariṇīṃ tām
kuvalayadalanetrāṃ cārumandasmitāsyāṃ
surucirakarabhāṣāṃ śoṇapāṇipravālām
suranuta caraṇābjām naumi durgāṃ hṛdisthām |

I salute Sri Durga

Who holds bow in her hand

Who destroys vicious people

Whose eyes are beautiful like water lily

Whose smile is so pleasing

Whose words are very sweet

Whose feet are red in colour like coral

Whose lotus feet Devas worship

Who resides in my heart

1. Poem expressing namaskars to Sri Durga Devi.

3[1]

कान्तो मद्दयितोप्यकालमरणं प्राप्तो विधेशासनात्
प्रागेवोपरतौ मदीयपितरौ भूयोप्यहं शोषिता ।
कानतान्वेषण तत्परं सहजयाः संप्राप्तयाः यौवनम्
चिन्ताचंचलितं मदीयहृदयम् शान्तं कुरु श्रीपते ।।

kānto maddayitopyakālamaraṇaṃ prāpto vidheśāsanāt
prāgevoparatau madīyapitarau bhūyopyahṃ śoṣitā |
kānatānveṣaṇa tatparaṃ sahajayāḥ saṃprāptayāḥ yauvanam
cintācaṃcalitaṃ madīyahṛdayam śāntaṃ kuru śrīpate ||

My beloved (husband), very much loved by me
Died immaturely by force of fate
Parents too passed away much earlier
I am in great distress due to these
Now I am in search of a spouse for my sister
Who has attained youth
My mind is restless due to this
So, O Lord of Sri (Mahalakshmi)
Bestow peace in my heart.

1. Poem to express her concern about her sister whose marriage was getting delayed.

Balakrishnan Serves at Nettayam Ashrama[1]

Smt. Indira Krishnakumar

Swami Tapasyananda Maharaj, as young Balakrishnan studying in college, did some service at Nettayam Ashrama.

On 7 March 1924, the 89th birth anniversary of Bhagavan Sri Ramakrishna, the consecration ceremony was conducted at Nettayam Ashram. The Ashram was dedicated in memory of Swami Brahmananda Maharaj.

During the summer vacation that year (in 1924), Balakrishnan and Appu, who were studying in different colleges in Madras, visited Trivandrum. Since Tulasi Maharaj [Swami Nirmalananda Maharaj] was in Kanyakumari then, they visited him there. After staying with him for a day, they returned to Trivandrum.

One morning, they walked from Trivandrum Fort to Nettayam Ashrama, and stayed there for some time with other inmates. Nettayam Ashrama is situated on a hillock. There was then no courtyard on the western side of the Ashrama. The western edge led to a slope down. The land on this side was to be raised and made in to a nice garden. For this, the soil had to be dug from a place nearby and brought to the spot carrying it on the head. Leveling the land there was the main work.

Apart from the inmates, fifty workers were also engaged in this work. All would work from morning till

1. The following narration is based on the notes written by Sri K.P.A Menon in his diary.

evening. Around 10 o' clock in the morning, they would stop the work for about half an hour to drink water and relax. It was then mango season and there was a mango tree bearing plenty of mangoes. So they would throw stones at the mangoes, pick up the fallen ones, eat them with some salt, gulp some water and resume their work. Since they were involved in hard physical labour, their appetite was good and whatever curries were prepared, it would all taste to them as heavenly. There was a stream flowing down the hillock where they would bathe. How pleasant had been their dips!

At dusk, all of them would bathe and assemble in the hall for prayer. After *arati, bhajans* would be sung. After japa, they would have their dinner. Balan and Appu and many others would lie down in the open verandah on the western side of the Ashrama. Sleeping there would be a joy for them. It was then peak of summer. But at nights, a cool and pleasant breeze would blow from the sea in the west. Due to hard physical labour during the day, they would only have to lay down on the bed to slip into a deep sleep. And at that young age, they had no other disturbing thoughts to interfere with their sleep.

When the rainy season began, all work came to an end. Then Balan and Appu went home to Ottapalam, after spending two months happily at Nettayam Ashrama.

When the college reopened, they returned to Madras. As their luck would have it, Mahapurush Maharaj visited Madras Math at that time. Both Balan and Appu received spiritual initiation from Mahapurush Maharaj on 23 December 1924. The rest is history.

What impresses one is that Swami Tapasyananda Maharaj worked hard for Trivandrum Ashrama even as a student. He also worked hard for that Ashrama after he became a monk. As a young boy, he had led a simple life in the Ashrama during that vacation. Later when he became the president of the Ashrama, he continued to lead a simple life. Some people, no matter how rich or influential, are still destined, nay, they choose, to lead a simplest of simple lives. Swami Tapasyananda Maharaj was one such person.

A Mother's Heart and a Hero's Will

Smt. Indira Krishnakumar

Smt. Parukkutty Amma was happy that her son Balan [Swami Tapasyananda Maharaj] became a monk. But she also wanted him to come home so that she could feed him. Her great concern for his food, health, mental strength and adherence to the path he chose ran concurrent to her sadhana. She used to make a jam using ripe jackfruit and jaggery. It is called "Chakka varatti" in Malayalam. Saying that it is a favorite delicacy of her son Balan, she would make large quantities of it and wait for him to arrive. But his arrival would always be delayed, for he had heavy responsibilities in the Ashram. Further, Maharaj, a monk after all, seemed unwilling to come home far too frequently.

The jackfruit jam would stay fresh for a long time if it was occasionally reheated adding ghee. Smt. Parukkutty Amma would do this periodically to keep it fresh for her Balan's arrival. Each time it is reheated with ghee, it becomes tastier and thicker, losing the water content. But the volume would decrease. When she made it, it would have filled a large jar, but finally, it would have been reduced to a small bottle. Still her Balan would not have arrived. This happened frequently. In fact, Maharaj's visits home were so few that it could be counted on fingers. She would send him money, medicines, health supplements, snacks and savories. Maharaj tried to dodge all attempts to have himself in the ambit of filial love. Going through the correspondence of those days, one would feel the situation was both highly noble and deeply touching.

Swami Shivananda

Part B

Reminiscences of Swami Shivananda A Direct Disciple of Sri Ramakrishna[1]

Swami Tapasyananda

It is in an apologetic mood and with a sense of diffidence that I put into writing the following reminiscences of the great disciple of Sri Ramakrishna, Sri Mahapurusha Maharaj, known also by his monastic name of Swami Shivananda. This feeling is due not only to an apprehension of his greatness and the littleness of my understanding to interpret him, but also due to the paucity of incidents of wide public significance that I have got to record.

I claim to be a disciple of Sri Mahapurush Maharaj in the fullest sense of the term. I received my Mantra-Diksha from him as also my initiation into Brahmacharya and Sannyasa. But yet my association with him was only for brief periods, and I have not got much to write about the incidents of his life and teachings he imparted. To start with, this requires an explanation. According to the Indian tradition, service of the spiritual teacher, and living with him, are considered the most important part of the spiritual discipline. The 'Gita' goes to the extent of saying that spiritual teaching is not to

1. Reproduced here from *Vedanta* 263 May-June 1955 & 264 July-August 1995. The last 4 paragraphs have been translated from Bengali version published in the Bengali book, *Shivananda Smritisangraha*, p 229-230 published by Udbodhan Press.

be imparted to one who has not undergone this discipline of serving the teacher.

In the tradition of the Ramakrishna Order, there are certain spiritual conceptions that have led to an amendment and extension of this great and wise rule sanctioned by age-long practice in India. Swami Vivekananda gave the idea that the Order he founded represented the physical being of the Great Master, Sri Ramakrishna, who is the real Teacher of the Order irrespective of the personality of the individual teachers through whom he functions. It is the service of the teacher of that wider conception that he primarily expects his followers to perform as a part of their spiritual discipline. In pursuance of this ideology, the monastics of our Order, often getting little opportunity to stay with their individual teachers, are put as workers in the far-flung centres of the Order – there to do all forms of work, physical and mental with a sense of responsibility, detachment and dedication. All the institutions and works of the Math and Mission are the responsibilities of the Head of the Order for the time being, and by sharing that responsibility one is serving the teacher in a literal sense too. But it is the wider conception of Guru-Sushrusha explained above that gives a special significance to the training in the Ramakrishna Order.

My first acquaintance with the name and teachings of Sri Ramakrishna was in my early teens when I was reading in the lower secondary classes at Calicut. It came about through some literature in Malayalam that my mother was reading. I had then gathered the idea that Sri Ramakrishna Paramahamsa was one who had seen God and that he had a disciple called Swami Vivekananda who was a great lecturer. I remember a hot boyish controversy I had with a school friend of mine on the question whether God can be seen – he maintaining that this is impossible and I advocating the opposite view. I recall how, in support of my contention, I mentioned the example of Sri Ramakrishna Paramahamsa, which my friend would not however accept.

My real acquaintance with the traditions of the Great Master began a year or two after when we went to reside in a new house, which by chance happened to be the residence of a great Ramakrishna-Vivekananda devotee, to whom for convenience I may refer here as Sri A. He was also the father of a close class friend of mine. It was my habit, along with some of the other boys of the house, to go for diving in a tank in the house of this particular class friend. Now Sri A, this friend's father, was one of the earliest in Kerala to have intimate contact with the monastic Order of Sri Ramakrishna. He had already received initiation from Swami Brahmanandaji Maharaj, had visited Belur Math and probably the birth place of the Master also, and was kept a Shrine in his house where the photos of Sri Ramakrishna, Holy Mother and some of his important disciples formed the main objects of worship. I had before that only attended Hindu temples where granite images of Gods and Goddesses were worshipped in a ceremonial manner by Brahmin priests, and this centre of worship, with its photos of human figures, was an entirely new experience for me. It had a great impact on my mind. I remember on most days, after diving for hours in the tank, I used to go with other boys into this Shrine of my friend's father Sri A, and sometimes witness there a simple waving of Lights too. It was there that I learnt that Sri Ramakrishna was looked upon by many as 'God', who has to be worshipped like

Rama, Krishna, Vishnu, Siva, the Divine Mother and other deities of the Hindu Pantheon familiar to me. Soon after, a similar Shrine of the Master, though on much simpler lines, was arranged in my house also. For my mother, who was already devoted to Sri Ramakrishna, became more intensely established in that line of devotion through association with the devoted inmates of my friend's house.

During this time an important incident, a landmark in my life, took place. That was the contact I had with the late Swami Nirmalanandaji Maharaj, known also as Tulasi Maharaj, while he was staying at the house of my friend's father, Sri A, during his sojourn in Kerala. Among the pioneers of the Ramakrishna-Vivekananda movement in South India, the Swami has a very prominent place. In later times a controversy arose about his discipleship – whether he was a disciple of Sri Ramakrishna himself or of Swami Vivekananda – but at the time I met him, the general understanding all of us in Kerala had was that he was a disciple of the Master. Though this has been disputed in later times, no one denies that he had contacted the Great Master as a young man, that he received his blessings, and that he had shared his life of the Sannyasin disciples of the Master from the days of the Baranagore monastery.

At the time I am speaking of, the Swami was in charge of the centre at Bangalore, and he, as also Swami Sharvanandaji of Madras, happened to be widely known among the devotees of Ramakrishna-Vivekananda of those days, because of the extensive tours they used to make in different parts of South India. Though Swami Nirmalanandaji's centre was Bangalore, he used to spend several months in Kerala almost every year. His method of work was to visit different places where there were devotees known to him, stay in the house of anyone of them who could accommodate him conveniently, and contact interested visitors through personal conversations. He had already established a centre of the Mission's work at Trivandrum, started the magazine 'Prabuddha Keralam', and arranged the visit of Swami Brahmanandaji Maharaj for laying the foundation of the monastery building in Trivandrum in 1916. At the time I am speaking of, though Swamiji had an influential circle of devotees at Trivandrum, the only person of some consequence who may be called an ardent devotee at Calicut was my friend's father, Sri A. Every time he visited Kerala, he used to come to Calicut and spend a few days at Sri A's house, giving an opportunity for all devotees as well as others to contact him.

The impression that the Swami made on my adolescent mind was tremendous. It may thus be summarized: Till then I had no positive idea of a spiritual personage, beyond that of legendary Rishis and sages of the Puranas. In daily life one came across only Brahmin Pandits and ritualists who expounded Puranas or officiated at temples and domestic rituals, and in their outlook and activities there was nothing to distinguish them from ordinary worldly man. The other types one associated with religious life were ochre-robed beggars who passed for Sannyasins and wandering ascetics who put on matted locks and weird dress and sat under trees before lighted fire to impress the credulous public with the idea that they were holy men with mysterious powers. None of these could in any way inspire or even impress one with the idea that the exclusive pursuit of a religion-centred life had anything ennobling in it.

I found a striking and startling contrast in Swami Nirmalanandaji's personality. He was so unlike the ochre-robed fraternity I had seen. With his athletic frame, his sonorous stentorian voice, his excellent command of simple, clear and well-articulated English and his astonishing capacity to give ready and crushing reply to mischievous questions, I found him more than a match for the self-accredited intelligentsia of the locality consisting of lawyers, officers, teachers, etc, who could take only a contemptuous view of a Sannyasin till then. To this inherent worth of the Swami was added the halo of association with Sri Ramakrishna and Swami Vivekananda. All these put together generated great reverence for him in one's mind, and the frequent contact I used to have with him from this time had a decided influence on the future development of my mind.

It was at the age of fifteen or sixteen that I began to read the lectures of Swami Vivekananda and the magazine, 'Prabuddha Bharata'. While all these impressed me very much, there was nothing that could equal, to my mind, the first edition of the Life of Swami Vivekananda by his Eastern and Western Disciples, now unfortunately out of print. The first two volumes of it, written in a simple yet fervent and inspiring English style, evoked a passionate admiration for Sri Ramakrishna and Swamiji in my mind and engulfed all other devotional allegiances I had till then.

It was just at this juncture, that I had my first opportunity of meeting Sri Mahapurush Maharaj. Swami Brahmanandaji Maharaj, the first President of Ramakrishna Math and Mission, the 'spiritual son' of Sri Ramakrishna – about whose lofty spiritual personality some information had reached even distant Kerala through the 'Gospel of Sri Ramakrishna' – had come down to

Madras in 1920-21, chiefly to open the Ramakrishna Mission Students' Home. His name was then very well-known to devotees in Kerala. He had visited Kerala, including Trivandrum and Kanyakumari, in 1916 when he laid the foundation of the present Sri Ramakrishna Ashram at Trivandrum and gave initiation to several devotees in the state. A few devotees from our place, including my mother, who was long aspiring to take initiation, started for Madras to meet Swami Brahmanandaji Maharaj, familiarly known as the Maharaj or Raja Maharaj. Swami Nirmalanandaji, who was intimately known to the devotees, was also expected to have arrived at Madras from Bangalore. As a youngster with some knowledge of English, the devotees considered that I might be useful as an interpreter, if none better was available at Madras. So I too had accompanied them.

When the party of devotees visited Madras Math, they were given a very kind and cordial welcome by Swami Sharvanandaji Maharaj who was the President of Madras Math then. Swami Nirmalanandaji Maharaj had also arrived at the Math, as expected. All of us, including myself, were admitted into the august presence of Maharaj. He sat on an easy chair with a hookah by his side. His face was calm and solemn, and eyes absolutely indrawn, though wide open and awake. He was very communicative but brief in speaking a few words of advice and assurance to the representations of the devotees. All of them were asked to come for initiation. The late Swami Siddheswaranandaji, then Brahmachari Gopal, acted as interpreter.

After the meeting with Maharaj, we were informed that there was present at the Math another venerable Swami, also a disciple of Sri Ramakrishna. This was an unexpected announcement, and we were immensely glad to be taken to the presence of this great personage, who was none other than Sri Mahapurush Maharaj, then the Vice-President of the Math and Mission. The Swami was occupying the southern upstairs backroom which is now the Holy Mother's Shrine. In those days, before the extension and remodelling of the shrine, this was a living room. Adjacent to it was a spacious staircase hall where Sri Mahapurush Maharaj was seated on a chair when we met him. The impression that now comes to my mind of him is in some respect one of contrast with the other great one, from whose presence we had just then come out. Unlike Maharaj, whose presence was forbiddingly solemn and elevating, and whose silence was more resonant than the spoken word, one saw in Sri Mahapurush Maharaj a more human yet transcendentally glorious figure, in whom a mighty personality combined harmoniously with an inviting and highly communicative disposition. His face was wreathed in gracious smiles, and his head nodded in an act of kind approval at the introduction of the new devotees. He seemed to be more elderly than Maharaj from the colour of his hair, but age had not made him old in any sense of the term. He was in good health, and his face, with somewhat high cheek bones, and elongated eyes that gave it a slight Mongolian touch, glowed with a reddish tinge and a sense of carefree cheerfulness and universal benevolence which made one feel absolutely relaxed in his otherwise august presence. He made kind enquiries about the devotees and said that uttering God's name with faith and devotion was in itself a potent means of men's spiritual development.

After that the party left the Math to see the new building of the Students' Home. It was to perform the opening function that Maharaj had come down from Calcutta. After the visit, before returning to their residence, the devotees stopped the car near the Math and sent me to tell Swami Nirmalanandaji Maharj that they would be coming again next day. As I approached the portico of the Math, I had an opportunity to witness an impressive scene that has so often come to my memory. Being late in the evening, Maharaj had come out of his room to air himself. He was just standing in front of the portico with Mahapurush Maharaj and Swami Nirmalanandaji Maharaj on either side. Maharaj, wearing a cap and holding a walking stick, stood in a rather absorbed mood, while Mahapurush Maharaj with his beaming countenance stood close by. On the right at a slight respectful distance was Swami Nirmalanandaji Maharaj. It was an extraordinary sight for me. All were impressive and venerable figures, both for their physical size and the dignity and composure of their deportment. Holy living had endowed their presence with a charming solemnity born of their universal benevolence and their poises in the Inner Self. I communicated the information.

The party stayed at Madras for about a couple of weeks and I had occasion to go to the Math with them on several days. On most of those occasions, I could pay my respects to both Maharaj and the Mahapurush Maharaj. We then returned home.

About a month or two after, I got more opportunities of following up these holy contacts. By that time I had finished my school education and left Kerala to join College in Madras. Maharaj and Sri Mahapurush Maharaj had not left South India. Swami Sharvanandaji had arranged for the celebration of Durga Puja at Madras Math in the presence of Maharaj with all the elaborate paraphernalia and rituals as in Bengal. The occasion was unique, as such a celebration was being held at Madras for the first time and that under such august and inspiring auspices. To add to the interest of the Celebration, another interesting personality, familiar to the readers of the 'Gospel of Sri Ramakrishna', had also come for the occasion. That was none other than Ramlal (known as Ramlal Dada in the Math), the nephew of Sri Ramakrishna. The celebration was a grand affair and attracted big crowds, besides devotees of Madras and those coming from other stations in the South.

I was a new comer to Madras, and being of a rather shy and timid disposition, I was a little backward in taking full advantage of the great occasion and the presence of such great personalities. However, I attended some of the important sessions of the worship and took 'Prasad' at the Math on those days. On a certain occasion, I saw Mahapurush Maharaj sitting before the image and reading the 'Chandi'. After the Kumari Puja (the worship of a small girl as Divine Mother) I saw Mahapurush Maharaj making Pranams (Prostrations) to the girl who was worshipped as representative of the Divine Mother, and the girl trying to run away from what she felt as an embarrassing situation.

After the Puja, Maharaj and Mahapurush Maharaj continued to stay at Madras Math for some time more. Off and on I used to go to the Math and offer my respectful Pranams to these great men. Maharaj often used to walk round the line of pillars. On several days I saw Mahapurush Maharaj going out for walk towards the beach. Often he went alone unaccompanied by anyone. During the time of the Durga Puja I had cultivated the acquaintance of a few young students like myself who had newly come to Madras and had started visiting the Math. Of these, one was Sri Krishnan Nambiadiri (afterwards Swami Agamananda) who had already taken initiation from Maharaj when he visited Trivandrum in 1916, and another was Chinnu (afterwards Swami Chidbhavananda), and the third was Sri T.S. Avinasilingam Chettiar, who later on became a noted political leader besides being a great devotee and worker in the cause of Ramakrishna-Vivekananda. I remember occasions when all of us met and sat together in the presence of Sri Mahapurush Maharaj who used to speak to us with a gracious smile and an expressive face. I now forget what formed the themes of those talks, but I remember he left a very deep impression on the minds of us all by his humane interest, his cheerful mood, and his communicability combined with quiet dignity. Some time after, the Presidential party left Madras, probably after a stay of about six months in the South.

Swami Brahmanandaji Maharaj did not live long after this visit to the South. Within a year he entered into Mahasamadhi in April 1922. He was succeeded by Sri Mahapurush Maharaj as the President of Ramakrishna Math and Mission, the second to hold that position.

Soon after he became President he visited Madras again, in 1923, probably. As a student visiting the Math I met him several times in those days. His stay in Madras was not however, long. He visited Bangalore also and spent some time there.

His next visit to Madras took place probably in 1925-26. I was then reading in my fourth year University class, the last year of my term at the Presidency College, Madras. Being a frequent visitor to the Math in those days, I met Sri Mahapurush Maharaj several times. We had all free access to him, and he made no distinction between youngsters like ourselves and man of status. He was staying in the western room at the front of the Math, now occupied by the President of the Math. He was this time accompanied by his three familiar Sevaks (attendants) who have since then become always associated in my mind with his memory. It was during this visit of his that I took initiation. He joyfully agreed to give me initiation for my mere asking, without being supported by the recommendation of anyone. The day fixed happened to be his birthday, quite unwittingly. That very day initiation was given also to my brother, who was then a student at Madras. It took place at the shrine of Madras Math as it existed before it was modified some years later during the Presidentship of Swami Saswatanandaji Maharaj. The chief difference then was that the present front ante-chamber of the shrine where devotees sit, was the shrine room proper, and the space occupied by the shrine at present was part of the spacious staircase hall, where I met Sri Mahapurush Maharaj for the first time. The initiation ceremony was short and simple but very impressive. The fervent manner in which he did Arati to the Master after worship, and his venerable and gracious figure with hands uplifted in a mood of prayer and blessing as it presented to my eyes on getting up after making prostrations, have always remained vivid in my memory. He instructed me that by repeating the Mantra he gave, Jnana (Knowledge),

Bhakti (Devotion), and Vairagya (Dispassion) will develop. Swami Akhilanandaji helped at the simple worship performed as preliminary to initiation.

That day, being the birthday of Sri Mahapurush Maharaj, was observed as a festive occasion at the Math. Quite a number of his disciples, besides devotees in general, had gathered to pay obeisance to him and to attend the service in the shrine and partake of Prasad.

The next visit of Mahapurush Maharaj to Madras took place about four years after, in 1930. I had by that time finished my college studies and started my monastic career, first as a humble worker in the Ramakrishna Mission Students Home at Mylapore, where Swami Saswatanandaji was then the warden (the monastic representative). The president of the Math at that time was Swami Yatiswaranandaji, Swami Sharvanandaji having left Madras about a year before after a long period of distinguished service and spiritual ministration, ever since the great Swami Ramakrishnananda, direct disciple of the Master and the pioneer of the Ramakrishna-Vivekananda movement in South India, had retired due to illness.

During this period I used to go every day, either in the morning or evening, to pay my respects to Sri Mahapurush Maharaj. He was still in excellent health, though the vigour of it as I noticed on my first meeting with him about eight or nine years back, was absent. But his face was still youthful, carefree and joyful. His manners were always so simple, frank and inviting that though you knew you were in the presence of an august and weighty personality, you also felt absolutely relaxed.

During those days, I heard a few remarks from Sri Mahapurush Maharaj that have always remained impressed in my memory. A representative of the Maharaja of Mysore had come, probably to invite the Swami to the Mysore palace at Madras. It was dusk, just after Arati. They were sitting in the big front hall of Madras Math and I was standing by. I heard him remark to the gentleman: "A man may be very wealthy and earn a big salary. But what is the use of it ultimately. Death comes and engulfs everything. The body is after all a 'rogamandiram'." The gentleman asked him: "As the head of a big organisation, you are directing all kinds of activities. Do you feel attached to them?" Sri Mahapurush Maharaj remained silent and indrawn for a moment and replied, "No".

Another day toward 4 p.m. I had finished saluting him and was standing in his room, when an educated middle-aged Tamil lady, a devotee from the rural area, probably employed in the education department, was brought in and introduced to him. In the course of preliminary personal enquiries he happened to ask her whether she had children. The lady felt confused and her face looked overcast by a sense of sorrow. Immediately Sri Mahapurush Maharaj understood the situation from the remark of the Swami who introduced her. She had been widowed in her early days and had no issue. Mahapurush Maharaj used the occasion to give her an exhortation: "Don't feel sorry", he said to her, "for being widowed early and being childless. After all, it has been a great blessing to you in your spiritual life. Consider what your condition would have been if you were burdened with a big family? You are now a free person and can follow your spiritual inclinations unrestrained. Many things which we consider to be misfortunes in a worldly sense, turn out to be fortunate circumstances afterwards from a spiritual point of view." These words immediately brightened up the lady's face, probably by the recognition of the truth that the Lord shapes the life of a devotee in many ways that look strange at first but turn out to be significant in the fullness of time.

One day I fixed a time with Swami Shivananda to talk on matters relating to spiritual practices, especially meditation. My mind was getting stimulated by the study of literature and feeling the need of explanations for many things that were till then taken for granted. I asked for the meaning of the Mantra he had given me, and he was gracious enough to explain it in a few simple words. Then I asked him about certain psychological implications of meditation. He spoke few words, but then cut short the talk, telling me that I would receive more light on these questions as I proceeded. I do not know how much of light I have got on these moot questions in the course of these years, but I have learnt that mind is a developing faculty, that ideas that seemed significant at one time cease to be so at a more mature period, and that trust in the guidance of the Spirit, provided that trust is genuine and not a mere smokescreen for whimsicality and instinctive impulses, is a much more ennobling and enlightening kind of trust in mere stereotyped forms and dogmatic assumptions. All the great teachers convey their lessons more through suggestions than lectures, putting more reliance on the reactive than the receptive role of the mind. Such were the great teachers of the Upanishads. When Prajapati was approached by Indra and Virochana with questions concerning the Atman, he only gave vague and indirect instructions, leaving their mind to react and develop in its own way in the course of years, before the real instruction was given to the deserving questioner. Equally significant was the instruction of Balaki to Satyakama Jabala when asked to be instructed on Brahman. He was merely asked to tend the cattle belonging to the teacher. The disciple's Shraddha (Faith) did the rest of the work. Great teachers teach through suggestions and not lectures. Sri Mahapurush Maharaj was one such.

I believe the 1930 visit was the last visit of Sri Mahapurush Maharaj to Madras, though he lived about seven or eight years more. So the next meetings I had with him were when I visited Belur Math on the occasions of my initiation into Brahmacharya and Sannyasa probably in 1932 and 1934 respectively. On the first of these occasions, I went with a small party of pilgrims from Kerala, one of whom was my mother. I feel it appropriate that I took my preliminary initiation into monastic life when she was with me. For she was the first of my teachers, being the one responsible for giving shape and direction to my devotional life from its earliest stage and later for introducing me to Ramakrishna-Vivekananda ideology. I have heard – but I cannot myself vouch for it – from Swami Siddheswaranandaji, who was the interpreter when she met Swami Brahmanandaji Maharaj and took initiation from him, that she prayed to him that one of her children may become a monk. Sri Mahapurush Maharaj knew her well, and she had met him twice at Madras and afterwards at Belur on the occasion now under reference. I had always seen Sri Mahapurush Maharaj very kind and cordial to her.

When I met him on this occasion, Sri Mahapurush Maharaj was still in fairly good health and he used to come down from his room to take a stroll. He was also present at the Homa ceremony at which the vows of Brahmacharya and Sannyasa were administered to the new initiates that year. But when I went for Sannyasa in 1935, I found his health completely broken down. He had had a touch of asthma for several years past but it had by this time become intensified, and high blood pressure too had now joined hands with it to undermine his health completely and reduce him almost to the condition of an invalid. But still, according to the tradition followed at the Math, all the monastics were allowed to go to the room of the President in the early morning to pay their obeisance to him. A remarkable difference I had noticed between Sri Mahapurush Maharaj and an ordinary patient is that there was no depressing and melancholy atmosphere about his sick-bed. His face remained always bright and cheerful in spite of a sleepless night from asthmatic spasms or from the uneasiness of high blood pressure. No physical ailment could make that face shrunken and depressed. I am told that this characteristic continued all through his sickness till the end. A sick man is the most selfish person one can see. He has nothing except his ailments to think about, and to everyone who goes to him, he pours out the story of his sufferings. Probably it is Nature's device to mitigate the sufferings by sharing them with others. Sri Mahapurush Maharaj's behaviour was quite different. To those who went to see him in the morning he looked cheerful, and he had nothing to say about his own sufferings even when enquiries were made. On the other hand he would make kind enquiries of your conditions in detail. Especially to people who went from the

South of India, he was particular to see that they got some dishes suited to their taste. I believe it was during his time, and probably due to his insistence, that Belur Math added Kolambu to its menu for the noon meal for the benefit of the sprinkling of South Indian Sadhus who stayed, off and on, at the Math. His solicitude in this respect was very appealing – almost motherly.

A man of spiritual realisation can best be distinguished from a worldly minded man when physical ailments attack him. When one is healthy, it is easy to lecture eloquently to others about the unaffectedness of the Atman and about the transitoriness and insignificance of bodily life. Any man with the gift of the gab could do so. But when illness and danger threaten, it is only the wise that can behave with equanimity. In the life of Sri Ramakrishna we find this most conspicuously. The painful and prolonged illness that brought his life, ultimately, to an end, failed to shake his mind. It was during this time that his spiritual powers were most manifest. By an act of his will, he conveyed spiritual inspiration and experience to devotees who flocked to him in numbers. The spiritual joy that emanated from him converted his sick-bed into a rallying point for aspirants. The great Master's behaviour makes one convinced that for the enlightened one the spirit is the substance and the body is only the shadow.

Sri Mahapurush Maharaj on his sick bed reminded one of his Great Master, whose name he always uttered with tremendous faith and inspiration.

I took Sannyasa that year with my esteemed friends Swami Tyagisananda (Krishna Menon) and Swami Nishreyasananda (Nambiar) along with others in that batch

besides others. On the previous day we performed the Sraddha ceremony for all ancestors as also for ourselves, indicating that a sannyasin is physically dead and the last rites for him have been done. Next day was the birth day of Sri Ramakrishna and there was the usual Puja and festival connected with it. But we had to fast the whole day and night, though the physically weak among us were allowed to take sugar candy water as a concession. Kalipuja was performed throughout the night and at early morning 4 o'clock, the Vedic ritual of Viraja Homa that precedes sannyasa was performed. The ideals of sannyasa and its inner meaning with the mantras were uttered by Swami Omkarananda during the Viraja Homa and we also repeated the mantras after him. We offered oblations into the sacred fire which is lit during the Viraja Homa. Sri Mahapurush Maharaj could not physically come to the temple as he was unwell. Early morning at 5.30, we twelve candidates who were seeking sannyasa went to his inner chambers to complete the last portion of the sannyasa ritual - to take the vows of sannyasa and the external insignia of sannyasa. We repeated the presha mantra and the mahavakya which were uttered by Swami Omkarananda and prostrated at the holy feet of Sri Mahapurush Maharaj. Sri Mahapurush Maharaj was seated on his cot; raising his hand, he blessed us with prayers to the Lord. We renounced the new clothes and other insignia thereby signifying the death of our previous lives and rebirth in a new spiritual existence. We got our new names and the two symbols of sannyasa, which are the ochre robe and the danda from the acharya and the guru. Both the symbols are indicative of knowledge: the ochre coloured robes are bright like the blazing fire and have the capacity to purify anything that comes into its purview; and the danda is a protection against worldliness and is the primary support in the path to realization of Brahman.

I was in Belur Math for about a month during this time. On the day of my return to south India, I approached Sri Mahapurush Maharaj to take his blessings. My guru was in his room and resting on his bed as he was suffering from asthma. But his face was calm and full of bliss, just as I had seen him on the first day when I arrived at the Math. When I got up after prostrating to him, he blessed me with his eyes still closed, by saying the following words: 'Maa bhaishih - there is no cause for fear. I am there with you always.' These words of blessing uttered by my revered guru have been a constant support in my life's tourney.

This is the last time that I saw my revered guru. He attained Mahasamadhi on 24th February, 1934.

Swami Vivekananda says in one place that if we compare Sri Ramakrishna to a tree, then his disciples are like the main branches of that tree. It is in and through the disciples of Sri Ramakrishna that the later generations like us will be able to grasp the spiritual greatness, divinity, love, renunciation, universal compassion and tolerance of other religions as were expressed by Sri Ramakrishna. In course of time, I have been able to understand that Sri Mahapurush Maharaj was one of the main torchbearers in spreading the spiritual ideal and tradition of Sri Ramakrishna. Among the direct disciples of Sri Ramakrishna, probably, Sri Mahapurush Maharaj had the blessed privilege of kindling the spiritual fire in the maximum number of sannyasis and lay devotees.

A Visit To The Maharshi[1]

The following article appeared as an appendix in the first edition (1937) of ***Maha Yoga****, in which it was prefaced by the remark: "The following passages are extracts from a letter written by a critically minded visitor, which once appeared in the* ***Vedanta Kesari*** *(Mylapore, Madras)."*

The Maharshi impressed me as a rare type of man. I do not know whether he is a *Jnani*, or what he is. For as the Vedanta says, a *Jnani* can be known only by a *Jnani*, and I am certainly not one. But this person, anyone can feel, is not of the ordinary run of men. We nowadays come across men everywhere whose one thought is world reform and things of that kind. But here is a man who is *perfectly aware*, as one can see from his conduct and movements, who has no such idea, who has in his opinion nothing to add to the sum-total of human happiness. He simply seems to exist, without waiting for anything, without being anxious about anything. On watching him I was powerfully reminded of the Gita passage beginning with `*Udasinavad*' (Like one that is unconcerned)[2]. He seems to take, as far as I can see, no interest even in the Ashram that has sprung up around him. He simply sits there; things are going on *as events and other*

1. This article, published in *The Mountain Path*, October 1982, p 266-268, was written by Swami Tapasyananda Maharaj.

2. "Nor do these actions bind me, O Dhananjaya, like one unconcerned, I remain unattached to these actions" – Bhagavad Gita 9.9; "Like one unconcerned, he remains unmoved by the gunas; knowing the gunas operate, he abides firm and moves not" – Bhagavad Gita 14,23 (Ed.)

Sri Ramana Maharshi

men shape them. The only activity of the Ashram in which he seems to take active interest is cooking. He cuts vegetables in the kitchen, and if there is any special cooking any day he is sure to try his hand at preparing some of the dishes for that day. Spicing and other processes of the culinary art are performed there under his directions.

Another point that struck me is his *silence*. We used to ask in fun among ourselves why eminent professors who crossed the seas did not deliver their Vedantic lectures through silence. But here is a person who actually does this as far as his teaching of the Vedanta is concerned. When I asked him to tell me something of spirituality, the first thing he said was that silence is the highest teaching! The beauty of the man is that he remains faithful to that idea to the utmost extent possible. His idea is that the *Advaitin* has no position to state, no siddhanta to propound. He regrets that in these days even *Advaita* has become a *Siddhanta,* whereas it is really not meant to be so. The reason for the existence of so much Vedantic literature is this. When doubts arise in the mind as our intellects are quickened such literature is helpful in dispelling them. In other words, the *Advaitin* speaks only to dispel a doubt that might have arisen in himself or in another. Our saint remains faithful to this idea. He is mostly silent, and speaks but a little if questioned on any point. Of course he jokes and speaks occasionally on other things, but he has no dogmatic teaching on Vedanta to deliver. He told me he says `yes, yes' to everyone who interprets *Advaita,* even to some of his followers who interpret his ideas in the book published under his name. When I asked, regarding a book that I purchased in the depot there, how far the ideas stated therein were his teachings, he said that it was very difficult to say that, as he had no definite teaching[1]. As people have understood they have written and they may be right from certain points of view. He himself, he says has absolutely no idea or inclination to write a book; but due to the entreaties of some people about him he has written he has written some verses, and he adds that he is often troubled by men who take a fancy to translate them into this language and that, and ask him about the faithfulness of the translation.

---

1. Refer to *Talks* No.107 (p. 103), where Sri Bhagavan says that teachings or instructions must "differ according to the temperaments of the individuals and according to the spiritual ripeness of their minds. There cannot be any instruction *en masse*". (Ed.)

So mostly, the Maharshi remains silent, and people come, make prostrations, sit before him for some minutes or hours and then go away, perhaps without exchanging even a single word! I have got my own doubts as to whether people benefit by this teaching through silence. But yet people come from long distances to hear this dumb eloquence and go back satisfied.

Though he speaks but little, it is very instructive to watch his face and eyes. There is nothing very prepossessing about his personality, but there is a beam of intelligence and unruffled calmness in his eyes that are unique. His body is almost motionless except when he occasionally changes his position or wipes his sweat in that hot place. I was carefully observing his face. I found him seldom winking and never yawning. I say this to show that I am sufficiently satisfied that the absence of activity in him is *not due to inertness*.

The third point that struck me was the absolute absence of vanity or self-importance in him. Except for his dress confined only to a *kaupinam* a visitor may not find it possible to make out Ramana Maharshi. He eats the same food as everyone else there; there is not even a single extra item or special dish for him. I specially noticed that in conversation he is not averse to using the first personal pronoun, unlike some other Vedantins who use 'he' and things of that kind. I point out this to show how unostentatious he is. His silence, I am convinced, is not to assume a gravity of disposition calculated to keep people at a distance. And when he breaks that silence, as he does when questioned, he appears to be *the sweetest and most friendly of men*.

He makes no distinction between man and man for their wealth or position in society. I saw peasants and gentlemen in motor cars coming and being greeted with the same silence. They all sit on the floor and receive the same hospitality. In fact the Maharshi seems to be quite indifferent to any financial gain that the Ashram may have by special treatment given to reach men.

I stayed in the Ashram for three days. The Maharshi talked with me very kindly and quite freely on the several questions I asked him. Although his manner of replying was not so impressive as I expected, *his thoughts are always clear, concise and free from all ideas of narrowness*. Though he has not read much, as he himself told me in some context, he has a good grasp of all the difficult points in Vedanta. My impression is this: Whether he is a *Jnani* or anything else I do not positively know. But I am convinced that *he is a sweet and lovable person who is indifferent to all things about him, who has no end of his own to gain, who is always alert even when he seems to be most deeply absorbed, and who may be said to be perfectly free from greed and vanity*. In seeing him I do believe I have seen a unique personage.[1]

1. The author of *Maha Yoga* concluded this article with the following comment of his own: "These very characteristics are according to the ancient lore, the distinguishing marks of a *jnani* – a perfect sage." (Ed.)

Swami Tapasyananda Maharaj's Message during his departure from Trivandrum to Madras[1]

I have been asked to give a message on the eve of my departure from Trivandrum to Madras after a stay of thirty years in this city as the head of the local Sri Ramakrishna Ashrama.

Sri Ramakrishna, the world Teacher from whom our movement has sprung, emphasized the idea that the unique value of human life consists in the possibility it offers to realize God and abide in HIS divine reality. To remove God from life will be like taking away the value giving figure one, two or three, as the case may be, from a line of zeroes. Without the figure, the zeroes became valueless. So also is life without an adequate conception of the divinity that is at the back of it.

The political & intellectual forces working in different parts of the world have been hostile to the acceptance of such a world view & would fain eliminate god and make a heaven of earth. But the disastrous consequences that have attended such efforts both in the collective and individual life of man are forcing all thoughtful minds to realize the utter futility of such an attitude. For all that such an attitude can ultimately achieve is to make man a mere exalted and

1. This text is reproduced here as recorded by Sri Achutha Menon in his diary. The time and place or the mode in which this message was delivered is unknown.

powerful animal in a collective sense and a restless unhappy being without any peace or tranquility in his individual life.

Is he then to abandon all efforts at improving the condition of life and making this a happier world? Far from it. It only means that if he lives with this truncated vision, the very methods he adopts will be self-defeating and will end in applying remedies that are worse than the disease he was to cure.

So if our endeavours are to be in the right direction, they must be based on an adequate conception of the spiritual possibilities of man and all our efforts at material improvement should not obscure from us these spiritual possibilities.

It is in this context that the importance of religion in its highest sense of yoga emerges. Religion is not an opiate as people hostile to it think. It forms the branch of human culture with the function of helping man in his higher evolution. With the perfection of the body and brain of man, nature has achieved the highest in the physical field. The rousing of the higher powers of understanding and insight are the possibilities in the next stage of evolution. Religion in its highest sense embodies the methods and devices arrived at by the greatest representatives of human culture in this regard.

We call it yoga in India. Yoga does not ask us to shun the social activities but only exhorts us to do all our works as action dedicated to God. If we recognize that all our powers, physical and mental come from the Supreme Being; if one grasps this idea through deep meditation and introspection then we would recognize that it will be a dereliction of duty if we fail to offer them all to Him. [By] Constant remembrance, we should use all our free time to the study of scripture meditation and devotional practices. By habituating ourselves to this kind of a balanced life in which devotion to God and discharge of duties go hand in hand, the human spirit will in the course of time emerge from the obscuring condition that stand in the way of recognizing its kinship with the Divine.

Human life can be lifted from the morass in which it is stranded in our times only if such a world view is made universally acceptable through a proper education system.

Extracts from *Apprenticed to a Himalayan Master – A Yogi's Autobiography*[1]

Swami Tapasyananda was quite different from both these souls. He was the then President of the Ramakrishna Mission situated at Sasthamangalam. The Ramakrishna Mission also ran a free hospital. I had read about the great Saint Ramakrishna Paramahansa and his illustrious disciple, the incomparable Swami Vivekananda, but did not know of the existence of a branch of the Ramakrishna Mission in Trivandrum. This is how I discovered its existence.

Not far from the Trivandrum Public Library where I had first read the wonderful set of books called *The Complete Works of Swami Vivekananda,* is a beautiful garden called the Museum Garden. It was my habit to walk from the library to the gardens and sit quietly on one of the benches there. One day, I met a young ochre clad sanyasin with a shining face. Curious, I asked who he was. He laughed like and a child and said that he was from the Ramakrishna Mission. It was not too far away. I asked him if I could visit the ashram. "Sure. You should," he said laughing again, "and you must meet our head, Swami Tapasyananda, great soul. Come sometime. My name is Golakananda [Golokananda]."

So I went, one Sunday morning. Swami Golakananda introduced me to Swami Tapasyanandaji. He was dressed in an ochre *kurta* and *dhoti* like all monks of the

1. Pp 65-67. The author of this book is Sri Mumtaz Ali Khan, also known as Sri M, currently heading Satsang Foundation in Madanapalle, Andhra Pradesh.

Ramakrishna Order, and the first impression one got was that of sternness and discipline. As days went by however, I sensed a tenderness and affection that was well hidden by a deliberately constructed faļade.

I learnt many things from him, especially about the Ramakrishna – Vivekananda movement, and for the first time, understood Swami Vivekananda's dictum that service to mankind is service to God. I realized how the loving heart of the great monk Vivekananda bled for suffering humanity. Tapasyananda enlightened me about the Ramakrishna movement and the stalwarts who worked tirelessly under the command of Swami Vivekananda, the greatest amongst Ramakrishna's disciples. He was himself a disciple of Swami Shivananda, better known as Mahapurush Maharaj, a direct disciple of Sri Ramakrishna Paramahansa...

It was Swami Tapasyanandaji who introduced me to Professor Balakrishnan Nair, who, according to him, had ascended the dizzy heights of Vedanta even whilst leading a family life with wife and children. Many a Sunday, on my way to the Shangumukham beach to practice *kalari,* I would drop in at Professor Balakrishnan Nair's house, and listen to him expounding the Vedantic teachings in simple language, mostly using the parables of Sri Ramakrishna Paramahansa.

Many years later, when Swami Tapasyananda was the head of the Ramakrishna Mission at Chennai and also the Vice-President of the Ramakrishna Order, he graciously initiated me into the Ramakrishna mantra which had evaded me even though I had spent some time as an acolyte of the Ramakrishna Order at the its different centres. I am eternally obliged to him for this.

Newspaper Clippings[1]

1

[The news that appeared at the time of Maharaj's transfer from Trivandrum to Madras][2]

(i). Swami Tapasyananda

Swami Tapasyananda who served as the president of Ramakrishna Mission, Trivandrum, for nearly 30 years is leaving the same. Though he is moving to a wider arena of activity in Madras his departure spells out a loss for Trivandrum. The Swami who had a deep knowledge of the Vedanta was a guide to those who were interested in the subject. But what made this karmayogi more endearing is the achievement he made in the field of care to the sick. It is from 'nothing' that he built up the great institution that exists at Sasthamangalam today. This first class hospital with all modern amenities is the embodiment of his selfless and ceaseless service and also a monument unto himself. People from all over the State are today beneficiaries to the contribution this great ascetic made to Trivandrum. We hope that his successors would follow in Swami Tapasyananda's footsteps and make this institution a treatment centre conferring solace to greater number of people. We wish all success to the Swami who first came to Trivandrum as a

1. Translated by Smt. Indira Krishnakumar.

2. The date of publication and the name of the newspaper are not known. According to Sri Udayanan, perhaps it is *Kerala Kaumudi*.

youth and is bidding audience as a person entering upon advanced years after incessantly serving for 30 years.

(ii). Swami Tapasyananda bids adieu to Kerala

Swami Tapasyananda is well-known to the citizens of Trivandrum. People who have gone to the Sasthamangalam hospital would not have missed this karmayogi working untiringly from dawn to dusk; they definitely would have spotted him seated at the window of the office-room of the Ashrama.

It has been three decades since The Swami came. One fine morning in 1940 a young ascetic arrived from Madras to take charge of this Sri Ramakrishna Ashrama. In these thirty years, he created history in Trivandrum.

Smt. Raman Thampi presents a bouquet when Tapasyananda Maharaj bids farewell to Trivandrum

That young sanyasi of yore has now entered upon the advanced age of his life. Still he has been enjoined upon to assume a more onerous responsibility and he will be bidding farewell to Trivandrum on 15th June immersing innumerable friends in grief.

He was born in 1904 in an ancient and famous family of Ottappalam by name 'Palat'. His mother who was of saintly qualities was the disciple of Swami Brahmananda who was a most meritorious disciple of Sri Ramakrishna Deva and the first president of the Ramakrishna Mission. The mother's tutelage created in the Swami 'shraddha' and 'viswasa' in God-oriented matters.

The Swami's high-school education was in his home town. He studied B.A. Hons. at Presidency College, Madras and passed out meritoriously. He came out of the college as a Ramakrishna devotee. In 1922, at the age of twenty-six, he became a brahmachari inmate of the ashram at Madras. In this matter he had received full approval and blessings from his mother.

That great soul, his mother had found great gratification in offering her son at the Lord's feet as a 'naivedya'. The president of the Madras Ashrama at that time was Sri Swami Yatiswarananda.

In 1935, he became Swami Tapasyananda, receiving sannyasa from Sri Swami Sivananda, one of the foremost among the inner circle of Sri Ramakrishna Deva's disciples and the second president of the Mission. The farsighted Guru must have sensed the strong quality of tapas in his disciple. For eight years from 1932, he undertook the publication of

The Vedanta Kesari, an English journal brought out by the Madras Ashram.

The Swami himself has said that it was the Madras Ashrama that had given the impetus to his spiritual self. In 1940, he was appointed as the president of the Trivandrum Ashrama.

During those days, only two rooms with thatched roof existed in the place of today's institution. This thatched structure was housing a dispensary started by the respected Sri K. Raman Thampi, a Sri Ramakrishna devotee, as a service activity. The great institution that we witness today is the result of the ceaseless efforts of Swami Tapasyananda who dedicated himself at the altar of service with all the commitment at his command, taking for himself only the bare essentials required to sustain life in the body.

The Swami's great and principled life and his affectionate behaviour have inspired several people to live scrupulously and undertake service-oriented activities. He took care of the institution as though it was a joint-family, taking care of the welfare of all concerned and at the same time focusing on the progress of the institution. He has been able to nurture the great and valuable qualities in each person and promote the well-being of the individuals as well as the institution.

The talks on spiritual topics given by the Swami, who was an erudite scholar both in occidental and oriental philosophies, were capable of igniting the listeners' thinking and appeasing their thirst for spiritual knowledge. Seldom had he recognized a dividing line between the spiritual and temporal.

Upholder of utmost simplicity in life, a yogi who fully adopted and lived the vow of aparigraha, the embodiment of sacrifice and asceticism, an advaitist yet a devotee to the core, a karmayogi who believed more in practice than preaching – this is Swami Tapasyananda.

It was during his stay in Madras Mission that the Swami wrote the life of Sri Sarada Devi in English. And the Math published this authoritative life which was for the first time written in English. Until then the Holy Mother's biography was available only in Bengali. With the publication of this life in English, people all over India and abroad got an opportunity to learn about Holy Mother.

Apart from this the Swami has written several articles in the *Prabuddha Bharata* and *The Vedanta Kesari*, the English journals brought out by Sri Ramakrishna Mission.

On 15th of June, the Swami will be saying good bye to Kerala, demitting office as the president of Trivandrum Ashramam to become the president of Madras Ashrama.

Mahasamadhi – Reports and Descriptions[1]

Mahasamadhi of Srimat Swami Tapasyanandaji Maharaj

WITH DEEP SORROW we record that Srimat Swami Tapasyanandaji Maharaj, a Vice-President of the Ramakrishna Math & Ramakrishna Mission, and President of Sri Ramakrishna Math, Madras, attained Mahasamadhi at 6.32 pm on Thursday, 3 October 1991, at BSS Hospital, Madras. He was 87.

The sad news was broadcast over radio and television that night and was carried by newspapers the next morning. The body was brought to Madras Math at 8.30 pm and kept for darshan in the library building. A large number of devotees and friends came to the Math to pay homage. There was continuous chanting from scriptures and devotional singing till 1.00 pm the next day when the body was taken in a huge procession to the Mylapore crematorium for the final rites.

Special Puja and Bhandara were held at the Belur Math, Madras Math and several other centres of the Order on 15 October in which many monastics and devotees participated. The Memorial Meeting held at Madras Math on the same day was presided over by Swami Gahananandaji, General Secretary of the Ramakrishna Math and Mission. A booklet

---

1. This report about Revered Maharaj's *mahasamadhi* was published in *The Vedanta Kesari*, Annual Issue, 1991.

containing a short sketch of Swami Tapasyanandaji's life was released on the occasion. Another Memorial Meeting was held on 6 November, in which prominent citizens of Madras paid homage to the departed soul. The meeting was presided over by His Excellency Sri C. Subramaniam, Governor of Maharashtra.

Known in his pre-monastic days as K.P. Balakrishna Menon, Swami Tapasyanandaji was born in 1904 at Ottapalam in Kerala. He came into contact with the Ramakrishna-Vivekananda Movement and its literature at a young age. In 1921 he met Swami Brahmanandaji Maharaj and Swami Shivanandaji Maharaj when they visited Madras. He received Mantra-diksha from Swami Shivanandaji Maharaj in December 1924. After completing his post-graduation in 1925 from the Presidency College, Madras, he joined the Order at the Ramakrishna Mission Students' Home in 1926. In 1928 he received Brahmacharya vows and was given the name Purnachaitanya. Four years later, in 1932, he received Sannyasa from his Guru. From 1931 to 1939 he edited the *Vedanta Kesari.* In 1940 he was appointed head of the Ramakrishna Ashrama, Trivandrum, where he spent the next three decades, developing the small dispensary there into a big hospital to serve the poor of the locality. From 1971 till the end he was head of Sri Ramakrishna Math, Madras. During this period there was a phenomenal growth and expansion of all the Math activities—spiritual, medical, educational, publication, and preaching. In November 1965 Swami Tapasyanandaji was appointed a trustee of the Ramakrishna Math and a member of the Governing Body of the Ramakrishna Mission. In 1985 he was elected one of the Vice-Presidents of the Order, and in that capacity he guided hundreds of earnest seekers on the spiritual path.

Swami Tapasyanandaji was an erudite scholar. His contribution to the Order's literature has been immense. He translated many Sanskrit scriptures into English, the most outstanding of which is his 4-volume translation of *Srimad Bhagavata.* Among the other translations he did are the *Gita, Adhyatma Ramayana, Sundara Kandam, Narayaneeyam, Bhakti Ratnavali, Sri Vishnu Sahasranama, Sri Lalita Sahasranama, Saundarya Lahari, Sivananda Lahari,* and *Kapilopadesha.* He also wrote short biographies of Sri Ramakrishna, Sri Sarada Devi, and Swami Vivekananda. His big biography of Sri Sarada Devi, published way back in 1940, continues to be the favourite among devotees. The last big book he wrote was *Bhakti Schools of Vedanta,* which is a masterly study of the philosophies of Ramanuja, Madhva, Nimbarka, Chaitanya, and Vallabha.

Swami Tapasyanandaji's departure is an irreparable loss to the Ramakrishna Order, and creates a vacuum difficult to fill up. He was an inspiring personality entirely dedicated to the ideals of the Sangha and was loved and respected by all for his austere life of self-discipline, dedication, service, and devotion. The devotees have lost in him a loving spiritual guide whose understanding, affection and sympathy were an invaluable asset to them.

Om Santih Santih Santih | |

Hari Om Tat Sat | |

Memorial Meeting – A Report

In the Memorial Meeting for Revered Swami Tapasyananda Maharaj held on 15 October 1991, Prof C. S. Ramakrishnan gave a very moving speech. He said that Swami Tapasyananda Maharaj embodied the two aspects of Shiva - one of asceticism and renunciation, and the other the Dakshinamurthy aspect of compassion and granting knowledge. And that despite a somewhat stern exterior, Revered Maharaj had a very soft and loving heart and a good sense of humour. His comparison of Revered Maharaj's character to the following lines of Visnu Sahasranama – *amaani maanado maanyo* – was so apt. Many people shed tears during his speech.

Many speakers at the Memorial Meeting dwelt on Revered Maharaj's the fact of Swami Tapasyananda Maharaj's renunciation, humility, scholarship and absolute dedication to the cause of Sri Ramakrishna.

Swami Raghaveshananda said at the meeting that Swami Tapasyananda Maharaj once told him, 'you have nothing to fear. You are working for Sri Ramakrishna. Hold on to Sri Ramakrishna and Holy Mother, and everything will be alright.' And then, Swami Tapasyananda explained to him, for almost half an hour, the first stanza from Swami Vivekananda's hymn to Sri Ramakrishna, *Hridaya Kamala Madhya,* which was one of his favourite stanzas.

Newspaper Report[1]

20th Oct. 1991

Swami Tapasyananda – A Memoir[2]

Swami Tapasyananda, Vice-president of the Ramakrishna Ashrama, who passed away recently was a person of outstanding capability in the spiritual and social fields. The Swami had given forewarning about the challenges faced by the Hindu Society.

The Swami who was an accomplished scholar and writer had served as the President of the Ramakrishna Ashrama for thirty years[3] from 1940. The Swami's translation of Mahabharatam[4], Sankara Dig-Vijayam, Narayaneeyam, Vishnu Sahasranamam, etc. from Sanskrit to English could be cited as his great literary achievements.

Swami Tapasyananda was the disciple of Swami Shivananda, a disciple of Sri Ramakrishna Paramahamsa. The Swami who had translated innumerable works like Mahabharata from Sanskrit to English was for a long time editor of the spiritual magazine `Vedanta Kesari'.

It was Balakrishnan, born in Ottappalam who had later become Swami Tapasyananda. He was born as the elder son

---

1. Translated by Smt. Indira Krishnakumar.

2. The name of the newspaper is not known. According to Sri Udayanan, perhaps it is *Kerala Kaumudi*.

3. The newspaper alludes to the Swami's tenure at Ramakrishna Mission, Trivandrum and has obviously omitted the Swami's tenure at Sri Ramakrishna Math, Madras. In Kerala, in common parlance, both the Math and the Mission are referred to as 'ashramas'.

4. Revered Maharaj had not translated the *Mahabharata*.

of Panangat Achutha Menon and Varode Palat Parukkutty Amma. It was his own mother who dedicated Balakrishnan to Sri Ramakrishna Mission. It so happened that she, who was fortunate enough to receive 'mantra diksha' from Swami Brahmananda, a disciple of Sri Ramakrishna Paramahamsa, had herself taken her son to Belur Math.

Swami Shivananda, who was a disciple of Sri Ramakrishna Paramahamsa gave Balakrishnan sannyasa with the 'diksha' name of Tapasyananda in 1935[1].

The Swami was not merely an expert translator. The Swami had also written books on Sri Ramakrishna paramahamsa, Swami Vivekananda, Sarada Devi, Sri Ramakrishnananda, etc.

When The Swami's mother and his younger brother Achuta Menon (Retd. Executive Engineer[2]) were living in 'Sarada Mandiram'[3], their family was a haven for the activities of the Rashtriya Swayam Sewak Sangha Vyasa Vidya Peeth Administrator Sri P. Udayanan who was the karya-vah of RSS Palghat Vibhag is Swami Tapasyananda's brother's son.

–Rama Nair

1. Revered Maharaj received sannyasa in 1932 and not in 1935.

2. Late Achutha Menon retired as Supdt. Engineer of the Government of Kerala and not as Executive Engineer.

3. 'Sarada Mandiram' is the name of a house in Sri Ramakrishna Nagar, near Palappuram Train Halt (near Ottapalam Railway Station in Palghat Dist.) where Maharaj's mother and brother lived from the mid-fifties till their end. Maharaj had visited this house when his mother was alive. This is close to Sri Ramakrishna Niranjan Ashrama founded by Swami Nirmalananda Maharaj and the Sarada Ashrama.

A Hymn of Remembrance[1]

Professor B. Sulochana Nair[2]

O Radiant Eminence,
Through ceaseless self-sacrifice
For the writhing humankind
Seared by the triple fires of misery,
You have crossed over to yonder shores
Strumming the strings of penance.
Did you not melt all your deeds into a melody?
Your mind and word were forever
In tender amity, ever radiant
You lit the lamp of compassion
In every careworn sick and weary heart.
The home of solace
Dedicated to the Master
Was an asylum
To those mired in misery
This abode of the joy of penance

---

1. Originally written in Malayalam, this poem appeared in the collections *Vilwa Patram* published by Southern Star Publications, Trivandrum. Prof. Sulochana Nair later published this poem in the Malayalam version of the memorial book on Revered Maharaj published by Madras Math, and released it at the fourth all Kerala Bhakta Sammelan in 2005 at Trivandrum under the title *Tapasyananda Swamikal.*

2. This poem is translated into English by a devotee.

Is the choice fruit of worship
A haven on the vast shores of compassion
The soul neither comes nor departs
This is known.
The fragrance of that lofty soul
Could be from afar or within call
The ascending notes of sweet melody in adoration
Are refrains of grateful remembrance
Showered at the feet of the great Yogi.
Let us place a *vilva* leaf at the altar of memory,
With folded hands let us offer our homage at his feet.

यतिवन्दनम्

(Yati Vandanam)

नमामि योगीन्द्र तपश्चरं सदा
श्रीरामकृष्णार्पित धन्यजीवितम् ।
लोकोपकाराय सुकर्मतत्परम्
नमाम्यहम् श्री यतिवर्यपादम् ।। १ ।।

namāmi yogīndra tapaścaraṃ sadā
śrīrāmakṛṣṇārpita dhanyajīvitam |
lokopakārāya sukarmatatparam
namāmyaham śrī yativaryapādam ||

I salute the lord of the yogis, who was ever austere, who has offered his blessed life for Sri Ramakrishna. I salute the feet of [this] great monk, who was engaged in doing good work for the sake of the welfare of the world.

कुलीनवंशे जननं सुमातरम्
लीनं सदा सद्गुरुदेवचिन्तनम् ।
चरन् पथे भक्तिविरागयुक्तम्
वन्दे तपस्यानन्दपदं मुहुर्मुहुः ।। २ ।।

kulīnavaṃśe jananaṃ sumātaram
līnaṃ sadā sadgurudevacintanam |
caran pathe bhaktivirāgayuktam
vande tapasyānandapadaṃ muhurmuhuḥ ||

I salute again and again the holy feet of [Swami] Tapasyananda, who was born in a noble family with a devout mother ever immersed in the thought of [her] holy guru, who travelled the path combining devotion and dispassion.

अनन्तपुरीनगरे गुरुस्मरणे
निर्माणं बृहदातुरालयम् ।
अश्रान्तमकरोत् दीनसेवनम्
वन्दे महापुरुषशिष्यरत्नम् ।। ३ ।।

anantapurīnagare gurusmaraṇe
nirmāṇaṃ bṛhadāturālayam |
aśrāntamakarot dīnasevanam
vande mahāpuruṣaśiṣyaratnam ||

I salute the jewel among the disciples of Mahapurush [Maharaj], who, in the memory of his guru, established a big hospital in Anantapuri [Trivandrum] to incessantly serve the destitute.

सद्धर्मनिष्ठं मतिः त्यागशोभनम्
वैराग्यसंशुद्धहृदिं वरिष्ठं ।
अध्यात्मज्ञानान्वितग्रन्थकर्तारं
तं योगिवर्यं प्रणतोस्मि नित्यम् ।। ४ ।।

saddharmaniṣṭhaṃ matiḥ tyāgaśobhanam
vairāgyasaṃśuddhahṛdiṃ variṣṭhaṃ |
adhyātmajñānānvitagranthakartāraṃ
taṃ yogivaryaṃ praṇatosmi nityam ||

I daily salute him, the best among yogis, whose mind was ever committed to righteousness, who was blazing with renunciation, who was purified with greatest dispassion, one who has written books on spiritual topics.

– Dr. Rema Krishnakumar

Books by Swami Tapasyananda Maharaj

Biographies

1. *Sri Ramakrishna: Life and Teachings*
2. *Sri Sarada Devi: Life and Teachings*
3. *Swami Vivekananda: His Life and Legacy*
4. *Sri Sarada Devi, the Holy Mother*
5. *Swami Ramakrishnananda: The Apostle of Sri Ramakrishna to the South*

Studies

1. *Bhakti Schools of Vedanta*
2. *The Four Yogas of Swami Vivekananda*
3. *The Nationalistic and Religious Lectures of Swami Vivekananda*
4. *The Philosophical and Religious Lectures of Swami Vivekananda*
5. *For Enquires About Ramakrishna Math and Mission*
6. *Spiritual Quest*
7. *Sri Ramakrishna's Thoughts on Man, World and God*

Translations

1. *Srimad Bhagavata (4 volumes)*
2. *Srimad Bhagavad Gita (Economy Edition)*
3. *Bhagavad Gita (Pocket Edition)*
4. *Adhyatma Ramayana*
5. *Sundara Kandam*
6. *Narayaneeyam*
7. *Bhakti Ratnavali*
8. *Sri Vishnu Sahasranama*
9. *Sri Lalita Sahasranama*
10. *Saundarya Lahari*
11. *Sivananda Lahari*
12. *Aratrika Hymns and Ramnam*
13. *Stotranjali*
14. *Sankara Digvijaya*
15. *Kapilopadesha*
16. *Prasnottara-ratna-malika*
17. *Laghu-Vasudeva-Mananam*